FIRE & ICE

EXTENDED EDITION

ROBIN LYNN

Idle Winter Press
Portland, Oregon
http://IdleWinter.com

Story first published 2020
This edition published 2024

The text of this book is in Adobe Garamond Pro

ISBN-13: 978-1-945687-19-8 (Idle Winter Press)

Acknowledgements

This book (and its predecessor) would never have happened if it weren't for the many people who pushed for me to put myself out there, coming through time and time again with the behind-the-scenes support, technical assistance, and love to make that happen. Thank you to the entire Clubhouse, especially Tabitha, whose willingness to format things (sometimes more than once) is the only reason I have published works. Thank you to Jen, who has been there from the beginning and stayed to drag me over every finish line since. And for both the expanded and audio versions of *Fire & Ice*, thank you to the incomparably generous and patient Supertwig (a.k.a. Sarah), who has thrown open doors I'd written off as locked(, barricaded, and hidden inside a house set on fire). I am firm in my belief that one day, you will be canonized officially as the Patron Saint of Transformative Works and Gay Audio Porn. Also, special thanks to my bestie Deb, for excitedly telling anyone who will listen that she has a friend who is a published author. I could sell a million books, but that would still mean more.

Love you all.

—Wings

Author's Disclaimer:

A good-faith attempt was made to depict the professional situations and references with as much accuracy as humanly possible. Department structures and standards may vary by location and leadership. Please note, specifically regarding medical interventions: EMS and hospital protocols vary by state and region. Some prefer or even mandate medication usage that others prohibit. Some may use different standards of practice or codes. There is no way to fully standardize this depiction. A glossary has been added to the end of the book to provide additional context and perspective on various terms and references.

Likewise, the BDSM community is not a monolith. All Dominants, submissives, and switches do not view or approach relationships and dynamics the same way, nor is there a single "right" way to approach them. This story aims to read accessibly and be equally enjoyable for folks with zero knowledge of BDSM or long-time veterans, but it is written through the author's personal POV and experience. It does strive to depict a safe, sane, risk-aware, consensual kink dynamic with an emphasis on self-awareness and personal responsibility. That shit is sexy, friends.

All scenarios and persons depicted during the course of this story are completely fictional. Any similarity to real life events is purely coincidental.

Chapter 1

The Halligan Bar *is crowbar-like, multipurposed tool that is widely considered to be the most versatile hand tool for a multitude of fireground tasks. It is not uncommon for some firefighters to be possessive over their favorite tool, or to show a particular one added affection.*

***

By the time the engine carrying Station Fifteen's crew pulls up outside the dispatched address, Tripp Truett—*noting the slight screech of the brakes and scratching a mental note to check the pads later*—can already tell that the house is going to be a total loss.

"You can leave your masks off for now, boys." Captain Gunnar's calm and even voice filters in over the headset Tripp's still wearing as he peers out the side window of the cab. As always, their platoon leader is both confident and reassuring, inciting the squad to follow his lead. Tripp's not worried. His eyes wander across the fireground, dancing over men in bunkers, precariously propped ladders, and trucks with flashing lights. They finally catch and linger on the brilliant yellow and orange tones of the flames erupting violently from the third floor of the little rowhome, unable to keep from noticing the way they lick and light up the dark, midnight sky above.

It's almost beautiful. *Almost.*

This is nobody riding Engine Fifteen's first rodeo, and as such, no one makes the rookie mistake of bolting from the truck before it's even been directed toward its final parking space. Out of the path from drafting hoses being laid (but still close enough to be useful), their engineer, Theo, throws the e-brake, which sends the truck into a high-idle to drive power to the ladder and pump panel.

As Tripp awaits direction (with his air pack wedged awkwardly between him and the seat and therefore digging obnoxiously into his back), his blood thrums hot in his veins. It's been many years and hundreds of fires both large and small since Tripp was new to all of this, but the shine has yet to wear off. This is what he *loves,* what he feels called to be doing, but that doesn't mean the reality isn't stressful.

Adjusting the straps of the pack where they press against the bunker jacket covering his chest, Tripp unconsciously double-checks every piece of gear he's wearing. Almost a nervous habit, the routine to do so is second-nature. His hands move assuredly over his uniform while his eyes watch the fire, his brain and ears remaining alert and tuned in for Gunnar's orders.

Most of Tripp's gear is still in standby mode—his air tank is full, his PASS device has fresh batteries, and his self-contained breathing apparatus is hanging from his neck. His hood and gloves are tucked inside the helmet bearing his name and rank on the front, and the helmet itself is cradled protectively in his lap. Those items all stay where they are, for the moment. Since Gunnar instructed them to hold off on packing up fully, Tripp's happy to oblige. He's not trying to turn himself into a human oven-mitt any sooner than necessary.

The rest of his checklist includes things that he could (and has) donned in his sleep: heavy, fire-rated turnout pants, coat, and boots, and all of it stacked over his regular duty uniform blues.

Tripp does have a secret, though. No one can see, but in addition to all of his regulation safety gear, he's *also* wearing his "happy hamburger" socks. Black, novelty tube socks, with red heels and little cheeseburgers stitched all over them. It's innocent—just the tiniest act of rebellion squirreled away beneath layers of clothing and fire-resistant Kevlar. Good luck socks are Tripp's *thing,* and sure, maybe no one actually *knows* they're his thing, but no one can take them away, either.

The engine Tripp's currently sitting in happens to be one of several trucks requested from his base, Station Fifteen, and since they were dispatched on an upgraded alarm, they're late to the party. As the third company to roll up to the active fireground, it's no surprise to see that the fight to beat the fire back is already going full-force. There's a crew inside the house executing an interior attack, a second engine setting up for exterior shots, plus the Rapid Intervention Team (RIT, for short) is packed up and standing by, hoping to remain unneeded.

Tripp's limited view from the truck's window tells him that a Battalion Chief is here, judging by the Sup vehicle abandoned halfway up on the sidewalk. There's also a handful of cop cars blocking traffic, and at least one ambulance curb-sitting a couple of houses down.

Distantly, over the crackling, snapping noise of the fire and people yelling to each other outside of the truck, Tripp hears Gunnar speaking into the radio clipped to his shoulder, communicating with whoever has scene command at the moment. Tripp assumes that would be one of the chiefs and the owner of that shoddily-parked Supervisor SUV—maybe Assistant Chief Walter, but probably Mickey Miller. Their Battalion Chief isn't exactly one to sit this kind of thing out.

"Alrigh' fellas," Gunnar starts, relaying the message through the headsets from his place in the passenger's seat at the front of the cab. "Chief Miller wants another stream on the northwest windows of the third floor, right where the visible flames are pushing through. There's a missing kid down on the first level, but Eleven is on it."

The 'Eleven' Gunnar is referring to would be the first-in crew—the company on the initial dispatch, and the one currently rushing through the front door of the rowhome with their hose line charged and at the ready. Even though everyone on Engine Fifteen knew this was coming, there's a murmur of disappointment-laced acknowledgment that ripples through the truck as Tripp and his crew nod and comply, exiting the vehicle with laden-down *thuds* as their boots hit the concrete.

The general dissent doesn't linger. It lasts for only a fleeting moment before evaporating completely as everyone springs into action. Jealousy forgotten, they move efficiently as a team, working to get their truck ready and their hoses connected, charged, and firing as much water as possible onto the burning house.

Tripp's eyes water when the smoky air hits them, but he blinks the discomfort away.

He gets the grumbling. He's right there with his co-workers, not that he'd ever *outwardly* let on. Every part of the job is important, every responding unit (and its crew) is as valuable as the next. There are no small tasks, everyone's a hero, and blah, blah, freaking *blah*. It's just that Tripp—and every other red-blooded, bunker-wearing human on this scene—*really* wants to be inside of that house.

That's just a fact. Firefighters do not sit around dreaming and longing for the day when they get to straddle a five-inch in the middle of a soggy street lit only by emergency lights, directing high-pressure water into a broken window high above their heads.

To be completely fair, that's definitely not the *worst* task in the world, either. Regardless, everyone wants to be the one on the nozzle. The hero leading the rescue team, the *guy—gender neutral—*in the absolute *fucking* thick of it. No one wants to be left hanging on the periphery, standing on the edge of the action and doing the necessary—but not nearly as exciting—firefighter version of busywork.

And yet, that's exactly where Tripp finds himself today. Orders are orders.

After just a few minutes, though, he ends up passing the hose off to a probie, Aydin, who's dying for it. Tripp's antsy, wanting to wander around and see what Mickey's doing, what his plan is for this whole show. Hey, if he can't get in on the real action, he can at least be nosy and find out what's happening inside the burn straight from the source. Nothing more he can do for Fifteen right now, anyway. Well, besides making sure that Aydin sprays straight, and keeping Theo company at the pump controls.

There's also the fact that in the several minutes Tripp was on the hose, there was absolutely no sign of Engine Eleven's crew. Not a flash of bunker jacket or a single radio crackle. That's sort of suspicious—makes Tripp's skin crawl. At the very least, the crew should be updating command via their radios, but there are no PASS devices alarming, so they must be alright. Vaguely, Tripp considers the friends he has at Eleven and wonders who, exactly, is manning their station tonight.

He rounds the truck and lets Gunnar know that he's going to take a look around, receiving the "A-OK" on his request without any kind of fuss. On the hunt for Mickey, Tripp has to pick his way around hose lines and the multiple hydrants being hooked up to help douse the flames—they're everywhere, crisscrossing the pavement like snakes. Other crews are busy soaking the adjacent houses to prevent the fire from jumping, but there's so damn many *people* on the scene that Tripp feels almost superfluous.

Maybe Mickey'll have something I can do, he thinks to himself, stupidly hopeful. Truthfully, smart money would be on Mickey calling him a dumbass and telling him to fuck off out of his hair so that he can concentrate properly, but Tripp's just bored enough to risk it.

Before he can even walk five feet away from his truck, though, alarms start sounding. A combination of PASS devices activating from inside the house, emergency buttons being pressed, and panicked yelling over the radios themselves pierces the distracted fog of his brain and fills the night air.

"Tripp!" Gunnar hollers out from somewhere behind him, and Tripp whirls around, ready. "Pack up, cupcake. Eleven's out, we're taking over the rescue. That kid is still in there."

In an instant, everything except for the task ahead of him flies out of Tripp's head. His focus sharpens and narrows as he mentally reviews what will be expected of him, visually assessing the burning house using his limited knowledge of the layout in order to develop a plan of attack. In his peripheral vision, the RIT team—already packed up and ready—is charging through the darkened front door, off to rescue whoever went down from Eleven and to bring their whole team back out safely. The RIT assignment is ninety-five percent standing around doing nothing, and five percent pure adrenaline.

Tripp doesn't pay them much mind. While he's definitely worried about Eleven (natural, when he has friends at every station in the city), this type of situation is a part of the job, and it's precisely what having a dedicated RIT team is for: rescuing the rescuers.

Less than two minutes after Gunnar's order, Tripp's standing outside the front door with a nozzle in hand and the rest of his newly-minted search and rescue team lined up on the pipe behind him. By that time, RIT is already extricating, leaving the house carrying two injured firefighters on Reeves. They move past Fifteen's hose team in a wave of smoke, bringing the victims over to where EMS is running rehab so that they can be assessed.

A quick glance towards the rehab tent tells Tripp that there are only two ambulances on scene right now. He frowns, pausing before entering the house to radio Gunnar and ask for status on a third. Thinking ahead is important, since the kid they're about to go looking for is more likely than not to need care, if not resus. Words the Chief told him during his probationary period years ago echo in Tripp's head: *Hope for the best, prepare for the worst.*

"On the way, sugar," Gunnar's Louisiana accent crackles next to his ear. "Coming from Central, ETA four to five. Everyone from Eleven is accounted for, you're cleared to enter the building. Make good choices, brotha."

Behind his face shield, Tripp can't help but roll his eyes at the sarcastic note in Gunnar's voice. He does know that the Captain means well, so he traps the return barbs that bubble up in his throat, instead zeroing in on what he has to do. A hand patting his shoulder says that his team is ready, and with it, Tripp advances forward. Easy, low and tight to the wall, assessing for structural integrity as he steps in through the blackened doorway.

The first floor is dark and thick with the odor of fire and smoke, but it's relatively clear. From the intel Gunnar received, there must've been some miscommunication with Eleven—the kid was never on the first floor to begin with. It's now up to Tripp and the rest of Fifteen to find him, wherever he might be hiding, somewhere on the second level. With the flames pouring freely from the third floor windows, Tripp doesn't allow himself to dwell on the implications of someone being stuck any higher in the building—they'll cross that bridge when they (hopefully don't) come to it.

As he and his team are climbing the stairs, their breathing loud inside their masks and their arms full of hose line, Gunnar's voice sounds again over the radio. "Idiot on Eleven tripped and took her buddy down with her. No one's seriously hurt, 'less we're talkin' ego. Only relaying so you don't get all up in your head—I know how you are. Evac wasn't even fire-related. Tripp, mother says the kid's name is Ben, room is a left off of the stairs and two doors down on the right."

"Ten-Four, Cap," Tripp replies after depressing the button on the speaker mic clipped to his epaulette. At the top of the stairs, he follows Gunnar's directions. The smoke pervading the second floor is much thicker, forcing the firefighters to get down on their knees and stay close to the ground, moving frustratingly slowly as they slog forward on all-fours. Tripp fumbles a little as he works to juggle holding onto the nozzle *and* feeling along the wall for molding or breaks that indicate doors.

"One," he calls out to the team members behind him, knowing that they heard Gunnar's message over their own radios. Normally, they'd be checking every room and clearing as they went, but time is of the essence here, and they're working with reliable intel that there's only one person to rescue *and* that he's likely in the second room. The house isn't particularly stable, either—drywall and beams creaking and snapping around them—and Tripp has no desire to be on the rescue-needing-end of a RIT team tonight.

"Two," he declares, holding out a hand to stop Aydin, who's right on his heels, from slamming a helmet into his ass.

Making quick work of a heat-check to the door, Tripp decides that it's unlikely there's fire behind it and turns the knob to shove it open. Sure as he was, the room *is* almost directly below where the fire is raging, so he still breathes a sigh of relief when it turns out the flames haven't spread. Unfortunately, while wet marks are steadily tracking down the walls from where hoses are flooding water into the house from outside, the fire is nowhere near controlled.

"Ben!" Tripp calls out, but there's no reply. They look to be in the right place, at least, if his bedroom is where Ben is hiding. Definitely decorated to be a young boy's room—sports posters on the walls that are curling and falling, shriveling in the heat and threatening to catch. A twin bed boasts a Lightning McQueen comforter and matching pillow, and toys and clothes are scattered all over the floor.

A quick glance around doesn't reveal anything overtly out of place, save for the smoky conditions that are worsening by the minute. From where he's crouched, Tripp can confidently clear the space underneath the bed—no Ben.

Within seconds, he clocks the closed closet door that's directly across the room and locks onto it. Tripp follows his instincts, standing and striding over to throw the door wide, feeling conflicting swells of relief and fear at what he sees inside as he drops back down into a crouch. Ben is curled up small and motionless in the farthest corner of the dark space, his skinny arms wrapped tightly around his legs, his head buried firmly in between them.

"Ben," Tripp repeats, this time more gently as he reaches out to touch Ben's arm. The closet wouldn't have done the boy any favors if the flames had spread to this room, but it actually seems to have kept some of the smoke out, or perhaps the clothing hanging above Ben's head provided some filtration. Tripp isn't sure, but whatever the reason, Ben is relievedly awake. Lifting his head, the boy blinks owlishly up at him, looking terrified and sleepy. He's got soot on his face, ash under his nose and around his lips, and while he seems to be compensating well at the moment, Tripp realizes that time is of the essence—much longer spent inside this house and Ben will be in deep trouble.

"Come on, buddy," he urges, opening his arms and wrapping them around Ben's little body as he eagerly climbs into them, clinging on tight. This close, Tripp can feel that his breathing is raspy and rattled. He stands and activates the mic with his free hand as soon as they're set. "Coming out with one, awake and alert but needs EMS, Mom can meet us."

Abandoning the nozzle, Tripp brushes past the rest of Fifteen's crew to exit down the stairs, knowing that his people will take care of the hose line and whatever interior attack Mickey orders next. Ben is the priority right now, and Tripp's extremely glad that he didn't have to warn Gunnar to keep the boy's mom at bay. It's nothing he takes pleasure in doing, and only would've happened if Ben was found in worse condition. Hurt kids are something no emergency responder wants to see—something that's almost universally dreaded and generally agreed upon to be nightmare fuel—and devastated parents are their own tragedy.

Not today, Tripp resolves, his gloved hand cupping the back of Ben's head protectively, the kid's face buried in the fabric of his bunker jacket.

Stepping out into the LED-lit front yard and emergency-vehicle-strewn street, Tripp blinks against the harsh, bright lights and looks around for the raised hand he knows will be there. *Gunnar.* Standing to one side of the scene, out by the curb, his Captain is waving wildly, trying to attract Tripp's attention. His eyes find their target just as Gunnar's voice comes over the radio.

"To your left, sugar."

It feels like every eye on location is following them as he and Ben exit stage left, but only for a minute, and then they're back to focusing on the project everyone was sent here to solve. *Rescue. Contain. Extinguish.* So far, so good, even considering Eleven's minor mistake.

Shit happens.

Out of the direct glare of the lights, Tripp's able to find and focus on the EMT standing next to Gunnar on the sidewalk—a familiar red-headed pixie that he's extremely happy to see. Marley, EMT-Basic extraordinaire and Tripp's best friend, grins as he steps up, turning Ben in his arms so she can eyeball an assessment.

Marley's holding an oxygen tank in a bag slung around her shoulder and has a non-rebreather mask inflated and at the ready. She's great with kids, and it takes very little coaxing for Ben to allow her to apply the mask. Despite that, he continues clinging to Tripp, even as his mother rushes to his side, grabbing at his torso and kissing his head from the side, sobbing into his hair. Sometimes that happens—kids are quick to bond to their rescuers.

"Thank god, thank god," Tripp hears the mom crying.

"Let's move this to the ambulance," Gunnar murmurs, more for the mother's benefit than anything else. He takes the distraught woman's elbow and gently guides her towards the box truck, idling with its lights flashing. She keeps looking over her shoulder to thank Tripp, crying and gushing profusely, but he barely notices.

In another world, this woman would be exactly his type, what with the dark hair and the dark eyes, and the yoga pants that leave absolutely nothing to the imagination. Maybe it'd be something to consider if everything in his life wasn't already in the process of changing.

Marley opens the side door to the ambulance and Tripp climbs in, Ben's positioning in his arms initially preventing him from seeing the paramedic who is occupying the back. Whoever it is must be setting up their gear, preparing for the worst while Marley went and retrieved their patient.

At the top of the three steps into the box, Tripp turns and nearly comes nose-to-nose with a pair of *very* familiar blue eyes. They crinkle at their corners at the sight of him, and in response, his stomach turns over, doing its best to tie itself in knots while *Tripp* does his damnedest not to let it show.

"Heya, Lee," Tripp says. The greeting comes out a little breathless, which he hopes can be attributed to his current situation and not the reality, which is that he's *always* a little too happy to see his best friend. Leander just smiles back, motioning for Tripp to hand the boy over, which Gunnar doesn't seem overly thrilled about, but allows. Gunnar's big on doing the heavy lifting for the ambulance crews whenever it's possible, and most of them love him for it, but not Leander. He mostly takes the rule as a personal affront to his biceps.

"Hello, Tripp," Leander replies, settling Ben onto the stretcher and introducing himself, immediately producing and handing over an inflated nitrile glove with a smiley face drawn in permanent marker on the palm. The endearment works— Ben gleefully accepts the gift, and does so with the untempered spark of someone who was not in life-threatening danger mere moments prior. Kids are heckin' resilient like that, though it's something that never fails to floor Tripp, seeing it live and in person.

Behind him, Gunnar is shutting the oxygen tank on Tripp's back off before moving to tug at his helmet and hood so that Tripp can move a little easier around the ambulance. He bats Gunnar's hands away, taking off his own mask before reluctantly allowing Gunnar to slip the tank from his shoulders, mostly so he doesn't accidentally destroy some of Lee's equipment in the process. Finally free from the worst of his protective gear, Tripp shakes his sweaty head and works his jaw before turning to give Gunnar the full attention he's waiting on.

"Stay with Lee," Gunnar instructs. "Do whatever he needs you to do—I'm assuming he's gonna want Marley in the back helping out, so you'll need to drive. Hit me up by radio if y'all need anything, you hear me?"

Tripp nods, reaching out a hand to fist bump his Captain in acknowledgement before Gunnar escapes back out the side door. He watches through the window as Gunnar returns to the active fire scene, checking in with Command and getting back to work. He takes Tripp's pack with him, but leaves the rest of his gear.

When Tripp turns around again, Marley has the back door open and is standing there with Ben's mother, who is still sobbing and bereft. Leander catches Tripp's gaze and raises an eyebrow, to which Tripp holds up an understanding hand.

"Say no more," he says, before exiting out the side of the ambulance, closing the door, and making his way towards the back. "I got her and I'll drive," he tells Marley, who eyes him gratefully before climbing in with Lee and pulling the doors shut behind her.

Plastering on his most empathetic face, Tripp wraps an arm around the petite woman's shoulders and moves to guide her towards the cab of the ambulance and the front passenger's seat. "What's your name, sweetheart?" he asks kindly, waiting patiently as the woman sniffles and wipes her nose on her sleeve. Tripp realizes belatedly that it's actually a bathrobe, which is not surprising, considering how the fire clearly caught this family off guard, flaring to life in the dead of night.

"Liza," she replies choppily, tipping her head to blink up at him with big, watery eyes.

Hoo, boy. Definitely in another time and place, Tripp thinks.

"Thank you," she tells him, stopping Tripp's arm as he reaches for the door handle like the gentleman he is. "Honestly, I can never—"

"You're welcome." Tripp cuts her off gently but genuinely, removing her hand from his arm—not unkindly—before opening the door, assisting when she struggles to climb up and inside. "It was my pleasure, glad we could be here. We're all just relieved that everyone is okay. Houses, clothes, even pictures—all that stuff is replaceable, you guys aren't." Liza nods as she looks down at him and Tripp offers her a soft smile, reaching out again to squeeze her hand briefly, a small gesture of comfort and reassurance. "It's all going to be okay."

"Okay," Liza echoes, nodding down at her lap as if she's trying to convince herself. "Okay."

"Seatbelt," Tripp reminds her as he closes the door.

Having been trained to drive all of the fire apparatus, maneuvering the box ambulance is a breeze. Although, Tripp does have to keep reminding himself that there are people in the back, that he can't take turns at sixty miles per hour and on two wheels—not if he wants Lee to make it to the hospital concussion-free.

On the way there, Tripp collects some basic info from Ben's mom, relaying the important pieces to Lee through the pass-through window cut between the cab and the box. Once at the hospital, he takes it upon himself to register the kid while Lee and Marley are transferring him to a room and giving report to the Emergency Department team assuming care.

When Tripp's done his part and then some, he meets the two EMS providers back at the ambulance where they're cleaning and restocking used supplies. Tripp props his booted foot up on the truck's fender, shivering a little in the chilly night air. He slipped his bunker jacket off before driving to the hospital—it was too warm and too confining for that particular task—but he kind of misses it now, since all he had underneath was a short-sleeved t-shirt.

"I told you to wear your long-sleeved tee," Leander grumbles, barely looking up from where he's organizing IV supplies back into the kit. His dark, messy hair is in a worse state than usual, looking as if each strand is determined to go in a different direction, just to piss off Tripp. It makes his stupidly handsome face look even more so than usual, and it's distracting enough that Tripp fails at coming up with a snappy retort.

"Geez, I knew you two were attached at the hip, but he's dressing you now, Truett?" Marley teases him as she slides the door to one of the storage cabinets shut, pumping some sanitizer into her palm and rubbing both hands together until they're dry.

"Fuck you," Tripp mumbles back, shoving a hand down inside his bunker gear to fish in the pocket of his regular pants and find his phone. Technically, he's not supposed to have it inside a live burn, but who's telling? Ducking his head to hide the flush in his cheeks, he drags up Gunnar's number and shoots off a text message: *Pick me the hell up, bitch.*

"No, he doesn't *dress* me. We were drinkin' last night and I passed out on his couch." It's a half-truth, but it's not like Tripp's about to disclose to Marley (or anyone else) what he and Lee were *actually* doing until two a.m., or what they have planned for tonight. Swallowing hard, Tripp struggles to compose himself after flashing back to that discussion, determinedly ignoring the interested twitch his dick gives, a movement that's thankfully hidden beneath several layers of *very* thick material.

When he finally glances up from his phone, Tripp's not remotely shocked to see Leander staring back at him and smirking openly. While Marley might be oblivious, Leander knows *exactly* what he's thinking about. Probably knows what his dick is doing in his pants, too, smug bastard. To make matters worse, Lee is now lounging against the ambulance wall with one foot propped up on the stretcher. He's oh-so-casual, infuriatingly calm, his crotch and the outline of what he's packing on easy display in his duty pants, and his piercing gaze challenging when it meets Tripp's.

Narrowing his eyes, Tripp replies without words as loudly as he possibly can.

"Will you be needing a ride back to the fire scene?" Leander asks, completely cool, totally nonchalant, but Tripp doesn't miss the way his fingers trail up the inside of his thigh, coming to rest scant inches from his groin.

"No," he manages to reply, voice slightly strained. "Gunnar, uh—" He checks his phone and bites back a grimace. Gunnar won't be able to come grab him for at least another thirty minutes, but no way is he going to let Leander in on that. If there's one thing Tripp is sure of right now, it's that he can't be stuck in a confined space with his best friend while they're both on work duty.

He can't—the teasing is cute, but if it keeps up, one of them is going to end up dead, fired, or worse. His thoughts slightly addled, Tripp pulls his shit together for long enough to remember the point he was trying to make. "You guys go on and head out, Gunnar's gonna come grab me." It's not a lie, and Tripp'll die on this hill if that's what he has to do.

"Alright," Leander replies easily, dusting off his pants as he stands. The devious smile on his face belies the fact that he knows *exactly* what Tripp is doing, and is more than happy to let him make his own bed *and* lie in it.

Very abruptly, Tripp realizes exactly how deep he is in this, that Leander doesn't think he even needs to be in the same *room* to torture and distract him. The truly awful thing is, he's right. Even worse, Tripp is *super* into it, wouldn't bail on this whole thing for all the bacon cheeseburgers in the universe *and* the metabolism to put them away.

As Leander steps down out of the truck, he drops a heavy hand to Tripp's shoulder, squeezing hard and for long enough to send a pointed message that Tripp and his dick receive loud and clear. Marley follows behind, jumping off the bumper and shooting each of them a concerned look in turn.

"Are you guys alright? There's something…" She narrows her eyes and waves an index finger back and forth, covering the charged space between them. "Something in the air, here."

"We're fine," Tripp retorts, waving dismissively as Leander wordlessly shrugs. They're saved from further prodding—and possibly the Spanish Inquisition, because Marley can be like a dog with a bone when she thinks she's onto something—by tones dropping over the radio clipped to Leander's hip.

"City Medic Four respond. 800 Park Avenue at Sunny Acres Retirement Home, Room 1501 for an ALS Medical."

Immediately, Leander's demeanor shifts, morphing into the consummate professional Tripp knows him to be. To be honest, watching that transformation only makes the situation in Tripp's pants increasingly dire.

"Marley," Leander says, all confidence and a take-no-shit attitude. "Please put our unit available and responding to that call. Ask Dispatch to leave Four on standby at the fire scene while they complete overhaul."

"Aye-aye, Captain," Marley affirms with a sloppy salute, holding that same hand up for Tripp to slap high-five as she passes by him before climbing into the truck. "Later, skater."

"Bye, nerd."

As Leander closes the back doors to the ambulance, he lingers inside Tripp's personal space bubble, only for a moment. "Will I still see you later?" he asks softly, his hand hovering *just* above Tripp's chest, and *God,* does Tripp ache to close the space between them. It's all he can do to remind himself that this is a *tease,* this is

Lee fucking with him, nothing more. It's not romance, it's not affection, it's just... foreplay.

Good foreplay, but still.

They are not a couple. They are not on their way to *being* a couple, no matter what the already-crossed wires in Tripp's head might want to believe. It's a mind-fuck, for sure, but sex and flirting? That Tripp can do. He would never have agreed to this—this *thing* that Lee suggested, if compartmentalizing wasn't already his strong suit.

Love 'em and leave 'em, that is his personal M.O., after all.

"You know it," Tripp replies gruffly, hoping that the rough scratch of his voice translates as pure arousal and not the mess of conflicted emotions that being around an openly sexual *Lee* unwillingly brings out in him. To both Tripp's great relief and incredible disappointment, Leander gives nothing away, just grins knowingly at Tripp before stepping away and disappearing around the side of the vehicle.

Tripp watches from beneath the neon-lit red and blue lettering that spells "EMERGENCY / TRAUMA" across the overhang as the ambulance pulls away, vanishing around the corner in a blur of flashing lights and wailing sirens.

What the fuck has he gotten himself into?

***

The final hours of Tripp's shift drag, and not only because he spends a chunk of it sitting on a freezing cold bench outside Central's ER with only a t-shirt on and absolutely nothing to do. It winds up taking longer than anticipated for Gunnar and Fifteen's engine crew to be released from the fire scene and to swing by the ER to pick him up. Long enough that Tripp has to hide around the corner of the building when Lee and Marley's truck returns to drop off the patient they transported from the nursing home, leaving him to reevaluate his life from the shadows.

Normally in a situation like this, Tripp would just text his younger brother Beau. Kid's a trauma surgeon here at Central, and—barring any surgeries getting in the way—is usually down to hang out in the cushy doctor's lounge for however long. His luck must be in the toilet, though, because Beau's not working tonight.

Humiliatingly enough, the waiting and hiding ends up being for nothing after all, since Leander and Marley wound up swinging by the fire scene to return Tripp's coat, the one he accidentally left in the cab of the ambulance. Back at the station, Gunnar hands it over with a questioning look, ultimately taking pity when the color drains from Tripp's face and he drops his forehead into a sweaty hand.

"Don't ask," he mumbles into his palm.

"Whatever you say, brotha," Gunnar replies easily, but Tripp catches him smirking as he saunters away across the fire bay. That reaction provokes a spike of anxiety in his gut, a baseless suspicion that Gunnar might *know* something, even though there's no possible way that could be true.

When the clock strikes midnight, Tripp's out of the station like a shot, freshly showered to ditch the residual smoke and sweat clinging to his skin, and dressed in clean clothing that was packed for this express purpose. He's in his car and halfway across town to Leander's apartment before the nerves really start to settle in, and the questions *(reservations?!)* begin running through his mind.

Is this really a good idea? What if Lee isn't actually into it, what if he's just humoring Tripp and his grossly-obvious crush? Worse, what if Lee is as into it as he claims, but Tripp turns out to be a big fuckin' disappointment? What if Leander regrets this thing in the morning?

What if they both do?

It's tough, because there's no question in Tripp's mind—he wants whatever pieces of Lee he can get. They're best friends and that's great, he wouldn't change that for the world. But Tripp's also an idiot, and he somehow let himself fall for the one guy who doesn't *do* romance, the one person on the planet who would never see him that way, even if he did.

It's too late for Tripp's feelings, that shit is a done deal. A smarter man, a *wiser* man would likely point out that getting physical with Lee won't make them easier to deal with, not by a long shot, but Tripp *wants*.

He wants to touch Lee, wants to know what it's like to be touched by him. With this offer, with the *knowledge* that Lee is open to it—how the hell is Tripp supposed to pass that up? Maybe other people are stronger or smarter than him, but when the dude he's been pining over for *years* offers to straight up fuck him 'til he passes out, all in the name of "stress relief," well. Tripp simply feels that hollering, *"fuck, yeah,"* in response is actually a really understandable reply.

Maybe it would have been easier for him to say no, or at least to hesitate, if they didn't have the whole BDSM thing working like padding to ease them into it. Lee has never hidden his life as a Dom—the opposite, really. In fact, he's *so* open about it, he's probably responsible for half of the City Fire & EMS crews being twice as satisfied with what goes on in their bedrooms than they were before he moved to town.

And while Tripp's never actually *done* any of that submissive stuff—or even admitted to anyone besides Lee that he *would*—he really wants to. The truth is, Tripp's long been interested in dipping his toes into those proverbial waters. That is, *if* he could find someone suitable and trustworthy enough to take him for a swim.

… Which isn't to say that he *meant* to suggest he'd be open to Leander doing exactly that, what with his experience, and the fuckin' *playroom* in his apartment, and his *very* big muscles that could maneuver Tripp around by the hair as he— *wait, what was he thinking about?*

Right. So maybe he struck up a couple of leading conversations. Maybe he asked a few too many pointed questions. Maybe he let the back-and-forth banter between him and Lee wander further into the dirty and sordid more often than he should have, for a guy who just wanted to be friends.

But hell—Lee was low-risk back when they started hanging out, no matter what the subject matter of the shit they talked might've been. At the time, the guy had a long-term, *contractually-bound* submissive, and while Lee was as vocal about his indifference to both gender and sexuality as he was passionate about BDSM itself, the sub *was* female, and Tripp didn't want to make any assumptions.

Especially when Lee *also* had no qualms in declaring publicly that his relationship with said sub was "exclusive, sexual-platonic", whatever the fuck *that* meant. After some probing, Tripp concluded that it was Lee's phrase for "fuck-buddies," or contractual friends with benefits, no other strings attached.

Sure. Whatever.

To be fair, it was *Lee* who brought up the idea of changing things between them, and only after he definitively ended things with said *fuck buddy*. Tripp isn't privy to the details of exactly what happened in that fallout, and he doesn't intend to ask. All he knows is that the chick, Autumn, wanted more emotionally than Leander was prepared to give.

Truthfully, the way Lee talked about her—the way he talks about romance and romantic relationships in general, actually—was always *cold*, and it made Tripp's heart sink every time. Not that he thought he had a shot to begin with, but it was still tough to hear reality stated so bluntly, so plain. Bottom line, Lee doesn't do romance, and that's fine.

Thing is, though, Tripp does. He's a damn romantic at heart, actually. Whether he *admits* that truth out loud to other people is neither here nor there, but being open about his feelings and being self-aware are two *very* different concepts. Tripp is unquestionably one but not the other.

For that reason alone, he's still not sure whether taking Lee up on the offer to let *him* fill the "subby fuck buddy" space at Lee's relationship table is the brightest idea. Sure, Lee has a point. They both could use the outlet. Stressful jobs and all, unprocessed trauma, and Lee isn't used to lacking someone he can turn to in that way. He actually told Tripp that he was feeling a little "lost and ungrounded" in his life since breaking things off with Autumn, and what the hell was Tripp supposed to do with that? He can't very well have his best friend feeling *ungrounded,* not when there's something *incredibly* simple that he could do about it.

Getting fucked by six feet of gorgeous hard muscle, pouty full lips, and magnetic blue eyes isn't exactly a hardship in Tripp's book, anyway.

So when Leander raised the possibility of trying it out, in the magic of the midnight hour, both of them tipsy and goofy from one too many frozen margaritas, yes, he jumped. Jumped on it so fast that Leander seemed surprised, and wasn't *that* embarrassing? At the end of the day, though, this is *Lee,* and Tripp can't help what he wants.

Pretty much from the day they met, Lee has been it for him, reciprocation be damned. Tripp would wait forever if he thought that would matter, would let Lee set whatever boundaries he needed, would accept *half* of Lee, or an eighth, because just being around the weird, nerdy, *freaky* confident paramedic makes him fuckin' happy. Happy in a way that nothing else has come close to reaching in years.

Maybe that's pathetic, but Tripp's accepted the situation for what it is. If this submissive thing is what he can get, if this is the most Lee is willing and able to *give,* Tripp will take it. He'll take it gladly and gratefully, and be damn thankful for it.

All's said and done, he's got a best friend who he can close down bars and shoot pool and drink beers and watch cowboy movies with, who can practically read his mind on emergency scenes, and who Tripp would trust with his very life. If they can add occasionally fucking—and maybe some other extra-dirty stuff, details of which he isn't overtly clear on yet—to the way they define their friendship, then that'll be a bonus.

Tripp can be content with that. He can. It's enough.

By the time he reaches Leander's soaring apartment highrise, Tripp is once again feeling calm and sure of his choices. He flashes back on the conversation he and

Lee shared the night before: the "kinks" list they pored over in excruciating detail, the safewords they picked, and the hard limits they set. Leander was *very* serious, ultra-methodical, and Tripp was both surprised and turned on by it, as much if not more than the teasing version of Lee he saw at the hospital today.

During that conversation, Tripp vocalized his suspicion that Lee would be a professional, career Dominant-for-Hire if he could, but his friend denied that, at first. When pressed, though, Lee admitted that he's held back from attempting such a thing based on his own inability to work with strangers.

"I need an emotional connection with someone in order to develop an interest in dominating them," Leander explained breezily, as if he was speaking about the way he takes his coffee. The pen he was using to mark up their contracts tipped and twirled between the lithe, thick fingers of his right hand, the only outward sign that he was nervous at all.

"Really? You couldn't just—"

"I *could*, yes, but it wouldn't be satisfying for me. I know that must seem strange, seeing as how it was my lack of romantic feelings for Autumn that prompted me to move on. I assure you though, Tripp, an emotional connection does not automatically translate to romance. Or love, for that matter."

That explanation made sense enough to Tripp, and it certainly helped explain why Leander would be interested in *him,* specifically. An "emotional connection" is definitely something the two of them have always shared—they just clicked, day one, right off the bat. Besides his own brother, Leander is far and away the best friend Tripp has ever had, no contest.

So cognitively, the whole thing tracks. Knowing more about Lee's needs, and equally, that Lee is very aware of Tripp's own stress and wants to help him, *as a friend,* it's reassuring. Those things allow Tripp to set certain boundaries in his own mind, to manage his expectations. This is an arrangement. A mutually beneficial, *stress-relieving* arrangement, between two otherwise platonic friends, and nothing more.

Tripp is fine with that.

If he wants this, then he has to be.

Tripp parks in the lot. He locks his car and strolls up the concrete sidewalk outside of Leander's building. Nodding a greeting to the doorman, he heads over to the elevator bank, enters the first open car, and presses the button for Lee's floor. As he does, it suddenly occurs to him that he wants this *very* badly.

Not just the sex and the opportunity for an excuse to be close to Leander, but the submissive aspect, too, even if—and despite the long-ass kinks list—he isn't *exactly* sure of what he's getting into. A new shiver of excitement ripples down his spine. It raises the hairs on his arms, even underneath the long-sleeved tee he's wearing and his heavy leather jacket.

Tripp watches as the glowing numbers cycle higher, anticipation rising along with the interest in his pants. Scowling, he glares down at his slightly-swollen groin and wills his dick to behave—the last thing he wants to do is appear over-eager or desperate. This is brand new territory for both of them and Tripp would never forgive himself for scaring Lee off by barging into his apartment with his traitorous dick already trying to run the show.

The idea of Leander rejecting him takes care of that issue like gangbusters, and by the time he's knocking on the guy's front door, Tripp's not entirely sure he could get it up if he wanted to. His nerves are flying back to hit him full force, heart pounding away in his chest like a drum. Is Lee going to open the door dressed head-to-toe in leather, maybe carrying a whip? Is he going to yank Tripp violently inside, shove him down to his knees and piss down his throat?

Ridiculous. The last sane brain cell Tripp possesses—thankfully—shows up to chastise him. First of all, he reminds himself, 'Watersports' is on both of your hard limit lists. Second, this is still Lee.

Despite that, when the door opens and Lee is there, dressed in soft, gray sweatpants paired with a navy blue t-shirt that has the City's EMS logo on the breast, Tripp can't help but breathe a sigh of relief. He's right, it *is* still Lee, his best friend in the whole damn world, and seeing him look so casually comfortable while *also* knowing what they're about to do makes Tripp want him more than ever.

"Hello, Tripp," Leander says warmly, stepping back to hold the door open as he enters. It's strange, because Tripp's been in Lee's space hundreds of times—passed out on the couch, next to the toilet, and even in Lee's *bed* more nights than he can count—but tonight, it feels new and different. In a good way, one that makes his fingers and toes tingle, but new all the same.

Looking around, Tripp cognitively understands that there's no reason for him to feel that way—he was here twenty-four hours ago and it's unchanged. Hell, there's an empty beer bottle with his DNA on it still sitting on a side table. Tripp wanders further in, the entryway bleeding into an open-plan family room with a step-up kitchen to the right and three closed doors across the way. From experience, Tripp knows that they lead to two bedrooms and the generous bathroom connecting them, all spaces he's extremely familiar with, except for one.

Also from experience, Tripp knows that the door on the left is Lee's bedroom, and the one on the right is their destination tonight.

"Tripp," Leander says softly, his hand on Tripp's forearm making him flinch and pull away. Even though it's a reflex, Tripp can see the hurt on Leander's face, no matter how quickly he schools it away. "We don't have to do this," Leander reassures him. "There's no pressure here. We could just have a beer, watch some TV."

Sucking in a deep breath and letting it out slowly, Tripp mentally slaps himself. This isn't the start to the night he was imagining, and he deeply regrets making Leander think that he's second-guessing things. He's on edge, not looking for an out. *Big difference.*

"No," he says firmly, punctuating his answer with a shake of his head. "No, Lee, I'm sorry, man. It's not you, I swear, I'm just… " Tripp raises his gaze to meet Leander's eyes, and surprisingly, finds only soft understanding and patience there. Lee smiles, and Tripp can't help but smile back. His friend's grin has always been contagious as far as Tripp's concerned, and their mirroring breaks the tension.

After another controlled, deep breath, he steps into Leander's space.

They stand there like that for a long moment, just breathing the shared air, eyes darting around each other's faces. On instinct, Tripp leans down to close the space between them, completely forgetting himself, forgetting that there are *rules* to what they're doing, that this isn't just some casual hookup or the start of a romance. It takes the gentle clearing of Leander's throat, and two fingers pressed against his lips to prevent their mouths from connecting, to bring him back.

"Tripp," Lee repeats. "I have no problem with—that is, I know that we discussed kissing, but I think we should set the scene first, for both of our sakes. Boundaries and limits, they're important." His voice wavers slightly, and it marks the first moment in *any* interaction Tripp has *ever* had with Leander—regarding BDSM and / or their potential relationship—where the man hasn't seemed confidently in charge, the dude with all the answers.

It throws Tripp a little, but Leander doesn't belabor the moment. He just steps away, over to the little table that holds his "catch-all" bowl, a crystal dish that's currently storing his keys, wallet, work ID, etc. From the built-in drawer he opens, out comes a small velvet box.

"Here," he says, holding out the parcel for Tripp to accept. Raising an eyebrow, Tripp looks the box over, unsure what to expect. It's fancy, like its job is to hold expensive jewelry or something, which is confusing.

"Just open it," Leander encourages. "When we spoke last night, you said that you'd be open to a collar and I—well."

Intrigued, Tripp does as he's told, discovering a thin, emerald-green leather collar resting inside. It's less than an inch wide and clasped by a metal O-ring that sports a hinge, and his breath catches looking at it. This is a tangible symbol of what he's about to do, but for the first time, he's not nervous or scared.

"If you aren't ready, I understand, but I thought—"

"Put it on me," Tripp says huskily, working hard to control his voice.

Leander blinks, retracting the arm he has stretched out, ready to whisk away the gift in the wake of Tripp's presumed rejection. "Yes?" he asks, sounding incredibly relieved.

"Yeah," Tripp replies with a nod, handing the box over and lifting his chin, waiting patiently.

As Leander works the clasp open, a pleased smile spreads across his face. "I found it very useful, back when I was scening Autumn, to utilize the collar as a signal of sorts. Its presence helped define the boundaries between our friendship and our interactions as Dom and sub. When you come over, you could put it on —or ask me to put it on, if you like—and when you do, you're mine. If you'd prefer to hang out as friends, or if you're not in the mood to play, then you leave the collar in its box, simple as that."

"I dig it," Tripp replies, and he does. This is exactly the reason he trusted Leander to guide him through this—his own inexperienced psyche would never have considered something like a collar; a visible, tangible signal to help separate their worlds. As Leander's deft fingers skate along the sensitive skin of his neck, securing the collar in place, Tripp swallows heavily, but he's feeling increasingly confident—increasingly *ready*—with every passing moment.

"Of note—you can remove the collar at any time, to the same effect," Leander elaborates. "It's less intimidating than safewording, and sometimes that can be a good thing. Of course, that option is always open to you, as well."

"Of course," Tripp murmurs, wholly distracted by the way one of Leander's hands lingers on his shoulder, the other just underneath his jaw, fingers firmly tilting Tripp's chin up while he very blatantly admires the way the collar looks against his throat.

"What is your safeword, Tripp?" Leander asks, his sparkling baby blues meeting Tripp's unflinching stare with hope and fire.

"Halligan," Tripp says clearly, refusing to feel even the slightest pang of shame about repurposing his favorite work tool for this.

"Good—if terribly cliché," Leander says, his hand soothing across Tripp's jaw to trail just below his ear and skate over the line where his hair meets the nape of his neck. "And are you using it right now?"

"Absolutely not," Tripp replies, flashing a cheeky grin that causes Leander to bite back his own amused smile.

"Don't be a brat," Lee warns, stepping away and motioning for Tripp to follow. He walks casually, and it would take a better man than Tripp not to gawk at the way his t-shirt stretches across the taut expanse of his back.

"Would you like to see my playroom? It's yours now, too. I want you to feel as welcome and at home there as I do. In fact, if you're open to the idea, it would be acceptable if—after putting your collar on—you would come in here directly, assuming that we have nothing else specific planned. If you are in the mood to scene, you may strip, kneel by the bed, and wait for me. If you'd like to wear your collar but need to ease into play or wish to begin with non-sexual submission, keep your clothes on and kneel next to the couch."

While he talks, Leander occasionally glances over his shoulder, but mostly, he leaves Tripp to listen and absorb, and for that, he's grateful. It takes him a few deep breaths and a small internal pep talk, but by the time Leander's holding the playroom door open, Tripp is fully on board and ready for whatever awaits him on the other side.

He's also quietly appreciative for the array of options Lee is giving him, the reminder that even stress-relieving submission isn't *always* overtly sexual. That's something they touched on briefly last night, but Tripp was left unsure as to whether Leander was interested in pursuing that side of things. It's doing a lot for Tripp's rollercoaster nerves to hear that he *is*.

As a show of equal trust and respect, on the spur of the moment, Tripp decides to return the favor. Before he can, though, he enters the playroom behind Lee and his attention is immediately stolen away. He gawks, struggling to take everything in—it's a *lot*. Even the architecture feels different, somehow, from the rest of the house.

Tripp's been in Lee's main bedroom, which—thanks to the apartment's corner unit status—benefits from windows on two walls, so he knew that this room would have some natural light. Despite that, he was not prepared for the playroom windows to be so dramatic, framed nearly floor-to-ceiling by blackout curtains made of what appears to be *velvet,* hanging from silver rings mounted near the top of the wall.

They're not the only silver rings the room boasts, either, that's for sure.

It's *classy*, though. On some level, even knowing Lee as well as he does, Tripp was expecting more, 'creepy sex dungeon' vibes, less, 'upscale downtown bar'. He was prepared for vampire-lair-energy, with dark walls and red-hued lanterns, thick carpet underfoot, the works—but this is not that.

The lights above are on sliders, able to be brightened and dimmed at Lee's will, and—probably for show-and-tell purposes—he shifts them all the way on. Between the bright lighting and the white walls contrasted with dark hardwood floors, the room couldn't be further from the goth-fantasy Tripp envisioned in his head. In fact, considering the elegant, four-poster king pushed up against the far wall, crowned with a gauzy canopy that reads, '*soft romance*' more than it does '*Mistress of Pain*', Tripp honestly can't decide *what* he's supposed to think.

Once the initial shock wears off, he begins to digest the details, and certain things start to coalesce and make sense. Sure, Lee's playroom bed looks like a dream to crash out on, but there are heavy-duty hooks mounted above (and all across the ceiling leading towards it). There is a Saint Andrew's cross propped against the wall facing the bed, perfectly stained to match the dark color of the wooden floor.

There are multiple side-by-side armoires to their right, all with closed doors and drawers, and a random, two-foot metal cube sitting innocuously on the floor. A couple of leather chairs and an upholstered ottoman are scattered around the space, and there's a small, leather-covered bench of some sort shoved flush against the wall with the windows. Tripp's fairly certain that the bench has restraints attached, although their location leaves him equal parts scared and aroused. He's pretty sure that thing isn't *just* for spanking, although he hopes that might be part of it.

"Holy shit," he manages to say, knowing that he's gaping and completely unable to rein it in.

Instantly, Lee is at his side, hand on the small of Tripp's back. The warmth of his presence is reassuring on its own, although Tripp isn't scared—not really. It's just a *buttload* to swallow, and he's processing.

"If this feels like too much, we needn't start in here," Leander offers, but Tripp shakes his head in the negative.

"No way," he reiterates after another minute, once his eyes have conquered the urge to continue roaming over each and every new item they land on. He blinks, finding himself easily able to focus on Leander's face instead. Lee looks curious and only has eyes for Tripp, so Tripp offers him the widest, most sincere grin he can muster.

"It's awesome, Lee. Seriously." Dropping his gaze for a moment, Leander nods, his shoulders lifting and squaring off as he takes his own deep breath before turning his back on Tripp and moving fluidly across the space.

"In this room, and when you have your collar on, you should address me as 'Sir'."

His reminder is gentle but firm, and Tripp instantly craves to obey. "Yes, Sir," he parrots back swiftly, watching in fascination as Leander stops dead in his tracks with his back still turned, and shivers. *Hot damn.*

"Good boy," Lee says quietly, and that's it—Tripp *and* his dick are definitely on board with *all* of this. "Also, just for your information and as we talked about before, I've replaced anything in this room used previously by anyone else."

"Thank you, Sir," Tripp tells him, and Leander makes a strangled sort of sigh that Tripp can only take as satisfaction, since he doesn't turn around. Instead, he busies himself with rummaging through the top drawer of one of the armoires, looking for God knows what. Tripp takes advantage of the moment, circling back to his original plan to repay Lee for working so damn hard to make him comfortable.

He strips quickly and dumps his clothing off to the side, kneeling quietly on the hardwood floor. It's not exactly a natural position for him, but Tripp forces himself to adjust, keeping his eyes down and his hands behind his back, just the way they talked about in last night's negotiations.

It's strange—Tripp's not entirely sure what he expected to *be* in this moment. Exposed or embarrassed, maybe. Self-conscious and awkward, definitely. But none of those feelings rise. Right now, waiting impatiently for Lee to turn around and notice his offered submission, all Tripp feels is *excited*. While this is a whole new facet of his relationship with Lee, something completely foreign and as-yet unexplored, Tripp is still perfectly comfortable with the man as his best friend, and he supposes that translates.

Weirdly, the only thing he can seem to focus on specifically at the moment is the vague hope that he'll have the chance to earn Lee calling him a "good boy" again —preferably soon. His dick agrees, plumping up against his thigh without permission, and Tripp wonders if Leander will mind. The thought that he could end up punished by Lee's hand is almost as thrilling and enticing as the alternative.

The shuffle of Lee's bare feet against the floor and the sharp intake of breath that follows are the only clues that his offering has been noticed, but they're more than enough. Tripp may be a newbie in practice, but over the course of their friendship, he's lost *hours* talking to Lee about the BDSM community and scening in general. Additionally, he's spent even longer parked in front of his laptop researching and reading, filling in the blanks Lee didn't (or couldn't) regarding what it means to be a submissive.

After all, when a topic truly catches his interest, Tripp can be an excellent student. Devouring each piece of new information, he'll then file it carefully away for some theoretical future moment that he assumes will never actually come to pass.

As such, today, Tripp is ready. He knows very well what Lee is looking for and what he wants to give. Eyes trained on the floor and head slightly bowed, he works hard to control his breathing, to keep calm and remain still. He can do this—he can be good for Lee, and in return, Lee will give him what he wants (and then some). Tripp believes that wholeheartedly.

The sound of soft footsteps is followed closely by Lee's feet appearing in Tripp's field of vision, and thankfully, Lee has *nice* feet. Well-kept toes and soft-looking skin, at least, what's not hidden by the drooping cuff of his sweatpants. That certainly fits with the image Lee projects to the world: he's neat and orderly, he takes care of himself in ways that *most* emergency service providers let fall by the wayside or never consider to begin with. Tripp's always known that about Lee, but kneeling naked and willing in front of the guy definitely gives him a whole new appreciation for it.

The fingers scratching through his hair are unexpected, and Tripp—for all his surety that he can be still and perfect for as long as necessary—breaks almost instantly. Internally, he curses himself for leaning into the touch, but the quiet growl that comes out of Lee's mouth suggests that he doesn't mind. As Tripp stares determinedly at the floor, Lee's fingers tighten and Tripp's head jerks back, his face abruptly tipping up towards the ceiling.

With the bright lights still set to full-blast, Lee is essentially haloed. Framed from behind like the angel he is, come to rescue Tripp, to pull him from his own mind and his own personal hell, in a way only someone with Leander's particular skill-set can. Tripp lets himself be tugged around, subconsciously wetting his lips and watching as the lust on Leander's face transforms his entire demeanor. It's hard not to react, because Tripp has *waited*, he's wanted for Lee to look at him like *that* since the first day they met.

Fuck me, he thinks, willing Lee to hear him. *Take whatever you want.*

Unfortunately, to Tripp's dismay, Leander releases his hair and steps away. Closing his eyes, he shakes out his head and hands, seemingly trying to center himself. Not that Tripp's ready to be hog-tied and fucked raw from both ends *just* yet, but the loss is still somewhat disappointing. The idea that Lee was close to losing control over just seeing him kneeling is intoxicating. It makes Tripp feel powerful, *wanted,* and he's not *too* far above considering acting up just to have Lee's laser-focused attention directed his way again.

In the end, he sits quietly, watching his friend pace and waiting for him to say something.

"I reviewed our lists again today," Leander says finally, almost conversationally, as he moves towards one of the three huge armoires up against the wall. Tripp watches with interest as he selects the middle one, opening both of the cabinet doors closing off the top half, sliding them back and out of sight so that the interior is fully-exposed. Inside is... *a stereo?* That's not exactly what Tripp was expecting, but it *is* interesting, he'll give Lee that.

While fiddling with the buttons and what looks like a freaking CD straight out of 2004, Leander continues speaking. "I struggled somewhat, to come up with a satisfying first scene. Something that wouldn't scare you or be too overwhelming, but would spark both your interest and mine. It's been longer than I would prefer since I've scened, and I fear that my desires may be clouding my judgment. So for first-time purposes only, I thought that I would ask: is spanking with a bare hand—"

Lee turns away from the armoire and holds up his right palm, flicking his wrist in demonstration as if Tripp might not be following. As if his *entire fucking world* hasn't narrowed to Lee and his *freaking* hand, *hello?!*

"—something you'd be amenable to tonight? Followed by penetration, so long as we both remain interested and consenting."

Tripp's mouth is suddenly dry as the Sahara, his brain supplying various images of how Lee's scenario might play out in rapid succession. Caught up in considering the possibilities, he nearly forgets to reply, forgets that Lee is *waiting* for him to do exactly that, to ensure that he's on board.

"Yes, Sir," he rushes to say, eager.

Leander nods with satisfaction. "Very good," he affirms and Tripp preens, even though it's hardly directed praise. Much more likely a casual colloquialism that Lee didn't even consider Tripp might take a certain way—he can still enjoy hearing it.

"Stand up, step over to beside the bed. Spread your feet apart on the floor, chest and arms down on the mattress. You may make yourself comfortable from there, however you like. Don't worry about whether you're positioning yourself 'correctly'." Here, Lee pauses to do air quotes, and the brief glimpse of the nerdy little dude Tripp is much more familiar with nearly whips him out of the moment and makes him snort. He catches himself just in time, managing to keep his amused smile to himself as he moves over toward the bed.

"Yes, Sir."

"If need be, I will move you myself," Leander finishes, and the commanding, assured tone of his voice wipes the smirk right off of Tripp's face.

Bending over the mattress—which has a raised frame lifting it high enough to make Leander's request slightly less awkward to carry out—turns out to be more intimidating than kneeling naked on the floor. The bed's fluffy comforter is folded down, revealing sturdy cotton sheets that slide cool and soft against Tripp's skin as he sinks forward. The feel of the mattress taking his weight suggests that he was right about this thing being a dream to sleep on—Tripp can't help but wonder if he'll get to find out.

It occurs to him that Lee probably keeps this second bed for exactly that reason. Having his submissives play and sleep here automatically creates needed distance between scening and the rest of his life, including his own private space. No risk of romance, no lines accidentally blurred or crossed. Tripp understands (and even subscribes), but the awesome mattress suddenly seems a lot less enticing.

As he spreads his legs and attempts to shift his weight more comfortably from foot to foot, Tripp is all too aware that he's *beyond* fully exposed. There's a large fan circulating the air above their heads, and the slight moving current feels like someone breathing on his hole—not at all unpleasant, but a *very* clear reminder that there's no hiding, not like this.

Hands clenching and unclenching in the sheets around him, Tripp tries to wait patiently, and thankfully, Leander doesn't keep him doing so for long. The sounds of Led Zeppelin's "Whole Lotta Love" fill the room—one of his favorites —and Leander appears by his side. "I thought this might make you more comfortable," he explains.

Tripp smiles, despite himself.

"Thank you, Sir," he says, making sure to lift his mouth away from the bedclothes so that Lee can hear him. He gets a firm squeeze to his bicep in acknowledgement and a teasing glimpse of a now-shirtless Leander, which is arguably the real prize. The defined muscles of Lee's arms and torso are begging for Tripp's touch, something he's not sure he'll even get to have.

Can't win 'em all, he tells himself.

When Leander steps up behind him, he hums softly before cupping one of Tripp's ass cheeks, pausing before pushing his palm up and over the expanse of his back. "Beautiful," he murmurs.

Tripp breathes a sigh of relief—over what, he isn't entirely sure. It feels good to have Leander's reassurance and praise, though, and Tripp gives himself permission to relax into it. He savors Lee's hands on his hips, on the insides of his thighs. Lee's foot nudges Tripp's where it's planted on the ground, carefully working his body into a better position for his purposes. It's not exactly sexual, but Tripp's body responds like it is, taking his cock the rest of the way from *interested* to rock-hard in-between his legs.

Satisfied with the way he's displayed, both of Leander's hands return to Tripp's ass, kneading his cheeks enthusiastically. "I think we'll do ten today," Leander muses out loud. "Five on each cheek, *after* we get the blood flowing. Three warm-up hits on each side first, how does that sound?"

"Good, Sir," Tripp replies breathlessly, struggling against the urge to shift and wiggle, wanting more than anything to shove back against Leander's groin and find out if his friend is as affected by all of this as he is. *What if he isn't?* Pushing his face into the sheets, Tripp decides that actually, he doesn't want to know— not yet, anyway. Lee sounds like he's enjoying himself, and that's enough for now.

"Color, Tripp," Lee demands.

Tripp nods, sucking in a breath and tipping his chin away from the sheets so that his reply is clear. "Green, Sir," he replies quickly.

"I am green as well," Leander replies good-naturedly. "Extremely so." He bends forward to nose at the space between Tripp's shoulder blades, left hand gripping his hip possessively, and once again, Tripp has to fight hard to stay still, to not shove himself over. He wants to, wants to flip straight onto his back, to grab Lee and yank him down to kiss, to wrap his legs around strong thighs. Wants to do all of those things and a million other stupid, impulsive moves that would undoubtedly ruin this *very* awesome thing they have going.

It doesn't help at all when Lee's groin presses flush against the crack of his ass and he discovers that, *fuck yes, Lee is hard. Yes.*

Tripp groans a little, he can't help it, and Leander chuckles. "Warm up hits should sting but not hurt. Do you trust me?"

"Yes," Tripp breathes, forgetting the formality, but Leander lets his faux-pas go unchecked as he straightens up and lands three light swats, delivered uninterrupted to Tripp's left cheek. As promised, they leave him stinging and a little breathless but definitely not in pain, and surprisingly, desperately craving more.

"Color?" Leander checks in, and Tripp nods into the sheets.

"Green," he affirms. "So freaking green."

Three swats to the right cheek, and Tripp has to actively stop himself from rocking back on his heels. He's biting his lip to hold back the demand threatening to roll off his tongue for *more, more, more.* Leander notices, probably sees him trying to chew off his bottom lip, and immediately shoves his own thumb into the warmth of Tripp's mouth without warning, prying it open.

"Say it," Lee orders, his still-clothed groin pressed flush against Tripp's thigh, teasing them both. "Whatever you're holding back, *say it.*"

Opening his eyes and from the angle he's laying, Tripp can just *barely* see Lee's face peering down at him, his expression a confusing mix of arousal and concern. The inside of Tripp's head is starting to turn a little hazy, but it's in a good way, and the last thing in the world he wants Lee to do is *stop.*

"More," he murmurs, his voice rough. "Please, Lee, more." To punctuate those words, Tripp rocks on his heels just a *little,* barely enough to give the man behind him some friction.

"Oh," Leander says softly, apparently surprised that *this* is what Tripp was thinking. He straightens up and returns to kneading his cheeks. "With pleasure. Count out loud this time, please."

The first real strike is more of a shock than it is pain, and Tripp relishes it. The feel of Leander's hand smacking his skin, the slight burn that settles in after he pulls away—it's far better than Tripp could've imagined.

"One," he says as he shifts against the sheets, sinking down both mentally and physically. Leander spanks him five times total on each cheek, just as he promised, alternating sides with each hit and sporadically kneading his cheeks in between. The variety and unpredictability of the sensations synergize to stack the pain versus pleasure in a way that keeps Tripp on his toes.

By the time they reach *"Nine!"* and *"Ten,"* Tripp is deliriously lost, barely able to vocalize the count and with tears pricking at the corners of his eyes. A rogue one spills over and tracks down his face, leaving a wet, cooling path against his fevered skin. Somewhere in the back of his mind, Tripp knows that he's not being as still as he should be, rocking into Leander's touch and often pleading for more without having been asked to speak.

Leander doesn't punish him for that. Instead, he responds to and even encourages it. The skin of Tripp's ass is on *fire* when Leander checks his color again, and even though Tripp has said "*Ten,*" and knows peripherally that the spanking is over, he's not ready to be finished.

"Green," he blurts out before Lee has even finished asking the question. "Fuck me, *please*, Sir," he moans, rubbing his cock against the side of the mattress, in desperate search of friction.

"None of that," Leander scolds, gently pulling Tripp's hips away from the bed and purposefully letting his thumbs graze over irritated skin, which only makes Tripp moan louder. "You've been so good, Tripp," he continues. "So very good, and good boys are always rewarded. You'll get what you want, I assure you."

Tripp sniffles somewhat pitifully as the sound of a lube bottle snapping open can be heard from behind him. Leander's fingers find his entrance easily, and the cool slide, the relief of penetration has Tripp gasping right out of the gate. Tangling both hands into the sheets, he squeezes his eyes shut against the onslaught of sensation.

Quiet, methodical, and efficient, Leander opens him up without fanfare or pretense, spreading thick fingers until they move comfortably in and out in a not-quite-enough glide. Tripp's happy as hell that he's not in charge right now, that Lee isn't asking *his* opinion about this—whether he's ready or needs more prep. It's all out of his hands and Tripp's *glad.* He lays there, raw, sore, and exposed but still wanting *more,* willing to take whatever Lee sees fit to give him.

The crinkle of foil is the only thing that catches Tripp's attention, aside from Leander's *perfect* fuckin' hands. They'd decided previously to use condoms (at least for the time being), and it's safe to say that Tripp has never regretted a decision more. He wants to *feel* Lee pressing against his walls, wants the slow drag of skin-on-skin as Lee fills him up, wants to know what it's like to have Lee dripping out of him when they're done.

Tripp's delirious mind tells him to beg for those things, but something stops him, tells him to let it go—this time. The words are gone, anyway, just like every other coherent thought in his mind the second Lee's cock pushes against his rim and pops inside. Leander groans and Tripp can't help but let a "fuck, *yes,*" slip from his lips.

"So tight," Leander murmurs, almost speaking to himself as he slides forward until his thighs are flush and his balls are knocking against Tripp's own. With some difficulty, Tripp swallows the demands that bubble up in his throat, buckling down and forcing himself to be patient. He's soon rewarded by Lee's hand carding through his hair, and that's worth the effort.

"So good for me," Lee says, his hips beginning to move and circle, dick dragging deliciously against Tripp's insides with every small stroke. "Go ahead," he says, "tell me what you want."

"God—"

"Sir," Leander cuts him off, voice tinged with amusement, though he doesn't stop teasing Tripp with those killer fuckin' hips. "Or Leander, but definitely not God."

"Sir, *please*—fuck me hard!" Tripp verbally pivots just as soon as Leander requests it, joke or not, and in response, he feels an approving hand tighten in the locks of his hair. To Tripp's great relief, the pace and depth of the thrusts both increase, and then Lee is threading an arm under his left thigh, encouraging his knee up onto the mattress.

The resulting angle is so much better, Leander nailing his prostate on nearly every thrust in or drag back out. Waves of pleasure shoot up Tripp's spine and down to his toes, mixing in perfect tandem with the sharp ache in his abused ass.

While Tripp's been fucked plenty of times before, it's never been like *this*. With abandon, so totally open and vulnerable, completely at someone else's mercy and because he *wants to be.* Tripp gets it, he *really fuckin' gets it,* and as Leander reaches around to strip his cock—making Tripp seize up and come violently all over the nice, white cotton bedsheets—he hasn't a single regret, not one. Not even that he's doing this with a guy he's so in love with he can't see straight, blinding orgasm aside.

As he floats back down to earth, Tripp lies blissfully sated and pliant on the bed as Leander yanks at his hair and chases his own orgasm. Thighs pound roughly against his stinging ass, nearly milking a second orgasm out of him via his prostate. Lee finishes soon after, grunting and grabbing at Tripp, ending up with an arm around Tripp's waist to clutch him tightly against his chest as he yanks them both down onto the bed to recover.

Tentatively, Tripp covers the hand splayed across his belly with his own, just for a minute. It's almost terrifying, how good it feels to be held by Lee like this after what they just did. So much so that Tripp is regretful when Lee pulls out of him, when he gets up immediately to tie off and toss the condom as he makes his way over to the open armoire. The stereo is playing "Kashmir" now, and Leander turns it off, changing the sound to something soft and instrumental.

Blinking up at the ceiling, Tripp wonders when the lights went down. They definitely have—dim in comparison to the brightness level Leander chose when he first brought them in here. Vaguely, Tripp's ears register a door opening and closing accompanied by some light clanking, like glass in a fridge. He wonders if he should get up, but then remembers about *aftercare* and the way Leander emphasized its importance. Tripp wonders what exactly that will entail, and selfishly hopes for more cuddling.

It's only seconds later that Lee appears back at his side, leaning down to press a kiss to Tripp's forehead and then cock his head towards the top of the bed.

"Come up here," he says gently, leaving a grounding hand on Tripp's shoulder that he feels strangely grateful for. With some difficulty—thanks to sore muscles and a fiery ass—Tripp drags himself more properly onto the mattress, only to collapse again face-down with his head on a pillow and his arms tucked underneath. Once settled, he releases a small sigh of contentment. Leander curls up next to him and soothes a hand down his back, stopping just shy of the reddened skin.

"Drink this before you pass out," he instructs, and Tripp cracks open an eyelid to see a bottle of orange juice thrust in his face. Somehow, he manages to prop himself up onto his elbows and to suck down half of the drink in one go. It tastes and feels good sliding down his dry throat, enough that he lifts the bottle again, finishing it off without having to be prodded.

"Good, Tripp," Leander praises. "You are so very good."

"Alright," Tripp grumbles before hiding his face in the pillow, as if *compliments* are the most humiliating thing he's faced in the last hour (or however long they've been in here).

To his relief, Leander just sighs, though Tripp can almost *feel* him shaking his head. "I'm opting to let that one go, because technically, the scene is over," he says. His tone isn't unkind, but it's still very firm. "But we will be working on your ability to accept praise."

"Fine," Tripp mumbles, directly into the pillow, and Leander pinches his ass. "Hey!"

"Don't be a brat," he murmurs, uncapping another bottle of something and squeezing a healthy portion of whatever it is into his hand. "This is arnica gel, it will help with any bruising." Leander's deft hands swipe the stuff over Tripp's abused skin, and it feels wonderfully soothing, enough that Tripp feels safe to relax down into the mattress once again. "I also brought ice," Leander continues, draping a soft cloth across Tripp's ass and resting what he assumes from the cold is a bag of ice over that. "Probably excessive, but you've never been spanked before."

After that, Leander hesitates, though his hand never leaves Tripp's skin. "Considering this was a first-time scene for you, I would feel much better if you'd stay the night. I'd like to sleep in here with you—close contact after an intense scene can help to ward off drop, something I'd very much like to avoid either one of us experiencing, especially so early on. But if you're not comfortable with that, I could be right next door…"

"Lee," Tripp says patiently, turning his head on the pillow so that he can look up at his friend. Immediately, Tripp registers the pointed cocking of Lee's eyebrow, the touch of his fingers to his own neck. "Sir," Tripp corrects, slightly sarcastically. "I know we've set some boundaries here, and I get it, but you and me have slept in the same bed plenty of times."

Leander still looks hesitant, his gaze darting over to the closed door of the playroom like he's thinking about bolting for an escape. Tripp sighs. Usually, he's the one boasting the shitty communication skills.

"I'd rather have you," he says, reaching out to drop a hand onto Lee's thigh, and *that* gets his attention.

The mischievous little grin that Lee is often seen wearing returns as he looks softly down his nose at Tripp. "Alright," he says simply, picking up a remote that Tripp hadn't previously noticed from the small table on his side of the bed. With a flick of his index finger, he's dimming the lights the rest of the way off, so that's one mystery explained.

When Leander relaxes down next to him and pulls the covers up over their bodies, Tripp doesn't think twice about accepting the invitation into his open arms.

This is dangerous, the single brain cell still operating in his head warns, but Tripp can't bring himself to care. Dangerous, but also exactly what he signed up for. Lee, warm and real, keeping him safe in the circle of his arms—however risky, it would take a much stronger man than Tripp to reject an offering like that.

So he stays, and they sleep.

Chapter 2

Leander dreams in color. Bright, startling technicolor that bursts into life behind closed eyelids and sucks him down into his deepest, wildest, most desperately secret fantasies. Unlike out in the real world, these fantasies aren't headlining a potent mix of sex and pain, dominance and submission. They aren't a manifestation of Leander's clawing attempts to keep hold of his sanity by wresting control of something—*someone*—in the bedroom.

No, these dreams are interminably soft, featuring one thing, and one thing only.

Green eyes. Freckles. Strong arms and a gentle smile, both wrapping Leander up in their warmth and carrying him away. In Leander's dreams, the entire universe comes to an end and rebuilds from scratch—over and over, millennia upon millennia reduced to stardust and light, imploding and exploding, collapsing in on itself before rushing outwards once again, all on endless repeat. The *only* constant, the *only* thing that matters in any of it, is that he and Tripp are together, always together.

In Leander's dreams, he can be honest. He can admit that he's in love with his best friend, because in these dreams, *Tripp* loves him back. He holds Leander's hand in public, rests a casual arm around his shoulder as they wait in line at the movies, offers to switch dinner plates when his order comes out looking like *exactly* what Leander didn't realize he was hungry for.

Most importantly, he *says* so. He puts his lips next to Leander's ear and whispers his affection softly, every chance he gets. He yells it across crowded rooms, wanting everyone to hear. In Leander's dreams, everything is perfect.

Especially tonight. Tonight, the fantasies are so vivid, he can smell the natural scent of Tripp's skin, the cologne he wears over it, and even the faint traces of spicy deodorant and silicone-based gel in his hair. It's not just smell, either—his brain had decided that he can *feel* Tripp, too. Shifting in his arms, nuzzling into the hollow of his neck, pressing their bodies together completely from cheek to toe. Warmth and devotion flow freely between them, a perfectly synchronous pair. Like a key that fits a lock Leander didn't even know he wanted to open.

It translates to one of the best nights of sleep Leander has ever experienced, and an unprecedented mindfuck when he opens his eyes and Tripp is actually there.

Abruptly wide awake, Leander shoves himself away from the other man so quickly that he nearly tumbles backward off the bed. Heavy sleeper that Tripp is, he barely notices, snorting a little and rolling over to snuffle into the pillow beneath his head. Leander sits stock still up by the headboard, barely breathing and with his legs curled underneath him, one hand fisted in his hair and the other in his mouth. His teeth create imprints on his index finger as he copes with a wave of shock and shame.

It's not until Tripp is safely snoring away again that Leander allows himself to begin to relax and to try and regain his bearings.

The truth is, he's not ready to see or interact with Tripp this morning, not yet. Not with his face still flushing red and his mind rushing like a mountain river in spring, overflowing with images from a night full of dreams like *that*.

There's some kind of irony here, Leander's sure of it. *Most* people feel embarrassment over boner-inducing, X-rated, pornographic dreams accidentally starring their best friends, but not Leander, he lives those outright. No, *he* has to be ashamed over *romance*. His mother always claimed he came off the assembly line with a crack; she'd be so proud to know how truly committed he remains to breaking the mold.

His plight might be funny, if it wasn't so damn lonely and confusing.

Regardless of all that, though, it's been a long time since Leander shared a bed with someone in this particular way. True, Tripp wasn't wrong when he pointed out that they've slept together previously—but that was different. Two platonic friends, passing out fully-clothed on top of the blankets after polishing off an entire bottle of whiskey is a *far* cry from curling up naked together after one of their dicks was buried in the other's ass.

And that's *solely* considering his experiences with *Tripp*.

The only other person Leander's shared a bed with in *this* way was Autumn, and doing so led directly to their undoing. Blurring the lines between aftercare and affection, Autumn could never properly separate the two, not in the way Leander wanted. Maybe that was unfair, but *he* couldn't control the fact that he never developed feelings for her beyond the physical. It didn't mean that she wasn't a valuable friend, that he didn't care immensely about her well-being, but Leander just couldn't make himself fall in love.

Can anyone?

Now, here he is, making the same mistakes but in the reverse. *That* is ironic—he knows that for sure. Perhaps this is karma, perhaps it's what Leander deserves after being so careless with Autumn's heart. Here he is, finally able to understand exactly what she was feeling, and it's because he's opening the door to have his own heart broken in precisely the same, terrible way.

Idiot, Leander chastises himself. He rubs both hands across his face before bracing them carefully on the side of the bed and standing up. The mattress barely moves (and Leander sends up a quick thank-you to whoever might be listening from above for that) before tip-toeing across the space on silent feet. As he moves, he skirts away from any floorboards that he knows will creak, easily making it out of the room without disturbing Tripp's slumber.

Inside the attached bathroom, Leander slumps against the door with a sigh of relief, grateful for the reprieve and the moment of privacy. In truth, there's nothing he wants more than to crawl back into bed beside Tripp and his warmth. To wrap arms around his slim waist and pull him close, to wake him with soft kisses to the back of his neck and a gentle hand cupping his cock.

Like lovers, Leander thinks. Like two people who might be falling in love.

He can't do that, of course, and those inappropriate thoughts and desires he's projecting onto Tripp are precisely the reason why. It's harder to *think,* to remember those boundaries when Tripp is lying next to him, looking tragically innocent and peaceful in his sleep. So soft, so beautiful and perfect, willing to lay in Leander's arms and—oh, *hell.* He has *got* to get his shit together.

In retrospect, the smartest thing Leander could possibly have done upon waking was precisely what he did: book it the hell out of that room before Tripp woke up. *Boundaries and limits,* Leander reiterates to himself. If he wants to keep this new dynamic with Tripp, he *has* to respect the fact that the man is not interested in a romantic relationship with him. That was made perfectly clear when they talked the night before their scene. It's not as if Leander didn't lay his cards on the table—after Autumn, how could he not? That's just not a mistake you want to make twice.

But Tripp seemed to retreat emotionally when Leander spoke about how he struggled to connect with Autumn, how he never developed romantic feelings for her, how he longed for someone who understood, who he could finally be on the same level with. It's true that there are times when Tripp looks at him a certain way, when he says various things and Leander wonders if he wasn't clear *enough,* if perhaps Tripp *didn't* get the memo, but ultimately, that's wishful thinking and he knows it.

He *has* to stop holding out hope that Tripp will somehow magically develop feelings for him, because that mindset will only get them both hurt.

At the end of the day, *this*—this beautiful dominant and submissive relationship that Tripp, by some miracle, has consented to—is what he gets. Staying with Tripp last night was the right thing to do, of course. Risking drop isn't worth it for either of them, but from here on out, Leander will have to be more careful. Tripp can stay over and sleep in the playroom bed whenever he likes, and Leander will just make it a point to relocate to his own room, once his sub has recovered and fallen asleep.

That is, if Tripp even *wants* to continue their new relationship going forward, something Leander can't assume. All the more reason for him to be happy and grateful for whatever Tripp is willing to offer to begin with.

It's enough. It has to be.

Turning his attention to his morning routine, Leander takes his time washing up. Meticulously brushing his teeth and styling his hair, he gives his face and body a quick, soapy wipe down before wandering naked into his actual bedroom to find some clean clothes. He ignores the empty bed standing cold and unused in the corner, and tries not to think about Tripp lying warm and pliant less than twenty feet away.

Rummaging through his dresser drawers, Leander remembers that he works tonight, so there's no sense in wasting a nice outfit on today. If he's being honest, once Tripp is gone, the only things scheduled on his docket are cleaning up around the apartment and mentally debriefing. His stomach twists when he inadvertently thinks about Tripp again, still sacked out peacefully, sated and unbothered. Determined to work through it, Leander ignores the tugging in his gut to return to the playroom bed.

Boundaries. T-shirt and boxer-briefs it is.

Out in the kitchen, he sets coffee brewing and cracks eggs into a pan, scrambling and seasoning them absently while he reviews the scene from the night before in his head. It truly was an excellent first encounter, and Leander feels good about his decision to go easy on Tripp, to start small and simple with something they both needed and could definitively handle.

Truthfully, touching Tripp for the first time—being granted full access to every part of his body, being handed *complete* control of his pleasure—was a lot for Leander, too. Being an experienced Dom makes a scene like that look simple on paper, but to add in the confusing emotions he's battling towards Tripp himself? That changes the entire game, and Leander is at least self-aware enough to recognize and account for that.

Still, he's pleased with his own performance, and Tripp seemed more than satisfied, as well. The fact that he's still unconscious supports that theory: Leander knows first-hand that the man rarely manages more than four hours at a time, especially when he's not in his own bed. Since they fell asleep around three a.m. and it's fast approaching noon, that's double what Tripp is used to getting.

If nothing else and at the barest minimum, it would appear that they did accomplish what they set out to do—blow off some steam, shed stress, and help each other unwind in order to achieve more quality rest and relaxation. That's great, and it's something for which Leander feels he can be proud. He just hopes that the tone he set was compelling enough for Tripp to be inspired to do it again.

An enthusiastic yawn from behind him has Leander whirling around, letting the hot pan he's holding clatter noisily down onto the stovetop. It's probably just as well, since the sight that greets him would've likely resulted in a loss of limb control, regardless. If ever there was a doubt in Leander's mind that the submissive is the one with all the *real* power and control in a relationship, Tripp himself would clear up that confusion simply by existing.

"Tripp," Leander exclaims, knowing full-well that it's useless to try and pretend he's not affected by a sleep-rumpled Tripp clad only in his boxers and his collar, standing easily in the middle of Leander's kitchen like he belongs there.

"Stole your toothbrush, Sir," Tripp says ruefully, shifting on his feet and rubbing at his forearms, like he thinks Leander might scold him and hasn't entirely decided whether he *wants* that or not. It does things to Leander—has him crowding Tripp bodily up against the breakfast bar without a second thought.

This is allowed, he tells himself as Tripp's hands find their way to his waist. Tripp is still wearing his collar. He's still playing by the rules, and so am I.

Still, Leander knows he should check. Perhaps Tripp was only being cheeky in using the honorific, and doesn't even realize that his collar is still on. Watching Tripp's face carefully for any change in his expression, Leander ignores the way their chests are pressed together, the way his groin is already stirring with interest, and lifts his hand to slip fingers underneath the thin leather wrapped around Tripp's neck.

"This truly looks lovely on you," he remarks, enjoying the way Tripp blushes under his attention. "Did you mean to leave it on? In the future, I won't ask. But seeing as how this is new for you..." Trailing off, Leander pulls his bottom lip in-between his teeth and peers up at Tripp with wide, innocent eyes. It's a dirty move, and Tripp's gaze goes predictably glassy upon receipt, which is satisfying.

"Oh, I meant to leave it on. Sir."

That's all the permission Leander needs. He reaches up to cup the back of Tripp's head and pull him in for a searing kiss that's more tongue and possession than anything else, but that's how it needs to be for Leander right now. To his delight, Tripp melts in his arms, allowing his head to be tipped and pulled in whatever direction Leander likes, moaning and sighing as his body is manipulated.

It takes every last ounce of strength Leander has in him to pull away, but he does it, stepping back with a hand on Tripp's bare chest and feeling thoroughly pleased with the way the man's eyes remain closed long after his mouth is gone.

"Go and kneel by the couch," he instructs. "You may take a pillow for your knees—the one on the side, there." He watches as Tripp goes, noting the way his boxers have ridden up slightly in the back, really highlighting the striations of muscle in the man's ass and thighs. Tripp is stunning from any angle, but walking away nearly nude turns him next-level, as far as Leander is concerned.

Ripping his gaze away, he turns back to the mess on the stove, grabbing a plate from the cabinet and transferring a sizable portion of eggs onto it. From inside the fridge, Leander retrieves a bowl of fruit salad, scooping out a hefty serving and piling it next to the eggs. He takes his time, pouring a cup of coffee and making it up the way he knows Tripp likes—black, one sugar—even though he personally prefers his coffee to resemble melted ice cream.

Once he's satisfied with the meal, Leander rips a paper towel from the roll and grabs a fork from the drawer. Picking the items up alongside the plate and his mug, he makes his way over to a compliantly-kneeling Tripp. Sitting down on the couch with the food in his lap, Leander places the mug on the side table and meets Tripp's gaze head-on.

He raises an eyebrow, making sure to take a moment and say out loud, "You don't need to do this. If you like, you can remove that collar, make yourself a plate, and join me here on the couch. However—" Leander pauses, shifting his gaze to the array of fruit and selecting a juicy-looking blueberry, grasping it between his thumb and forefinger. Raising the berry to Tripp's eye-level, he holds it out. "I don't want to be unclear. I would very much like to feed you, exactly like this."

Tripp's face does several things very quickly, and Leander can tell that he's thinking, which allows him hope that he isn't pushing too hard. Hand-feeding *was* on Tripp's list of "yellow" kinks—items that weren't known to him specifically, but that he was open to trying. However, part of Leander's job as the Dom is figuring out appropriate *timing* for such introductions to new things. They've only begun their exploration together within the last twenty-four hours, and equally, only decided to *keep* exploring within the last ten minutes.

It's too much.

He's about to give Tripp an out, to let him off the hook without consequence, when Tripp surprises him. Leander watches in abject fascination as Tripp leans forward, parting his lips and closing them around his fingertips, sucking the offered blueberry into his mouth in a *much* more erotic fashion than is strictly necessary. It leaves Leander wholly affected, cock stirring to life unbidden in-between his legs. Technically, this is *his* party—Tripp's only doing what was asked of him, and yet, he's so easy and free about it, the act could be mistaken for something he does *every single day*, by choice.

Not for the first time, Leander finds himself in awe of the man kneeling before him, and incredibly interested in pushing him to the edge of his limits. For now, he simply pops a strawberry in his own mouth and chews thoughtfully, trying to appear more together than he feels. After several bites of fruit—and Tripp learning that he can absolutely get away with using his tongue to swipe any juice dripping from his fingers—Leander starts gathering some eggs onto the fork and offering them to Tripp directly.

Interestingly enough, Tripp looks disappointed by the change in utensil, but Leander sticks to his guns and doesn't sub out the fork for his fingers. Part of training Tripp in the lifestyle will be teaching him that he doesn't always get to dictate the terms. That it isn't a given for him to get whatever he wants, not if what he *wants* isn't in line with what Leander *needs*. The reverse is true as well, of course —Leander's not selfish.

While he adamantly refuses to feed Tripp eggs with his fingers, he does pause to allow him to drink, with Leander holding the mug, naturally. Tripp seems surprised to find the coffee made to his liking and he says so, dropping a delayed "Sir," at the end of his remark, nearly forgetting. The interaction suggests to Leander that he should set up a punishment structure, just in case this continues to be an issue in the future. He files that away to muse over later.

"A good Dom puts his sub's needs first," Leander says, answering a question that Tripp doesn't actually ask. The look Tripp gives him in return is full of both wide-eyed wonder and open appreciation, and Leander finds himself enjoying watching his friend discover what it's like to be a submissive, to be *Leander's* well-cared-for submissive.

"I'm entirely pleased you let me feed you, Tripp," he says casually, moving the empty plate to the table and carding fingers through Tripp's messy hair. "Selfishly, I'd love to keep you like this all day. You look incredible, and I'd love to see you on your knees with your head on my thigh while we watch TV, or let you warm my cock for as long as you can stand it before coming down your throat."

Tripp's pupils visibly expand as Leander talks, but he sits calmly with his hands folded in his lap—*so* patient, *so* perfect. Leander clears his throat before continuing, trying to hide how affected he is. "However, just this once, I think that we should debrief, instead. While it pains me to ask you to remove your collar, I think it's for the best. I cannot put into words how much joy it brings me to see you wearing it, but for this conversation, we must be equals."

Obediently, Tripp tips his head back, intending to allow Leander access to the clasp. "No," Leander says gently, shaking his head in refusal. "You are solely in control of removing your collar. That's very important to me. I can request for you to put it on or take it off, but to actually do so *must* be your choice. Especially right now, considering what I'm asking. Do you understand?"

Tripp looks Leander straight in the eyes and nods solemnly. "Yes, Sir," he replies, and Leander's heart clenches in his chest as Tripp fumbles with the buckle sitting over his Adam's apple. For a moment, Leander worries that he won't be able to undo it, but then it slips free and Tripp peels the leather from around his neck. The box is still sitting inside the catch-all bowl in the entryway, so Tripp returns the collar to it before taking a seat next to Leander on the couch.

"It's weird," Tripp says almost immediately, pulling a leg up and wrapping his arm around it protectively, which Leander finds immensely interesting. Tripp's never been shy or ashamed of his body, so perhaps he's feeling vulnerable. Leander will have to keep an eye on that—their interactions are supposed to improve Tripp's self-esteem, not damage it.

Oblivious to his internal musings, Tripp continues talking, which is a good thing. "Not like I haven't sat on your couch a million times before. Shouldn't feel any different, right?"

With a shrug, Leander helps himself to a gulp of the remaining coffee before passing it over to Tripp. It's cold and could use a refill, but Leander senses that Tripp needs something to do with his hands more than he needs a drink.

"I think it's fine to feel however you do right now. Our dynamic has changed, it makes sense that your feelings towards me and being in my space may have shifted as well. There's nothing wrong with that, but we should talk about it. The last thing I want is for that shift to impact our friendship, Tripp. Losing what we already have because of missteps surrounding sex and submission, that would be…" Leander trails off and shakes his head. "Unforgivable. Meaning, I would never forgive myself."

Predictably, Tripp nods and then shoves his face into the mug, taking an exaggeratedly long sip while Leander waits patiently. He swallows when he surfaces, licking his tempting pink lips and flexing fidgety fingers across the curved ceramic. "Well, I hear you, but for whatever it's worth, I had an awesome time and I wouldn't take any of it back. Hell, you want my honest opinion on all this? Here it is."

Tripp pauses, waiting for Leander to meet his gaze before laying out his thoughts. In typical Tripp style, no punches are pulled. "It helped. Did exactly what you said it would, and I want more. I liked getting out of my own head. I liked not knowing or having control over what was coming next. And I want... I want to do *all* the stuff we matched on, the things on the kinks list." He stretches out a hand, beckons with his fingers like, *come at me.* "Bring it on, baby."

"Really?" Leander speaks without thinking, but Tripp's phrasing is both surprising and relieving—it hits him hard. Of course, he suspected that his friend enjoyed himself, considering the way he essentially passed out from the orgasm, but that was no guarantee he was *in*. No promise that he wouldn't wake up and decide that being a submissive wasn't for him, or that being with *Leander* wasn't, either.

Despite what Tripp has said in the past about only being interested in exploring the scene with someone he trusts unconditionally, it's no secret that the world is full of other Doms and Dommes. Most of whom would wait in a *line* for a shot at handling someone like Tripp.

Truthfully, a not-small part of Leander *did* wonder if Tripp wouldn't simply use him to get his feet wet, to take the edge off of the terror that giving up control for the first time brings. A test-run, so to speak, before swiftly moving on. It's a weight off of his shoulders—perhaps more than it should be—to hear directly from Tripp that, at least for now, this isn't the case.

Wanting to appear genuine, Leander pivots his body to face Tripp more fully. It takes him a second or two digesting his friend's concerned eyebrow raise before he realizes how his blurted-out reply must have been received. "I didn't mean—" Leander cuts himself off with a sharp exhale, shaking his head before offering Tripp what he hopes is a reassuring smile.

He continues, "I'm *very* happy to hear you say that, because I also found our encounter to be extremely satisfying. I was hopeful you'd want to do it again, to continue our contract for as long as scening remains both enjoyable and beneficial for both of us." In response, Tripp's cheeks turn pink and he ducks his head, focusing on obtaining what has to be the absolute dregs of that coffee, but Leander doesn't call him on it. He just waits, and when Tripp lowers the cup, Leander's still staring, catching his eye and smiling encouragingly.

They look at each other dopily for nearly a full minute before Tripp clears his throat, puts his cup down, stands and stretches. It's a lost cause—Leander's unable to even pretend that he isn't gawking at the way Tripp's muscles move when his body changes position, and Tripp smirks openly when he notices. Wanting to regain the upper hand in the conversation, Leander stands up with him, carrying the dirty dishes over to the sink and refilling Tripp's mug from the carafe.

"Are you off this weekend?" he asks, aiming for casual conversation, something closer to their usual dynamic.

"You know I am," Tripp replies easily, trailing behind and leaning forward over the breakfast bar using his elbows, propping his chin in his hands.

Brat, Leander thinks, suppressing the urge to spank him, collared or not.

"We work the same rotation, sunshine."

"I didn't know if you picked up any OT," Leander retorts, holding the mug out. "I'm not your keeper." Tripp snorts and Leander tips his head to the side, one corner of his mouth inadvertently ticking up. "Poor choice of words?"

"Awesome choice of words," Tripp declares, accepting the refreshed coffee with a wink before downing at least half of it in one go. "Depending on what our next scene is." A thrill shoots down Leander's spine at those words (and the images that whip tantalizingly through his mind to accompany them).

"About that," Leander says carefully, not failing to notice the way Tripp's eyes follow his fingers as they walk their way across the countertop. Perhaps Tripp is not the only one with anxiety soothed by keeping their hands busy.

"I have some thoughts. I believe that we're on the same page regarding *trying it all,* and for starters, I would like to increase our next scene's intensity level. I don't want to do that if you have somewhere to be the next day, for safety reasons. I work tonight and then am off Friday through Sunday, back in on Sunday night. That would mean I'd be available to you for that entire time period, as well. There wouldn't be any pressure for you to leave my apartment, and I could care for you, if necessary."

The reaction Leander gets to that bit of long-windedness is unexpected, especially since Tripp has been so easygoing about everything thus far. On the other side of the counter, he fidgets, and a discontented noise finds its way out of his throat. It's a bit unnerving, but Tripp holds up a hand to stave off Leander's worry, which is unquestionably showing on his face.

"Okay, two things," Tripp says suddenly, shoulders straightening. "One, all that sounds great. Whatever you want, buddy, I'm here for it. Seriously. But on the flip side, are we gonna… " Tripp motions clumsily with his hands, gesturing between their bodies as Leander cocks his head to the side, confused. Clearly exasperated, Tripp sighs and shakes his head, pinching the bridge of his nose between his thumb and index finger.

"All this *talking*, pal," he blurts out. "You're not gonna make me do this every time, are you? 'Cause buddy, I gotta be honest, this analytical shit isn't really my thing."

Narrowing his eyes, Leander taps his lips thoughtfully with the pads of his fingers. It's not as if he was intentionally trying to turn this into a roundtable discussion, just keep the flow of communication open between himself and his new sub. "Comprehensive debriefing is important in any Dom / sub relationship, but especially one like ours, where you are very new to this and we have our underlying friendship to consider."

Tripp scratches at the back of his neck and shrugs, letting his arms drop and both of his hands clap loudly against his bare thighs when they do. "I know, Lee, I get that. I'm not saying that I don't want you to check-in, I do. I appreciate the due diligence—I can tell how seriously you take this stuff and, you know, it makes me feel safe, or whatever. But the whole, not *having* to talk, it's part of what I signed on for, and maybe I wasn't clear enough about that. What I *want* is to hand the thinking, the decision-making, over to you. All of it. I want—fuck."

Abruptly, Tripp turns away, dragging a hand over his face and allowing it to linger on his chin with the other planted firmly on his hip. The set of his shoulders and the dip of his head conveys self-disgust and embarrassment, which makes Leander feel terrible.

This is hard for him, Leander realizes. It genuinely never occurred to him that it would be, that this type of debriefing could be asking way too much of his emotionally-constipated friend. For Tripp, this conversation is apparently much closer to "feelings" territory than Leander would have placed it himself, in addition to likely hitting his shame buttons, specifically in regards to *asking* out loud for things that he wants and needs.

Tripp can't separate the discussion from the act—not yet. They can work on that together, sure, but to jump in this way was a *big* miscalculation on Leander's part. Thankfully, it's been caught, and it's an easy fix.

"I understand, Tripp," he says quickly, reaching out to touch Tripp's shoulder and getting shrugged off for his efforts. Instead of being offended, Leander softens his tone and tries to sound as reassuring and nonjudgmental as possible. He's not entirely convinced that some of Tripp's current attitude isn't a form of drop, but more importantly, it's not inconsistent with *Tripp* in general, and the trouble he has giving voice to his desires and emotions.

"I hear you," he tries again. "These discussions, the planning—they're all things you would prefer for me to handle and that's *fine*. That's perfectly fine, there's nothing wrong with that at all. I didn't—It didn't occur to me that's what you meant when we discussed debriefing originally."

The tension infusing the hard lines of Tripp's body begins to bleed and soften, and he glances over his shoulder like a petulant toddler who's being offered candy, but thinks he might have to take a nap to cash in.

"Yeah?" he asks warily. "Just like that?"

"Our contract stipulates a check-in once per week. For many reasons, that's not something I would feel comfortable eliminating completely, but I think a once-weekly chat is plenty for the time being. Anything else, we'll play by ear. If there's something I feel truly requires discussion, I'll try to save it. Alternatively, if *you* ever change your mind and need to talk, the offer is always on the table. Take off your collar and say so, I will always listen.

"Aside from that, I will take full control of our new relationship dynamic going forward. I will tell you what to do and when to do it, including how much recovery time will be needed. If your schedule can't accommodate my plans, you'll need to inform me so that I can adjust, but that is the extent of the input I'll ask from you."

Having turned around again fully, Tripp's face is visibly painted with relief. Leander only wishes he was still wearing his collar, so that he could comfort him physically. It's achingly difficult to be so close to a Tripp that's struggling and not be able to touch, but these boundaries are *vital* to what they're building.

Still, something seems not quite right. As Leander watches, Tripp shivers a little. The apartment is not cold, which is concerning.

"Tripp," Leander says carefully, not wanting to alarm him. "Would you like to go put your collar back on, at least for the time being?"

The effect is instantaneous—Tripp releases a haggard breath and nods, his eyes nearly going glassy before he turns away and Leander can no longer see them. *Incredible,* Leander thinks, strangely proud as he watches Tripp stride determinedly across the room. For a man who has never actually been a submissive before, his entire being positively *screams* with the need for it.

Not for the first time, Leander thinks that he and Tripp might be a lot more alike in that respect than he'd initially thought. His own need to take control is hard-wired into his personality, into who he *is* as a human. When he can't, when he doesn't have an outlet and a sub to care for, Leander feels lost at sea. Unfulfilled, like a boat with neither a mooring nor a captain at its helm. Watching Tripp, he can see that hunger, those desires of his own mirrored so perfectly in the man's deep-seated yearning to submit, to be cared for. To have his needs looked after and the burden of *choices* and responsibility lifted completely from his shoulders for any period of time.

Perhaps Leander should have seen this coming, the way Tripp reacted just now, but in his defense, it's been a long time since he's encountered another person who is built from the ground up to *either* command or serve. This not-quite-earth-shattering revelation makes him feel drawn to Tripp even more strongly, like there's something connecting them, two sides of the same coin. A perfect pair with an extremely special bond—they understand and complement each other in ways that other people can't begin to understand.

Of course, he can't *say* any of this to Tripp, and not solely because his emotional state is slightly fragile at the moment. It's too much, too soon, and may very well always remain something that Tripp isn't ready to hear.

That's fine.

Leander can do one better, anyway. He can fix this misstep with touch, since it's very clearly what they *both* need right now. When Tripp returns with his collar in place, Leander takes him by the wrist and leads him over to the couch. Sinking into it, he pulls Tripp down on top of him without any hesitation. Leander relaxes back against the cushions, stretching his parted legs out in a vee to make room for Tripp's body.

He's unsurprised but pleased at how easily Tripp obeys the direction, allowing Leander to shift and maneuver his limbs until he's comfortably placed. The end result has Tripp lying on his stomach and draped across Leander's chest, head tucked deftly underneath his chin.

Once they're settled, Leander flips the blanket he keeps folded on the back of the couch over both of them for warmth, though Tripp's feet stick out the far end. He pushes his fingers through Tripp's hair, scratches nails across his scalp, and soothes both hands down the length of his back. He resists the urge to verbally reassure Tripp about anything they discussed earlier, thinking that might not be the best way to assuage his bristly embarrassment, considering.

Tripp calms.

Not that he was overly worked up to begin with, at least not outwardly, but Leander's been around the block with submissives, and he's good at reading body language. The longer they lay together, the more relaxed Tripp becomes. His heartbeat slows, his breathing evens out, and his muscles unclench beneath Leander's touch. It's a beautiful response to an irritated submissive simply being held by their Dom, and Leander feels both proud and grateful. Any shadow of a doubt that doing *this* with Tripp is rewarding enough to be worth the struggle with his emotions all but dissipates—dust in the wind.

Later, when Tripp uncollars for good (for the day, anyway) and redresses in his own clothes, he leaves Leander warm and hopeful, flashing a bright smile over his shoulder. It's nothing flashy or dramatic, just a squeeze to his shoulder and a "thanks, Lee," but the way they part ensures that those feelings don't fade, not in the least. Leander stands with his back to the apartment door for a very long time, smiling at nothing as he stares down an empty hallway, thinking about how damn lucky he is to have found a submissive like Tripp hiding inside his very best friend.

***

It's five minutes past six in the evening and Leander has barely managed to punch his timesheet into the machine or drop his overnight bag in the bunk room when his phone starts lighting up with messages.

Ding. Ding. Ding. Ding. Ding.

Tripp: Whatcha doin?

Tripp: Lee

Tripp: Lee

Tripp: Lee

Tripp: Leeeeeeeeeeee

Against his better judgment and *only* because Tripp can't see him, Leander smiles down at his message-flooded screen as he replies.

Leander: Bratty behavior will
not be rewarded.

Tripp: Brat? Me? :-P

Tripp: C'mon, Lee, I'm bored. Entertain me. I know you're not on a call, I'm sitting right next to the scanner.

Leander: I am not on a call, but that doesn't mean I am without work to do. Go and annoy Gunnar, I need to do a rig check. Zavier has been playing this ridiculous game where he plants expired medications just to see if we're actually looking at the dates.

Tripp: :(i'm bored

Tripp: how quick do you think you'll regret choosing chores over me

Tripp: try not to think about my ass too much

Leander: you're not funny

Tripp: I am objectively adorable

Leander: you're distracting me, i have a very important job, as you know

Tripp: i'm worth it, baby.
C'mon, talk dirty to me

Tripp: talk anything to me

Tripp: send me a dick pic

Leander: you know, it is true
that we never talked about
your lying to me yesterday.
The way you ran and hid and
spent an hour outside the ER,
rather than risk you and I
being alone together. If
you're this bored, we could
certainly discuss that. At
length, and in excruciating
detail?

Tripp: uh i think i hear our
tones gtg

It's unnecessary to check the scanner to know that there are no tones and that Tripp is definitely not going on a call right now.

Closing his eyes, Leander locks his phone and slips it back into his pocket before taking a slow, deep breath, letting it back out while he prays for strength. He has to remind himself several times that Tripp is just being *Tripp*. In fact, that entire virtual interaction was completely on par with their usual relationship, long before any discussion of sex and submission came into play. If Tripp had asked for a dick pic two weeks ago, Leander would have shot back a photo of an anonymous, dismembered body part (courtesy of Google) without so much as a second thought.

The fact is, they aren't in Dom / sub mode right now, and if he takes a step back, Leander can see that this is exactly how Tripp *should* be behaving. While it presses his buttons, that's *normal*, and it shows that Tripp is adapting. That he's not so affected or bothered by the shift in their relationship that it's seeping into their usual back-and-forth banter.

It's a good thing, Leander thinks.

"Meditating, boss?" Startled, Leander whirls around to find Marley leaning casually against the doorframe of the crew room. He moves towards her, heavy boots squeaking against the tile floor of the kitchen section of the common space, where he apparently forgot he was standing, in plain sight of anyone who might wander by. The whole room isn't more than twenty feet by twenty feet, a functional space divided straight down the middle by the shift to carpet.

On the side that doesn't host a full working kitchen (plus a table and chairs for eating), there's a hodge-podge of mismatched couches and recliners, plus a coffee table and a TV mounted above a bookcase that mostly holds DVDs. The far wall of the room plays host to a long countertop, currently cluttered with an assortment of chargers and empty holsters meant for various pagers and radios, plus a hanging literature organizer functioning as mailboxes, each slot labeled with someone's last name.

"Marley," Leander exclaims, clapping a hand to his chest. "You startled me."

His partner looks amused as she crosses the room to flop down on one of the ratty couches, bright red hair spilling artfully over the arm and swaying gently in the air. "'Sup, El Capitán? You seem… " She squints and raises her hands the way a director framing a shot might, thumbs and index fingers creating a window. Scouring his demeanor with what can only be described as suspicion, she eventually shrugs and tucks both hands behind her head.

"*Something's* weird with you. You *and* Tripp, actually, now that I think about it. You know, he was supposed to meet me for drinks last night. Never showed, didn't even *text*. Weird behavior from such a reliable guy, right? And now you, Captain Anal Retentive, are, what? Playing Candy Crush and getting zen in the kitchen, instead of checking your truck to make sure every gauze pad is in its place? What gives?"

Ignoring the lowkey insults, since he knows that coming from the *equally* anal-retentive Marley they're actually compliments, Leander runs a hand through his hair and nods, starting for the door.

"You're right, I should—"

"Don't bother." Marley cuts him off with a dismissive wave of her hand. "I did it already. Came in early to finish a chart from last night and jumped right into work when I finished. Changed the onboard oxygen, too. Oh—Zosia's switching your expired drugs out, including your narcs, so you'll just have to sign off on the new count when she's done. I wouldn't bother her, you know how she is with that stuff. All jokes aside, I think it *is* like meditation for her, you know?"

Nodding, Leander changes course, shuffling back into the crew room and sinking down into one of the recliners. He shifts to avoid the springs needling his ass and picks at the stuffing sticking out of the elderly chair's arm, avoiding Marley's shrewd gaze.

"So, you're really not going to tell me?" She pouts obnoxiously and crosses her arms with a loud and pointed, "*Humph.*"

"I'm really not going to tell you," Leander replies evenly, fishing the remote out from under the cushion he's sitting on and absently flipping through channels until he finds something suitably mindless. With any luck, it will serve to distract his partner and divert her endless curiosity. "And if you keep bothering me about it, I will assign you the entirety of the B.L.S. chart pile to Q.A. for the rest of the month."

"Whoa, shots fired," Marley replies, flipping onto her side and tipping her head up to affix Leander with what he's sure she believes is a charming grin. "So, what I'm hearing is, it's juicy."

"Marley," Leander warns.

"But—"

Whatever Marley's going to say is miraculously interrupted by the house system activating above their heads. Claxons blare, tones drop over pagers, and a staticky voice comes across the building's speakers as well as every device attached to belts and slung around shoulders in the vicinity. The feedback from his and Marley's pagers catches on the house system and makes Leander cringe. He misses the beginning of the dispatch, at least until they both get fingers on the squelch buttons, quieting their mobile devices and making it possible to hear the overhead.

"…an MVA with entrapment, multiple victims, possible Class 5… "

That's all Leander needs to hear before he's off of the couch like a shot, followed closely behind by Marley as he charges into the ambulance bay, mind already working overtime. On a scene like this, Leander has to manage so many things —responding units, prioritization of patients by severity, allocation of resources —the list goes on and the situation is, by nature, constantly evolving. Should he have a helicopter on standby? Should he try to resuscitate a pulseless, entrapped person when two other human beings need his attention? Are there enough medical providers to go around?

Nature of the beast—none of those questions can be answered, not yet. Not until they arrive on the scene, or if a cop gets there first and provides a radio update.

As he and Marley make their way across the bay, Zosia pops out from the back of their truck and slams the doors behind her. "Drugs are good. Put your narcs back, didn't have time to switch 'em before the call came in. They're expiring today, so use 'em if you can! You wanna lead?"

"Yes," Leander replies shortly, squeezing his Lieutenant's arm in thanks as he moves past her towards the cab. "Echo?"

"Already in the truck."

Of course, Leander realizes, internally facepalming. Both bay doors are open and Zosia's truck engine is running. Marley fires theirs as Leander hops into the passenger seat and clocks Echo, buckled and ready to drive the other truck. She shifts into gear as Zosia climbs in beside her, flashing him a smile and a wave, and then they're off. Echo's face disappears swiftly from Leander's peripheral vision as Marley pulls their ambulance forward.

On the way to the scene, Leander communicates with dispatch and learns that there are two victims already out of their vehicles, both up and walking, and an additional one who is reportedly unresponsive in the driver's seat. While the police officer on scene doesn't say so outright, Leander suspects from reading in-between the lines that the driver will not be a candidate for resuscitation. Based on that, he decides not to call for a third ambulance to join them.

It's not yet seven in the evening on what turned out to be a rather temperate spring day. One that successfully tempted a fair number of locals out and about, called to enjoy the sustained respite from the cold winter still chasing them. It's the same weather that had Tripp forgoing his long-sleeve tee at work the other night, and vaguely, Leander wonders if he made a better choice this evening.

Leander himself is wearing a sweatshirt with the City EMS logo on the breast, monochromatic navy from head-to-toe—it's all navy, all the time here, minus the white lettering—and the same color t-shirt underneath. In a few hours, even that may not be warm enough.

The thing about spring days and the increased outdoor activity they bring, is that trauma inevitably comes with them. People—lay people—tend to view rain and snow and sleet as the harbingers of terrible motor vehicle accidents, but no, it's the sun. The sun brings everyone out in force, crowds the roads, makes people feel innately safe and therefore act recklessly. The first nice days after a long, cold spell nearly *always* spell disaster on the roads and work for EMS. Motorcycles ripping carelessly around curves for the first time since fall. Elderly couples out for leisurely drives. Teenagers who earned their brand-new licenses over the winter and have been begging their mothers to let them borrow the car for *months,* finally cruising with the windows down and music up, laughing with friends, not paying attention.

As his ambulance pulls up to the scene and Leander registers the wreckage, he can almost *feel* the crash happening, replaying automatically in his mind's eye. It's not difficult to put the pieces together, not with how many vehicle accidents he's seen in his career, and honestly, Leander isn't sure that's a good thing. It certainly doesn't help him to sleep at night, when everything is said and done and the accident he wasn't even *in* repeats over and over behind his eyelids.

The car sitting smashed and totaled, leaking fluids like a sieve into the middle of the roadway, would have been turning left. From the angle it's pointed now, it had to have been coming out from a side street—*there,* Leander finds it—onto the main thoroughfare. This intersection (if you can call it that) is notorious—people have been lobbying for a stoplight here for years, to no avail. It's at the bottom of a steep hill, one that has nowhere convenient for police to sit astride and monitor speed, and as such, people fly down it traveling up to twice the legal limit.

Inside his head, Leander imagines the car pulling out, driver looking left and then right, waiting patiently for a fast-moving vehicle to finish blowing down the hill. It's probable that they forgot to recheck their left before ultimately pulling out into traffic.

The impact of the Ford F-150 that hit them would have been head-on, slamming directly into the totaled car's driver-side door. Whoever was operating the truck would have had no time to react, no chance to brake or swerve. His mind supplies the sensory details as Leander's eyes fall closed: the sickening crunch of metal-on-metal, the screeching of rubber tires against unmoving asphalt, the *pop* of airbags deploying violently—and it *is* violent.

Clouds of powder would have exploded over the car's interior, coating the upholstery and invading the mouths and nostrils of any passengers unlucky enough to be riding along. The sharp scent of gasoline and the burning smell of the destroyed engine would have mixed with the copper tang of blood in the air and on tongues, bitter as it pooled with saliva and God knows what other bodily fluids.

The car would have spun, the people inside would have been jerked and jolted from side to side, thrown about like rag dolls even with their seatbelts on. Leander's fingers tighten on his own thighs, envisioning—almost against his will—the force of the impact, the sound of glass shattering, the feel of it raining down over his face.

The smell he doesn't have to imagine at all: it's still lingering in the air. Stale and burning, a unique combination of oil and gas, smoke and fear. Most vehicle accidents smell exactly the same, just like this, and that produces a strange sense of deja vu each and every time Leander arrives at one.

Marley eases the truck's brakes to a full stop just shy of the edge of the scene, not wanting to drive into the middle of the mess. For practical reasons, but also, should the event actually produce a fatality, the immediate area will require the state police to conduct accident reconstruction—best not to disturb the evidence telling the story, if possible.

Produce a fatality. What an odd, detached way to refer to the violent snuffing out of someone's life. It's so cold, so callous, and yet, that's exactly what Leander has to be right now, so it's apt. He has a job to do.

"Dispatch, Medic Three and Medic Four are on location."

Fire is already here as well, an engine and a heavy rescue unit from two different stations, no Chief's vehicle yet. Both of their trucks are parked so as to create a barrier between the accident scene and approaching traffic, shielding both the first responders and the victims. From memory, Leander knows that there are two firehouses close by in opposite directions down the road, and that one of them is Tripp's. Despite that, Leander isn't looking for him, not right now.

The responding fire units beat EMS by several minutes, and consequently, there are a handful of bunker-gear-wearing firefighters distractedly milling around. Two are peering into the totaled car and yelling for something—Leander can't quite discern what that is over the ambient noise of trucks idling and traffic being redirected. Two more are crouched near the curb on the other side of the street, their helmets and gear blocking Leander's view of what must be the ambulatory victims.

There's a familiar face walking brusquely his way as he approaches the crash site. A petite blonde police officer who's normally sporting an unshakeable smile and a terminally-sunny attitude, something Leander would welcome immensely on a scene like this. She's likely come to give him report.

"Darla," he greets her warmly, but Darla's face remains taut and grim. Of all the ominous signs this scene boasts, that might be the most sobering.

"Captain," she replies formally, and Leander's stomach knots up in his abdomen. "Car full of teenagers, older brother taking his girlfriend and his sister on a ride to the mall." She points over to where the two firefighters are crouched by the curb and jerks her chin. "Driver of the truck is fine, doesn't want EMS to touch him. I have the girlfriend and the sister sitting down, they were both wandering around when I pulled up. Both are pretty shaken and bruised, younger one might be confused, hard to tell. Figured I'd leave that up to the professionals to decide."

"And the brother?" Leander asks, already dreading the answer but still not entirely prepared for Darla to shake her head and pull her uniform hat off, placing it over her heart. "God bless him—I'm no medical professional," she starts, "but even I know you don't survive your head exploding all over the window like that."

"Right," Leander acknowledges, the breeze feeling that much cooler as it whips across his face. "Thank you, Darla." He turns to his team, gathered a respectful step or two behind him, but nearly bouncing on the balls of their feet to jump into action.

He continues, "Zosia, see to the girls. Both of them need to be transported, regardless of injuries. It'll be much better for their parents to get the news about the boy in the safety of the ER where there are resources to support them. Marley, Echo, grab collars and boards and use Fire to help secure and load them. None of you need to be near the car, and I expect you to keep the girls away, too. It sounds as if they probably haven't realized what's happened yet. I'll pronounce and call for the coroner."

There's relief on everyone's faces as they split off from their little huddle, hurrying to carry out Leander's requests. Darla pats him on the arm, her face contrite and apologetic as he steps away towards the car. In his peripheral vision, the gold-plated "15" on the side of the engine glints dramatically in the dying evening light, making Leander squint.

Tripp is here somewhere, he remembers absently, now wishing more than anything that his friend was *right* here, by his side. But that's a luxury and a comfort Leander just isn't going to get today. As Tripp would say, "It's 'Big Girl Panties' time."

This is the worst part of the job, without question. This is the thing most of the EMTs and paramedics Leander knows have nightmares about. Before it happens, because of the fear, the anticipation of it, and then afterward for *years*, because of the scars it carves into your psyche. This type of situation represents the ultimate failure for a first responder—the victim they were too late to save, the person who is beyond their ability to help, even before they arrive on scene.

It's never *easy*. No matter the victim's age, gender, or the way in which they died, death is never painless to bear witness to. Some deaths are easier than others, of course. The ninety-year-old grandmother who dies peacefully in her sleep—Leander doesn't know too many medics waking up in cold sweats over calls like that.

But this... Darla slipped him the victim's license as he walked away—how she got it, Leander's not willing to think too much about. The boy's picture—vertically placed, since he's under twenty-one—shows a floppy-haired teenager with a dorky smile and acne. The birth date printed to its right lets Leander know that he only turned eighteen a month ago.

Eighteen.

These firefighters are on the ball. As Leander nears the car, he recognizes his niece, Chloe, standing alongside Station Eleven's Captain Reina Harrington. Reina gives him a solemn nod and tips her head towards Chloe, who's holding a folded tarp and looks as serious as Leander's ever seen her. They can't tarp the car until they have a medical go-ahead, and that's on him. Even though it's obvious, even though everyone already knows, no one on this scene can decide that it's officially over for this boy—no one except for Leander.

That reality weighs heavily on his shoulders, and he tries equally hard not to show it.

The actual physical assessment takes less than thirty seconds total, even counting the time it takes for Leander to climb into the passenger seat and lean over the boy's skinny body. He places two fingers on the boy's neck, because he has to. He presses his stethoscope to his unmoving chest, because he has to. Neither are necessary. If anything, Darla was downplaying the severity of the head trauma in her succinct description, and it's one of the hardest things Leander's ever had to look at, which is saying something.

Eighteen years, gone in the blink of an eye.

As he exits the still-smoking car, the whole scene seems to slow down and blur, voices going muffled and fading into the back of Leander's mind as he forces himself to go through the motions. Together with Chloe and Reina, he pulls the bright blue tarp up and over the car so that gawking bystanders can't see inside. Blue plastic waves in the wind and has to be weighed down by bags of sand in order to stay in place.

Leander turns away. The two survivors are already on backboards, secured to stretchers that are being loaded into each of the ambulances, and he follows, numb.

Using his portable radio, Leander requests the coroner. He speaks to Darla. He climbs into his ambulance and takes report on the shaken-up but mostly-uninjured little sister from Marley. They drive to the hospital in a hazy fog of red lights bouncing aimlessly through the deepening darkness outside the windows, sirens echoing off of towering buildings as they fly through the city unhindered.

He starts an IV. He asks the fourteen-year-old girl questions about her pain level, about what she remembers happening. He checks her vital signs, covers a shallow laceration on her arm, gives her an icepack for the blossoming bruise on the side of her face. When she questions him about her brother, Leander doesn't lie, but he doesn't tell her the truth, either.

"We should wait for your parents," he suggests. "At the hospital, they'll be there."

Someone called them. Darla, probably—Leander thinks he remembers her saying as much.

He's off the hook, anyway. The girl doesn't push for a better answer. Either she already knows and wants to stay in denial for a little while longer, or more likely, she hit her head and isn't completely capable of putting two plus two together right this second.

Leander calls report to the hospital and when they arrive, both his patient and Zosia's are taken directly to the double trauma bay. *Injury potential,* is the reasoning. *Death, same vehicle.* He and Zosia orate their reports clearly and competently to a crowded trauma room full of gowned and gloved professionals before leaving both girls in good, capable hands. The Chaplain is already present, ready to help deliver the bad news alongside the doctors and nurses.

It's cowardly, but Leander feels relieved to know that particular burden won't be down to him. At least, not this time.

As he strips off his gloves and washes his hands, Marley pats his back and instructs him to "go get some air," while she restocks their supplies. She knows him, knows how much he takes these sort of calls to heart, and considering the situation, it's likely that she's also extremely grateful he didn't make her look inside the car. Somewhat mechanically, Leander thanks her and turns away, automatically flicking his badge at the sensor lock to key open the ER doors.

Outside in the ambulance bay, there's a fire truck idling. The familiar gold "15" on the side looks colder since the sun has fully disappeared. Zosia must have taken one of their firefighters with her to help in the back, the engine is probably here to pick up whoever it was.

The air is chilly, the wind outright brisk, and Leander can't help but reflect back on his earlier ponderings regarding the likelihood that his sweatshirt wouldn't be warm enough tonight. He was right, but there's nothing to do about it now.

He's dazed. So much so that he doesn't realize he's been standing in the middle of the parking lot, staring blankly at the engine for several embarrassingly long minutes. It's not until the side door opens and someone gets out that Leander even makes an attempt to blink himself back to reality.

Tripp, clad once again in only his bunker pants and a fucking t-shirt, hits the ground moving and strides towards him with a worried look on his face. Despite everything, Leander can't help but smile at Tripp's stubborn stupidity, his ridiculous predictability, and his lack of simple common sense. It's inane, and Leander loves him for it.

"You look cold," he comments smugly, but Tripp isn't fooled, reaching out to grab Leander by the bicep and yank him into his chest, hugging him fiercely and clapping him firmly on the back, twice. Tears burst violently into the corners of Leander's eyes, and he chokes and gasps a little while doing his best to force them back.

"I know," Tripp says gruffly, rocking them both from side to side as Leander clings.

"I really need you," he mutters, soft and rough, and Tripp gets it immediately, pulling back and holding him at arm's length, but in a reassuring, possessive sort of way.

"You've got me," he replies, looking Leander straight in the eyes. "I promise. Tomorrow night, soon as we get off shift, I'll be there." Tripp squeezes his shoulder while Leander works to put his emotions in check and his face back in order, searching for the right thing to say. Tripp is a miracle, and Leander already owes him so much. What would he have done if they hadn't gone down this road? That's not even something he's capable of contemplating at the moment, so he shoves the thought away.

"Thank you," he settles on saying, his voice coming out used and gritty. He swipes roughly at his eyes and nods. "Tomorrow, then."

The fire engine revs and rumbles behind them, like someone has stepped on the gas without first releasing the brake. Clearly, the crew inside isn't trying to be obnoxious or insensitive, but someone wants them to get a move on.

"Text me," Tripp says, pointing a finger in Leander's direction as he walks backward towards the waiting truck. With a last nod and a wave, Leander agrees, and lets him go.

When he returns to his own truck, parked carefully in-between the next set of white lines beside Zosia and Echo's, the patient compartment is nearly back to its formerly pristine state. "Thank you, Marley," Leander says quietly, thumbing through his paperwork and the patient demographic information that Marley has kindly retrieved from registration.

"Dude, I should be thanking you," Marley quips, zipping up the first-in bag and plopping it on top of the stretcher for next time. "If you need—"

"I don't," Leander cuts her off quickly and then offers what he hopes reads as an appreciative look when she glares back at him disapprovingly. "I'm fine," he assures her.

"Oookay, if you say so," Marley concedes, shrugging as she hops down out of the truck and makes her way to the driver's seat. Before Leander follows, he takes a second to poke his head into the back of Zosia's rig, only to find Echo doing the same cleaning routine as Marley.

"Hey," he says. "You should text Chloe. I don't know how much she may have seen, but I thought she looked... " Leander trails off and presses his lips together. Echo will understand—she's been dating his niece for over a year now and knows the interminably stubborn Chloe better than just about anyone. In some ways, the two of them remind Leander quite a lot of him and Tripp: complementary pieces that shouldn't fit together, but somehow do.

Except, of course, for the fact that Chloe loves Echo back, and she shows it openly.

"Thanks for the heads up," Echo replies sincerely, stopping what she's doing to lean an elbow against the cabinets and eye Leander with concern. "And you? You don't look so good."

"I'm *fine*," Leander grumbles, ducking back out of the box and heading for his own truck. "Besides having to reassure everyone else that's the case."

"That's what Chloe always says when she's not fine," Echo yells after him.

"It's what *everyone* says when they're not fine, Echo," Leander shoots back, noncommittal and evasive as ever. He slides into the cab of the ambulance and motions for Marley to get going before Echo can so much as reply (or before Zosia can show up and pile on him, too). That's the last thing he needs right now. He *is* fine. Or at least, he will be.

Tomorrow night.

***

Twenty-four hours stuck off and on in various enclosed spaces with three smart, intuitive women who are *determined* to make Leander talk about his feelings turns him itching and anxious in an entirely different way. By the time six p.m. rolls around the following evening and Leander's shift ends, he's feeling marginally less distraught about what he saw at the accident scene, but a *lot* more interested in getting the hell away from his well-intentioned co-workers. He gets it —they're grateful he took one for the team, they want to support him, but none of them are any good at accepting that a roundtable discussion is simply *not* how Leander copes.

No matter what the experts claim, simply *talking* things out is not an effective tool for every person to deal with every kind of stress. Rehashing trauma in that way has always functioned in the reverse for Leander, causing him to feel worse. Unpacking what's in the rearview tends to paint a vivid picture of all the things that were and are out of his control, placing the value of words and intention above action and outcome in all ways. It's not something that's ever made sense to him and it's not a coping method he can relate to.

Working things out in a BDSM scene, though—a place where he controls the *intention,* the action, and the outcome—now, that's useful. However twisted someone else may find it to be, in Leander's mind, the importance of being able to *see* and *feel* his wins can't be overstated, and that's where being a Dom comes in. Talk can be valuable, of course, and there is a time and a place for it. But when it comes to processing and coping with trauma, talk simply doesn't work for Leander, and insofar as he can tell, it doesn't work for Tripp, either.

No one else needs to understand. They have each other for that.

As Leander is loading up his car to head home, he receives a text from Tripp advising that he's coming straight over, the minute the clock chimes six. Do not pass go, do not collect two hundred dollars—or in this case, do not shower and change. Logistically speaking, Leander knows that he should probably tell him to go to *his* home and do all that, but put plainly, he simply doesn't want to.

Since their brief encounter in the hospital parking lot the night before, he hasn't seen Tripp at all, and they've barely spoken. Both of their shifts were busy, leaving little time for texting. The result is an anxious Leander who is quite desperate to get on with their plans, and in general, to have Tripp in his arms.

Besides, he reasons to himself, it's well-within the sphere of their relationship for Leander to order Tripp—once he's collared—to get cleaned up or to prep himself in whatever way he deems necessary. In fact, the idea of Tripp *doing so* in Leander's own bathroom is an enticing thought all it's own, not to mention, one that's easily tacked onto the scene he has in mind.

Excited all over again (perhaps even more so now), Leander bids his co-workers a rushed goodbye, completely ignoring Marley's suspicious line of questioning regarding why he's suddenly smiling.

"Are you seeing Autumn again or something?!" She calls after him hopefully, her voice carrying loudly across the parking lot. But Leander just slides silently into his car, thrusting a hand out the window to wave at her as he pulls away. Marley doesn't need any inadvertent clues about how close she's accidentally wandered to the truth—knowing her, it's only a matter of time until she figures it out.

Leander wonders if Tripp realizes as much, and how he'll react when she inevitably does, because it's almost *certainly* a 'when,' and not an 'if.'

The drive home feels endless, though in actuality, it takes less than fifteen minutes. When Leander turns to maneuver his car into the parking area beneath his apartment complex, he notes Tripp's Chevelle already parked in the visitor's lot outside, and his extremities tingle with anticipation. Overnight bag slung over his shoulder, Leander takes the elevator from the garage up to his floor, beginning to slip into Dom-mode even before it dings his arrival and the doors slide open.

He's still unprepared.

Leander's breath catches in his chest because Tripp—Tripp looks even better than usual. Perhaps it's all of the anticipation and the build-up, the coalescing stress and emotions piled high on top of something Leander *already* wanted and needed very badly over the last twenty-four hours, but he's fairly certain he's never seen such a welcoming sight.

Tripp is still in his t-shirt, of course, paired with his blue uniform pants and heavy black duty boots, essentially the same thing Leander is wearing. Except, Tripp looks like he's modeling for a catalog, not coming off of a long work shift, and Leander probably has "just rolled out of bed" vibes. To be fair, he did—he took a nap from about four-thirty to six, and likely retains the crease lines on his cheek to prove it.

The way Tripp leans so casually against Leander's door frame, arms folded across his chest as he absently scrolls his phone, is artful perfection. His toned biceps push against the fabric of his t-shirt and the hem rides up a little near his hip, exposing skin that Leander has to physically restrain himself from dropping to his knees to lick.

Was he always this thirsty over Tripp? Leander finds himself having to wonder, and the answer is a resounding, *absolutely not.* Of course, he's been interested. He's found Tripp impossibly attractive, even, but it appears that getting a taste of what actually *having* Tripp is like has sent him tumbling over a cliff, the edge of which he didn't even know that he was standing on.

Cracking his neck, Leander ensures that he appears outwardly composed before approaching Tripp and sliding his key into the lock, which he does without a word. They both know why they're here, and—for many reasons—it's best that Tripp has access to his collar as quickly as possible.

Boundaries, Leander emphasizes to himself, for the hundredth or so time since their debriefing discussion yesterday morning. Excessive, perhaps, but important to him all the same.

As the door shuts behind them, he finds out swiftly that he has no reason to worry. The lock has barely clicked into place before Tripp is extricating the thin strip of leather from its box, threading it around his neck as Leander bends to put his bag on the floor. Doing his best to appear nonchalant (and not as if he thinks he might explode waiting for Tripp to give him the green light), Leander stands quietly with his fingers laced together behind his back.

Once again, Tripp doesn't disappoint, heading directly for the playroom after flashing Leander a cheeky wink that he gladly lets slide—just this once—because he really *is* thrilled with Tripp and the complete lack of prompting he's needed.

As he watches him go, Leander has the distinct feeling that he may need to remind himself from time to time that Tripp is *not* an experienced sub. He's clearly something special—his demeanor, his attitude, and the easy way he slips into the role, the willingness to accept everything Leander asks of him—he could fool even the most experienced Dom. But that doesn't mean that he knows his own limits, and Leander needs to maintain awareness of that.

He supposes they'll find out, if those things carry over to some more intense scenes, and the mere suggestion of doing so has the hairs on his arm standing up wildly.

Remembering himself and his plan for the night, Leander clears his throat. Instantly, Tripp stops dead in his tracks. The swiftness of his response and the incredibly clear desire to please nearly result in Leander's abandonment of the request on the tip of his tongue, and it would have—because he has very little restraint left in him tonight—but he does need a few minutes to prepare the room, so in the end, it's easiest to follow through.

"Instead of heading to the playroom, you're going to strip in the bathroom today. Leave your clothes in the hamper, then shower, clean up, and prepare yourself for me. There are enema kits underneath the sink, and lube in the top drawer of the vanity. In fact—wait one moment, please."

Leander's tone is clipped and efficient, and for the first time tonight, he sees Tripp falter a little, which is amusing. It's good that he's surprised and caught off-guard—scenes like this *should* be somewhat unpredictable for him, that's what Tripp wants. As Leander moves past his sub, he drops a hand to Tripp's lower back, allowing for a gentle caress, something grounding between them. Opening the door to the playroom, he heads over to the closest armoire and pulls the top drawer open, removing a still-packaged item from inside and handing it over.

"Clear?"

Tripp is still standing in the doorway, obedient as ever. Leander doesn't miss the flush that colors his cheeks when he accepts the brand-new plug, but to his credit, his posture straightens and he flashes a wide, cocky smile.

"Yes, Sir," he answers confidently. "Anything else, Sir?"

"No," Leander replies with a roll of his eyes and a mild swat of his hand to Tripp's ass as he passes. "Don't be a brat."

The door to the bathroom closes and Leander waits until the shower turns on, just on the off-chance that Tripp might need something. Satisfied that he'll have a few minutes alone, he moves about the playroom, meticulously setting up and fussing over details.

Even though Tripp doesn't wish to discuss or debrief on the daily, Leander's already decided that he's not willing to compromise on being the kind of Dom who doesn't blindside his sub with something—or a combination of things—that he may not be interested in. Kink worksheets are all well and good, but for the most part, all scene participants should have a *general* idea of what's coming on any given day, otherwise, there's no ability to ensure ongoing consent.

Perhaps that concept will evolve as they grow to learn and trust each other more fully within these new roles. After they find and press their own limits, both together and individually, and once Leander feels confident in reading Tripp's nonverbal cues. For now, though, they're building a foundation, and he's determined to ensure that it's solid.

As such, when Tripp finally exits the bathroom, naked, damp, and fresh, his skin pink and his hair wet but re-styled, Leander is waiting for him with a plan. He has Led Zeppelin playing again, knowing that the familiar chords will put his sub at ease, although it's much quieter tonight than last time—truly background music. Already stripped down to his boxers, Leander meets Tripp halfway across the room and cups his cheek, briefly considering dragging him in for a kiss but deciding at the last second that it would be too intimate under these circumstances. Instead, he reaches around and uses his fingertips to search for the base of the plug, humming approvingly when they brush along its curve.

"Lovely," he approves. "Thank you, Tripp."

"You're so welcome, Sir," Tripp replies quickly, and Leander preens.

"Truly, such a good boy," he murmurs, placing a hand on Tripp's shoulder and pushing down lightly in suggestion. "Kneel."

Once Tripp is on the ground, Leander steps away towards the bed, where numerous supplies have been laid out. "Tonight, my goal is for you to learn to trust me with your pleasure. You already know, of course, that I am in control of your body, but unless you earn a punishment or we agree in advance on complete denial, I *also* want you to trust that I will always take care of you in the end. Do you believe me, Tripp?"

Raising his eyes from where they've been trained on the floor, Tripp nods. "Yes, Sir."

"That's good," Leander says almost conversationally, nonchalant as he selects a slim vibrator, fresh out of its package, lifting it up from where it's been sitting on the bed. Once he's sure that Tripp's eyes are tracking, he runs a loose fist over it, intentionally teasing.

"It's good, because you won't come tonight until you're begging for it, until you've nearly given up on release. Your whole body will be screaming for deliverance, but only I get to decide when you've earned it. I'm going to tie you to this bed, blindfold you, tease you relentlessly, and fuck your mouth the way you wish I'd fuck your hole. Does that sound amenable?"

Biting back a smirk, Leander tips his head to the side and watches as Tripp's mouth falls open slightly, his tongue darting out nervously to wet his lips before he sucks in a breath. "Y-yes, Sir," he replies, fumbling over the words, which is very much the reaction Leander was hoping for. To his delight, Tripp remains kneeling with his hands behind his back, wide-eyed and unflinching as he awaits his next instructions.

Leander's blood warms in his veins to see it, thinking about all the ways he can't wait to positively *ruin* this man.

"Safeword, Tripp?"

"Halligan."

"And are you using it?"

"No, Sir."

Interesting. A much less cavalier response than the last time—Tripp is appropriately nervous now, and Leander is extremely pleased. "Stand. Lay on the bed, face-up, with your head just over the edge of the side I'm standing on—yes, exactly like that. Good boy." Leander praises Tripp as he clamors to obey, appreciating the curve of his ass and the flex of the muscles in his back as he climbs onto the elevated mattress and works himself flat.

Part of this scene involves keeping Tripp on his toes by forcing him to hold his head up. He *can* allow it to fall back, of course, and it won't even be particularly painful or much of a punishment if he does, but it won't be comfortable, either. With nothing underneath to support it, Tripp will be constantly pulled to thinking about his head and neck, to the blood rushing in opposite directions and deciding whether to endure the strain or let it drop. It's an additional mess of sensations that he'll have to war with, in addition to the rest of the onslaught Leander is planning.

Once Tripp is in position, Leander tugs loose a cuff that's attached to the post at the bottom of the bed, and another from the post at the top. He secures the first to Tripp's left wrist and the second to his right. When that's done, he adjusts each restraint length so that Tripp's arms are extended straight out to the sides. They stretch parallel along the line of the bed, only an inch or so of mattress separating the tops of his arms from empty space.

"Comfortable?" Leander murmurs, slipping a finger beneath the bindings and assessing Tripp's fingers to ensure that the cuffs are secure, but not so tight that function or circulation is impeded.

"I guess," Tripp huffs, clearly just being difficult and not actually unsure, but Leander grabs him by the hair anyway.

"You *guess?*" he growls. "Color, Tripp."

"Green, Sir," Tripp replies quickly, contrite as Leander raises his eyebrows and casts him a warning look. "I'm sorry, Sir."

"Better," Leander allows, before returning to his work.

It's entertaining to watch Tripp wriggle in place, testing his restraints and simultaneously trying to figure out what to do with his head, although Leander tries his best not to show exactly how amused he is. Instead, he grabs the silk blindfold left out for this purpose and folds it slowly, intentionally, drawing out the moment. He patently ignores the way Tripp squirms below him, starting to show the budding signs of impatience.

Sweet, summer child.

When the fabric has been secured around Tripp's eyes (and tested), Leander moves to the other side of the bed. There, he shoves a pillow underneath Tripp's ass in order to elevate it for easier access, before securing both of his ankles in a similar fashion to his wrists. Satisfied, he steps back to survey his kingdom, a thoughtful hand stroking his chin.

Just seeing Tripp tied up and helpless, willingly putting himself at Leander's mercy, *does* things to him. The feeling is far from unexpected and it isn't wholly unfamiliar, but it's also not *exactly* the same as his Dom experiences from the past. Sometimes with Autumn, Leander would work through an entire scene without so much as getting hard. Sometimes, he would get her off and completely forget about himself, because it was the *control* he was there for, first and foremost. The sex was always a bonus or a side-effect—and an unnecessary one, at that.

This, though. This is something different. Tripp's body is *interesting* to Leander in ways that no one else's has ever been. It produces sensations in his own being, awakens feelings and instincts he was never entirely sure he possessed. Just seeing Tripp naked—*knowing* that he's allowed to have him, to *take* him, any way he might desire—not only has Leander hard in his boxers, it forces the blood to flow definitively away from his brain.

It's very possible that lack of oxygen is making him hazy and silly, but just for a moment, Leander wonders why they're bothering with all this other stuff when they could just be *fucking*.

Thankfully, he comes back to himself before he does something stupid. After all, that "other stuff," is what Tripp is here for, and Leander *needs* to stay on track. This is where his own BDSM experience becomes salient, allowing him to easily pivot back to the task at hand, completely second-nature, as well as serving to keep him focused on what's important. Leander can do this—he can definitely do this, he was *made* for it.

Climbing up onto the bed, Leander straddles one of Tripp's thighs and runs a single finger down through the valley separating his pecs. Splayed out beneath him, Tripp shivers a little and pulls his bottom lip in-between his teeth.

"Color, Tripp?" Leander asks.

"Green, Sir," Tripp replies breathlessly, biceps flexing as he inadvertently tugs on his restraints.

"Hmm," is all Leander replies. Glancing over the remaining items he has laid out on the bed, Leander selects a small feather duster, flipping it over in his palm to tickle the soft end across Tripp's bare skin. It has the intended effect—at first, it makes Tripp laugh, loosening him up a little, but after a minute or two, the too-light sensations have him squirming and sighing, murmuring about being ticklish.

Down on Tripp's thigh, his shy-from-nerves, half-hard cock begins to plump up fully with the distraction. Leander doesn't even need to touch it to get him all the way there, he just flicks the duster around Tripp's various sensitive areas and grins at his own cleverness.

"I enjoy seeing you like this," he tells Tripp, who exhales pointedly. "So docile and compliant. So open and beautiful. Your body," he continues, leaning down to press a kiss to Tripp's sternum, to let his open mouth drag greedily over Tripp's firm abdomen, leaving a wet trail from his tongue and lips in its wake. "It's stunning," he tells Tripp's belly button, "You are an incredible creature, so deserving of my affection, my attention."

Unsurprisingly, Tripp grunts dismissively beneath him. Leander suspects that his face has turned fire engine-red, his lip probably close to bleeding from biting down hard enough to resist talking back. Amazingly, he does manage to keep his mouth shut and Leander rewards him, knowing full-well how hard that must have been for his self-deprecating sub.

"Good boy," he says approvingly, before opening his mouth and taking Tripp's erection in nearly to the root, swallowing firmly around him not once, but twice.

The muscles in Tripp's thighs spring taut and he groans, not expecting the intense stimulation and therefore, not remotely ready for it. Leander pulls off with a wet pop, wipes his mouth, and says, "Don't you *dare* come." He sits back on his heels and watches with satisfaction as Tripp struggles and pants but wrests himself back under control rather impressively quickly. Running a hand up Tripp's thigh, Leander decides that he's ready to move forward.

"Don't forget," he reminds Tripp. "You may come *only* when I say so, but you may beg all you like. In fact, you must, if you want to obtain my permission."

"Yes, Sir," Tripp acknowledges, his words already breathy and wonderfully needy.

After obtaining the lube and the vibrator again, Leander gets his fingers around the base of Tripp's plug and toys with it a little, working it against his rim. In and out, occasionally leaning forward to swirl his tongue over the crown of Tripp's cock, just to be a tease. Tripp responds beautifully, sighing and moaning quietly, tugging at his restraints and wiggling his ass as best as he can. There's no reason to admonish or encourage him to stay still—Leander's rather enjoying how affected Tripp is, and besides, there's quite literally nowhere for him to go.

The plug slips out and Leander sets it aside, slicking up his fingers and prodding Tripp's hole himself, wanting to draw out the teasing before allowing him the vibrator. He slips two digits inside easily, sweeping them around until he locates Tripp's prostate. A firm press of his fingers has the man arching right up off the bed—as much as he's able—and Leander draws the moment out, entertained.

"That was impressive, for being tied up," he teases, and Tripp moans, doing his best to rock down onto the fingers but getting absolutely nowhere. "Now, now," Leander scolds. "Patience. Or, at least tell me what you want."

"Want *you*, Lee," Tripp moans throatily, and if Leander wasn't hard before—*fuck*. His dick blurts precum onto his thigh and Leander blinks down at the mess in surprise, his hand automatically moving to provide some relieving pressure, unfamiliar with having such a strong reaction in a sexual situation.

"Sir," he corrects Tripp, but his reaction is delayed and he's almost remiss to issue it for the way '*Lee*' sounds coming out of Tripp's sinful mouth. Despite his hesitation, he does lift Tripp's leg to slap him on the ass, hoping that'll be received as sufficient reproach. Tripp is... *so* much more distracting than Leander could have anticipated.

"*Sir,*" Tripp moans, not missing a beat. "Sir, please, I need your fingers. Please touch me again, ple—" His rambling is cut off by another moan when Leander obliges—since he asked so nicely—pushing two fingers inside again and giving Tripp the pressure he's asking for.

"You like that, hmm? That's excellent news, because I have so much more to give you." Without waiting for a reply, Leander swaps his fingers for the lubed-up vibrator, turning it on and angling the device so that it rests directly against Tripp's prostate. At this point, Tripp's cock is rock-hard and looking a little purple, practically begging for someone to touch it. Tripp clearly agrees, rocking his hips and squirming, desperate little noises spilling from his throat.

Pleased by what he's created, Leander hops down off of the bed and watches for a moment, enjoying Tripp's writhing and the sounds that are steadily increasing in both volume and need. He readjusts the vibrator's depth when it slips, and eventually, rounds the bed to where Tripp's neck is having the roughest time of all.

It's clear from the tension in Tripp's strong shoulders that keeping his head up is becoming a strain. He's frequently letting it drop, which makes Leander's timing all but perfect. Anticipation thrumming, he shucks his boxers and stands to Tripp's left, at exactly the right height thanks to the elevated nature of the bed— one of the best design decisions he could've made regarding this room.

Reaching out to slide a bracing hand underneath the base of Tripp's skull, the overstimulated sub can't help but sigh in relief. He tries to relax into the soothing grasp, but Leander clicks his teeth in reproach. "Oh no, you don't," he says, carefully tipping Tripp's head to the side and using his free hand to grasp his own cock, rubbing the tip across Tripp's parted lips.

The sight is obscene. It looks almost nonconsensual, with Tripp stretched out and tied down, the blindfold covering his eyes, the way he's sweating and tensing from the vibrator in his ass. He's gorgeous, truly a work of art, and Leander is over the moon about every single detail. Not only the aesthetics, but the way the scene as a whole makes him *feel*—body hot and so aroused that he has to work to keep himself in check, in control. It's way beyond what he's used to, what he *expected* to feel, but in a truly spectacular manner that he wouldn't change a bit.

Another dribble of precum leaks from his cock, and this time, Tripp's tongue is darting out to taste, his mouth opening and neck straining to take Leander in, and who is he to deny such a perfect, desperate request? *Except—he can't.* Leander's so enthralled, he nearly forgets to pause and roll on a condom, remembering at the last possible second. Tripp looks disappointed, but he waits patiently.

As Tripp's lips finally close around him, Leander releases a hum of satisfaction, allowing himself a long, quiet moment where he closes his eyes and just holds Tripp's head, relishing the hot, wet heat enveloping him. With one hand grasping Tripp's jaw, he can feel the muscles there relax, see the saliva drooling from Tripp's mouth as he cautiously pushes all the way in, past his hard palate and into his throat.

To his credit, Tripp—shaking and clutching at the bedsheets with his fingertips —just breathes and takes it, moving air through his nose and letting Leander do whatever it is he wants.

That produces an incredible rush of power and emotion, and when Leander pulls out and Tripp gasps, he can't resist crouching down immediately, fisting both hands into Tripp's hair and kissing him passionately—thorough and deep, even as the man is still catching his breath.

"Perfect," he mumbles, right into Tripp's mouth. "You're perfect."

"Please," Tripp rasps, as Leander kisses the corner of his mouth, his jaw, as he nips along his neck and reaches down between his legs to adjust the vibrator. Tripp's body jerks violently beneath his chest when he does, and he cries out.

"Fuck, Sir, please, please," he begs.

"Soon," Leander replies, pressing his thumb into the soft flesh of Tripp's chin and encouraging his mouth open again. He complies, of course, with tears in his eyes and a sob in his throat, and Leander slides back into his mouth, more gently this time. He doesn't fuck Tripp's face like he promised, or try to deepthroat him again, he just rocks there for several minutes, alternately reaching down to fix the vibrator and murmuring encouragement for Tripp to swallow or to use his tongue, which he does flawlessly on command.

When he pulls out again, Tripp has had enough, and Leander can *see* it this time. He recognizes all of the signs that this scene is nearing the point where it will tip for Tripp. That's perfect, because he's ready, too. Supporting Tripp's neck, Leander removes the blindfold before hitting the quick releases for the restraints at his wrists, pushing him to a sitting position so that he can follow him up onto the bed and release his ankles, too.

Once free, he shoves Tripp down onto his back where he flops like a ragdoll, as glassy-eyed and pliant as Leander can imagine it's possible to get. It's an incredible, beautiful thing to see, and Leander soaks up every second of it.

"Gorgeous," he murmurs, sliding both hands up the tender skin of Tripp's thighs before pushing them apart to crawl in-between and pull the vibrator, tossing it aside. He elaborates on his praise to buy himself a couple of seconds.

"You are incredible, Tripp. Everything I hoped for and more."

When Leander pushes inside his body, Tripp groans loudly in abject relief and reaches out to touch, retracting his hand just as quickly, unsure as to whether he's allowed.

"Go on," Leander encourages, thrusting shallowly. "Touch whatever you like, you've earned it." To his surprise, Tripp immediately threads both arms around his neck, pulling him down so that his own legs are bent up nearly against his chest. He wants skin-on-skin, wants them to be as close as possible, and Leander *knows* he shouldn't allow it, but can't bring himself to deprive this version of Tripp anything.

Instead, he sets about fucking him hard, going fast and deep, making Tripp cry out and dig fingers into his shoulder blades with every thrust. "Please, Sir, please, please, please let me come, *please*, I—"

"You can come, Tripp," Leander replies fervently, doing his best to shut Tripp up because it's *too much,* for *him,* and oh—Leander realizes far too late that he should have fucked him with the blindfold on, because his *eyes*—

He is way too late to stop Tripp from finishing while looking straight up at him, eyes brimming with lust and longing, at least until they squeeze shut with pleasure, and isn't that some kind of bizarre relief? Still, with Tripp clenching around him and the memory of the *desire,* the *want,* the *trust* in his green eyes, in his expression—Leander groans into Tripp's shoulder as he spills inside of him, filling the condom and wishing it wasn't between them.

He steals only a second to catch his breath in the warm, inviting crook of Tripp's neck before sitting up, very aware that Tripp is sore and will need a significant amount of care and attention before they can collapse tonight. That's obvious when Leander accidentally leans on his shoulder to sit up, and Tripp winces before blinking up at him, wide-eyed and unsure.

"Sir?" he asks timidly, and he's very quiet, very *un*-Tripp-like, which makes Leander start, despite his exhaustion. "Was that...uh, okay?"

Despite himself and the fact that he knows Tripp is serious, Leander can't help it —he bursts into laughter. Only for a moment, and then he reins it in. Cupping Tripp's cheek and leaning down to kiss him softly, he smiles. "I don't lie to my subs, Tripp," he says. "When I told you that you were perfect, I meant it." Tripp still looks unsure, so Leander sighs and takes his chin between his thumb and forefinger. "Do you believe that I would lie to you?" he asks sternly, and Tripp looks surprised.

"No," he says, after a moment. "Of course not."

Releasing him, Leander pats the side of his face. If only he could reassure Tripp with the truth, the fact that he's never had a more satisfying, a more *arousing* sexual encounter in his *life,* but clearly, Tripp would not appreciate that. No, Leander needs to keep those feelings and revelations under wraps, but that doesn't mean he can't reassure Tripp as best he's able.

"I'm extremely pleased with you, Tripp," he says. "If you'll roll over onto your stomach, I'm going to retrieve some juice and some lotion, and then I'll be happy to show you how much."

As Leander makes his way over to the armoire that houses his mini-fridge, he chances a glance over his shoulder and finds Tripp already on his stomach, watching. He flashes Leander a sleepy smile and then yawns, and Leander's heart nearly stops.

Damn, but he is so, so fucked.

Chapter 3

Tripp is fucked.

And not only in the literal, obvious way that's currently making his throat and ass ache in equal measure, although that's true, too. Ironically, that's also the one thing between him and Lee that's going very, very right.

Alright—*fine.* Tripp's man enough to admit that it's *possible* he's being a little dramatic, in that respect. After all, he and Lee are technically fine, at least as far as Lee has any idea. Tripp is the one that's messed up in the head, the one who's feeling guilty for enjoying this whole "aftercare" thing a little bit more than he should.

It's just that Lee gave him a free pass to press up against his chest and to tangle their legs together. To lean into Lee's caressing fingers as they slip through his hair while another soothing hand runs down his flank. Doing so is definitely not assuaging his mental turmoil, but it isn't like Tripp's turning it down, either.

No, he's definitely doing this to himself, but at least his cover is solid. If Tripp's going to lie here risking his sanity just to revel in getting Leander's affection exactly the way he's always dreamed of having it, he can at least take comfort in the fact that this is technically what he's *supposed* to be doing. As far as Lee is concerned, Tripp is simply taking what's on offer, accepting the care that *Lee* believes he needs following their scene. The end result—*cuddling on steroids*—is both the worst and best situation he could imagine, and it would *once again* take a stronger man than Tripp to turn it down.

Another complicating factor is that Tripp is so damn new to this whole scene. By default, he isn't familiar with what *"aftercare"* normally involves or should entail, and he's been relying on what Lee has told him and what he's read about online to gauge his own boundaries and limits. He can guess, but he really wouldn't know if he was going too far or being too obvious about his secret desires in the first place.

Regardless, Lee clearly believes that everything he's doing is important—necessary, even—which kind of makes it easier to accept. That's definitely something to fall back on, should the guy ever become suspicious of Tripp's intentions and motives. The whole, "Shit, sorry, I dunno what I'm doing here, man," dumbass shuffle is as perfect an excuse as Tripp could hope to keep in his back pocket.

Push comes to shove, though, Tripp's fairly certain that these internal conflicts—the things he can't stop himself from wanting or from taking when they're offered, no matter how much guilt it piles on his conscience—aren't even blipping Lee's radar.

The guy is *focused*, Tripp will say that much. While he was busy basking in the afterglow, toes still tingling from the mind-numbing orgasm gifted to him, Lee was practically *jumping* off of the bed and back into action. He was adamant about rubbing Tripp down thoroughly, meticulously working even the *memory* of strain from his shoulders and arms, and he spent nearly an hour following their scene doing exactly that.

Not that Tripp is complaining—far from it. Hell, it was one of the best massages of his life, and he enjoyed every damn second of what felt like pampered luxury. Lee's hands are magic, and the weight of his body, his knees bracketing Tripp's hips from behind—well, Tripp would be hard-pressed to think of any other place in the world he'd rather be than the meat in that thick-slice sandwich.

And then there was the *touching*—that was nothing to sneeze at, either. As if he could sense Tripp's needs, Lee barely left him alone on the bed. Less than a minute, in fact—only as long as it took him to grab a pack of clean-up wipes, a bottle of juice from the little playroom fridge, and some massage oil. Then he was back, and ever since, some part of his skin has been in constant contact with Tripp's. It's impressive, how careful and thoughtful Leander can be, how he *always* is when it comes to Tripp.

It's just that—well, Tripp can't help but suspect that most of those things were items Lee had on his *agenda*. Things he planned for and was prepared to deliver in advance. They don't amount to anything more than a BDSM checklist, stuff Lee felt like he *needed* to do, not because they were specific to Tripp's wants and needs or rooted in actual concern and affection.

Leander performs aftercare because it's *right*, and necessary.

Perform is a good word for it. Unlike Tripp, Lee's post-sex, post-scene actions aren't based on any emotional desires or a desperate need to touch, to hold Tripp close in the same way Tripp himself craves being held. He knows that, but with the orgasm hormones raging, it messes with his head a little. He has to repeatedly remind himself that Lee is his *friend*, and he does care in his own way. Even if it's not the way Tripp wishes he would.

Those intrusive thoughts kept popping up during Lee's rubdown, annoying and preventing him from relaxing completely, and to Tripp's chagrin, Leander took notice. Fortunately, he assumed that the uneasy discomfort was related to Tripp's pain level, force-feeding him a handful of ibuprofen and setting him up with alternating ice and heat for his shoulders, no matter how vehemently Tripp protested that he was *fine*.

Tripp has been learning rather quickly that Dominant Lee isn't someone you argue with. Not for fun and definitely not for keeps, and in the end, it seemed patently easier to just let Leander fuss over him. So Tripp gave in, allowing himself to savor the touching and the attention, and to be fair, the pampering wasn't anything approaching terrible. If Tripp's being honest, he might even admit that he liked it more than the sex.

Hard to regret.

While Tripp was laid up with his ice packs—definitely unnecessary, but it did feel good—Leander ordered them delivery from Tripp's favorite burger joint. He brought the food into the playroom spread out on a fancy-looking lap tray and plated with real utensils, like he was trying to mimic a five-star restaurant. At Lee's own insistence, he hand-fed Tripp the entire meal, kissing his mouth between bites and praising him generously, as though by opening his mouth and chewing Tripp was doing something difficult and burdensome, not literally being finger-fed like a spoiled, lazy prince.

Aftercare that was arguably as intense as the actual scene initially made Tripp feel somewhat uncomfortable, but Leander won him over. He just seemed *so* pleased, so damn into what he was doing, that Tripp couldn't help but follow the vibe. He found himself (slowly) relaxing into it, enjoying himself, smiling dopily and kissing Leander back without overthinking it. Despite his lingering embarrassment over just how *much* aftercare Leander apparently thinks he needs, Tripp has to admit, it's not the worst feeling in the world—being cared for so thoroughly.

Almost like he's special or important, words he struggles to apply to himself in any way outside of this liminal space.

Here, Leander's easy way of making moments like that feel natural, his fierce determination to treat Tripp with care and respect—it spills over into Tripp's inherent ability to accept those things for what they are. And maybe, *maybe* a tiny part of him can admit that he wants to do precisely that, but only inside his own head.

Hey, Rome wasn't built in a fuckin' day.

At the end of *this* day, though, here Tripp is, laid out on Leander's playroom bed with his belly full, his mind and muscles sated and relaxed, staring aimlessly up at the ceiling and feeling borderline euphoric. At some point, Leander slipped on a pair of sweatpants, but Tripp hasn't bothered. He's enjoying the feel of crisp, clean sheets against his back and the gentle airflow from the overhead fan whispering across his bare skin.

Leander is sitting propped against the headboard, his legs crossed casually at the ankles and Tripp's head in his lap, where it's been for at least the past half an hour.

All told, they've easily spent twice the amount of time recovering from their scene as they did engaging with it tonight, and Tripp wonders somewhat absently whether that's normal or not. It's not like he has any frame of reference to know, and he's *just* about to open his mouth and ask when Leander clears his throat, thighs shifting underneath his head.

"How are you feeling, now?" he asks, one hand moving down to smooth over Tripp's chest before cupping his chin. "Still sore?"

"I'm good," Tripp replies honestly, tipping his head back in time to catch a glimpse of Leander's soft smile directed his way. "Really, I swear. *Sir*," he adds smugly, tacking the moniker onto the end of his reply like an afterthought, intentionally bratty.

"I believe you, Tripp," Leander assures him, ignoring Tripp's dangling bait, and then it's silent for a moment while Lee's finger traces over his collarbone and down the line of his sternum. "I know you don't wish to debrief, but may I at least ask whether or not you enjoyed yourself?"

Caught off-guard by that particular twist in the conversation, Tripp barks a laugh and grins up at his Dom when he's able. "Uh, yeah, you could say that," he replies, pulling his lip slowly and provocatively through the cage of his teeth. Lee seems pleased with that answer, his face practically glowing in the dim light, and Tripp likes the look on him, wants more than anything to be the reason Lee looks like that all of the damn time. All because of *him*.

"It's late," Leander tells him gently, soft fingers continuing to stroke across his chest and the curve of his face. "Time… got away from us this evening, not that I'm complaining. However, I may fall asleep on you shortly if I don't admit that between my difficult shift and tonight's activities, I'm quickly running out of steam. And we wouldn't want that."

"Oh," Tripp says weakly, surprised and unprepared for Leander to be kicking him to the curb after everything, but he sits up and moves to start gathering his things all the same. It makes sense. Lee is tired, Lee deserves some time to himself. The last thing he needs is a high-maintenance sub hanging out in his space, sapping his energy, and—

"No, Tripp, wait—" Leander reaches out an arm and catches his wrist, tugging him back down onto the mattress. "I wasn't attempting to subtly suggest that you should leave. On the contrary, if you're interested in doing another scene tomorrow morning, I would very much like for you to stay."

The earnest look on Lee's face, paired with those wide blue eyes practically pleading for Tripp to accept his offer, have him feeling like putty in his best friend's hands. Who on earth could deny someone who looks like *that* when they want something?

"You know, you can pretty safely assume that the 'yes' reply to a 'wanna do it again?' is a given with me," he replies, pasting on his best smirk, if only for Lee's benefit.

"Be that as it may, the scene that I have in mind is exciting but intense, and I—well, you said that you didn't want any spoilers. Now that I know you're up for it, I suppose I have what I need, and can let you be." With that, Leander works his way off of the bed, sauntering over towards the door, and Tripp doesn't need to see his face in order to know that Lee is wearing a smirk of his own.

"Oh, that is cold, Le—*Sir*," he corrects himself, just in time.

When Leander twists at the waist in the doorway, he's sporting a full-on predatory grin, and Tripp can't help but marvel at how *he's* supposed to be the brat in this relationship. *Damn.* But then he sees Lee stifling a yawn, and Tripp's instantly back to wishing he hadn't left the bed, that they were about to curl up together and just *be*—no rules, no boundaries, no expectations. They've only really done this twice, and it's already becoming difficult for Tripp to switch gears, to turn his outward desire towards Lee off and on like a lightswitch.

"So you'll stay?" Lee is asking, when Tripp tunes back in.

"I'll stay," Tripp allows, scooting back onto the bed and spreading his arms wide on the pillows. "You know, this mattress *is* huge," he adds, shooting for casual. "Plenty of room for two. No reason we can't sleep in the same place again, right? I thought it was pretty nice last time. I mean, you know, if you wanted company."

To Tripp's dismay, Leander's face does about a thousand things all at once, none of which mean anything good for him. *Oh fuck,* he thinks, realizing with some horror that he's just made a huge mistake that's about to turn things incredibly awkward. Lee doesn't want to sleep next to him—of course he doesn't. That's not what this is, not what either of them agreed to, and now, thanks to Tripp's selfish idiocy, Lee thinks he has to figure out how to *say so* without coming off like *he's* the major-league dick.

Shit.

So Tripp does what he does best—he rushes to make a joke.

"Dude, relax," he says, offering what he hopes is an easygoing laugh as he tucks his hands casually behind his head. Lee is so obviously distraught that he doesn't even catch the slip, doesn't remind Tripp that he's wearing his collar, and that it's '*Sir*' right now. "You should see your face. I was just messing with you, didn't think you'd take it so seriously. Go on, get out of here. Tripp Truett does not cuddle." He punctuates the last sentence with a pointed finger and an equally sharp look that has Leander's expression melting into one of pure relief.

After that, Lee can't seem to bolt from the room fast enough, although he does take the time to remind Tripp that there's more juice in the fridge, and that he's welcome to come out and watch TV if he can't sleep, or to utilize anything else in the apartment to make himself at home. It's cute and unnecessary, and it makes Tripp's chest tight to watch Lee try and compensate for not wanting to stay in the same bed with him overnight.

When the door finally clicks shut, leaving the room dark and empty, the smile Tripp's wearing immediately drops from his face. Inwardly, he vows to be more careful, to never let something like what just happened do so again. Lee is in this for one thing and one thing only, and that shit was on the label. Like *fuck* is Tripp going to allow his inconvenient emotions ruin this for the both of them.

Before Leander ran away, he also let Tripp know that he could remove his collar if he wanted, for sleep. That he was under no obligation to stay in "sub-mode" overnight or into the morning—not if he didn't want that. If he's being honest, for the first time since Leander presented him with him the collar, the temptation to take it off is *there*. Seeing his best friend reject the offer to stay in the same bed was tough, and Tripp would be lying if he claimed that a little distance from the whole arrangement didn't sound good right now.

On the other hand, his emotions are on the edge. He hasn't experienced any sort of "drop" for himself yet, nor has he seen any signs of it on Leander, but the potential is certainly there—Tripp can feel it. While he may not fully grasp all the specific minutiae of aftercare or the details particular to '*Lee*' versus '*Doms in general*', Tripp definitely gets the importance of the process. And Lee did do a stellar job with him tonight, but there's still… something. A lingering instability in the back of his mind, a crawling worry or fear that he can't quite articulate just yet.

Tripp's not an idiot. He knows perfectly well that those feelings are an indicator of drop, but they're not overwhelming him, not taking over or monopolizing his thoughts in any way that he can't control. So instead of tracking Lee down and filling him in—*especially* knowing how much Lee wants to be in his own bed, not trapped in here with an annoying sub—Tripp fights off the creeping gloom.

He goes over to the armoire containing the fridge, grabs a juice, and retrieves his phone from the pocket of the pants he left crumpled and kicked to the side of the bathroom. Settling uneasily back into bed, he thumbs through a mindless internet game, and after popping virtual soda bottles for the better part of half an hour, Tripp feels a little more solid. Better, but not fully like himself.

He lets out a sigh and glances around the darkened room. His widened pupils take in the shadows of various pieces of equipment, his gaze drawn to the armoires towering overhead. They look at least twice as big with the deep pockets of darkness reaching like arms to envelop them.

The collar sits weighty on his neck. It itches and feels tight, whereas usually, it makes him feel free. Right now, there's nothing Tripp would like to do more than rip it off, but just the *idea* of doing so has him feeling worse. What if he wakes up in full drop and can't find his collar? Or shaking hands keep him from buckling it back together? What if he goes to the bathroom to piss, panics, and his collar isn't nearby? Lee made the rules crystal clear—he won't touch him when he's not wearing it, and Tripp *can't* risk that right now.

As he scoots down into the mattress and pulls the blanket up over his shoulders, Tripp grumbles quietly to himself. It's frustrating, having these emotions swirling around inside of him, but most of all, he's annoyed. Annoyed that he's feeling some type of way at all, annoyed that he needs Leander and can't have him, annoyed that Leander would apparently rather be anywhere else than by his side.

Tripp closes his eyes and pushes a few slow, calming breaths through his lungs. The irritation, the prickly attitude—none of it passes or starts to ebb away. Ultimately, Tripp is cognizant enough to come to terms with what's up and not coming down here, but that doesn't mean he's about to ruin Lee's night over it.

Instead, Tripp decides to go deep. Squeezing his eyelids tight, he thinks back on their scene, on the adoring way Leander looked at him, and some of the things that he said.

"Good boy," Leander had murmured, his voice warm and rich and appreciative. Tripp can still hear the words ringing in his head, feel Lee's breath soft against his skin.

"Perfect. You're perfect." That one was whispered against Tripp's mouth, leaving him greedily swallowing every word, gulping them down desperately, flaming with embarrassment to hear such praise directed his way, and yet—it all felt *so* damn good.

He treasures the memories now, digging for more, and there are so many. Tripp drowns himself in each recollection, savoring them one at a time.

"An incredible creature," Leander had called him. "So deserving of my affection, my attention."

Those are the words Tripp clings to, here in the lonely dark. He lets the tone of Lee's voice in his head, the memory of the gentle caress of his hands soothe and pacify him. When the impact of those things starts to fade, Tripp moves on to thinking about how Leander cared for him after the scene finished. The way he spoke softly, the way he tipped juice into his parched mouth. The incredible massage, the ice packs, the heating pad. His favorite burger ordered from memory and fed from Lee's fingertips—*bliss.*

It works.

The tendrils snaking out from the darkest corners of Tripp's mind retract, dissipating slowly but surely back into the ether. His mood evens out and stabilizes, no longer setting his teeth on edge or making him clench his fists in raw irritation. In fact, the entire day starts catching up with him fairly quickly, making Tripp's eyelids heavy and his thoughts turn fuzzy. Even as he drifts off to sleep, Tripp continues to wish that he wasn't alone, but there's nothing he can do about that now.

The best he can hope for at this point is more of whatever Lee is willing to give, tomorrow.

Tripp already knows he'll take it, whichever parts of his friend end up on offer.

Tripp will take it all.

***

Waking up is confusing. The warm body pressing flush against his back is something Tripp feels *extremely* sure was not there when he went to sleep. A quick glance towards the covered windows reveals the barest fringe of bright light leaking out from one curtain's edge—*morning.* Despite the fuzziness in his head, Tripp's dick is having none of the same qualms, fully on board with the big, warm hand stroking it firmly.

"Hello, Tripp." Leander's sleep-rough voice rumbles in his ear and against his skin, warm breath ghosting over the curve of Tripp's shoulder and down the back of his neck. There's a knee nudging its way in between his thighs, and Tripp finds himself parting his legs instinctively, letting Leander manipulate him in whatever way he likes.

That includes, apparently, mouthing at his collar, nosing at the leather, and nipping the sensitive skin just beneath. Even in Tripp's sleep-groggy state, the possessive show has him rolling his eyes.

It would be going too far to say that Tripp doesn't like his collar—*hell* no, he loves it. Loves how free he gets to be while wearing it, loves everything that it represents. At the same time, he would be lying if he claimed that Lee's obsession with the thing wasn't starting to grate. Waking up to his friend worshipping the little strip of leather first thing in the morning automatically brings Tripp *right* back to the negative headspace he worked so hard to rid himself of the night before. Being left alone with his thoughts was no freaking picnic.

Still, it's hard to argue with being jerked off in Lee's arms, his hand functioning as an alarm clock, though how that happened Tripp can't begin to figure. He supposes—like everything else lately—that he should probably just sit back and enjoy, and not question it.

Just when he's finally starting to relax and sink fully into Leander's grip, it disappears completely, as does the man's reassuring presence behind him. Unable to suppress the urge in time, Tripp groans and smacks the mattress with his palm, growling his friend's name as he buries his face into the bedding.

"*Lee,*" he grunts, voice muffled significantly by the pillow's bulk, but not enough. Leander catches the slip and swats him—*hard*—right on the meat of his ass. "Ouch!" Tripp yelps, rolling over swiftly and sitting up, rubbing a hand protectively over his stinging skin as he does.

The lights are on, causing him to blink groggily against their glare, still not entirely awake. Small mercies, they're dim, but plenty high enough for Tripp to see the room and that Leander has been busy while he slept. Narrowing his eyes, Tripp glowers at the man as he strides—buck naked and clearly very pleased with himself—around the bed to stand at his side.

"What the hell," Tripp mutters, rubbing at his eyes and trying to figure out why there's a foam mat on the floor to his left and a *hefty*-sized dildo sticking jauntily out from the wall above it. He's sure—well, ninety-five percent—that particular monstrosity wasn't there when he drifted off to sleep, any more than Lee was in his bed.

"What was that?" Leander asks smugly, cupping a hand around his ear to blatantly mock Tripp while simultaneously assessing exactly *how* much of a brat he's intending to be. When Tripp doesn't answer, Leander hums and cards a hand through his hair, tightening his fingers at the back in subtle warning before abruptly letting go.

"You kept your collar on," he says, tone thoughtful but pleased. "And you're familiar with the rules, yes?" It's an olive branch, an out (or at least a last chance of sorts), but Tripp is grumpy this morning, and while he *does* want Lee to fuck him six ways 'til Sunday, he's irritated enough to fuck around and find out what happens.

Glaring up at his friend through his lashes, Tripp licks his lips and holds steady eye contact while he carefully annunciates, "Fuck the rules, *Sir.*"

Tripp's cheek is stinging before he even fully registers what happened, his head whipping violently to the side as Leander's palm makes sharp contact with the side of his face. No time for recovery—or even to take a breath—given that Leander grabs his chin in one hand and forces him to make eye contact, his own blue eyes glinting with both amusement and promise.

In the aftermath, Tripp has zero—*count 'em: fuckin' zero*—regrets.

Hit me again, his brain supplies, and Tripp wants it so badly, he can taste blood on his tongue—he nearly says so out loud.

"Color, Tripp," a righteous Leander demands, and even if Tripp didn't have a front-row seat to the guy's dick filling out against his thigh *right* beyond the tip of his nose, he'd be able to see the arousal, the *intention* coloring his face.

Before answering, Tripp works his jaw back and forth and then pauses, just to piss Leander off. "Green," he says finally, right as Lee is opening his mouth to do God-knows-what, Tripp's never going to find out. Against his better judgement, he smirks a little, and Leander grabs him by the thighs, yanks him towards the edge of the bed, and then tosses him over onto his stomach in one *incredibly* swift—and *hot*—motion.

"Fuck!" Tripp yells, mostly in surprise, because he's certainly not hurt. Actually, the way his face smarts from Lee's hand feels seriously fuckin' awesome, and Tripp's not entirely sure what to do with that information.

Sure, he's messed around with mild masochism in the past—a tweaked nipple here, some biting there, even a little spanking once in a blue moon (though nothing like what Lee dishes out). He's always known that he *likes* it, that razor's edge where *hurt* cuts into the sweetness of pleasure, amping it up, but he's never sought out or experimented with *pain* as a concept. Not until now, anyway.

Seems like Lee might be the one to change all that, and Tripp's body thrills at the possibility. He decides not to overthink it—he'll trust Lee, stay in the moment, and worry about the details later.

Good thing, because Tripp has barely three seconds to grapple with the fact that Lee can throw him around like an inflatable pool toy if he so chooses before the sound of a tube snapping open behind him can be heard. Soon after, Lee's hand is pressing between Tripp's shoulder blades, holding him down while he pushes not one, but *two* fingers inside of him. They're slippery and cold, and Tripp wriggles beneath his Dom, just because he can.

"Color," Lee demands, his fingers stilling inside Tripp while the hand on his back bears down more firmly and Tripp grins into the bedsheets, forgetting that Lee can't see him.

"Green, *Sir*," he replies enthusiastically, and Leander's answering murmur of acknowledgement sounds positively *predatory*.

"You're still fairly loose from last night," he declares, and Tripp fists his fingers into the sheets, somewhat embarrassed by that announcement, although Lee seems pleased. "Very fortunate for you, since I'm not in the mood to reward your brattiness with careful prep." Despite his words, Lee lingers where he is, scissoring his fingers and running them along the edge of Tripp's hole. It's partly perfunctory but mostly teasing, which Tripp only realizes when Leander dips his fingers in far enough to brush intentionally over his prostate, making him gasp and jerk.

The laugh Leander lets out at his expense is low and dark, and perhaps for the first time, Tripp wonders if he *really* knows the man at all.

The insistent weight of Lee's knees against his thighs vanishes suddenly, alongside the fingers toying with his ass, and the mattress shifts as the Dom moves away.

"Stand up, *boy*," Leander demands, and the way he says it makes both the hair on Tripp's arms and at the back of his neck prickle and raise.

Disobedient mood aside, something tells him to stow his bullshit, at least for a minute. As such, Tripp scoots backward off of the bed without a word, turning to find Leander wiping his hands off with a towel and scrutinizing him with focused interest. He steps forward, well into Tripp's space, and touches a finger to his own lips, his other arm wrapped across his naked chest. Cocking his head to one side, he says nothing as his eyes search for something in Tripp's face, in his *posture*, and fuck if Tripp knows what the hell he might be looking for.

Shifting uncomfortably beneath Lee's gaze, Tripp does manage to keep his mouth shut, but it's a close thing. As Lee's eyes continue to roam, he struggles not to blurt out, "See something you like?" Or, "Take a picture, it'll last longer," but he does think about it. If the glint in Lee's eye is any indication, he knows it, too.

Fuck that, Tripp thinks, obstinate. If that's what Leander wants to provoke, he'll fuckin' give him the opposite. After several minutes, though, the silence gets to be too much for his emotional energy, and he breaks.

"Sir?" he asks warily, struggling to maintain eye contact and not glance away from Leander's unrelenting, unapologetic stare.

Abruptly, the tension in the room breaks, Leander's reaction to Tripp's unsure question entirely unexpected—he grins. Finger still tapping against his lips, Leander *grins,* and yeah, Tripp was right about the laughter, because that sound is *definitely* predatory.

"Oh, *now* it's '*Sir*?'" Leander taunts, rocking back on his heels before stepping forward so that they're toe-to-toe. He relocates his finger from the pad of his lips to the middle of Tripp's chest, just lightly touching.

Barely two inches shorter, Leander tips his head up, and he's so beautiful, he's almost ethereal. Dark eyelashes contrast softly against his cheeks, blinking wide to reveal rings of dark blue that Tripp's stupid brain wishes he could drown himself in forever. He's close enough now that Tripp *could* lean forward and kiss him, but in all honesty, Leander's never felt more untouchable, never seemed more out of his reach. He's all effortless power and control in the way he holds his body, emanating confidence and security that Tripp can't even fathom owning for himself.

The way Lee is looking at him right now, Tripp wouldn't lift his hands from his sides for all the money in the world. *This* version of Lee—from the way he moves, to the way he speaks, to the way he pins Tripp in place with just his gaze —is something a guy can't help but respect. To Tripp's surprise, he finds his bratty attitude evaporating like an early morning fog, replaced by the pure, burning desire for Leander to give him another chance to kneel.

Fuck, he really wants to kneel for this Lee.

"I could make you submit," Leander says softly, so quietly that Tripp almost misses it. "I *could* and I will, if that is truly what you desire. But... " He hesitates, cupping Tripp's jaw with a surprisingly gentle hand, considering the still-throbbing print it recently left on the side of his face. "For today, at least, I'd prefer if you'd go willingly."

And that would have been enough. Tripp absolutely would have dropped to his knees right then and there, but Leander apparently isn't done.

As soon as he stops talking, he leans forward, one hand on Tripp's shoulder and the other on his waist as he presses an impossibly tender kiss to his lips. It's so in contrast with the threat, with what Tripp *expected* to happen next, that he's essentially rendered powerless to do anything except kiss back. The only thing Tripp manages to keep control of in the situation are his hands and his feet, which he only *barely* stops from first grabbing Leander by the sides of his face and then walking him backward towards the bed.

Focus, Truett, he scolds himself internally, keeping his eyes closed for a moment in order to gather his shit while Leander steps away. When he opens them again, Leander's staring at him in amusement, tapping his mouth and pointedly raising his eyebrows.

"If you're ready," he says, the ghost of a smile flitting across his lips, there and gone. "Over on the mat, next to the armoire. Kneel and face me."

Taking a deep breath in and letting it out slowly, Tripp complies, this time without argument or complaint. How could he not, after all of that? As he walks over, he digests the way the mat is pushed all the way up against the wall, the way the enormous dildo is secured only a couple of feet—*not even*—off of the ground, and then it clicks.

Oh.

Unable to fully believe how slow on the uptake he's been, Tripp fails to control the flush in his cheeks when he thinks about the scene that Leander is setting. In fact, for once, he's struggling to *not* allow the litany of questions currently flying through his head to fall from his lips, but on the other hand, he really *doesn't* want to worry about any of it. So, instead of leaning into the rising anxiety and mounting anticipation, Tripp simply turns away from the dildo and faces Lee, sinking to his knees and letting it all go.

One more deep breath: five seconds in, five seconds out, and Tripp is ready.

"Very good," Leander praises, and Tripp—with his eyes closed—lets him, nearly sighing with relief when he feels Lee's hand in his hair after that wave of jittery apprehension. "There's my good boy. Now, get down on all fours."

The vinyl of the mat is cool against his palms, slightly sticky on his skin, and Tripp already knows that if he's stuck in one place for a long period of time, he's going to be peeling himself off of this thing later. Whether that's an intentional slight on Leander's part or not, he has no idea, but he works himself into place without a word. No longer in the mood for games, Tripp doesn't make any bones about spreading his legs and backing himself up into position, the wide head of the silicone cock bumping against an ass cheek as he does.

"Do you like it?" Leander muses, the question obviously rhetorical as he trails a hand over Tripp's shoulder and down his back, grabbing the fake cock and teasing it into his crack, but no further. "It's screwed to the wall, so we can be as rough as we like, it won't come off. I'll bet you didn't notice the various mounting hardware I have all over the place, hmm?"

It's clearly a suggestion and Tripp obliges, opening his eyes to glance around the room from this new angle. From down here, he sees what Leander is referring to —an assortment of inconspicuous, tiny holes in the wall interspersed with screws sticking out less than an inch, all at varying heights. The display is not as intimidating as his friend maybe means for it to be, but Tripp for *sure* makes a mental note to ask Lee to review *in detail* all of the shit he has hidden around this room at some point. Preferably soon.

For now, though, Tripp's got other things on his mind, like how the fuck that giant cock is going to fit inside his ass. Lee is big, and his fingers this morning felt like nothing but a good time, but the fake dick-on-a-stick is no joke. While Leander rummages in an upper drawer of the armoire to his left, Tripp works on breathing and centering his mind, understanding fully that relaxation is going to be the key to making Lee's plan work.

Strangely, he's not nearly as concerned about the potential pain or discomfort as he is with the possibility of disappointing his Dom, or worse, giving Leander the idea that he's not actually trying. Now *that's* a terrifying thought. Thankfully, Lee returns to distract him, hovering above his back to prod some more at his rim, and Tripp reflexively jerks away when he feels an item being inserted. It's not the dildo, though—it's something thin and slick that barely registers, except that Lee uses it to *inject something cold* inside of him.

"Lube," Lee explains easily, as if this is a thing Tripp should have expected, and okay, yeah. Technically, he's *read* about it, but being bitch-slapped by the reality of functioning as a well-basted turkey is genuinely fucking confronting.

"Jesus Christ," Tripp murmurs as Leander spirits the syringe away. Shifting and clenching, he wiggles his hips in protest against the feeling of lube settling inside him.

"Still just 'Sir'," Leander replies with amusement, and then he's back kneeling at Tripp's side, wrapping an arm around his waist to take hold of his flagging erection and stroke him hard again. While he does, Leander turns soft and affectionate, kissing over Tripp's shoulders and spine, propping a hand next to the one he has braced on the mat, presumably to keep as much surface area of their bodies touching as humanly possible.

"I can't wait to see you take this cock," he murmurs quietly, *plainly*, like he's innocent, like this isn't one of the dirtiest things Tripp's ever done. "You know, I'd love to see you take a real one besides mine, but I'm far too possessive to share." Tripp shivers at the suggestion, his body relaxing minutely, because that *does* sound really hot. Not that he'd want to bring someone else into this messed up thing he has going with Lee and his wayward emotions, but even Tripp can admit that the fantasy is sexy as hell.

"You like that, do you?" Leander takes notice, because of course he does, pushing himself upright so that he can stroke a hand down Tripp's flank and over his ass to finger his rim, teasing the head of the fake cock against it. "Perhaps we'll explore the concept more, then. From your list, I know that you're not interested in sharing, so is it more the idea of being watched? Is that a fantasy of yours, Tripp?"

Nailed it, Tripp thinks, but he bites at his lip instead of speaking, because Lee is lubing up the cock and guiding him back onto it, just the tip pushing slowly past his tight ring of muscle. He moans a little as the head pops inside, struggling past the pressure to breathe deeply, fighting to relax against the significant intrusion. The thing feels even bigger than it looked, and it didn't look small.

"I think it is," Leander continues, undeterred by Tripp's lack of participation in the conversation. "I think that you would get off on the idea of someone—anyone—watching me take you, of being naked and vulnerable beneath my hands in public, or where others could happen by and see us. I wouldn't let anyone touch you, you know that well enough. You know that I'd protect you, surely, but do you know that I'd show you off? I'd be so proud, Tripp."

Leander hums, his giant hands soothing tracks up and down Tripp's sides, encouraging him to slide back, to take more of the dildo, to rock against it until he can.

Tripp, for his part, just lets it happen. He revels in Leander's dirty talk, flexes fingers against the mat beneath him, moans low and long when the dildo finally brushes against his prostate. Eyes falling shut, his mouth drops open and he pants as he adjusts to being so increasingly full. It doesn't hurt—not really, but it's not *easy* to accommodate something this big, so it takes time and patience for Tripp to find himself ready to *move*.

All the while, Leander just kneels beside him, watching and touching him gently, adding lube when he thinks he needs it, and *talking*. It's his voice that's grounding the scene, leading Tripp, spurring him on.

"Yes," Lee encourages, a thumb dragging over Tripp's lip as his own very noticeable erection bumps against Tripp's thigh. "I would be so proud of you, taking my cock so easily, letting me bend you over the nearest surface with every eye in the room focused solely on us. You'd be gorgeous, a work of art, just as you are now—ass cheeks pink from my hand, of course, eyes glazed over, just perfect. Perhaps I'd grab your hair—"

Reflecting his words, he does exactly that, yanking Tripp's head in a way that jerks his body backward and settles him nearly all the way onto the dildo. Using his hair to steer, Lee tilts his upper body this way and that, like he's really showing him off.

"—Let them see your face, how hungry and desperate you are for my cock, what a slut you can be for *me,* only me. Would there be tear tracks running down your cheeks? I do love when you cry. Think of how jealous they'd be, that they can't have you. Think of how their eyes would roam over your body, watching greedily as I slid in and out of your holes. Oh, the *envy* they would feel when I stroked your cock, just like this."

The mewling whine Tripp lets out when Leander touches him again is truly pathetic, but he can't care, so lost in Lee's praise and flagrant appreciation, he can hardly focus on anything but hearing more.

At this point, the dildo is moving fairly easily in and out of Tripp's ass, its girth wide enough and the angle hitting just right to provide his prostate with some major stimulation on nearly every stroke. While he hasn't before, Tripp's seriously starting to think that he could maybe come like this, especially if Lee keeps talking.

But then, suddenly, Leander moves, leaving Tripp's side to shuffle over and kneel in front of his face. There's no warning, but Tripp is still one step ahead of him, mouth already open and seeking when Leander deftly rolls a condom over his dick and offers it up.

"My God, you are perfection," Leander praises, and Tripp revels, eyes drifting closed as he takes whatever Lee sees fit to give him. Letting his mind float away, Tripp fucks his body on the dildo while sucking and swirling his tongue around the cock in his mouth, handling it all like a goddamn pro. The condom tastes like ass, and a nearly completely-spaced-out Tripp knows that he's probably drooling, but if the increasing thrusts, the tight hand in his hair, and the one cupping his cheek are any indication, Lee likes what he sees, and that makes Tripp happy.

It also makes him work harder, the toy creating slick sounds as it slides in and out of his ass, the pressure building deep in his gut and at the base of his spine. It's clear from the way Lee's tumbling words begin to slur that he's close, too—Tripp can't even make out what he's saying anymore, but that doesn't matter. The pattern and the tone are soothing, and the message is clear: Lee is pleased, Lee is proud, Lee thinks he's a good boy—that's all Tripp needs to know right now.

His orgasm sneaks up in the background, building and cresting slowly, making him moan and cry and shake as his vision goes blurry and he comes in spurts with nothing but the fake cock milking his prostate. Even after he orgasms, Tripp doesn't stop moving, because Lee didn't say he could.

That's probably because Lee is busy gasping and shoving his cock into the back of Tripp's throat one last time, shuddering and releasing spend so hot, he can feel it through the latex. Twisting the hair wrapped around his fingers more securely, he holds Tripp's head in place as he finishes. Ready and willing, Tripp swallows around him, wishing desperately that he was sucking Leander dry, continuing to lick around his (annoyingly) condom-covered shaft instead, at least until Leander releases a pained noise and pulls away.

It's strange how—sore and exhausted as Tripp might be—he misses him already.

"So good, Tripp," Leander is saying, gentle as he stops Tripp's rocking motions with a firm hand to his shoulder, carefully guiding him off of the dildo and into his arms. "Are you able to walk with me to the bed?"

Things are slightly hazy. Tripp is still *very* spaced-out, and Lee's chest is warm and inviting. He's tired, so instead of answering, he sinks into it, following his base instincts. "Whoa, whoa," he hears Leander say, and that snaps him out of it —at least enough to lift his head and register the pair of sensitive blue eyes looking down at him, crinkling at the edges and softer than he's seen them appear at all today.

"Hello, Tripp," Lee says, and Tripp manages a weak smile in return. "The bed?"

"Right." Tripp grits the single word out, his voice rough and throat sore, but the next time Lee tries, he allows himself to be pulled to his feet. They stumble together over to the bed, the strong line of Lee's body barely adequate to keep him upright.

"'M fine," he mutters, letting Leander dump him onto the mattress and step away to retrieve the things he likes to use for aftercare. "Just tired." He yawns, as if to punctuate the point.

"Yes," Leander agrees, returning with a cracked bottle of orange juice and tipping it high so that Tripp is forced to drink at least half of it in one go. At the very least, it washes the plasticky aftertaste of the condom away.

"It's early yet. Probably around eight, now," Lee is saying. "We can nap together as aftercare, if that sounds agreeable to you. I woke this morning in somewhat of a mood, as you may have noticed. I planned to clean up and only came in here to retrieve the items we used last night, but I saw that you kept your collar on… " He trails off, touching the side of Tripp's face with a soft, appreciative expression that Tripp isn't sure he's ever seen on Lee before.

"I couldn't resist, and somnophilia was on your list of things you were very interested in trying."

"It was great," Tripp says sincerely, leaning back against the pillows and stretching. "All of it. Best damn way to start the day." When Leander just stands there staring down at him, Tripp smiles and jerks his head toward the empty space next to him. "You comin'?"

Seemingly shaking himself off, Leander returns the smile and rounds the bed to slide in beside him. "Anything particularly sore? I could massage you again, if you'd like."

Finishing off the juice, Tripp leaves the bottle on the side table and turns into Leander's chest, tucking himself flush against the man's side without shame or hesitation. Fuck it—Tripp's starting to get the hang of this give and take thing, and after last night, he's not about to set himself up for failure in the form of major drop. If Lee is willing, then Tripp's going to grab what he needs and hold on, and right now, what he *needs* are some extremely unmanly cuddles. It's just a fact, and he's too damn tired to pretend that it's not.

For a short moment, Leander tenses beneath him, leading Tripp to think that perhaps he's made a mistake. Thankfully, after a second or two he relaxes completely, wrapping both arms around Tripp's body and pulling him close. Lee settles back into the pillow with a contented sigh, and the way he curves into Tripp's shape is both welcome and reassuring.

This is good, Tripp thinks. This is what I need.

Damn right, he's going to take it.

***

Contrary to what Tripp expects after falling asleep in Lee's arms, the next time he wakes, he's completely alone. As he pushes himself to a sitting position and runs a hand through the disastrous state of his hair, he can't help but feel just a little bit frustrated. If this was a normal relationship, he'd ask Lee outright, like, *hey man, is this hot and cold bullshit you're doing intentional? Is this just how these kind of things go? Are you an asshole or am I just needy?* Maybe just, *Am I seeing shit that isn't there, or what?*

But what they're doing isn't "normal", at least, not according to what Tripp is used to, and because he can't think of a single, concrete example to point at in order to explain how Lee might be acting outside of their agreed-upon boundaries, calling him out feels dangerous.

So instead, he keeps his mouth shut, showers quietly, and pulls yesterday's clothes back on his body. They're the ones he changed into at the station, just something to ditch his work uniform, and they were off mere minutes after entering Lee's apartment. By every reasonable standard, they're basically clean, and yet somehow, they make Tripp feel a little bit dirty.

Because he's heading home, he avoids using Lee's toothbrush again, opting to simply swish some mouthwash around his mouth and hope that Lee doesn't want to kiss him goodbye. Or maybe it's an excuse to get out of doing exactly that—Tripp's not exactly in the best mood for self-reflection. As he stares at himself in the mirror, he makes the abrupt decision to take his collar off and to not give Lee the option, period.

Fully-dressed and fairly clean, Tripp finds the man in the kitchen, putting the finishing touches on two enormous sandwiches that look stuffed to the brim with meats and cheeses. That offer alone would normally be enough to drop Tripp to his knees all over again, but standing here, considering it, he just feels... itchy.

He *should* be hungry. He hasn't eaten anything since Lee hand-fed him last night, and it's—*what the hell time is it, anyway?*

Checking his phone, Tripp realizes that it's later than he expected, nearing three in the afternoon. That explains the sandwiches and probably Lee being out of bed, but Tripp can't focus on anything logical right now. All of a sudden, he feels claustrophobic and *caged*. He wants to be anywhere but here, in Leander's space and under his thumb, whether he's wearing his collar or not.

It's an unpleasant sensation, and while the rational part of Tripp knows that he wouldn't trade the things they've done for all the normality in the world, there's another part of him that just wants his friend Lee back.

"Hey," he says, doing his best to sound casual and put together when he feels anything but those things. Across the kitchen and facing away, Leander starts at the noise, but he's boasting a big smile on his face when he turns around. Better believe Tripp is looking for it, and he has to fight back a grimace when his top worry manifests, Lee's eyes flicking to his neck and registering the missing collar, his smile dimming accordingly.

It shakes Tripp—more than he'd like, and while he's *pretty* sure Lee doesn't actually feel this way, it makes *him* equate his self-worth to the collar and this submissive role he's taken on.

Somewhere in the back of Tripp's mind, he knows this isn't right. Knows that the feelings and emotions coursing through him are something off-kilter, something he should communicate with Leander about and lean on him to fix. On the flip side, Tripp *also* feels embarrassed and unsure, because how much of this is *normal* sub-drop, and how much is intrinsically tied to his stupid emotions, the feelings he has for Leander that he's been hiding and lying about almost constantly over the past few days?

Isn't there a good chance he did this to himself? That he's at fault here, for being stupid and selfish enough to jump into this type of relationship with a dude he's secretly *in love* with? Whatever the truth is, Tripp knows one thing for sure. He has to get the hell out of this apartment, right the fuck now. In fact, he barely registers Lee's "good morning," or any of the other small talk he's attempting to make. Heading straight for the front door, Tripp gives him the blatant brush-off and hopes that it doesn't come off as harsh as it feels when he mumbles something about having places to be today.

"Oh," Leander replies, disappointment clouding his face as he stands there in the little foyer, still shirtless and fiddling with his hands as Tripp pulls on his boots. His entire subdued demeanor only makes Tripp feel worse and more determined to leave, before he makes a serious misstep or blurts something out that he can't take back.

Leander clears his throat. "I was only—well, it's just that you took your collar off and I thought, perhaps you might like to go to the bar tonight? You know, as friends, like we—"

"Yeah, no, not tonight, Lee." Tripp cuts him off swiftly, breezily, though he pauses when he sees the obvious hurt on Leander's face. "I've got plans with Beau," he adds, trying to sound apologetic, relieved when Lee nods with supposed understanding.

"Of course," he says, before patting his pockets absently—he's wearing pajama pants and doesn't have any—then looking around like he's misplaced something. There's a box sitting on the table beside the catch-all bowl, smaller than the one to which Tripp returns his collar, and Leander retrieves it. He holds the item out until Tripp accepts, albeit warily and with an eyebrow raised.

"It's just something that I thought you should have," Leander rushes to explain, suddenly looking shy.

Inside the box is a key. It's a normal hardware store copy, but it features a cute version of the Maltese Cross and the fire symbology printed on both sides. It's not hard to figure out that this is a *house* key, that it was specifically made for *him*, not just anyone Lee might need to give one to. The gesture is thoughtful and miraculously does aid in assuaging some of the irritation bubbling beneath Tripp's skin. This means that Lee has been thinking about him and his potential needs, and Tripp genuinely does appreciate that.

The gift forces him to stop for a moment, to slow down. To haul in a deep breath and then let it out slowly, to look Leander in the eyes at least once before leaving. When he does, what he finds there is somewhat surprising—Leander looks unsure, too, and if Tripp didn't know better, he might even use the word *vulnerable.*

The realization has him stepping forward and tugging his friend into a hug, the significance of which should not be understated. Contact like this between them was rare before their arrangement—even the hug he gave Lee at the ER the other night was somewhat out of character, though he'd do it again in a heartbeat. Didn't take a genius to see that Lee had really needed someone, there.

But this—a hug just because? Tripp is treading into dangerous waters, putting risky toes over the line in the sand, the boundary between their *contract* and their friendship as it's already been defined.

And yet, he can't deny that it feels incredibly fucking *good.* Incredibly *right.* Leander is solid and warm in his grasp, and he hasn't showered so he smells musky and just faintly like sex, which is not unwelcome. More than that, he clings to Tripp, similar to the way he did the other night, his embrace full of both need and relief at being given something that he didn't know he wanted.

When Tripp pulls away, Leander seems a little reluctant to let him go, but less sad overall. That change is enough for Tripp to feel comfortable putting himself first, which he really feels like he needs to do at the moment.

"Alright, Lee," he says gently, extricating himself from Lee's grasp and stepping away. Raising his hand to wave as he opens the door, Tripp offers up what he hopes reads as a kind smile. "I'll talk to you soon."

"Of course, Tripp," Leander replies, already back to tugging on his fingers as he holds himself back, looking a little bit lonely, a little bit lost. Tripp just can't deal with that right now—he can't. He lets the door slam closed behind him and walks away, the key weighing heavy inside his pocket.

On the ride down in the elevator, Tripp swipes open his phone and shoots off a message to Beau. Thankfully, his brother is on a similar rotation as him and Lee, and he *should* be off work tonight. So long as he's not already tied up with Briana—and doesn't *that* invasive thought make Tripp cringe with unwanted mental imagery, considering what he's been up to himself—he'll probably be into hanging out.

A guy can hope.

Even though they still live together—hey, city living is expensive—both Truetts have their own lives, plus Beau and Bri are planning a wedding. That doesn't always leave an assload of extra time to just hang out and be brothers. In fact, Tripp's pretty sure that it's been over a week since he and Beau shared more than a cup of coffee in lieu of a meal, or exchanged any words beyond bleary good mornings.

Maybe *that's* why he's all off-kilter and weird. Yeah, that must be it. He just needs some family time to help relax and unwind. Needs to bounce a few things off of Beau's big brain and make fun of his too-long hair over a couple of beers.

By the time he's stepping out the front door of Leander's apartment complex, Tripp's already feeling moderately better. The wind is cold and sharp as it whips and stings at his face, but the fresh air helps, too. He sucks it in, driving home with the windows down, despite the cold.

As he's pulling into the parking lot adjacent to his and Beau's building, Tripp's phone buzzes twice in a row. Throwing his car into park, he fishes in his pocket and swipes the text message open without pause. He's inordinately relieved to see Beau's reply, even more so when he reads that Beau is at Bri's but wants to hang out. His brother suggests that they meet up at their usual haunt, the Hot Plate.

The Hot Plate is a shitty dive bar just down the street from their place, but it's close to Tripp's heart. The place is owned by Station Eleven's Captain, Reina, and it's a regular hub for off-duty fire, police, and EMS personnel, for obvious reasons.

In fact, a lot of the EMTs and firefighters that work for the City also take shifts waiting tables and working the bar there: it's Reina's way of giving back to the community that can't afford to pay them the living wage that they deserve. No firefighter or EMT should have to work two, even three jobs just to make rent and put food on the table, but such is the world they live in. Tripp himself has been known to do the Hippy Hippy Shake behind the bar a time or two, but only when he's desperate enough to be scrounging between couch cushions for spare change.

Honestly, he's got better things to do on his nights off, like drink or binge soapy medical dramas. Or hang out with Lee. And that was *before* they were fucking.

Speaking of Lee—how the guy affords such a kickass apartment on a medic's salary, Tripp will never understand. He has a working suspicion that Lee comes from money, that he has a trust fund or stocks, maybe some other kind of inheritance or passive income Tripp wouldn't know anything about. Whatever it is, Lee doesn't talk about it. Doesn't share about his family at all, actually, ever. Tripp's known the guy for the better part of a decade, and he always spends his holidays alone or with Tripp and Beau, and previously, with Autumn and her crew.

Within that oddball group, they're all very different people, but the one thing the five of them have in common is their distinct lack of blood-related parents. Whether by unfortunate circumstance like Tripp and Beau, or choice (definitely Autumn and presumably Lee), the outcome is the same. It's part of why Tripp never disliked Autumn as much as he maybe should have—she was alright to Lee, and from what Tripp knows, life didn't hand her the greatest shake, either.

Still, Tripp's pretty fuckin' glad she's out of the picture. Not that she ever had a chance with Lee in the long run (or Tripp wouldn't be in this mess), but his complex emotions about Leander are screwed up enough without adding *that* into the mix.

Those thoughts about Lee start to make him itchy again, so Tripp shoves them away and refocuses on his excitement at getting to see Beau. With a renewed spring in his step, Tripp jogs up the stairs to their shared apartment on the second floor and quickly swaps clothes, runs a brush over his teeth, and throws some gel in his hair.

While looking in the mirror of their tiny bathroom, he can't help but notice that there's a trail of hickeys running down the side of his neck, towards his collar bone. Scowling at his reflection, Tripp buttons the front of his flannel a little higher and it (mostly) does the trick—bruises hidden. The twinge in his ass when he takes a seat isn't so easily ignored, but at least no one can *see* that.

Despite the cold, Tripp opts to walk the five or so blocks down the street to the bar. Parking's a bitch outside the Hot Plate at this time of night, and Tripp's not keen on leaving his vehicle on a busy street outside of a rowdy bar in the bad part of town, anyway. Or maybe all of those things are excuses to avoid admitting to himself that he's planning on getting so smashed he can barely walk, because apparently, that's the only way *Lee* is going to stop popping into his goddamn head uninvited.

Letting out a frustrated growl, Tripp stomps a little heavier than necessary down the street, his breath puffing clouds of white into the frigid evening air. A few people eye him curiously or worriedly, giving him a wide berth as he passes on the sidewalk, and he wonders what kind of angry expression he must be wearing to merit that.

Sighing in defeat, Tripp rubs at his face and runs a hand through his hair, but that only makes him think about Lee doing the exact same thing in various but equally appealing ways. Traitor that it is, Tripp's dick twitches in his pants, and he directs his scowl towards his crotch, albeit with lackluster results.

There's a decent-sized crowd loitering outside the bar, which isn't surprising for a Saturday, even so early in the night. Tripp catches sight of a few of his platoon members talking and laughing, and it drains him. Theo and Mac are hanging out next to the door sharing a smoke, so he basically has to engage, even though small talk with his co-workers is pretty low on the list of things he wants to be doing right now.

"Trippster, haven't seen you around in a few days," Mac comments, the slight glaze over his eyes and the tang in the air suggesting that the smoke he's puffing on is not a cigarette. When Mac offers it up, Tripp hesitates, but ultimately decides, *what the hell?* He did come here to get fucked up.

No, he scolds himself. *You came for Beau.*

"Thanks," he says anyway, taking a small puff and handing the joint off to Theo, who surprises Tripp somewhat by partaking. Then again, Theo's always been kind of a 'rules are for when they benefit me,' sort of guy, so maybe it's not surprising at all. Truthfully, Tripp doesn't really care what anyone else is doing to cope.

"So what's up?" Mac prods, jerking his head towards the door before accepting the joint back from Theo. "Saw your bro come in a few minutes ago. You guys up for a game later?"

"Pool?" Now *that,* Tripp can get behind. "Hell yes," he replies enthusiastically. "For money, right?"

"Ain't no other kinda game here," Mac says, shooting him a grin and a knowing nod.

"Sure you can afford it, Truett?" Theo teases. "I've seen those boots you drag your sorry ass to work in, they've sure seen better days. Maybe you should keep your money and buy some new ones, before you walk right out of them soles. Or are you saving up to finally buy Leander that diamond engagement ring he's always wanted? Let him make an honest woman out of you?"

Tripp just rolls his eyes, outwardly unfazed. The guys he works with teasing him relentlessly about his feelings for Lee—that's nothing new. The resulting sharp pang that stabs him straight through the heart and wraps icy tendrils around it to squeeze, however—*that* is. He's not upset, though, not really. His co-workers are decent enough to only bust his balls when Lee isn't around, and Tripp's more grateful for that than he could ever say.

On the other hand, he sure wishes he could get ten goddamn minutes without his brain being sucker-punched and cornered and basically drop-kicked into thinking about *Lee, Lee, Lee* all over again.

Fuck.

"Forget Lee, your mom rocked my world last night, maybe I'll give that ring to her," Tripp shoots back airily. He can play this game in his sleep. Flashing his widest, most unbothered smile, Tripp tips his head to the side and rocks some disastrous finger guns in Theo's direction.

"*Someone* rocked your world last night," Mac comments, waving the joint around. "Shit, it's been years since I had even one hickey that big, and here you are with a whole fleet of 'em." He whistles, leaning away from the wall and into Tripp's space, trying to get a better look, but Tripp bats him away and tugs his collar back into place.

Rookie move, dumbass, he tells himself, stumbling over his own feet in his haste to move towards the entrance to the bar.

"So I'll catch you guys inside," he replies evasively, purposefully ignoring Mac's comment and the hollered complaints about "*details*" that chase Tripp inside the Hot Plate as he slips through the closing door. Thankfully, Mac's bitching is lost to the din of the bustling bar, and Tripp breathes a sigh of relief as he looks around. Sure, it's dark and dirty with shitty lighting and a layer of stickiness on the floor that no amount of mopping is ever going to remove, but the Hot Plate is as much a second home to Tripp as his station.

Not just the place, but the people, too. Mood already improving, Tripp waves to several friends right off the bat, catching Reina's eye from where she's surveying her territory behind the bar. He raises an arm in greeting, and in return, she offers a warm smile and a hollered demand to come talk to her before he leaves.

The walls of the Hot Plate are covered with police, fire, and EMS paraphernalia: patches, flags, photos of big, local incidents, and framed gear belonging to fallen firefighters. In the middle of the rear wall is a giant tribute to Bill, Reina's late husband and both the former City Fire Chief and the one who opened the Hot Plate with her, way back when. He died in a fire going on ten years ago now, back when Tripp was brand-new to the job. Tripp wasn't working the day that it all went down, but like every firefighter in this town, he can recite the story like he was, and like it happened yesterday.

Scanning the room is a formality, since Tripp finds his brother seated in their usual spot, the booth set right below Bill's montage. Beau is relaxing on the bench beneath his framed bunker jacket, leaving the seat across from him—the one under Bill's picture and the hook that holds his helmet—open for Tripp.

Same as it ever was. The familiarity is welcome tonight.

Tipping his head in greeting, Tripp shucks his jacket and slides onto the worn vinyl covering the bench seat easily, sighing with the kind of happiness that only comes from being in one of his favorite places, with one of his favorite people. There's a cold beer dripping condensation onto the table in front of him, matching the one sat opposite in front of Beau, and if Tripp knows his brother the way he thinks he does, dinner will be along shortly.

Best guess: rabbit food for health-freak Doctor Beau, red meat for him, if he's lucky. Beau hasn't been in his presence enough this week to bitch about his diet, so there's a good chance he's just going to let Tripp have what he wants without picking a fight.

Left upside down on the table, Tripp's phone buzzes, but he ignores it.

"Hey," Beau says, a big smile gracing his face that reminds Tripp of *home* and *family* and everything that's freaking good with the world. Not that he'd ever admit that shit out loud, even under penalty of death. "So, what's up with you?"

"Same old," Tripp says with a sigh, and although there are a million things he wants to blurt out, to beg Beau's advice on, to just unload from his shoulders, not one of them makes it past his lips. Two minutes in and already halfway through his beer, Tripp sees Ro (Reina's daughter and another firefighter at Eleven), passing by with a tray, catching her eye to signal for a refill. On the table, his phone vibrates again.

"You… gonna get that?"

"Nah," Tripp replies, shaking his head before reaching across the table and smacking Beau's arm with the back of his hand. "What about you, how's wedding planning?"

"Dude," Beau says, with a meaningful look and a long sip of his own beer. "I've never been happier to get a text from you. My eyes are crossing from looking at flowers and favors and *fabric* samples all day. Do *you* know the difference between crimson and claret? 'Cause I do, now."

"Uh, no, Bozo, my manhood is intact, thanks for asking." Tripp fiddles with the glass in his hand, smirking but softening when he sees the dopey expression on Beau's face as he stares down into his glass. "All worth it, huh?"

Lovesick. That is, without question, the only way to describe how Beau looks when he raises his eyes to meet Tripp's. He scoffs a little, maybe even blushes, and Tripp's heart swells with genuine happiness and pride for who he's become.

"Yeah," Beau replies dreamily. "I get that it's dumb, but you know, after the way we grew up, always out on the road and without Mom... I dunno, Tripp. This was something I always dreamed about, but never thought I'd get to have." His eyes flick somewhat anxiously between his beer and Tripp's face. "Silly?"

"Nah," Tripp reiterates, because he gets it, more than he can ever let on. Except, in his case, there's no happily ever after on the horizon. No obnoxious wedding planning, no flowers or favors or colors Tripp secretly *does* know *way* more about than he'll admit (claret is superior). All that's ahead in Tripp's future is a bunch of really good sex for as long as it lasts and a few stolen moments he'll—pathetically—carry with him and think about constantly for the rest of his life, once Lee has moved on.

With impeccable timing—since Beau is starting to look like he's *way* too intuitive about what Tripp is thinking—Ro appears next to their table, tray full of an assortment of food and drinks balanced on her shoulder. As she sets the whole thing down on a collapsible stand, Tripp's phone vibrates yet again.

"Dude, pick that up," Beau tells him, shooting Tripp a skeptical side-eye. "What, you avoiding someone? Accidentally give your number out to the dregs of last call and now suffering buyer's remorse?"

"Psh," Ro interjects as she sets their beers down on the table before sliding a chicken-topped salad in front of Beau and a truly monstrous, onion-laden burger in front of Tripp.

God bless Bozo, Tripp thinks, rubbing his hands together with poorly-concealed glee.

"Tripp hasn't been here in days," Ro continues, complaining. "Whoever's texting him ain't someone he picked up at the bar." She pauses and reconsiders. "Unless you're cheating on us, is that it? You got something going with that flashy new place down the street? The one with the little umbrella drinks and the neon lights in the windows?"

To be fair, Tripp *does* like those fruity umbrella drinks, they friggin' come with *pineapple* and a cherry, but he's sure as hell not admitting that to Reina or Ro. And anyway, if he is having an affair, it's the bar's fault. It totally seduced him, all flirty and sexy with its Air Supply soundtrack and its clean floors.

Trampy bar, Tripp thinks, accusatory. "You're high," he scoffs back. "What, a man can't take a few nights to himself? Grab a bubble bath, get in touch with his feelings?"

"Whatever, Tripp," Ro says with a shrug before turning to Beau. "I'm pretty sure he only puts up this act when he's been hooking up with dudes and thinks we're gonna judge him."

"I don't care what you douchebags think of me," Tripp fires back around a half-chewed mouthful of burger that makes both Beau and Ro cringe.

"Right." Ro rolls her eyes and tucks her serving tray underneath her arm. "The real mystery here is how you attract *anyone* with manners like that. We're all heathens here, but you are truly disgusting, Tripp Truett."

In response, Tripp just grins toothily, food in his teeth and all. "Thank you, sweetheart," he says with a wink as she ruffles his hair roughly and saunters away. For a minute or two, he continues munching happily on his burger, still ignoring the buzzing of his phone. It's only when Tripp realizes that Beau is sitting stock still, staring him down from across the table, that Tripp pauses and sets what's left of his nearly-demolished meal back down on the plate.

"What?" he asks. "Do I have sauce on my face?"

"Uh, yes," Beau says flatly, his eyes narrowed, "but that's not my issue."

"Okay," Tripp replies. He wipes inelegantly at his face with the napkin that came wrapped around his silverware before shrugging and digging back in, speaking again around another giant bite. "What is your issue, Bozo?"

"Lee," Beau says slowly, deliberately, and Tripp nearly chokes on his food. "Nice," Beau adds as he recovers, swallowing and trying (failing) to look nonchalant.

"What about Lee?"

"Well," Beau says pointedly, drumming his fingers on the tabletop. "I just watched you do a non-ironic spit-take at the mention of his name, so why don't you tell me?" Silence being the only defense Tripp has left, he keeps his mouth shut, except to shove the last bite of burger in-between his teeth.

"Fine," Beau continues. "Then I guess I should tell you that I talked to Lee about some groomsman stuff this morning and he said you guys 'hung out' last night. That you stayed over."

"Okay, first of all," Tripp replies, wiping both hands on his napkin and propping an elbow on the table so he can point an accusatory finger in his brother's direction. "Were those *actual* air quotes? Because, seriously, don't pick up Lee's dumb habits. Bad enough I have to deal with it from him. Second, I don't like what you're implying. And third, me and Lee hang out all the time, so whatever 'gotcha' moment you think you're pulling here, it ain't gonna work." Tripp realizes way too late that he did the air quotes himself and silently curses Leander's name.

"Tripp," Beau says, wholly exasperated now and leaning forward over the table to emphasize his point. "I'm a *doctor,* you walnut. I'm a trauma surgeon, my specialty is literally trauma. It's my *job*. Do you really think there's any bruise on any human walking this planet that I can't stage and identify from a passing glance?"

Confused, Tripp's mouth drops open slightly before snapping closed again in horrifying realization. His hand flies reflexively to his neck, where he can feel that his shirt is hanging open just a *smidge* too wide.

"Ro's right, you know," Beau continues conversationally, stabbing at his salad with a fork, but not even pretending to eat. "This is exactly what you do when you're on a Grindr kick. Disappear from the Hot Plate scene for a few days, sleep away from home, show up weirdly satisfied and think none of us can put two plus two together on why. Except—"

"Don't do it, Beau," Tripp pleads, closing his eyes and shaking his head.

"I *know* where you were last night, *all* night," he persists, undaunted. "And now —" Beau flips Tripp's phone over without asking, and sure enough, Tripp can see without even directly looking that there's a string of text messages from '*Lee Grigori*,' the only angel in Tripp's life. Although, he's starting to think *that* name might be an ironic coincidence, since right now, he feels like Beau is about to uncover his deal with the devil.

Frustrated, Tripp throws his hands up in the air before crossing them over his chest defensively and saying nothing. "Tripp," Beau continues, puppy-dog eyes out in full force. "Dude, I'm happy for you! You know I've always thought you and Lee had a good thing going. I dunno why you're hiding it, everyone we know would be thrilled to hear you guys finally—"

"Just shut up, Beau," Tripp mutters miserably, fixing his gaze on the door at the far end of the room. "Seriously, you don't know what you're talking about."

Deflated, Beau sits back and raises his hands in defeat. "You know what? Fine, Tripp. I was trying to be supportive, but if that's how you want to act—"

"It's just a hookup," Tripp announces blandly, finally turning his gaze to meet his brother's and hoping he's at least semi-suppressing his shame. He shrugs. "Okay? You happy? Lee and I are hooking up, but we're not... anything else, nothing like whatever you thought you Nancy Drew-ed into a conclusion there."

To his credit, Beau looks genuinely confused, as if he's never heard of the concept before. "But I thought—"

"Dude," Tripp groans. "Why are you doing this to me, man?" He slumps back against the booth and glares at Beau, irritated all over again, worse than when he left Lee's apartment. There's an itch crawling beneath his skin and something calling to him, something strong and unrelenting that he's determined as fuck to ignore. Also being ignored are his previous thoughts about confiding in Beau, because right now, being a bitter asshole just feels more satisfying.

"You know that I don't do the touchy-feely crap, alright? Just leave it." There's a long pause while Beau looks Tripp up and down and considers the totality of whatever he's projecting right now, but ultimately, he nods, raising his eyebrows as he sighs.

"Sure, Tripp," he relents. "It's your life." It's quiet again while Beau pokes at his untouched salad and then, "One thing. Just one, and then I'll shut it, I swear." Reluctantly, Tripp makes the 'proceed' motion and waits, but Beau hesitates, staring down at his plate for so long that Tripp almost checks to see if he fell asleep. "I wasn't kidding, earlier," he says finally.

"About what?"

Beau looks up. "About how good it feels to have someone like Bri in my life. About how I never really thought I would. You shouldn't give up on yourself, Tripp. You shouldn't shut Lee out because you think... whatever it is you think."

Tripp just snorts and averts his eyes. "Alright, well, thank you for the pillow talk," he mutters, picking up his phone and scrolling absently without even realizing what he's done.

> **Lee:** I hope you're having a
> nice night with Beau

Lee: Just so you know, I
spoke to him earlier and said
you were here, perhaps
ensure your bruises are
covered.

Despite the discomfort twisting inside of him, Tripp snorts again and has to bite back a smile. Figures—he should've checked his messages, after all. Considering that, he keeps reading, but the next few lines wipe the happy look right off of his face.

Lee: I'm going to have
dinner with Autumn later.

Lee: As friends, of course,
there is no ambiguity in our
relationship status. I just
wanted to tell you, in
advance of it getting back to
you some other way.

Whatever good mood Tripp had grappled with and nearly recovered dissipates immediately, replaced with something sour and vexatious that churns his stomach and makes his skin feel like it's too tight. He shoves his phone into his pocket without replying and slides out of the booth, heading directly for the bar. Beau will follow—Tripp knows him well enough to be sure that he won't take any of this personally—but before they can get on with the night, he's going to need a *lot* more liquor dulling his system.

That, at least, he can fix. That, he can take care of and control. In fact, Tripp plans to exercise said control to the fullest extent.

In his pocket, his phone is finally silent.

Chapter 4

Leander is unsettled. From the moment Tripp stepped out of the playroom, it was obvious that something was *off*. The change was woven into the way that Tripp carried himself, how he avoided any real eye contact, and the way his answers to questions were short and stiff. It bled from the extra work he poured into trying to appear casual, like his actions were nothing but normal and fine. In and of itself, the way Leander's garbage-disposal of a friend completely ignored a *sandwich* was an undeniable, massive red flag.

Having been around this block many, many times before, it all screamed loudly, pointing towards exactly one thing—a thing that normally, Leander would rush to correct. He would *never* let a sub leave his sight or his presence until he was *sure* beyond measure that they were not experiencing some form of drop.

With Tripp, though, things are complicated. There are lines in the sand, there are boundaries he has to respect and refrain from crossing, for both of their sakes. And Tripp *can* be moody. Leander's been on the receiving end of an unearned tongue-lashing from the man more than once, so he certainly knows that's true.

Tripp also has moments where he withdraws into himself, where the *last* thing he wants is for other people to *see* him, to know that he's feeling weak or vulnerable. It's a nuanced situation, an extremely fine line to walk when mixing existing friendship with domination and submission, and Leander only wants to be cautious.

So he hesitates, in a way that he normally never would, never has before when engaging with a submissive. In the end, his play comes down to the way Tripp softens after he pulls on his boots, the manner in which he accepts the house key and pulls Leander into a hug that's obviously not for Tripp's own benefit but for *his*. He seems more like himself in that moment, and Leander's worries lessen significantly.

If Tripp *was* dropping, surely he wouldn't have bothered with such things? Or even been *capable* of them? No, in Leander's experience, this is very much a Tripp who is just being *Tripp,* difficult as that may be for him to personally understand. At the end of the day, Leander is not Tripp's person. He's not his partner or boyfriend, and he can't expect the man to lean on him that way—or even as a friend—if that's not what Tripp decides that he wants.

This morning, Leander had been overcome with joy and affection for his sub, sparked when he popped into the playroom and saw him sleeping with the collar on. At the time, he only intended to slip quietly in and out, to gather the used equipment and take it to the kitchen for cleaning, just something productive to occupy his hands while sleep eluded his mind.

But seeing Tripp lying there, so beautiful and absent of any stress or worry on his face, just *knowing* that he chose to fall asleep still marked as *Leander's*—it was an offering too alluring to pass up. Tripp's collar was permission to touch, an outward sign that Tripp was happy with him as a Dom, that he *continued* to be pleased with what they were doing, and that he wanted more. It thrilled Leander to see, and he truly couldn't resist the urge to try and show Tripp how much. The kissing and nuzzling at the leather—that was Leander wishing terribly for the words to explain just how much it meant to him that Tripp kept it on.

The collar *is* their line in the sand, and as much as its presence on his neck is a green light, likewise, it being off is a hard limit. Tripp came out of the playroom this afternoon with his signal light on 'red', and that's a boundary Leander needed to respect.

Which is why he let him go.

It weighs on him, though, after the fact. Enough that Leander is distracted away from going through the motions of cleaning and putting the playroom back together, of restocking the mini-fridge and changing the sheets that still smell like Tripp—not that he stops to shove his face into the wadded up bundle in his arms, because that would be truly pathetic.

Enough that he strips the bed and gets lost on the way to the washer, winding up listlessly slumped on the living room couch, soiled linen piled up next to him, bereft. Without ever really considering why he's called to do so (or if it's even a good idea), Leander scrolls his phone contacts for a particular name and selects "Send Message".

Before he can lose his nerve (or think better of his life choices), Leander fires off a text message and then waits, impatiently tossing his phone from hand to hand. Perhaps this last-ditch effort to cope won't even reply, or she'll rightfully tell him to fuck off, or she'll be busy, or—

Ding.

> **Autumn:** Sure thing, Simba.
> Meet me at our favorite
> place in an hour?

The breath Leander sucks in while reading that message is shaky, haggard. He feels worn to the bone and has absolutely no idea why. The *last* thing he wants to do tonight is dress, leave his home, and interact with other people like a normal, functioning human being. The thought alone has Leander feeling exhausted. Still, he forces himself to reply in the affirmative to Autumn's message and to drag himself up off of the couch. After all, he's the one who contacted her, and he's certainly done enough yanking her chain—no pun intended—for one lifetime.

As the water for his shower heats up, Leander contemplates the screen of his phone some more, ultimately shooting a text message over to Tripp before getting in. While he understands that Tripp wants his space and probably isn't keen on hearing from him so soon, Leander isn't taking any chances with his evening plans.

The fact is, the emergency services community is small, gossipy, and incestuous. Someone seeing him and Autumn together again in public would *rip*-whisper through the grapevine, eventually filtering its way back to Tripp. By that time, the story would be distorted and dangerous. There's nothing to hide here, so Leander should act accordingly and get ahead of it.

Unfortunately, his texting skills leave something to be desired, and Leander's roundabout way of trying to start a casual conversation with Tripp goes completely unaddressed. Either Tripp isn't paying attention to his notifications, or he's not impressed. As the bathroom becomes increasingly steamy, Leander shucks his clothing and stands in front of the mirror, naked and frowning at the string of one-sided messages filling his screen.

Frustrated, he sets the phone down and glances up, blue eyes meeting their reflections in the mirror. He looks even more tired and sad than he feels.

Leander allows his gaze to drift, scanning the length of his own body and noting with some disappointment that there isn't a single bruise or scratch mark on him. No indentations from Tripp's teeth or fingernails, no physical sign of *anything* that happened, some token Leander could look at and relish knowing that it was the equivalent of body graffiti proclaiming: *Tripp was here.*

Almost incidentally, that thought drags his focus back to Tripp himself. Scrutinizing his own unmarked skin, Leander abruptly recalls the line of bruises marking the side of Tripp's neck from what was *perhaps* an overzealous reaction to discovering that his collar was left on overnight. In turn, he's reminded of the exchange he had with Beau earlier, shared when the younger Truett texted about tuxedo fittings and bachelor party plans. It was a conversation Leander was wholly intending on relaying to Tripp over lunch so that he'd be aware.

He forgot, plain and simple. Tripp left and Leander was thrown off-kilter, and it fully slipped his mind. *Damn, damn, damn.*

Hurriedly, Leander snatches up his phone and taps out yet another message in the thread. He details what, exactly, he shared with Beau, and encourages Tripp to keep the bruises hidden with a shirt. Nothing to do after that but pray that his warning comes in time for them to synchronize stories, though a quick glance at the time suggests that he's probably too late. All he can hope is that Tripp isn't too pissed, and that his conversation with Beau didn't inadvertently out their situation to Tripp's brother (and one of Leander's best friends).

This whole situation is a lesson in tightrope-walking, that's for sure.

When Tripp *still* doesn't reply, Leander gives up on trying to be either socially savvy or diplomatic, explaining plainly over the course of several additional texts about his plans with Autumn. The two of them hanging out shouldn't bother Tripp, anyway, since they've had *several* very frank conversations about her, stretching all the way back to when she was still Leander's sub. Tripp certainly knows that their relationship is long dead and buried, with no chance of resurrection in this lifetime.

In that same vein, Leander feels *sure* that Tripp couldn't possibly be suffering any delusions that there might be something left between him and Autumn besides friendship—and a tentative one at that—not after the way things ended, and moreso, the reason *why*. He's probably overthinking this, but better safe than sorry.

With a disappointed shake of his head, Leander puts his phone down and steps into the shower. He's resigned to the fact that Tripp isn't going to answer him tonight, but understandably uneasy and wishing that he would. If what Tripp needs is space, though, Leander will give him it. He's already pushing the limits Tripp has set with all of this texting, so the least he can do is wait to contact him again until the man decides that he's ready to reciprocate.

The ball is in your court, Tripp, Leander thinks to himself, blinking against the water as he wets his hair and soaps himself up into a lather. He tries his best not to worry that Tripp has simply taken his ball and gone home.

After an extended, thirty-minute affair in the shower where Leander mostly stands and stares blankly at the white tile wall, he steps out and shaves off the last two days' stubble. Freshly smooth, he wrangles his hair into something semi-styled and presentable before spritzing on some cologne. At least he'll look and smell decent, even if his attitude and mood don't match.

It takes longer to pick out an outfit. Leander rejects a lot of his staples because they're things Autumn has, at one point or another, indicated she enjoyed seeing him wearing. No need to add fuel to the fire or insult to injury—whatever the correct saying there would be, Leander's too mentally exhausted to unmix his metaphors.

In the end, he chooses something simple: black jeans, black duty boots, a long-sleeve gray Henley, and his trusty black leather jacket. The resulting vibe definitely *does* match his gloomy disposition, and that gives Leander a perverse satisfaction. The debate between his car and a ride-sharing service takes less than thirty seconds and is a no-brainer, the easiest decision of the night by far—*Uber it is*. Leander's going to need a drink or seven for what he's about to do, and while his car may be a piece of junk (at least according to Tripp), he's not keen on leaving it overnight and halfway across town when he inevitably can't drive home.

The city feels stark and bleak tonight, the biting cold that's settled in over the past twenty-four hours not helping matters in the least. It's almost too chilly for the outfit Leander has chosen, but when he steps outside to the wind cutting straight through his clothing to his skin, his Uber is already parked and waiting by the curb. Knowing that if he turns around now, he probably won't be able to force himself to come back, Leander forges on.

"Tempt-Pura?" the driver asks, confirming, and Leander nods.

This particular sushi restaurant is a place that he and Autumn used to frequent on a twice-weekly basis, mostly due to its proximity—close to both her apartment and Leander's EMS station. Traveling through the city tonight on this once-familiar trek, Leander finds himself melancholy. As they cross into his ambulance's first due area, the car passes location after location filled with memories of calls and patients past, and he can't seem to turn off the film reel.

A fire scene, where a former diner suffered a devastating arson event, and the sidewalk outside where Leander spent nearly ten straight hours doing fire rehab. Dead on his feet, cycling equally exhausted firefighters in and out of the blaze, taking vital signs and tending to minor injuries.

There's the cross-street where Leander responded to his first major pediatric trauma—a six-year-old hit by a car while riding her bike. Patently terrifying, but the child lived, so there's that. Next is the subsidized housing highrise that towers above them at a stoplight: Leander's been called here more times than he can count. Multiple elderly men with heart failure, a frequent flyer who goes into diabetic shock on the regular (both high and low blood sugars, she's not picky), and chronic bronchitis requiring CPAP on the third floor. Down on the first, there's a vet with a below-knee amputation who's never learned to use his prosthetic properly—he falls constantly, and often only needs a hand up off of the floor.

So many dwellings and businesses they pass evoke similar memories, both public and private spaces Leander is all too familiar with for all the wrong reasons. He can see the ghosts of the past replaying scenes from his mind like a movie: patients being carried out on stretchers or in stair chairs and in varying states of distress. He can see himself, tending to the wounded and the gravely ill, some of whom will live to see another day because of his interventions, and some who won't.

Despite the streets being empty and cold, in Leander's mind, the red lights flicker, casting the nearby buildings in an eerie glow, both a warning and a reminder.

None of this is unfamiliar to him, these ghosts that follow wherever he might go. They're always there, a few steps behind and lurking in the back of his mind. People he couldn't fix, patients he worries that he didn't do enough to save, in one way or another. The ghosts are something Leander's become accustomed to seeing, something he's accepted that he'll always carry with him.

In all fairness, though, normally they don't weigh *quite* as heavily on his psyche.

With some effort, by the time his Uber pulls up in front of the restaurant, Leander has managed to effectively push those thoughts aside. Ironically, his work woes aren't problems he needs to hide from Autumn, either—she's a nurse over at Central, and she certainly understands. On the other hand, Leander's professional trauma is not what made him send that text, and it's definitely not the focus of their meeting tonight.

"We're *here*," the Uber driver snaps impatiently, and only then does Leander realize that they've probably been parked for several minutes.

Embarrassed, he mumbles a rushed apology and a thanks. The man just grunts and probably annihilates his star rating for being as anti-social and oblivious as they come, but he can't do much about that now. Stepping out into the cold, Leander suppresses a shiver and regrets the lack of additional layers between the leather and his bare skin.

The restaurant is fancier than he would have chosen for tonight, and he nearly grimaces at the heaviness of the front doors, the cool sophistication practically emanating from the place. His usual haunts are more, 'stale beer smell and sticky floors' (or maybe that's Tripp's influence), but *this* is Autumn's purview. She is doing him a favor, though, so Leander will deal.

The atmosphere inside is subdued: candlelight on the tables as the primary illumination, deep shadows around cozy booths that offer the illusion of privacy. A low, respectful din of patrons socializing politely while eating, and ice clinking in glasses.

To be fair, it's a relaxing sort of place, and Leander does feel some of the stress sliding off of his shoulders as he moves inside and gives the host Autumn's name. That, or perhaps it's the nostalgia setting in, triggered by sensory recall tossing him back to all the nights they spent together here in the past. Either way, Leander can admit that Tempt-Pura wasn't a *bad* choice for somewhere to meet, to hopefully unpack the particular issues weighing on his mind.

"Right this way," the hostess tells him with a charming smile, and Leander follows her slim figure, bouncing ponytail, and high-heeled feet as they turn and lead him into the depths of the restaurant. It's plenty warm in here, so he loses the jacket and drapes it over his arm, ignoring the piqued glances of several women and at least one man as he passes by their tables. Autumn is seated all the way towards the back, at a table that—once upon a time—even Leander might have referred to as "theirs."

"Simba," Autumn says warmly, though her grin is smug as she rises from her side of the booth to greet him. "My little 'Lion Man'."

"You know that I hate when you call me that." They watched the stupid Disney movie *one* time by accident at the beginning of their relationship, and—drunk on endorphins—Leander had casually mentioned the meaning of his name. Autumn has never let him forget it.

"You'll always be my Lion King, hot stuff." Somewhat stiffly, Leander allows her to draw him into a hug and to kiss his cheek, because that's just Autumn's nature. He'd be shocked if she didn't invade his space and act overly personal. Even after everything they've been through, there's no changing her, nor would he want to do so. She is unapologetically herself and exactly who she's always been, and Leander could never fault her for that.

"So, to what do I owe the pleasure? And I don't just mean those kickass arms you have on display, there."

"Autumn," Leander replies easily and with a small smile, sliding into the booth across from his old friend and accepting the menu from the hostess. She looks somewhat disappointed by their interactions, and Leander finds that very amusing. If she only but knew.

He watches her go, in some ways almost resentful that he isn't remotely interested in flirting or taking her on a date—it would be nice to feel 'normal' for once, to understand *instant attraction,* as it were. It must be unspeakably blissful to be able to feel a romantic or sexual spark upon meeting another human being, to not be required to nurture an established connection simply to have enjoyable sex or be comfortable engaging as a Dom. To fall in love, or at least to *grow* to love someone else in a predictable way… it must be nice.

In an attempt to distract himself from his own thoughts, Leander immediately turns to sipping on the glass of ice water set in front of him, but under Autumn's piercing gaze, he's a mouse in the tiger cage. Outside of the bedroom, no one ever would have guessed their dynamic, not when they were actively involved with each other and definitely not now.

Back then, Leander got off on it—thought it was hilarious that other people assumed Autumn had him under her thumb, that people thought he was quiet and awkward and mousy. Their friends would joke, and Autumn would smirk, and Leander would shrug and sip his drink knowing that Autumn's provocative hip-sitting was only because she had as-yet unscabbed whip marks on her ass that he *personally* put there.

Now, raising his eyes to meet Autumn's twinkling brown ones, Leander *almost* misses when things were as easy as that. He definitely misses the feeling of having the upper hand, the one that comes along with *not* being the unfortunate dumbass who fell in love with the one person he definitely can't have.

It wasn't always so complicated. In fact, scening with Autumn began very similarly to the way he and Tripp have taken up: casual, *fun,* stress relief, and nothing more. They even met in a similar way, and Leander looks back on those days .fondly. Technically, he saw Autumn—many times actually—long before they ever spoke. Autumn was a smoker back then, and took so many breaks it felt like she haunted the security-camera-free hiding spot outside of Central's E.R. like a ghost.

Leander would catch sight of her lurking there practically every time his truck came to drop off a patient, and—he can't lie—she was *interesting* to him. Most nurses put their hair up for a shift, but not Autumn. Long, thick, ringlet curls down past her shoulder blades, dark against her skin and constantly falling in her eyes—he often wondered how she managed to complete patient care without it becoming soaked in bodily fluids. She wore expensive, custom scrubs that hugged her ample curves, and while Leander wasn't necessarily attracted to them, he certainly found her look aesthetically pleasing.

And she always had a cigarette in her hand.

One day, she called out to him as he passed. Leander was oblivious and busy, solo-dragging their litter towards the truck while his partner (pre-Marley) remained inside, restocking their gear. This woman, smirking and leaning sideways against the cement wall of the E.R., called him handsome and asked for a light, her cigarette already burning between two fingers. By that time, Leander was fascinated enough by her entire schtick and constant presence outside the hospital to take the bait. They talked for at least fifteen minutes that day.

The truth is, Leander found Autumn's personality to be just as captivating as her image, and her tendency to be an open book about anything and everything revealed a history rife with experiences that he could heavily relate to. Shitty parents and shittier coping skills, estranged siblings, and a drive to help others that neither of them have entirely made sense of, even now. Becoming a health care provider to try fulfill that calling, but then drowning under the weight of responsibility—Leander understood exactly why Autumn was always smoking.

Time went on, and eventually, they exchanged numbers so that she could coordinate her breaks with Leander's drop-offs. They'd talk while he cleaned the back of the ambulance, or he'd lean against the wall and keep her company through her last drags. It went on like that for months, before they "took things extracurricular," as Autumn called it, before his partner casually mentioned Leander's penchant for bondage and effectively outed him.

It was meant to be a tease, of course, his partner trying to embarrass him in front of a girl it was assumed he was crushing on, but Autumn was intrigued. The conversation immediately switched tracks, Autumn mentioned that she was looking to quit smoking, asked slyly whether Leander had any suggestions regarding healthier methods of coping or relieving stress, and the rest is history.

It's difficult to feel regret for what they shared. Autumn was an incredible sub. A natural, and since Leander truly cared for her as a friend, their scenes were some of the most fulfilling of his life, up to that point. Her body was beautiful, she was adventurous and responsive, plus she communicated both frankly and openly. Autumn always told him what she needed, and therefore, Leander exited their scenes feeling satisfied, knowing that he was truly helping her.

But easy as it might have been to get his needs met with her and *without* all of the messy intimacy, Autumn simply doesn't hold the same allure for him anymore. Even aesthetically, the idea of tying her up, dripping wax all over her body and then stepping back to admire his work feels lackluster and uninspiring. It's not just Leander's emotions that are tied up with Tripp—it's *everything*. All of his needs, every single one.

Reaching across the table, Autumn pokes his bicep with a manicured finger, playful but uncharacteristically serious as she persists in coaxing him to share. "I know that face, Leander. And I didn't really think you called me here because you missed me. You know, you break a girl's heart, that's one thing. You break her Saturday night plans and don't deliver something juicy, she might have to kill you."

Without missing a beat, Autumn lifts a hand and catches the attention of their server, ordering drinks for both of them and nailing Leander's usual: a double ten-year whiskey, two rocks. He smiles at her gratefully before sighing and leaning back, tacking on a few appetizers and sushi rolls to the order, because if he's doing this, it's not going to be on an empty stomach.

Said stomach twists a little as he thinks about the two abandoned sandwiches still waiting futilely for their intendeds back home on his countertop. He hadn't been able to muscle up the strength to put them away.

"So?" Autumn prompts, once the server is gone, resting her chin on the back of one hand with genuine interest.

Leander nods and takes a deep breath, struggling with where to begin. "The truth is—and I realize that this is extremely awkward and unfair of me—"

"But that's not stopping you." Autumn winks to soften the barb, so Leander continues.

"—I was hoping you could give me some, well, pointers, I suppose," he says hesitantly. Autumn's eyes narrow in confusion, and her lips part (undoubtedly to sass him), but Leander cuts her off before she's able to speak another word.

"I need to know what I could have done to make things better for you, emotionally, when I was your Dom. Or, on the flip side, if there is anything you wish that *you* would have done to create better boundaries while still ensuring that your needs were met with me. I'm… " Leander lets a small growling noise escape from his mouth and runs a frustrated hand through his hair before throwing it up into the air and letting it slap down on his thigh. "I'm floundering."

There's silence from across the table, and Leander can't bear to rip his eyes away from the Swedish Ivy plant that is for some reason placed between their booth and the one next to it on Autumn's side, as it has abruptly become extremely fascinating. He's *just* about to call this whole night off, dub it a failure—it's too much to ask of this woman, it's unfair that he did so in the first place—when Autumn finally speaks.

"Are you telling me that the Tin Man finally convinced the Wizard to give him a heart? Seriously? *The* unfeeling Leander Grigori? Mister 'I Don't *Do* Love, Autumn,' has fallen prey to Cupid's bow and arrow? Oh, this is delicious. This is *too* good."

Struggling not to roll his eyes, Leander drags them back to his dinner companion and scowls, especially when he clocks the amused expression on her face. "I don't know that I'd call myself *unfeeling,*" he protests.

"I would," Autumn replies quickly.

"I feel things *very* strongly, in fact. It's just that love has not traditionally been—"

"Yeah, yeah, spare me the sermon, Little Lion Man. You do remember who you're talking to, hmm? I'm the original one-eyed chicklet in the kingdom of the blind, baby. You can't fool me, so don't even try. Who is it?" Autumn sits back and folds her arms over her chest, tongue running across her teeth as she surveys Leander with what can only be described as smug superiority. She raises her eyebrows and waits while he resists the urge to point out that it would've been far more on brand for her to make a crack about him being the Cowardly Lion.

Miraculously, their server picks that moment to show up with their drinks, and Leander buys time by savoring several long sips, but Autumn isn't remotely put off. She tastes her own cocktail—something mixed and fruity with an umbrella, Tripp would love it—while continuing to stare him down, gaze relentless and knowing. Honestly, if Leander ever had a mind to switch, he'd be curious on a purely scientific level what Autumn as a Dom would be like, because he has to admit, she has the attitude *down*, when she wants.

"It's Tripp," Leander says simply, once he decides that he's ready, figuring he owes Autumn that much. To his surprise, she barely reacts, dropping back against the booth with her fingernails tapping away against the table.

"Huh," is all she says. When Leander raises his eyebrows in question, she just shrugs. "Makes sense." Somewhat put out, he stares and blinks at her in disbelief, but she just raises both hands as if to say, *what do you want from me?*

"You can't be serious. After everything you mocked me for lacking."

"It's relieving, really," Autumn tells him, somehow holding a straight face. "I mean, for starters, you're obviously a big 'mo, so that doesn't actually reflect on me at all." Leander furrows his brow and opens his mouth to lecture her about the spectrum of sexuality but this time, Autumn cuts him off. "Whatever, don't give me the identity speech again, it was just a joke. No, that isn't it. You're going to hate hearing this, I can guarantee it."

"All I'm hearing so far is you making fun of me."

Autumn snorts and shrugs with one shoulder. "Fair." She swirls her straw in her drink for a minute before nodding to herself. "If it was going to be anyone, it was always going to be Tripp," she says frankly, before taking a long sip from the glass she's still toying with. "We can pretend I only thought so because of how well I know you, but the truth is, you're not subtle, Lee."

Leander can only imagine that the furrow in his brow is getting deeper as he stares back at Autumn in abject confusion. "You'll have to explain this to me further at some point, because I certainly wasn't aware that I had romantic feelings for Tripp until very recently," he says, and then promptly drains his glass, because this is a *lot* more than he anticipated hearing. "On second thought, don't."

Smirking as she puts her hands up in mock-surrender, Autumn's face softens a little. "Well, all of that aside, you know I care about you, Simba. So yeah, I think I can help a fellow lost soul out. No guarantees on outcome, though, and there's no magic button you can press to keep those pesky romantic feelings separate. What I *can* offer you is a shoulder to cry on and an ear to bend, and a big mouth that doesn't know when to keep her thoughts to herself."

"Thank you, Autumn," Leander says in relief. "That's more than I deserve from you, I know that."

"Believe it," Autumn retorts. "Although speaking of deserving better, I hope you know that you do, too. If Tripp doesn't feel the same way, you don't *owe* him to stick around for sex or submission, no matter what you promised him to start with. Cutting yourself open and bleeding the contents of your heart all over the floor—and not in the fun way—for someone who doesn't appreciate it gets harder by the day. That is a thing that I learned the hard way."

Leander ducks his head and fiddles with his empty glass. "Tripp is very deserving," he says quietly, and Autumn laughs a little in response, though the sound isn't judgmental or cruel.

"Oh, Little Lion Man, you got it bad."

He doesn't deny it. There's no reason to, now. The waitress comes with a tray full of food and sets each item down in front of them, but all of it suddenly looks gray and unappetizing to Leander's palate. The things that have been weighing on his shoulders aren't all out there yet, and the worry and regret is starting to leave a bad taste in his mouth.

"Autumn," Leander says tentatively, watching as she uses chopsticks to pop a piece of California roll into her mouth and chew. "There's more. Specifically, I think I may be falling short in giving Tripp what he needs with regard to after-care. I've been leaving his side, denying myself certain affections for self-preservation purposes. Only after he seems to be fully recovered or has fallen asleep, of course, but I'm concerned that it's not enough. I fear—"

"Psh," Autumn replies, her mouth still half-full. "You ain't worried about him. You," she jabs her chopsticks in Leander's direction, "are worried he's gonna realize you're head over heels in love with him if you show it too much."

"Yes," Leander says, relieved at being understood. "I am."

But Autumn just shrugs. "You're stupid," she replies easily.

"Excuse me?"

"Lee," she says, dropping the food pinched in her utensils back onto the plate while she addresses him, patient but exasperated. "You have a frickin' free pass. Trust me, *he* will tell you if you're doing too much. If you ask me—and you did," she reminds him, scooping up some rice and inhaling it like a vacuum. "You're way more likely to send him into drop doing what you're doing than you are to protect yourself in any kind of way that's gonna matter. Running out on a sub early because you're scared of your own feelings is bad frickin' news, lovemuffin. Let me tell you, there were plenty of times it hurt like hell for me to sleep in your arms."

Autumn swallows and stares down at her plate, refusing to make eye contact with him for the first time this evening, and Leander's guilty conscience swells in his chest. Both for what he's definitely done to Autumn and what he's potentially been doing to Tripp. Before he can apologize—not that he thinks Autumn will like that, either—she continues talking.

"But the thing is, Simba, I'm smarter than you, and I'm definitely smarter than the Ken-doll you're fucking. I've been subbing since I was eighteen and I've had *all* the bad Doms, plus I *know* what I gotta do to avoid drop. Does Tripp? Would he tell you if what you were doing wasn't enough? I dunno, Lee. I've met the guy, and I can't say that I have any confidence in his ability to own his vulnerability and to share his feelings with the class.

"Point being, yes, sleeping with you like we were lovers—after you made it clear more than once that we would never be any such thing—was hard, really hard. The best thing you ever did for me was to break things off when you did. But baby, *you're* the lover in this equation, and Tripp is the one in need. What you're doing is just selfish. If you can't be what he *needs*, you've gotta cut ties with him as a sub."

Stunned, Leander just sits there, digesting Autumn's words. They're honest, brutally so, and it takes him a minute of grappling with his own defense mechanisms to keep from firing back. She's right, of course, and that is the hardest pill to swallow.

Selfish.

Her words ring inside his head, rattling his brain. Leander has been going about this all wrong—he's been too selfish, too caught up in *having* Tripp the only way he believed Tripp would allow, too focused on the *having* itself and chasing his own desires to acknowledge any of the potential fallout, and now Tripp is paying the price.

Jesus Christ, he's been a fool, he's put Tripp in danger, he's—

"Autumn," he says, voice as full of apology as he can muster at the moment. "I need to go, I need—"

"Thought you might say that," she replies wryly, spearing a piece of chicken with her chopstick and waving it absently in the direction of the front door. "Go on, get out of here, you responsible, caring Dom, you. Do the right fucking thing, for once."

"Thank you," Leander says earnestly as he stands to throw on his jacket. He steps away and then quickly turns back, pulling out his wallet to toss a handful of twenties down onto the table, enough to cover the meal and several additional drinks for Autumn. "I owe you, truly."

"Uh, yeah," Autumn replies emphatically, bristling before softening again. "But Simba, do call me if you need to, okay? Everything else aside, like I said, I care about you, and I—well, no. I don't care about Tripp, but I care about *you* and I don't wish the guy any harm, so, you know. Call me. I mean it."

Backing up towards the door, Leander barely avoids running into another table of diners as he nods and touches two fingers to his lips in a distant goodbye kiss.

"Thank you!"

On his way out of the restaurant, Leander briefly considers ordering another Uber, but the wait times are peak and much longer than he'd like. Now that he's come to his senses, he feels anxious to rectify his mistakes, and the idea of delaying any attempt to do so for longer than necessary makes him almost physically uncomfortable. Standing alone on the sidewalk, Leander barely feels the cold wind whipping at his skin, his attention fully focused on finding Tripp and putting things right.

A quick scroll through the one-sided conversation they had earlier fills him with even more dread. If Tripp *is* dropping, if his off-kilter behavior this afternoon winds up being what Leander fears and not just Tripp being *Tripp*, then there is a zero percent chance his recent messages didn't add fuel to that fire.

Sad and ashamed, Leander considers how he would react if he were on the edge, and instead of comfort, received similar messages from his scene partner. Nonchalant ones, about covering bruises and his sub going to meet up with his former Dom. Especially when Tripp may have been experiencing feelings of rejection already, that *can't* have felt nice. Even if Tripp understands cognitively that Leander would never trade him for Autumn, drop isn't logical or sensical: it's *emotional,* it's hormonal. Looking at the situation now and with a clear head, Leander honestly can't believe how badly he's failed them both.

How could he be so ignorant? So short-sighted and self-involved. Leander curses himself and glances around, just on the off-chance that there's a taxi or a bus nearby. Anything else useful, actually—even a bicycle he could steal, because fuck it, why not? Unfortunately there's nothing, and he just can't risk waiting around any longer.

He runs.

Bolts, really, the soles of his heavy boots smacking loudly against the pavement as they propel him forward. Leander doesn't need a reply from Tripp to know exactly where he and Beau are hanging tonight. There's only one place they ever retreat to for solace, and Leander heads straight for it.

The Hot Plate is nearly five miles from the restaurant where he left Autumn, but thankfully, Leander is a regular runner and plenty capable of hacking it. Regardless of the lack in flexibility of his jeans, the way they chafe against his thighs as he sprints, Leander doesn't stop. Ignoring the way the sweat builds beneath the leather of his jacket despite the cold, he doesn't slow down.

Less than a block from the Hot Plate, he regains some sense of rational thought, forcing himself to cool off and to rein his wild energy in. It wouldn't do to show up there like a tornado, exploding into a bar where everyone knows his name and will certainly have questions as to why he's so desperate to find Tripp Truett. The last thing Leander wants is to embarrass the man, or worse, out their situation to the public as a whole.

Running full-speed into the Hot Plate while screaming Tripp's name at the top of his lungs would be an excellent way to announce definitively that there's something fishy going on, and neither of them needs that drama.

The half-speed remainder of his trek also allows Leander a minute to catch his breath and to formulate a plan: it's simple, first and foremost, get Tripp alone.

Once in private, he'll ensure that Tripp isn't dropping, and if he is, get him out of the bar, bring him home, *make this right*. He'll apologize, he'll get on his knees if he has to, because Tripp *trusted* him, Tripp put his sanity and safety in Leander's hands and he failed. He fucked this up, he let Tripp down.

The plan seems easy and close to foolproof, but in the end, nothing goes right.

Bursting inside the Hot Plate more excitedly than he intends, Leander almost immediately spots Beau sitting at the bar. Tripp isn't on a stool beside him—or anywhere else to be seen, for that matter—so Leander bypasses the entire restaurant and heads for the restrooms, hoping to get lucky. There's a couple making out in the corner by the sinks, but the stalls are otherwise clear, and Leander doesn't run into Tripp either on the way there or back.

Growing concerned, he chews his lip and surveys the bar floor again. The Hot Plate is busy—it is Saturday, after all—but it's not so packed Leander can't be sure that he's scanned the crowd sufficiently. Normally, he'd call this a wash, but after everything his eyes have been opened to tonight, he can't bring himself to be so dismissive. At this point, it feels worth the potential risk to approach Beau, so that's exactly what Leander does.

"Hey!" Beau exclaims in surprise, grinning widely when Leander appears at his side and taps him on the arm. "Nice to see you, man, pull up a stool. Reina's making... uh—what are you making, Rei?"

"Buttery Nipples," Reina declares with a wink, capping her cocktail shaker and making it live up to its name. "You in, Lee? On me."

"Hello, Beau," Leander replies stoically. "Reina. And thank you, that's very generous, but not tonight." He turns his attention fully back to the younger Truett and leans in so that he can't be incidentally overheard. "Actually, I'm looking for Tripp. It's—" he hesitates, unsure how to convey the gravity of the situation without oversharing their business. "Well, it's somewhat of an urgent matter. Is he here? Did he go back to your apartment, by chance?"

The sympathy that fills Beau's eyes is out of place, and Leander doesn't like it one bit. "Uh, you just missed him, Lee," he says carefully. "He headed out maybe twenty minutes ago."

"Alright," Leander persists impatiently. "He's not responding to my messages, should I just check your apartment? Or—"

"He left with a girl," Beau interjects, not even trying to hide the apologetic note in his voice. "I'm sorry, Lee, I—"

The shock that Tripp would seek out a random hookup after the past twenty-four hours they shared together short-circuits Leander's wiring for a moment, but he shakes it off just as quickly. He and Tripp have not promised exclusivity in their contract. In fact, they specifically decided against it, although Leander had *thought* they exchanged a moment of mutual understanding that it would be a goal, something to work towards and consider seriously, if they were each able to meet the other's needs.

The reality that Tripp doesn't feel as if he's doing that stings, although that *is* what he came to correct, isn't it? This doesn't change anything—he still needs to find Tripp.

"Could you message him, Beau? Please. I normally wouldn't ask, and I wish I could explain to you why this is so important, but I'm afraid I've let Tripp down enough for one day." As an afterthought, he turns on what Tripp would undoubtedly refer to as 'puppy dog eyes,' widening his gaze and blinking innocently down at Beau while attempting to look *extra* sad. Tripp always claims that no one could possibly say no to him with that face on—no better time to find out.

"Jesus," Beau replies. "Who taught you *that?* Never mind," he adds, holding up a hand. "Stupid question. Hang on." Beau slides his phone over from where it's resting on the bar and taps out a message before pressing send. They wait, but nothing happens. Without having to be asked, Beau then calls Tripp, putting the phone to his ear and raising an eyebrow at Leander, who tries to appear as immensely grateful as he feels.

"Yeah, Tripp, it's me," Beau says, after the disappointing sounds of Tripp's voice-mail filter out through the tiny speaker, just barely making it to Leander's ears. *Damn.* "Give me a call back as soon as you get this, it's important." He hangs up and shoots Leander an apologetic look. "Sorry, man. We could still have that beer?"

Blowing out a stream of frustration from his lungs, Leander pushes a hand through his hair and shakes his head. "Any other night, I would be glad to, Beau. I know we haven't had much time together lately," he adds regretfully. "But I can't—I *have* to find Tripp."

"Lee, no offense, but he could be anywhere in the city by now, and Tripp not answering his phone usually means that he wants to be left alone. Or, alone with whoever he's with," Beau tacks on meaningfully, with an eye roll and a swig of his beer. Doesn't matter—Leander's already halfway to the door by the time the bottle makes contact with the bartop again, as Beau's words go in one ear and out the other.

"I'll find a way," he says, determined, more for his own benefit than anyone else's, since there's no way Beau could hear him now, anyway.

And Leander tries, he does. He scours the whole damn city as best he can, well into the early hours of the morning. He starts and ends at the Truett's front door, knocking and listening for movement but coming up empty both times. Beau must have gone over to his fiancée's place after leaving the bar, and Tripp—Tripp never came home.

In between lurking somewhat creepily outside their apartment, Leander checks all of Tripp's usual haunts: the fancy bar he thinks no one knows that he likes, a handful of all-night diners and restaurants, the donut place he often stops by on the way to work to pick up treats for his crew.

Desperate, Leander even drops by both Station Fifteen *and* Station Eleven, since occasionally and if his friends are working, Tripp will wind up there in the middle of the night, wanting to hang out or sleep off a bender. That happens more often if he's been out drinking or went home with a hookup on the wrong side of town, but tonight, Leander is out of luck.

Tripp is nowhere to be found.

When his wristwatch shows nine a.m. and his phone screen is still black and silent, Leander is ready to admit defeat. His bottom is sore from sitting on the shitty, trodden-down carpet that lines the hallway outside of Tripp's door, and he begrudgingly calls it a night.

Even as Leander drags his feet down the stairs and patiently waits on the sidewalk for his Uber, his drooping eyelids still blink open in fierce determination, glancing around with waning hope that Tripp will suddenly appear. His *car* is in the parking lot, for God's sake. He *has* to come back *sometime*.

But Leander has to work tonight and so does Tripp, and he can't very well do the job on no sleep at all. Much as he may hate it, the reality is that Tripp has made himself inaccessible, and Leander has done all that he can do for the moment. Fixing things with his friend will just have to wait.

With any luck, though, he'll be able to at least speak to Tripp once he's sober again, hopefully before work. Leander makes a mental note for when his brain is less fuzzy to come up with a more condensed version of the speech that he was going to give when he finally found the man in person. Something that will encourage Tripp to *not* hang up during Leander's pressured attempt to blurt it out. In his physically and mentally exhausted state, nothing comes to mind, but perhaps with some rest.

Heartbroken and disappointed, Leander climbs into his Uber and returns home. Walking into his apartment, his *last* remaining hopes are dashed when Tripp isn't there, waiting for him inside. Numb, Leander strips to his boxers and climbs into bed, barely remembering to set an alarm before allowing the creeping darkness to pull him under.

***

There's no answer on Tripp's phone when Leander tries before heading into work. It rings this time, at least, and that's an improvement over the "straight-to-voicemail" situation he was getting earlier. Or perhaps it isn't, since that means Tripp has charged his phone, turned it back on, and is still ignoring Leander's attempts at contact. If he previously thought that he couldn't feel worse, he was wrong.

Unfortunately for Leander, his twenty-four-hour EMS shift continues fueling the dark cloud hanging over his head. Call after call after call keeps him busy, and then there's the charting and the station chores, his Captain's duties—all of it amounting to very little free time with which to do anything else. The few hours that he does manage to steal for himself are spent sleeping, urinating, or eating, and Leander's never felt more like human needs are cursed.

At one point, he hears Station Fifteen go enroute to an automatic fire alarm at a warehouse downtown, not in Leander's local. From the back of his rig (where he's regretfully sitting and checking I.V. medication expiration dates), Leander cranks the volume dial on the radio and listens in. Gunnar's unmistakable voice puts the squad responding and on scene, but the crew sent in to clear the building is led by someone else—*Tripp*.

It's difficult not to breathe a sigh of relief at being presented with solid evidence that his friend is alive and well, but it also hurts. This is definitive proof that he's being ignored, and Leander can't quite figure out what to do with that. The ignited flame of desperation and adrenaline that pushed him to his limits on Saturday and well into Sunday has flickered and been extinguished, but now Leander can't be entirely sure that forcing Tripp into a confrontation remains the right thing to do.

Surely if Tripp had been dropping, he would have spun out by now. Since he hasn't, Leander can only assume that the situation, while regretful, isn't entirely emergent. While he's loathe to make any *more* assumptions, he's not positive what other choice Tripp has left him. Bereft, Leander spends every spare moment of his shift—when he's not focused on patient care or another task requiring his full attention—wavering between the idea of showing up in person at Tripp's station, or leaving him alone completely, providing time and space for Tripp to come to him.

That seemingly-impossible decision is made for him when a text message from Tripp arrives at 17:52, eight minutes before they both are set to go off-duty for the night.

Ding.

> **Tripp:** sorry for blowing you off. Just need a little space. I'll hit you up soon, cool?

It *pains* Leander to accept the neutral note, but at this point, he's sent countless messages pleading with Tripp to hear him out. He's asked for a mere five minutes of the man's time, either on the phone or face-to-face, he's been clear that he needs to apologize and that he feels he's made a mistake, but the details beyond that aren't appropriate to convey via text. The bottom line is that Tripp isn't currently interested in hearing what he has to say, and it would be invasive and disrespectful to keep pushing.

> **Leander:** My offer and request both stand. Use your key anytime you like or feel up to seeing me, I am always here for you. I care about you very much, Tripp.

It's the best he can do, for now.

Tripp doesn't call and he doesn't use his key. Leander works the next two nights, twelve-hour shifts that stretch from six in the evening to six in the morning, and the reversal of his normal routine is jarring and frustrating. Those feelings are multiplied further by both his continuing worry about Tripp, and his own lack of an outlet to process and release them.

While he does honor Tripp's request to leave him alone, Leander is weak, and he can't help checking in on the older Truett via his brother, at least once. Beau doesn't seem even moderately surprised by his message, but he's evasive. All told, he doesn't really give Leander a satisfying answer as to how Tripp is doing, which leaves him wishing he hadn't contacted Beau at all.

Also, the text conversation that follows quickly turns to wedding favor options, which is basically the last thing on earth Leander wants to discuss, and something he doubts he'd have an opinion on, even if it was for his own wedding.

Tiny bottles of alcohol, he suggests, and apparently, that's the sort of helpful feedback Beau is looking for. All Leander cares about is that it gets him out of any further interaction.

Early on Wednesday, Leander arrives home similarly blearily and burnt out, the same way he has the past three mornings prior. *I'm getting too old for this,* he tells himself, slumping defeatedly against the mirrored wall on the elevator ride up to his floor. He's practically half-asleep, allowing his head to loll to the side and his eyes to drift closed for a blissful moment of peace.

Need to see about switching to dayshift permanently, he thinks.

When the elevator dings open, Leander yawns heavily before trudging over to his door. Small comforts, he now has a couple of days off with which to recover and regain his bearings. While he's still holding out hope that Tripp will appear —even if it's only to hang out, get drunk, and watch trashy TV—Leander is so damn tired that a part of him feels relieved to be able to simply pass out for as long as he desires. He's *bone*-tired, in every way a person can be worn-out, so much so that his brain is barely online enough to help his hands fit his key into the lock.

Which is why, when he stumbles into his apartment and locks the door behind him, kicking off his boots and wandering sluggishly into the living room, his reaction to the scene that's awaiting his arrival is perhaps somewhat less than ideal.

There, in the middle of the hardwood floor, wedged between Leander's wrought iron and glass coffee table and the wide, sliding doors leading out to the balcony, kneels Tripp. He's naked, save for his collar and a gorgeous pair of matching green panties complete with satin bows and lace side panels that, at *any* other time, Leander would be, frankly, unapologetically obsessed with getting to know on an intimate level.

Right now, the sight only brings him heartbreak and a near-blinding sense of exhaustion.

As Leander stands frozen, Tripp smirks down at the ground, his head only bowed *just* enough to give the illusion of submission while his fingers twist restlessly into each other at the small of his back. If Leander wasn't looking for it, he might not have noticed, but he *is*—he's been waiting for days to see Tripp in person, to find out if his fears are justified.

They are. Tripp didn't just *drop,* he's been dropping, he still is. His posture and the way he curls into himself but still leans unconsciously in his Dom's direction, his fidgeting, his facial expressions—it's all so obvious and horrifying, because Leander *did this to him.* If Tripp wasn't someone he already knew inside and out, Leander wouldn't be as confident in his assessment of the situation, but this isn't *some submissive.* This is *Tripp,* and Leander is first and foremost Tripp's best friend.

Emotional drop. Leander has never seen it, never engaged with a sub who was prone to it, or suffered from anything similar during their time together. Emotional drops can last for days, weeks even, and the cure to the fall sure isn't orange juice and a massage, though those things don't hurt. Constant contact, strong boundaries and routines, reassurance from a trusted Dom—basically, everything Leander has failed to give and hasn't been allowed to even *try* to make up for these past few days is the solution.

Now, Tripp's reaching out in the only manner he feels he can, which is surprising in a way that Leander knows it shouldn't be. Of course, Tripp in a spiral would see his self-worth tied to being a sub. Of course, Tripp would think that the only way he could obtain the affection and validation he's so desperately craving would be to submit, like this. And to be fair, he probably needs this end of things, too—God knows, Leander does.

Tripp needs something else first, though, and it's time for Leander to give it to him, whether he likes it or not. Whether Leander has the *energy* for it or not. He owes Tripp so much more than that, but it's a start.

"Get up," Leander barks shortly. He strides over and makes it into Tripp's space just as he's straightening up, the faint but razor-sharp ghost of whiskey unmistakable on his friend's breath. "You've been drinking," he says flatly.

"I'm not drunk," Tripp replies defensively, recovering quickly to tack on a sincere, "Sir," that makes Leander's heart ache for how much Tripp clearly wants and *needs* him to be better than he's been. Not that he's likely even aware of Leander's failings—no, knowing Tripp, he's surely blaming himself.

Leander clears his throat. "We don't have rules requiring you to abstain from drinking prior to a scene, so you are not in trouble with me. For that."

Perhaps Tripp is tipsier than he lets on because he snorts and averts his gaze, leaving Leander to raise a brow, grab him by the chin, and force eye contact. "What was that?"

It's not unexpected when Tripp breaks, twisting away from Leander's grasp like it burns and wrenching himself to his feet, stumbling a few steps away to fist a hand in his hair and swear. "Shit. I shouldn't have come here. I don't know what I was thinking, Lee. I gotta—"

"Sit," Leander commands.

Tripp, with desperation in his eyes, hesitates but then finds his way over to Leander's couch and plops down. He slumps forward, crossing both arms over his body self-consciously, and Leander doesn't think he's ever seen his friend look less like his overly-confident, proudly arrogant self. In response, Leander perches on the coffee table's edge just in front of him, close enough that their knees touch. He pulls the blanket from the back of the couch, draping it around Tripp's shoulders and encouraging him to pull it closed if he wants. He does.

"It's Wednesday," Leander says casually.

"I know. I know, Le—*Sir*. I'm sorry for blowing you off, or whatever, I just—"

Leander holds up a hand, and Tripp's mouth snaps closed. "Good boy. That was not commentary on your behavior, it was a reminder that we agreed to a weekly discussion regarding our terms. Last Wednesday was the last time we did so. This week has been... challenging, to say the least, and I don't think I can overstate the importance of this conversation."

Tripp's eyes dim slightly, but he nods, resigned, as Leander continues, "Normally, I'd ask for you to remove your collar, but I feel as if today, that is not a good idea." Tripp just shrugs listlessly.

"This whole thing is about what you want, anyway," he mutters, and while Leander strongly suspected he might feel that way—or at least, that the drop was feeding him those negative thoughts—it's difficult to hear the accusation spoken aloud.

He controls his emotional response, and instead of chastising Tripp, Leander reaches out to take his hand where it's white-knuckling the blanket. Thankfully, Tripp lets him, though he keeps his eyes fixed on the gas fireplace built into the far wall behind Leander's head.

"I've really let you down," Leander says quietly. "If you're amenable, I'd like to share some things with you, and then you can respond however you see fit. For the purposes of this conversation only, you may call me whatever you like, and that includes insults and derogatory names, if they represent how you feel. Tripp," Leander says, using his free hand to touch Tripp's chin and feeling relieved when the man's glassy eyes flicker to meet his own. "When you first put that collar on, I believe that it made you feel free. Something changed, *I* made a misstep here. I need to help you understand that none of this is your fault."

The set of Tripp's jaw twitches minutely, and he blinks fiercely against what Leander would be willing to bet is a burning sensation behind his eyes. "Tripp, do you know that you're in sub drop?"

The lines crossing Tripp's forehead and in between his eyebrows deepen, and Tripp looks adorably confused. He opens his mouth to speak and then closes it again, apparently unsure, but Leander just waits patiently. "I don't... uh, no? How is that even possible? We scened like, three days ago. I thought—"

"This is happening because of me," Leander says bluntly. "I should have recognized that you were struggling on Saturday morning. I should never have let you leave. Trust that all I wanted was to respect your boundaries and the limitations set for both of our relationships, but that is *not* an excuse. I should have known better. I should have erred on the side of caution. I didn't meet your emotional needs as my submissive, and now you feel... "

Leander narrows his eyes and regards Tripp carefully. It would be immensely damaging to Tripp for him to project another incorrect assumption his way. However, knowing Tripp the way that he does, the last thing the headstrong man will want to do is give voice to his own perceived weaknesses. So Leander *must* do it for him, must hit the nail on the head so that Tripp can begin to process that he is not broken, that he *can* feel better, and that Leander may be relied upon to help him do exactly that.

"Rejected," he finally offers, squeezing Tripp's hand reassuringly. "Unworthy, perhaps. Like your value is tied up in your submission, and not who you are as a person. That those things are mutually exclusive, when they never, ever were. You're irritated and cranky, everything in your life feels exponentially exhausting and more difficult to handle than usual. You are worried that you're a burden to me, that you ask too much, that I feel trapped and possibly even tricked into showing you affection."

As Leander finishes speaking, Tripp's face transforms into an expression of pure *grief*, a single tear spilling out of his right eye and rolling slowly down his cheek. Leander wastes no time—he surges forward, climbing into Tripp's lap to straddle his hips and frame his face with both hands.

"Are you my sub, Tripp?" he demands. "Are you?"

"Yes," Tripp chokes out, nodding against Leander's palms. "Yes, Sir."

"I have one task for you, just one, and I need you to perform it perfectly, do you understand?" Tripp's eyes slipped closed, but he nods, and Leander is so proud, so in awe of Tripp, considering their circumstances. "You are to tell me honestly and clearly, the truth about what you *need* from me as a Dom, Tripp. I *know* there is something that you have been afraid to ask for, but I am telling you, I *want* to give it to you. You *deserve it,* Tripp. Whatever you've been resisting giving voice to, you say it now. *Let* me give you what you need, Tripp. That is an order from your Dom. Do you understand?"

Sniffling and inhaling roughly around a swallowed sob, Tripp nods again as the tears spill freely, making beautiful tracks down his lovely face and turning Leander's fingers damp. Tripp is so *soft,* so vulnerable, and Leander *aches* to be this close to him, to have him in his hands, so damaged and still so perfect. If it wouldn't be totally inappropriate to what he's trying to accomplish, he'd lick Tripp's tears from his face and take him right here, just like this. Show him exactly how much he's loved and cherished.

"It's just," Tripp starts and stops, letting his eyes flutter shut, wet lashes dark against his pale, freckled skin. "You don't. You say that, but you don't want this." Leander shifts back on his heels, just enough to release Tripp's face and grab his wrists instead, bringing them together between their chests.

"Tripp," he says patiently. "Your thoughts are corrupted by the drop you're experiencing, so I'll forgive you this once for telling me what I do and don't want. I will promise you this—*if* whatever you ask for is something I truly cannot do, then I will be honest with you about it. This is a two-way street." After a brief pause, Leander borrows from Autumn and sends up a silent prayer of thanks to her for the assist. "I'm not new to this. I *know* how to ensure that my own needs are met. Do you trust me?"

"Yes," Tripp hisses through gritted teeth, eyes pinched closed like he's fighting some great, internal battle, and this is Tripp, so that may not be far off. He takes a deep breath and blows it out before opening his eyes and visibly steeling himself. "Lee," he says cautiously. "Everything else you do for aftercare is great. But —I need you to *stay.* With me."

"The night?" Leander replies quickly, unable to believe his ears. *That* is what Tripp wants? What's caused all of this turmoil? Something Leander was denying himself because he assumed it wasn't an activity Tripp was interested in, that it was a toe across the line he needed to draw in the sand—for *both* of them. *Seriously?!*

"That—that's all, are you sure? Be honest with me, Tripp." He levels a stern glare down his nose and those bright green eyes blink back honestly as Tripp nods.

"I swear, Lee. I know it's needy and annoying and there's gotta be a million other —"

Leander cuts him off with a kiss, cupping his jaw and letting his tongue dart out to barely brush against the tip of Tripp's before pulling away, leaving the man breathless and searching for more.

"I am *so* proud of you. I think I should just speak plainly, Tripp. I was leaving for the night because I thought that was what you wanted. And other, more arbitrary reasons, none of which mean anything now. I apologize for not being in tune with your needs and for not asking outright. It will *not* happen again. Likewise, I expect that you'll be equally honest with me in the future. If you feel upset or uncomfortable, if you need something that I am not providing you—keeping in mind that *want* is different than *need* and that this is not an excuse to be a raging brat—you will be frank. Understand and agree?"

"Yes, Sir," Tripp replies, brighter and more enthusiastic than Leander's seen him since early last week. It's relieving, and as he slides back off of Tripp's lap and onto the coffee table, he breathes out a sigh that reflects that feeling.

"So," Leander says conversationally, as he folds his hands in his lap. "Regarding our contract, is there anything else you'd like to discuss before I take you to bed and keep you there until we both have a non-negotiable elsewhere to be?"

"Uh… " Clearing his throat, Tripp looks a little sheepish, his cheeks pinkening slightly and his feet pressing up onto their toes against the floor. "Beau told me he saw you. At the bar." Leander raises an eyebrow but doesn't comment, allowing Tripp to get whatever he needs to say out.

"I know I shouldn't have—I'm sorry for avoiding you, and for making it look like I was hooking up with someone else. I wasn't," Tripp clarifies, "for whatever it's worth. She was just an old friend, and I thought… " He shrugs. "I knew there was a good chance Beau would talk to you, that you'd find out."

"You thought you'd try and make me jealous," Leander surmises carefully.

"I wanted to piss you off," Tripp adds helpfully, more lively and colorful by the second, and *God,* it's so wonderful to see. "I didn't understand why I felt like stomped over horseshit, and you were with Autumn, and—I don't know. I'm not gonna pretend I have a good reason."

"I see," Leander replies thoughtfully, dragging a finger slowly across his mouth and filing the '*you were with Autumn*' comment away for later. "Well, as we've discussed, much of that was my own fault. I can't blame you for your avoidance of me, based on your conflicting feelings. However, I certainly think a punishment is in order for the *girl*. For trying to bait and mislead your Dom, who cares about you and is trying his best to meet your needs."

"Guilty," Tripp admits with a shrug. "I didn't do it, though." Suddenly, his expression turns earnest as he stares into Leander's eyes. The intensity and insistence woven through his words are startling, and Leander is surprised by this particular reaction. "You believe me, right?"

"Of course, Tripp," Leander replies. "I will always take you at your word. This is a discussion we badly needed to have, and I would hope that you wouldn't lie to me now, after all we've been through."

"No," Tripp says firmly, shaking his head and letting the blanket drop slightly off of one bare shoulder. It's distracting and enticing, and Leander's interest in focusing on that newly-revealed skin nearly distracts him from what Tripp says next. *Nearly.*

"Um, on that topic, I actually think I might have another... need."

"Oh, really?" Interested and eager to show Tripp that he's taking his communication attempts seriously, Leander tears his eyes away from the curve of his collar and shifts them over to Tripp's face. "Do tell."

In his lap, Tripp's hands are fiddling with each other—*he's nervous.* "So, I was wondering what you thought about us maybe being exclusive, as far as both the BDSM and sex in general goes. I wasn't going to say anything before, but it's like..." Tripp trails off and motions toward his head with a single finger. "All these pieces just sort of clicked into place with the stuff you said. Things I've been feeling over the past few days. I mean, I get it if you're not into the idea, but for me, I think that I need to be focused on *you.* I think that would help me, knowing that you're—"

He cuts himself off and stops, throwing his shoulders back and straightening his spine, blatantly searching for the right word to use while Leander's heart thumps excitedly in his chest. Finally, Tripp concludes, "That I belong to you, just you. Does that... does that sound stupid?"

Struggling to control his voice and keep it from either shaking or belying how entirely thrilled he is, Leander nods before he speaks. "You know that I don't seek out random sexual encounters," he says and Tripp nods in return. "And that I require an emotional connection to dominate someone. You are the only person I'm interested in doing this with right now, Tripp. I'm... " Leander trails off, unsure whether he's taking things a step too far, but then deciding, *to hell with it, Tripp said he needs this.* "I'm thrilled that you want to be exclusive. I'm thrilled you want to be mine."

The smile he's rewarded with makes the risk feel paid off tenfold. "Great," Tripp tells him. "Damn. That's great, Lee. Oh, um. So, since we're doing that, do you… have any interest in revisiting the whole condom thing?" Tripp is doing his best to sound indifferent and nonchalant to the idea, but his tone betrays him, and it's Leander's turn to smile.

"Very much so," he replies. "I was tested a few months after Autumn and I ended things, and I haven't been with anyone since, present company excluded. I have copies of my paperwork and can show them to you, if you like."

Tripp's eyes widen and he waves Leander off. "Yeah, no, that's *not* necessary, dude. I trust you. Um, I haven't been with anyone since the last time I was tested, either. After I broke up with that stripper, for reasons. I definitely don't have the papers, but I'm sure I can call the clinic and—"

"Unnecessary," Leander replies with amusement. "I trust you, as well." He pauses and tilts his head, narrowing his eyes a little at Tripp. "Really? No one besides me in the past six months?"

"Didn't realize you were keeping track of my conquests." Tripp snorts, evading the question, and Leander lets him. "So… just like that? We can skip the rubber?"

"I'm open to it if you are," Leander says with a punctuated lift of his shoulders. "We'll amend the contract. I'm also going to include the basics of our aftercare plan going forward, though you should *not* feel as if these are hard boundaries or limits. They are simply a guide, a visual so that you can see that I hear you, that I'm taking your concerns seriously."

Tripp blushes and ducks his head. "Dunno if we need all that," he mumbles, but Leander ignores him, standing to make his way into the kitchen and retrieve both their kink lists and the contract from one of the drawers. He sits back down on the coffee table, twisting his body to the side so that he can write after first handing Tripp his version of the list and asking for him to review it.

"Change anything you feel differently about, for any reason," he suggests, and Tripp nods. "These lists are as fluid as the owner wishes them to be."

In the aftercare section of their contract, Leander leaves an elaborate note detailing his improved promises. Extended skin-to-skin, sleeping together in the same bed, Tripp staying overnight unless otherwise requested, and Leander not leaving before they're both awake in the morning. All of those things should go a long way towards soothing Tripp's feelings of rejection and abandonment, towards preventing this sort of drop and distress moving forward. As an afterthought, Leander adds a blurb about checking in (and equally, Tripp *answering*) at least twice per day should they need to be apart for some extended length of time following an intense scene.

All told, he feels good about the alterations, and even better when Tripp looks positively relieved at seeing them in writing. It's strange, the feeling curling inside his chest. All of this time he's been avoiding doing the *one* thing Tripp really needed, and that was to both of their detriments. Is it possible things could really be this simple? That they *can* both find solace and satisfaction with each other?

On some level, Leander still feels guilty and even slightly worried. After all, Tripp doesn't *know* what he's taking away from this experience, how it's different for him because of his feelings. Leander supposes it doesn't matter, though. He should probably consider himself lucky to have this excuse to be open and affectionate, to touch and care for Tripp in the ways he's so desperately wished that he could.

He's been handed a free pass to basically live the boyfriend experience, and if there's one thing Leander *does* know for sure, it's that he's not going to waste it this time.

***

"You have a choice, today," Leander tells Tripp. His sub is bare again, save for the collar and his lovely panties, which Leander openly admires again as he presses against Tripp's shoulders to encourage him down onto the playroom bed. They haven't talked about the scene yet, but there's a vibe flowing between them after that intense conversation, and Leander's instincts tell him to follow it through. The panties were Tripp's bait tactic, but much as Leander's a sucker for him in lace, they'll have to wait.

"I know that things have been difficult for you," he says. "I don't wish to push you too hard. In fact, if it were up to me, I might forgo the scene completely, take you to bed and hold you for the rest of the day. Feed you from my hand, perhaps draw us a bath and wash you from head to toe. I'm a *very* thorough scrubber, and my bathtub can easily accommodate two, as you've seen."

As he talks, Leander wanders over to the middle armoire, opening the cabinets to reveal a huge array of impact toys hanging from various hooks. When he turns around again, Tripp's eyes are wide and wanting, his tongue darting out to lick at his lips without thinking, and Leander smirks. "So here's the part where you make a choice. We could do that, all of the things I just listed, but then you don't get to come. Not today, and perhaps not tomorrow."

Casually, Leander lifts a paddle from its hook and turns it over in his palm, making a show of examining the integrity. "Or," he says, "I can issue you your punishment, the one you earned for taunting me. For making me imagine you fucking some nameless, garden-variety barfly who didn't possess the slightest clue what a find, what a *treasure* she had lured into her bed." He makes a concerted effort to keep his voice nonchalant and even, but his words definitely land with Tripp, who struggles to keep still where he sits.

"And then, after I've spanked you red and your ass is burning, I'll turn you onto your back and ride you, hard and rough until I come all over your stomach. Perhaps I'll even let you finish, inside me at that, as a reward for taking your consequence like the good, obedient submissive I know you are."

Leander bites his lip as he steps forward towards the bed, flipping the paddle teasingly in his hand. He crouches down in front of Tripp and lays a gentle hand over his bare thigh, skin hot between them. "How much would you like to be inside me, Tripp? Impossibly tight, wet, hot—could your girl from the bar give you what I can, Tripp?"

"No way," Tripp breathes, his eyelids heavy, and Leander can see that he's well on his way into subspace, despite the fact that he technically hasn't made a decision yet. The sight raises his own confidence, knowing that he *was* able to recognize Tripp's needs even in a heated, stressful scenario. Because he's being gentle tonight, he doesn't backhand Tripp for the blatant lack of respect.

"No way… " he leads him, instead.

"Sir," Tripp adds quickly, raising his chin so their eyes meet as Leander straightens back to his full height. "Please, Sir. I want my punishment. Thank you, Sir," he adds without being asked, and Leander has to fight not to melt into a puddle on the floor like a popsicle in the mid-July sun. He threads fingers into Tripp's hair, leans down to kiss him—gentle but firm, because he just *can't* resist—and hums.

"Such a good boy," he murmurs, allowing his lips to graze Tripp's temple as he stands. "I feel so very lucky." Without warning, Leander tightens his fingers and jerks Tripp's head around by the roots of his hair. "Color, Tripp," he demands, Tripp's head tilted back at an awkward angle, his mouth parted and his breath coming quick.

"Green, Sir," Tripp replies easily.

"Stand up." As he and Tripp switch positions, Leander quickly casts off his original plan to have his sub count the strikes. It's very clear to him that Tripp wants to drift, to let Leander control the scene completely and just reap the benefits. Despite the fact that this is technically a punishment, Tripp *needs* this, and Leander is happy for him to take it however he wishes—today.

Not for nothing, the idea of Tripp hazy and lost to the pain, draped across his thighs, moaning and sighing and totally pliant while Leander turns his ass red— well, it's certainly no hardship for him to endure.

Tripp crawls over his lap and into that very position with barely a verbal sugges- tion needed, presenting himself for Leander's hand without so much as the bar- est flinch of hesitation. This sort of ability and desire to slip into subspace so ea- sily can be dangerous, and therefore, Leander is on high alert for Tripp's reactions to the scene. Contrary to what he promised, this whole thing is more of a show to give Tripp what he deserves, rather than to teach him a lesson. As zoned-out as Tripp already is, his ability to safeword isn't something Leander can take for granted.

When they begin (*"Green, Sir"*), Tripp responds beautifully. Leander slips fingers underneath the waistband of his panties, tugging them down to mid-thigh and leaving them stretched taut. He warms up each ass cheek with the palm of his hand before switching to the paddle when Tripp grows used to the contact (*read: stops squirming*).

The smack of leather-covered-wood on skin is satisfying to Leander's ear, as are Tripp's corresponding noises. With every strike, Tripp cries out, wiggling some- times but never protesting or complaining. As time goes on—*four, five, six*—his cries turn into moans and his cock fills out completely against Leander's thigh, leaking precum so enthusiastically that it drips onto the floor.

"Color, Tripp," Leander asks after strike number seven, but Tripp only moans without a coherent reply. "Color, Tripp," Leander repeats, reaching down to grab his chin and tug it skyward so that he can see his eyes.

"Green," Tripp murmurs dreamily, but Leander's seen enough to know that they're done with the paddle for tonight. He hauls Tripp upright and into his lap, one leg bracketing either side of his thighs. Leander cups Tripp's head and drags him down into a languid kiss, squeezing one of his reddened ass cheeks roughly and making Tripp moan into his mouth. It's heavenly—Tripp is loose and pliant, cock hard against his abdomen, and Leander would *love* to throw him down on the bed, push his legs back and sink inside of him.

That isn't what he promised Tripp, though, and Leander is nothing if not a man of his word. With a grunt, he wraps both arms around Tripp's waist and stands up, barely long enough to turn and dump Tripp down onto the bed. Bending to scoop his legs up, Leander urges Tripp to scoot towards the middle as much as he can.

To Tripp's credit, he complies without question or complaint, lying there naked and sprawled out, with heavy-lidded eyes that lazily track Leander's every movement. Satisfied and entirely aroused, Leander strips in record time before retrieving the lube from his bedside table drawer and wasting no niceties when it comes to prepping himself.

Climbing up and over Tripp, Leander leans down to kiss him. His lips trail across Tripp's cheek, whispering praise and dirty little things in his ear, enough to make Tripp arch up against him and whine. He keeps things perfunctory, and as soon as his ass is anywhere close to ready, Leander turns the lube on Tripp's cock, slicking it up like crazy before grabbing the base and sinking down.

Tripp—Tripp is a fucking revelation beneath him. The perfect, patient sub, desperate to near quaking, shivering from arousal and the undeniable pain of the fiery skin of his ass cheeks, but still trying so damn hard to please. He groans and tips his head back as Leander's body envelops his cock, briefly flustered about what to do with his hands until Leander grabs them and places them firmly on his hips.

"Touch me, you can touch me," Leander pants, his own eyes fluttering closed as he pushes himself down to fully-seated. It's been a minute since he's done this, and while it's pleasurable and it's *Tripp,* it's also a not-small dick up his not-used-to-it ass, and Leander finds himself curling forward into the chest in front of him for a moment to adjust. To his surprise, Tripp's hands fly to his back and drift gently down over it, nails scratching blissfully then followed by flat, soothing palms.

"Feels so good, Sir," Tripp whispers, and Leander clenches his muscles in response, dragging another moan from his sub's lips. "Thank you," he adds, and *that's it*—Leander has to slap a hand over Tripp's mouth before he loses it. To lean into the moment, he keeps it there, straightening up only to look down his nose and rock his hips into Tripp's pelvis.

Just above Leander's hand, Tripp's eyes are wide but still plenty glazed, beautiful and piercing as they hold unflinching contact with his own.

Tipping his head back, Leander lets out a groan as he moves, riding Tripp enthusiastically, sliding up and down his cock and rolling his hips in a circle. The more he moves, the better he feels, and planting a foot next to Tripp's flank gives him the leverage he needs to hit his own prostate.

He *uses* Tripp, fucks him hard, chases his own pleasure and relishes the way Tripp shakes and sweats and fights to hold on beneath him.

"You—you can come," Leander gasps out, knowing that he's less than a minute from finishing himself and not even remotely attempting to hold back. As he grinds down and swivels his hips, Leander gets a hand around his cock and strokes until his orgasm flows through his body, nearly sending him to a higher plane as he spurts hot and wet all over Tripp's stomach, as promised.

Tripp isn't far behind, Leander's permission unlocking some kind of floodgate he was barely holding shut, and his hips jerk up while his hands pull down.

Even through the fog of his own afterglow, Leander *loves* feeling Tripp let go, relishes the gripping of his hips in both need and desperation, and Tripp's hot seed spilling so satisfyingly deep inside him. It feels like a *mark,* a brand, and while the man doesn't know it—Tripp thinks he had to *ask* to belong to Leander, to be *his,* when the opposite is true—Leander has always belonged to Tripp, whether either of them realized it or not.

Cleanup is faster than usual this time, perhaps in part because Leander has something to look forward to when finished. Today, he doesn't have to worry about getting out of the room, or what he *should* be doing, *should* be feeling. He just gets to *be* with *Tripp.*

He cleans himself up in the bathroom just to steal a quiet moment to control his shaking hands, to wrestle his excitement under control before slipping back into the playroom bed with an orange-juice-flavored Tripp and pulling him close. It can't be more than ten in the morning, but Leander is now the kind of exhausted that a person can't fight, no matter how much they want to enjoy the moment. His eyelids fall closed with the weight of something much heavier pressing down on them.

It's *good* to know that he doesn't need to fight. That he's *meant* to stay, that Tripp wants him to do so. As he falls asleep, he pulls Tripp just a little bit closer, savors the puff of warm breath on his neck. He delights in every tiny aspect of the moment—from the way Tripp's ribcage expands into his side, to the contented sigh he exhales following. The hand resting in the middle of Leander's chest and the way Tripp's lips graze gently over the hollow of his collarbone bring him close to a state of euphoria.

Drowsy and completely relaxed, Leander *almost* slips and murmurs to Tripp that he loves him, managing to bite the words back at the very last second. It's not as painful, today, the way they're swallowed down into his chest, because Leander has every chance in the world to put his feelings into action in a way that he already knows Tripp will accept. In a way that Tripp not only *wants* but *needs.* He revels in the heat of Tripp's body, the way his torso feels resting half on top of his own—it's *good.*

Leander hangs on, holds him that much tighter.

It's enough.

Chapter 5

Waking up next to Lee never gets old. It's only been a little over three weeks since Tripp showed up half-drunk and dropping, wholly unsure of what he was doing, dressed in panties and trying to bait Lee into showing him affection by way of an ass beating. In that time, though, Lee has been damn true to his word. Now, after they scene, he reliably stays the night in the playroom bed with an attitude that Tripp might even be coaxed to call "enthusiastic." Through every one of those nights, Lee either does the holding or lets Tripp hold him, and he tries his best not to be the first one up and at 'em in the morning, before Tripp can wake up and register that he hasn't left.

With each passing day, Tripp can feel something loosening inside his chest. The tendrils of that deep-seated fear he can't help but cling to, the idea that Lee is resentful and simply placating him, begin to release and disappear. Tripp can hardly believe it himself, but all of those insecurities are slowly but surely whittling themselves away, and doing so without him ever actively working through the issues that put them there in the first place.

The way Lee saw straight through his bullshit that morning was a little scary, though. At least he had the decency to explain about the "meeting of the minds" (i.e. dinner with Autumn) later that night, allowing Tripp to shelve his suspicion that his friend was actually psychic. Of course, if Lee *was* some form of mind-reader, Tripp would have a whole other set of issues to deal with, wouldn't he?

Regardless, Lee is keeping his promises, and better than that—from where Tripp is sitting, anyway—he seems pretty damn happy about the changes himself. There are even times when Tripp has lowkey thought to question his own assumptions about Lee and his (in)ability to develop feelings for other people. Honestly, he'd be a fool not to consider it, with all of the signs that seem to be cropping up left and right.

For starters, there's the way Lee reaches for him totally unprompted in the middle of the night. There's the way he seemingly jumped at the chance to stay overnight with Tripp in the playroom bed. And there's how, when he thinks Tripp isn't looking, Leander *stares,* his face morphing into his sappy expression, the one that usually only crops up after sex.

There's also the fact that—even with their freshly-relaxed boundaries—Lee hasn't tried to put up any others. He hasn't distanced himself from Tripp's friendship, hasn't suggested that perhaps they should try and keep their relationship to one thing or another, for clarity's sake. New to this whole thing as he is, Tripp can't help but think that would be the *most* logical path, for someone so concerned about bleeding the perilously thin barriers between friendship and sex.

But Lee doesn't seem concerned, so Tripp isn't about to waste time worrying either. They continue to have movie nights (sometimes with Tripp's collar on, sometimes off), visit the bar with Beau and their co-workers, and generally, live their lives the same way they always have, just with some new and improved *extras.*

Still, Tripp wonders. Distantly, and only from the safe space known as the inside of his own head, but he does. It's nothing he can bring up at this point, even if he wanted to, but surely, if Lee *was* developing feelings, he'd share them.

He *must* know that Tripp would never make the first move, not after everything Lee has told him about Autumn and how *her* unreciprocated feelings drove them apart and then straight into the ground. It's those thoughts and reservations that have Tripp questioning his own judgment, pondering whether the things he sees can just as easily be explained by the care and patience of a good Dom and a great friend.

Probably that, he tells himself. That's probably all it is.

On the other hand, their sex has never been hotter, and their scenes only seem to be getting better. More intense and fulfilling each time they're together, if still fairly "safe," as far as BDSM can be, at least in Tripp's opinion. Getting there, though. Last night, Lee wove a full harness over Tripp's chest and thighs with rope before suspending him from the ceiling and fucking him in mid-air. It made Tripp feel like he was flying, or maybe tumbling around in outer space like a sexy, intergalactic porn star.

Fuckin' hot.

In short, Tripp has no complaints, and maybe he shouldn't let himself get so hung up on wondering what all is going on in that weird little head of Lee's, lest he push the wrong button and mess up the great things they do have going. Whatever it is Lee's feeling, it's translating to Tripp spending a crap ton of time on Cloud-Fucking-Nine, so really, he'd be some kind of walnut to do anything that might put that in jeopardy.

The *only* thing he sort of wishes that he could voice to Lee freely and without consequence isn't anything related to that complicated emotional bullshit, but everything to do with his own desires. Bringing up anything scene-related to Lee feels like a Big Deal, though, in part because he's made such a production out of not wanting to be involved with either designing them ahead of time *or* debriefing them afterwards.

It's just that the more comfortable he becomes with Lee, the less difficult the concept of discussing things feels, even with concepts he previously would have balked at (heavily). On the other hand, Tripp's not stupid—he knows that if he's bringing something up, Lee's going to take it seriously. If he portrays whatever it is as a *need,* he's absolutely getting exactly what he asks for, which in this case is as terrifying as it is enticing.

So for that reason, Tripp has been stewing and chewing on his thoughts *much* more carefully than he ever has about *anything* he's sought out in his entire life.

At the end of the day, he's not afraid to tell Lee about what he wants because he's worried the guy won't be into it or won't give it to him. On the contrary, Tripp is nervous because he *knows,* instinctively, that Lee has been holding back on some of the more dangerous, more *specific* kinks on their lists. Maybe he's protecting Tripp, taking things slow after what happened at the beginning of their relationship. Or maybe he's waiting for Tripp to be able to find the balls to ask for what he really wants.

That would be such a *Lee* thing to do, Tripp's definitely not ruling it out.

Plus, there's no rush. It's not like what they're currently doing isn't meeting his needs—it definitely is. Submitting to Leander, handing over control of his body and his pleasure, it's a high and a relief like no other Tripp's ever experienced. The way he feels when he comes out on the other side of an intense scene is nearly indescribable: floating and free, unburdened, cared for, *light.*

So why can't Tripp stop circling back to the conversation he and Lee had at the beginning of things? The one that happened way in advance of them ever laying a hand on each other, back before there were contracts and kink lists—just him, Lee, some beers, and a movie that was too dull to keep either of their attention.

That night, Tripp had been fidgeting something fierce, and Leander called him on the carpet for exactly what he was: touch-starved, horny, unable to get out of his own head. Frustrated and antsy, Tripp had all too easily spilled his guts on how the stresses of his job felt like they just kept building. Unlike when he was younger, these days, things never seem to mellow. There's no reprieve, no emergency release valve for the pressure he's under. Too many victims, people he can't save, not to mention the *friends* he sees going under around him for the same reasons he's struggling to keep his own head up.

Emboldened by Leander's understanding gaze, Tripp even admitted to having nightmares. Nightmares in which he's forced to relive different emergency responses that didn't go well, calls he wishes he would've done something different to handle but didn't in the heat of the moment. Something that—in retrospect —feels like it could have changed the game and resulted in a better outcome.

When Tripp was younger, all those issues still existed, still *happened* on the job, regrets and all. The difference is, they rolled easily right off of his back. A few whiskey rocks, a quick roll in the hay with a hot stranger he picked up at a bar, and *boom*—good as new. With a sigh and a drag of his fingers through his hair, Tripp had complained to Lee that those coping mechanisms hadn't been cutting it, not for quite some time.

… *aaand* that's when Leander set down his beer and made Tripp an offer.

At the time, it was so unexpected that it probably took Tripp the better part of half an hour just to wrap his head around the basics, which came down to *his best friend* suggesting that the two of them have sex. *Together.* On a regular basis!

That would have been wild enough, and Tripp would have been in like Flynn, no questions asked. Fortunately, his brain caught up with his dick in time to beat his downstairs brain into submission and take over again—*temporarily*—at least, for long enough to parse out a few of the more *specific* aspects of Lee's proposal.

Obvious stuff aside, one such aspect happened to be the way Leander talked about pain, freely and as if there was no innately associated taboo to speak about. It was fascinating and alluring, and Tripp was captivated from the jump, not that he had the guts to say so back then. Now, though—it's what he comes back to constantly, the thing he's been fixating on for days.

That's his secret, so to speak, the dirty-dark thing he's been working up the courage to ask for his Dom to give him. It's the need he's both unabashedly terrified of confessing and desperate to try on for size—the temptation and the possibilities call to him like a siren.

In fact, the deeper he and Lee travel into their shared world of submission and domination, punishment and pleasure, the more Tripp *wants*. It's complicated— all of it twisting together, intoxicating and delicious, swirled and blended with love and lust and fear—but Tripp is *ready* for Lee to take both of them to the next level.

It was clear from the things Leander said and the examples he gave that first night, that *Lee* doesn't get off on pain, or even causing it, necessarily. No, even so early on, Tripp understood very clearly that *Lee* gets off on making his subs feel satisfied. *Lee* gets off on meeting his sub's needs. That's *part* of what Lee's own needs are, really, which is a whole separate train of thought, albeit one that Tripp finds equally fascinating, mostly because it's entirely different from how his brain works.

Despite that distinction, Leander still managed to make the idea of inflicting and receiving elevated, intentional pain sound seriously exhilarating. He described a kind of eyes-rolling-back-in-your-head experience that could transform a scene —and a subsequent orgasm—from '*awesome*' to '*soul-temporarily-left-my-body*' levels.

And Tripp *wants* that. Sure, maybe he doesn't have any real clue what he's asking for beyond some broad concepts courtesy of Google, but it's not as if this is out of left field. Tripp's fairly certain Leander knows perfectly well that he enjoys a little pain with his pleasure, he's just not entirely sure whether, as a Dom, Leander grasps the *extent* of Tripp's curiosity, or even his desire to explore his own limits.

Therein lies the problem.

Squirming against last night's slightly-crusty sheets, Tripp tips his head to the side and contemplates Leander's peaceful expression. The lines in his forehead and around his eyes smooth out to nothing when he sleeps, taking years off of his handsome face. Right now, Lee's laying on his left side, right hand tucked below his cheek, pillow completely lost to the nighttime shuffle. Warmed by the sight, Tripp chuckles a little as he imagines the way Lee's for sure waking up pissy, his left arm almost definitely gone numb thanks to the awkward angle it's tucked beneath him.

Smile fading, Tripp bites at his thumbnail and tries to summon both the courage and the words to ask Leander to hurt him.

Hurt him? Is that really what he wants? It's hard to say. It's not *solely* the pain— Tripp's scened enough at this point to know that—it's the *escapism* the pain provides. The way it forces Tripp out of his head in a way that nothing else can. Actually, the amplified orgasm is a bonus, really, and he's experienced the phenomenon enough with lighter types of domination to feel comfortable in saying as much.

If pressed, Tripp would say that it's *that* aspect he's really interested in—the *distraction*. And yes, on some level, he does feel that he deserves it. Pain, that is. Punishment. There are things in Tripp's life that he feels guilty about—people he should have been better able to help, victims and patients he let down by not being *his* best, by not being able to deliver on his promise to protect and save them.

In that same vein, of all the things Tripp is unsure about when it comes to Lee, *this* is a big one. Part of him thinks Leander will understand those haunting thoughts completely, and part of him worries he'll be rebuffed outright. That Lee will insist that he's being unfair and ridiculous by berating himself in that particular way, by carrying these regrets and perceived failings about things he could *never* control, whether it's logical to do so or not.

Tripp scoffs at himself. He knows that his issues aren't logical. If they were, he wouldn't need to resort to alternative methods to cope, he'd just reason his way back to sanity and emotional peace. Stealing another glance in Leander's direction, his mouth twitches up reflexively when Leander sighs and snuffles down into the mattress in his sleep. After taking a snapshot with his mind, Tripp blows out a breath and refocuses his gaze on the rotating ceiling fan.

He knows what he has to do—what he *wants* to do—but first, he and Lee have something much more serious to deal with today. Something that's going to take *all* of their combined strength and mental fortitude to endure.

"You look stressed." Leander's sleep-rough voice rumbles soft in his ear, and Tripp can't help but turn into him, to curl into Leander's body as he stretches briefly and then snuggles back into his side. As they come together, Tripp automatically tucks Lee's face into his neck the way that he knows he likes, curling an arm around his waist just because he can. The hum of approval and brush of lips over his collar is affirmation enough, and Tripp smiles into Leander's hair, relishes the way their legs tangle automatically together underneath the blanket.

"I'm okay, Sir," he replies, not having to look to know that Lee is making an epic expression of disbelief. Before he can protest, Tripp amends, "I, uh, wanted to run some stuff by you. Later. After this torture session we have planned in—" He rolls over just far enough to reach his phone and squint at the screen. "—An hour. Ugh," he groans, tossing the device down onto the bed and twisting himself around Lee, burying his face back into his hair. "Permission to stay here, be tied to the bed, and devastated for hours by my Dom instead, Sir?"

In response, Leander grunts something that might be a laugh into the space beneath Tripp's jaw before abruptly sitting up and wrapping lithe fingers around Tripp's throat. His grip lands *just* over the dangerous side of teasing to flirt with threatening, his thigh hot against Tripp's hip and the place he vacated at his side far too cool. Lee's blue eyes flash dangerously in the strip of morning light slipping through the generous break in the curtains.

"You will behave today," he warns, the pads of his fingers pulsing nearly imperceptibly against the sides of Tripp's neck while his dick *very* quickly hops on board with wherever this is going.

Unfortunately for Little Tripp, Leander grins wickedly and then takes his hand away. Hopping out of bed in one smooth movement that Tripp tracks with his eyes (fine, he watches his ass), Leander heads for the bathroom before any sort of bratty act can be pulled from Tripp's arsenal to try and trap him into staying or convince him to follow through.

Grumbling to himself, Tripp reluctantly sits up and shoots off a text message related to their impending doom before lazily rolling free of the mattress and scooping up the clean clothes he brought with him from home yesterday. All told, it's a salty way to start the day.

That is, until Leander changes his attitude with the most welcome invitation in history. The shower is already running when a messy shock of bedhead appears in the open bathroom doorway and Lee clears his throat.

"Brush your teeth and join me," he commands, and Tripp's never spun on his heels so fast. By the time he's spitting into the sink and washing the remnants down the drain, Lee is well on his way through washing up, body only half-visible through the frosted glass pane of the shower door.

Despite having heard the instructions clearly, Tripp lingers for a moment by the sink, enjoying the show Lee is putting on whether it's intentional or not. His eyes follow the outline of his Dom's muscled arms as they raise to scrub the shampoo from his hair, the subtle shift of his hips as he enjoys the hot spray against his shoulders. Lee's head tips back until water streams down his face, a satisfied little hum escaping from parted lips, and Tripp marvels at how naturally sexy he is just going through his daily routine.

There's no pretense here, and he appreciates seeing Leander stripped so bare in a different sort of way.

When he finally does open the door to the shower, Tripp hesitates, caught up in admiring the way Lee shakes the water from his face and eyes before blinking them open. As usual, his gaze is sharp, intense, and it burns straight through Tripp as steam rises around his tanned and wet body like a dream. If he's being honest, it's hard to recognize the man who has been his friend for so many years —in this context, Leander looks unearthly, ethereal, even God-like. It's a hell of a sight.

"You're going to regret standing out there and staring at me instead of obeying my order," Leander says off-handedly, pouring some body wash onto the cloth he's holding and lathering it up. He nods at a second washcloth, left folded over a little bar built into the shower wall. "Clean yourself up, quickly."

"Yes, Sir," Tripp acknowledges, rushing to oblige as little lightning bolts of excitement zap through his fingers and toes at hearing Leander's tone. It's full of promise and something more to come, which Tripp *really* freaking needs before facing this damn day. While he washes, Leander rinses himself, but he doesn't close his eyes again, and he doesn't speak, either. He just stares at Tripp, openly appreciating the way the soap suds and water droplets sluice down his body, smirking when he discovers Tripp getting hard, presumably in response to his hungry gaze.

"See something you like, *Sir?*" Tripp quips, and Leander's eyes narrow, giving him less than a second to register his world being turned upside down before he's slammed against the shower wall face-first, a hand fisted tightly in his hair and the other wrapped around his torso, squeezing the base of his cock.

"Don't think I don't know what you're doing," Leander hisses in his ear and Tripp swallows heavily, forcing himself not to struggle in his Dom's grasp. Moderately successful, he then fails completely at suppressing a moan when Lee's teeth sink into the meat between his shoulder and neck. The bite isn't hard enough to break skin, but the threat is there, and Tripp's *really* fucking glad Lee is squeezing his cock and keeping him from doing something embarrassing, like coming all over the shower wall. As it is, he can't help chasing the urge to shove his ass back against Leander's groin, and *damn,* he's really turning into a needy slut for this guy.

No regrets.

"I'm going to give you what you need, Tripp," Leander continues, grinding his own hard cock against the crease of Tripp's ass, where it slips and teases in the slickness of residual soap. "But I am not going to reward you for insolence. I think, perhaps, what '*need*' includes today is motivation. Motivation to behave, to be good, to not ruin this day for people who are important to you, simply because you can't stop being a brat. Do you understand?" Leander's fingers tighten pointedly, the resulting stinging in his scalp nearly making Tripp's eyes roll back in his head.

"God, *yes*, Sir," he replies huskily, and to that, at least, Leander chuckles.

"I know you can be good for me, Tripp," he says softly, dropping Tripp's cock in favor of trailing a wet hand over his hip and across his flank, making him shiver against the tile. "Can't you, beautiful boy?" Lee's lips press insistently against his neck, just above where the bite mark falls and below his collar, and Tripp nods, letting his eyes fall closed as a small whine escapes from his lips.

An intelligible, "Yes, Sir," is almost more than he can manage.

"Good," Leander replies, and just like that, his hands are gone, leaving Tripp to nearly flail into the wall as he stumbles to regain his balance. When he turns around again, Leander is smirking. "Switch places with me," he commands, placing a hand on Tripp's hip as they dance sideways so that he's moved under the arc of the spray, sending any remaining body wash swirling away down the drain.

"Kneel."

Tripp does, without protest or complaint, and even though the water beating down makes it somewhat uncomfortable, he lifts his face to blink up at Leander. With his bitten lips slightly parted, lashes wet, and cock flushed and heavy between his legs, Tripp knows *exactly* what the fuck he looks like. This move is purposeful and it lands, Leander grabbing him again by the hair and dragging his face forward towards his groin.

"Color, Tripp," he demands impatiently.

"Green, Sir," Tripp replies immediately, and the words are barely out of his mouth before Lee's cock is filling it, shoving all the way in and past his hard palate so that Tripp has to consciously relax his jaw and breathe through his nose. They hold like that for a minute, until tears are pricking at the corner of Tripp's eyes and mixing with the water trickling down his face. A small stream of drool joins the mix right before Leander pulls out completely, patting Tripp's cheek as he goes and practically glowing with satisfaction.

"Good boy," Lee tells him, selecting his razor from the small built-in shelf and holding it out for Tripp to take. "We will return to that momentarily. First, you're going to take care of some maintenance for me." Expression smug, Leander props his foot up on the same shelf and raises an eyebrow as he looks down at Tripp, motioning with a wide circle to his pelvic area. Water from the shower still streaming freely over his face, it takes Tripp a minute to figure out what he's being asked to do, but when he does, he's eager.

"I know you enjoy a clear workspace," Leander quips with a twinkle in his eye, presumably by way of explanation.

The thing is, Leander is typically good about manscaping, way better than most of the dudes Tripp has been with in the past. Even still, he tends to keep things trimmed and neat, never bare. Not that Tripp has any complaints—it's Lee's body and however he wants to rock his shit is what he should do—but if he's *offering*, then Tripp is definitely all in on this one. In fact, just imagining being allowed to worship at the altar of the end result has his dick pulsing with interest.

He glances up at Leander, unsure, because this definitely feels like a reward and not a challenge.

"Do you... have any other instructions for me, Sir?"

Visibly pleased, Leander runs a gentle hand through Tripp's hair, approving. "Whatever you would like to do," he says, and even though it's blanket permission for Tripp to proceed how he likes, Leander's words somehow still carry a weight and authority that has him anxious to get this right, whatever *right* means.

"Just don't cut me, or there will be serious repercussions."

Tripp nods, and refocuses on his canvas. Licking his lips and tasting water, he decides to use some of the body wash to soften and smooth the way, lathering Lee up and ignoring the way his cock fills out further under his touch. He checks the razor and finds it to be a brand-new, five-bladed, expensive thing that makes Tripp feel a lot better about using it on someone's sensitive parts.

Carefully, he drags the razor against the grain, over the short hairs above Lee's cock, glancing up partway through for approval and finding only amusement peering back at him.

Since Lee is trimmed already, it's not exactly a tough job, though Tripp finds himself holding his own breath while he works on shaving Lee's balls. It's not the potential punishment he fears as much as knowing from experience what a nick down there feels like. He stretches the skin carefully, holding it taut against the razor and managing to guide them both through the process in one piece.

When he's finished and Lee is both smooth and nick-free, Tripp makes a pleased noise and tries to flip the razor in his hand, though with the water in his face, he winds up dropping it with a clatter onto the shower floor. He's more careless than he should be when reaching down to pick it up, the stream flowing into his eyes and obscuring his sight as he closes fingers around the razor's head instead of the handle. The result is a thin cut to his index finger and a yelping, "Ouch!" spilling from his own mouth.

Lee is there immediately, crouching down to take the razor before reaching for the injured finger Tripp's instinctively popped into his mouth. Raising his eyes to meet Lee's, Tripp notes the way the man's pupils dilate to see him do so, but only upon pulling his finger out through his lips does it register that there may be more to this than just Tripp making a suggestive gesture that reminds him of cock-sucking.

"I think you'll live," Leander tells him, but he barely glances at the injured finger, pressing down over the cut with his thumb and watching Tripp's reaction with interest. It *does* sting, but Tripp doesn't hate it, and he's pretty sure the way he pulls his bottom lip in between his teeth tells Leander as much.

"Interesting," Leander murmurs before standing again and putting the razor away. "Unfortunately, we don't have time to explore this particular pursuit at the moment, but we will talk later. Right now, we need to give you your motivation so that we can get to our scheduled appointment on time. In fact—"

Pushing open the shower door, Leander wipes his hand on one of the towels hanging from the rack before reaching over to press the home screen on his phone, which is sitting on the counter next to the sink. "You have exactly three minutes to get me off using only your mouth. You are *not*, under any circumstances, allowed to come. If you can get me to finish in time, I won't put you in chastity today. If you don't… "

Leander trails off and flashes him a wicked smile, the fucker. *No one* is getting off in three fucking minutes. What are they, seventeen and new? Tripp sighs and dutifully edges forward, still being soaked by the shower as he does, opening his mouth wide for Leander to slide into. His knees are really getting sore, and that shit is punishment enough, if anyone cared to ask his opinion. Doesn't matter— if there's one thing Tripp's learned the hard way, it's that arguing with Leander will get him nowhere except frustrated and horny.

It's not as if he has anything to complain about, though—Lee's freshly shaved skin is deliciously smooth and soft against his nose, his cheek, his lips. It's pretty fuckin' heavenly, and Tripp does his best to show his appreciation with enthusiasm, dipping into a top-tier assortment of the best tricks and techniques he knows.

Unfortunately, despite pulling out all the stops—deepthroating and swallowing around nearly Lee's entire length, licking around the shaft like a lollipop, sucking as if his life depends on it—he doesn't succeed in dragging Lee over the finish line before time gets called. While Tripp expected this outcome—and is highly suspicious Lee did, too—he's still disappointed.

Notably, Leander himself doesn't seem remotely upset.

Of course he isn't, Tripp thinks as he raises a water-and-tear-streaked face to watch Lee finish jerking himself off with one hand, closing his eyes as cum lands hot on his nose and cheeks. *He's off, he's way off. I'm the one getting my dick shoved in prison.*

Grumpy about it, Tripp pouts as he dries off, using the towel to obscure his expression from Lee's scrutiny, but he's sure he knows. Leander finishes before him, sweeping off into the playroom to rummage in the middle drawer of one of the armoires. Tripp follows reluctantly, standing quietly with his head down and his hands behind his back.

"Tripp," Leander says softly, appearing at his side somewhat suddenly. "I want you to know that you can say no to this request. I'm aware that you're going to take your collar off before we leave regardless, and that we will be in friendship-mode as far as the world is concerned. If you want to maintain those boundaries, you may. I've no right to insist you disregard them. However... I believe we've come a long way."

Tripp lifts his head to find Leander standing ridiculously close and looking up at him fondly. "I think that we can handle this, and if I'm being honest, on a purely selfish level, I'd love to see you do it."

Never one to back down from a challenge, Tripp bounces his eyebrows and spreads his arms. "Then lay it on me," he replies. "Sir."

The grin that splits Leander's face is heart-wrenchingly gorgeous, and it's so un-fair—Tripp would do *anything* to be the reason for that smile. A little chastity? This is nothing. A freaking walk in the park. Tripp is *in*.

***

Tripp has made the greatest mistake of his life. Why the fuck he ever thought Lee would make this *easy*—maybe because of the newness, or the fact that they were sceneing in public for the first time—the absolute *delusion* in which that assumption was rooted is truly beyond his current comprehension.

How it never occurred to Tripp that Lee would absolutely seize *every* opportunity to press his buttons, to rile him up, and to generally put that cock cage to the test, he has no idea. He's pretty sure he's not an idiot, much as his decision making and thought processes today might indicate otherwise, and yet, here he fuckin' is.

At first, things seemed to be going pretty smoothly.

Tripp's anticipation about wearing the cage took care of any lingering arousal that might have prevented securing it in place, so at least he had that going for him. As the two of them left the apartment—his collar tucked safely away in its box but his *mind* still very much in sub-mode—the cool, circular metal actually felt alright.

Good, even, to Tripp's surprise and intrigue. Not to mention, it felt pretty ex-hilarating to be under Lee's control in public, even if (for starters) *public* only meant the elevator in Lee's building and the uninspiring front seat of Tripp's car.

During the drive to their destination, Lee didn't mess with him. He just sat back and let Tripp adjust, focus on driving, and cope with *not* leaving his role at the door to the apartment. He looked pretty pleased with himself, though, glancing between Tripp and his window, relaxed back into his seat with his favorite ratty trench coat on and his legs spread, exuding all the confidence of a man who has the entire world in the palm of his hand and damn well knows it.

He's got one thing in the palm of his hand, that's for sure, Tripp thinks, only slightly rueful.

Pulling into a parking space outside of the building where their appointment is, Tripp throws the car into park before turning toward Leander. "You know I'm gonna have to call you Lee, right? Sir," he tacks on belatedly, since they are still in a private space and Tripp is not about to go into this thing with Lee's handprint waving hello from the side of his face.

"Of course, Tripp," Leander replies easily. *Too* easily, which is suspicious—or maybe it's not, Tripp's not exactly swimming in familiar territory. "Consider it like… roleplay."

Barely stuffing down the *'are you fucking kidding me, I'm roleplaying being myself?!'* that practically begs to be blurted out, Tripp shakes his head in disbelief and holds up a finger, the one with the cut on it. "Can we, uh—yellow," he says weakly, and the change in Lee is instant.

The cocky smirk drops immediately from his face and he turns fully in his seat to face Tripp, practically kneeling to do so. Reaching out to take Tripp's closest hand between both of his own, Leander doesn't so much as blink when Tripp tugs it away with a frantic glance around the parking lot.

"Go ahead," Lee reassures him, blowing straight past his paranoia. "Speak freely, you're just Tripp right now."

Tripp can feel a flush creeping into his cheeks but has no idea why or what's causing it, so he covers. Dragging a hand over his mouth, he ducks his head under the pretense of adjusting his ass in the seat. Small miracles, Lee doesn't say shit about it.

"Okay," he says. "Okay. So, here's the thing. I wanna do this, Lee. A lot, if you really want to know." He pauses to wait for Lee's acknowledgment and gets it in the form of a subtle nod and patient smile. "I'm just—um." Anxious, he shakes his hands out and raises both eyebrows at Leander, searching for words and failing to find them. "*Beau,*" he finally hisses, like Beau is sleeping in the backseat and might overhear.

"Well," Leander replies with a shrug, his own gaze drawn briefly to the view from the window before snapping back to Tripp. "All I can do is ask for you to trust me. I would never intentionally out you and our relationship to Beau, nor would I embarrass you in public, since humiliation isn't on your kink list." Lee says the last part so blandly, Tripp isn't entirely sure whether it's a joke or not, and then equally can't decide whether the sentiment is concerning or not.

"About Beau," he starts, but Leander keeps going.

"Beau knows that you and I are having sex, but not the particulars. He also thinks we're both in denial about harboring feelings for each other," Leander says flatly, like it's the world's smallest deal and not Tripp's heart being ripped out of his chest and trampled on, right there in his own fucking car. He imagines his face reflects the same, which Leander must notice, as his carefully blank expression twists with sympathy. "Apologies. I thought it best to just cut to the chase. You know Beau and I talk regularly—"

"Well, yeah," Tripp replies, gesturing out the window to the place they're parked and waiting to enter. "Duh."

Leander shoots him a warning look and Tripp shrugs. "*Beau*," he continues, with carefully-measured cadence, "has never held back on his thoughts about you when speaking to me."

Well *that* is new information, something Tripp *really* would have rather known and had time to come to grips with more than sixty or so-odd seconds before—

A rap on the window startles them both. Tripp cranes his neck to glare at his brother's stupid-ass, Frankenstein-looking face peering in at them with a *way* too knowing grin slapped across it. Considering the information he's just learned, that irritates the hell out of Tripp, and he's not above showing it.

"Fine," he grunts, in the same heartbeat shoving the door open and straight into Beau's side, intentionally rough.

"*Oof,*" Beau huffs, stumbling away.

"We can do it your way," he mutters to Lee, "don't make me regret it."

"Don't tell me what to do," Leander replies, so low and so quiet that Tripp *almost* misses it, and then abruptly, as he's stepping out of the car, wishes he had.

It's late November, and the weather isn't above reminding them of that. The warm spell that followed the city's transformation from summer to fall all the way through October has officially worn all the way off, and in Tripp's opinion, "cold as fuck," doesn't even begin to cover it. Not that he's some delicate flower who withers and ceases to be able to function when the temperature drops below sixty degrees, but the bite in the air and the way his nose begs to be tucked into the collar of his jacket—*or Lee's*—has even Tripp wishing for spring.

A respectful ten or so feet away from his car, the remainder of Beau's gaggle of groomsmen lurks, and Tripp hates this whole thing already. As he waves politely, doing his best to ignore the stinging cold whipping across his cheeks and causing his eyes to water (cue the flashbacks to this morning's shower, and *nope*—the warning pinch in his groin is enough to bring that train to a screeching, grinding halt), he takes inventory of the faces.

There's Bri's brother, a nice enough kid named—of all things—fucking *Sandalphon,* though Bri and everyone else call the poor sucker Sandy, for obvious reasons. As the kid waves back, Tripp makes a mental note to send Leander over to commiserate with him over faux-religious parents who hate their children enough to name them after obscure angel-lore. True, Lee is only burdened with 'Grigori' as a weird surname, but it's still relatable childhood trauma. Tripp can't help but look at *that* and feel like his own parent loss and early promotion to adulthood both pale in comparison.

Beside Sandy—and standing close enough together that Tripp wonders if he's not the only one who got the deviant gene in the family—are his douchey cousin Christian and Beau's equally douchey college and med school buddy, Brett. Tripp can't think of another person in the entire known universe that he enjoys being around less than them, except for *maybe* the current City EMS Chief, Zavier. That dude is a Class-A prick, and he's always fucking with Lee. Tripp lowkey considers setting fire to his car at least once a week.

Play nice, he reminds himself.

Holding out a hand to each of them in turn, Brett shakes it reluctantly before wiping his fingers on his coat, and Christian slaps his palm so hard it turns red. *Asshole,* he thinks, as Christian smirks, clearly hoping that Tripp will give him an opening to question his manhood or something equally ridiculous. Excuse him, but Tripp isn't the one with his hand in the coat pocket of his "platonic work buddy".

Well, he thinks, stealing a glance over at Lee. *Not currently, anyway.*

"What's up," he says flatly. Internally, he's cursing Beau for liking these guys enough to even *invite* them to the wedding, never mind crowning them people Tripp will have to be in close quarters with for extended periods of time until this whole thing is over. Brett is one thing—Tripp gets it, Brett and Beau lived together all through pre-med and college is a weird time, *whatever*. The guy's a jerk, but it's mostly because he's pretentious and thinks he's better than lowly, non-doctorate-holding losers like Tripp.

Christian, on the other hand, Tripp doesn't get at all. Not as a person, and definitely not what Beau sees in him. Despite technically being cousins on his mother's side, Tripp adamantly denies any family resemblance. Christian, in his opinion, is an irredeemable asshole.

Growing up, Tripp and Beau were too busy being dragged around the country by their grief-stricken and usually intoxicated father in the years before his death to have many typical childhood experiences. After their mother was killed by a drunk driver in a hit and run, Teddy Truett became a man obsessed. Convinced that he was on a holy mission of righteous vengeance, following breadcrumb trails in a supposed attempt to track down whoever murdered her.

Every move was, "one step closer to the truth," a proclaimed fresh lead that would buoy them to a new town, full of bars that old Teddy wasn't banned from entering and pool tables full of unsuspecting assholes he could hustle for his next drink. The motels were always the same. Stale, musty, too hot in the summer and cold in the winter. Tripp never had his own room.

It took Tripp years to figure out that his dad wasn't looking for anyone at all, not unless that person was hiding at the bottom of a fifth of whiskey. Half the time, Teddy seemed to forget that he and Beau even existed. Tripp was left to figure it out on his own, stealing boxed mac and cheese and dry cereal to feed his little brother, because their dad was just *gone,* but fuck his twelve-year-old self, right?

All that said, when it came to attending extended family functions, making a cross-country trip for Cousin #4's birthday just wasn't on the "how to survive to next Tuesday" to-do list.

For some reason or another, Christian seems to have branded that *Tripp's* fault. Sure, *maybe* Tripp could've made more of an effort after his father finally kicked it (liver cirrhosis, anticlimactic as hell), but he was still a *kid.* Sixteen years old and dumped on Mickey's doorstep, a guy who, at that point, he and Beau had only seen once a year *max* for the past decade. He was a brand-new orphan and living with virtual strangers! It wasn't like *Christian* was Tripp's top fuckin' priority.

The worst thing is, Christian knows what they've been through and still sneers about their childhood. Condescends to Tripp, as if that mess is something he had *any* control over whatsoever. He exalts Beau for "rising above it," and regularly reminds Tripp that—in his mother's family's opinion—he's still gutter trash, just like his dad.

The mere reminder has Tripp clenching his hand down by his side, willing it to *not* find its own way into the sharply-sloped cartilage of Christian's nose.

Fucking Beau just *had* to go and match for his residency at the same hospital where their estranged cousin was an attending. And of course, Beau being *Beau* (and a much better man than Tripp), he then had to go and mend fences with the guy. Not solely to maintain a working relationship, either, but to try and patchwork-together the larger family the two of them never got to have.

For that reason alone, Tripp can't even be openly resentful about it. In his opinion, *Mickey's* the guy who stepped up to the plate when the situation called for it. Mickey's the person who took them in, who taught him what a parent *should* be, who put a roof over their heads and helped Beau apply to college. He was the first man to tell Tripp that his father's shit wasn't *his* to drag around, the reason he got his GED and enrolled at the fire academy in the first place. Mickey and his family are all the kith and kin Tripp cares to need, *thanks*.

But if Beau wants to form relationships with his blood, Tripp would be the ultimate dick to ice him out for doing so. Especially when it *is* maybe a little bit his fault that they don't know each other in the first place. Just a *little*. Look, no one can accuse Tripp of not doing his best where Beau's concerned. It's just that distancing himself from Theodore Truett's stain and gaining redemptive approval from his mother's side of the family wasn't ever something he cared to do.

"Hey there, Tripp," Christian says, his eyes sweeping over Tripp's cheap jacket, his old jeans, and his scuffed boots with a raised brow. "I see you came with your little guardian angel. Surprise, surprise. You winged-creatures like to stick together, don't you?"

Oh good, a fairy joke. Tripp was really hoping this event would kick off with some old-fashioned homophobia and a fistfight. He grits his teeth and catches sight of Leander squinting and sizing Christian up with a thoughtful tilt of his head. Well, best-laid plans—Tripp gives Christian thirty more seconds 'til Lee lays him out on principle. Never, *ever* underestimate the hot, nerdy dude in a flasher coat, that's what Tripp always says.

Luckily for Christian's face, Beau pops up in-between them, timely and slinging an arm around each of Christian and Tripp's necks before sweeping them towards the front doors of the building. "Alright, alright, you guys are here for me, not each other, try and remember that. It's my day and I want you *both* up there by my side, got it? We're family. So no fighting," he emphasizes with a chuckle that makes Tripp want to reach down into his throat and rip out.

Ugh. He hates how his brother acts around these two, but he's right about one thing—it's Beau's day. With that in mind, Tripp rolls his eyes and settles for quietly wishing that his brother would go back to being his normal, dorky self, not this wanna-be mess he's putting on to impress.

"Fine, Bozo," he mutters, using the childish version of Beau's name on purpose, knowing he hates it.

"Burnout," Beau replies, giving Tripp the finger.

"Clown."

Leander opens the door for the group and everyone walks through, though he grabs Tripp's arm and holds him back for a moment until the rest of them pass. Beau glances their way but ultimately doesn't say anything as he disappears into the relative darkness of the shop, and Tripp's grateful. The reassuring squeeze Leander applies to his hip goes a long way towards cooling his fiery edges, and he sighs, yanking a hand through his hair in frustration.

"I hate those two," he tells Lee.

"I know," Leander replies, standing close enough for their toes to touch. "You're doing just fine." The wind ruffles his dark, gel-spiked hair, and the concerned, caring look he pegs Tripp with as he looks up into his eyes has Tripp working *really* hard to keep from kissing him. "Whatever you do, don't hit him." Tripp scowls, but doesn't promise anything. "If it's needed, I'll do it. Beau will be more inclined to forgive me."

Lee's unexpected remark has Tripp laughing, even as Lee pats his arm and moves past him into the store with a crafty smile on his face. In his pants, the cock cage bumps against Tripp's thigh, reminding him of his future reward if he can make his Dom proud.

Alright, maybe he can get through this after all.

Tripp inhales a deep breath of the crisp air before following his brother and his... *Lee* inside, wrinkling his nose against the too-clean scent of new clothing and fancy shoes.

Tuxedo shopping.

One step up (barely) from the kind of clothes shopping Marley drags him along for every couple of months—i.e., Tripp plays the part of the gay bff, sitting in uncomfortable chairs while Marley blasts one-hit-wonders from her phone and pretends she's in a makeover montage from the eighties. At least here there's champagne, and Tripp manages to down four flutes before Lee gently takes away the fifth and pinches his flank in silent warning.

Tripp's tipsy brain digs it.

Somewhere between having his inseam measured by a way-too-handsy attendant and actually getting into the fitting rooms to try things on, Tripp somehow stops hating this whole thing. Sure, Brett and Christian are up to their normal douchebaggery, but Beau seems *really* happy, glowing even, and *damn,* does Lee look mouth-wateringly delicious in formalwear.

So delicious, that Tripp doesn't even bother to make a token attempt to control his face when Lee emerges from a fitting room to strut in front of the group. When he comes out, Christian and Brett are still changing, and Tripp is sitting with his legs spread between Beau and Sandy in the line of chairs facing the mirrors. The three of them are just waiting their turn, shooting the shit about the various shades of red and where each of them appears in major league sports logos.

Which is probably a blessing, since there's no *way* the asshole twins would ever let Tripp *or* Lee hear the end of it, had they been there to witness the way Tripp's jaw dropped like a cartoon character at the sight of his friend all glammed up.

To be fair, Lee looks like he just strode off the cover of GQ, a transformation worthy of Jack Dawson in *Titanic*—broke-ass scrub to regular first-class swell, with nothing but some starched fabric and a nifty-looking bowtie. Damn, but he wears it well.

Lee knows it too, judging by the way his eyes find Tripp's immediately, all-knowing and crinkly at the corners as he winks and steps up onto one of the little podiums before turning to face the mirror. His eyes find Tripp's there, too, and he turns this way and that, admiring his own form as the attendant moves to adjust his cummerbund and then crouches down to do some pinning.

The cut of the tux does *everything* to accentuate Lee's trim waist and broad shoulders, the muscles in his arms, and the swell of his ass and thighs, and Tripp *knows* he's basically drooling, can't find it in himself to care. He knows one thing, though. Lee is a *bastard* of a tease when he wants to be.

Before Beau can let go of the comment that's clearly dancing on the tip of his tongue—or Tripp's dick turns this outing into the most awkward family moment in history—he snatches up his tux and hightails it for the room Lee vacated, pulling the curtain shut with more emphasis than is strictly necessary. As he dresses, Tripp simultaneously wills his dick down *and* lets his mind wander, even though he knows that's a terrible, terrible idea.

It's not that he's afraid of being called out for ogling—let these fuckers know he's doing Lee, Tripp's not the least bit ashamed of the facts. The man is *hot,* and anyone who's got a problem with the idea of two dudes hooking up isn't someone whose opinion Tripp gives a rat's ass about. No, if anything, so long as Lee doesn't care about people knowing, Tripp's pretty damn proud to be able to say that he's hitting that.

No, the problem is—once again—*Tripp* and his inconvenient, unwanted *feelings* popping up and rearing their ugly heads at the worst time.

Yes, seeing Lee in a tux makes him want to get down on his knees (*plural*) right there in the middle of the shop, audience and all, but it also hurts like it has *no* goddamn right to do, and he's an idiot for even entertaining that. Tripp wishes more than anything that he could simply be happy with what the two of them have, that these fleeting thoughts about *what if* and *if only* would leave him the hell alone and stop waltzing through his brain, but he's not in control of when they come and go.

The fact is, seeing Lee in a wedding tux reminds Tripp that this is the *only* way he'll ever see the man looking like that. That no matter how happy he is with their current relationship status, that reality still blows. It's worsened by the fact that Tripp never even considered himself a "picket fence and two-point-five terriers" type of guy before, never imagined *wanting* to give up his wild and free single life to commit to one chick or one dude.

With Lee, though? Fuck, Tripp can't even pretend. He'd sign on that dotted line tomorrow if Lee was an option, if Lee wanted it too.

But he's not and he doesn't, and Tripp needs to knock off the sappy, self-pitying BS and get with the program before somebody catches on. He sighs as he pulls his crisp dress pants into place, tucking the overly-stiff button-down he's already wearing into the band as he settles it around his hips. If there's one upside to all of this angst, it's that the risk of his dick going wayward and making things painful for everyone has effectively dropped to *zero*. Any arousal he might have felt over seeing Lee all dolled up has been quenched, like a bucket of ice water thrown onto a campfire, courtesy of Tripp's errant emotions.

As he twists to check his angles in the small mirror, trying in vain to secure the snappy cummerbund, there's a knock on the wall just outside the curtain and Lee's voice following close behind.

"Everything alright in there? May I help with your band?" Rolling his eyes, Tripp *almost* sends Lee away, but then he figures, *what the hell?* He's already in this deep, might as well try on some of that masochism for size, let the guy torture him in private.

"Yeah," he calls back, voice slightly unsteady, enough that he hopes Beau's jerk friends aren't listening. The second he receives permission, Lee slips inside and pulls the curtain behind him, which thankfully, extends all the way to the floor.

Tripp has to hand it to him—he doesn't fuck around or carry on with some fake pretense for why he's here. *Nope*, he just slams Tripp up against the wall so hard the mirror shakes, plastering himself flush to his back.

Instantly, whatever Tripp was thinking before? That bunch of bull about his arousal being doused? Yeah, *scratch that*, he's in *big* fuckin' trouble. His breath puffing cloudy condensation onto his own reflection, Tripp gives a token struggle, but that just prompts Leander to grab his wrist, twist it behind his back, and hold on tighter.

"Fuck," he murmurs, as the obvious bulge of Lee's erection makes itself known in the crack of his ass. "This is cheating," he complains, the cage swiftly growing tight and painful around his own cock.

"Is it?"

"Ungh," Tripp moans, using his free hand to press down on his crotch. His mind flips desperately through every disgusting, dick-deflating image he can summon while an undeterred Lee nips gently at the shell of his ear.

"You look incredible," Leander growls, apparently uncaring about Tripp's discomfort, or perhaps enjoying it, probably the latter.

"I *know*," Tripp replies defensively, shifting uncomfortably against the wall as Leander grinds into him enthusiastically and without shame. "Listen, it's a damn miracle all the blood in my entire body didn't rush to my dick when you walked out, I could've ended up rolling around on the floor screaming about my balls, right in front of Beau! You get that, right?"

"I really do," Leander replies thickly, and with blatant appreciation for the imagery. "Perhaps I should be insulted that you didn't."

"I ran back here, didn't I?" Tripp mumbles, his dick finally giving up the ghost under the pinching pain and pressure it's been getting in response to the multiple failed attempts to stand up and say hello. Alright, so the details of his escape are *slightly* different than he's claiming, but Lee doesn't need to know that.

"Hmm," is all Leander says in return, busy nosing at the nape of Tripp's neck, kissing his skin softly and then pulling away without warning. When he stands back, Tripp realizes that his cummerbund is secured perfectly in place and Leander is grinning from ear to ear, looking like he just won the giant stuffed animal at the county fair.

"Sneaky bastard," Tripp grunts, pressing a rough kiss to the side of Leander's face before slipping out from behind the curtain and going to face the music.

The rest of their appointment runs smoothly, and they all manage to make it out the door with tuxes ordered and no one's face being rearranged by Leander's fist, so Tripp figures the day a success. Before the group splits, he and Beau solidify plans to meet for dinner the following night since they're both off, and Lee mentions something about seeing him in the hospital the following week.

Apparently—according to the casual chatter Tripp only half-listens to because he's busy thinking about his dick—Lee is scheduled for his annual intubation skills review and subsequent O.R. demonstration with Cornell Reading, City EMS's Medical Director. Tradition holds that this would-be ten hour assignment winds up with Lee intubating two people and then Dr. Reading taking him out for an extended lunch, one that involves cocktails and neither of them returning to the hospital for the rest of the day.

Man, Tripp thinks, jealous. Christian might've been right, after all—drinking in the middle of the work day? He *is* in the wrong profession.

During their ride back to the apartment, Lee is quiet, contemplatively gazing out the window as they drive. Try as he might, Tripp can't figure out if he's having some kind of a moment, or if this is an intimidation tactic. Either way, he'd be lying if he said it didn't make him uneasy. Lee's silence continues all the way through their walk across the underground lot (where Tripp's car can lately be found hanging out in the second space assigned to Lee's apartment, and with his very own keyfob access to the garage, thank you very much), through the journey up in the elevator, and Lee's unlocking of his front door.

It lasts through Lee picking up the box that contains his collar and offering it up, through Tripp accepting and threading it back around his neck, and even through Leander retrieving beers from the fridge and motioning with his hand for Tripp to sit down on the couch. When he speaks, it isn't what Tripp expects.

"If I asked you something, would you be honest with me?"

"Yes, Sir," Tripp replies easily, despite the lump rising in his throat. It's not a lie, not for ninety-nine percent of the questions Leander could *possibly* ask. The only things Tripp would lie about at this point are his feelings regarding the man himself, and *only* if Lee asked him point-blank, in a way that Tripp couldn't possibly dodge or divert.

Not a cell of his being wants to be untruthful with Leander, not anymore. Not after everything they've been through together and the incredible series of gifts Lee has given him. But *that*—those feelings? Tripp thinks this topic is perhaps best summed up with lifestyle-speak: Lee has taught him everything he knows about hard limits, and this is just one of his.

"When we were in the dressing room together," Leander begins, and Tripp barely stops himself from breathing an obvious sigh of relief.

When you were fucking with me, he wants to interject, but doesn't, because while the cage has been fun, Tripp *is* looking to get both it and himself off tonight. "When you became aroused and the cage began to cause physical discomfort, did you... enjoy the actual *pain* aspect of what was happening?"

Tripp opens his mouth to reply, but Leander holds up a hand, so he stops.

"I'd like you to take a moment and really think about what I'm asking. There's a difference between *appreciating* the pain and enjoying it. There is a line between understanding hurt and *craving* it. I saw something in your face, when you cut your finger in the shower, and I'm... curious."

Working his jaw a little, Tripp slumps back against the couch and regards Leander skeptically. *Is* his friend actually a mindreader? This wouldn't be the first time Tripp's wondered. It definitely isn't the first time Lee's seen through to his covert desires so easily, which *would* be worrying, mostly because in what universe does Tripp get to *have* this?

To have someone who understands and validates him like it's a *given*, who's always one step ahead of the sometimes-scary things Tripp wants and struggles to give voice to. If he was a lesser man, the whole damn concept might bring him to tears, and—oh, fuck. Who is he kidding?

"Oh," Leander says immediately, turning to grab a tissue from the box on the side table. "I'm so sorry, Tripp. I didn't mean to—please don't be upset, there's no pressure for you to like something that you don't. I was wrong, I—"

"No, stupid." Tripp sniffles, snatching the tissue from Leander's grasp and swiping roughly at his traitorous eyes.

"Tripp," Leander says warningly, but it's Tripp's turn to hold up a hand, still pressing the tissue against both of his eyes using his fingertips.

"Sorry," Tripp says brusquely, tone covering desperately for the quiver he knows is present in his voice. "Just—one minute. Let me try, please? I'm trying." He manages to look up and make eye contact, because he's figured out that's what Lee responds to best, what makes him feel respected and like Tripp is being sincere. It works: Lee nods and relaxes minutely, allowing Tripp the space to move what he needs to say from his brain down to his tongue and then out into the world.

"You're not wrong," Tripp begins, and this time, his eyes are focused on the knit fabric of Lee's couch cushions. He'd love to look his Dom in the eye, but he just *isn't* that together or confident, not by a long shot. The fact that he's even doing this, when only a few short weeks prior he wouldn't even debrief a scene with Lee, feels like monumental progress. He hopes that Lee sees that, too.

"You remember this morning, when I said I had some stuff I wanted to run by you? Well… "

Tripp's courage starts to run out, so instead of searching up some better words, he raises his cut finger and wiggles it, then uses the digit to point between himself and Lee. "Guess you beat me to the punch." Feeling lighter, Tripp chances glancing over to gauge Lee's reaction, able to do so only because he already knows that he won't find judgment there.

He's right, of course—Lee is leaning against the couch with his arm on the back and his head braced on his hand. His eyes are thoughtful and the gears are clearly turning, but there's nothing scornful in his expression. If anything, he looks intrigued. While Tripp watches him, nervous and twisting his fingers together in his lap, a small smile spreads across Leander's face.

"You know that I couldn't ask for a more perfect, more lovely, willing, and inspiring submissive," Leander says bluntly, and Tripp flushes, because who the fuck *talks* like that? About him, no less. "If you want to explore this," he continues, easy as if they were discussing whether or not to go out for dinner, "I'm not only game, I'm excited. And if you decide—at any time—that it is not for you, or even that a particular type of pain is not for you, you should know in advance that you will *never* disappoint me by saying so."

Breathless, Tripp can only nod.

"We will make it up as we go," Leander offers, leaning forward and well into Tripp's space. It's not only intention and promise that are written all over his face but plain and obvious affection, too.

"Thank you, sunshine," Tripp says softly, tipping his head to the side and his mouth forward in a silent request. Leander reaches out, crooking a finger under Tripp's chin to pull him the rest of the way in for a gentle kiss. The sweetness of his touch and the promises he's just made sit in stark contrast, but Tripp eats it up, can't ever get enough of Lee's hard and soft edges. The way he can make him twist and scream and beg for mercy, and then right after, pet his hair for over an hour while Tripp lays boneless in his arms—both sides of Lee are his favorite.

In fact, it's *all* a lot more than he deserves, more than he ever could have dreamed of having.

Leander clears his throat. "While both adorable and appreciated, 'sunshine' is not quite appropriate right now," he reminds Tripp after pulling away from his lips. "Nor is 'stupid,' but you know that. I would have slapped you, but it felt incongruous with the conversation." Lee is only half-serious, Tripp can tell by the way he's suppressing a smile and the way he looks towards the balcony doors instead of making eye contact, presumably so as not to undermine himself.

"Besides," he continues. "Considering the subject matter, it seems as if I'll have satisfaction in that department soon enough." He shrugs. "I'll find a way to work it in." He winks as he stands, holding out a hand for Tripp to take and then leading him to the playroom when he does.

"Strip," he commands.

***

What follows is the longest inside-the-bedroom kink negotiation Tripp and Leander have ever tried, up to this point. Going down the S&M road blindly seems like something Lee just isn't willing to do, and Tripp is fine with that—maybe even secretly relieved, just a little.

While Tripp kneels on the bed, a fully-clothed Leander sifts through his various toys and implements, holding different options up and explaining what they're for, what they *will* do to Tripp's body when used, and then watching his face for a reaction.

Tripp, for his part, is struggling a little.

Sure, the *idea* of pain inside a scene sounds all sexy and exciting in his head, and God knows Tripp is confident in chasing his dreams, but there's nothing sexy about what Lee is doing tonight. Hearing the nitty-gritty details—the mechanical, clinical explanations of what *this* flogger and *that* whip feel like, the harm *this* pinwheel and *that* clamp might cause him—*outside* of any existing arousal or stimulation that's designed to mitigate anxiety and extend payoff isn't the same.

Without corresponding physical sensations to guide Tripp in what he's looking for, Lee's questions are difficult to answer and his presentation feels a lot like pure intimidation. It's not exactly putting Tripp in the mood. Ironic, since his cock has finally been freed for the negotiation, and subsequently branded itself uninterested in taking advantage of the situation.

Thankfully, Leander seems to catch onto this and changes tack, though not before Tripp considers at *least* throwing up his yellow flag or maybe bailing out altogether. His mind is already half-gone, more focused on going in search of more beers than making a memory.

As he shifts uncomfortably—*restlessly*—atop the sheets, Leander very suddenly just stops. Stops talking, stops examining his collection of toys and tools, stops trying to solicit Tripp's input on the best way to wreck his shit without scaring him off of ever scening again. Quietly, he closes up the armoire he's been rummaging through and turns around to face Tripp, the thoughtful look he's been wearing off and on all day returning to his face.

"This isn't working, is it?" he asks bluntly.

"No, Sir," Tripp replies, rather emphatically shaking his head while his shoulders deflate in relief.

"Alright," Leander agrees. He presses a finger to his lips as he paces a little before once again rounding on Tripp. "Shall we start over?"

"Please, Sir." Tripp doesn't hesitate to answer, licking lips that have gone dry with his building anxiety.

Leander nods. "Sit up against the headboard." He points for emphasis and then moves back to the middle armoire, the one that Tripp has learned contains the most practical items—restraints, plugs, a friggin' endless supply of lube that Tripp suspects rivals the Astroglide Twitter intern's personal stash.

When Lee returns, it's to toss his favorite plug onto the mattress next to Tripp's hip alongside a bottle of lube. "Prep yourself," he says simply. "I'll be right back." On his way out of the room, Leander dims the lights and presses play on his sound system, releasing some soft, nondescript music to float through the air.

Slightly less unsettled now after the changes in both energy and atmosphere, Tripp sinks back against the headboard and squeezes some lube into his hand, stroking himself gently. Lee didn't say he *couldn't* touch his cock, and Tripp really needs his buddy to get back into the mood for what they're about to do.

In the end, it's not a difficult mindset to shift. Without Lee's (slightly terrifying) lecture-slash-show-and-tell dampening his arousal, just being in the playroom and in this bed easily fires his libido back up. In turn, Tripp allows his mind to drift, thinking about Lee and Lee touching him, shivering a little when the cool air from the fan blows across his naked skin, letting his eyes fall closed as his fingers make their way down and inside himself.

It's not long before he's sighing and moaning quietly, riding his own hand with the other still slipping slowly around his cock, biting his lip and tipping his head back against the wall. In fact, Tripp gets a little lost in the feeling, nearly forgetting where he is and what he's meant to be doing. At least, until he hears a soft growl from above and opens his eyes to find Lee staring down at him with the *most* heated look on his face.

"I regret not staying for the show, now," he says, as Tripp blinks and hums and pulls his fingers free, accepting the damp towel Leander readily offers to clean them off. Without a word, Lee leans down and shoves the plug inside his ass, no warning save for the brief glimpse Tripp catches of some lube being squeezed onto it. Even still, the plug is a welcome sensation after losing his fingers, and Tripp can't help but bite at his lip, making eye contact as Lee toys with it, tugging the bulb against his rim before letting it sink back in.

"Hands relaxed against the sheets, for now," Leander instructs, *finally* peeling off his own long-sleeved Henley and undoing his belt while Tripp's gaze lingers lazily on his bare chest. Mid-strip, Lee gets distracted and moves back over to the nightstand where a handful of candles have appeared alongside their typical aftercare supplies… and a first aid kit.

Jesus, how into the moment *was* Tripp that he didn't notice all of the apparent back-and-forth activity? *Holy hell.*

He blinks quizzically up at Leander, who just smiles and lights the candles, adding a romantic sort of glow to this side of the room. Without any further hesitation, Lee kicks off his boots, drops his pants, and climbs up into Tripp's lap. Reaching down, he takes one of Tripp's hands and directs it to his own ass. Tripp's fingers curve naturally around a cheek, tips coming to rest on something skin-warmed and metal nestled in between them. He raises his eyebrows in surprise and Leander nods.

"You wore the cage, I wore the plug," he says easily, and a less horny version of Tripp would probably stop to wonder when the fuck Lee had time to do *that,* but as it is, he doesn't really care. He's slightly surprised that Lee didn't demand to be fucked in the dressing room, but Tripp figures he must have his reasons.

"I had a different scene in mind when we got up this morning, something to do with riding your cock while choking you into near-unconsciousness, but—" Leander shrugs. "—the mood shifted."

"I'll say," Tripp murmurs, taking full advantage of Leander's lack of instruction to finger the plug in his ass and pry it out playfully before pushing it back in with intention. Virtually unaffected, Leander rolls his eyes from above him like a God on high and slaps Tripp's hand away. "I'm still going to ride you," he says, almost conversationally. "I'm also going to fuck you, but later. And in between…"

He settles in Tripp's lap, muscular thighs heavy over Tripp's own, knees pressed tight against his hips. Lee's well-toned chest looms teasingly close to where Tripp's mouth is watering to taste it—in fact, he barely resists the urge to close his lips around a nipple as Lee leans over to pick up a small box from the side table before sitting back on his heels. The box snags Tripp's attention—not a fancy or decorative thing, just some cardboard and tape, hardly bigger than a matchbox.

In his distraction, Tripp finds himself absently running a hand down Lee's thigh, yanking it away and pushing a fist frantically down into the mattress before Lee can realize what he's done. Whether he does or doesn't, nothing is said about it as Leander opens the little box and pulls out what appears to be a tiny envelope.

Alright, color Tripp confused. What the fuck is Lee playing at?

Before he can ask, Leander flips the envelope open and extracts something that makes Tripp's heart jump into his throat. It's a brand-new, straight-edged razor blade. Lee's gaze flicks from the blade's edge to Tripp's face, his eyes sharp as the tool he's holding as he carefully analyzes Tripp's reaction.

"I thought perhaps it would be easier to try something that we know you had a positive response to in the moment, when you were already on your knees. Also, light scarification was marked as an interest on your kink list, so this feels apt."

Dry-mouthed, Tripp nods, maybe not entirely sold, but definitely willing to see where this is going.

"Relax, Tripp," Leander says softly, leaning down to press a kiss to the side of Tripp's neck. "It's important that you know this is not a punishment. This is me giving you something you feel you need. You can slow things down or bring them to a stop anytime you like, and if you do, you will not be disappointing me. There's nothing to live up to here but the expectations you set for yourself. What is your safeword?"

Tripp has to clear his throat, and in an unprecedented move, Leander exchanges the razor between his fingers for the orange juice, cracking the lid and offering Tripp a sip before they begin.

Licking the sweetness from his lips, Tripp nods and says, "Halligan."

"And are you using it?"

Another deep breath. "No," he replies firmly, clearly, surprised to find that he means it. Tripp's eyes are drawn to the glint of the nearest candle's flame and the way it reflects off the metal sitting atop its little box. Setting the juice down, Leander fits a hand to Tripp's cheek and redirects his wayward gaze to his own face.

"Focus on me," he commands, leaning forward to kiss Tripp slow but thorough, licking his tongue into Tripp's mouth and grinding down in his lap. It's exactly what he needs in the moment, and he finds himself melting into all of Leander's touches.

This might be the softest his friend has ever been with him during a scene—in fact, if Tripp closes his eyes and lets himself pretend, he could *almost* buy that they're a normal couple. Just two boyfriends, about to make love and swap undying declarations of devotion afterward, or whatever it is normal couples do, Tripp wouldn't fucking know.

But Leander—he's *gentle,* tonight. He threads hands through Tripp's hair, cups him around the neck, works his body up to a needy frenzy with his hands and his hips like the two of them have all the time in the world. Eventually, he slicks up Tripp's cock and pulls his own plug before sinking down onto it, settling in Tripp's lap and pulling his body forward so he can tuck his legs behind, wrapping himself fully around Tripp's torso.

Once again, Tripp takes full advantage of the moment, pressing his face to the curve of Leander's neck and against the top of his chest, nipping at his collarbone and leaving open-mouthed kisses on his skin. No marks, because Lee didn't say that he could, but he also didn't say that he *couldn't.*

For a few minutes, they rock like that, Tripp's hands finding their way to Leander's hips as he circles his pelvis, teasing. It's nice, but the stimulation and movement aren't *nearly* enough to even come close to getting either of them off.

When it happens, Tripp is neither looking for nor expecting the complete one-eighty Leander does, though in hindsight, that feels a bit naive on his part. The hand tightening in his hair, yanking his head back—that, at least, is familiar territory—and Tripp relishes it, moaning happily as Leander jerks him around by his roots, dipping down to bite at his neck, *just* over the line to where it hurts. When he does let go, Lee immediately drops his hand to wrap it around Tripp's bicep, and it stays there.

"Color, Tripp," Leander demands, and Tripp, still achingly hard inside him, aroused as hell and fully fired up for whatever comes next, doesn't so much as blink.

"Green, Sir."

"Good boy." The next sensation is cool and wet on his skin, replacing Lee's hot palm on his upper arm for just a brief few moments before it returns. "Alcohol swab," Leander murmurs softly. "Cleanliness *is* next to Godliness, you know." He laughs at himself and then clenches the muscles in his ass intentionally, and not for the first time, Tripp wonders what kind of a lunatic his best friend really is.

The first drag of the razor's edge against Tripp's skin doesn't feel like much of anything at all. Just a scratch—Tripp's had more painful stubbed toes. Nonetheless, he jumps a little, and Leander pauses what he's doing to kiss him reassuringly on the mouth.

"Color?"

"Still green, Sir," Tripp replies, if a little breathlessly, flexing his fingers against Leander's hips to ground himself in the moment. He fills his lungs slowly and deliberately as Leander brings the razor down again, letting the corner of the blade sink into his skin only *just* enough to draw pinpricks of blood before pulling it along.

In Tripp's mind, the conflicting sensations start to war and blur and blend, in a shockingly delicious way that surprises him quite a bit more than he expected. His hips start moving of their own accord, flexing up into his Dom more and more with every stinging swipe of the razor while his torso relaxes back, allowing the man above him to do whatever he wants and trusting him completely.

Lee lets him cope, doesn't comment on Tripp's touching or his movements, except to occasionally ask him to keep his left arm still, if he's able. The more Lee cuts, the more it hurts, and yet, the more excited Tripp becomes. He doesn't hold back any moans and groans, and when tears prick at the corners of his eyes, he lets them fall.

A particularly long drag of the razor has him reaching for Lee, winding an arm around his back and gripping his shoulder before deciding that isn't enough. Pulling that hand back, he trails it up Lee's chest, over his jaw to thread fingers in his hair, and *that* feels good. *Intimate.* The whole thing is so weirdly intense and bizarrely romantic—Lee in his lap, his focused face only inches away from Tripp's, the heat building steadily between them and the pain in Tripp's arm becoming layered and complicated, all of it laced with the pleasure of Lee trying to make him come.

The superficial stinging in Tripp's bicep morphs into a deeper throbbing, and contrasted with the tight, wet heat surrounding his cock, Tripp would easily call this *bliss.* In the back of his mind, he even feels relief. There are so many things he carries with him, so much guilt over victims and families he couldn't save, couldn't help, and it all just builds and builds with *no* outlet, *no* escape, *no* pressure relief valve to *vent* and help him let it all go.

And yes, right or wrong, on some level Tripp *wants* to be punished for what he views as his failures, his short-comings. This pain—it's more than an enhanced orgasm to Tripp, it's a fucking benediction. It's a way to atone, a reason to forgive himself, and he can't forget that Lee is *giving that to him.*

Somehow, as Tripp slips further into subspace, Leander works them down to the bed so that Tripp is no longer leaning against the wall and he has more leverage to ride him. Tripp barely even notices when the cutting is finished, only registers the hot trickle of blood running down his arm, and it's so fucking *good*—he feels so good, so free, so unencumbered for the first time in *so* very long.

Leander goes back to yanking his head around by the hair while he picks up the pace on Tripp's dick, riding him hard and murmuring a very *Lee* mix of praise and dirty talk that has Tripp nearly short-circuiting with arousal and desire, and —fuck it—*love*. He gasps and reaches behind him to grab at the headboard as his orgasm builds and crests, the burning heat in his arm and the waves of pleasure washing over him sending his eyes rolling back in his head, making him call out with every ounce of breath he has left and then leave him sobbing.

Lee is merciless then, grabbing Tripp by his uninjured bicep as he slides off of his softening cock, only to haul him up and over, throwing him down onto his stomach.

"Ass up, shoulders and head down," Leander demands, and Tripp complies as well as he can, still rippling with the aftershocks of his orgasm, still crying openly into the sheets his face is unceremoniously shoved into by Lee's hand curved firmly around the back of his head.

The plug comes out and Lee wastes no time in replacing it with his cock, no niceties or time for adjustment, just sliding all the way in to the hilt with what feels like half a bottle of lube slicking the way. He grunts as he fucks Tripp hard and fast, making him wail when he strikes his prostate, but for the most part acting generally indifferent to his sub's existence.

He chases his own pleasure and Tripp adores it, *loves* feeling like Leander is using him like a toy when they're like this. Half-out of his mind, Tripp relishes every damn semi-dehumanizing moment of Lee nearly ignoring him completely, even as his eyes continue to leak and his arm oozes blood onto the crisp, white sheets.

At the last second, when Leander is tensing up behind him and moaning as he starts to come, he grabs Tripp's newly-marked arm and squeezes. The action brings a new rush of tears to Tripp's eyes and causes him to cry out with yet *another* conflicting wave of pain and pleasure as Lee's cock rams repeatedly into his prostate at the same time. Valiantly, Tripp's dick twitches between his legs, blurting another round of cum onto the sheets, and he's never been more regretful that the refractory period is a thing that exists.

Behind him, Leander slumps forward, one giant hand coming to rest between Tripp's shoulder blades as he struggles to catch his breath and presumably, his bearings. When he slides free from Tripp's ass, he pauses, and almost as an after-thought, fumbles around in the sheets for the plug and shoves it back in, which —*damn*. Tripp's dick also attempts to take an interest in that (incredibly hot, deliciously possessive) move, too—*holy hell*—and the idea that Lee's spend can't leak out.

No dice.

When Leander turns him over again, he's gentle, and the look on his face is slightly anxious and concerned. "Hello, Tripp," he says softly as Tripp blinks up at him, desperately hoping Lee doesn't want to *talk* about this, because words are not a thing that's possible for him right this second. Hoping to ward that off, Tripp does the only thing that he can think of, which is to flash Leander the big-gest grin he can muster, and along with it, shoot him an enthusiastic thumbs up.

Surprised, Leander chuckles and pats his flank. "You still have to drink your juice," he says. "And I need to tend to your injuries."

Tripp nods while stifling a yawn, accepting Lee's assistance to sit up against a stack of pillows enough to drink the juice without dumping it all over his face. He uses his right arm to do so, since Lee is busy examining his left, dabbing io-dine from the first-aid kit in a strangely specific pattern. His motions pique Tripp's curiosity, despite the exhaustion he feels and the impending hormone crash that is about to vehemently insist he nap by simply turning out the lights.

"Can I see it?" he asks gruffly, tipping his chin in the direction of his bicep, which Leander is currently obscuring with a piece of blood-riddled gauze.

"Of course," he answers. "Though, I will warn you, as far as scarification is con-cerned, I'm not sure this one will take. I used a very light hand, and honestly, I believe these marks will heal without leaving any reminders behind."

The way Leander looks at Tripp when he says that makes him abjectly wary of what he's about to find on his arm, but when Leander lifts the gauze, Tripp can't help but draw in a sharp breath. *Holy hell is right.*

It's a tracing of Leander's hand, the outline of where his fingers were wrapped ar-ound Tripp's bicep. The fresh cuts are thin and angry, most of them still oozing tiny droplets of blood. The skin around the actual wounds is reddened and ir-ritated, striking in its unapologetic rawness. It's an incredible sight, and the resi-dual burn-throb Tripp feels makes his chest a little tight, makes his mind spin with how much he *likes* it. Tripp can hardly *believe* how much he likes it.

Lee's handprint, cut into his skin. It better not fuckin' fade.

"I hope it does scar," Tripp says, eyes still glued to the way the marks look marring his skin. It's beautiful in its own right, and Tripp can't believe that he thinks that. "Otherwise, you'll have to do it over again." He winks as Leander glances up at him in surprise, a smile spreading across his face and—if Tripp isn't mistaken—a slight blush. He's so stunning and perfect, fucked-out and exhausted himself, and Tripp *so badly* wants to keep him.

He shifts his gaze down to his arm. At least now, he'll get to keep a part of him.

Another yawn from Tripp breaks their reverent moment, and Leander quickly resumes what he was doing before Tripp's request. He spreads antibiotic cream meticulously over the cuts he made, and bandages Tripp up with expert hands that have done this so many times before, both in and out of the bedroom. Fuck, but Tripp's *never* going to be able to look at Lee in the back of an ambulance the same way again.

"Thank you, Lee," Tripp murmurs, only after Leander has shut off the lights and slid back into bed with him, gathering him up and holding him close, careful not to press down on his arm. "Not only for... what we just did. But for not judging me, not treating me like shit for being into some weird stuff. For feeling like I need it. I just—I know some people would think that me liking what we just did is really fucked up."

"I am not 'some people'," Leander interjects fiercely. "You are aware of who I am and where you are... ?"

"Shh, ugh. I'm trying to—" Tripp wiggles around at Lee's side in a mix of annoyance and frustration, glad that it's dark and Leander can't see his glaring face.

"I understand. Go on," Lee says, and Tripp doubts it, so he sighs.

"Yellow—hear me out. Dom Mode off, just for a minute, opposite of this morning with the collar?"

"Alright," Leander agrees.

For a moment, Tripp struggles with both what to say and how to phrase it so as not to come off *too* obvious or pathetic.

"You're a good friend, Lee," Tripp settles on. "You're, you know. You're my person." It's a monumental effort just to eke that out, so Tripp manages to forgive himself for not doing better, for not saying *more*. Anyhow, Lee seems to get the gist, as the arm he has wrapped around Tripp's body tightens, and he drops his face into Tripp's hair.

"Thank you," he mutters, suspiciously heavy in tone and barely audible. "I needed to hear that tonight."

"Cool," Tripp says, going for casual and pretending to stifle a yawn when he says, "Dom Mode on, then."

Neither of them speaks again as they both drift off, but Tripp feels Leander relax beneath him in a way that he usually only does after he's sunk into a very deep sleep. It's all so strangely comforting, so starkly contrasted with the way they played and got each other off earlier, and Tripp—if he's being honest, and when did *that* become a theme in his own mind?—has never been happier in his entire life.

Nothing has changed between them, and yet, for some reason, Tripp feels a spark of hope about the future that he's never let himself consider before.

And he hangs on.

Chapter 6

For the next few months, as far as Leander is concerned, life is pretty damn perfect. Having a regular, reliable outlet in the bed(play)room for any frustrations and failings goes a long way towards stabilizing his emotions, and it shows. Having a sub who needs him, who Leander can pour his heart and soul into caring for and watch as Tripp benefits from all the things they do together, makes him feel like a whole new person.

His nightmares let up, his overall mood improves, and the number of times he sinks into a melancholy funk over memories and situations that were out of his control drops significantly.

The weeks fly by one after another, the holidays coming and going in their usual fashion. This year, Leander speaks to his one brother, Lawrence, and his niece Chloe via phone, since despite living local, they travel to see Lawrence's in-laws in Ohio. Leander appreciates the chance to wish them well, but spends all the special days with the Truetts, Chief Miller's family, and the Harringtons, and that just feels right. It would appear that he's become an adopted member of the extended Fire family at this point, and for that, he is exceedingly grateful. That phenomenon may exist independently of Tripp, actually—the little ragtag group he's fallen in with was stitched together from the same lack of having anywhere else to go that Leander boasts in his own life.

Still, being accepted into the circle means sitting next to Tripp at a holiday table, laughing and feeling included, exchanging presents in front of Reina's fireplace on Christmas Eve, and then falling asleep in Tripp's lap with *Elf* playing on the TV. All that instead of spending the night drunk and alone in his too-big, empty apartment, picking at takeaway Chinese. Things could be worse.

By the time February rolls around and Beau's wedding looms large in front of them, Leander could almost talk himself into believing that he and Tripp are in a pattern that could hold indefinitely. That, against all odds, this thing they've built *might* be satisfying in a way that could actually *be* enough for both of them.

At the very least, Tripp hasn't given him any reason to suspect that he doesn't feel the same. More importantly, Tripp seems to be benefiting from their arrangement in the same way Leander is: he's happier, healthier—mentally, at least. Internally, Leander is fairly certain Tripp's arteries are filled with bacon—and at the end of the day, that's what matters most.

With the two of them settling into a routine, it also feels to Leander—*dare he say it?*—almost easy. The way their lives intertwine so naturally, with work and play and their respective but overlapping social circles. The way he and Tripp have *always* fit together so effortlessly—it all just *works*.

Strange as it may sound, his relationship with Tripp really does feel meant to be. In fact, if Leander didn't know better, he might be inclined to call it fate or destiny, or something equally ridiculous and non-existent that, as a recovering churchgoer, he definitely doesn't believe in... except, it's hard *not* to believe, every time he looks at Tripp.

Well, not right *now*, perhaps, since Tripp is driving him up the proverbial fucking wall, and he'd sooner knock him out cold just to shut him up than pee on him if he was on fire.

It's four in the morning, and the fire scene for which Leander is coordinating the EMS response has been raging for over two hours. As if sitting outside in the dead of night, taking blood pressures and listening to lung sounds on endless repeat while the temperature hovers just below freezing isn't enough, Station Fifteen is first due, and therefore, Leander also has *Tripp* and his randomly rotten attitude to deal with.

On top of that, the house system at the station activating for the call rather rudely interrupted a *very* pleasant dream, and the kind of deep sleep that Leander rarely achieves while on duty. Being jolted awake *and* out of a mental scene in which he had Tripp tied up and making the most delicious noises while dripping wax all over his body—it was jarring, to say the least.

Hours later, those images *still* refuse to leave his head, which isn't particularly helpful when Leander *needs* to focus. Needs to pay attention and ensure that he isn't sending at-risk firefighters back inside to combat the blaze when their bodies can't handle it. Fire rehab at a low-risk scene like this is dull as all get-out by nature, but it's necessary and important, too, as so many boring things are.

EMS isn't always excitement and glamour.

In addition to boring, Leander's job is also occasionally infuriating. Like, for instance, when he's the paramedic in charge and he has a bull-headed firefighter who sits down for a routine vital sign check, only to get benched for having a too-high blood pressure and pulse. *Fifteen minutes* of rest is all that's being asked of him, but the walking hero-complex will absolutely not accept that he *isn't fucking Superman,* and that sometimes his body needs a damn break.

"There are three other members of your crew sitting here with you," Leander argues, his face set firmly in a scowl as he goes physically toe-to-toe and chest-to-chest with Tripp. "You've all been inside that blaze for nearly an hour, you need to *rest.*" For some bizarre reason, Tripp seems to be under the false impression that he can intimidate Leander into giving him his way tonight. "You don't see any of them complaining or talking back. Stop being a stubborn bastard and sit on your ass until your heart calms down!"

"*They* aren't Lieutenants," Tripp sasses back, unfazed by Leander's proximity in a way he wouldn't *dare* pull in private, and the warring thoughts in Leander's head both love and hate the challenge. Mostly, he wishes he could slap Tripp across the face before turning him over his knee, but he supposes keeping his job is worth tabling that particular inclination for the time being.

Still, it's tempting. Tripp is a *sight*—red-faced and sweaty, his hair sticking up wildly in all directions as he holds his helmet casually underneath his arm. His bunker jacket is tossed onto the floor of the ambulance, draped halfway over the truck's license plate in the way it falls down through the open back doors. Without it, Tripp is left wearing only his bunker pants and suspenders with a plain white t-shirt underneath, and despite the extreme chill, his bare arms are a rosy color from working inside the burning building.

"Lee, a hose line to the third floor might be the difference between these people having homes to come back to or not."

"A fifteen-minute break might be the difference between you spending the night in the hospital or not," Leander challenges, raising his eyebrows and holding Tripp's eye contact without flinching.

"Wow! Wow, wow, wow*wee!*" Leander's niece, Chloe, pipes up loudly from where she's sprawled out in a camp chair nearby, one leg over the arm as she accepts her temporary benching from Lee much more gracefully than Tripp. Which is really something, since Chloe is frequently a disrespectful little shit—just like her father, his brother—though Leander loves her endlessly.

"Rawr," she continues, making a claw with her hand. "You could cut that sexual tension with a knife." She laughs, and Tripp's second, Mac (also benched beside her), joins in so enthusiastically he nearly falls off of his chair.

Ignoring them all, Tripp just narrows his eyes and tips his head, the unspoken message he's sending to Leander crystal-clear. But this is Leander's *job,* and neither Gunnar nor Mickey is going to be so dumb as to overrule a medic—*a*

Captain—who says that a firefighter needs a break, so Leander's unclear why Tripp even thinks there's a battle to fight here. After another tense minute of staring, Tripp sighs and relents, sinking down onto the truck's bumper and ripping the radio mic off of the belt loop where it's been clipped since he shucked his jacket.

"Lieutenant Fifteen to Fire Command," he says, after depressing the 'talk' button and waiting for the channel to click open. Gunnar answers in short order, and Tripp rolls his eyes. "I'll be with EMS for fifteen," he says grudgingly.

"Ten-four," crackles the reply, and Tripp slumps back against the truck, folding his arms across his chest, defeated. Totally because it's his job and not at all to rub the salt of his moral victory into the wound, Leander makes his way to Tripp's side and drapes a hospital blanket around his shoulders.

"There, there," he says blandly, biting back his smirk as Tripp glares. In his peripheral vision, Leander's attention is caught by another team entering the apartment building with an additional hose line. "Look at that," he says. "A line for the third floor."

The bottle of water in Tripp's hand crackles as he crushes it into his palm. "You're such a dick."

"I'll remember you said that," Leander tells him, squeezing his shoulder as he uses it for leverage to climb up into the ambulance and retrieve some more linens. "Later." Thrillingly, Tripp's eyes go slightly wide and he drops his head, shifting against the bumper in a way that Leander recognizes easily as Tripp feeling arousal while wearing a cage. Nylon, of course, because fire, but still.

Delightful.

"Whoa," Mac says suddenly, prompting Leander to glance over his shoulder, only to find the mullet-sporting firefighter leaning forward in his chair, intent. His eyes are narrowed and he's moving his hand back and forth as if he's trying to suss out the energy between Leander and Tripp. "When did the two of you end the mating dance and get physical?"

Having picked that very moment to take a drink from his semi-crushed bottle, Tripp sputters water and Leander barks out a laugh. Unsurprisingly, Chloe swiftly comes to their 'rescue', because mocking her uncle is one of her favorite pastimes.

"Are you serious, Mac? Where do you live, under a rock? They've been fucking for months," she declares, only somewhat derisively.

"Chloe," Leander snaps. "Don't be crass."

"Sorry, Uncle Lee," she murmurs as she sips her own water, apparently appropriately chastised.

It's Tripp's turn to laugh, relaxing back against the truck and shaking his bottle in her direction. "You got owned," he says, amused.

"No more than you," Chloe shoots back without missing a beat. "At least my girlfriend has the decency to get me off when she fucks me over like that. Ooh, *burn*." She smirks and Tripp blinks, clearly taken aback.

"Chloe," Leander admonishes again, but he's weak and has to turn away, busying himself with pretending to rearrange supplies in one of the cabinets so that Tripp doesn't see him fighting hard not to smile.

"He's *not* my boyfriend," Tripp mutters petulantly.

"Fine, fine," Chloe says with a sigh, holding her hands up in mock surrender. "Uncle Lee, if I stop teasing your *not*-boyfriend over how whipped he is, can I go?"

Jumping down from the ambulance box, Leander dons his stethoscope and goes through the motions of checking Chloe's vital signs once more. He records them in the neat list he's keeping that's secured to his clipboard, updating Chloe's column just below her previous measurements and her name, and then nods.

"Be careful," he instructs. "Your father will have my head if something happens to you. You know that he still asks me to bench you for entire fires, on principle." Chloe just shrugs as she pulls her long blonde hair back into a ponytail, slips her bunker jacket over her shoulders, and dons her helmet.

"He's a good dad." She stands on her toes to kiss Leander's cheek, and he pretends he's not entirely warmed by it. "So are you. Later. Later, Fireman Sam. Enjoy riding the pine." As Chloe steps over the leaking five-inch line and disappears around a drafting engine parked between them and the actual fire, Leander sighs.

"I'm not whipped," Tripp protests from somewhere behind him, and Leander raises his eyes to the sky. Lord help him. Is it six a.m. yet?

***

06:30 A.M

Much as Leander enjoys having Tripp in his space and would never, *ever* turn him away, he's secretly relieved when Tripp doesn't come home with him in the morning. The night was long and cold and exhausting for both of them, and uninterrupted sleep is a necessity, considering what they have planned for later. Still, as Leander hauls his overnight bag from the warmth of the EMS station out to his running car, the way his breath puffs clouds into the freezing morning air makes the quiet of the still-sleeping street feel that much more lonely.

All around him, in row homes and apartment buildings, families are just beginning to stir, waking up to a new day and to each other. Secretly, Leander wants that, but has no idea how to go about getting it. Solitary as he must seem to others, he always feels least alone when he's with Tripp, secondarily when he's working or out with his EMS family. Increasingly as of late, returning to his empty apartment feels less like sanctuary, less of a reprieve from the violent, hectic hustle and bustle of the world. These days, it feels more like a punishment for demiromantic failures who can't force themselves to snatch the first warm body they can reasonably tolerate in order to fulfill the goal of *not* ending up alone.

The door to the station bangs open behind him, sent flying into the outside wall by the sole of Marley's boot, culminating in a noisy crash of metal on brick. She staggers out, full-handed with a stack of books, her laptop and charger, and the fluffy blanket and pillow she insists on carting along to every shift. Leander pauses to watch as she blinks tiredly against the low-set morning sun. After pausing to indulge an enormous yawn—complete with eye-closing and some extremely dramatic noises—Marley waves awkwardly without removing either arm from around her pile.

"See ya, Lee," she mumbles sleepily.

"Are you alright to drive home?"

"Taking the bus," Marley replies. "Always take the bus. Cars are for flush paramedics, I can barely pay rent in this city on my salary."

Leander scrunches up his face and narrows his eyes at her. "You regularly skim off of the R.N.C.'s fundraising efforts *and* you live in a rent-controlled walk-up with your 'mother'," he reminds her, putting the last word in air quotes. Marley's mother passed away years ago, but her greedy landlord doesn't need to know that.

"True," Marley replies brightly. "Still, girl's gotta save for Comic-Con."

"Get in," Leander tells her, gesturing toward his passenger seat as he slides behind the wheel.

"Well, if you *insist*. Girl's also gotta save her strength for *da club* tonight!!"

During their ride, Marley seems to gain her second wind, chattering on about Beau's impending bachelor party and how awesome it is that he and Bri are hosting a combined outing that still includes a trip to the strip club. By the time he lets her off a good ten blocks from his own place, Leander's even more exhausted. Oblivious to his state, Marley thanks him and waves goodbye enthusiastically, still yelling about plans for the night when Leander drives off.

Finally back inside his apartment, Leander only gets as far as his living room couch, stripping off his multiple shirts and dropping them carelessly on the floor before collapsing down onto the cushions. It's just one of those mornings, and he's not in the mood to walk even one step further. With his duty pants on and boots still firmly in place on his feet, Leander passes out cold, an arm slung across his face and a leg trailing over the side of the sofa.

Beep! Beep! Beep! Beep!

Groaning, Leander unsticks his forearm from his face, rubbing fingertips into eyes that are still heavy with sleep. If ever there were a day to turn over and let blissful unconsciousness sweep him away again, this would be it. Unfortunately for Leander, he has plans.

Stupid plans.

Beep! Beep! Beep!

The alarm on Leander's phone is relentless and irritating, buzzing against the glass of his coffee table what feels like a *very* distant two feet away. Without so much as opening his eyes, Leander throws an arm out to grab for the device and blindly turn it off. Unfortunately, his hand never makes it to the table, colliding instead (and with *oomph*) into something that feels worryingly flesh-and-bone-like.

Oh, dear.

"Oof—oh, fuck!" Tripp grunts as Leander's eyes fly open and he bolts upright, finding his lovely submissive kneeling and naked, save for his collar and those *gorgeous* lacy green panties. While welcome, their presence does have Leander beginning to wonder if they're perhaps some sort of cursed item.

Down on the floor, Tripp is wincing, pressing gingerly with the tips of his fingers at the curve of his cheekbone and around his left eye socket, because apparently, Leander has just cold-clocked him in the face.

"Oh, Tripp," he sympathizes, reaching out to cup Tripp's face and tip it towards the dying evening sunlight for better examination. No red or purple is blossoming beneath the skin just yet, so with any luck, Leander didn't hit him as hard as the impact felt against his knuckles. *Oops.* "I am so sorry, darling. Come with me, let's put some ice on that. Quickly, so that it doesn't bruise."

Once he's up off of the couch, Leander bends down to scoop an arm underneath Tripp's bicep in order to help him stand. He's a bit slow to straighten, and his knees both crack in protest, which suggests to Leander that he's been on the floor for quite some time.

"This was a very considerate and welcome surprise," he offers, an ironic little smile playing over his lips as Tripp glares up at him, struggling to get vertical.

"I spend over an hour on my knees tryin' to apologize for my shitty attitude last night and I still get punched in the face," he grumbles half-heartedly, before gesturing to his own ass. As previously noted, it's beautifully-encased in lace and silk, and it flexes as Tripp limps ahead of Leander towards the kitchen. "Wrapped up your present all pretty and everything."

"I adore it," Leander assures him, pulling a bag of frozen peas from the freezer and wrapping it up in a dishtowel. Instead of placing the bundle in Tripp's outstretched palm, Leander crowds him up against the counter and steps between his legs. He holds onto the makeshift ice pack himself, pressing the compress gently to the side of Tripp's face. Difficult as always, Tripp makes a face at the contact and tips his head away, but Leander fusses and insists, squeezing Tripp's ass cheek in warning with his free hand when he doesn't immediately comply.

"Alright, alright," Tripp mutters, settling for covering Leander's hand with his own until he slips it out and lets the stubborn brat hold the ice himself. "Only because I don't need to hear the jokes Christian will *definitely* make if he sees me walking in with a shiner."

"I will never understand what Beau sees in him," Leander agrees, still fully invading Tripp's space, both hands on his ass now and mouth freely trailing over his neck and collarbone with increasing interest. "Speaking of which—if you'd woken me when you arrived, we would have actually had time to give these gorgeous panties the attention they deserve. Unfortunately for you, I had that alarm set for the absolute last minute, which means that we need to be out the door in… "

Leander pauses and pulls back from Tripp's skin for long enough to glance down at his watch. "Less than half an hour."

The pout that appears on Tripp's face is all the confirmation Leander needs to feel like he might be open to another outside-the-playroom scene. They haven't attempted anything since the tuxedo fittings, even though he's personally been dying to try. Especially since—as far as Leander's concerned—that whole situation was fairly mild, and Tripp got off extremely easily. Figuratively *and* literally.

Time to up the ante.

He licks his lips before glancing the scant few inches up at Tripp, unsurprised to find him staring back intently. "Are you up for an uncollared scene tonight?"

The change in Tripp is immediate, and positive—his entire face lights up. "Absolutely, Sir," he replies. Leander opens his mouth and then closes it again, thoughtful.

"Actually," he says, tapping a finger against his lips as he steps back and looks Tripp over. "Humor me. Take off your collar for a moment and let me see it." Tripp complies without hesitation, handing the strip of leather over easily, likely since he knows that it doesn't genuinely mark an ending to their dynamic. In turn, Leander flips Tripp's wrist over and wraps the collar around twice, securing it like a bracelet.

"Hmm," he says, intrigued. "I'm not exactly a font of fashion knowledge, but this seems relatively on trend. And you do wear jewelry, on occasion."

"I do," Tripp agrees. "Sir."

"Thoughts?"

"I like it, Sir. I'm on board. Thank you, Sir."

"Good," Leander acknowledges with a smile and another squeeze to Tripp's ass before he steps away definitively. "Then retrieve your plug from the drawer, go into the bathroom, clean yourself up, and get ready. I expect those panties to be on underneath your jeans when you're done."

Watching with poorly-concealed amusement as Tripp scurries away, Leander leans back against the countertop for all of thirty seconds before realizing his error. "Fuck," he murmurs to himself, looking down at his bare chest and the remainder of his duty uniform that he *still* has on from last night. A quick whiff under his arm has him recoiling, and he sent Tripp to the only bathroom his apartment has to offer. With a sigh, he heads into his bedroom and raps on the adjoining door.

"Quickly, Tripp," he calls out, not sticking around to try and decipher Tripp's muffled reply.

Oh well, Leander thinks as he rifles through his drawers, trying to find clothing that's both club-appropriate and also guaranteed to rile Tripp up. Strip joints aren't really Leander's thing, but screwing with Tripp all night *definitely* is. Beau will forgive them if they're slightly late, anyway. Lately, whenever he and Tripp turn up together somewhere, Beau reliably gets it into his head that they're one step closer to declaring their mutual undying love and tying the knot.

Beau clearly doesn't know his own brother very well.

… *Not* that Leander thinks for even one second that Beau *wants* to know all of the dirty details he's tucked away, regarding what makes Tripp tick.

Smiling wickedly, Leander slips the remote for the plug—the one that's innocuously replaced Tripp's usual one—into his pocket. Deviously left in the former plug's place in the armoire drawer, it was positioned for an opportune moment such as this. Leander doubts very much that Tripp even noticed a difference when he picked the imposter up. Without question, the results of this set-up will be *well* worth their little delay.

Fifteen toe-tapping minutes later, Tripp emerges from the steamy bathroom flushed and damp, wearing the ripped jeans Leander *loves* on him and a plain white Henley that hugs his toned biceps and chest like a beautiful dream. The necklace Beau gifted him when they were kids hangs on a leather cord around his neck, and his emerald green collar looks—as Leander suspected it would—fittingly stylish around his wrist. With his hair spiked up and a fresh, new-looking pair of black combat boots on his feet, the whole package is positively mouth-watering.

Briefly, Leander considers whether Beau would still forgive them if they were *very* late, subsequently forcing himself to dismiss the pantheon of ideas that parade through his mind of all the ways he could ruin Tripp's outfit before they even step out the front door.

What he's thinking must show on his face, because Tripp smirks—he knows he looks good. Leander would punish him for the insolence, but they *are* running behind, and besides, his revenge is already in his hands, in more ways than one. Knowing that, instead of acknowledging the attitude, Leander brushes by Tripp without a single word and shuts himself inside the bathroom. He showers and shaves in record time before quickly throwing on his own clothes and gelling up his hair.

Checking his look in the mirror, it's Leander's turn to smirk. Dark jeans, a charcoal gray collared button-down with the sleeves rolled up, topped off with a solid black waistcoat and a deep red tie tucked smartly behind the buttons.

Forearms? Check. Broad chest, trim waist? Check. Ass? Double check.

Tripp is toast.

Spritzing a little of the cologne that he's noticed Tripp tends to sniff on his skin with heightened interest, Leander jams his feet back into his duty boots (because Tripp loves those, too, but also because they're already dirty from work, so a strip club floor probably won't make them worse). He laces them tight and then strides out into the living room like he hasn't the faintest clue why Tripp's jaw nearly hits the floor.

"*Lee,*" Tripp whines, hands tucked between his thighs as he squirms like a hooked fish on Leander's couch. Thankfully, his face still appears to be bruise-free.

"*Lee?*" Leander repeats with intention, his tone incredulous and his eyebrow raised challengingly.

"Sir," Tripp amends, easily chastised and shrinking in on himself slightly while still eyeballing Leander's form with open desire. "I'm sorry, Sir."

Checking his watch for the umpteenth time, Leander sighs. They *are* already late, what's another few minutes? "You know," he says, pacing slowly across the room until he comes to a stop directly in front of Tripp, where he turns a sharp forty-five degrees on his heel to face him. "I let you slide with that *often,* don't I?"

"Yes, Sir," Tripp mumbles, swallowing visibly, his cheeks turning pink.

"And you'll be calling me *Lee* all evening, by mutual agreement. That's a *gift,* from me to you. As such, you would think you'd have enough respect for me not to do it here." Leander taps his foot as Tripp raises his eyes guiltily. "Either we can end the scene now, or you can accept your punishment."

Right away, Tripp shakes his head and blows out a breath based in what is *very* clearly relief, just as Leander knew he would. "Oh, I—Sir, I accept whatever you see fit to give me. Sir. Please."

So predictable. So wonderfully willing.

"From your mouth… " Leander says with a shrug, like he couldn't care less (*he cares).* "Alright, as you wish. Stand up, pull your jeans down to your thighs and bend over, hands on the arm of the couch." Tripp complies swiftly and Leander struggles to hold back a groan of arousal when the panties appear once again. Stretched tight over the curve of Tripp's ass, the jewel-toned fabric accentuates the freckles on his skin, making them stand out. Adorable and enticing, all in one.

"Safeword," Leander requests softly, running gentle fingers over one of Tripp's cheeks, dipping down under the satin just to feel the plug nestled in place there. This whole scene provokes a wildly intense wave of possessiveness over his sub, and Leander feels very pleased with himself that he's found a way—*an excuse, if you will*—to mark him up before they venture out in public.

"Halligan," Tripp replies dutifully, his words slightly muffled by the way he has his face buried in his own arms.

"And are you using it?"

"No, Sir."

The first smack to each cheek is reasonably gentle, just warming the skin up. Leander loves this part, would linger here a lot longer if they didn't have other places to be. *Alas.* Five strikes on each side: that's what Leander decided on before Tripp even accepted his punishment, and it's what he doles out accordingly. When it comes to strength of impact, he doesn't hold back—Tripp can take it, he's practically a pro by now—and after ten, his own hand is smarting something fierce.

When he's finished, both of Tripp's cheeks are delightfully red. They're stunningly contrasted against the pretty green panties, and it takes *every fucking ounce* of Leander's self-restraint and practiced control of both his body and mind to stop himself from yanking Tripp's plug and taking him right then and there. God knows, Tripp wouldn't protest.

In the end, it's the fact that this was supposed to be a punishment—a *deterrent* even—for Tripp that stops him, but Leander's still slightly regretful. By his own estimation, there's less than a five percent chance they're going to make it back to this apartment tonight without him coming at *least* once, preferably inside Tripp and hopefully while finally getting his hands on those damn panties.

Leander indulges in the possibilities that lay ahead regarding that very thing while he considers whether to put gel on Tripp's ass (no), ultimately yanking him to his feet from behind and tucking him back into the jeans himself.

The cage Tripp was wearing last night is gone, Leander can't help notice, though he *did* give permission for Tripp to take it off before going to sleep this morning. In truth, *not* having it on will likely make this night much harder for a sub new to public play, which is interesting, and not something Leander is going to point out. He's anxious to see what Tripp does with it.

Adorably, Tripp gasps a little when Leander turns him around, but he goes pliant when Lee fists a hand in his hair and tugs him into a pretty intense, brutal kiss that's mostly tongue in his mouth and teeth against his bottom lip. The effect is pleasing to Leander's eye when he pulls away—Tripp's still plenty put together, but *just* mussed enough that a discerning eye could guess what he's been up to.

Tonight, Leander's feeling reckless. Most of their friends know by now that he and Tripp are hooking up, and Leander *wants* people to notice, wants them to ask. Wants them to be aware that in nearly every way that matters, Tripp is *his*.

Fuck propriety.

***

As it turns out, Beau did not forgive them for their lateness *quite* so easily. In fact, when Leander and Tripp didn't show up at the designated meeting spot outside the Truetts' apartment building for a full thirty minutes *after* they were supposed to arrive, *and* neither of them were answering their phones, Beau instructed the rented party bus to leave them behind.

That alone was enough to wreck Tripp's good mood, sending him into a spiral of moping and grumbling that Leander tires of *extremely* quickly. It's nearly enough to prompt him to bust out the secret weapon in his pocket, but they *are* driving, and Leander isn't interested in spending the remainder of his evening being pried off of whatever tree he and this bunch of metal become forcibly wrapped around.

"Marley doesn't drink, Tripp," Leander finally interjects with a heavy sigh, interrupting an endless rant about Beau's expectation that Tripp would leave his beloved vehicle overnight downtown for "just anyone" to come along and "violate".

The wrinkles in Tripp's forehead deepen and he looks honestly confused. "So?"

"Sooo, she can drive us home. Back to my place." Leander corrects his misstep quickly and casually, and thankfully, Tripp doesn't seem to pick up on it. Or at least, he doesn't say anything if he does.

When he chances to glance over at him again, Tripp is still scowling, but he doesn't look quite so miserable, and Leander recognizes that the night might yet be salvaged. If not, then the hell with it, *he* will stay sober and drive the damn car home. He'll do anything to stop this whining.

"Fine," Tripp grumbles eventually. "I'll find her when we get there, make sure she's cool with that."

"She'll be the one buried beneath the largest pile of ladies, of that I am sure," Leander replies mildly before turning his attention back to the passing scenery.

As they're pulling into the club's parking lot, Tripp suddenly clears his throat, his tone taking on the particular hesitant twang that only appears when he knows he's about to say something Leander won't like. Well, when he knows he's about to say something Leander won't like *and* he's not excited about it. Let's face it, sometimes Tripp is an asshole.

Luckily for Tripp, this is not one of those times.

"You do know that this is my ex's club, right?"

"Suzy works here?" Leander's slightly surprised, but not overly put out. Tripp's past is his own business, it's not as if either of them thought the other was a pristine, blushing virgin when they started hooking up.

"Yeah, well." Tripp pulls the key out of the ignition and fiddles with it in one hand before shrugging. "Not a lot of choice around here. Pretty sure this is the only club within fifty miles where you aren't risking some kind of disease just by walking in."

That, Leander can't argue with. He knows of at least two additional strip joints —one in the depths of the city and one on the outskirts—but both have a reputation for unsavory activities occurring on the premises. Leander himself has taken several overdoses out of the bathrooms in both places, and responded to at least one stabbing. To be fair, that was in the parking lot.

Regardless, Suzy being present tonight doesn't bother him. If anything, he's much more surprised by this venue's proximity to the BDSM social club he's visited on rare occasion, and is busy wondering if there's any overlap in clientele. The idea that Tripp is nervous because he *wants* to flirt with Suzy or because he's concerned about Suzy flirting with him—those possibilities hardly register, never mind faze Leander in the least, but then again, he's perhaps overly practical in that way.

If Tripp wanted to be with Suzy, he would undoubtedly still be with her. If he wanted boring, vanilla sex with a hot female stripper, he wouldn't have thrown it away when he had it grinding in his lap. What is there to be jealous *of?* For Leander, it's easy as anything to shrug Tripp's warning off and head inside to get on with the night.

Somehow, none of those very common-sense-infused, very *logical* thoughts translate when Leander actually *sees* Suzy, mostly naked and with her ass raised high as heaven in her stiletto heels, straddling Tripp where he's sprawled in a chair next to Beau.

It's less than an hour into the party at this point, and Beau, drunk and happy as he is, was already completely over Leander and Tripp's fashionably late entrance by the time they arrived. Tucked back into the booth beside Tripp's chair, Bri is perched on Beau's lap, their friends scattered around them, all laughing and talking and oblivious to Leander plotting the murder of a stripper at the bar.

He only even came *over* here to surprise Tripp with a glass of expensive whiskey, and now he's regretting it. Leander supposes he'll never know what would have happened had he been sitting next to Tripp, perhaps with their ankles intertwined beneath the table, when *Suzy* came over to say hello. Would Tripp have introduced him as his... his what? They aren't boyfriends. Leander scratches his head, completely aware that he's being unfair and petulant, and all of the many things he regularly scolds Tripp for being.

Instead of acting the part of a well-adjusted adult, he gulps the thirty-five dollar glass of whiskey in front of him like it's a two dollar shot and pulls the remote free from his pocket. The club is dark but relatively airy and cool, not overly sticky or hot or smelly. Leander's glad for that as he tries his best to melt into the shadows off to the side of the bar, hoping that none of *Suzy's* probable sticky-sweet perfume or her glittery sweat will cling to Tripp once she's gone.

Across the room, 'Candy'—*Suzy's* stage name, Leander is... sixty percent sure—undulates her hips in Tripp's lap, her arms wrapping lazily over his shoulders and around his neck. She's breaking the no-touching rule so casually, so *intimately*, like it's nothing. Like Tripp is something special *to her*, so he's an exception.

A semi-drunk Leander sees red, especially when Tripp's head tips back slightly, *seductively*, to make eye contact with his ex and smile, his hand brushing the small of her back.

With a roll of his eyes, Leander switches the remote in his hand to "on," cranks the voltage up, and watches with barely-concealed glee as Tripp jerks violently in his chair and sends Chastity-Cinnamon-whatever-her-name-is tumbling down onto the ground.

Feeling merciful, Leander dials back the intensity on the vibrating butt plug as Tripp doubles over, struggling to wheeze out an apology and simultaneously help Tiffani Amber Annoying back to her feet. As Leander cocks his head to the side and swivels on his stool in amusement, Tripp sends the dazed stripper on her way before whipping his head around the room until his eyes land on their target, narrowing dangerously.

Busted.

Before Leander can so much as grin back at him, a redheaded blur appears in front of his face, forcing his eyes to blink and refocus. It takes him several seconds to do so, his vision not quite as clear as it was when he and Tripp walked into the bar. Whether that's from jealousy, whiskey, or a lethal combination of the two, Leander can't be entirely certain.

"Hiya!" Marley says brightly, fixing him with a knowing look and bouncing her eyebrows as she gestures to the remote. Leander glances down at it guiltily, having failed to conceal the device swiftly enough in his pocket to escape her keen notice. "Petty revenge? One step away from a public claiming, there. Hmm, you never seemed like the jealous type to me, but it's always the quiet ones."

"I don't know what you're—"

"Psh, save it, Leander," Marley interrupts in a huff as she slides onto the stool next to him and waves down the bartender. "Two of whatever the fruitiest, most ridiculous thing on the menu is, please," she orders before turning her attention back on to him. "Listen. There's not a thing about battery-operated sex toys your girl doesn't know about. For both of our sakes, let's assume I'm telling the truth and leave it at that."

"Fair enough," Leander agrees with a nod, flipping the remote to its lowest setting and tucking it away. Once again, he finds himself grateful for the low lighting, hoping it's enough to mask his rising blush at being called out.

"So?" Marley persists, and as much as he could use an ear, she's Tripp's friend too, so Leander decides to play dumb.

"It's just a game," he deflects. "You know Tripp and I... " He trails off as the bartender produces two enormous hurricane glasses filled with blue liquid swirled in purple, *plus* what appears to be a sampling of every fruit the bar has on offer, and then some. Each monstrosity is delicately-topped with a colorful little umbrella.

"Oh, I *know*," Marley assures him, rolling her own eyes and patting the bar with her open palm. "Hey, I gotta get back. Ro's keeping my seat by the stage warm, and there's a really hot girl dancing next. She came by the table earlier, flirted like *crazy* with Tripp."

"Oh?" Leander replies, doing his best to sound casual, keeping his eyes focused on the neon alcohol in front of him and the way it shimmers as he plunges the accompanying straw further into the glass. *I don't care,* he tells himself.

"Mmhmm," Marley says, punctuating with a nod before continuing. "Right after you two came in. Not that Tripp had any clue, or even noticed her at all. He was busy watching some oblivious, tall, dark, and dreamy dude apologizing to Bri halfway across the room." Startled, Leander's head snaps up to find Marley beaming at him. She sighs, all pretend-exasperation before ruffling his hair and hopping down off of her bar stool. "Yes, *you*, doofus. God, if you two weren't so deliciously perfect together, I swear I'd wash my hands of you both. The angst!"

"Hey," Leander calls after her as she starts to walk away. "You forgot your drink."

Marley throws him a wink and a cocky finger gun. "I don't drink, remember? But I know someone who does, and I think you owe him an apology." With that, Marley saunters away, back to the splintered group from their party hanging out by the stage. They're chatting and spilling drinks, preparing to throw some bills, and Leander clocks Christian and Brett sitting among them, feeling secretly glad that they're nowhere near Tripp.

After shooting a glance in Tripp's direction and finding him very guardedly sitting with his arms folded, legs crossed, blatantly *not* looking his way, Leander sighs and picks up the two glasses. With absolutely no intention of apologizing —for this or anything else he's going to rain down on Tripp's head tonight—he makes his way over and slides into the booth next to his friend, where Tripp has relocated from his former chair. Leander supposes that it's probably easier to hide any discomfort, sunk back into the bench seat the way that he is.

Across the table, Bri and Beau are making out enthusiastically, groping at each other in a more graphic manner than Leander's ever seen from either normally-reserved person in public.

Good for them, he thinks, a small smile tugging up the corner of his lips. Without a word, Leander slides Tripp's drink in front of him and then slips a hand beneath the table to squeeze his thigh. Still pouting, Tripp leans forward and drinks half of the concoction in one go, unable to resist letting a pleased little noise slip from his throat. It's terribly, painfully endearing.

"Hey Leeee," Beau slurs, finally surfacing from Bri's embrace and taking notice of the new arrival at the table. "Havin' fun?"

"Yes. And I don't think I've ever seen you this drunk," Leander points out good-naturedly, as an equally intoxicated Briana drops her head to Beau's shoulder. After beaming happily at Leander, she then switches to sloppily draining some water from a random glass on the table, before ultimately returning to mouthing at Beau's neck. Tripp wrinkles his nose in disgust.

"I need to piss," he announces loudly, shoving at Leander's shoulder in an effort to get him to move out of the seat. It's not the need, but the way he goes about it that has Leander swearing internally he'll make the man pay. He growls quietly in warning, even as he stands, but Tripp's only response is to nearly fall over him in his haste to escape the booth. Lee's hand drifts across his ass as he goes, mostly accidental, the low key vibrations only noticeable because he's checking.

As Leander sits back down, his eyes never leave Tripp's retreating form—watching, waiting for a sign, and—*there.* Right before he disappears inside the unisex restroom, Tripp glances back over his shoulder, making pointed eye contact that absolutely cannot be mistaken for anything other than what it is.

An invitation. The implications of that look, that *offer,* steal Leander's entire brain capacity, and only after Beau has said his name several times does Leander even realize anyone was talking. With reluctance, he tears his eyes away from the still-closing bathroom door, redirecting his attention to the pair of tipsy lovebirds openly laughing at him.

"Wow," Bri remarks, lolling against Beau's side as she waves her index finger vaguely in Leander's direction. "You… you're…" She trails off and squints, tipping her head up and slapping Beau's cheek gently. "What is he, again?"

"I'unno," Beau slurs back. "A dumbass, just like my brother." He laughs, loudly, and then smacks the table hard, rattling the glasses. "Lee, don' hate me for telling you the truth, alright?"

"Never, Beau," Leander replies automatically, sipping at Tripp's abandoned drink, since he's already emptied his own. His brain is starting to turn extremely fuzzy, so it's probably time to slow down, but a few more swallows of what seems to be mostly sugar won't hurt.

"Tripp… " Beau slurs. "He is *so* gone on you. And you," Beau says more firmly, sitting up in a way that causes Bri to fall over and planting his elbow on the table so he can jab an accusatory finger across it. "You're not any better."

"Perhaps you're right," Leander replies noncommittally, still stirring at his drink.

"Well, aren't you going to go after him?" Bri pipes up, smiling knowingly, and Leander glances over at her, surprised.

"Oh, just go," Beau chimes in, waving Leander off and turning back into his bride-to-be's embrace to continue making out. Pretty soon after, Leander might as well be sewn into the vinyl of the booth, for all the attention he's being paid. He squints at the still-closed bathroom door, chews his lip for a moment, and then makes a break for it.

Leander barely has a foot through the narrow opening when his shirt is grabbed and he's yanked the rest of the way inside, Tripp's hand in his hair and a tongue down his throat. Making a surprised noise, Leander reacts immediately, ripping Tripp away and slapping him across the face before shoving him up against the wall from behind. With a hand twisted in the hair at the crown of Tripp's head and the other pinning the hand Tripp was using to grope his crotch to the door, Leander uses the length of his body to keep a struggling Tripp still.

"You really think you call the shots, don't you?"

Tripp doesn't respond, just wiggles valiantly beneath him, and that ass moving against his groin isn't doing anything to slow things down. "I know what you're doing," Leander continues, dropping Tripp's wrist in favor of yanking his jeans to his thighs, keeping his own shoulders pressed against Tripp's so that he's still effectively trapped.

"Teasing me, trying to make me jealous, now baiting me into fucking you. Fine," Leander snaps, yanking Tripp away from the door by his hair, pants low enough to make the move awkward. Predictably, he stumbles, and Leander is there to catch, recalibrating them both in front of the sink and the mirror above it.

Tripp is beautifully messy in his reflection, pupils dilated from both the alcohol and arousal, hair destroyed, cheeks pink and lips parted—Leander couldn't say no to him if he tried.

"I'll give you what you want, *and* I'll make you regret it."

The skin peeking out from beneath green lace is still slightly pink, and Leander kneads both of Tripp's cheeks greedily before tugging the fabric to one side. After that, he doesn't mess around. Leander unzips his pants, pulls his cock out over his boxer briefs and then removes Tripp's plug, holding it in his hand.

"Don't you dare touch yourself," he murmurs. "Or you won't be coming at all tonight."

In his drunken state, Leander's a little unsteady, and it takes him two tries to line himself up and push inside. Tripp doesn't seem to notice or care, rocking on his heels and whimpering with need. His rim is wonderfully slick and relaxed when Leander nudges at it, allowing him to sink inside easily, sliding until his hips are flush with Tripp's gorgeous ass.

With his free hand, he wraps fingers around Tripp's neck from behind, forcing the man to keep his head up and to look himself in the eyes as Leander fucks him, slow and deep. "Don't bait me, Tripp," he warns, tightening his fingers just enough to make Tripp's eyes go wide and his lips part, before relaxing them again. "Tell me, who do you belong to?"

Tripp works to catch his breath, moaning as Leander punches out a particularly emphatic thrust against his prostate, but Leander only leans in, plastering their bodies together from shoulder to thigh and nipping at Tripp's ear.

"Who do you belong to, Tripp? Whose ass is this?" He removes his hand from Tripp's throat for *just* long enough to give said ass a little spank. Not fighting the visceral urge to expose his sub further, Leander grabs at the bottom hem of his shirt and pulls it upward, shoving the material through the opening around his tanned, collarless—*but not ownerless*—neck. He likes the way it looks, Tripp's body on display, the fabric bunched at his nape.

"Tell me, Tripp!"

"You!" Tripp gasps out, "Yours! Oh, God, *yes, Lee!* I'm yours, Lee!"

"You're damn right," Leander replies, picking up the pace with his hips and chasing his own orgasm, tempting and powerful on the horizon. He'd love to yank

Tripp's thigh up, really bend him over and push his head down onto the counter, but they're limited by the constraints of Tripp's jeans, so what he has will have to do.

He settles for twisting a hand into the knot of Tripp's rucked-up shirt, admiring the way he appears mostly naked despite all of his clothing still technically being on. As his peak approaches, fueled by Tripp's gorgeous little noises and moans beneath him, Leander fucks him hard straight through it: no warning, no mercy.

He's so overcome by pleasure and the sight of Tripp totally wrecked in the mirror, that Leander barely reacts when the door to the bathroom clicks open and *Suzy* is standing there, her lipstick-painted mouth frozen in a perfect "O".

It's ludicrous and delicious, and Leander loves every second of watching her react and flee. He's never laughed his way through an orgasm until now, but there's a first time for everything. At the very least, Leander still has the presence of mind to grab the base of Tripp's cock and stop him from coming, since by the sound of it, he was working up to a pretty amazing finish.

As soon as he's milked himself dry in Tripp's ass *and* he's sure that releasing Tripp's dick won't result in anything besides raging disappointment, Leander pulls out and replaces his cock with the plug. Meanwhile, Tripp catches on, all too quick to start crying and begging, pleading his case.

"No, no, no, Lee, please, *please* let me come," he sobs into his folded arms, awkwardly still bent over the counter next to the sink.

Since Tripp is in no state to do so—and they'll be in here all night if they wait until he is—Leander rights Tripp's underwear and jeans, buttoning them up and turning him around to cradle him in his arms. Tripp's still-hard cock strains against the unforgiving material of his pants and he looks positively *destroyed,* just how Leander likes him.

"Lee," he whines, as Leander kisses the side of his neck, his jaw, and finally, his lips. "This is so cruel."

"Oh, baby," Leander soothes, flashing a devious grin as his palm caresses softly down the side of Tripp's face. "You haven't seen anything yet."

As he's leading a reluctant (but no longer mopey, surprisingly) Tripp back out onto the club floor, Tripp seems to abruptly remember the details of what happened in the bathroom. He stops Leander with a hand on his chest, looking horrified. "Please tell me I imagined Suzy walking in on us," he says, eyes wide, and when Leander simply grins in return, slaps a hand over his mouth. "Jesus Christ. What a way to out yourself to an ex."

"I thought it was spectacular," Leander tells him, resuming their walk back to the table. "Now we *all* know who you belong to."

As he not-so-subtly adjusts his pants, Tripp snorts. "Yeah listen, I'm into this, but if it's all the same to you, let's not repeat that display with Christian. Dude already hates me enough for one lifetime."

Leander snorts derisively but doesn't promise anything. Truthfully, he'd appreciate the loosest excuse to rearrange Tripp's cousin's features, although part of him suspects that the man really only hates himself. Tripp is simply a convenient target, someone who reminds him of all the things he wants but is too damn cowardly to reach out and take.

"We'll see," is what he settles on saying aloud, releasing Tripp's hand so that he can drag over a chair and motion for Tripp to sit in it. He does, albeit with a wary eyebrow raised, like he's just catching on that Leander still has some major tricks up his sleeve regarding the rest of their night.

"Welcome back," Marley says smugly from her place on the bench seat Tripp was occupying earlier. To Marley's right, Ro is tipping the last of her beer out of the glass and into her mouth, and barely-legal Sandy is essentially smushed into the wall on her other side. He doesn't look as if he minds, though, glitter and a bright smudge of lipstick visible on one rosy cheek, the hazy glow of alcohol glazing his eyes.

"Another round!" Ro yells, haphazardly flagging down a waitress by waving her empty glass around in the air. Across the table, Beau and Bri are still busy with each other, and Leander doubts they even realize that he left and was replaced.

"Alright," Leander begins, clearing his throat as he looks around and beckons for the first unoccupied stripper he sees to come over to their group. He's already aware that the no-touching rule at this club can seemingly be bent at the dancer's discretion, courtesy of Tripp's ex's display and possibly Sandy's cheek, but a quick conversation with the lovely girl he's engaged confirms that's the case.

Stepping to the side so that Tripp can't overhear, Leander holds a brief but pointed discussion with his new friend about what he would like and what he expects from the house before handing over a *very* large wad of cash.

With a knowing wink, the girl agrees and disappears, promising to be return shortly, and Leander thanks her with a smile. Turning back to the group, they've all barely even noticed his distraction, probably assuming he's just doing what normal men do at a strip club and enjoying the talent. In a way, that's true.

Bending down, Leander places his lips adjacent to Tripp's ear so that only he can hear when he says, "Remember, you are not to come tonight until you have my permission. Will that be a problem?"

Tripp makes a dismissive noise. "I've got it under control, Lee, thanks," he replies, patting his crotch. "System standby, I think I'll make it."

"Sarcasm doesn't become you," Leander murmurs before he pulls back, catching the eye of the dancer as she approaches again, a friend by her side. Hiding his smile, Leander moves a chair so that it's almost perpendicular to Tripp's, his left knee nearly touching Tripp's right, but not quite. They're in perfect line of sight to each other, which is exactly what Leander wants.

"You wanted a lap dance?" Leander asks casually, conversationally. "You've got it."

Before Tripp can protest, the recruited dancer is straddling his lap, grinding down on him. She's good, Leander can tell from where he's sitting. Just the right kind of pressure, just enough tease and torment. While she gyrates in Tripp's lap, her friend waits patiently nearby, and after fifteen or so minutes, the girl gets up and Tripp looks abjectly relieved, flushed and adjusting himself where he sits, clearly thinking that he's survived.

Unfortunately for Tripp, this torture session is far from over. The girl that's waiting in the wings takes the previous one's place in Tripp's lap, and this one is topless. Now, Leander may be jealous, but he's not an idiot. He knows that Tripp is attracted to him, has zero insecurities about what he offers and what Tripp needs in the bedroom. On the other hand, he's known Tripp for many years, and the man *enjoys* looking at women, especially naked women. It's just a fact, and in this situation, Leander's wielding that attraction like a weapon.

It's a beautiful thing to witness.

Seated catty-corner to Tripp, Leander laughs—he can't help it, Tripp's face just looks *so* pained. As he watches the endless lap dance progress, something hits him softly in the side of his head before tumbling into his lap. It's a wadded-up napkin, and its wielder is Marley, who's looking over at him rather incredulously.

"Baller," she says, nodding in Tripp's direction with what seems like awe. "Mad respect. Didn't know you had it in you."

"You'd be surprised what I have in me," Leander replies evenly, shooting her what he knows is a devilish smirk. A waitress stops to drop off their refill pitcher, and Leander accepts the glass of beer Ro offers with thanks. He sips it, the crisp, cold liquid immensely satisfying gliding down his throat after the last hour's activities.

Impatient for some reason, Marley raises her eyebrows and leans in. "Well?" she prompts. "Did you like my present?" Confused, Leander cocks his head to the side and shakes it slightly as if to say, *I don't know what you're talking about.* In response, Marley's eyes fixate on something just over his shoulder, and she tips her chin at it. When he turns around to see what's so interesting, Leander finds Suzy walking past. While he watches, the girl shoots Tripp a brief glance, her cheeks pinkening up as she drops her gaze to the floor and hurries by.

But she—*oh.*

Turning back to Marley, Leander doesn't know whether to try and look appreciative, or skeptical, or *what.* Ultimately, he goes with the night's theme and just laughs, truly shocked, which is not an emotion that Leander feels very frequently.

"*You* did that?" he remarks, leaning forward to clink his beer against Marley's when she holds it out in a toast.

"Did what?" Ro chimes in, visibly confused, but neither Marley nor Leander answer, both waving her off with mutually conspiratorial giggles. Luckily, another couple of dancers wander by at that moment and stop to chat, sufficient distraction for the table. That includes Beau and Bri, who have finally surfaced for air. All of them slip into easy conversation, talking and laughing and passing bills, continuing to drink and dance and party until Bri finally falls asleep with her head on the table.

During that time, a number of Beau and Bri's co-workers stop by, many of whom Leander is also peripherally acquainted with, thanks to the ER overlap. That's very pleasant, and he enjoys feeling like a part of the team. Even Christian and Brett seem to be on their best behavior tonight, or perhaps they're simply occupied with harassing the dancers instead of Beau's other friends and family.

The only person associated with their group who is not having an easy, laid-back sort of evening is *Tripp,* since Leander ensures there's an attractive stripper in his lap for the entirety of the event. By the time his allotted money runs out and the last girl bails, Tripp is visibly struggling. He's not only half-drunk, he's clearly so aroused it must be painful. His hair is a mess and damp at the edges from sweat, his face is red and he's damn near panting, crossing one leg over the other just as soon as there's no one straddling them.

It surely has not helped that Leander's been sitting close enough to touch, occasionally—*alright, frequently*—leaning in to whisper filth. Or that he's been working the settings on the remote in his pocket like it's personally offended him. It's all been *very* entertaining, but Tripp is starting to look increasingly miserable by the minute, and Leander doesn't want to push him *too* far.

The minute Tripp closes the space between their chairs, leaning over to brush lips across the shell of his ear in order to whisper, "Please, Sir," Leander jumps into action.

At that point, it's all too easy to excuse both himself and Tripp from the group, since Marley knows pretty much exactly what he's been up to, and has already agreed to take them home. Leander owes her big, he really does. Like, *riding in a four a.m. knee pain,* big, but that's a conversation for another day.

No one else seems to take particular notice of Tripp's state. In all likelihood, they probably believe he's simply drunk and horny, which is a pretty average state for a living, breathing man at a strip club bachelor party to be experiencing. The two of them walk out with arms around each other—necessary, due to Tripp's wobbly legs—to a chorus of 'thank you's and 'goodnight, be safe' type-sentiments from their friends.

"Lee," Tripp mumbles in his ear, sounding truly pitiful. "Lee, please don't make me wait. I'll do whatever you want, all night, I swear. Dude, it *hurts.*" He does his best to tug Leander towards the bathroom they visited earlier, but Leander is much more sober now (though not entirely), and has no problem resisting.

Steering them back into Marley's wake as she heads for the exterior doors of the club, Leander smiles and tightens his grasp around Tripp's waist. "You're being *very* good for me, Tripp," he reassures the man softly. "All this restraint, without so much as a cock ring to help you out. It's very impressive. I'll make you a deal, since you've endured so beautifully tonight, and it's been a true pleasure to watch."

Tripp's long-suffering expression peers mournfully up from where he's (somewhat dramatically) planted his face into the curve of Leander's neck. Their walking suffers a bit for it, but Leander doesn't mind. In his tipsy state, he can't be bothered to worry about the way they're blurring lines like crazy right now. His *friend* Tripp Truett would never drunkenly wrap himself around Leander in public, would never be so blatantly needy and affectionate.

This *is* dangerous—this is not *friend* behavior, and it barely qualifies as part of their scene. It's certainly not *necessary.* And yet, Leander hasn't the slightest inclination to put a stop to it.

As soon as they're out of the club and into the frigid night air, Leander allows his reckless side to hijack the reins completely, at least for a minute.

"Whoa, holy shit," Marley squeaks as Tripp gets slammed against the side of the building, Leander pushing both of his arms up next to his head and kissing him slow, *deep.* "Hey!" She protests, edging close enough to nudge Leander's hip with the toe of her boot. "*Hey!* Yo, let's get something straight. I love the two of you like the brothers I never wanted, and I *totally* ship you as my O.T.P., but this?"

She circles a hand in their general direction as Leander breaks away from Tripp's mouth, biting his own lip to see Tripp's desperate, dazed eyes staring back and filled with want. His lips are shiny from Leander's spit, and he *would,* he absolutely would take him *right here* and right now, if it were not for Marley hovering in the background.

"*This* is not something I ever want to see," she continues as they resume their walk towards Tripp's car. "Got it? And don't even *think* about desecrating the back seat while I'm driving. I'm serious, Leander, I will put itching powder in your boots the next time we're on duty together, I swear to *Gaia.*"

"Of course," Leander replies easily.

Clearly skeptical of his word, Marley makes him swear to God, Buddha, Scout's honor, and General Leia Organa before she'll let them in the car, never mind into the rear seat together. To be fair, Leander never had any intention of finishing off this night in the back seat of Tripp's car—that would be terribly anti-climactic—so it's an easy promise to both make and keep. It doesn't stop him from running fingernails down the inside of Tripp's thighs as they drive, though, or from pressing open-mouthed kisses to the side of his neck.

"Hey," Tripp says suddenly, just as they're pulling into the building's garage and Leander is finishing an Uber order for Marley on his phone. "You said you'd make me a deal. What was that about?" Not wanting to upset the friend doing them a favor with further sex talk, Leander glances up, ensuring that Marley is fully occupied in navigating the narrow path between parked cars to his apartment's assigned space.

"Why don't you guess?" he murmurs quietly. "What could I possibly be leaving up to you, at this point in time?"

Before Tripp can answer, Marley's pulled in, shifted the car into park, and they're all exiting, repeating the "*thank you and goodnight*" furious exchange of words and hugs previously shared with their other friends back at the club.

"I owe you," Leander tells Marley, right before they part.

She waves cheerfully, pulling her earbuds out of her bag and inserting them before shrugging. "I'll find a way for you to make it up to me," she says with a wink. Another wave and then she's gone, leaving Leander and Tripp *finally, finally alone.*

They don't even make it all the way to the elevator before they're pulling at clothing. By the time they're tripping over each other's feet struggling down the hallway that leads to Leander's door, both of their pants are undone and Tripp's shirt is off, hanging from his forearm. Thankfully, it's the middle of the night and no one is out and about, so they make it inside the apartment without scarring any children, giving little old ladies heart attacks, or having the police called.

They lose the remainder of their clothing on the way to the playroom, save for Tripp's panties—which, if Leander had his way, he would always have on—and somehow, Tripp ends up flat on his back on the hardwood floor. Unwilling to wait, Leander finds himself straddling Tripp and rutting their groins together.

While he knows that Tripp is in pain and on the edge, Leander can't help but relish the way he hangs on for dear life. Tripp's searching fingers slip from sweat as they scrape against the smooth floor, desperately seeking something to grab onto. His jaw is clenching and his head tosses restlessly from side to side, collar still beautifully bright against the pale skin of his wrist. Even the scars on his shoulder—that Tripp picked at incessantly while healing, working to ensure they'd stick around—in the shape of Leander's handprint seem to stand out in stunning clarity tonight.

"What do you *want*, Tripp?" Leander demands. "Tell me, I want to give it to you."

"That… that's the deal?" Tripp manages to ask, choking on a gasp as his head tips backward when Leander purposefully slides their groins together.

"Delicious," Leander murmurs, hips gyrating in a way that's playful for him and must be torturous for Tripp. "Yes, that's the deal. You may come however you like. Tell me, Tripp."

"*Ung*," Tripp groans. "I—fuck me? And…the fleshlight?"

"Done," Leander agrees easily, sitting back on his heels before standing up. He reaches down to grasp Tripp around his forearm and yank him vertical, with *force,* so that he slams against Leander's own chest. They stare at each other for a moment, Tripp breathing hard and their forearms pressed together between their bodies.

Tripp makes the first move this time, Leander's sure of it. Normally, he'd scold him for the presumption, but—well, he *did* say that Tripp could have whatever he wanted, and so sue him if Leander fucking *loves* feeling like Tripp wants *him*.

Right now, Tripp's kissing like he's a man on the verge, and therefore, Leander wastes no time in steering him towards the bed. He only breaks away for a brief moment, necessary to retrieve the fleshlight from the armoire containing the lion's share of his casual toys, making it back to Tripp's side in record time. They're both a little unsteady and sloppy, and Leander's not sure that he could handle anything overly complicated right now anyway, so he shoves Tripp down onto his back and pours lube into the toy without pretense.

Normally, he'd warm the insert up with water, but there's no way Tripp is going to sit around and wait for that, nor does Leander care to make him. Removing the plug in Tripp's ass reminds him that it's holding his cum inside, some of it immediately leaking out and dripping down Tripp's crack. The sight leaves Leander grabbing his own dick and trying not to come, his possessive streak showing through in spades.

"Oh, *Tripp*," he murmurs, wiping the leftover lube smeared across his hand over the length of his cock before pushing Tripp's thighs back and apart even further.

For his part, Tripp barely seems to notice, fumbling at the sheets and mumbling to himself in what Leander's fairly certain is an incoherent mix of pep-talk and desperate begging meant for him. He's so gorgeous and pliant like this, exactly how Leander *always* wants him—broken down and desperate, pure, unspoiled *perfection*.

Leander pushes inside him without pretense, and Tripp cries loudly with relief, his back arching and his cock blurting a steady stream of precum that dribbles down onto his belly, cock itself purple and angry at the head. Leander's not an idiot—this will not be some drawn-out event. As tears leak from Tripp's eyes and his lip gets sucked in between his teeth, Leander slides the fleshlight down over his cock and works it carefully, imagining that the pleasure is borderline painful, in and of itself.

Tripp's response to his gift is nothing short of stunning, so much so that Leander nearly forgets to actually fuck him. In awe of his sub, he opts to mostly watch—watch the way Tripp's hips swivel and meet his gentle thrusts, watch the way his muscular chest expands with corresponding choppy breaths and moans, watch the smooth length of his throat and the droplets of sweat that pool in its hollow.

Leander does his best to catalogue every moment, to file each one away and save it forever in his mind. All in all, there are only a short few minutes of him moving the fleshlight and providing soft encouragement to Tripp's ears before he's coming, body shaking and trembling and clenching around Leander's cock as he cries out with unfettered relief and satisfaction.

Once he's done, Leander tosses the toy aside and gathers Tripp up, pressing his thighs to his chest and fucking him hard, arms wrapped tightly around Tripp's back and shoulders. It's incredibly intimate, and a still-vaguely-intoxicated Leander feels like he's inside of a dream. Tripp is wonderfully boneless beneath him; kissing back passively when Leander licks into his mouth, compliantly allowing himself to be manipulated this way and that.

When Leander comes, it's with Tripp's name on his lips and their bodies as close as two people can possibly be. The orgasm is *almost* as good as the way Tripp's arms tighten around him, the way he sighs into his ear, how he nuzzles just beneath it. It's stupidly soft, and Leander can't even bring himself to worry about the way they're *barely* toeing the party line anymore. In fact, it's all he can do not to shove his fingers into Tripp's hair, to pull him close and confess all the ways that he loves him, is *in love* with him.

Instead, Leander forces himself to pull away, to clean them both up, to bring water and aspirin and juice for Tripp over to their bedside table before succumbing to the urge to pass out. Even as that's happening, Leander finds himself blinking against his heavy lids, staring in awe at Tripp's peaceful face and his closed eyes, the way he drapes himself so easily over his chest.

What is he even *doing* with this man?

Any other time, Leander would probably fall down the rabbit hole agonizing about it, but tonight, he just can't do it. Thinking back on everything they've done, Leander has no regrets, can't bring himself to even pretend. Especially right now: he's still tipsy, he's satisfied, the mattress is inviting, and Tripp's embrace is warm and comfortable.

Perhaps he should be more concerned with how often he tables these particular fears regarding his relationship with Tripp. Perhaps he will try to be better or more careful with his boundaries in the future, whatever that might mean.

But not tonight.

Chapter 7

"*Sir, yes!*" Tripp can't help but cry out as Leander thrusts into him from behind, pushing his bare belly up against the railing of the balcony where the edge digs mercilessly into soft flesh. Between that and the cutting cold of the air whipping around them up here on the twentieth floor, Tripp's already lasted a lot longer than he might have bet. Thankfully, the sliding glass doors to Leander's apartment are thrown open behind them, a wide swath of warm air wafting out and offering *some* semblance of relief, a slight buffer against the early morning freeze.

"If you can't—*ugh*—keep that pretty mouth shut, I will shut it for you, *and* I will take away your hand," Leander admonishes, his pace slowing to something deep and frustrating as he wraps himself around Tripp's back. That's enough of a warning for Tripp to bite his lip, to tuck his chin down against his chest, and concentrate on finishing. With his eyes closed, it's much easier to forget the cold *and* the fact that he's completely naked, being fucked in plain sight of anyone who cares to look.

The view from Leander's apartment looks out over the city and is fairly high-set, which means that from the street below, one would really have to be straining to catch sight of the two of them. Nonetheless, the balcony faces several other apartment buildings and corporate offices across the way, and even in the pre-dawn, five a.m. stillness, there are plenty of lights illuminating various windows to make the risk substantially real.

The thought of being watched, whether purposeful or accidental, is something Tripp hasn't been able to stop thinking about since his brother's bachelor party and *Suzy*. It's led to several interesting discussions and offers from Leander, including a possible trip to some kink club he knows about downtown, which sounds intimidating as hell. This—this brutal fuck on Lee's balcony—seemed like a pretty harmless way of testing the waters.

So far, Tripp loves it. Maybe not the cold—that's less than thrilling, and not doing much for his ability to keep it up, either. Also, the fact that Lee is in sweatpants and an unzipped hoodie behind him is just so *Lee,* Tripp wouldn't even know where to start, but being exposed and violated in public is fucking *hot.* In his mind, Tripp imagines the people across the way looking out their windows, watching him getting railed, or maybe Lee's nextdoor neighbors hearing his badly-bitten-off moans and just *knowing* what's happening to him.

Between that and Lee's torso pressed warm and inviting up against his back, his own hand jerking his cock, and Lee's dick nailing his prostate, the whole situation escalates towards a peak fairly quickly.

"Stunning," Leander praises when Tripp manages to finish, despite his shivering. The thrusting slows for a second, and at first, Tripp thinks he's going to get to go inside. But then Lee reaches underneath his armpits to cup his shoulders for leverage and sets about fucking him harder, rougher than he was before. Despite the prickling chill and the icy metal of the railing against his skin, Tripp can't help the way his eyes roll back in his head, or the noises that are punched out of his throat at the overstimulation.

It's *just* on the right side of too much, and a tear—*fine, two*—escapes from one eye, trickling wetly down his cheek as Leander groans and finishes achingly hot and even more so for the cold, inside of him.

Before Tripp can even straighten up fully, Lee's hoodie is already around his shoulders and he's being helped back inside, a strong arm wrapped steadyingly around his waist. The balcony doors slide closed and then Lee is leading him to the kitchen for orange juice and a warm cloth. Same as it ever was, whether they're heading back to bed or not.

They're not, unfortunately—not today, and as Tripp watches Leander rinse the used rag off in the sink, he regrets that fact more than usual. The lighting is low inside Lee's space, just a single lamp in the living area casting a dim glow out into the apartment as a whole. It's quiet as they move around each other instinctively, in routines that have now become second nature. This feels domestic, what they're doing, and every time Tripp has to leave or break one of these moments in particular, he worries that it won't happen again.

Sure, it's a little sad, a bit desperate, but that's what Tripp's life has come to these days. Clinging to every scrap he can steal with Lee, holding on for dear life to any glimpse of what *might* lie beyond this power dynamic relationship they have —if they could ever get there.

Tripp sighs and leans back against the countertop, still naked save for Lee's hoodie, and scrubs a hand over his tired eyes.

"What?" Leander asks softly, wringing out the rag and dropping it into the basin to sit until he throws a load of laundry in later. The sheets from the playroom and yesterday's uniform, probably. He's predictable that way—*Tripp* can predict his movements, because he's in Lee's space so often now, he just knows. Tripp hates how much he loves that he just knows.

"Nothing," he replies off-handedly, forcing a yawn, the façade of which Leander's all-seeing eyes undoubtedly pierce through directly, though he doesn't call Tripp out. "Just tired. Thinking about how friggin' long this day is going to be."

With a low hum of acknowledgement, Leander nudges Tripp's arm away from his side so that he can step in and press up against him, hugging him around the waist before dragging a gentle hand down over his cheek. The result is Tripp's face turning into his, their lips meeting softly, affectionately. Leander kisses him long and slow, not too deep but plenty intentional, and Tripp can't say that he doesn't enjoy it as much as falling asleep in Lee's arms. It's a good close second, anyway.

Lee takes a long time to pull back, probably longer than Tripp has to spare, considering the hour. He *should* be the one to cut it off, Tripp knows damn well he should, but it's hard to say no when Lee is like this. While his logical side is certain that his friend is just being careful—yes, Tripp is *fully* aware that's all that's happening here—since he has to leave so soon after a scene, his goofy brain insists on floating the suggestion that Lee is seeking comfort and affection, too.

Really, in *theory*, he supposes it could be both. Who the hell knows? These days, Tripp finds himself increasingly unsure of what's right or real anymore at all. He's finding it harder and harder to parse out what the truth is, at least where Lee's feelings for him are concerned. It's not easy to distinguish between what's true tenderness and what is ultimately a fantasy that his own hormone-addled body dreamt up just to torture him.

"I gotta go, sw—Sir," Tripp tells Lee, barely managing to stop himself from calling Leander 'sweetheart,' and spitting out the appropriate moniker. "Duty calls," he adds apologetically, extricating himself from Leander's grasp before unbuckling his collar and making his way to the hallway leading to the front door.

Luckily, he thought ahead last night, leaving his folded uniform out there in preparation for this very moment. Tripp knew that he'd want to spend every second up to this point with Lee and *belonging* to Lee, so why not make it easy on himself? Briefly, he wonders if he should shower again but then decides, *fuck it*. Plans on the docket are to spend the entire day packed up and training in the County's burn building, so he's going to smell like absolute ass by the end of it, anyway.

While Tripp dresses in the relative darkness of the hallway, Leander leans one shoulder on the edge of the doorway to the kitchen and watches. He looks stupidly inviting with his wild bedhead and his soft gray sweatpants, bare chest radiating warmth the way Tripp knows it does, strong arms just begging for him to crawl back into them.

It's tempting. He *could* call off sick...

No. Tripp dismisses that idea outright, or at least before it can grow roots and take hold, because *damn,* does he want to do that. But he can't bail on his crew today: trainings are important—they're the difference between a newbie panicking and bailing during a live burn, or taking a deep breath and moving forward to save someone's life. They're the line between an interior attack crew going in prepared and competent, and someone's home burning to the ground.

As a Lieutenant, it's Tripp's job to hand the collective knowledge he stores in his head (a lot of it learned the hard way) down to the next generation, the firefighters who might very likely someday be the difference between *his* own life or death.

No calling off allowed, seductive as the reasoning may be. Anyway, he'll see Leander tonight. *All* night, and it's gonna be a big one.

"Take my sweatshirt with you. Wear it under your coat," Leander instructs, and Tripp can recognize from his tone that it's not a request. He complies, but also shoots his friend a rueful look.

"I'm fine," Tripp assures him, though after zipping up the maroon hoodie, he has to admit that feeling and smelling Leander all around him is *not* a bad thing. Not at all. Truth be told, Tripp's glad he has an excuse to accept the offer so readily. "I promise, I'll text you if I'm feeling off. Swear," he says, holding up three fingers like a Boy Scout.

Eyes narrowed, Leander stands in the middle of the hallway and chews his thumbnail, concerned and skeptical, as usual. After what happened early on in their relationship, Lee *hates* for either of them to leave quickly after a scene and without extended aftercare. While it doesn't happen often—and the few times it has, they've kept in close contact and everything has been fine—Leander still worries, and he makes no secret about it.

"Promise me," he says eventually.

Tripp laughs, but it does feel good that Leander cares so much. On his way out of the apartment, Tripp winks as he tosses his keys and catches them in his hand before waving. "Cross my heart, sunshine," he quips, skating swiftly out the door and letting it slam shut behind him before Leander can say anything about *"inappropriate nicknames, Tripp"*.

During the ride down in the elevator, Tripp finds himself whistling, and (despite the lingering twinge in his ass), really feeling great. Before he even reaches his car in the garage, Tripp's phone is buzzing in his pocket, and he smiles when he sees Lee's message lighting up the screen.

Before starting up the vehicle, Tripp fires one back, assuring Leander that he's doing *just* fine and promising to contact him immediately if anything changes. His fingers stumble over the sign-off, wanting to say something more, some message of affection or similar to show Lee how much he appreciates him, but at the last second, Tripp reels himself in.

He winds up sending a cocky, *"Laters, Baby,"* which Leander will either be totally appalled by or not understand at all. Considering the nearly-nonexistent pop-culture database the man has to draw on, Tripp is betting on the latter, though who knows. In addition to being oblivious to most major media produced in the last fifty years, Lee is also wildly protective of the BDSM community's integrity, so *50 Shades* feels like something he should definitely know and hate.

By the time he arrives at Station Fifteen, Tripp has already put his and Lee's exchange out of his mind, focusing fully on the work he has ahead of him. Their station is going out of service for most of Tripp's twelve-hour shift today, the entire crew heading out for a scheduled training at the County fireground. While they're off-status with the dispatch center, Station Eleven will cover any calls that come in.

Shifting his car into park, Tripp steps out and stretches, waving good morning to Theo, who salutes casually as he rounds the side of the building and enters through the open bay doors. Max and Lisha are only a few steps behind him, bickering about something Tripp can't discern from the distance and doesn't try.

Sibling bullshit, he deduces, as Max catches Tripp's gaze and rolls his eyes before he and his sister disappear inside. Tripp's all too familiar with *that.* Probably for the best that Beau didn't wind up a firefighter—one of them would have undoubtedly ended up secured to a backboard and tied to the top of the ladder truck by now. Heck, *weekly.*

It's cold out this morning, though thankfully not as bitter as the week prior, when they had that all-nighter three-alarm blaze. Even still, Tripp can see his breath in the crisp pre-dawn air, but maybe after the sun comes up it won't be so *biting.* He's going to be spending the majority of the day inside a controlled burning building, so at the very least, the low temperature will be relieving when he comes back out.

"Hey, Gunnar." Tripp nods to greet his Captain when he strolls into the bay, glancing around to survey the scene. The rest of his crew are already shuffling around, packing up the trucks and getting ready to move out.

"'Sup, brotha?" Gunnar tips his chin in Tripp's direction as he slings a bag of gear into the front passenger seat of Engine Fifteen's cab. "You're awfully cheery for this early in the mornin'. What's gotten into you?"

Tripp grins widely as he reaches the gear racks and kicks off his duty boots in favor of stepping into his fire-rated ones, stomping them on before pulling up his bunker pants. He collects his jacket and helmet and throws them into the back of the engine's cab, behind Gunnar's seat before answering. "Who says I'm not the one getting into someone else?"

The laugh that explodes heartily from Gunnar's chest should probably be insulting, but Tripp's unbothered, lets it roll right off his back. He got laid this morning, who cares what the fuck anyone else thinks about it? "They say if you can dream it, you can achieve it, sugar," Gunnar declares with another guffaw and a rough slap to Tripp's shoulder. "It's downright adorable you think any of us believes you're a top."

"Shut up," Tripp grunts, shoving Gunnar as hard as he can manage and barely budging him. Fuck Gunnar and his stupid-huge muscles. It's not as if Tripp's small, but Gunnar's a brick shithouse. He chuckles as he shrugs Tripp off, turning away to walk towards the middle of the bay, where he can address everyone more effectively.

"Alrigh', let's get a move on, slackers," Gunnar yells, clapping his hands together. "Fire ain't gonna start itself."

The ride to the training grounds is relaxing for Tripp, as much as being at work can be when he'd rather be at home, buried under the covers with Lee. The city flies by outside his window, turning first into sprawling industrial complexes and factories before becoming increasingly rural as they reach the outskirts. The slowly-rising sun in the winter sky is reflected off of towering windows and still-sleeping cars, pink and lazy in its journey to wake up.

Around him, Tripp's fellow crew members shoot the shit and laugh, but Tripp's content to sit quietly, running through drills in his head and thinking about everything he has to do, both today and tonight. He feels oddly comfortable, secure, even. Looking forward to seeing Lee later and spending the night with both him and his brother at Beau and Bri's rehearsal dinner, but not desperate for it or needy.

Just... *happy.* Content with the way things are. His life is damn good right now. Tripp can't even imagine returning to the way things used to be before he and Lee jumped into this whole thing they have going together, wouldn't know what to do if he suddenly had to try.

In the pocket of his pants, Tripp's phone vibrates, but it's too much of a pain to reach *under* his bunker gear and dig it out when he'll just have to put it back. Leaving any device in an outer layer would be a great way to end up with a melted hunk of plastic and be out a few hundred dollars for a new phone, so… no. It's probably just Lee checking in on him, anyway. He's such a mother hen after they scene. That thought makes Tripp smile, makes him grateful. He turns his nose into the hood of Lee's sweatshirt that he's still wearing, closing his eyes and inhaling the scent deeply.

Damn, Tripp thinks approvingly. Why doesn't he steal Lee's shit more often?

The County's fireground is available for any company in the local area to use for live burn training, City fire services included. It only has to be reserved ahead of time, and whatever potential scenarios approved by the County Commissioners. Not that those talking heads know anything about fire safety, and Tripp snorts when he thinks about them "approving" anything. As a Lieutenant, his own worries are mostly operational and practical, he steers clear of anything that would require wheeling and dealing with upper, *upper* management in that way.

That's Chief shit, so Mickey and Walter's gig, or maybe Gunnar's, if he's extra-unlucky that week.

When Theo pulls the engine to a stop about a hundred feet from the main burn building, Tripp glances out the window and spots Chief Mickey right away. He's wearing his white helmet and leaning against the Sup vehicle impatiently. On the ground next to him are several huge stacks of wood pallets, bushels of hay, and some assorted other "Class A" materials they'll use to stoke up a rager. All of the fire-fodder has to be brought inside the buildings, and no way is Mickey carting that stuff up multiple flights of stairs himself.

As Tripp listens to Gunnar taking them off-status with dispatch, Station Fifteen's ladder and rescue trucks both pull to a stop behind the engine. Crews from the platoons scheduled opposite Tripp's and an entire truckload of academy-fresh trainees soon to be turned loose on the department as a whole are packing them full, and they spill out like ants fleeing a smoking hill.

Ironic.

Every single person is here to participate in the planned drills—more specifically, they're all here to learn from Tripp.

Damn, is he glad Lee let him blow off the lion's share—*ha*—of his nervous energy before facing this shit.

Hopping down out of the truck—and noting disappointedly that the risen sun hasn't remotely burned the chill from the air—Tripp waves hello to Mickey and then rounds on the burn building to assess his canvas, internally reviewing his plan of attack.

"Coffee's on the picnic table," Mickey grunts in his direction, before leaning sideways to holler around him at a gaggle of trainees socializing and dawdling awkwardly in front of the ladder truck. "Hey, you rookies just planning on watching while a real house burns to the ground, or what? Stop actin' like spoiled princesses and haul this junk up to the second floor."

From over at the picnic table—one of several placed beneath a pavilion structure meant to shelter onlookers from rain, water, falling debris, and sun—Tripp stifles a laugh. He turns away so that the newbies don't see him smirking as he pours himself a coffee from one of the many Boxes of Joe littering the aged wood. There's a giant stack of donuts there, too, and Tripp wastes no time in shoving more than a mouthful's worth of powdered deliciousness into his face.

No question, this is the best part of any training—free food. With any luck, they'll get hoagies for lunch, hopefully from that place he loves down the street. *Fuck, yeah.* Once his belly is full and there's caffeine enroute to his veins, Tripp turns his attention back to the fireground.

The "burn building" they're working out of today is actually two adjacent concrete structures, built specifically to train firefighters and rescue personnel using simulations that mimic real life as closely as possible. The wing closest to Tripp's engine was constructed to resemble a three-story rowhome, a residential dwelling, hundreds of which are found all over the city. Alternatively, the complex to the right of the house mimics a four-story commercial or industrial structure. Both are important to master, and each requires an entirely different approach to do so.

For Tripp, the teaching struggle lies in where to start and what to focus on as the major touchstones. On deciding what is *most* important, what the priorities are to drive home, especially when handling a bunch of wet-behind-the-ear probies. There are a million things they could do during a live burn today, *hours* worth of exercises and training using either structure, and Mickey's left it completely up to Tripp to pare their maneuvers down to the essentials.

He takes a deep breath and lets it out. *Alright,* he thinks, *Let's do this.*

"Not gonna make us run sprinkler drills on the industrial side, are you?" Aydin appears at Tripp's side, helping himself to a cup of coffee. "Fuckin' cold out."

Tripp scoffs. "In this weather? What, you think I want my balls to fall off after I unpack? Don't ask stupid questions. We'll do those in the spring. Bus here yet?"

"Yep," Aydin replies with a nod, gesturing off towards an area of the parking lot Tripp can't see, thanks to all the fire trucks taking up space. "Medic-1 just pulled in. Your boy on today?"

"My—" Tripp startles, accidentally cuts himself off as he nearly spills his coffee, and then glares. "What did I say about stupid questions?" Leaving Aydin looking confused and sort of pitiful with his hands still raised, trying to pacify Tripp's attitude, he stomps off.

Your boy.

Tripp wishes.

Focus. "Probies to the second floor," Tripp hollers, swirling his hand over his head like he's rounding them up, cowboy-style. "Time to see what you're made of."

Having collectively graduated from the academy and received conditional employment offers from the city, none of the newbies Tripp's dealing with today are *brand* new to either fire ops or training evolutions. But everything they know is controlled—and nothing about fire in the real world is nearly so cut and dry. *This* is where these kids will start learning how to apply what they've memorized from books and in class: how to think on their feet, how to translate the theoretical to the practical, how to react when everything goes wrong and nothing that exists is how you expect it to be.

For starters, Tripp gathers them all inside the second floor of the residential side, packed like sardines into the bonfire room as Mickey lights the flame and then immediately bails. He'll run command via radio from outside the building, just like during the real deal. Everyone that's left inside is fully-masked and packed up at this point, except for Mac, who is stoking the fire completely unbothered by the increasing heat and smoke. He's hanging out by the door to the fire escape, so Tripp isn't overly worried, but he expects Mac to be forced from the room within the next few minutes.

Fire doesn't care how tough you think you are.

Elsewhere in the two buildings, Gunnar is putting the seasoned crews from Fifteen through their paces, sending them floor-to-floor on last checks for anything out of place or unsafe. Specifically, they're looking for crumbling walls or large cracks permeating the cement structure. It's good practice for firefighters to spend time existing in SCBA gear with no actual risk present, but the checks are also important for safety purposes. The buildings were walked through last night and they're regularly maintained by the company who built them, but even concrete has its limits when it comes to fire and heat.

Everything does, and the last thing any of the officers want is to douse a training fire and have the resulting steam put pressure on an already-stressed crack, resulting in half the building coming down on top of their heads.

It could happen. Nothing is *truly* safe or risk-free when it comes to live fire—that's just the nature of the beast.

Tripp reminds his trainees of that fact like a broken record, using the room they're all currently huddled in to make his point. "Stay low," he reminds them, when a firefighter or two try to lean on the sills of closed windows to make themselves more comfortable. Hardly any of them have radios, so Tripp has to raise his voice to be heard through his apparatus and over the crackling of the fire, which means that the resulting grumble of complaints he gets in return are almost completely stifled.

"Fine, stand if you want. Your brains will roast inside your skulls, but clearly, you're not using them for anything, anyway. This is Firefighting 101," Tripp yells from his crouch on the other side of the blaze.

"Two hundred degrees near the floor means up to *two thousand* near the ceiling. You think that difference doesn't matter when it comes to how long you'll last inside a real burning building? Be my guest, try it out. All the faster I can weed your asses off my crew. Trust and believe, you do not want someone who doesn't respect the danger that fire presents holding *your* life in their hands. Not when they're at your back, and not when you're trapped under burning rubble. Don't be that person, got it?"

Clipped to his shoulder, Tripp's radio mic crackles to life and Gunnar's voice can be heard saying, "We're in place, brotha. Whenever you're ready."

"Alright," Tripp announces, clapping his hands together once as Mac hauls another pallet in through the doorway and throws it on top of the bonfire. The blast of oxygen from outside fuels the flames and makes them surge like a wave, licking up the closest wall and onto the ceiling. "Search and rescue drill—hand to foot chain, clear the second floor. There are at least two victims. *Talk to each other.* Go!"

As the trainees crawl awkwardly through the only door leading out of the room-turned-oven, Tripp watches them move with a critical eye. Each has one gloved hand on the gear-covered ankle of the firefighter in front of them, and the other alternately used for balance and to clear the ground around them.

"Echo," he snaps, and the EMT-turned-potential-firefighter visibly jumps, even under all of her gear and down on all-fours. "You're not clearing the space as you go! You could have easily missed a downed victim moving the way that you are.

Don't cut corners, don't think of this as 'practice.' You want victims brought to you, go back to the ambulance and stay there. Rescues are on *your* head now, so here's your first lesson—" Tripp pauses dramatically as Mac punctuates his sentence by tossing another broken pallet onto the blaze. "It's *always* real."

The day is exhausting. They wind up doing five full evolutions, which is an aggressive effort. The trainees participate in the first four, and then the experienced firefighters do a coordinated, advanced interior attack to combat a progressed fire on the industrial side of the burn building.

When he's not stoking the flames, Mac is filling air bottles, one after another after another, so the training can continue uninterrupted. Slowly but surely, the newbies learn to manage their oxygen better, learn to calm down, to breathe through the stress, to relax enough to use critical thinking instead of just their automatic fight or flight reflexes and whatever passed for competency during "Essentials" class.

Under Tripp and Gunnar's direction, they run hose line, hook up hydrants, throw ladders, learn to break into windows several stories up, rescue their fellow firefighters, and practice extinguishing blazes from both inside the structure and out. Every one of them improves, enough that by mid-afternoon, Tripp's no longer adding to the short-list in his head of the recruits Mickey needs to fire immediately.

In fact, some of them turn it around so hard, Tripp actually feels honored to be leading them. He hopes that Mickey feels the same way about the job he's done organizing this thing.

Echo is the real surprise. The pride Tripp feels in his chest when he sees the timid EMT leaning halfway out of a third floor window, successfully carrying a firefighter heavier than she is over her shoulder, threatens to rip his heart in two. From down on the ground, he can see Echo start to struggle, so Tripp quickly begins clapping and whipping Cody, Max, and several of the other trainees standing and watching below into a mad frenzy. They root loudly for her as she holds her own trying to get the "unconscious person" out the window and safety into the Aerial's raised bucket.

As Echo finally succeeds in passing the boneless firefighter on her shoulder over to the two crew members waiting in the bucket with absolutely *zero* help from inside, the noise around Tripp is deafening. Everyone is screaming and jumping around, cheering Echo on. As soon as he's in, the 'downed' firefighter stands up and pulls off his—*oops, no, that's definitely Chloe, her*—helmet, and Echo yanks off her SCBA mask to reveal a face-cracking smile.

Tripp can't even bring himself to reprimand them when Chloe leans across the space between the bucket and the window to drag Echo into a *very* approving kiss.

"Fuck yeah, Echo!" Tripp yells up at her, pointing his finger and nodding with approval. "That's how we do it! Alright, you talented sons o'bitches—gender neutral, obviously—we're changing it up. Trainees, tear down the residential structure setups, unpack, and then head to the hill where you can watch the rest of us rock out a commercial demonstration. Chloe, stop pretending to be a pro-bie and get down here."

Up in the bucket, Chloe kisses Echo one last time before smashing their hands together in an energetic, congratulatory, gloved high-five. The affectionate, adoring looks they continue to exchange as the bucket comes down and Echo rests her elbows on the windowsill suddenly have Tripp's chest aching for a whole different reason, and *God,* is he excited to see Leander tonight. He only wishes he had a minute to strip his gear down and find his phone, to check in, but as it is, his crews are waiting for instructions on the big demo they're facing.

Mickey sits this one out completely, allowing Gunnar and Tripp to run the entire advanced drill by themselves. It's definitely an evaluation, for sure, but it's also a show of trust, and one that Tripp appreciates. This final evolution includes a monster fire and a not-small amount of real danger, but under Gunnar and his leadership, the whole thing goes professionally smooth. All told, the crews put on an exhibition that Tripp feels immensely proud to have the newbies witnessing.

Sprawled out on the grass nearby, the exhausted trainees sit sweaty and red-faced with their air packs and jackets piled around them, the cold breeze a welcome reprieve after everything they've been through today. Tripp's pretty sure he even sees some of them taking *notes.*

Once the last fire is out and the complex is cleared, the remainder of Station Fifteen's crews file out of the damp, smoking building. They're pulling off helmets and hoods, masks and jackets, checking in and ensuring that every person is accounted for before so much as sitting down. Everyone is visibly tired, but it's the *good* kind—this was a productive, successful day for all involved. The new recruits are learning, one step closer to being considered reliable and dependable in the field. The existing crews, likewise, had a chance to brush up on their skills and reaffirm trust between co-workers, which goes a long way for both practical proficiency *and* morale.

The burn building will take almost a full day to cool down before it can be checked for new damage. Normally, that task would fall to Mickey—and by extension in this particular case, Tripp—but both of them are otherwise occupied tomorrow night, so Walter has volunteered to take care of it. Tripp supposes he'll have to thank Bozo for getting him out of that one, however unintentionally.

Speaking of which, as they're finishing packing up their gear and readying the trucks to return to the station, Tripp glances at his watch for the first time in hours. *Four-thirty.* Only an hour and a half until his shift is over and Lee will be meeting him at the station to head to the rehearsal. As Tripp pulls himself up and into the engine's cab, he realizes that he should dig out his phone and find out whether Lee is going to take the bus or leave his car at Fifteen overnight.

Either way is fine, but they're both meant to head back to his and Beau's place with the other groomsmen after dinner, and Tripp isn't keen on him and Lee splitting up while Christian is around. Plus, one car instead of two means one less designated driver necessary, and Tripp isn't trying to be sober for this.

Lee will probably take the bus anyway, he thinks. Lee's always ten steps ahead of him, not that Tripp is complaining.

Just as he's about to shove his hand down under his bunker pants and go fishing for his phone to make sure, Tripp hears Gunnar put the entire station back on ready status with the 911 Center. That's standard procedure, since they're now capable of responding to calls if needed. It's neither responsible nor considerate to the covering company to keep them tied up longer than necessary—after all, they have their own territories to worry about.

They've also been lucky (or rather, Eleven's been lucky, depending on your point of view), since the radio-designated fire bands have been quiet all day. As far as Tripp knows, the only things Eleven responded to in their stead were a minor accident with fluids down on the roadway (not serious and no injuries), a report of a fuel odor in a residential neighborhood (unfounded), and an automatic fire alarm at the local Walmart (accidental activation, i.e., some asshole teenager pulled it).

Really, Tripp and his crews didn't miss out on a thing.

Of course, now that he could *use* some quiet—or at least some easy-to-deal-with bullshit—things go haywire. Tripp barely has his fingers wrapped around his phone in his pocket when Fifteen's tones drop over the radio, and their activation comes alongside the station that houses the city's high-angle rescue truck.

A ladder truck is a ladder truck and a heavy rescue is a heavy rescue, but the city is lucky enough *($$$)* to have a special, well-equipped technical rescue unit that's built specifically for certain extreme situations. It's not tapped for action very often, and usually only by officer request, so the dispatch itself has Tripp sitting up ramrod-straight and listening intently to what comes over his headset.

"...for a rescue, caller states the victim fell approximately twenty feet over the cliff side and has a visible broken leg. Victim is conscious, unable to move, EMS has been dispatched."

Tripp exchanges an excited glance with Max—this is definitely the real deal. As their lights and sirens activate, he mentally switches gears, putting the rehearsal completely out of his mind. Instead of evening plans, Tripp's immediately running through various protocols for high-angle rescue, adjusted for the need to backboard or for the victim's inability to assist due to major injury.

Since he's trained as an EMT and has high-angle certification, it's a near-certainty that Tripp will be one of likely two responders that will be rappelling down to rescue this person. The other will probably be from Station Ten, where the technical rescue is housed and coming from.

Just like that, all thoughts of Lee and checking his phone are shoved unceremoniously to the backburner. He's not worried—Lee will understand, Tripp knows because their positions have been reversed more than once.

The engine carrying Gunnar, Tripp, and the rest of his crew comes to a stop on the shoulder of the highway that borders the southern side of the city. Just ahead, the roadway passes over a river that's bordered by steep rock face on both shores. On the brush side of the shoulder's guardrail, there's a wide dirt strip and a path of trampled-down weeds that leads off into the woods. From experience, Tripp knows that beyond the treeline, the path runs directly adjacent and over fifty feet above the river.

In the summertime, the cops are constantly chasing kids away from this place. There's an overlook further down that's hidden from view of the highway, a place where teenagers like to gather and hang out, to do whatever it is kids do when no one's watching. Drink, get high, have sex, whatever. That part isn't so troublesome and problematic—hey, Tripp was young once, too—it's what they tend to do with the river itself that's worrying.

At the edge of that favored clearing sits an outcropping of rock that juts out over the river, and it's become somewhat of a magnetic draw for daredevils to treat like a diving board. If Tripp had a nickel for every water rescue he's been forced into because someone jumped into that river in the wrong spot and got fucked, he could pay for Bozo's wedding. So many things can go wrong: getting sucked into the current at the bottom, breaking a leg by jumping onto a submerged rock, even hitting your head on the water and getting knocked unconscious—surface tension is hard as concrete from that height.

Hell, he's even seen his fair share of idiots who didn't realize they'd have to *swim* once they jumped in. Always interesting.

What anyone's doing out here on a day like today, though, is beyond Tripp. Jumping would be suicidal—the water's fast-moving so it doesn't ice, but it's dangerously cold, colder than the air. Anyone feeling froggy enough to jump would be paralyzed as soon as they plunged in—like a thousand knives stabbing you all over, the shock alone might take someone out. Tripp's been in the river at this time of year exactly once before—in a *drysuit*, of course—out of necessity, and he wouldn't wish the experience on his worst enemy.

Well, maybe Christian.

As their crew gathers equipment and makes their way down to the scene, the situation becomes clear pretty quickly. Tripp hikes his way down the dirt path as fast as his boots will carry him, emerging from some brush out into the clearing to find a sobbing teenage girl, still clutching her cell phone to her ear.

"Yes, they're here now. Thank you. Thank you," the girl cries, presumably to the 911 dispatcher doing their best to keep her calm.

"What happened?" Tripp asks, though when he looks around, it's obvious.

"It broke!" The girl replies tearfully, right before dissolving into full-fledged sobs again, anything said after that indiscernible to Tripp's ear. He pats her on the shoulder and moves closer to the cliff's edge. Sometime between last summer and now, the city must have tried installing a railing, thinking it would curb the jumping. It's a good thought and Tripp approves, except whoever installed it didn't do the greatest job. From where Tripp's standing, it kind of looks like the thing gave way under the slightest pressure. Poor kid probably leaned against it and went right over, never stood a chance.

Yikes. No fuckin' way this isn't gonna end up in court, Tripp thinks, dropping to his hands and knees before peering over the edge.

About twenty feet below, a teenage boy lays moaning and terrified, sprawled on his back across a perilously small outcropping of rock. Below *him,* at least twenty additional feet down, the river rushes mercilessly, white-capped and threatening. It even *looks* cold, gray and sharp as it is, cutting around the rocks that crop up in its way. Despite himself, Tripp shivers.

Evaluate the scene, he reminds himself, forcing his mind back onto the task at hand.

The boy is wearing a bright orange puffy vest and jeans that are splattered with blood, ripped straight through just below the knee by a bone that's no longer inside his lower leg where it belongs. Cringing, Tripp suppresses his instinctual repulsion by putting himself in the kid's shoes—*don't make this about you, asshole.*

"Hey!" he calls out. "Hey, buddy! Can you hear me?" In response, the kid just moans and nods. "Can you tell me your name, bud?" There's no reply—the kid just squeezes his eyes shut and cries out in pain, lolling his head against the rock face, which is concerning. Tripp can't be sure that he didn't smack his dome, that he isn't altered and out of it. On the positive side, the break in his leg *could* be in a worse location. The kid definitely got lucky there, but this rescue needs to get a move on.

"Okay," he calls out again. "That's okay, you're okay. Just stay still, stay real still. I'm coming to get you."

Tripp confers quickly with Gunnar, but they're already on the same page. The technical rescue is pulling off of the road and onto the site, firefighters cutting down brush with chainsaws to make way for it to pull as closely as possible to the edge. That's great, but Tripp can't imagine they're going to be able to work it close enough to use for leverage. He pulls a hand over his mouth, relieved to see Jesse Martinez hopping down from the passenger's side of the cab while the truck is still moving, nodding at Tripp and making a beeline in his direction.

As soon as he's close enough, Jesse grabs Tripp's hand and yanks him into a back-clapping hug. "Was hoping it'd be you," he says gratefully. "We doin' this?"

"Harness up," Tripp says in agreement, filling Jesse in on the scene that awaits them while Jesse grabs his harness from the truck and fits it around his own waist. Without asking (and while multitasking, nodding along to Tripp's words), he steps in to check the fit of the one Tripp's donned, and he's grateful for it. Tripp may have his certification, but Jesse is the expert, and he's happy to defer. No dick-measuring contests on scenes like this, especially not when someone is literally about to throw themselves over a cliff.

Practiced and proficient, Jesse's team works together flawlessly, anchoring ropes to trees and to each other before clipping first Tripp and then Jesse himself into the knots using carabiners. The plan is for the two of them to rappel down, splint the kid's leg, address any other life-threatening issues that can't be seen from twenty feet up, then roll him carefully onto a backboard. Once he's secure, they'll clip the backboard itself to even more ropes, and then it'll be a coordinated effort between Tripp, Jesse, and the crews above to raise the board, followed by the two of them. Climbing will most definitely be involved.

Just before they drop over the edge, Jesse reaches out with his fist, Tripp bumping it with a lot more confidence than he feels. As he arranges his ropes, Tripp looks up to find Chloe hovering near the treeline, watching intently.

"Don't you dare tell your uncle what I'm doing," he calls out to her, even as he's bracing his feet against the crumbling edge and leaning back into open air. The rushing water is loud below.

Chloe's eyes widen comically. "Like hell I want to deal with that," she yells back. "But he's probably listening to this cluster over the radio. Echo said he was at the station when the ladder got back." Something about Chloe's tone pricks at Tripp's spidey senses, but he simply doesn't have the bandwidth to sort it out at the moment, being halfway over a cliff and all.

"Great," Tripp mutters to himself. Lee *hates* when he puts himself in 'unnecessary' danger, and most definitely will have something to say about Tripp volunteering for this particular gig. Somehow he doubts, "Comes with the territory, Lee," will be an adequate response. That's a problem for future Tripp, though. Present Tripp is busy not careening to his death in the wild and freezing river forty feet due south.

Despite his dramatic thoughts, the rescue goes smoothly. The kid definitely did knock his head, but he's the type of confused that just wants to go to sleep, not the kind that gets combative and punchy when you try to help them. No miracle too small, and all that.

Tripp and Jesse work well together, communicating via radio with their crews above and stabilizing the patient efficiently in what feels like an *impossibly* small space to work within. There's no room for both firefighters to fit on the ledge with the injured kid lying there, so Tripp spends as much time hanging over the river with his toes on the rock as he does standing on solid ground.

Oh, yeah. Lee would hate this.

They get the boy spinal-immobilized using a cervical collar and the backboard that's carefully lowered down, his lower leg splinted to a shortboard (with minimal screaming) and then to the backboard itself. It's times like these Tripp wishes he was a paramedic—this kid *deserves* pain management, but there's nothing that he, as an EMT-Basic, is authorized to give. All Tripp can do is handle him gently and get his ass topside as quickly as possible. There, the medic is waiting, ready to administer a nasal atomizer full of fentanyl just as soon as the patient is within reach.

By the time the crews above them are yelling to each other and hoisting the board up and over his and Jesse's heads, Tripp is sweating profusely, despite the cold. He's also experiencing the kind of exhaustion he suspects might be what marathon runners feel around mile twenty. He's sore, burned-out, already come *so* far but with miles to go before he sleeps. Miles that suddenly feel a *lot* longer than they actually are.

While they wait for the go-ahead to start climbing, Tripp slumps against the blood-stained rock by Jesse's side as they congratulate each other on a job well done. For a few minutes, they sit in silence, just looking out over the river, and then Jesse pipes up with something completely out of left field.

"Hey," he says, elbowing Tripp in the ribs good-naturedly. "Congrats on Lee, man. Heard through the grapevine you two finally got your heads out of your asses. Always knew you would be good together."

Whether it's the exhaustion he feels settling into his bones, the daunting thought of both the climb ahead and the entire *night* still looming in front of him, or something else completely, Tripp's standard slew of protests die on his tongue. "Thanks," he replies weakly. "I—yeah. Lee is great." He's saved from having to say anything further by their radios activating, letting them know that the team is poised and in position, ready to bring them home.

The climb is worse than Tripp imagined, but hand over foot—and a lot of help from whoever's reeling him in up top—he makes it. Lungs wheezing and arms burning, Tripp pulls himself over the ledge with some crucial help from Gunnar and Max. Both of them rush forward to grab and drag him over the finish line, an arm under each of his, even as his toes scrabble and lose grip against the loose rock and dirt.

As soon as he's vertical, there's a bottle of water being pressed into his hand and a bunch of people clapping him on the back, offering praise and congratulations. Jesse's close behind and receives the same treatment, applause all around.

All Tripp wants is to *sit down.* And not on a ledge carved into the side of a cliff.

Naturally, the ambulance is long gone, and Tripp can't wait to be a fuckin' memory here, too. He says a blurry and worn-out goodbye to Jesse, somehow finding himself agreeing to poker night with Lee sometime in the near future, because Tripp can't be trusted with his own best interests when he needs a nap. Despite that fact, he's belted to his seat in the engine's cab before anything else dramatic can happen (and before he does something *really* dumb, like imply to more casual acquaintances that Lee loves him back).

On the way to the station, Tripp falls fast asleep, drool on his shoulder and everything. Having shucked his bunker jacket, he curls up in Lee's hoodie, which unfortunately now smells a lot more like smoke mixed with his own sweat and a lot less like *Lee.* Hoodie aside, the nap is a knockout, dead-to-the-world sort of thing, and Tripp only wakes because the backup alarm blasts discourteously in his ear as the engine finds its place in the fire bay.

As he blinks sleepily and wipes wetness away from the corner of his mouth, Tripp hears Gunnar's familiar "Ho!" yelled to Theo as he spots the engineer's parking job from behind the truck. He feels the air brakes engage before the engine finally stops and goes silent, and they're home.

What a relief.

Tripp's still yawning as he stumbles out of the cab, kicking away his fire-rated boots and stepping sleepily out of his bunker pants. There's maybe twenty minutes left in his shift. The oncoming crew should already be in the building, and no doubt, if a call comes in, he won't be expected to take it.

Maybe, if he's lucky, he can sack out on the couch for thirty minutes or so before Lee shows up and forces him to get presentable. Beau's rehearsal doesn't start until seven-thirty, buffered specifically for Tripp's work schedule, since being on duty today means having the rest of the weekend off. That's plenty of time for a nap and a quick shower.

First, though—all of the gear worn inside the burn buildings today needs to be laundered, which is a chore. Tripp's thankful that a few of the other city stations volunteered to take some of the newbies' stuff, or Fifteen's crews would be cycling shit straight through until Tripp returns again on Monday. Officer gear takes priority, anyway, so Tripp doesn't bother checking in with Gunnar before emptying his pockets and dumping his pants, hood, and jacket straight into the open industrial washing machine at the side of the bay.

His gear tops off the load, so he closes the lid, checks the settings and detergent level, and sets it to work, patting the top when he's done. Out of the corner of his eye, Tripp sees Gunnar chatting with someone, maybe one of the guys from the oncoming crew, which isn't unusual. What *is* unusual are the covert glances they're both shooting in his direction, and the subsequent way Gunnar saunters over—*way* too casually, at that—while Tripp is still trying to put the unwashable parts of his gear back on the rack.

"Dude," Tripp says with a heavy sigh, scrubbing a hand through his sweaty hair as he turns to face Gunnar. He motions with his hand for his Captain to just give it to him. "Out with it, come on. I'm too fuckin' tired to play games right now."

Gunnar lifts an eyebrow as he leans casually against the rescue truck, arms folded across his chest. Around them, their co-workers continue about their business, laying hose line across the floor to drain and dry, checking tools—generally putting the vehicles, the station, and themselves back in order.

"Lee is here," he says simply, face giving nothing away.

"Okay?" Tripp replies, somewhat confused. So Lee is early, big deal. Or maybe he's just visiting—they all do that, all of the time, medics and firefighters alike. When your friends are also your co-workers and downtime is baked into the job, it kinda follows that work sometimes becomes a place to play.

Hell, Tripp's passed out here and at Station Eleven more times than he can count. It's fun to end the night shooting the shit with friends, plus it's safer than trying to drive home tipsy, or worse—staying the night with a bar hookup. Gunnar acting weird over Lee being in the building is *much* stranger than the fact that Lee is here.

"He's upstairs in the bathroom of the men's bunkroom, folding laundry."

Alright, so that's a little bit odd, but Tripp's not one to judge. Maybe Lee got bored waiting for him and was just being considerate. There's a regular washer and dryer in that bathroom, there for the crews to wash bed linens or uniforms. The laundry basket was probably overflowing and Lee is—first and foremost—a team player, a good guy.

There's a nudge at the back of Tripp's mind that tells him he's working pretty hard to paint this scenario as perfectly normal, but is there *really* a reason not to do that?

"So?"

"Sugar, he's washed and sorted every piece of linen we have in this entire building. Maybe the whole city, I dunno. Towels, bedsheets, dishrags—you name it, Healing Hands up there has folded it. Twice. Something's going on with your boy. Better go find and fix it before he figures out he can't fold his way back to sanity and has a full-on breakdown in my bunkroom."

"Right," Tripp replies distractedly, pulling a hand over his mouth. Before Gunnar can finish talking, he's already backing towards the stairs that lead up to the second floor, where the crew and bunkrooms are located.

Gunnar clears his throat. "Tripp," he says pointedly, following Tripp across the room with a worried look on his face.

"Yeah?" Tripp blinks and does his best to focus on his Captain. He *is* still on the clock, after all, but he's unprepared for Gunnar to reach out and grasp the edge of his t-shirt sleeve, tugging it up to reveal most of Lee's scarred handprint on his bicep. The weather's been cold since Lee put it there, so Tripp's made a habit of wearing long-sleeve shirts, generally not needing to worry about accidentally showing off his scabs when they were healing. These days, though, the handprint is fairly inconspicuous and mostly white, but still obvious if you're looking either for it or directly at his arm.

"Fuck off," he snaps reflexively, jerking away from Gunnar's touch. Tripp glares defensively, but Gunnar doesn't react, just hesitates for a moment before shaking his head and waving him off. Thank God, because Tripp does *not* have time to cope with this bullshit right now.

"Be careful," is all Gunnar says, and Tripp nods automatically before turning on his heel and heading up the steps. He'll deal with Gunnar later.

Halfway there, Tripp remembers his phone, pulling it out to find an astronomical number of missed calls and messages. There's exactly one text from Beau—he was the trauma surgeon on duty at Central's E.R. today, and he got to hear about Tripp's heroics first-hand from the rescued kid with the broken leg. His message is lighthearted, something about Tripp not needing to throw himself off a cliff to get out of having dinner with Christian and Brett, and any other time, Tripp would have found it hilarious.

Unfortunately, his mind is focused on the twenty-or-so-odd other messages, all from one person.

Lee: I know you're busy, just checking in.

Lee: Please let me know that you're doing well when you have a free moment.

Lee: Apologies for the messages, you know how I worry.

Lee: Hope your day is going well. Text me when you have the chance, it would be nice to know that you're feeling okay.

Lee: My day could be better. If you have a moment, could you call? Two minutes, no more, I promise.

Lee: I know you're busy. I'm so sorry.

Lee: Tripp, I hate to be a
bother, but I really need to
speak to you. It's urgent.

There are a few more, all similar, and Tripp's stomach drops. It's not difficult to figure out what's happening here, unusual as it may be for Lee. The last unread message causes a wave of fear and nausea to roll through his body, and goosebumps to rise on his arms. If he wasn't already aware that Lee happens to be safe and sound less than fifty feet away, he might actually panic.

Lee: If you

That's it.

"*If you*", and nothing else. Tripp can't remember the last time he received a text from Lee with so much as a typo, never mind a thought that wasn't even finished. It's one of those weird, nerdy little quirks he loves about the guy—who the hell bothers to punctuate their texts before sending, or refuses to shorten words on principle?

It all amounts to one thing, and that's the unavoidable fact that Lee is dropping. Lee is dropping and likely has been since they were together early this morning. Which means that Tripp ignored him for almost *twelve hours*. Jesus Christ, he's an asshole.

Despite the way that his eyes ache and his muscles still burn from the day's activities, begging him to sit the fuck down already, Tripp puts it all aside for Lee. It's damn near torture to sprint up the remaining stairs two at a time, but he does it, bursting through the door at the top and patently ignoring the chorus of greetings that erupts from his various coworkers scattered around the crew room.

With a grunt and a half-hearted wave in their direction, Tripp doesn't so much as pause, never mind stop. He bolts directly into the hallway that leads past the charting room and the offices, practically sprinting down to the bunkrooms.

There's a light on in the windowless bathroom ensuite to the men's bunk, and Tripp beelines straight for it. As he rounds the corner from the hall, he stumbles, having to grab onto the frame of the door for balance because he's moving too fast, nearly sending himself tumbling headfirst over the twin bed closest to the door. Once he's steady, Tripp takes exactly two seconds to ease off and drag exactly *one* deep breath fully into his lungs.

Calm, he reminds himself. He has to be calm for Lee because Lee needs him.

All day, every damn day, Lee worries about Tripp and puts his needs first. He's *there* for him, in ways that no one in his life has ever bothered to be. It's devastating to Tripp that this is how he's repaid the best person he knows—by completely missing the boat the *one* time Lee needed him to do the same.

If he wasn't so busy cursing himself out for his mistakes, Tripp might be more concerned about what, exactly, he's going to do when he finally gets to Lee's side, but as it is, he doesn't give himself the chance to dwell. He'll figure it the fuck out.

The muted yellow glow of cheap incandescent lighting spills out around the partially-closed door to the bathroom, and Tripp reaches to push it open without hesitation. Despite Gunnar's warning and his own internal self-flagellation, he's fairly unprepared for the sight that meets his eyes.

Lee's back is to him, dressed simply in dark jeans and a blue-gray button down. He looks… okay, at least from behind. Like he's showered and reasonably well-put together, which Tripp can't say that he expected. When he was dropping, he barely had it in him to swipe some deodorant on.

Still, there's a tenseness in the buff line of Lee's shoulders, a stilted awkwardness to how he's folding the flat sheet in front of him. As Tripp stands there and watches, still unnoticed, Lee finishes with the sheet and places it gently atop the pile closest to him. Gunnar wasn't exaggerating about the linen, that's for sure—there are multiple stacks of towels and bed clothes lined up across the washer that all go the better part of the way towards the ceiling.

Heck, Tripp can even recognize a bunch of the oil-rag junk towels they keep down in the bay for spills and maintenance—Lee would have had to sniff those out and drag the bin of scraps all the way up here *just* to wash and fold them. *What the fuck?* As he stares, Leander pauses in his motions, and Tripp thinks that maybe he's finished. His eyes are drawn to Lee's hand as it brushes over the exterior of the pants pocket at his hip, fingers tracing the outline of his phone before clenching into a fist at his side.

Oh, Lee.

Before Tripp can react, Lee reaches out and uses one finger to mechanically tip a stack of towels onto its side, undoing all of his (pointless) hard work. Swallowing the intense urge to call Leander 'sweetheart,' Tripp steps forward and places a gentle hand on his friend's shoulder.

"Lee," he says softly.

Once again, Tripp's unprepared. The look on Leander's face when he whirls around is sad and desperate, his eyes red-rimmed and dark underneath. As soon as he sees Tripp, the puppet strings snap, and Lee loses whatever tenuous grip on his composure he was clinging to.

"Tripp," he mutters, voice filled with obvious relief as he flings himself into Tripp's chest, and Tripp takes back his initial assessment—there's nothing put-together about this.

"Hey," he soothes, letting Leander octopus around him and returning the gesture by wrapping one arm tightly around his back, the other hand cupping his head. "Hey, shh. It's alright. I'm here, Lee. I'm here. Lee, I'm so sorry," he murmurs into Leander's ear, feeling the way his friend's body shakes beneath his hands. "I'm so, *so* sorry. I should've checked my phone. There's no excuse, I didn't even think—"

"It's not your fault," Leander says quietly, pulling back *just* barely enough to look Tripp in the eyes. There's more to his expression than what should be obvious, and Tripp abruptly realizes that there's something going on here other than hormones. That's as far as he can get on his own, though—he's got no fucking clue what Lee might be feeling, and beyond that—*comforting a Dom? Where to even start?*

Tripp's way, *way* out of his depth. The only thing he can do—*and he can do this for Lee*—is use his goddamn words like an adult.

"Lee, talk to me," Tripp says sharply, grabbing Leander by his biceps and steering him over to the toilet. Using his foot, Tripp kicks the lid down and sits Leander on top. It's unnerving how easily Lee lets himself be maneuvered, how little resistance he puts up. If Tripp didn't know any better, he'd think that his cocky Dom who hates demands and loves being obeyed had been body-snatched.

Crouching down in front of the toilet, Tripp rests his hands on Leander's thighs. "You *have* to talk to me," he says. "Listen, sweetheart, I want to help you. I'm not going to leave you, or judge you, or whatever the hell else you're worried about happening, but—buddy, I'm treading water here. Understand? Tell me what you need and it's yours, but *I* need something… " He trails off, tapped out on that analogy.

"To hold onto," Leander finishes weakly, nodding before sighing with apparent exhaustion. For a second, he looks like he's going to launch into some long-winded explanation, but then he just stops and thrusts his hand out, looping a finger through Tripp's belt hole.

"Can you… "

This, Tripp doesn't need to be told twice, and even though it's awkward and there would be a *thousand* better places to do this than the seat of a toilet in the men's sleeping quarters of a firehouse, that's what they have to work with. So he goes—because *this* isn't something he needs explained—straddling Leander easily and drawing him in to his chest.

"Got you, Lee," Tripp murmurs, stroking nails down his back, and finally, Leander relaxes. It's minute, and he can tell that they still have a long way to go, but Tripp can feel Lee melting incrementally into the warmth of his body, pressed tightly between him and the porcelain water tank. God, Tripp hopes that some-day they can look back on this and laugh.

"You smell like fire," Leander observes quietly, mumbling into the fabric of Tripp's shirt, and he sounds a lot more like himself, which makes Tripp smile but also tear up, just a little. Not that Leander can see—he's busy doing his best to make a permanent imprint of his face on Tripp's neck.

"I smell like ass," Tripp retorts, working his roaming fingers against Leander's scalp and hoping that what he's doing is helping, that it's working, that he's be-ing what Lee needs right now. "Showering was pretty high on my list of things to do before you showed up. Is this... ?"

"It's good," Leander replies quickly, arms tightening around Tripp's waist. "Tripp, I am so—" The way Lee is plastered against him, Tripp can see how he shakes, can *feel* the sob that catches in his throat and rattles his chest.

"I'm sorry," Lee manages to blurt out, after a minute that Tripp spends horrified and frozen, unsure of what to do. Still hiding his face, he continues, sounding completely broken, defeated, and miserable. "I'm sorry that I neglected our after-care, and I'm sorry I pestered and didn't trust you to know your own feelings and limits. I'm sorry for showing up here and bothering you now."

"Lee," Tripp starts, but falters. Fortunately, Leander doesn't seem to notice, busy clinging and running hands up and down Tripp's back as he is.

"I *am* sorry, but also, I'm so very relieved you're safe."

"I was fine," Tripp protests. "I wouldn't have left your place if I wasn't. And I wouldn't have hid that from you, if something came on later. Lee, why are you talking like you did something wrong, here?" When Leander just shrugs and sniffles, Tripp abruptly decides that he's had enough. He wraps both hands ar-ound Lee's shoulders and gently pushes him back so they can look each other in the eyes.

Damn, he looks sad. Tripp wants so badly to kiss him, to tell him how much he's wanted and loved. *If ever there was a time...*

But he doesn't give in. Reluctantly, Tripp settles for circling his arms over Leander's shoulders and scratching soothingly into the hairs at the nape of his neck.

"Dude," he says gently. "If anyone fucked up here, it's me. I should have checked in with you at least once. I should have made sure you knew that I was fine. Next time, I will, I promise. I'm glad you came here."

Leander's face flushes with obvious shame. "I shouldn't have *had* to. I know better than this, I—" He breaks off with a frustrated, rough exhale and shakes his head. "I understand that you felt fine today, but I *still* believe I dropped the ball by not allowing for proper aftercare. It's part of why I spiraled. And then I—oh, Tripp, I've been such a mess." The tears well up in Leander's eyes again, and Tripp dries them swiftly with some toilet paper ripped off of the roll to their right.

"Spiral seems like the right word," Tripp offers, trying to be open and neutral so that Leander keeps talking and gives him some sort of clue about where to go with this.

As he watches intently, Lee closes his eyes briefly and nods. "It's very apt. Please believe me Tripp, I trust you to know yourself. I trust you to communicate with me." He motions to his head. "It's… hard to control, as you know, once you're in it. I kept telling myself that I needed to wait, to believe that you were fine and would come to me if you weren't, but I *worried.* And I started thinking about worst case scenarios, how if you *did* drop and perhaps even injured yourself at work because of it—how that would be all my fault. How I would have failed you, how I don't deserve—"

The barely-choked-off sobs threatening to overtake Leander's already questionable composure finally get their way, and he breaks down, shoulders slumping and chin dropping to his chest. He doesn't lean forward to seek comfort from Tripp, and Tripp understands why—Lee is still deep *in* this spiral, still berating and blaming himself. Logic isn't going to cut it, won't work to pull him out.

"I should *never* have pushed to do that scene this morning," he cries as Tripp yanks him close and holds him tight, rocking them gently. "I don't deserve you, Tripp," he continues, barely audible, into Tripp's shirt.

"Whoa, hey, first of all," Tripp interjects, because that's *bullshit,* all of it. "I *wanted* to scene this morning. I asked for it and you gave me what we both thought I needed. Lee, this isn't new territory for us. We tried something, it didn't work. We won't do it again. This ain't any different then any other time that's happened. Buddy, I can't even count the times you stopped a scene or changed the vibe because it wasn't working for one of us. I don't agree that you made a mistake, but if *you* feel that way, you know, I'm not gonna tell you not to feel your fuckin' feelings. They're yours to be wrong about."

In his arms, Lee actually chuckles a little, and Tripp smiles against his hair, pleased that he's not, at least, blatantly making things worse. "I—" *love you, love you so fuckin' much, you idiot. Let me love you, love me back. You deserve love, asshole.* "—need you, Lee. So don't be trying to get rid of me with this, 'don't deserve you' crap, it pisses me off."

"You trusted me," Leander mutters, turning his head so that his ear is against the top of Tripp's chest, but at least what he's saying can be understood now. "You trusted me, and I did... this. I hear you, Tripp, but I still feel... " He trails off, a hand coming up to cover his face. "This drop is telling me that I don't deserve you, that I shouldn't be a Dom at all. When I think about what I put you through when we got together, and *now...* " Leander shrugs sadly, but doesn't resume crying. He just sags listlessly against Tripp's chest and clings.

"Alright," Tripp says slowly, thinking through his next move carefully. "Listen, I could tell you how dumb that is until your ears bleed, promise that you won't feel this way forever, but I know what it's like to be all up in your own head. How about this, you trust me?"

When Leander nods, his hair brushes against Tripp's jaw, tickling it.

"'Kay, give me a minute."

Without getting up, Tripp extracts his phone from his pocket and fires off a text message. Less than five minutes later, there's a knock on the bunkroom door, and Leander jolts upright, alarmed. "Don't worry," Tripp soothes. "It's just Gunnar dropping off my bag. I'm going to get up and grab it, and then I'll be back, okay? It's six o'clock, I'm off duty. I'm not gonna leave you, Lee, you hear me?"

In a role reversal that has even him spinning, Tripp grabs Leander's chin and forces him to look up. "Sir," he adds softly, and Lee's eyes well up again almost immediately, but he nods.

As quickly as he can move, Tripp grabs the duffle bag from where it's been dropped outside the door, not bothering to glance down the hallway and see if anyone's gawking or trying to snoop on them. It's a firehouse, so Tripp's sure there's someone, but fuck 'em. When he steps back inside the bathroom, Leander's still sitting on the toilet, blowing his nose and generally looking like he's working *really* damn hard to keep his shit together.

Closing the door behind him, Tripp drops his bag, turns on the shower, and then strips before dropping into a crouch and removing Lee's shoes and socks.

He doesn't ask permission before taking Leander by the hand and hauling him to his feet, finally following the instincts that tell him to lean in and kiss him softly.

It's meant to be nothing more than reassuring, and Leander seems to take it that way, making a sad little noise in the back of his throat when their lips meet. Wordlessly, Tripp relieves him of the rest of his clothing, folding each piece neatly and leaving them in a pile at the edge of the sink.

By the time they're stepping into the shower—Tripp leading and Leander following him so trustingly—the usually confident Dom is looking slightly less devastated. It's enough of the old Lee peeking through that Tripp feels comfortable in deviating a *smidge* from the panicked *comfortcomfortcomfort* mode he's shoehorned himself into, out of necessity.

Under the hot spray, he drags Leander close and rests one hand at the small of his back, grabbing Lee's wrist with the other before lacing their fingers together.

"Are we… dancing?" Leander asks, a small smile gracing his handsome, if still mournful, face. Tripp just grins down at him and shuffles them around the small space as best he can until Leander gives in and laughs, wrapping an arm around Tripp's neck in tacit approval. The silly dancing evolves into holding each other close, turns into Leander soaping Tripp up, to Tripp kissing Leander against the shower wall, and doing so without even particularly worrying about what it is he's doing.

It's only after, when the water's turned off and Leander is visibly feeling better, when they're dry and buttoned-up into their nice clothing for Beau's rehearsal, that it even occurs to Tripp that what they did in the shower was *not* necessarily within the parameters of their negotiated contract. It *definitely* wasn't platonic friend behavior, either, so what does he do with that? Where does that leave him?

Where does it leave *them*?

Maybe he's thinking too much. Lee needed him, Tripp gave him what he needed. He supposes it's as simple as that. Speaking of which—

"C'mon," Tripp says, looping an arm through Leander's. "You've been in here folding shit for hours, you've gotta be starving. We'll get you a burger on the way to the church, alright?"

Instead of replying, Leander stops him at the bunkroom door, right before Tripp can pull it open. "Thank you," he says simply, letting his arm drop so that he can slip a hand into Tripp's and squeeze. "Not just for—" he motions towards the bathroom. "That. But for trusting me. For believing in us."

Surprised, Tripp squeezes back readily. "I told you," he says. "I need you."

"Yes," Leander replies, holding Tripp's eye contact this time, all on his own, and Tripp finds himself feeling not only relieved, but proud. "I need you, too."

"Then let's go, sunshine."

Chapter 8

It's a wonder what a little food and some affection from Tripp does to turn Leander's mood around, though the bad energy lingers. The inside of his head is still a bit of a jumbled mess, riddled with guilt and the shadows of things that he knows better than to believe in, though they haunt him nonetheless.

It's been years since Leander has experienced a drop like that, not since he first began experimenting in the scene and tried some casual submitting, just to learn what it was like to be "on the other side." While he didn't particularly enjoy the experience of being dominated, it was useful to understand the spectrum of things his potential subs might go through, the emotional highs and lows. For that, Leander is glad that he did it.

Still, he encountered some real assholes in the process, predators branding themselves "Doms" who were really just horny bullies with consent issues wanting to be called "Daddy." These were people who didn't seem to understand that submission is a gift, a privilege, and that *all* subs deserve both respect and something in return for the things they offer up freely.

Thankfully, and perhaps by pure luck, Leander never found himself in a situation where he was in danger, never had an encounter violate his boundaries or escalate further than he was willing to go. He would be lying, though, if he said that his early experiences weren't a significant factor in not wanting Tripp dipping his toes *anywhere* near the local scene. Not on his own, anyway.

Yes, Leander's initial offer to act as Tripp's Dom *was* partially selfish, but on the other hand, he's always been open with Tripp and their mutual friends about the scene and his involvement in it. He's had plenty of conversations with Tripp in the past—both with and without others present—to notice Tripp's interest, to see where it was leading. Especially now, Leander truly believes that if he *hadn't* offered to take him under his wing, it would only have been a matter of time before Tripp sought a Dom for himself.

All of those things came back to bite Leander in the ass today. Never particularly experiencing drop as a Dom (though, now, he's wondering whether some was happening at the beginning of his and Tripp's relationship and he was too focused on *Tripp* to realize it), the intense wave of emotion took him by surprise, to say the least. The feelings themselves were recognizable, sure, but they were also intertwined with guilt and self-recrimination in a way he had no reason to feel back when he was a sub. Thus, it was a lot harder for him to cope.

This crash was centered around *Tripp,* because what isn't when it comes to Leander, these days? More specifically, the drop flooded his brain with all of the times Leander perceived he failed Tripp, the ways he let him down—whether logical or not.

From the very start, Leander promised to keep Tripp *safe.* That was his base reasoning, the concept that pushed him into offering himself up, into looking past the threat of having his secret feelings exposed. It was all for *Tripp's* sake, *Tripp's* well-being. *Leander: Experienced Dom and Caring Best Friend,* was supposed to be the better choice, the *safe* option, the one who would always put Tripp and his best interests first: purely, reliably, and without hesitation.

After today's events, it's clear to Leander that the trust Tripp placed in him to do that very thing has been blown to smithereens. Not once, but *twice,* at that. Firstly when he didn't recognize that Tripp was dropping, or pick up on what Tripp needed to *not* feel that way, and secondly when he didn't trust his gut on *always* creating space and time to *give those things* to both of them.

The hard truth is, they played with fire this morning. Whether Tripp did or didn't actually drop after he left the apartment is irrelevant. That is what Leander has ultimately decided, after copious hours agonizing over the matter, folding laundry and brooding angstily while waiting for Tripp to show up. Facts are facts —regardless of things working out, Tripp *could* have dropped, and if he had, it would have happened because *Leander* relaxed the strict boundaries for the affection and reassurance he *knows* Tripp needs after a scene.

All in the name of, what? *Getting off?*

Sure, Tripp wanted something this morning, perhaps even needed it. That's not in dispute. But Tripp always wants things, always needs them, and it's not *just* Leander's job to deliver, it's his damn obligation to do so *safely.* And if it can't be done safely, it shouldn't be done at all. That's supposed to be rule number one in his own damn playbook.

Admittedly, Leander got caught up this morning. Tripp does that to him, but it's not an excuse.

Around four a.m., Tripp had woken up anxious and flailing around in the bed, very unlike his usual motionless sleep of the dead. Usually, he knocks out like a rock after they scene, hardly rolling over until morning, especially when Leander is curled around him, or vice versa.

Not today.

Most assuredly, Tripp hadn't meant to wake Leander up, but with all of the huffing and flopping he was doing, that was probably inevitable. Some minor coaxing convinced a reluctant Tripp to admit that he was stressed about the day ahead—mostly regarding his leadership role in the fire training scenarios, especially when it came to the new recruits. But that wasn't all—those worries were also piled on top of the self-inflicted stress that comes with being the best brotherly support system he can possibly be, while simultaneously tiptoeing around the two assholes Beau insists on calling his best friends.

At the time, the solution to all of this had seemed obvious to Leander. And to Tripp, of course. Expending stress and anxiety is what he and Tripp *do* together, it's the major purpose their altered relationship serves in Tripp's life. It's what keeps Tripp coming back to Leander's home and his bed, night after night.

And so what if they were pushing the window for decent aftercare? It wasn't the first time. They'd risked a few casual scenes before this, times when one of them had plans to be somewhere else soon after. Although, when Leander reflects back, he *does* realize that none of those scenes ended with *zero* cuddling, and *maybe* he overlooked that, just a little, because it wasn't convenient to his in-the-moment desires.

Selfish.

The bottom line is, Leander truly believes that he put Tripp at risk (again), whether Tripp agrees with his assessment or not. That knowledge makes him feel terrible, like the worst person in the world, *especially* because of how much he loves Tripp. *Especially* because of how he made the man specific promises to never take advantage, to never do this very thing.

The enormity of what he had done overwhelmed Leander. The feelings compounded and dragged him down into a shame spiral, one that made his need to see Tripp—to feel with his own hands that he was *alive* and *okay*, to hear with his own ears that Tripp still *wanted* him, regardless of whether that was right, or smart, whether he should or shouldn't—impossible to ignore.

But once he was *there*, the whole concept of invading Tripp's space at work, of showing up uninvited, of adding to the burden already on his shoulders, of embarrassing Tripp and humiliating himself, and *everything else*—

It wasn't good.

Hence, the folding and the isolation. Channeling his anxiety and rage at himself into something mundane and rote, away from other people but as close to Tripp as he could get for the time being. It worked, enough to get Leander through the fraught and endless hours until Tripp showed up, anyway.

And Tripp—sweet, intuitive, forgiving Tripp—was perfect. Leander is entirely certain that he can never repay him for this. One thing is for sure: if he didn't already love Tripp with every fiber of his being, today would surely have sent him tumbling headfirst over the cliff.

Whether Tripp agrees or not doesn't matter, because Leander *knows* with absolute certainty that he does not deserve this man. While he may get to keep him regardless of that fact, it doesn't make it any less true, and Leander will spend the rest of the time Tripp gifts him with making that (and everything else) up to him.

As he crumples the empty cheeseburger wrapper in his hands, making sure there are no stray crumbs littering the otherwise pristine seats of Tripp's vehicle, Leander can't help but glance over at his friend. His heart races in his chest to find Tripp already smiling back, the lines at the corners of his eyes giving away that he's *truly* happy. He's not playing for Leander's sake, not simply acting because he thinks it's what Leander needs right now (although, that's not incorrect).

All too soon, Tripp has to turn his gaze back to the road, but Leander can't stop looking, can't stop marveling at how *unbelievably* lucky he is to have someone like Tripp in his life. Something twists in his gut, enough that he physically has to put a hand on his stomach. From the moment Tripp walked into the bathroom, to the sweet dancing moment they shared in the shower, to Tripp's kisses and their unexpected exchange of "*I need yous*" back in the bunkroom—Leander might be crazy, might be dreaming, might be straight up seeing what he wants to see, but something *feels* different.

It doesn't help him sort out that question to know that Tripp *was* quite obviously giving everything he thought Leander needed to pull him out of a major drop. That is definitely true, and it *could* explain away the entirety of Tripp's behavior and all of their affectionate interactions. On the other hand, following his gut is something Leander has *always* regretted not doing when it comes to Tripp, both today and any other time that he's resisted or second-guessed himself.

And his gut says something is shifting between them. Something good. Something Leander *wants* more than he can put words to and is afraid beyond measure to name, at least where it concerns Tripp, and how *Tripp* feels about *him.*

If it *is* true, then Leander needs to tread carefully, slowly. Much of his relationship with Tripp, even before they added the BDSM and the sex, was one step forward, two steps back. That's just how Tripp is, and it's taken Leander years to learn how to handle him. This—this *change* in whatever's happening between them—can't be treated any differently.

One agonizingly slow minute at a time, then onto the next.

On a lighter note, Tripp looks positively stunning right now, behind the wheel of his car. Despite his impossibly long day and evident exhaustion, he's beautiful. He's also surprisingly bright, his five o'clock shadow looking intentional and roguish, the tight fit of his button down perfectly accentuating his lovely body, even under his (*not* weather-appropriate) leather jacket.

Of course, Tripp always looks beautiful, but tonight, Leander can't pry his eyes away from him. So much so that he's nearly gawking as Tripp exits their vehicle, stepping out into the evening chill and the dim light of a nearly-set sun looking like a model at a photoshoot.

They're parked at the curb in front of the ornate church where Bri and Beau are tying the knot tomorrow afternoon, and—likely due in part to the near-freezing temperatures—no one is waiting outside to greet them. In fact, the street itself is oddly quiet, traffic low and slow and no one walking on the sidewalks. Perhaps it's the negligent risk that makes Leander brave, but reason aside, when the urge strikes him to reach out and slip one hand into Tripp's, he doesn't think twice.

The residual static in Leander's head, the whispering ghosts repeating that he's *not* good enough, *not* worthy, poof and evaporate like dust in the wind when Tripp turns his face towards him and *smiles.*

Blinding, absolute sunshine, and the light at the end of Leander's sometimes very dark tunnel, he finds himself barely able to breathe with that look directed his way. Whistling and happy as a clam, Tripp fails to notice anything off in his demeanor, and plows ahead. Dragging Leander determinedly up the stone steps of the church, Tripp pulls open one of the *very* heavy wooden double doors and sweeps him inside ahead of himself without pause.

On the other side of the door, Beau, Bri, and their squads of bridesmaids and groomsmen are gathered in the lobby. Leander scans faces and accounts for all of their friends plus Bri's parents. The elder Baileys are lingering off to the side of the main group, standing with Mickey Miller and Reina Harrington. The latter pair are standing in for father and mother of the groom, respectively, and Leander knows personally that Beau is both grateful and proud to have them do so.

Still holding Leander's hand, Tripp waves and grins at everyone, echoing greetings and one-arming hugs, first with Bri and then Beau, angling his body so that he doesn't have to let go. Watching that happen and feeling Tripp's grip only tighten around his palm nearly has Leander losing it all over again. He truly does not deserve someone so *good,* so considerate and constantly giving of himself.

Tripp isn't even wearing his collar, nor did they negotiate anything like this ahead of time. He's just… *Tripp,* holding Leander's hand, because he wants to.

"'Bout time," Christian scoffs when Beau and Tripp separate, despite Beau being nothing but smiles and good cheer at the arrival of his brother. Leander can almost *feel* the room drop twenty degrees just from the icy sneer in his voice, the chilling disdain in his tone. "You two are really making a habit out of being late, huh? No respect for your brother and his wife, always getting up to some bullshit together that's more important than your commitments, aren't you? Wonder whose turn it was this time?"

He's openly mocking, and even Brett puts a hand on his shoulder, mumbling something under his breath that Leander can't hear but makes Christian roll his eyes. Before things can escalate, and they're close—Leander feels Tripp's entire body tensing and radiating anger beside him, so it's just a matter of time—Beau and Bri's officiant sweeps in from the sanctuary and unwittingly saves the couple's rehearsal from devolving into a bloodbath. At least, for the time being.

"Good evening to my happy couple, welcome to all of their beloved family and friends!" The priest is an older man with gray hair and kind eyes, casually dressed in his black clerical shirt, pants, and collar. Seemingly grateful for the distraction, everyone pivots physically to hear what he has to say, budding spat forgotten.

Everyone, that is, except for Tripp, Christian, and Leander. And Mickey, actually, Leander notices—the fire chief is eyeing up Christian with a furious expression that suggests he might actually be more of a danger to the guy than Tripp is, should shit actually hit the proverbial fan. It's only Reina's insistent tugging at his elbow that seemingly keeps him where he is, but Leander's fairly certain that if Christian doesn't knock it off, they all might be attending a funeral tomorrow instead of a wedding.

Even as the priest talks, reviewing the procedures for the next day, the relevant parts of the ceremony, and what each of their roles will be, Tripp and Christian continue shooting daggers at each other with their eyes. Tripp is eventually required to let go of his hand when they pair off to walk down the aisle, but he's escorting Ro, who touches Leander's arm and quietly assures him that she'll have Tripp's back, and that she "has a knife in her boot," a statement that Leander isn't sure whether or not he's supposed to be comforted by.

For his part, Leander's paired with one of Bri's nursing friends, Avery, and the way she eyes him up is the *last* thing he needs to deal with right now. Doing his best to politely blow her off, Leander genially offers his arm and then hums quiet, noncommittal acknowledgment to any comments or flirtations directed his way. The two of them are following directly behind Tripp and Ro in the procession, and Leander goes through the motions of thoughtfully practicing their part, all without dragging his eyes away from his best friend.

"Really gone on him, huh?" Avery murmurs, when they're halfway down the aisle.

Up ahead, Bri's wedding coordinator is hollering at Tripp to, "slow down, take your time, it isn't a race!" from the front of the church.

"What? Oh," Leander replies distractedly. "No, I—" He lifts his eyebrows and shakes his head. "Just hoping to avoid this whole thing turning into a bad tribute to a *Game of Thrones* episode." Avery laughs and leans into his side, very clearly turning on the charm. She's conventionally attractive, and maybe in another time and place, Leander could be interested in getting to know her, but she couldn't hold a candle to Tripp on her best day, and today is *not* that.

At the foot of the altar, he and Avery separate, and Leander takes his place beside Tripp, very intentionally keeping his back turned to the two troublemakers behind him. The rest of the rehearsal flows flawlessly. Tripp producing ring pops from his pocket in place of the real thing, which makes everyone laugh and lightens the lingering tension significantly.

Beau and Bri are adorable. They can't stop touching each other, or smiling and laughing stupidly, the way two people who are madly in love tend to do. Their priest is charismatic and has a good sense of humor, everyone seems relaxed and confident in their roles, and by the time they're all walking out the front door of the church, things actually seem like they might work out. Most importantly, Christian keeps his damn mouth shut.

"You're doing fine," Leander reassures Tripp, as they descend the steps back to his car. The group has temporarily split with the goal of relocating to a restaurant several streets over, and Leander's not unhappy to have a moment alone.

"You can't let him bait you," he continues as they both slide into the car and Tripp turns it around. "Had we not both been through so much today, I'd suggest a bit of 'stress relief' in the back seat before heading inside to eat, but honestly, I think that might be tempting the Gods at this point. If it were up to me, we'd certainly be in bed together right now, but sleeping, not fucking."

That makes Tripp laugh, loud and unexpected, and after he's parked, he reaches out to cup the side of Leander's head, firmly holding his gaze. "Thank you," he says sincerely, his expression sobering. "Dunno how I'd get through this without you. Beau deserves better than me losing my cool over some douchenozzle and his badly-dealt-with internalized homophobia."

Leander just smiles and peels Tripp's hand from his head, threading their fingers together once they're settled in his lap. "I hope you know that I feel the same," he says, and then rolls his eyes. "About you, not regarding the self-hating asshole. Though, I do agree with your assessment."

Something outside the window distracts Tripp before he can reply, catching his attention and making him growl under his breath. Unsurprisingly, it's Christian, flipping them two middle fingers as he passes by the car on his way towards the restaurant.

"Down, Tripp," Leander says immediately, kind but firm as Tripp bristles. He squeezes Tripp's hand. "Be my good boy."

Next to him, Tripp visibly struggles before relenting, relaxing slightly as Christian and Brett head inside and out of sight. "Good boy," Leander reiterates, and Tripp blows out a breath, nodding like he's psyching himself up.

"Yeah," he says, still staring at the restaurant door, and Leander can almost see his mindset shifting, watch the gears turning. Is he—*really?* "Alright. I can be good for you, Sir. That's what Beau would want."

Leander's *floored.* Tripp's slipping into sub-mode by mere suggestion, just to get himself through a difficult moment where he feels as if he *may* lose control. If the two of them hadn't been blurring lines left and right all night, Leander might stop him, might drag him out of it, but this—this is something *new.* This has nothing to do with sex, and it isn't even about *Leander* at *all.* It's a risk, for sure, but it wasn't his suggestion, and maybe it's not his choice to make. If this is what Tripp wants, Leander can support him through it, can look out for and protect him while he works the problem.

After all, that's what he's meant to have been doing all along.

"Let's go inside, Tripp. You can show me how good you can be."

Dinner proceeds smoothly, and Leander is both surprised and impressed at Tripp's motivated demonstration of self-control. Beau and Bri are completely wrapped up in each other, too immersed in their own vibe to be any kind of in tune with what *Tripp* is doing way across the table, but Tripp is fine. Great, even. He's calm, collected, polite, charming. He lets Christian's occasional snide comments roll over his shoulders and off of his back without giving even the slightest indication he's heard them.

Christian hates it. In fact, by the time their salad plates are cleared away, he's seething openly and becoming restless. Still, Tripp doesn't react.

In fact, right before the entrees come out, Tripp actually stands up and gives a lovely, touching toast to the almost-newlyweds, one that brings his future sister-in-law to the brink of tears, and has Beau jumping out of his seat to drag him into a fierce, back-clapping hug. After that and throughout the remainder of both dinner and desert, Tripp continues to be stunning. He makes appropriate jokes, drinks sparingly, and eats politely.

He's *perfect,* he's a vision, and Leander has never been prouder.

Behind the scenes, Tripp is relying heavily on Leander to help him through every move he's publicly executing, but there's no shame in a submissive leaning on their Dom for support. It's support that Leander is more than happy to provide, at that. The truth is, Tripp's doing a lot more via his own sheer willpower than he's likely giving himself credit for.

Every so often, though, he'll turn to Leander, meet his gaze, and something unspoken will pass between them. In return, Leander will hold his hand beneath the table. He'll squeeze his thigh in warning, or lean in to whisper a soft word of encouragement (or reprimand) in his ear, whatever he feels Tripp needs to hear at the time.

It works. They make it through the entire meal and all of the socializing, and the only fight that erupts is a good-natured one over the bill. In the end, Mickey and Reina emerge victorious, and the only threats exchanged are very clearly jokes between family, banter fueled by love as the driving force behind it.

For a minute, Leander thinks they're actually going to pull this off.

And then Christian drops his whiskey on the floor.

It's not an accident—that much Leander understands immediately. Christian is *sloshed,* so drunk that he's unsteady on his feet, which leaves Leander hard-pressed to believe the guy wasn't already half in the bag during the rehearsal. When it happens, everyone is chatting, pulling their coats on, discussing sleeping arrangements for tonight and plans for the next day. Bri and Beau are over in a corner of the restaurant's private room they're all currently occupying, exchanging an extended, sappy goodbye.

On the other side of the table from him and Tripp, Christian raises his tumbler in the air, making brief but pointed eye contact with Leander before slamming it down onto the ground, glass and watered-down whiskey spraying in every direction. Several of Bri's bridesmaids screech and jump away, everyone collectively creating space to avoid both the mess and becoming the target of Christian's sudden, uncontainable wrath.

"No, fuck that," Christian is slurring at Brett, who appears to be trying to talk him into simply putting his coat on and leaving (or perhaps just leaving, fuck the coat). On their side of the table, Tripp pushes his chair back to get to his feet, but keeps hold of Leander's hand. He watches the proceedings with interest but resists jumping in head-first the way that he normally would.

"Tripp," Leander says urgently, standing and leaning in close to Tripp's ear. "You have to trust me, please. Don't react. No matter what happens, I think it's best that you stay out of it. In your current state—"

"See, this is what I'm talking about," Christian interrupts loudly, coming to face-off directly opposite them. Slamming his hand against the table, his fist makes it —and all the glassware on it—rattle and shake. Very slowly, Leander puts a bit of distance between his and Tripp's face, but he doesn't drop his hand. Why should he?

"These two fuckin' *faggots*," Christian continues, gesturing wildly, like everyone in the room *obviously* agrees with and supports his assessment. "Flaunting their disgusting relationship all goddamn night. In a *church,* at that." Christian pauses to make a face and spit on the floor, and Leander marvels at the irony, unable to stop himself from cracking a smile. "Oh, you think that's funny, faggot?"

At his side, Tripp is palpably about to lose it. Leander can tell, and he's not under any delusions—the only reason he has yet to rearrange Christian's face is because *Leander* asked him not to, but he's barely holding on.

A good boy, but not one with endless patience, nor should he be.

"Nothing I am is any of your business," Leander replies evenly, a lot calmer than he feels, even as Mickey takes a menacing step forward.

"Pretty clear you've had too much to drink, son. I think it's time you clear out before I have to go and get ugly, you hear me?" Mickey's tone brooks no argument, but Christian doesn't even acknowledge him, doesn't tear his eyes away from Leander and Tripp—specifically, their joined hands—for *one* fleeting second.

"You're right," he says, presumably to Leander, since his eyes are still locked on their target. "Don't give a shit about you, ambulance driver. It's this *weak*, candy-ass *bitch* giving this family and *Beau* a bad name—"

Except for the short time Tripp was standing to give his toast, Leander has steadfastly held onto his hand since they exited the car. He's terribly remiss to drop it for the first time now, but needs absolutely must. Before anyone else can react, Leander leans across the table, snatches Christian by the tie, and lands a wicked right hook to the side of his face that drops the man cold.

"Talk about me all you like, but don't come for Tripp," he says flatly, watching curiously and with his head tilted to the side as Christian flops bonelessly to the floor, apparently unconscious.

"Holy shit," Beau exclaims from somewhere across the room. He's still hovering in front of Briana, shielding her from the theoretical fight Leander just ended in one fell swoop. Brett has stepped back to cower over by the wall, and the fact that he doesn't even try to come to Christian's defense is enough for Leander not to go out of his way to engage with him.

"Damn, boy," Mickey says with an appreciative whistle, stepping forward to peer down at where Christian continues to be out for the count. "Someone should probably check on him. Or call a bus." He stares for another second before turning on his heel and cheerfully looping an arm through Reina's. "Well, we'll see you all in the morning. Beau, I expect you'll need someone to fill a space at the altar—I'd be honored to stand up for you, boy."

A visibly overwhelmed Beau is nodding, opening his mouth to presumably thank Mickey, but whatever he's about to say is interrupted by Ro bursting breathlessly into the room, back from wherever she's been.

"Lee," she says urgently, "The restaurant is calling the cops."

Beau makes a noise, turning towards where Leander and Tripp are still standing together uncertainly and waving them off. "Go," he says. "I'll talk to you both at home. Go, before they get here."

"I'll handle it," Mickey assures them. "He's right, though. Better that you're not here when they show up."

Leander nods, having full confidence that the beat officers will defer to whatever account Mickey gives them regarding what happened. As City Fire Chief, Mickey holds a lot of clout in this town, a lot of pull with the rank and file in every emergency services department, should he choose to use it. He doesn't throw that influence around lightly, which should make him even more believable today. While it's unlikely that what Leander did will have any lasting impact beyond this room—besides, perhaps, for Beau—he's not about to roll the dice, not when he's being offered a clean exit.

"Thank you," he says gratefully, as he and Tripp toss their jackets quickly over their shoulders.

"Don't thank me," Mickey says gruffly. "You're family. And not just because of that idjit," he adds, nodding towards Tripp, who rolls his eyes. Tripp's been inordinately quiet through this whole thing, and looks surprisingly calm, but as Leander grabs his hand and yanks him towards the restaurant's rear employee exit, Tripp turns a heated expression on him that Leander would recognize anywhere.

They tumble through the back door to the sound of sirens already filling the air, approaching swiftly.

"Car's parked at the front," Tripp points out. "They'll see us, maybe stop us from leaving." He's right, and Leander hesitates, glancing around furtively as the cold wind slips in under his dressy trench coat, making him shiver.

Where can they go?

Behind the building, there's not much. The usual tiny parking lot, dumpsters, some crates for employees to sit on during breaks. The restaurant itself is situated back-to-back with another eatery that faces a city street on the other side, and as such, there's an alleyway in-between, and several more running perpendicular in both directions. Flipping a mental coin, Leander takes his pick, dragging Tripp down one and then another—lather, rinse, and repeat until it feels like they're finally a safe distance away.

He brings them to a stop just below a steam vent, one that happens to be exhaling warm, laundry-scented air. Feeling like a fugitive, Leander turns to look at his friend, to check-in with him and see how he's really doing, now that they're alone. But when he makes eye contact with Tripp, not a single word is needed.

Before Leander even really knows what's happening, he has Tripp pressed up against the cold brick of the alleyway wall and is kissing him soundly. This press of lips is a revelation, so chock-full of relief and desire and every other emotion that Tripp provokes in him regularly, and Leander is *amped* from what went down inside the restaurant.

His knuckles hurt, his heart races, his blood hums hotly in his veins. He's worried and maybe a little scared, angry about the things Christian said, and jazzed that he was finally able to honor the promise he made to Tripp when all of this began. He protected him. Not solely by defending his honor, but by doing the dirty work so that Tripp didn't *have* to. Tripp deserves that and so much more, and *finally,* Leander did something right.

If the way that Tripp is kissing him back is any indication, he agrees. "So fuckin' hot, Sir," he mumbles as Leander's mouth leaves his to bite at his jaw and suck on the tender skin of his neck. "God, Lee—*Sir,* that was so—" He growls and shivers, grabbing Leander's hand and pressing it tight against his groin, where he's *rock*-hard in his pants.

"*Yes,*" Leander murmurs back, unable to come up with anything more articulate, and truly, '*yes*' really does cover the spread.

"Fuck me, Sir, right here, please," Tripp pleads. "Lee, I want you so fuckin' bad."

Too caught up and aroused to correct Tripp's bullshit—aside from a sharp tug to his hair—Leander fumbles with his belt and the closures on his own pants while Tripp yelps in excitement and does the same. Within seconds, both of their cocks are out and sliding together between their bodies, Leander yanking Tripp's thigh up around his own as much as their (*stupid, useless*) pants will allow.

"Lick," he commands, holding up his right hand in front of Tripp's face, having to drop Tripp's thigh so he can use the other to brace his weight against the wall. Tripp complies enthusiastically, drooling spit onto Leander's hand in a way that leaves his mouth shiny-wet and tempting. *Gorgeous.*

"You're a work of art," Leander says softly, and Tripp blushes, shy expression turning wrecked as Leander closes his hand around both of them and strokes.

This is what he loves most about being with Tripp—watching him fall apart. Even out here, in this cold, dark, nasty alley, he's like something that tumbled off of a cloud and fell straight from Heaven into Leander's lap. So bright, so wonderful, so perfect, his pretty mouth falling open as his eyes drift closed, head dropping back against the wall with a quiet thud.

I love you, Leander thinks, and so badly wants to say. I love you endlessly, ferociously, would lay down my life for you in an instant and not think twice.

To stop himself from blurting such things out loud, he leans forward and nips at Tripp's lower lip, sucking it into his own mouth before letting go.

"Kiss me, please," Tripp pants, his eyes cracking open hazy and lovely, and *how* —how *could that make Leander love him more?*

They rock together, somehow both rushed and desperate, clinging to each other and chasing a high that's rooted in violence and discord, but also exceedingly gentle and soft. Tripp comes moaning and sighing with Leander's tongue in his mouth and then drops to his knees, swallowing him down and carrying him over the edge in under a minute.

When it's over, the two of them stand in the cold with foreheads pressed together for entirely too long. Their pants are still unbuttoned, and both of them are beginning to shiver and freeze in the unforgiving night air. Tripp is the first to look up, meeting Leander's gaze with one that's so full of varying emotions, Leander doubts he could trust himself to list them. What he says, though, is the real surprise.

"I'm *so* fuckin' tired," Tripp declares with a bitten-off laugh, which makes Leander laugh, which breaks whatever weird tension might have been hanging between them.

"I've never agreed with you more," he says mildly. "I'm sure the cops have gone by now, and if not—we'll cross the street and come from that direction, I doubt anyone will pay us any mind."

"Thank God," Tripp groans as he does up his pants, and Leander follows suit. "I can't wait to get into bed."

They begin their walk down the alleyway towards the main street, slightly apart. "I can't wait to get into bed with *you*," Leander says softly, reaching out his hand. Tripp pauses, glancing from Leander's face to his fingers and back again, wearing an expression that can't easily be deciphered. Just as Leander's about to worry, he not only accepts the offer, he uses Leander's hand to yank him bodily into his side and kiss him soundly.

"I needed that," is what Tripp tells him when they part, all soft eyes and a tired smile, so Leander simply nods, somewhat dazed. More to the point, though, Tripp doesn't let go of his hand.

New, Leander finds himself thinking. *This is new.*

"Tripp," he says carefully, after a minute, as they continue making their way towards the street and the car. "What... what are we doing here? You and I?"

Next to him, Tripp licks his lips and shrugs, but to his credit, he doesn't rattle off some bullshit answer about 'stress relief'. "I don't know, Lee," he replies, tone revealing nothing. "You got any ideas?"

"No," Leander readily admits. "But, I... I'm not unhappy with it. I like... " He trails off, searching, not wanting to say something he regrets and can't take back. This day has been a *lot* for both of them, and the worst thing Leander could do right now would be to push Tripp into confronting something that he isn't ready to deal with.

But Tripp just nods and brings Leander closer to his side by way of their joined hands. "Alright," he says easily. "I'm good with that."

Leander supposes that for now, he'll have to be good with that too. Surprisingly, he is.

Chapter 9

A morning like this after a night like the last should *not* feel so good. Or maybe —*fuck*, is this how it feels to have a *real* partner? In life, in crime (literal, this time), in—*nope, not there yet,* Tripp thinks to himself, wiggling down into the mattress and refusing to open his eyes, pupils protesting against the tendril of sun leaking around the far edge of his bedroom curtain.

Next to him, Leander is snoring, heavily enough that Tripp can't imagine him waking anytime soon. *Good,* he thinks. It's not that he doesn't want to interact with Lee, he's just *basking* right now. He isn't ready to break this feeling yet, this sense of peace, tranquility, and relief that's infusing the morning stillness. Reasonably sure that he won't be caught, Tripp cracks one eye open and checks out the situation in his room. What he sees has a smile spreading across his face that he couldn't suppress if he tried.

An unconscious Leander is wrapped around Tripp's spare pillow, treating it like a life preserver floating in the middle of the ocean. Usually, that's Tripp's job in the bed, and actually, he's not entirely convinced Lee doesn't think the pillow is him. Especially since their legs are tangled together underneath the covers, leaving Leander sleeping at a weird angle, one that has his body taking up the majority of the mattress space.

Tripp doesn't even care. Fuck, he'd let Lee starfish on top of his face (*mind out of the gutter, Truett*) if that's what he wanted, if that's what was *needed* to make him *stay.* Not that Lee has even remotely required something so lame as a *reason* to spend the night beside him, not for a long time now.

Even last night, outside of a scene and absent any good excuse other than a severe lack of beds, Leander didn't blink. Tripp honestly wasn't sure what he might do, since after all, the surprise lack of groomsmen meant ample couch and floor space were available. Separating was never on the table in Lee's mind, though.

The two of them stumbled into Tripp and Beau's shared apartment long before the rest of the groomsmen—well, whatever was left of them, anyway—made it back from the scene of the crime. In all likelihood, the group was either stuck cleaning up the mess at the restaurant, or drinking away the memory of it over at the Hot Plate. Beau isn't him, though, so Tripp's betting on the former. It sucks that this is how the night before his brother's wedding went down, but Tripp only feels minutely guilty about that. After all, Beau is the one who brought that douchebag into their lives, and Tripp has *zero* regrets about the way Leander effectively escorted him out.

And *damn,* did he look good doing it. So much so, that when they found the apartment empty, Tripp still had Lee's furious, *'I'll smite you,'* expression burned into his brain, and therefore had *plans.* He was *all about* baiting Leander into a little scene, into taking advantage of their alone time before they both knocked out or the other guys came home. Unfortunately, after stripping down to his boxers, Tripp accidentally fell asleep on his bed (*sweet, sweet memory foam)* before Lee even made it back from the bathroom.

To be fair, he *did* have one hell of an exhausting day.

Excuses aside, that meant that not only did Tripp *not* get laid a second time, he also has yet to encounter Beau. The two of them haven't spoken since Tripp left his brother nodding dazedly at Mickey, while he and Lee bravely fled the scene.

By nature, Tripp therefore has *also* not yet faced up to any possible consequences of what he and Lee did, all in the name of… of *freedom,* and—and social justice, and—*oh hell,* Tripp just wanted to watch that asshole take one to the face. Pretty much since the day Beau re-introduced them as adults, aiming for family unity, or whatever. It's bunk, but if that other stuff helps Beau to not be mad at him, then Tripp's not above a couple of little white lies.

Stretching carefully so as not to disturb the sleeping and righteously bed-headed Leander at his side, Tripp slowly extricates his legs and swings them over the edge of the bed. There's barely a token reaction from the pillow-hogging octopus, save for a quiet grumble directed down into the bedding. Watching that, Tripp barely resists the urge to leave a kiss on some part of Lee's plethora of exposed skin.

He scratches an itch on his stomach instead.

Stifling a yawn, Tripp pads down the hall and finds Beau easily, taking up the majority of the space in their tiny kitchen with his giant frame. His brother's not only awake, he's dressed and unpacking ribbon-tied boxes from an oversized, plastic take-out bag marked with the logo of the bakery from down the street that Tripp loves. Behind him, there's a percolating pot of coffee on the counter, and Tripp heads straight for it.

As he passes Beau, Tripp shoulder checks him *hard,* making the Bigfoot-imposter masquerading as his younger sibling grunt and stumble to the side.

"Clown," Tripp grunts, like everything is totally normal.

"Ow," Beau complains, rubbing his bicep for what feels like a goddamn eternity before cracking a smile. "Burnout."

Coffee pot in hand, Tripp stops what he's doing to return Beau's semi-uncertain look with his own grin and a nod of affirmation. To his relief, Beau relaxes in kind as something unspoken passes between them, and whatever tension might have been simmering breaks and dissolves.

Despite the sigh of relief he exhales upon replacing the coffee pot, Tripp knows in his heart that he has no reason to worry. He and Beau may bicker, may piss and moan and make mistakes with each other, but they're *true* family, and they've *always* worked things out. Whatever Beau's reasons were for wanting Christian around, Tripp's already decided that it's something he can and will get past. Beau will talk about it when he's ready, or he won't, and the two of them will be just fine.

It's silent in the kitchen over the next few minutes as both Truetts move around each other easily and in practiced rhythms. It's different for Tripp than at Lee's place or with Lee in general—this sort of familiarity is the kind that feels like *coming home,* like stepping into somewhere safe and familiar after being away for months on end. It's like sitting at a shared table in a childhood home on Thanksgiving, or putting up a tree filled with sentimental ornaments at Christmas.

It's the memory of years and years of shared experiences, both happy and sad, and the way he and Beau have carved *each other* into a place that's so much deeper than DNA or material things they never had.

It's a feeling that's beyond words, and it's not until they're both settled in front of pastries and bagels at the crappy breakfast bar, fake-marble-laminate peeling worse than Tripp remembers at one corner, that Beau breaks the quiet.

"I'm really sorry, Tripp," he blurts out, setting his coffee mug down a little too forcefully.

Black liquid sloshes over the side, and Beau curses under his breath. He reaches for a novelty napkin, plucked from a stack that says, "I need my bro when I marry my ho," which has Briana written all over it. As far as Tripp's concerned, Beau is marrying up. Bri has a *way* better sense of humor than his brother does.

"Ugh," Beau exclaims, wrinkling his nose as he reads the message for himself, which makes Tripp laugh out loud and also feel increasingly relieved. This is *Beau.* They were never not going to work this out.

"Anyway," Beau continues, crumpling the napkin in his hand, "I really messed this up, Tripp, I know it." He pauses, staring down at his plate, so Tripp does the same, never being particularly good at showing his own emotions. "I know this doesn't make it right, but the hospital is cutthroat, man. Back when I was a resident, there were five of us competing for *one* attending spot the next year. Christian—"

Beau cuts himself off, groaning in frustration. He ruffles his own hair before sighing and letting his shoulders droop. "It was more than just *family* with him, more than obligation. He took me under his wing, he had my back. Whether you believe it or not, he's a really good doctor, Tripp."

Tripp snorts but otherwise remains quiet, reserving airing his thoughts out loud for another time. Beau's entitled to his opinion, and Tripp's no doctor himself, but he's *reasonably* sure that being empathic and non-judgemental when it comes to others' differences are important qualities for one to have. Factually speaking, those are traits that Christian is sorely lacking. A person can have all the knowledge in the world, all the technique and skill in the palm of their hand, but if they don't care about *people,* they're missing the entire point of saving lives.

Doctor or not, Tripp knows all about that, firsthand.

He clears his throat. "So, he made you feel like part of the team. Had your back with the big bosses. Got you that cushy, six-figure job you like so much. Pop a shoulder back in place, buy a new Lexus. Gangbanger with a knife to the gut? Couple stitches, bam! Money in the bank." Tripp knows he sounds like an ass, but it's intentional banter between them, testing the waters, and Beau passes. He rolls his eyes, elbowing Tripp in the ribs.

"Earlier this week, I repaired a bullet wound that caused cardiac tamponade. Red Room activation, open chest, *in* the trauma bay, with none of my usual OR support staff or equipment. Guy's wife is pregnant."

"Alright, alright, you're a fucking hero. Don't have to tell me twice."

Beau laughs, but his smile fades quickly. "Tripp, all of that aside—it's not an excuse. Listen, I knew Christian could be an asshole, but I thought—okay, I don't know what I thought. Sometimes two people just don't get along and it's not deep, you know? I figured your personalities didn't mesh. I knew he could be a jerk, but honestly, Tripp, until last night I didn't know he *meant* it. Sometimes guys like that, they say stupid things."

Tripp stops chewing mid-bagel-bite to bestow an incredulous, *are you fucking serious?* look on Beau that he's sure would make Leander proud. Or maybe earn him a spanking—either way's a win. Beau glances over, his shoulders drooping again as he registers the face, while Tripp tips his head to the side in order to make his nonverbal message even more pointed.

"I'm serious, Tripp!" Beau persists, despite his defeated stature. "Yeah, I hear you, it sounds stupid. But it's the truth."

Tripp opens his mouth and sticks out his tongue loaded with chewed food to express what he thinks about that. Beau just sighs and drops his fork, because he's been cutting his bagel into tiny pieces like he's eighty. *Good luck, Briana.*

"You're right. You're right. It's not like I haven't been thinking about the same shit all night, ever since you guys left the restaurant. You're good, by the way," Beau tacks on, hitching a thumb over his shoulder in the direction of Tripp's room, and presumably, his criminal best friend. "Mickey took care of everything, and Brett didn't say one damn word to argue with his version of events."

Brett. They're definitely circling back to that dude later. Tripp makes a mental note, as Beau continues talking.

"But I just kept thinking, *how* did I not realize he was that kind of person? That he was *serious* when he put you down, when he made jokes about *patients…* " Beau trails off, looking a little green around the gills and genuinely upset, his hacked-up breakfast now completely abandoned in front of him. And maybe Beau's made mistakes, sure, but Tripp would forgive his little brother anything, least of all this. The majority of the mess is all on Christian's head, anyway.

"Beau," he starts, reaching out a hand to squeeze his brother's bicep, but Beau shakes him off.

"No, Tripp," he says firmly. "I'm not looking for your sympathy, or whatever. I fucked up. Christian is family and he's done a lot for me, but I never should have let those things overshadow what a goddamn *asshole* he is. Tripp, I've always thought I was pretty smart, practical."

"You are—"

"I wasn't, though," Beau interrupts, turning on his stool to more fully face Tripp, and he's angry now, very clearly at himself. "Christian showed me who he was and I didn't believe him. Even before last night—I told you, he said things about patients, too." Beau goes quiet for a second and then raises his eyes, looking resolved.

"I'm going to make this right, Tripp. I'm done with him, first of all, I don't care what anyone else from their side of the family says about it. *Our* family comes first. And shit, if *they* accept his behavior, that says it all, doesn't it? But beyond that—I'm going to talk to our superiors about his attitude, about my concerns regarding his bigotry and how it may be affecting patients. Can't guarantee they'll do anything—he's a surgical star at Central—but I'll try, and I won't stop trying."

Beau looks so fervent, so desperate for his absolution, that Tripp can't help but give it to him. It's what he's always done for his baby brother, and it feels kind of right that they're getting back to their roots on his wedding day. Anyway, so what if Beau got lost? No one's perfect, least of all *Tripp,* and if he has faith in anything, it's that Beau will be true to his word. Tripp absolutely believes that he'll do everything possible to make things better.

"'Course you will, Bozo," he replies around another mouthful of bagel, reaching out again to clap Beau on the back. Swallowing and dusting off his hands, Tripp struggles as the bagel goes down a little rough, his bite too big. "So, about Brett —"

"He's not like Christian," Beau rushes to reply. "I mean, maybe he's not *great,*" he amends. "At least, these days. But he was never the way you've seen before I introduced him to Christian. I feel like it's sort of my fault. He's here," Beau adds, nodding his head towards his own room. "Slept on my blowup mattress. Not that you should feel any obligation to hear him out, but he told me that he wants to apologize to you and Lee. Not that—I mean, Tripp, I wouldn't blame you if you didn't forgive *me,* never mind some guy you barely know, but—"

"Listen," Tripp interrupts, sensing that his brother is about to dissolve into an unfixable ramble. He stands up and puts his plate in the sink before returning to Beau's side and resting a hand on his shoulder, one finger pressed pointedly into his chest. He waits until his brother makes eye contact before continuing.

"Shut up. I heard you, and I promise I'll think about everything you said. Maybe. Alright, I'll at least listen if you need to talk about it sometime in the future. But you and me? We're good. Everything else? Gravy. This is your day, Bozo. I'm your best man, it's my job to do exactly three things. One, keep a beer in your hand. Two, Bri's ring in my pocket, and three, steal the whole damn show with my good looks and the best wedding toast in history. Simple as that. You just find your way to the altar and I'll be right behind you. Got it?"

Like the big, sappy, gentle giant he is, Beau's eyes rapidly fill with tears as he nods, and Tripp isn't remotely surprised when he stands up to drag him into a hug.

"Alright," Tripp says gruffly, patting Beau's shoulder blade and acting mock-grumpy. Secretly, he *loves* every second of having his brother back, rescued from the jaws of that homophobic piece of shit for good.

Actually, he thinks, fuck it. It's Beau's day, he deserves to hear the truth.

"Love you, man," Tripp grunts at a nearly inaudible decibel, attempting to pull away and flee before Beau can—

"Dammit, Tripp," Beau sobs, yanking him back with a grip that Tripp is not nearly strong enough to break. "I love you, too. So much. You're the most important family I have, and—"

"Oh Jesus, Beau, don't make it weird," Tripp groans, finally extricating himself from the soggy Sasquatch and high-tailing it back to his room. "Don't follow me, we've hugged enough for one decade."

"You can't take it back!" Beau calls after him, like the unrepentant brat he's always been. "You love me!"

"I do not," Tripp grumbles, slamming the bedroom door behind him.

***

Hours Later

"I have a surprise for you," Leander says, when Tripp returns to the bedroom with both of their tuxes, each hanging in its respective garment bag. They still have the better part of two hours until the wedding, but the photographer will be here soon, and the limo to take them to the church should be arriving shortly after. So much for Tripp's plan to talk Lee into letting him blow off some steam before having to behave in public.

Oh, well.

There's always Plan B, and Tripp's got the commitment to prove it. In fact, he's already wearing his collar wrapped around his wrist, and under Lee's instruction, he prepped and popped a plug in when he showered.

Dear God, he thinks. Please never, ever let Beau find out we used his wedding as elaborate foreplay.

"What's that?" Tripp asks Lee, doing his best to both refocus (for Beau's sake) and sound nonchalant (for his own).

Currently, Leander is hanging out on the other side of Tripp's bed, wearing nothing but a threadbare t-shirt and boxers, and he looks ridiculously angelic haloed by the noonday sun streaming in through the window. While Tripp hangs the two garment bags over the door to his closet, Lee rummages inside his duffle, surfacing with a coiled length of thin, white rope raised triumphantly in one hand and his eyebrow deviously quirked.

"Oh, *hell* yes," Tripp agrees immediately, pulling his own shirt swiftly over his head without an ounce of hesitation. "Boxer-briefs?"

"Take them off," Leander instructs, patting the edge of the mattress next to him, and Tripp nearly trips over his underwear trying to lose it, stumbling in his hurry to obey. Leander's stern expression turns amused but fond as Tripp sits down, back ramrod-straight, eager to please.

"I thought you might appreciate some grounding today," he explains, pulling lengths of the soft rope absently through his hands, like he has no idea what it's doing to Tripp, having to sit still and watch.

Tease.

"Yes, Sir," Tripp replies eagerly, and then more calmly, "thank you, Sir."

Rolling his eyes a little, Leander steps between Tripp's legs and cups the base of his skull, gripping his hair for leverage to tip his head back so that they're making eye contact. "One thing I would like for you to think about," he says, "is whether you'd be open to taking some pictures later. I would love to add onto the harness I'm going to tie for the wedding, to suspend you from the ceiling and push you to the edge of your limits. And I would *love* to take some pictures of how incredible you look while that happens. Something for us to have, to look back on. Perhaps even frame and hang in the playroom."

Up until that point, Tripp was all-fucking-in for *whatever* kinks Leander wanted to break out tonight, but that last sentence has him tripping inside his own head and nearly choking on his tongue. *"Frame?"* he sputters, holding up a hand. "Let me get this straight. You want naked pictures of me on the walls of your house?"

Leander just smirks and shrugs, releasing Tripp's hair to loop the soft, satiny rope around the back of his neck, twisting each side together across the middle of Tripp's chest, dead-center over his sternum. "If you're self-conscious, perhaps we should have some taken together. Then we can both be on the walls of my house."

That proposition makes Tripp's mouth go completely dry for more than one reason, and thankfully, that seems to be Leander's intention, because he doesn't look for a reply. Instead, he sets about weaving a fairly simple diamond harness over Tripp's torso. It's just as well—there aren't many non-sexual aspects of his and

Lee's relationship that Tripp enjoys more than this, and he relaxes easily into Leander's touch, relishing the feel of the rope sliding across his bare skin.

"Comfortable?" Leander murmurs as he nears the bottom of Tripp's abdomen, touching his hip in a nonverbal directive to stand, which he understands and obeys intuitively.

"Yes, Sir," he replies, his voice breathy, and if this was anyone other than Lee, that would be embarrassing. By this point, he and Leander have dabbled in shibari quite a few times, and suspension is a favorite for both of them, but Tripp's not yet had the opportunity to wear one of his Dom's woven creations in public. They've discussed it, mostly as an option for Lee to *'be with'* Tripp when he isn't physically able, but the majority of the time they spend apart lately is for work.

Everything else aside, wearing something like that underneath firefighting gear could be a safety risk, a hazard to Tripp's health. If something disastrous were to happen where seconds matter, the paramedics having to cut through his harness could be the difference between life and death for Tripp. And God forbid that paramedic be *Lee*—neither of them had to say it aloud to understand that Lee wouldn't survive that happening on his watch.

Suffice it to say, shibari at work isn't an option for Tripp.

Today, though, Tripp can't *wait* to be out there with his and Lee's little secret tied beneath his clothing. Maybe he should be more worried, more careful—after all, he'll definitely be expected to do a shit ton of hugging, all day long. But the rope is thin, and his dress shirt and jacket are thick, which should take care of hiding the goods. Plus, anyone who *does* feel something will probably just assume he's holstered and carrying discreetly, because everyone around here does.

After the business with Christian last night—which Tripp is positive has ripped through the emergency services community like wildfire—no one would blame him, either. Regardless, if anyone has something to say, that's the lie Tripp's prepared to serve cold.

Oblivious to his inner monologue, Lee is busying wrapping loops around each of Tripp's thighs, adding a few twists that result in the rope wound snug at the base of his cock and around his balls. A careful tie-off is situated near his hip so that it won't stand out, and then they're done.

"I know that I specified 'later'," Leander starts, openly admiring his work and the way Tripp's dick has plumped up significantly from the incidental contact. "But could we circle back to the photography question early? I would love—"

"Do it," Tripp interrupts, catching Leander's surprised gaze head-on and with confidence. "Sir."

Fake it 'til you make it, right? He can do this. He *wants* to do this. Still, Tripp's unprepared for Leander to surge forward and knock him onto his ass on the bed, to straddle his hips, grab him roughly by the hair, and kiss him like his life depends on it. Their positioning makes it easy for Tripp to rock up into the sweet friction of Lee's barely-clothed groin, moaning into his mouth without reservation, and *hoping.*

But Leander's a man with a plan.

"No, Lee, come *on,*" Tripp pleads when Leander slides backward off of him, his stupid white grandpa boxers tented fully now, but Lee doesn't even seem to register the change. Without responding to Tripp's whines, he snatches his phone from the nightstand and swipes open the camera, centering Tripp in the frame with focused intent. Tripp doesn't bother to hide his disappointment.

"You can pout," Leander tells him, unbothered. "You're very sexy when you pout." Tripp rolls his eyes and Leander glances up sharply. "Do *not* ruin this by turning into a brat," he warns.

They really don't have the time for Tripp to test Leander's patience, so he nods and grabs the base of his dick, looking towards the camera through the fan of his eyelashes. He's not naive—Tripp knows exactly what he looks like all tied up and splayed-out, propped on one elbow against messy, unmade sheets. That's gonna be one hell of a picture, and suddenly, Tripp finds himself warming to the idea of Lee maybe taking a *few* more featuring only him, after all. He's already all-in for the rest of Lee's suggestions, no convincing needed.

Without warning, there's a loud knock at Tripp's bedroom door, followed by Beau's voice filtering in from the other side. "The walls are *thin,* you know," he yells, less irritated than Tripp would expect, but clearly exasperated. "You think you two could keep it in your pants for *one* day? Just one."

"Sorry, Beau," Leander calls back, sounding apologetic. "We're behaving, truly. Although, you were right not to come in."

"Uh-huh. I'm sure. Photographer is here, by the way, and whatever 'getting ready' you guys are doing isn't something I was looking to capture for the wedding scrapbook, so. If you wouldn't mind?"

"Be right out, Bozo. You *sure* you don't want pictures of this, though?" Tripp chimes in, unable to help himself. Both he and Lee suppress laughs while listening as Beau shuffles away, grumbling loudly.

"Ironic phrasing," Leander says, holding up his phone. "Do you want to see?"

"*Hell* yes," Tripp replies enthusiastically. "But I'm also kind of worried that if I look, we aren't going to make it out that door without Beau's soul leaving his body. So—"

"Raincheck," Leander agrees with a nod, reaching for the garment bag with his name on the front and tugging open the zipper. "Tonight."

"Tonight," Tripp echoes, returning Leander's smile with a genuine one of his own.

***

The next few hours are a blur for Tripp. The photographer takes candid photos of all of the groomsmen, half-dressed and scattered around Beau and Tripp's apartment. Shots of them fixing bow ties and clinking beers together, supposedly looking casual while being weirdly posed. Tripp hates it, but he doesn't say a single word, because Beau is *so* damn happy his cheeks must hurt from smiling.

Tripp's pretty sure the photographer catches the moment that Beau walks out of his bedroom looking like a groom, and Tripp loses it like he's pretty sure only the bride and the mother of the groom are supposed to do.

Well fuck it, Tripp thinks. *He's* Beau's mom, much as anybody is. *And* his dad, *and* his damn big brother, and for well into Beau's teen years, he was Santa-freaking-Claus, too. Tripp's pretty sure he's entitled to a couple of sappy tears on today of all days.

After multiple checks to ensure that they have everything that needs to come along to both the church and the reception venue, Beau's entire entourage heads outside. To Tripp's dismay, the casual-force-posed picture-taking is repeated under the sun and in front of random trees, next to the limo, and—by Tripp's insistence—in front of Engine Fifteen when the crew stops by to wish Beau well.

At least when things get tedious, Tripp has the reassuring comfort of the ropes hugging his body to soothe and calm him, tempering his natural tendency towards impatience and irritation.

Plus, Lee is by his side pretty much the whole time, which also helps a *not*-small amount. The limo ride to the church ends up being a lot more fun than the picture taking, and includes as much beer as Tripp can drink during the twenty-minute trip (four). By the time they're all lining up in the back of the church, he's feeling pretty damn good. Pretty damn *happy.*

In fact, Tripp is relatively sure that he could put up with nearly anything this day might throw at him, all in the name of being the most stellar Best Man Beau could freaking ask for. He deserves it.

Even when Beau heads off down the aisle on Reina's arm, and the doors to the main church swing closed behind him so the girls can file in and pair off, Tripp manages to hold it together. *No emotion, no tears.* Not with such a giant audience waiting on the other side to judge him. Even Tripp has his limits.

Right before the music starts and the wedding coordinator motions for him and Ro to start the long walk towards the altar, Tripp glances back over his shoulder to send a tipsy wink Lee's way. Lee must be feeling pretty good himself, because he doesn't even admonish or scold Tripp, just smiles softly and shakes his head before mouthing the word, "Behave."

Tripp does, save for a few devilish winks at elderly ladies in pews, and the entire party makes it to the altar unscathed.

The ceremony is beautiful. Flowers everywhere, lots of that white, gauzy shit draped over the seats and the altar itself. Tripp digests the display from Beau's side, deciding that Bri did a bang-up job on the place.

The whole church stands when "Here Comes the Bride" plays and Briana enters, and Tripp, fully-prepared, has a handkerchief ready to hand off to the emotional groom. Hundreds of Beau and Bri's family and friends line the aisle, but the two of them only have eyes for each other. As Tripp watches his baby brother tear up seeing his almost-wife make her way towards him, it's a much more sobering moment than he thought it would be.

Beau is *grown,* and somehow, that's *startling.* It's not as if Tripp didn't know that already, he's known it for years. And yet, it's never been demonstrated—never been shoved in his face—*quite* so clearly as this.

Bri, with her starry-eyes and bright smile that's for Beau only—*she* is Beau's future, not Tripp. While he and Beau will always be family, always be irreplaceable in each other's lives, they aren't the *only* thing each of them has to lean on any longer. Beau has Bri, and Tripp—Tripp's alone.

Except, no.

No, he isn't, Tripp realizes, feeling the barest tips of Lee's fingers nudging at the edge of his palm. It's a gentle, careful reassurance, designed to make Tripp feel safe and supported but not to steal the show. Lee *knows* him, likely knows exactly what he's feeling right now, and he cares enough to reach out. And while Tripp can't bring himself to tear his gaze away from his brother exchanging his vows, he does have the strangest thought go through his mind, one that he can't quite shake loose.

It's the idea that—if he *did* turn and look at Lee—he might find him looking back with the same expression that Bri is wearing while smiling up at Beau, right now.

That thought scares and excites him so much and in equal measure that Tripp can't bring himself to glance Leander's way at *all*. At least, not until Beau and Bri have been pronounced "husband and wife," and the whole party has paraded back down the center aisle of the church, ushered off into one of the side rooms so that everyone in the cheap seats can exit and form their rice-throwing lines outside.

Inside the cramped holding area, Tripp gets about four seconds to congratulate Beau before his newly-hitched self is swept away by other members of the bridal party, a whirl of back-slapping, face-kissing, and loud cheering erupting before the happy couple manages to break away and steal a moment for themselves in a far corner.

As Tripp watches them cup each others' cheeks with a wistful little smile on his face, an unmistakable presence appears by his side, accompanying giant hand coming to rest at the small of his back.

"Hey, Lee," Tripp says, finally glancing over to find Leander looking back exactly the way he always stares at Tripp, and somehow, that's even more confusing.

"Hello, Tripp," Leander replies, holding his gaze from just a *few* inches too close for two (otherwise) platonic (fuck) buddies, and it's right then when Tripp realizes that *maybe* the answer is that Lee has been looking at him this way all along.

"Alright, everybody line up! Opposite order as the procession, please. Bride and groom, you'll be bringing up the rear." The wedding planner calls out instructions from where she's popped only her head into the too-small space. Tripp can't help but think that if Christian was here, her remark would have definitely been turned into a dig at him and Lee, so thank *fuck* he isn't.

Their exit from the church is cliché and cute, rice raining down over all of their heads while the crowd cheers and the girls yell and try in vain to cover their carefully-styled hair. With the procession reversed, Tripp and Ro are following Lee and Avery to the limo, and *Lee* is the one who turns to wink over his shoulder this time. He's all bright smiles and perfect, rice-strewn hair to match his gorgeous tux, everything Tripp ever wanted all wrapped up in a fancy, bow-topped package for today.

Tripp's chest aches.

There are more pictures. *Lots* more pictures at multiple locations, and no alcohol to make the taking of them more tolerable. Tripp grins and bears it, because it's for *Beau,* but even inside the limo, he's not having any fun. The beer and champagne have long-since run out, and Lee gets stuck several seats away from him, no matter how Tripp tries to position them otherwise, each and every time they pile in and out of the vehicle.

By the time the bridal party makes it to the reception venue, Tripp's harness isn't doing jack shit for his mood, and he's ornery enough to consider making amends with Christian if the reward would come in the form of a double whiskey on the rocks. Things get better once Mickey makes that wish come true for both of them, and Tripp's never been more grateful for his and Beau's surrogate father. That's saying a lot, considering this weekend alone.

Bri and Beau's reception is being held at a swanky hotel downtown, and the ballroom the party is set up in sits right off of the hotel lobby. Just inside the open double doors to the room, the lights are dim, the disco ball is spinning, and the DJ is talking, getting ready to announce the wedding party's big entrance. Furtively, Mickey and Tripp gulp down their drinks in a far corner of the hallway, and then ditch both empty glasses in a decorative ficus.

Looking significantly happier, Mickey wipes his mouth and claps Tripp on the shoulder before taking his place in line behind Brett and in front of Lee. Ahead of them all, Sandy and one of Bri's friends are already dancing their way into the ballroom to the sounds of "Marry You" by Bruno Mars.

Tripp rolls his eyes—*talk about cliché.*

The two fingers of whiskey hit his bloodstream in a rush, mellowing him out more and more the closer he gets to the door. The alcohol also serves to relax his limbs and smooth his rough, antsy edges, which is *maybe* why he misses the covert glances being exchanged between Ro and Avery, right over Leander's shoulder.

Minutes later, when Lee and Avery are up to bat and the DJ is calling their names, Tripp's feeling pretty damn good again. He's dancing in place, swaying his hips to the music and bopping his head along to the beat. Ro is hanging casually on his arm, more or less doing the same by his side, until very suddenly, she's *not.*

As Tripp stands there and gapes, she friggin' *bolts,* rushing forward to hip-check Lee aside and take Avery by the arm. Even *more* surprisingly, Avery laughs openly and lets herself be swept out onto the floor, where she and Ro break it down like the two scheming assholes they are.

To his credit, the DJ pivots easily, announcing the correction with humor and grace, and the girls wave their bouquets and lean into each other affectionately as they skip happily off to the right of the dance floor. Tripp's so busy being confused and then watching the show they put on that he doesn't even realize he's been set up until it's *way* too late to do anything about it.

And then there's Lee, looking twice as surprised as he feels, but still offering up an arm, and—*God damn it, and now he's the* girl, *too. Fuckin' Ro.* Tripp's gonna put a laxative in her martini.

Oh, hell.

With a shake of his head and a resigned sigh, Tripp takes Leander's arm and allows himself to be led out onto the dance floor, under the sparkling disco ball. He leans into the buzz he has going, biting his lip and shaking his ass to the beat, like the rhythmless white boy he knows he is.

Of course, that isn't good enough for Lee, who gets a wild hair up his ass and takes Tripp by the hand, sending him whirling and twirling underneath his own fucking arm until suddenly he's falling—and humiliatingly, *screeching*—backward. Lee catches him in a dip, grinning down at Tripp's answering scowl with poorly-concealed smug satisfaction.

"Dick," Tripp grumbles, but that only makes Leander's smile widen as he sets him gently back on his feet.

"Kiss!" Someone yells out from the crowd, and the rest of them laugh while Tripp jumps back hastily, abruptly realizing that he's standing *way* too close to Leander.

"Whose wedding is this?" Beau calls out from where he and Bri are lingering in the open doorway, just as the Bruno Mars song is coming to an end. It's clearly good-natured, but as an apology, Tripp darts back across the dance floor to grab his brother's face and lay a sloppy kiss on his cheek. He waves apologetically to the crowd as he skates away again, finding his way back to where the bridal party is lining the edge of the dance floor and sliding in between Ro and Lee.

"That was *so* not cool," he mutters to Ro as the room explodes around them, everyone cheering and clapping for *the new Mr. and Mrs. Truett!*

Ro gestures vaguely to her ear and smirks. "Sorry, can't hear you!"

While his friends are definitely assholes, Tripp's seething over their plotting against him lasts only until the end of Beau and Bri's first dance. The adorable sappiness of his brother's pure, palpable joy succeeds in melting the ice cube Tripp assumes he has in place of a heart, at least enough that he's once again ready to get his drink and party on.

Several drinks, what feels like a thousand hugs, dinner, and a round of semi-memorable toasts later, the reception is in full swing, and Tripp finally feels like he can relax. While most of the guests are out jumping around and grinding on the dance floor, Tripp's lurking by the bar, stealing a few quiet moments with his old friend, Mister Macallan. The whiskey is smooth and hot in his throat, and Tripp savors every drop, so much so that he doesn't notice the figure sidling up beside him until it's too late to escape.

"Fancy meeting you here, Acid Tripp." Autumn's sultry voice cuts into Tripp's peaceful reverie, making him grimace. "Oh, relax," she says, presumably when she notices his eyes start to roll. "I'm not your enemy, you know."

"Why are you even here?" Tripp doesn't make eye contact, just signals the bartender for a refill and drinks half of it way faster than a whiskey of that caliber deserves.

"I transferred to Bri's floor at Central earlier this year," Autumn explains and Tripp nods, already sick of the small talk, but she doesn't leave. "We're friends. Seriously, relax, dewdrop. I just came to say hello. Figured Lee would be with you, but I don't see him."

"He's around."

"Hmm," Autumn hums noncommittally, sipping from her own drink and leaving a bright red lipstick smear on the rim. It twists Tripp's stomach a little to see, makes him wonder—however irrationally and against his will—if she ever left marks like that on Lee. *Damn,* but he's becoming a possessive son of a bitch, not that he has any right to it.

"Anyway, like I said, no need for the cold shoulder." Autumn continues talking, oblivious to his inner turmoil. "You know, you and me? We have a lot in common, not the least of which is wanting the best for our boy."

"Yeah, well," Tripp replies, dropping his tumbler onto the bar just a *little* harder than necessary before scanning the crowd for the *boy* in question. "Wanna get technical, Lee isn't my boy or yours. He isn't anybody's anything, not like that. Guess that's another thing you and I have in common—getting bitch-slapped by that reality the hard way."

Finally, Tripp's eyes alight on his target. He's on the dance floor with Marley, being cajoled into learning the robot. Lee is stiff, awkward, and way too serious as he goes through the stilted motions Marley demonstrates and then prompts him to copy. There's no sign of the dapper dancer who flung Tripp around so easily earlier—*this* is a lot closer to the Lee that he knows and loves. Teaching the guy the robot is a little on the nose for Tripp's taste, but Marley and the other girls gathered nearby are laughing uproariously.

In Tripp's peripheral vision, Autumn shifts so that her elbow is on the bar and she's facing him, smirking, waving her hand like she's reading his aura. "I know you're all… uptight or whatever with your little feelings, but the pissy anger you're throwing my way is *so* misplaced. That's all I'm saying. Between the two of us, I'm not the danger to Simba. You are."

That gets Tripp's attention, and he snaps his gaze back to his uninvited company, incredulous and touching a finger to his ear. "Gonna have to run that one by me again, because I *know* you did not just imply I would ever intentionally hurt Lee."

Autumn wiggles a little against the bar, her smile never faltering as she scrutinizes Tripp's face. "You're right, I didn't. I *implied* that you *could* hurt him. Never said anything about intention. And if you're really as oblivious as you're playing right now, then I was right to say so. Honestly, you two dumbasses can't see what's right in front of your adorable little noses." As if to make a point, she reaches out and boops Tripp on his, making him reflexively scrunch his face in response.

"Hey," he protests.

With a shrug, Autumn grabs her drink and saunters off. "If you geniuses ever manage to pull your heads out of your asses and stick with each other for the long haul, feel free to call me up when things get boring. I think the three of us would have a magical time together."

Normally, Tripp would respond with something snarky, but even *his* repertoire is empty for a snappy comeback to the man he's in love with's *ex* propositioning them for a threesome. Probably for the best—some things are better just left alone. Shaking himself off, Tripp returns to his drink and finishes it up.

Having been at the bar for the better part of an hour, Tripp is once again pleasantly drunk, but his interaction with Autumn has him on edge. Well, that, and the way the stool he's been occupying shifts the plug in his ass every time he moves, but mostly the first thing. It's not as if Autumn *implied* anything Tripp wasn't already beginning to suspect regarding Lee, but still. It's definitely more unsettling hearing the speculation from a third party.

A third party, who—arguably—knows Leander better than most other people on the planet. Who has no reason to lie, much as it may pain Tripp to admit that (and he never will out loud).

Still conflicted, Tripp gets to his feet and starts wobbling across the room towards the dance floor. On his way, he passes the dessert table and does a double-take because the spread is a wet-friggin'-dream. Bri and Beau cut the cake a bit ago, so there are copious slices of richly-frosted marble pastry laid out, but there are also pie squares, a chocolate fountain, and candy in bowls with big metal scoops. Tripp's liquored-up brain suddenly can't decide what he wants more, Lee or sugar.

Sugar with Lee, his brain decides helpfully, and Tripp pivots back in his original direction, vowing to grab his friend and drag him back to plunder the table.

As he approaches the dance floor, the current upbeat song ends and a slow one begins. The crowd circling Leander looks visibly bummed, most of them dispersing, breaking off to head back to their tables for well-deserved drinks and a rest. By the time Tripp reaches his friends' sides, Marley and Lee are slow dancing like two Catholic school kids at a middle school social. Rocking awkwardly at least two feet apart, afraid the sisters are going to smack them with rulers while insisting they "leave room for the Holy Spirit!"

When Marley catches Tripp's eye, she grins and drops her hands from where they're resting high on Leander's shoulders. "Don't mind me," she squeaks, stepping away and melting into the crowd before Tripp can so much as get a word in edgewise.

"Hello to you too, Marley," he says to the empty space Marley's vacated, and Leander chuckles, stepping into it and dragging Tripp close. Without hesitation, Lee's hand finds its way to the small of Tripp's back, the other confidently interlacing with one of his. Very sexy, very *not* Catholic-middle-school-dance. Uncaring of who's watching, Tripp wraps his free arm around Leander's neck and allows their torsos to be pressed together, shoulders all the way down to their groins.

Now, Tripp's drunk, but he's not *so* drunk that he doesn't realize how intimate, how *publicly intimate* that move is.

And yet tonight, Tripp's feeling brave, so he lets whatever is happening here happen, and just settles in to enjoy the ride. The song that's playing is ultra sappy and romantic, your standard wedding fare, really, and Tripp can't take his eyes off of Leander. They sway together, soft and slow, eyes locked and foreheads nearly touching. Lee's pupils are a little dilated, and Tripp wonders if it's from alcohol, or something else.

"You look good tonight," Tripp says softly, even though he's already done so at least ten times since Leander first put on his tux back at the apartment. Even though he's heard the sentiment a million times since, Leander's eyes still crinkle at the corners and he smiles widely, like the fact that Tripp finds him irresistibly hot is brand new information.

As they sway, Leander's hand releases Tripp's to come up and cup the side of his face, so Tripp drops his newly freed one to Lee's waist. He can't help it, blame the alcohol or whatever else, but his eyes slip shut and he leans into Lee's touch easily, not remotely missing the way Lee's breath hitches in response.

"Tripp, I've been meaning to—" Leander starts, but he's cut off by the music fading out and the DJ's voice booming loudly overhead, announcing that it's time for the bouquet and garter toss. All of the single women are ordered to the dance floor first, so reluctantly, Tripp forces himself to pull away from Lee and clear off towards the edge to make room.

Despite the hours of drinking, dancing, and mingling, Briana is still a vision. Standing in the middle of the floor with her bouquet in one hand and half of her dress bunched up in the other, she looks straight at Tripp and gives him a wink. That's kind of odd, in his opinion, but then again, Bri looks drunker than he feels, so Tripp doesn't think too much of it. He and Lee are off to one side, nowhere near the gaggle of pretty bridesmaids and guests in evening gowns, which is why Tripp couldn't possibly have foreseen what happens next.

"*Oof,*" Tripp grunts, stumbling backward and ultimately plopping down on his ass as Bri's bouquet hits him squarely in the stomach. *Fuck,* those things are heavier than they look. Blinking and confused, Tripp holds out the bouquet for someone to take and return to the bride for a redo, but Bri is busy jumping around and cheering, and no one will *take the fucking flowers* from his hand.

"I think you were set up again," Leander stage-whispers conspiratorially from behind one hand while Tripp struggles to his feet. That suggestion has him glancing around wildly, taking stock of his friends and their varied reactions to this utter *bullshit*. Beau is over at Briana's side now, grinning like a jackal, and when Tripp's eyes find Ro, all she does is shrug and raise her eyebrows innocently. Even Reina has her face buried in Mickey's bicep, her shoulders shaking with laughter, and Mickey looks like the cat who caught the mouse. He's red-faced and straining, trying and failing to hold his amusement in.

Fuck all of them, Tripp silently fumes, but he's a gentleman, so he raises the bouquet a bit sheepishly and waves it in the air to a chorus of cheering approval from the rest of the crowd.

"Hmm," is all Leander says, stroking his chin. "Let's test this theory."

"No, Lee, don't—"

That's all Tripp manages before the 'single men' are heralded onto the dance floor by order of the DJ, although most of them look a lot less excited than they might've been a few minutes prior. Tripp can't blame them, though he secretly kind of does, because who the hell *wouldn't* want a piece of this fine ass?!

It's all irrelevant anyway, because despite the fact that Leander stands *far* on the outskirts of the crowd, Bri's garter gets shot directly his way and he catches it easily, Beau barely even pretending to act surprised when he does. True to form, Leander just stands there awkwardly, looking down at the frilly, satiny thing in surprise, like he doesn't quite understand.

"Ha, ha," Tripp says loudly, mockingly, waving the bouquet around and rolling his eyes. "Oooh, you really got us now. Guess we have to get married. Tou-fuckin'-ché, assholes."

"You don't have to marry him," Marley interjects, popping up behind Tripp from out of nowhere, only to escort him forward onto the dance floor, where a chair has materialized. She plucks the garter from Leander's hand as they pass and presses it into Tripp's palm. "You just have to let him take this off of you. With his teeth," she adds pointedly, this time to Leander.

"Do it, do it, do it!" Bri cheers excitedly, jumping up and down while holding onto Beau's hand, which, because of his height, yanks him haphazardly all kinds of around. Like the dutiful new husband he is, Beau doesn't complain at all, just raises his eyebrows at Tripp and gestures to his bride like, *better do what she says, it's her day.*

With a long-suffering sigh, Tripp looks down at the garter and then up at Lee, who's still just standing there, wide-eyed and nervous. It would appear that he's only now realizing what he's gotten himself into by "testing his theory." *Dumb-ass.*

Still, what the bride wants, the bride gets. Who is Tripp to deny his new sister-in-law her entertainment? *Time to put on a show.* With new resolve (and without looking at Lee), Tripp steps up on the chair and waves his arms, hyping the al-ready-rowdy crowd to near-feral levels. He jumps down, stumbling and nearly falling over while tugging on the garter, all the way up to mid-thigh.

The room goes wild.

When Tripp sits, the guests only grow more enthusiastic as Lee follows him down, getting on his knees and shuffling his way forward like that's a *thing* Lean-der's ever done before in his life. *If they only knew.* When he's *just* between Tripp's knees, Lee very pointedly and dramatically spreads both of his arms, wrapping them behind his back with one hand grasping the opposite wrist to hold them there.

Whatever the crowd sees, whatever they're screaming, Tripp barely notices, hardly cares, because his entire world has ground to a halt. All *he* can see is the way Lee's eyes lock onto his, all he can *feel* is the hot puff of air from Lee's mouth on his inner thigh, even through the fabric of his dress pants. Lee's teeth barely graze him as they catch the garter, but Leander never looks away, not for one second.

By the time the garter is slipping down over his shoe, Tripp is gravely worried about his ability to stand up without humiliating himself, and wondering where that whiskey dick that he usually resents so much is hiding.

Thankfully, as soon as the garter is free and Lee is standing up, twirling the thing around on his finger in smug success, the DJ switches gears and throws some dance music on. As everyone crowds their way out onto the dance floor, Tripp grabs his chair and lets Leander escort him off of the makeshift stage, holding it strategically in front of his crotch while willing his dick to deflate.

"I believe our friends are trying to send us a message," Leander murmurs into Tripp's ear, as he's dropping the chair at the first table they come upon. Wayward cock sufficiently settled, Tripp allows Leander to slip an arm around his waist, reciprocating in kind as they wander away from the mob scene that's now dancing wildly to "Jump!"

Usually, this would be the part where Tripp would deflect, where he'd make up some reason as to why their friends are circus material and no one should listen to them ever, about anything. But tonight, taking in the way that Leander is staring up at him, so soft and hopeful, Tripp can't do it.

God, this is a risk. This is so much harder than fighting or fucking Lee for fun and in the name of *"stress relief"* could ever be. In fact, it's harder than *anything* Tripp has *ever* done in his entire life not to throw up walls, not to try and protect himself from what *feels* like obvious, inevitable rejection, and the ensuing heartache.

… but what if?

"Yeah," he manages finally, completely dry-mouthed and anxious, the weight of his lack of denial sitting heavy on his shoulders. Despite his fear and the pounding of his heart in his chest, Tripp doesn't look away. "Guess so."

And then he and Lee are kissing, hands on faces, sloppy because they've both had more than their fair share of alcohol, but hot and delicious all the same.

"What—" Leander starts, but Tripp cuts him off with a tongue in his mouth, a nip to his top lip, and Lee growls a little in the back of his throat. When Tripp pulls away, his friend looks positively predatory.

"When does this party end?" he asks, blue eyes dark, lips slick and kiss-bitten, and *right the fuck now,* if Tripp has anything to say about it.

He starts to reply with exactly that sentiment, but groans and reels himself in at the very last second. This is his little brother's *wedding*. Tripp is *not* going to bounce early just to get laid. Even if he does have to repeat that phrase in his head two more times before it fully sinks in. Once he has a handle on himself again, Tripp steps forward, grabbing Leander by the hips and sighing.

"Soon," he replies, and then actually looks at his watch. "Half-hour, tops. Newlyweds are leaving, they're staying the night at some B&B out in the 'burbs, something about banging in proximity to relatives... I dunno."

"No honeymoon?"

"Schedules didn't sync for extended time off until next week. Whatever, who cares? Are you going to fuck me? When we get home?"

"I'm going to do unspeakable things to you," Leander replies softly, *way* too gentle for the absolute promise those words hold, and *damn it,* Tripp's pants are tight again. He *wants* to take Leander into a dark corner of the room right now and investigate this—whatever they fuck they're doing—further, but there are giggling girls nearby, whispering and definitively pointing in their direction.

Again, Tripp sighs and throws up a middle finger towards Ro and Marley (and probably fuckin' Avery—*he doesn't even* know *Avery*), looping his arm through Leander's and dragging him away to the only adequate or available replacement for sex.

Sugar.

That turns out to be somewhat of a mistake, since watching Leander lick chocolate off of his dexterous fingers does nothing to settle Tripp's once-again-dire pants situation. Lee notices—*because of course, he notices*—and grins, something feral and knowing, and he puts on a real show of finishing cleaning off his index finger. Tripp keens, but Leander makes it up to him by finding a piece of cake and hand-feeding it to him with those same fingers, letting each one linger in Tripp's mouth so that he can tongue around it.

"Been awhile since we did that," Tripp observes with his mouth still full, all faux-casual as Leander wipes his wet fingers off on a napkin.

"Mmm," he agrees. "We should rectify that tomorrow morning. Breakfast in bed, I'll feed it to you and then ride your cock. Perhaps I'll feed it to you while riding your cock."

"Jesus Christ, Lee," Tripp swears, crossing one leg over the other and glancing around to see if anyone heard him.

Leander just shrugs, undoing his work with the napkin by sticking another strawberry under the spill of the chocolate fountain and failing to keep his fingers out of the way. "Most everyone here is certainly asking for it. They're the ones who keep shoving us together, rigged wedding games and all. If they happen to overhear the fruits of their labor, that is exclusively on them."

Tripp just blinks back at him, mid-chew.

"Besides," Leander continues, eating the strawberry himself and sorely disappointing Tripp. "That was meant to be motivation. A theoretical reward. You only get it if you behave tonight, and survive everything I have to throw at you."

"Fuck," Tripp swears. "I'm going to go see if Beau and Bri's ride is here." He turns on his heel, needing to press a hand against his crotch as he tries to appear nonchalant in his saunter away. The low laugh that follows in his wake suggests that he is not very successful, and Tripp doesn't care at all.

***

The door to the newlywed's limo is barely closed behind the poofy train of Bri's giant dress when Leander's still-sticky fingers are twisting into Tripp's. Without asking, Lee high-tails it in the opposite direction, yanking Tripp along after him.

"Wait," Tripp protests, digging in his heels. "Shouldn't we say goodnight to everyone? Offer to help clean up, or whatever? I got no idea how this fancy shit works, the last wedding I went to was in a fire hall and everyone was supposed to bring their own chairs."

Leander snorts, but doesn't slow down or even so much as glance back over his shoulder. "I said our goodbyes while you were speaking to Beau, and our bags are already in the car. Trust me, Tripp, no one is expecting us back."

While the concept of Leander saying "their" goodbyes to all of his friends and family sinks slowly into Tripp's head, Lee leads them directly to a waiting black sedan. It's idling by the curb with a driver already seated at the wheel.

"No regrets on skipping out on the hotel stay?" Tripp asks, as they both slide into the back seat. "This place is pretty swanky."

After confirming his address with the driver, Leander turns and raises an eyebrow at Tripp. "The hotel doesn't have heavy-duty suspension hooks driven into the ceiling joists," he remarks. In front of them, the driver does a double-take into the rearview mirror that has Tripp thanking God it's too dark for the guy to make out the blush surely staining his face.

Despite the sexual tension that has been following him and Leander everywhere they roamed—especially the dessert table—all damn night, the ride home in the car is surprisingly low-key. Both of them are exhausted, spending the majority of the trip slumped back in their seats and staring aimlessly out the window. Leander's hand finds Tripp's in the middle of the seat, though, tracing patterns over his palm with a warm thumb before working open the button of his cuff and absently fingering the collar that's still wrapped around his wrist.

As they pull onto the street where Leander's apartment building sits, they both happen to tear their eyes away from their respective windows at the same time. The look Leander gives him is heated, purposeful, and Tripp instantly feels wide awake. As Tripp gathers their things, Leander tips the driver with barely a glance in the guy's direction or down at his wallet. Hopefully, he doesn't regret that later.

Inside, Leander nods a greeting to his doorman as he sweeps Tripp through the lobby and into the waiting elevator, and seriously, Tripp's gotta ask about Lee's money situation, because this place is bananas. His own building barely has a damn lock on the front door.

It's quiet on the ride up, but Leander stands *right* at Tripp's side, invading his personal space with confidence, despite the otherwise emptiness of the elevator. Tripp can tell by his energy and the way he's holding himself that he's shifting into Hardcore Dom Mode—not that Leander ever really leaves it. Tripp snorts a little at that thought, and Lee looks at him sideways, eyes narrowing like he can read Tripp's mind.

Fuck, that's hot.

"When we get inside the apartment," Leander starts, and his words come out slow and deliberate, enough to prick the hairs on the back of Tripp's neck up to full attention. Lee's nose dropping to his shoulder doesn't help, either. "You're going to head directly to the bathroom. Remove the plug, clean up, but don't take off your harness. Obviously," he adds as an afterthought, exiting the elevator rather abruptly and leaving Tripp to trail behind him with the bags.

Tripp eyes his friend suspiciously once he's dumped their things on the living room floor, but Leander just folds his arms across his chest and raises an eyebrow. "Was something I said unclear?"

"No, Sir," Tripp replies quickly, shaking his head before slipping into the bathroom and locking the door behind him, because *some* things are just not sexy to walk in on, no matter how into someone you might be. He does as he was instructed, leaving his tux pieces folded a bit haphazardly on the sink. They'll be sent for dry cleaning—no need to be precious there.

Clearly, Leander wanted him out of the way so that he could set something up, that much was apparent. Despite knowing that, Tripp is *not* prepared to walk out of the bathroom and into the scene that's awaiting him. In fact, he stops dead in the middle of the doorway, completely forgetting that he's supposed to both be kneeling *and* keeping his eyes down.

No, Tripp's definitely staring, but who could blame him?

On top of the bed, Leander is standing barefoot on his toes, suit jacket gone and long dress sleeves rolled up to his elbows. His bowtie is also missing, and the first few buttons of his shirt are undone, but his waistcoat's still there, accentuating his broad chest and trim hips. No *way* is this look anything but extremely intentional—it's pushing nearly every button Tripp has that Leander knows exists (at least in the clothing department), and if Lee is planning on teasing him by looking like *that,* Tripp might as well grab a white flag now, because he's not going to last very long.

"Kneel," Leander says dismissively, otherwise failing to acknowledge Tripp's existence at all as he reaches up to clip an already-threaded pulley onto a ceiling hook. Tripp obliges, but can't help noticing the way Lee's shirt pulls slightly free from where it's tucked into his pants, watching with interest as it separates between two of the buttons.

Why that particular tease is so hot, Tripp will never know, but here he is, drooling over the *barest* flash of tummy skin. *Woe.*

When Lee finally jumps down from the bed onto the ground, he lands softly, crouched directly in front of Tripp where he reaches out with one finger to tip his chin up. It all happens in one smooth motion that Tripp can't quite process. God knows *he's* still tipsy, and if he tried that move, he'd be down for the count. True, he's got no idea how much Lee actually drank tonight, and maybe he's basically sober. That's not impossible, per se, but Tripp has his suspicions that Lee's dismount was curated specifically to keep him from falling on his ass. From breaking the tension or the *tone* he's gone out of his way to set in the room.

Watching Lee straighten up, Tripp lets him have it. While he's unquestionably a brat, those aren't the kind of buttons he cares to press when it comes to their dynamic. He's smart enough to leave well enough alone and just blink innocently up at his Dom.

From this close, Lee smells *good.* Not that too-fresh sort of clean that comes with hopping out of the shower, but a manly, musky scent that mixes with the expensive material of the suit he's wearing and into his cologne—*intoxicating.* It's all Tripp can do not to lean into it, to bury his face in between those spread legs and mouth there until he can feel Lee filling out. With any luck, that's on the guy's to-do list, because Tripp's mouth is watering at the mere thought.

"Safeword?" Leander prompts gently, the crinkles around his eyes deepening as he stares down at Tripp. His gaze is soft and hard at the same time, like he's looking right through him, straight into his soul.

Holy shit, he's really drunk.

"Halligan," Tripp replies, his voice cracking a little. Embarrassed, he flushes and tries to duck his head, but Leander is quicker—grabbing Tripp's chin between his thumb and forefinger, forcing him to maintain eye contact.

"Don't look away from me," he commands.

"Yes, Sir," Tripp replies, keeping his voice soft and quiet, because he knows that Lee loves when he's compliant and submissive, but also so that it doesn't crack again. *A man can only take so much.*

"And your safeword, are you using it?"

"No, Sir."

Leander nods. "I'm not going to gag you. I want you to let me hear every pretty noise you feel compelled to make tonight." Starting to move and then thinking better of it, Leander settles back into a crouch as he looks pointedly down his nose at Tripp.

"Noises," he clarifies, because he knows Tripp all too well. "Not words. No back-talk, no questions, no talking at all unless you're feeling unsafe. As usual, you may say 'yellow', 'red,' or safeword if that's the case, and I will respond accordingly. Otherwise, *noises* only. Am I understood?"

The still-tipsy part of Tripp's brain just can't help itself.

"Mmhmm," Tripp hums, barely suppressing a smirk as he stares wide-eyed back at Lee. After all, he's only following instructions. Before he can so much as blink, Tripp's cheek is smarting and he's looking at the floor instead of his friend. The *smack* of Lee's hand making contact with his face sends a thrill through Tripp's body—he's *so* fucking ready, *so* desperate for this.

His hands clench behind his back as he breathes, *in and out,* closing his eyes and allowing himself an extended second to relish the sting of his skin before Lee is grabbing his hair and yanking his head up.

"Brat," Leander growls. "We don't mess around with safety. Answer my question immediately or I'll stop the scene right now."

"I understand, Sir," Tripp gasps. Lee's grip on his hair is more ferocious than usual, and when he releases it, he does so with a little jerk that has Tripp toppling over from his knees onto his hip. "I'm sorry, Sir." He's not sorry, and Leander knows it, judging by the roll of his eyes he gives in return as he stands and beckons for Tripp to do the same.

"Up. Feet slightly apart, arms straight out, like you're reaching for the walls." As Leander saunters over to the far armoire, the one that holds all of his bondage supplies, Tripp complies with his instructions. While he watches Leander rooting casually around in the top drawer, he regrets doing it so quickly, realization slowly dawning that holding his arms out in this way was not necessary positioning for shibari, it's punishment for his sass.

When Leander finally turns around, several lengths of rope in hand, he looks smug. As he returns to Tripp's side, he quirks an eyebrow. "Comfortable?" he asks. Tripp stays silent, recognizing *that* trap for what it is, but in the quiet, the noise his teeth make when he clamps them shut is *loud,* and Leander's smile widens.

"Alright," Lee relents. "As fun as you're making this for me, it's not exactly what I had planned. You can rest your arms and lay down on the bed. Ass at the very edge, please."

This time when Tripp does what he's told, Leander watches, making his own pleased little noises as Tripp splays himself out without an ounce of shame. As soon as he's down, Lee is between his legs, hands all over Tripp's body, threading rope this way and that. He's soft, gentle, pressing kisses between the twists, scraping fingers down over Tripp's sides, tying ropes off to the loops that already hang from one end of the pulley.

He disappears once, only to return with something that makes a *thump* and a *clank* when he sets it down on the floor. Unable to look and see what it is, Tripp's heart races, his nerves over what might be coming next preventing him from fully relaxing and enjoying the remainder of Leander's hands working to tie him up.

"This is new," Leander says suddenly, startling Tripp out of his nervous daydream, making his eyelids pop open and his pupils focus on the silhouette towering over him in the now-dim light. Lee is holding a spreader bar, one with four limb restraints attached, and Tripp's already hard, but seeing his Dom with *that* in his hand spikes the arousal he's feeling significantly.

It's difficult for Tripp to ask plainly for what he wants and needs, it always has been. And even though he's gotten better about it, feels more at ease around Leander than ever before, Tripp still has his hangups. This kind of bondage is something he's lusted over Leander putting him in for a *long* time, but *asking* to be made powerless and vulnerable? It's just not something Tripp's been able to give voice to wanting. Maybe that's silly, considering all of the things he and Lee have already done together, combined with the fact that Lee has *never* judged him, but that's just the way it is.

Tonight, though, all Tripp can do is whine and nod as his dick sells him out completely by drooling precum all over his stomach. After pressing a kiss to the inside of Tripp's knee, Leander is quick to oblige. Pretty soon, the bar's end restraints are fastened around Tripp's thighs and it's positioned to press into the flesh just above his knees. After that, Lee's onto securing the cuffs near the middle of the device to each of Tripp's wrists. The final result is him on his back, legs in the air, hands caught uselessly somewhere in between.

His abs *burn* within minutes. This would be a sadistic as hell position if Leander didn't help Tripp out by securing each of his ankles to the suspension system he's already rigged, taking the burden off of his limbs to hold himself up. It's still not entirely *comfortable,* but it's better.

"We're not trying to dislocate your shoulders," Leander explains, and despite the fact that Tripp's slipping quickly into subspace, *that* he understands. Without the ankle support, he'd have to either use his thigh muscles to hold his legs up, or strain his shoulder joints trying to give them a break. This way, he's restrained, he's exposed, he's at Lee's mercy, but the carefully-tied ropes are doing most of the heavy lifting.

"Color?" Leander checks in again before putting the suspension rigging he's so carefully tied to the test.

"Green." Tripp sighs dreamily, tugging gently against his restraints, testing his limits, enjoying the way he's held captive, the way nothing even remotely budges. Leander can truly do *whatever* he wants to him now, and there's *nothing* Tripp can do about it. That thought *should* terrify him, and it does leave goosebump-chased chills running down his arms, but not because he's afraid. Trusting someone so completely, the way he's learned to trust Lee? It changes *everything.*

Tripp doesn't feel restrained, he feels *free.*

As Leander manipulates his torso and moves him around—checking ties and circulation before eventually lifting Tripp's body the rest of the way off the bed and into the air by way of the pulley—that feeling only multiplies. The actual act of suspension isn't as dramatic as it sounds, in fact, Tripp's only hovering a few inches above the mattress, his ass slightly higher than his head. If he *really* works hard to arch his back, he can actually skim the top of the rumpled sheets below with his hair.

"I also need to know," Leander says, so casually they could be discussing plans to meet up at the Hot Plate after work, "—and you may use your words to answer —what you've decided regarding the taking of pictures."

"Take whatever pictures you want," Tripp replies immediately, even as he feels himself moving further into the air, watching Leander secure the ropes so that he stays there. "I trust you."

"I appreciate your trust in me," Leander replies, coming to stand in-between Tripp's legs again, and it's suddenly clear why he didn't pull the ropes higher. He's now suspended at the perfect height for Leander to fuck him without bending down or having to lean on the bed at all, and Tripp is *so into this.* The anticipation, the *excitement*—it's causing his breath to come fast, making his cock twitch against the plane of his abdomen.

Things become a bit hazy and blurry after that—mentally, Tripp commits to letting go, succumbing to the submissive headspace he's begun to crave so badly. It's been too long since he and Lee have done something *this* intense, and Tripp suddenly remembers *why* they started playing and sceneing to begin with. It's been easy to forget lately with how he's been stressing, worrying over the possibility of things between him and Lee changing emotionally.

This scene is a reminder—they're *so fucking good* together this way, too. Just this. It's more than enough.

One minute bleeds into the next, and while Leander is definitely talking, murmuring explanations and sweet reassuring praise, Tripp doesn't always hear the words. There are wax sticks—hot, burning drops that Leander drips all across his body while Tripp moans and twists beneath, and he drifts, focusing on the sensory ride.

Lee doesn't stay between his legs, either—he's *everywhere,* all at once. He's biting Tripp's collarbone, he's rubbing still-warm wax into the skin of his tender inner thighs, he's pressing Tripp's face into the bulge of his crotch, just the way he hoped for earlier. As much as he can, Tripp mouths at the fabric enthusiastically, leaving damp spots behind as his way of saying '*thank you'* to his Dom before Leander pulls away.

At some point, Leander breaks out a vibrator, sticks it inside Tripp's ass, and levels it directly over his prostate while continuing to torment and tease the rest of his exposed body. First the wax, then clothespins on his nipples, clipping them on and then flicking them off while deftly stroking his cock. Lee keeps that up until tears stream from Tripp's eyes and he's *this close* to breaking the rule about *words,* if only just to beg for mercy.

He doesn't need to, not in the end, because Lee is *so fucking good* at reading Tripp's body language, at anticipating both his desires *and* his limits, that he's already soothing a tongue over one abused nipple *right* as Tripp is teetering on the edge of losing it.

And then, like the master torturer he is, Lee switches the game up completely, abandoning pain for pleasure completely as he gets down between Tripp's thighs and presses the flat of his tongue unabashedly to Tripp's rim. Right around the edge of the vibrator, teasing and aggressive, Leander licks and sucks in a way that makes Tripp twist and shake and cry out without shame, jerking in the air.

"Fuck, *Lee!*"

Damn it—he slipped, he knows he slipped, *fuck,* but Tripp's half out of his mind, nearly delirious, couldn't have helped it if he tried. "Sorry," he half-mumbles, half-gasps as another tear leaks from his eye and tracks down over his temple and into his hair. "Sorry, Sir," he repeats, but Leander is already taking his sweet, sweet mouth away, making clicking sounds with a tongue that should be working on *other things,* and Tripp can't do anything but groan to hear it.

"Naughty, naughty," Leander chastises as he climbs onto the bed, shuffling towards Tripp's head on his knees. As he does, his hands are already unbuckling his pants and pulling his cock out without ceremony. "Open," he says, pressing a thumb to Tripp's chin to encourage him to comply while rubbing the crown of his cock across his barely-parted lips.

Even in Tripp's floaty, altered state, it's not hard for him to tell what Leander wants, what he's trying to do. With the vibrator shoved far up his ass, it's hardly a punishment, but Tripp's certainly not going to say so. He opens his mouth wide, moaning and relaxing his jaw as Leander slides in deep, giving a few gentle, testing thrusts before pulling him in by the back of his neck.

Breathing carefully through his nose, which winds up flush to the crease between Lee's groin and thigh, Tripp goes pliant as much as he can. He swallows when he's able around the intrusion in his throat, allowing saliva to otherwise run freely down his cheek. He'd love to grab onto Leander's thighs for leverage, but he can't, just has to let whatever his Dom wants to happen, happen.

Like always, Leander remains perfectly poised and unaffected in his control, even as he ravages Tripp, using Tripp's hair to set the speed and rhythm more than his own hips. It's likely in part because he just loves to pull hair, but also (probably) because he knows that Tripp enjoys it too. Leander thrusts in and out of his mouth and Tripp follows along as best he can, sucking and licking and trying *so* damn hard to be *good* after accidentally messing up.

A mere handful of minutes later, he's rewarded, and it feels like turning his face up to the sun.

"There's my good boy," Leander croons, smoothing a hand over Tripp's cheek, even as he chokes a little, the head of Leander's cock bumping against his soft palate. Despite that, Tripp is still, he doesn't pull away. "So good for me when he wants to be." At that, Leander withdraws. He shifts backward on the mattress, creating room for him to bend down to Tripp's eye level.

"Answer me, Tripp," he demands softly. "Are you mine?"

Somewhat dazed, Tripp has to suck in a deep, steadying breath to even process the question. His eyes are suddenly exhausted and heavy, struggling to remain open as he stares back at Leander, knowing he must look exactly how he feels—completely undone.

"Yes, Sir," he manages, the sound rough and used, even to Tripp's own ears. For a minute, he thinks that Lee is going to close the distance between them and kiss his mouth, but he only dips his head to nose at the pulse point of Tripp's throat before pulling away.

It's a loss. Tripp's close, he's *really* close, despite not having been fucked yet, despite the lack of consistent attention to his cock, despite a *lot* of things. He's so hard that it's painful, so needy and desperate for Lee to take him over the edge that it's becoming increasingly difficult to stay silent.

He *wants*, God, he *wants*. But, he also wants to be *good*. He *is* good, for Lee, Lee said so. Fixating on that thought instead of giving into his desire to break the rules and beg, Tripp exhales a stream of air from his lungs and tips his head back, very slowly counting to ten inside his head. Silently, Tripp does his best to center his mind and regain both a modicum of patience and some semblance of control over his body.

He's so preoccupied with maintaining that control that he *almost* misses Leander removing the vibrator and saying, "I think we've both earned this," right before he spreads Tripp's cheeks and slides home.

After so many hours of wearing a plug, stacked with the way Lee has played with, tortured, and toyed with his body all night long, there's nothing but near-agonizing relief when Leander's cock pushes inside. Tripp expects him to use the spreader bar for leverage, but he doesn't—he grabs Tripp's hips, grips *him* tight, and fucks him mercilessly. Tripp's hands flex in his restraints and his head falls back, eyes closed and mouth open, unable to even pretend that he has the strength to hold it up anymore.

And *Lee*—he's an animal.

Suddenly, Tripp is flashing back to the Dom's little speech about noises and wanting to hear them all, because Lee is *loud*. Not that he's usually quiet, but this is next level. He growls and grunts, propping a foot on the bed so that he can thrust more forcefully. He moans and cries out, and Tripp is *shaking*, he's so fucking overwhelmed, struggling to believe that he could really make someone— *Lee*—feel this way, especially while tied up and doing virtually nothing except clenching his ass.

Seeing him unravel makes it so much easier for Tripp to let go, to return Lee's moans with his own. There's nothing subtle or slow about his orgasm tonight— no, this one barrels down the track like a thundering freight train.

When Tripp comes, it's with Leander's fingers shoved down his throat, Leander's hips grinding figure eights into his pelvis, and his own cock untouched. The sensation is so powerful that Tripp's vision whites the fuck out, his legs are shaking relentlessly, and he feels like he actually stops breathing for a moment. By the time he sorts himself out, his ass feels warm and wetter than before, and Lee's thrusts are slow, lazy—he's already done.

Holy fuck, did they finish at the same time? That's a thought Tripp's going to have to circle back to at a later date, when he can actually think, because—yeah. No one *actually* does that. Climaxing at the same time is for porn flicks and romance novels, but here Lee is, slipping out of him like that's what the fuck happened here.

As Tripp dazedly muses over his mini-revelation, Leander gently lowers the rigging and starts undoing his bindings. Everything in reverse, and it takes longer than Tripp would like, considering how tired he is. Also, because Lee is Lee, he insists on working each of Tripp's joints out individually, testing their range of motion and checking for any injury, tenderness, or other signs of a problem.

Thankfully—because Tripp just wants to go the fuck to *sleep*—he passes whatever tests Lee is giving and earns his reward of orange juice, a banana, and a warm washcloth to the groin, which for some reason feels *extra* enjoyable tonight. He also gets Lee leaning up against the headboard and insisting Tripp lay back against his chest, for the sole purpose of continuing the massage Tripp grumbled his way out of after being initially released from his restraints.

It does not escape Tripp's notice that he's still covered in wax, but the patches that pull at hairs are easily picked off, and the rest aren't terribly uncomfortable. Therefore, they can wait until a time when his eyes don't have sandbags weighing them down to be dealt with.

When he's finally allowed to pass out, even half-asleep, Tripp has to admit that there's nothing wrong with being pampered like this. As he's drifting off with Lee surrounding him—Lee's hands on his skin, Lee's lips in his hair—it occurs to Tripp that there was *something* Lee wanted to talk to him about earlier. He can't quite put his finger on it, he's *so* fucking tired, but he could swear—they were definitely interrupted at some point, and there was *something* Lee wanted to say.

Oh, well. If it's important, Lee will come back to it, he thinks sleepily. Lee is the responsible one, after all. If he's got something to say, he'll say it.

Right?

Chapter 10

When Leander wakes, he's alone. That's not entirely unusual—there's no unspoken agreement regarding *Tripp* remaining in the bed until both of them are fully conscious—it's just that more often than not, Leander simply beats him to the punch. Out of the two of them, he's also the least petulant about mornings, not that Tripp will ever admit to being such a bear. In fact, before Tripp began staying over regularly, Leander would frequently wake long before the sun in order to go down to his complex's gym and knock out a treadmill session before work.

Speaking of which—Leander lifts his head, looking down guiltily as he pokes at his stomach in the dark. To anyone else, there would hardly be a difference to notice there, but *he* can tell, and that's what matters. Too many nights of extra drinks and decadent dishes, too many mornings spent stealing extra minutes with Tripp rather than doing the responsible thing and exercising. Still, Leander would be faking modesty if he claimed he thought he didn't look *good,* despite all of the recent indulgences. He merely needs to phase regular workouts back into his routine, preferably before that actually changes.

Across the room, there's light spilling from the cracked door leading to the attached bathroom. Through it, Leander can hear Tripp grumbling quietly about something, but he can't make out any specific words. Lazily, he stretches, yawning dramatically while pressing both palms flat against the wall, in-between the intricately-carved twists of the headboard. With a sigh, Leander glances skeptically towards the drawn curtains. No light leaks out from around their edges, which means that it is *far* too soon for Tripp to be out of bed. Everything else aside, Leander wants him back.

They both have to work later tonight, which means there are approximately fourteen hours left for them to make the most of the remaining weekend. Thus far, it's been one for the books, and Leander can't remember a time in his life that he's ever been happier.

He *was* fairly intoxicated at the reception the night before, though. Sober enough by the time they reached his apartment to not be wholly irresponsible in dominating Tripp, but perhaps not *quite* as sober as would have been ideal. Not that he has any regrets—their scene was beautiful and intense, and Leander's cock perks up at the barest thought of how Tripp responded so perfectly to everything he asked him to take. Tripp *is* perfect, and the more Leander tastes of him, the hungrier he feels.

But did he almost ruin everything with that near-declaration of love? The mood had felt so right—the wedding, the music, the way their friends were unceremoniously shoving them together all night long. With the way the alcohol was flowing freely and clouding his mind, it's hard for Leander to be *fully* certain now, looking back on it.

At the time, he'd been *so* sure that Tripp was right there with him, giving as much of a green light as Leander thinks he'll ever get from the man. There was one moment in particular, after the garter ceremony—Tripp hadn't shied away from acknowledging their friends' scheming, and then that *kiss*—even in the harsh light of day, that sequence of events is hard to paint as anything but tacit approval.

It's just so hard to believe. Leander could, in theory, come to terms with the idea that Tripp's feelings *may* be changing. That they *may* have morphed into something more in his mind than simple friendship and lust. It's certainly not that he doesn't *want* to acknowledge it, to ask Tripp and find out for sure—no, that's no longer the problem. Now, it's that Leander just wants to go about things the proper way, lest he move too quickly or sharply and scare Tripp off for good.

In truth, he has no idea what's going on in that man's head. Even if true feelings for Leander are rattling around in there somewhere, *Tripp* has yet to say so—and wouldn't he?

Just as Leander decided that night after the rehearsal dinner, he must continue to tread lightly. There will always be more time. In fact, if there's one important realization Leander has had, it's that Tripp doesn't seem interested in going *anywhere*. It would appear that the two of them have all the time and space necessary to feel this thing out slowly and to work through it properly, whatever that might mean. Leander only has to be patient and let Tripp show him what he needs, just as they've been doing.

Except—*screw* patience when it comes to early morning cuddles. Leander's not a saint, after all.

Fed up with waiting for Tripp to return, he kicks off the covers, wincing at the stiffness in the movement of the linen and making a mental note to change the sheets once Tripp departs. At the bathroom door, he raps but doesn't wait for a reply before pushing it open—if Tripp truly wanted privacy, he would have closed it. Besides, he's cursing up a storm on the other side, and Leander doesn't want to give Tripp the opportunity to deprive him of finding out why.

It takes Leander a minute for his eyes to adjust to the comparatively bright light of the bathroom, and he blinks against the discomfort. When Tripp comes into focus, he's naked and scowling back at him via the mirror above the vanity. Leander tips his head to the side, momentarily confused but then abruptly understanding when Tripp's fist opens above the sink in front of him and releases a flutter of tiny wax pieces. They drift down like snow and stick in the basin.

Upon more careful inspection, Leander notes all the many tiny reddened marks littering the front of Tripp's body. They're not burns, just minor irritation from where the leftover wax has adhered to the tiny, fine hairs on Tripp's skin. Leander suppresses a smirk and plasters himself (in what *he* feels is a cleverly ironic fashion) to his friend's back, wrapping arms around his middle and tucking his chin over Tripp's shoulder.

"You're being very dramatic about all this," he scolds good-naturedly. "My tough, strong, pain-loving submissive, moaning and groaning over a bit of wax that's *meant* for this very purpose." Leander tsks and shakes his head slightly, taking the opportunity to nose at Tripp's ear. "Whatever shall I do with you?"

In his arms, Tripp softens, and no matter how many times Leander watches his demeanor change in that fashion, it *never* gets old. What a profound effect they have on each other, he and Tripp. In ways that no one else can, Leander is able to make Tripp *soft,* pliable, subservient. And Tripp—Tripp can make him *love.*

Tripp clears his throat, and Leander recognizes the gesture, the hesitation—Tripp has something to say, there's something that he wants. So he waits, and lets Tripp work it from his brain down to his tongue.

"Sir," he starts, and *oh, yes, this is promising.* "I know that you had plans for a scene this morning, with the—the feeding, and riding me, and, uh—don't get me wrong, okay? That sounds fuckin' awesome."

"Mmm," Leander agrees when Tripp pauses, tipping his head down to kiss at his neck, an idle distraction that will hopefully assist Tripp in admitting to whatever it is he's working towards. "But?"

Huffing a small laugh, Tripp reaches behind them both to grab Leander's ass and bring their bodies together flush. The way he does it has Leander's semi-hard cock nudging *just* between his cheeks, not enough to brush his hole. Seemingly in direct response, Tripp releases a disgruntled sound, leaning forward against the vanity to present his ass more effectively.

285

"Hello," Leander says, surprised, but not displeased in the least.

"Get up in there," Tripp grunts, prompting Leander to glare disapprovingly at him in the mirror. "Don't worry, I cleaned up again. Just *feel*, okay?" His elbows are on the marble countertop and he's looking over his shoulder expectantly.

Quirking an eyebrow up, Leander obliges, brushing two fingers firmly over Tripp's hole and understanding immediately what he's getting at. Despite being dry, Tripp's rim is soft and gives easily, though Leander doesn't press inside, just touches gently. Clearly embarrassed, Tripp ducks his head, but not before Leander can catch the pretty flush staining his cheeks.

"Are you worried, or—?"

"No," Tripp replies quickly, *too* quickly, and *ah*—that isn't all he was trying to say. *Interesting.* Leander waits, his index finger still lazily circling Tripp's rim, while Tripp takes a deep breath and then lets it out.

"I've been thinking," he continues, finally, "about... *doublepenetrationinonehole.*" He says the last part so quickly, like it's all one word, and Leander struggles not to crack a smile. The phrasing, of course, is lifted directly from their kinks negotiation list, where Tripp rated his interest in *this* particular activity an unenthusiastic "maybe."

One of the least compelling selections possible, aside from "No," it's a significant reason as to why Leander has not ventured to test-run that particular kink just yet. That, combined with the fact that each Wednesday when they review their lists, Tripp never waivers in his answer to that section—he hasn't exactly been flashing green lights. Until now, that is.

"I'm stretched the *fuck* out from last night," Tripp explains bluntly, rubbing at the back of his neck, which, like his cheeks, has turned a rosy shade of pink. "I dunno what you did back there, but I'm pretty sure I could shove a baseball up my ass if I wanted to right now. At *least* a tennis ball."

"What a sight that would be," Leander replies, struggling and failing miserably at not picturing Tripp as one of those machines firing balls in cages for people to practice hitting. It's incredibly unfortunate that this is a sensitive subject and he can't share. Tripp would undoubtedly get a kick out of that joke made at anyone else's expense. Somehow, Leander doesn't think he'll feel the same when the punchline is his own ass.

"So?" Tripp prompts, breaking Leander out of his ridiculous reverie, only to see him hesitate.

If Tripp had been a 'hard no' previously, Leander wouldn't even consider diving in like this, but he knows Tripp pretty well these days. It seems likely to him that Tripp's 'maybe' response was rooted in both fear of the unknown and anticipation, perhaps a few other things that aren't quite as important as those. The bottom line leaves Leander fairly certain that Tripp was never disinterested, exactly —just perhaps not ready.

Not to mention, there's no reason for Tripp to go out of his way *now* to ask for something he isn't completely sure that he wants. Something he clearly finds embarrassing to admit aloud, at that.

Other issues aside, Leander needs to reward Tripp for using his words, for communicating his desires so effectively the way that he has. Leander's proud and wants him to know that, wants to give him the world in return. On the other hand, he also takes a *lot* of pleasure in teasing Tripp, so.

Without first replying, Leander pulls one of Tripp's cheeks to the side before taking his own steadily-filling cock in hand. He rubs the smooth crown of it against Tripp's hole, leaving wetness behind and Tripp gasping, still bent over the counter next to the sink.

"Eager," Leander remarks offhandedly, right before letting go of Tripp completely, stepping to the side, and grabbing his toothbrush from its holder.

"So tell me," he says casually, squeezing some toothpaste onto his brush like he and Tripp are discussing nothing more controversial than the weather. Meanwhile, Tripp gapes up at him in disbelief. "What is it that you want me to do?"

"Sir, please," Tripp groans, turning his face into his forearms so Leander can't watch it flush as he scrubs away at his teeth, creating a foamy mess that drips into the sink. Mouth occupied, he doesn't bother to dignify Tripp's complaint with a response, just continues about his business and waits. Tripp will answer, he always does.

From beside him, there's a long-suffering sigh. "Fuck me," Tripp tells the countertop. "With your dick. And a fake dick. At the same time. Please. Sir."

Leander spits into the sink and rinses out the basin, filling a Dixie cup with some water. "Any fake dick? We have that Jeff Stryker model—" Before he can even finish that sentence, Tripp's head shoots up with alarm in his eyes. At least, until they meet Leander's and subsequently narrow.

"I cannot believe you're fucking with me right now! That is *so* not cool, dude— *Sir.*" Tripp flinches a little, clearly prepared for Leander to punish him for the slip, but Leander just laughs. In fairness, Tripp's not wrong, that was somewhat cruel. The Stryker dildo is… true to size. Leander finishes rinsing his mouth, replaces the toothbrush, and tosses the little paper cup into the trash before slipping an arm under Tripp's and helping him stand, pulling him in tight to his body.

"Tripp," he says sincerely, once Tripp is secure against his chest and can't look away. "I'll take care of you. I promise you that."

***

As stretched and loose as Tripp might already be, it's not enough to comfortably take two cocks (or a tennis ball, no matter what Tripp thinks). So Leander lays him out on the bed, stepping away briefly to grab a particular toy that he's long had in mind for this, *should* the occasion ever arise. It's a realistically-shaped dildo that has vibration capability and a very natural, skin-like feeling when touched. Slightly smaller in girth than an average-sized cock, which seems about right for Tripp's first time with two.

In truth, Leander is definitely suspicious that Tripp would gladly consent to (and enjoy) being fucked by more than one man (or woman) at a time, but that is not on the menu in their dynamic. It has nothing to do with trust, either. Ultimately, Leander's never going to be the sort of person who can *share,* never going to be comfortable with casual strangers in his playroom. It's a hard limit—no, more than that, it's part of who he *is*—and he doesn't see that changing in the future. In light of those things, the least he can do is try to make experiences like this mimic the real thing as much as possible. For Tripp's sake, but also his own. Monogamy should be as interminably spicy as a person cares for it to be.

If Tripp winds up enjoying this, perhaps Leander will obtain one of those torsos meant for riding—that would certainly push things to the next level, as far as realism goes. And perhaps they could take this scene to the BDSM club, allow others to participate with them in a controlled and safe manner, one in which they're both comfortable engaging.

Tripp has responded more than favorably to the semi-public sex they've had, as well as the times they've discussed it, and Leander has absolutely no objection to watching or being watched—they just haven't made time to actually *go* down to the club yet. It's something to prioritize, though—Tripp deserves to explore his kinks and his limits. Perhaps the next weekend they're both off, they can make a night of it.

Returning to the bed, Leander smiles down at his wonderfully patient sub. Tripp is *so* good when he wants to be, splayed out exactly where he was placed, ass propped up on some pillows and his arms above his head.

"I don't want to restrain you for this," Leander says. "But I'm going to give you the cuffs to hold onto, something to pull on, should the need arise."

"Thank you, Sir," Tripp says softly, and nothing more. Leander recognizes the nerves kicking in high-key, so he sets the items he's holding down on the mattress and crawls between Tripp's legs, covering Tripp's body with his own. He kisses him, soft and deep, smoothing a hand over the side of his head and into his hair, reassuring and sweet, until Tripp relaxes beneath him.

Once he does, Leander grabs the restraints from where they're each already locked onto a respective post at the top of the bed, closing Tripp's fingers around one cuff at a time.

"You won't *need* them," he assures his anxious sub, adding a cheeky wink. "But you may want them. I'm going to make you feel so good, Tripp." As Leander sits up again, he pauses. "Having your hands free is a gift, so don't make me take them away. Keep them above your head until I instruct you otherwise."

"Yes, Sir," Tripp agrees, still sounding more subdued than normal, but that's not unusual behavior for him when they're trying something new. Leander expects that Tripp will come apart beautifully beneath his hands, just as he always does, and the thought makes his own cock twitch.

"Safeword?"

"Halligan."

"And are you using it?"

"No, Sir."

"My good boy."

Tripp preens, and Leander has a strange thought. "Tripp," he says carefully. "You know that using your safeword is the right thing to do, if you need to?"

"'Course, Sir," Tripp replies, shifting a little against the sheets and blinking up at Leander curiously.

"And that being good has nothing to do with the fact that you are *not* using your safeword?" Something flickers across Tripp's face, and Leander is suddenly glad that he followed his instincts on this. He grabs Tripp's chin, forces him to maintain eye contact.

"Tripp, you are wonderfully good and sweet, and will never be less so for enforcing your boundaries and limits. Please assure me you understand that."

Leander softens his tone on the last sentence, wanting Tripp to comprehend that this is important to him, personally. That he truly cares whether Tripp accepts and internalizes what he's saying.

He must look upset, because Tripp's brow furrows and he visibly slips back into his normal persona, self-dissolving any subspace that might have been creeping in. As Leander stares down at him, Tripp struggles up onto his elbows, balancing on his left so that he can reach out and touch Leander's face with his right.

"Yeah, Lee," he says pointedly, voice full of solemn empathy. "I hear you. I promise."

The little smirk Tripp then immediately offers is enough to snap Leander right back into Dom-mode and the scene, proving so by shoving at Tripp's shoulders so that he flops down flat on the bed with a pleased gasp.

"Fuck, yes," Tripp whispers.

Leander doesn't waste any more time getting busy in between Tripp's legs. He starts with two fingers, lubing them up and slipping without resistance inside Tripp's hole, watching his face for any reaction. Tripp doesn't disappoint, biting his lip and letting his eyes flutter closed, flexing his hips down onto Leander's hand. If they didn't have an end result in mind, Leander could do this endlessly —just touching and teasing Tripp until he falls to pieces and begs for release. He's beautiful that way.

Today's playtime has a goal, though, and they will not reach it like this. Even four of Leander's fingers aren't going to cut it for where they're headed, which makes it time to up the ante. When he withdraws his hand, Tripp writhes against the mattress and complains—*as expected*—but Leander pays him no mind. He *wants* Tripp lost to the sensations, wants him *really* into what they're doing. Swallowing a small dose of brattiness will be a necessary rub.

"Sir, come on, don't treat me with kid gloves!"

Again, Leander ignores him, except to say, "All good things in time," which makes Tripp snort and drape an arm dramatically across his forehead. Leander responds by shoving the fake cock he's holding inside of him in one go, and Tripp abruptly stops mouthing off.

The dildo helps move things along, and Tripp is relaxed enough that Leander is fucking him easily on its length within a scarce two minutes. Feeling bold, he adds more lube and starts to test Tripp's limits, fitting first one finger and then the next inside his ass around the silicone. In working him open, Leander's been both careful and patient, and Tripp's rim is therefore stretched but willing, allowing both to pop past with little issue.

On the receiving end, Tripp's breath is coming short now, and Leander has to stop working the dildo to soothe a hand up his abdomen and chest several times. "Breathe," he commands softly, leaning down to kiss Tripp, keeping it open-mouthed and deep until he has no choice but to slow himself down and un-clench his muscles again.

They proceed like that for a while, a cautious give and take while Tripp's body and mind adjust and accommodate. Any time his cock begins to flag alongside a new intrusion, Leander leans down to suck him off until it's hard and leaking again. Tripp remains wonderfully pliant in his hands, taking everything he's given and still crying out for more. It's a beautiful sight.

It's therefore a struggle, a testament of will, for Leander to hold out on swapping the fake cock he's wielding for the real thing, but he is nothing if not a profes-sional. The angle and the slip of the silicone both make it much easier to work his fingers inside, so he resists. Still, he's not hesitant when he *does* deem it time, and Tripp's pleas to feel Leander inside of him fuel the already roiling heat in his stomach into an unruly blaze.

Pushing inside Tripp feels like coming home, and despite what they're doing, despite the fact that this is a *scene,* Leander can't help but indulge his desires—just for a minute. He rolls his hips gently into Tripp's warm, wet heat, feels the rumble of Tripp's answering groans echoing through his chest when he covers the man's body with his own.

As Tripp's arms close around his back to hold him tight, Leander sighs into the crook of Tripp's neck, presses a kiss to the sensitive area just below his right ear. Tripp's skin is warm and soft, and Leander *craves* this feeling, the way it is when they're pressed together infinitely like this. It doesn't happen very often during sex—not the way he and Tripp do it—and so now that it is, the sensations are nearly as intoxicating as the alcoholic drinks consumed in excess the night be-fore.

Beneath him, Leander can feel Tripp's stomach muscles tensing and relaxing as he rocks his own pelvis to take the cock inside of him deeper. Leander can feel the hard planes of Tripp's chest, his racing heartbeat, and the way Tripp's head tips back in ecstasy against his cheek. He relishes Tripp's thighs tightening ar-ound his hips, the way Tripp's ankles lock and his heels dig into his ass, urging him on. Leander could drown in every delicious sound Tripp releases, could suf-focate in the exhaled rush of breath from his chest through his lips, and *oh*—Le-ander loves him so.

It's perhaps one of the hardest things Leander's ever done, drawing back from this exhilarating, heady, fucking *boring, totally vanilla* sex they're having, but he does, because Tripp—Tripp has expectations, and... *and?* Leander fumbles, even in his own head, to come up with solid reasons why he *needs* to pull away. He's *sure* they're there—just slightly out of his conscious mind's addled, Tripp-drunk reach.

Once he's straightened up and has Tripp's thighs in his hands, the look on Tripp's face nearly has Leander diving back in all over again. Truly, he's a wonder to behold—drowsy and aroused, heavy-lidded, swollen-lipped. His lush green eyes are dark, nearly all pupil, and his freckles stand out brightly against the flush in his cheeks.

"Sheer perfection," Leander murmurs, dragging his own thumb down over Tripp's mouth. He lets it catch, reveling in the way Tripp's breath subsequently stutters on its way past. "The things you do to me."

Trapping his bottom lip in-between his teeth, Tripp's eyes fill with mischief and he bucks his hips. "Show me," he demands, and then cheekily adds, "Sir."

With a low chuckle, Leander resumes thrusting into Tripp, languid strokes that make it easy for him to reach down and work fingers around his cock once again. It's all Leander inside Tripp now, and he *almost* wants to keep it that way, out of some bizarre, possessive notion that hardly makes a lick of logical sense.

Tripp slips back into the rhythm easily, and after a few brushes against his prostate that have him incredibly loose and whining, Leander picks up the dildo again. Slicking its length, Leander pulls almost all the way out, enough that he can line the fake cock up alongside his own and they can press in together. Slowly, carefully, and with Tripp alternately tensing and forcing himself to relax, Leander guides them both inside.

It's a tough thing, being a Dom in a situation like this, because the pleasure on *his* end is *fucking* exquisite. Between the vice-like tightness, the heat of Tripp's walls, and the pressure-sensation mix from the veiny silicone sharing his space, it's all Leander can do not to let his eyes roll back in his head and ram them both home. It's only through years of depriving himself gratification and practicing the extremes of self-control that Leander is able to grit his teeth and resist the urge to buck his hips and chase the stimulation he craves. Against every baser instinct, he ignores the way his body ripples with fire, sweat rolling over his shoulder blades and down the sides of his face.

"*Tripp,*" he murmurs. "Are you alright? Color, Tripp."

Both cocks are nearly fully-seated, and Leander stops moving until Tripp pulls himself together enough to murmur, "Green." Cuffs forgotten, his right hand is wrapped around Leander's bicep, nails digging into the muscle, but Leander's not about to chastise him for touching before he gave the go-ahead. Not now, and not when he so conveniently ignored the issue when it was serving *him* to indulge his vanilla whims.

Below him, Tripp's chest heaves and glistens with its own thin sheen of sweat, and he pants, licking his lips while his eyes roam wildly across the ceiling. "Tripp," Leander repeats. "Talk to me, sweet boy."

"'M good," Tripp manages with a nod, head tipping back as he tries to force his hips down the rest of the way, but Leander holds firm and doesn't give it to him just yet. "C'mon, Lee, I can take it," he begs. "I want it—please, *please*, Sir."

Leander obliges, *how could he not?* He's so pleased and proud of Tripp, so turned on by the way he's spread out and willing to do almost anything Leander desires of him. When both cocks can go no further, Leander gives Tripp another moment to adjust and then starts to move. He's careful to hold the dildo in place, to not be too rough or demanding, but there's plenty of lube in the mix, and Tripp's rim is doing just fine. Leander fingers the edge admiringly as he rolls his pelvis forward, and Tripp moans, flexing his hips up for more.

With his ass so full, Tripp's prostate has to be receiving fairly constant stimulation, and it's not long before he's completely undone, near-sobbing and clawing at Leander's shoulders, begging for contact, for release. Not that Leander has any intention of denying him such, but Tripp *can* come untouched, and Leander definitely thinks that this is the right time to do so.

A few more drawn-out internal strokes have Tripp tensing up all around him, and just like the night prior, that's enough to wrest Leander's last ounce of self-control from his grasp. While Tripp cries out and grabs a handful of his hair, Leander is burying his face into Tripp's chest, second dildo forgotten and slipping out as he shoves himself deep, shaking and finishing with a final thrust against Tripp's body that is anything but gentle.

The world turns hazy for a few minutes as Leander sighs into Tripp's skin and slowly comes back to his senses. Usually, he's fairly alert once a scene ends, jumping up and out of bed right away, grabbing aftercare items for Tripp and generally ensuring that his sub gets what he needs.

Today, Leander is wiped. Whether from the alcohol or the multiple rounds of intense sex, or something completely else, that last orgasm did him in. When his arms stop tingling and his brain stitches itself back together enough that he can process a coherent thought, Leander realizes that Tripp is holding him and petting his hair.

"Apologies," he says swiftly, casting Tripp a rueful look as he tries to shove his way up and off of the bed. "Let me just—"

"Hey." Tripp stops him, reaching out to cup Leander's jaw and drag him back down for a deep, unhurried kiss. That's new, too. "No worries," Tripp says when they part, Leander feeling slightly dazed and off-kilter all over again, especially at the brightness of Tripp's smile. "I only needed that."

Leander smiles back before glancing down at the way their torsos pressing together has smeared the sticky mess on Tripp's stomach around. He sighs, narrowing his eyes at Tripp and gesturing towards it.

"Look what you did. Who's going to clean that up?"

Mere suggestion is all Tripp needs, green eyes flashing before his head dips down, mouthing enthusiastically over his own spend as Leander works fingers into his hair encouragingly. "Use your tongue," he suggests, and Tripp huffs a laugh against his skin but complies. When he's done, Tripp drags said tongue all the way up Leander's chest and neck, nipping at his jaw before capturing his mouth one more time.

The cooling, wet trail and the feeling of Tripp's lips against his own have Leander shivering, wanting to grab at Tripp again, to throw him down and see what else he can wring from his body, but the truth is, he's also *pretty* fucking tired.

With great self-restraint—which is apparently today's theme—he forces himself to go retrieve a warm washcloth, some cream, and Tripp's juice. On his way back to the bed, Leander stops at the beside table and taps at the screen of his phone. After checking the time, he's pleased to discover that it's barely approaching seven—they have *hours* with which to sleep and then share a shower, followed by a greasy brunch together.

Perhaps Tripp would even like to watch a movie after that, before they go their separate ways. After all they've been through this weekend, some extra cuddling and contact is certainly in order.

Tripp seems to feel the same, anxious as he is to drag Leander back underneath the covers before he's done even a passable job of cleaning up and caring for him. Though he has to hold the glass himself and tip the liquid into Tripp's mouth near-forcibly, Leander does manage to get most of the juice into his belly before Tripp's adamant twisting of their limbs together wins out and he has to set the cup down or lose it.

"You need to drink that," he admonishes sternly, which is hard to do with a sappy smile on your face.

"I need *you*," Tripp counters, eyebrows raised, and if that isn't a *checkmate, game over,* Leander doesn't know what is. Poking Leander in the ribs, Tripp grins and waggles said eyebrows. Leander rolls his eyes, because he certainly can't admit that he's putty in Tripp's hands.

"C'mon," Tripp wheedles, "Give me something good to think about tonight when I'm all alone and stuck in the shitty bunk by the door with the janky frame."

"I believe I've already given you *many* 'good things' to think about, greedy. Also, Station Fifteen's mattresses were at least replaced sometime in the last decade," Leander reminds him, as Tripp settles easily into his arms, head pillowed on his chest. "I'm fairly certain that ours were purchased in the estate sale from that defunct nursing home over on Fourth Street."

"That's maybe the most disgusting thing you've ever said, Lee."

"It's true," Leander replies defensively. "At least, I think it's true." Tripp snorts and buries his face into the side of Leander's neck, one arm slung casually around his torso. Leander's eyes slip closed as he feels Tripp inhaling a deep, satisfied breath, holding his own as his friend blows it back out, hot on Leander's skin.

It would be so *easy* to tell him, right now. The moment even feels right.

I love you, he would say, and Tripp—what *would* Tripp say in return? Leander *hopes,* prays, *feels* the way Tripp holds him so tenderly, and it's hard to imagine a situation where he *wouldn't* reply in kind.

This can't be imagined, he thinks. Socially awkward as he may be, this is *Tripp,* and Leander *knows* Tripp. Why is it so hard to fully believe that he might be right about this, too?

But then, *why* doesn't Tripp *say* so?

Sucking in a deep breath and exhaling in measured motion, Leander pushes those thoughts aside. There's no reason to taint their afterglow or the rest of their day together with confusing '*what if*'s. Later, when they're away from the playroom and on even footing, when they're not staring down the barrel of several nights in a row spent apart, Leander will consider testing the waters.

Not now. The worst thing he could do would be to send Tripp away on another misunderstanding or miscommunication. One that they'll both have to stew over alone, inevitably twisting and blowing up into something that it was never meant to be. So, later it is. *Not today.*

In his arms, Tripp sighs blissfully, and Leander wraps both arms even tighter around him as he turns more fully to face his friend.

"I'm very grateful to have you, Tripp," he ends up saying, because he just can't leave well enough alone.

In response, Tripp nuzzles back, his hair tickling Leander's lips and nose, making him smile. "'S'me too, Leeee," Tripp slurs, clearly having journeyed the better part of the way to unconsciousness already, so Leander stops needling at what's between them and joins him.

***

Domestic. That's the word for what they're doing, the explanation behind the warm, fluttery feeling in Leander's chest when he looks down and sees Tripp sprawled between his legs.

They've retreated to the couch, now, after waking lazily, showering slowly, and cooking a meal that's going to take several hours on the treadmill to burn off. As much as Leander enjoyed the wedding yesterday, from the public play to the teasing, and—*yes,* he can admit it—the *romance* of it all, this is something different. As much as he wishes *every* night and every morning could be filled with the kind of wildly satisfying sex and submission they've shared, it's these last few hours spent with Tripp that Leander has enjoyed the most.

And isn't that bizarre? Despite the fact that Leander can recognize (now) that he's harbored budding feelings towards Tripp for quite some time, since long before they ever slept together, *this* is an outcome he could never have foreseen. Having someone in his space who feels as if they belong, like they're some kind of piece to his puzzle that Leander didn't even realize he was missing. He can't imagine attempting to return to a life without *this* version of Tripp in it.

Even when Autumn was around, she never stayed for this part—not that Leander wanted her to do so. The two of them were exclusively Dom and sub in the playroom, and in public, they were friends. They didn't shower together outside of scenes, didn't kiss for no reason at all, didn't share the burden of chores and clean-up. Perhaps most notably, they did not spend *days on end* enjoying each other's company, simply because they *could.*

This is brand-new territory he and Tripp are exploring, and it frightens Leander a little at how much he *loves* it. How desperately he yearns for this to be his everyday reality, and for Tripp to want the same thing. The boring, the mundane, the rote. Leander wants to be dull and domestic *with Tripp,* and he can't quite figure out how and when that happened.

He wants today on repeat: stripping soiled bed sheets with Tripp standing on the other side of the mattress, cracking terrible jokes and acting entirely carefree. The way Tripp so easily gathered the dirty sheets and dropped them into the hamper before making his way over to the usually-covered windows and pulling the curtains, lifting the sash to circulate fresh air through the room. He's so *natural,* so comfortable in Leander's home.

Of course, Tripp has always been that way, hasn't he? He just hasn't been that way wearing nothing save for Leander's collar, Leander's fingerprint bruises, and Leander's teeth marks.

That thought alone was enough to bring the rest to a screeching halt, Leander having to closely examine whether it was *possessiveness* over Tripp that's been driving his feelings of late. Of course, that devastating thought was easy enough to discard as he watched Tripp finish re-making the bed, kneeing his way onto the crisp, fresh sheets with a mischievous grin plastered across his face.

"Wanna mess these up too, Sir?" he asked, and Leander melted.

Tripp is already his, and what Leander feels for him—what he craves *from him*—goes far beyond simple jealousy or the desire to *keep* him. No, Leander wants *all* of this. Wants Tripp here all of the time, wants this space to be *their* space, and for Tripp to always move around it as freely as Leander has watched him do today.

Because none of it stopped with the scene. It's certainly not new territory for the two of them to forgo leaving their roles at the playroom door, but *nothing* they've done since stepping outside of that space earlier this afternoon has been about sex.

Service, perhaps. Submission, definitely, but not *sex,* and sex is what their relationship—*their contract*—is predicated on. Sex is *all* that contract is, really, at the end of the day. So the spillover *must* come from one of two things: either Tripp's novice nature to the BDSM community is making him confused, or this is something that he wants, too.

Perhaps that's the segue I need, Leander thinks. He could bring these things up in the context of their weekly contract review, test the waters that way and see how Tripp responds. It would be… *safer,* for both of their hearts and their friendship. That is, if Leander has somehow misinterpreted the signals he believes with increasing certainty that Tripp has been sending. In a review setting, Tripp will have an easy out, if he wishes to take it. He can simply say that he didn't understand the boundaries and limits of a Dom / sub relationship and their contract. If that turns out to be the case, then they can fix it going forward, and Leander will let the rest go.

But *God,* Leander prays he isn't wrong. He'll bend to Tripp's wishes, he'll do whatever it takes to keep the piecemeal parts of Tripp that he's allowed to share, but—it would be crushing. The *first* time he's truly felt romantic love, to have it rejected and scorned—well, that possibility is not something Leander is able to look at too closely, not while Tripp is in kissing distance, anyway. It's a devastating concept.

So Leander just *hopes,* hopes *so* badly that Tripp wants his love as much as he wants to give it.

This certainly feels like love. The way they move so easily around each other while cooking in the kitchen, the way Tripp thinks nothing of invading Leander's space as he pushes eggs around in a frying pan. The way Leander's coffee is made exactly to his liking and kept filled until they settle down together, and the way Tripp kneels at Leander's feet without him even asking.

Hand-feeding Tripp *could* be sexual and certainly has been in the past, but today, it feels different. Tripp holds Leander's eye contact, lingers while licking and sucking the food from his fingers, but the air between them is charged in a way that has nothing to do with simple arousal and *getting off.*

As Tripp settles against Leander's thigh and between his legs, Leander keeps a hand in his hair while he's there. Several times, he nearly sticks fingers into his coffee, all for his inability to look away. It's worth it, though—it *feels* worth it. This feels like love blossoming between them, as much as Leander has any clue, any *guess* as to how 'Love' with a capital 'L' is supposed to feel.

Tripp is so unlike his usual self, or perhaps Leander has that backward. Maybe *this* Tripp is the true Tripp, the one who's been granted permission to shed his tough facade and be the soft, gentle boy that lives inside of him. The part of Tripp that's usually deemed weak and sequestered away where no one is allowed to see, set free. He's so quick to take *care* of Leander, looks so entirely *happy* to be tasked with mundane chores and routine activities that Leander himself would usually loathe doing on his own.

Today, it all feels like some kind of magic.

Chores done, bellies full, and kitchen cleaned, they settled on the couch together to tackle the entirety of the *Star Wars* franchise. That was several hours ago by this point, after Tripp fussed excessively about the importance of watching the movies in a particular order. They have been, technically, but all Leander has to show for that is the hope that Tripp never asks for an in-depth analysis of his thoughts, because he's barely glanced up at the screen.

In fact, he's been so taken with the way Tripp looks and feels in his arms that he truly can't conjure even one good reason why he *should* watch anything else. The miraculous rise and fall of Tripp's chest is all the entertainment Leander thinks he could ever need.

Plus, they're *snuggling*. Over Tripp's bare stomach, their right hands are twisted together, and the blanket Leander keeps on the back of the couch is draped lazily over Tripp's hips and his own legs just below that. When Tripp hums in quiet satisfaction, Leander resumes petting his hair from where his free arm has fallen away in distraction.

Absently, Tripp shifts and reaches out from under the blankets towards his phone, which is sitting next to them on the coffee table. He presses the home button and groans when the screen lights up.

"Gotta take off soon," he says softly, the reluctance clear in his voice, and privately, Leander savors it.

"I know," he replies, unable to resist pressing a soft kiss just behind Tripp's ear.

"Hmm," is the only response, save for Tripp wiggling some against Leander's chest and groin, which makes him smile.

"Don't start," he warns. "We do not have the time."

"I didn't start shit," Tripp retorts, and he's not exactly wrong, there. "But you're right. Hey, lucky you—get to lay around doing nothing for another hour at least before it's time to get moving. You're already home."

Just barely, Leander resists the urge to tell Tripp that he could be home, too, if that's what he wanted.

Not the time.

When Tripp leans forward and stands with a luxurious stretch that highlights every carved muscle in his back and shoulders, Leander can hardly enjoy it. Apparently, he'll be playing the role of "petulant brat" in their relationship today.

Tripp should spank *him*.

Not the time!

As he pouts and Tripp wanders about gathering his things, Leander tries halfheartedly to identify the plot of the movie that's still playing, but it's too far in, and he's irredeemably lost. Instead, he watches as Tripp reverently replaces his collar in its box before dipping over to Leander's bedroom, emerging wearing one of his old t-shirts and a pair of sweatpants that fit him like sin.

Somewhat belatedly, Leander realizes that he must have made some sort of face at the sight, because Tripp grins, flashing the smile that means he's truly amused, the one where he presses the tip of his tongue just behind his teeth.

Someone stab me in the heart, it would be less painful, Leander thinks.

Wednesday cannot come soon enough. And yet—

"Hey," Tripp says off-handedly as he's pulling on his boots, snapping his fingers like he's just recalled an important thought. "Wasn't there something you wanted to tell me? Something you wanted to talk about? I could swear we got interrupted last night, but I'll admit," he pauses to tap his temple, "It's all kinda fuzzy." He straightens up, and suddenly, his expression becomes weirdly intense.

Leander fidgets. Almost everything in him is screaming to just *tell Tripp* how he feels, and *something* about Tripp's faux-casual-bullshit is setting off alarms in Leander's head. On the other hand, every worrisome thought from earlier comes flooding back, along with the hauntingly frightening possibility that Tripp *doesn't* love him the way he loves Tripp.

That sends Leander's anxiety flaring, has him clutching nervously at the blanket in his lap, has him scared. Scared enough that he freezes and can't do *anything* but default back to his previously-made plans to test the waters surrounding this in a way that ensures Tripp has an out. An out that might be the difference between preserving what they *do* have, or losing it completely.

Losing *Tripp* completely. That, Leander can *not* risk.

He swallows heavily and tries to look innocent, blinking back at Tripp with wide eyes and shaking his head. "No idea," he lies. "I'm sure I did, at some point, but… I also had too much to drink." Leander licks his dry lips and watches Tripp's face carefully. To the casual observer, it would appear that Tripp has virtually no reaction, but Leander knows him so much better than that. The light in his eyes dims slightly, and his smile becomes just a *little* tight.

Right away, Leander starts to panic for an entirely different reason, wondering if that *was* the opening he's been waiting for and he just—*oh, no.*

Tripp is already turning towards the door when Leander jumps off of the couch and follows. "Tripp," he calls out. "Tripp, wait."

"No worries, Lee," Tripp says, huffing a little laugh and turning to face him. Up close, Tripp just looks tired, but his smile is genuine again, and Leander wonders if he imagined the strain being there at all. It's certainly possible, the way he's been all up in his own feelings about this mess. As a test, he opens his arms imploringly, and Tripp moves so quickly, he nearly falls into them. Squeezing Leander tight, he rocks them both back and forth, from side to side.

"Alright," Tripp says, reassuring. "We're good, pal."

When he pulls back, Tripp winks and claps Leander on the shoulder. "Text me when you get to work. Lemme know who you're on with and stuff. If my guys are up for it, I'll see if they wanna grab coffee and donuts, bring the engine down, we can all hang at your place. Play cards or something. Cool?"

It's been a while since they've done anything like that, and Leander finds himself nodding enthusiastically. It would be a real pleasure to see Tripp socially at work, and it would probably go a long way towards soothing his own frayed nerves and fear of some potential misunderstanding brewing between them. Plus, poker and company will make work seem hardly like work at all.

"Yes," he agrees. "That would be wonderful. I'll look forward to it."

Tripp waves as the door closes behind him. "I'll see ya, Lee."

Despite their apparent resolution, the click of the lock leaves Leander feeling totally unsettled. No one is dropping and everything, on paper, is fine. And yet, something doesn't feel right. Leander can't help but worry that he's made a huge misstep, missed an opening he was too busy looking for to actually *see*.

That would be so like him, Leander is reluctant to dismiss the possibility.

He stands in the middle of the entryway, wiping his suddenly-sweaty hands against his pajama pants and angsting over the possibility. Hopefully, if he did screw this up, it's nothing he can't fix in time.

***

"And your medical history, tell me again about that," Leander prompts. He's balancing his clipboard on his thighs while bracing his feet against the bars of the stretcher to keep himself from sliding around on the bench seat. Sirens wail in the background, not so much out of necessity for their patient, but the need to get the ambulance back in service quickly—all of the area's trucks are tied up on calls.

"Well," begins the slight, frail, elderly woman who is currently strapped to Leander's stretcher. "There's my high blood pressure." He plasters on a practiced, 'interested and empathetic' expression, but inwardly, he's sighing. Mrs. Baxter calls 911 several times a month complaining of chest pain, but in reality, she's just very lonely and prone to indigestion. Still, Leander's job isn't to judge—everyone with "chest pain" gets the same workup, regardless of his opinion on it.

Thus, for the second time in two weeks, Mrs. Baxter is riding in the back of City Medic Two, hooked up to a cardiac monitor, blood pressure cuff, and pulse ox, having been given aspirin and a nitroglycerin tablet left to dissolve under her tongue. She particularly dislikes that part but always says that it helps with her pain, so Leander can't even get away with skipping it.

He taps his pen on the side of the clipboard and cycles her blood pressure again, absently glancing out the back window to see the lines on the highway whipping along through the ambulance's tail lights before disappearing into inky blackness.

Mrs. Baxter is rattling on about her diabetes and the stent she had placed in 2002, but Leander's only half-listening. Nothing about her medical history has changed in the five or so days since he brought her in last, and the hospital will have an accurate record to print for him. His question was mainly to give Mrs. Baxter something to chat about, since left to her own devices, she's eternally trying to set him up with her (supposedly) very accomplished and attractive single granddaughter.

They're headed to the smaller, rural hospital just beyond the outskirts of the city, so the ride is slightly longer than Leander is used to. When they're five minutes out, he calls report in to the Emergency Department over the radio and transmits a copy of the EKG (normal, nothing acute going on that he can identify) along with it. Since Mrs. Baxter seems to be the very picture of stability, Leander disconnects her from the monitor to take her out of the rig and wheel her inside upon their arrival.

The ED is busy tonight, especially for the smaller hospital which tends to see less traffic, but the board above the EMS entrance has them already assigned to a room. Leander waves and nods a greeting to some of the staff members as he and Marley navigate the litter through the heart of the emergency room and then down a side hallway. As they're transferring Mrs. Baxter from their bed to the hospital's, both of their pagers *and* Leander's radio simultaneously activate, creating an obnoxious clash of beeping sounds and static.

This far inside the hospital, the dispatcher's voice is muffled and broken, but after squelching his pager and dimming the volume on his radio, Leander is able to discern that they're being called to standby at a building fire.

Distractedly, he gives report to the ED nurse and kisses Mrs. Baxter goodbye on the cheek—as annoying as she might be, she's basically family for how often Leander sees her—and wishes her luck. Marley replenishes their supplies and grabs a demographic print out from registration for Leander's chart while he heads outside and clarifies with dispatch who is needed on the incoming call.

The unexpectedly dramatic bottom line turns out to be that *everyone* is needed. This is a multi-story blaze in an abandoned, industrial building on the south side of town. There are reports of homeless encampments inside, which will need to be checked for and cleared by the firefighters. Only one victim—a night security guard with complaints of difficulty breathing after smoke inhalation—has been reported. Several fire companies are already on their way, and Medic One, staffed with Zosia and Echo tonight, is clearing from Central and enroute as well.

Leander places Medic Two responding as Marley gets them back out on the road, flipping on their lights and sirens and putting the pedal to the floor. Over text message, Zosia and Leander coordinate a decision to request two other ambulances from the county to come and assist their efforts. There's always a possibility that the extra support won't be needed, but it's infinitely better to have too many hands and nothing to do, rather than too many patients and not enough help.

At the very least, this looks to be an all-night sort of event, and one of their trucks will be grounded at the scene, unable to leave, overseeing both firefighter rehab and any necessary patient triage. Better to have the option of an additional transport truck, or even local 911 coverage.

Better safe than sorry, Leander decides.

Once all of that's settled, there's nothing to do but get there. He and Marley are quiet, listening to scene status updates over the fire band as they drive.

So much for poker night, Leander thinks dejectedly. He knows he shouldn't be petulant. After all, this is his *job,* and he and Tripp had a wonderful weekend together. But Tripp's been short with him over text messages this evening, not the warm and affectionate version of the man Leander's become spoiled with lately.

He scrolls through their text thread anyway, sending off a, *"Be careful,"* message that he doubts Tripp will even see. In fact, Tripp may already be packed up and inside the burning building—likely, even, since his station is located right down the street.

Earlier, Leander *was* harboring some concerns that Tripp's distant attitude meant that he was dropping. Unfortunately, they were both so busy, a physical check-in was patently out of the question. Leander's learned from his past mistakes, though, so after transferring care of his patient and before putting the truck back in service, he stepped around to the side of Central's ER for some privacy in order to make a call.

Upon hearing Tripp's voice, Leander could tell that wasn't the case, that he wasn't dropping, and that, at least, was a relief. Something still seemed *off* about the man, though, and whatever it was, Tripp wasn't sharing. When they hung up, Leander didn't feel much better than before they spoke.

The twisted knot in his stomach hasn't unclenched, either, and Leander knows it's related. He's fairly certain about what's going on with Tripp, and it's not something that can be fixed over text or a casual phone call. Part of him is remorseful, thinking that if he could rewind time and do this afternoon over, he *would*—he regrets letting fear control his response, now—but another part of him is irritated.

Tripp could certainly say something, too, instead of pulling this passive-aggressive, "I'm fine," bullshit Leander thought that they were long past.

It's a sore enough subject that he hasn't really *tried* to make amends (or even made plans to make amends) over text, because if Tripp is going to play games, Leander's not going to make it easy for him to do so. That doesn't mean he isn't worried as hell about Tripp's well-being, though.

The box-frame ambulance turns a bit roughly onto the darkened side street that's home to the building they're headed towards, smashing a pothole with the right front tire. The jolt has Marley grimacing apologetically as the truck bounces from side to side, trying to right itself. Grumbling nonsense, Leander grabs onto the handle above his head so that he doesn't get tossed into the window, and narrows his eyes at his partner before focusing them out on the scene ahead.

The night is dark but the sky is almost glowing with the way the fire has engulfed half of the top floor of the sprawling building. It's big—three stories high and spanning a good third of the block just in width. Leander recognizes the place to be a now-defunct battery manufacturing company with questionable scruples—the locals say the groundwater within a mile each direction is permanently tainted from their activities, but no one seems to know if that's actually true. Regardless, the inside remains full of everything from giant smelters, to various production machinery, to empty corporate offices. It's going to be an absolute *nightmare* to control and clear.

On the plus side, it's a new enough building that it should have sprinklers, though Leander guesses they're likely partially defunct from lack of maintenance. Perhaps they've been able to keep the flames somewhat contained, though. Maybe that's why it appears that only the back corner of the top floor is on its way to fully engulfed. Out on the street, there are tons of assorted fire apparatus lining both curbs: engines, ladders, at least one rescue, and as such, there's charged and leaking five-inch hose line everywhere.

Leander instructs Marley to follow the direction of a police officer—Darla— wearing a reflective vest and waving them through a particular path to the heart of the whole scene. On the other side of the street, safe from being parked in by apparatus and gear, Leander clocks Medic One sitting with their flashers on and back doors open. Inside, Zosia and Echo are visibly working on a patient.

They must have plans to transport, which is why Darla is stranding Medic Two in the middle of the fray. Leander sighs and reluctantly gets on the radio to assume EMS command. They're stuck here for the duration, now, might as well accept his fate.

It's not long before his phone is buzzing in his pocket—Zosia, confirming his suspicions—Medic One is going to Central with the smoke inhalation guy, and then they'll be back. As he exits the ambulance, Leander acknowledges both her and Echo as they wave from the back of their truck before pulling the doors shut.

While Leander would love to sweep an eye over the scene, to spend a few moments looking for Tripp and his crew just to obtain visual affirmation that he's okay, there's no time. Even as Leander is yanking the side compartment of the rig open and pulling out their fire rehab supplies, more trucks are arriving to help fight the blaze, which means even more people whose health and safety it's his job to monitor and protect.

Sooner rather than later, he's going to need to begin cycling them all through periodic vital sign checks and water breaks. He's in over his head and he hasn't even started.

Better get to work.

The next two hours pass in a blur of blood pressure cuffs and lung sounds, the roar of fire and engines idling, the heavy scent of smoke and diesel and sweat mingling in the night air. Despite the cold, no one complains or falters, everyone does exactly what they came here to do. Leander keeps only one of the ambulances that he requested from the county—a couple of firefighters end up being transported for minor issues, and it's hard to run a rehab of this size with just two people.

An hour or so in, a handful of the city's new EMT-certified probationary firefighters show up to help, and that's a huge burden lifted.

Eventually, hours in, the Red Cross arrives, bringing their own emergency assistance unit. They're handing out food, hot drinks, and providing a place for people who need it to get warm, which takes some additional strain off of Leander and his team's shoulders.

The fire is aggressive, its location in the building making exterior attacks difficult and ultimately ineffective at eliminating the source. Despite multiple hose lines directed at the flames, they just keep coming, keep spreading, eating away at more and more of the building that still isn't fully cleared. Everyone is weary— some of these firefighters haven't worked a long-haul scene like this before, but

Mickey certainly has, and he wields control of the fire scene with a careful, capable, iron fist.

As EMS command, Leander confers with him briefly early on, walking over to where Mickey is running things out of his Chief's vehicle. Various ideas are exchanged, but Mickey makes one thing clear—he wants to know if his people are tired, if they're wearing out. Once the building is confirmed empty and any of the homeless people holed up in there are evacuated, if they can't get the blaze under control, then Mickey isn't afraid to let the thing burn.

He clearly wants Leander to understand that he'll do that in a heartbeat, rather than risk his people's health and lives. It'll be controlled, of course: a surround and drown operation with continued exterior attacks to prevent the flames from jumping or spreading. At the end of the day, though, that amounts to the same thing—they'll burn this whole thing to the ground, if that's what needs to happen.

Since Tripp is leading one of the main interior attack crews, Leander sees him come through the EMS rehab station several times. Each time, he's more ornery than the last, snapping at Leander and barely tolerating having his vital signs taken. The first couple of encounters, Leander lets him go, doesn't even address his attitude. Tripp is stressed, he's worried that there are still victims inside the building, he's pissed at having to interrupt his search and rescue for rehab, and he's pissed at Leander himself, that much is clear.

It's not hard for Leander's cooler head to prevail, and for him to simply table the entire thing. They'll work through it tomorrow, when no one's life is at stake.

But the third time Tripp is ordered by Mickey to sit through rehab, he mouths off, is an asshole to Marley, and that is Leander's breaking point. He wouldn't put up with that behavior from *anyone,* never mind *Tripp.* Tripp, who is a leader, a mentor, and owes his entire crew a better example than that. Never mind what he owes his *friends.*

When it happens, Leander is standing across from him in the little campfire-style circle they've created just off the back of the open-doored ambulance. He's distracted, crouched down and taking Ezra's blood pressure. Ezra is a new recruit to Tripp's station, a bright, sunny personality that Leander finds somewhat shocking and better in small doses. Despite that, he's perpetually pleasant, always smiling, and so when Leander glances up from where he's been focused on the gauge of the cuff to find Ezra frowning, he pays attention.

Following Ezra's gaze, he registers Marley and Tripp engaged in a visibly heated discussion, glancing over just in time to see Tripp *smack* Marley's arm away, snatching and tossing the pulse ox she's been trying to slide onto his finger to the ground with a worrying crunch.

"I'm *fine*," Tripp snaps, and Marley recoils.

In an instant, Leander's between them, carefully curling an arm around Marley's body to push her behind him while he glares down Tripp.

"Oh, don't you start too," Tripp scoffs, throwing his hands up before folding them across his chest, and Leander has had enough.

"Sidebar," he growls, curling a hand around Tripp's sweaty, t-shirt-clad bicep, only possible because his bunker jacket is currently shed, slung over the back of the camp chair he's been occupying. "Now." Tripp sighs heavily but doesn't resist as Leander yanks him roughly around the side of the ambulance, where they have at least some semblance of privacy.

"What's wrong with you?" Leander demands.

True to form, Tripp just rolls his eyes and tightens the way he's hugging himself, but Leander detects a flash of—*something* behind the arrogant facade. They're at an impasse—Tripp is silent, and Leander is seriously concerned. A distracted Tripp is a reckless Tripp, and he can't send him back into an active fire like *this*. He has two choices right now: get through to Tripp, or bench him. While Tripp would deserve it, Leander doesn't think that making him angrier will serve any-one in the long run (himself included), so he softens.

"Tripp, this isn't you," he tries. "Marley is one of your best friends. At the very least, you owe her an apology. And you owe your work *focus*."

"Fine, I'll apologize," Tripp replies shortly, staring intently at the gold lettering on the side of the truck and not at Leander at all.

Time to bring out the big guns.

"Tripp, please," Leander says softly, stepping forward into Tripp's space, close en-ough that their chests are nearly pressed together. "You're scaring me, this fire is not something to trifle with." He trails a hand tentatively up Tripp's arm and Tripp grumbles a little but dips his head, as close to Leander as he's allowed him-self to get all night long. If Leander tipped his chin up, he could kiss him. "I un-derstand that you're off your game, that I made a mistake earlier, that you're an-gry with me—"

It's the wrong thing to say. Tripp rips himself away like Leander *is* the fire and he's just remembered that flames burn. "Tripp," Leander tries, but Tripp holds out a hand: *stay back*. His fingers curl slowly into a fist, except for one that stays pointed somewhat menacingly in Leander's direction.

"Not everything is about sex and submission," he says icily.

Leander furrows his brow. "I know that."

"Yeah," Tripp replies, nodding tightly. "'Course you do. You know so much about me," he says, and Leander can't figure out whether he sounds more angry or hurt. Neither are good signs. "Just—" Tripp ducks his head and shakes himself off. "Lemme do my damn job, Lee." His radio crackles, and Leander sees wetness shining in Tripp's eyes. "I gotta go."

Before Leander can say another word, Tripp is stalking off and taking the rest of his team with him. Leander *could* pull rank, could call him back and demand that he stay, but he saw Tripp's vitals earlier and there really wasn't anything concerning. It would be a power move, and one that he has *no* doubt would go over like a lead brick in a pool. After he wanders back into his makeshift camp and exchanges a look of disbelief with Marley, Leander lets Tripp go.

More firefighters cycle through for checks, and Leander goes through the motions of his job but his mind is elsewhere. He *should* have proceeded more carefully, should have predicted that Tripp would be hyper-sensitized over a perceived rejection. Of *course,* he perceived Leander's reply earlier as a rejection.

You idiot, Leander admonishes himself.

The fact that Tripp won't even give him the opportunity to make it right smarts, but Tripp's mocking of him was fair. Leander *does* know Tripp that well, and he should have followed his instincts. Bereft over his shitty decisions, Leander struggles to focus on simple tasks like taking a pulse, never mind paying attention to the fire scene as a whole.

It therefore takes a moment to register with him when panic erupts over the radio. Marley rushes to his side, cranking the volume high on the portable at Leander's hip so that they can listen in. The ominous sounds of multiple emergency buttons activating drowns out all other noise as several radios with hot mics war for air priority, waiting for the dispatch center to make sense of the cacophony. Marley's nails dig into his bicep, pinpricks of pain keeping him grounded amidst the crashing sounds and screams echoing over everyone's handheld devices.

When the words hitting his ears finally begin to make sense, Leander goes numb from head to toe, unable to feel his limbs any longer as he struggles to process what's happening.

"Structural collapse second floor... backdraft... multiple firefighters down... trapped... no visual... RIT team activation... "

Around him, firefighters are jumping into motion, swarming the building with all sorts of rescue gear and intent. Mickey is yelling, Leander can hear him without aid of the radio, and Assistant Chief Walter is standing on top of an SUV, directing squads and acting like a human repeater.

All Leander can do is stare blankly as the whole world seems to grind into slow motion. Only one thing really sticks in his mind, and that's Ezra's voice filtering over the wire through the chaos.

"Firefighter down! Lieut—Tripp, Tripp Truett, he fell through the floor, Mickey! He fell through the fucking floor!"

Chapter 11

There's a strange pressure around Tripp's face when he begins to wake. His eyes blink slowly, heavy lids sticking together in protest before he manages to get them all the way open. For a moment, he can't for the life of him figure out where the fuck he *is*. Last Tripp can recall, he was at Lee's place. They were fucking and cooking and being pretty disgustingly domestic together—Tripp had been thinking that it was a good thing he needed to go to work, otherwise he might've developed a cavity from all the *sweetness* passing between them.

Lifting a hand to his face, Tripp realizes that he's looking out through dirty, smudged plastic, staring at a fire-rated glove. He closes his eyes for an extended minute, and then everything comes flooding back, albeit in clips and flashes.

Searching the building for ages before *finally* stumbling upon the homeless encampment initially reported to be there. The heat of the fire, and how the floor shivered ominously before collapsing underneath his feet. The way his arm muscles strained, tossing that unconscious, presumably homeless teenager to safety in Gunnar's arms, seconds before the fire sucked him down. Gunnar's screaming face and outstretched hand, useless as Tripp slipped away into the burning pit.

All of that comes flooding back, yes. But so does everything *before* it.

Arguably, recovering the memory of Lee awkwardly dodging his question—when both of them knew *full well* what the hell Tripp was asking about—hurts a hell of a lot more than the fiery plunge into the depths of the burning warehouse.

Groaning, Tripp tries to rub at his face, abruptly being reminded that he's wearing an SCBA mask, responsible for piping in the fresh(ish) air he's currently breathing. As if on cue, the little alarm that monitors the level in his oxygen tank begins beeping a warning in Tripp's ear. He hits the button to silence the sound —it's not as if there's anything he can do about that now. Either he has enough air to survive until he's rescued, or he doesn't.

Above him, the hole Tripp fell through isn't even visible anymore, the entire floor caved in directly overhead, creating a hovel of broken concrete, pipes, and duct-work. The dust hasn't even fully settled, so he can't have been down here that long. On the other hand, the throbbing in his head tells Tripp the helmet he's wearing didn't completely protect him from knocking it but good, so who the hell knows?

As he glances around and takes stock of the situation, Tripp's budding fear begins to compound. With everything in his immediate vicinity partially collapsed, there's no way to identify which direction is which, and if Tripp remembers correctly, he and his team weren't even searching *in* a room that was bordered by an exterior wall.

He might be in some real trouble, here.

The visible flames are weak, which is a small miracle. They're busy at the edges of the room, eating up some of the insulation and drywall packed into the rubble above Tripp's head and piled to his left. The result is a low-level glow that at least allows him to see at all, but Tripp's not soothed—those flames are only going to get bigger, and as he's experienced so many times in the burn building, concrete holds heat like an oven. He'll cook to death if he stays put, and that's if he doesn't run out of clean air to breathe first.

Wincing, Tripp pushes up on the assortment of debris and broken concrete that he's landed on, fumbling around and struggling until he's finally sitting relatively vertical. In the process, he cries out in surprise pain not once, but twice. The first happens when he puts pressure on his left hand—his wrist, he's pretty sure—the second when he tries to move his left leg. Safe to say, that side of his body must have taken the brunt of his fall.

Great. That's just great.

His vantage point from sitting upright isn't much better, unfortunately, but it does give Tripp access to the portable radio clipped to his pants that he was previously lying on. Cradling his injured arm across his lap, Tripp grimaces as he uses those sore fingers to tug off his right glove, freeing his hand so he can reach across his body and work the radio's controls. The first thing he does is activate his panic button, a little orange circle on the top of the radio that will—theoretically, if he's not out of signal range—temporarily truncate other transmissions so that he can patch through.

Once it's pressed, a whole lot of *nothing* happens, and it takes Tripp a few seconds to realize that his volume is flipped all the way down. As soon as he twists the dial to turn it up, the air in the increasingly stifling room is filled with the end of the emergency notification alert, and then, relievedly, Mickey's anxious voice.

"Tripp! Boy, you better come in right now and tell me you're alright."

Clearing his throat a little, Tripp finds himself oddly thankful that Mickey can't see the way tears are welling in his eyes at the familiar sound of his surrogate father speaking. Shaking the emotion off, he squeezes the button on the mic that's clipped to his shoulder in order to open the channel. "Can't get rid of me that easily, old man," he retorts, though his snappy comeback comes out far less cocky than Tripp was hoping.

"Thank God for that," Mickey replies, and then there's a muffled exchange Tripp can't quite make out in the background, though he strains to hear. "Noted," Mickey says to whoever is beside him, and then, "Tripp, go to Four, will you?"

With practiced fingers, Tripp switches over from the Fire Ops channel he's utilizing to the more private one Mickey requested, presumably so that communication about the active fire scene can continue on the main band. When he gets there, though, Tripp wastes no time in attempting to gauge the severity of his situation more fully. "C'mon, Mickey," he demands with a sniff. "Don't keep me in the dark. How bad is it?"

There's a brief pause and then, "We're working on it, Tripp. There are two teams on their way to you, both coming from different directions, but—it's complicated." Mickey hesitates. "Lot of rubble we can't clear out of the way. Plus, where you are, it's just not as simple as blowing a hole in the wall and pulling you out."

Apparent unfortunate location aside, Tripp understands the logistical struggle all too well, in a way he maybe wishes he didn't. In fact, he can bottom line it for himself: the building's integrity is deteriorating by the minute. Taking out a wall could bury both Tripp *and* the entire rescue team in the process. It's not encouraging news, but that doesn't mean he can't fight his own way out.

"Mickey," Tripp says, glancing up. "I got a wall here, has huge lettering on it. Says, 'LR-12,' any idea if that's useful?"

"Standby, Tripp. Hey—how're you on oxygen?"

This time it's Tripp's turn to hesitate, eventually deciding that there's no need to worry Mickey more than he already is. "'S'alright. Just… I shouldn't waste it."

All Tripp hears in reply is a huff and a swear that's probably going to earn the Chief a reprimand from the commissioners for saying it over the radio, but it's doubtful Mickey gives a rat's ass. More to the point, imagining Mickey chewing that group of balding suits out for bitching about language while he was busy trying to save a life is funny as hell, and Tripp laughs.

Too quickly, his smile fades away again. The silence that fills the room while he waits for Mickey's voice to return feels more ominous now, increasingly hot and filled with the determined crackling of a fire that's got a mind of its own.

Left alone with his thoughts, Tripp can't help but let his own mind wander, and it goes where it always goes, like a moth to a flame. *Lee.* Despite everything, Tripp still loves him—of course he does. And even though Lee hurt his feelings earlier, Tripp regrets being such a dick to him about everything. If the way Mickey is *not* talking is anything to go by, that shitty interaction might end up being the *last* one he ever has with his best friend. Might be the way Leander will be stuck remembering him for the rest of his life, and Tripp can't *believe* he left it the way that he did.

That's morbid.

That's life.

Tripp barks a depressed little laugh, raising his watery eyes to the wrecked ceiling and blinking wildly until tears track down his cheeks on the inside of his mask.

Lee.

Every single one of Tripp's reasons for staying silent, for *not* sharing his true feelings, seem so fucking stupid now. He's going to die here, in this goddamn dirty hovel, without ever telling the love of his life that that's what he is.

At the end of the day, Tripp is pretty damn sure of what Lee feels in return, but that's irrelevant, isn't it? Tripp could have been the bigger person in all of this, just as easily. Could have been the one to step out on that limb, instead of waiting in the wings like a coward.

Let's be real, Tripp thinks to himself. A person can worry, or they can act, and he's *always* been a *doer*. Not a 'sit around and drown in his feelings' kind of douche, but here he fuckin' is, drowning.

Looking back, Tripp wishes more than anything else that he'd been better than that. That he'd taken what he learned so painstakingly over the last few months, through BDSM and with Lee as his Dom, and applied it to their relationship as a whole. It seems so obvious in retrospect, with everything he's practiced so faithfully as a submissive—all that open communication and building of trust— he should have run with it.

Lee ain't off the hook, either, not in Tripp's mind. He could have done that shit too, that's for damn sure.

314

Both of them are idiots, that's what Tripp thinks. If he ever gets out of here, the *first* thing he's going to do is—

"Tripp, you there?" Mickey's back, and he sounds friggin' excited, which perks Tripp up immediately and helps him refocus. Parts of the precariously-stacked rubble are starting to crack and shift, and Tripp's no stranger to this part of a working fire. Sooner rather than later, this whole room is going to cave in.

"I'm here, Chief," Tripp replies reflexively. As he does, his eye catches on a particularly large concrete beam that appears to be holding up the majority of the stacked debris. It's probably the reason he isn't already buried, but it also has a worryingly-aggressive stress fracture creeping down its middle that's only growing wider by the minute.

"Good catch on that wall, son. There's a couple like it in the building, but we're gonna make a best guess as to which one you're near. Can you get over to it? There should be a door in the northwest corner, and if you can get through that, it'll move you further away from the main blaze. Buy the boys some time to get to you."

"Roger," Tripp acknowledges, feeling slightly more hopeful now that they have a plan, tenuous as it may be. Tripp's not a quitter, he's not just going to lay down and die. *Hell* no, he's going to fight with everything he has in order to survive—this, and any other wild thing God or Fate or whatever else sees fit to throw his way. All the same, though…

Tripp stops right before starting to drag himself over towards the wall and presses the 'talk' button on the mic again, licking his dry lips before speaking. "Mickey," he says. "Beau?"

"I called him," Mickey replies gruffly, and of course he did. He knows Tripp all too well. "He was over at Central, he's on his way. Should be here soon." In equal measure, that knowledge fills Tripp with both relief and dread. If this rescue mission fails, he *wants* to be able to talk to Beau one last time, but on the other hand—

"Mickey, you gotta promise me, something goes wrong, you keep Beau away. Don't let him see—" Tripp breaks off mid-sentence, choking on his own words.

"Boy, I'm gonna smack you silly for even talkin' that way once your ass is free," Mickey growls back, but Tripp can hear the emotional edge marring his voice. He softens, then, and that scares Tripp more than anything else has yet. "You just worry about you, Tripp, and I'll—I'll take care of Beau." There's so much stuffed into that promise that it would break Tripp if he let himself think about it too much, so instead, he lets go of the mic and gets to work.

Cramming his hand back into his glove, Tripp leans heavily on his right hip—the intact one—and starts pulling himself across the floor. It's awkward and difficult and it's slower progress than he'd like, but Tripp doesn't stop. Pushing with his undamaged foot and reaching out with his good hand to pull, steadily, Tripp propels himself forward. It's rough going, and he's forced to use both injured limbs more than is tolerable, but there's no alternative.

There's no door, either. Tripp knew that as soon as Mickey mentioned it. It's either not there or covered by rubble: either way, it's of no use to him. He'll just have to find another way, and if he can't go around, then *through it is*. Hell, he's always been a 'to the point' sort of dude, so why not?

When he makes it to the wall, Tripp allows himself a break. Just a brief moment's rest, leaning against the hot stone and breathing heavily, squeezing his eyes shut against the pain coursing through his body. Because he doesn't have enough going on, the alarm on his tank picks that moment to begin sounding again, and *this is it,* this is his last warning. His oxygen is nearly out.

With any luck, the room on the other side of this one will be slightly less hazardous. If not, Tripp's done for.

Running a gloved hand over the smooth drywall in front of him, Tripp zeroes in on a crack in the surface, picking and then yanking until a chunk comes free. Underneath is concrete cinderblock—not a surprise, considering the state of the rest of the room. Biting his lip, Tripp glances around frantically for anything he might use, and comes up with a busted section of metal pipe. He's broken through cinderblock before during drills, but always with *real* tools, like crowbars and sledgehammers.

Also, he had two working arms, which Tripp can't believe how much he's taken for granted.

Never again.

He's got no choice but to work with what's in front of him, though, if he wants to survive.

Bracing himself for the onslaught of pain, Tripp picks up the broken pipe and holds it firmly in both hands. Taking a deep breath, he slams it full-force into the block and immediately rears back to go again, pushing himself to repeat the action before the jagged bolts of lightning-hot pain that are ripping up his arm can really sink in.

Again. He brings the pipe down over and over, over and *over* again, and miraculously, the cinderblock steadily chips away.

It's working.

Tears stream freely down Tripp's cheeks, his left arm so sore that it's practically numb, and his right not faring all that much better. Still, Tripp doesn't stop. With repeated, unrelenting blows landed one after another, he manages to break a hole through the wall, and to hack away at it until it's nearly big enough for him to squeeze through.

With a gasp that's partially from pain and equally from lack of oxygen, Tripp chucks the pipe aside and resorts to using his hands to pull away larger chunks of rock. When the breach in the wall is finally wide enough for him to crawl through, Tripp unclips his airpack and lets it fall from his shoulders, ripping his helmet from his head and tossing it through the hole. His hood and mask follow carelessly after, but he leaves his pack behind. It's no use to him now, it's heavy, and he's exhausted.

Steadying himself mentally, Tripp tries to prepare for what might be on the other side—life or death: this is the moment of truth.

He crawls through head first, bad leg snagging on some cinderblock and dragging a yelp from his lungs, but he makes it. On the other side, there's about a foot and a half drop to the ground, but it's *much* cooler and *much* clearer. The air is lighter, more breathable, and the room is far wider than the space in which Tripp was trapped, so it'll take longer to become smothering.

Tripp uses the adrenaline he's built up from hacking through the wall to buoy himself forward, dragging his broken body as fast as it will go across the floor, just trying to move as far away from the blaze as he can get.

Right as he reaches the middle of the room, Tripp hears an ominous creaking noise following behind him. He reacts just in time to look over his shoulder and see through the hole he came through that the hovel has collapsed in on itself, a puff of smoke and dust the only other thing making it out.

Tripp's mouth goes dryer than it already was, uncomfortable with how close he came to being buried alive. Breath coming short and fast, he fumbles for the mic and activates the radio again. "Mickey," he croaks. "I'm through. I'm through, but—it's spreading fast. I dunno how long I'll be safe here."

Peering around, Tripp registers yet another disappointing, windowless space. There's one set of double doors at the far end, but Tripp's fairly certain they point towards where the epicenter of the blaze lies. He thinks he might be in a basement, which is *really* a worst-case scenario, and likely why Mickey hasn't suggested he access those doors at all. The fact is, there may not *be* any way for him to move that won't lead directly into the bowels of a fully-engulfed fire.

He still has to ask.

"Should I—should I try the doors?"

"No," Mickey replies sharply, his voice slightly staticky now. Radio signal must be weaker here. "Tripp, I've got the blueprints for the building in front of me—do not go through those doors. Just—sit tight, alright, son? Don't—don't you go giving up on me yet." That spiel would have been a hell of a lot more convincing if Mickey bothered to take his finger off the mic before barking, "Get Lee," at someone in the background.

Tripp's heart sinks.

Mickey thinks he's going to die. Mickey wants him to be able to say his good-byes.

A normal person would probably panic, and Tripp knows that he should, but he's too damn exhausted, in too much pain, and so *broken* about everything he's about to lose. It hurts like hell to think that he'll never wake up in Lee's arms again, never see Beau's smile when he cracks a joke at Tripp's expense, never get to know the joys of being an uncle—or a dad.

Devastated, Tripp lies flat on his back on the dirty concrete floor, doing his best to breathe shallowly and to stay as low as possible, away from the rising smoke and heat. A single tear makes its way down his cheek and into his sweaty hair, and Tripp doesn't bother to wipe it away. *What does it matter, now?* For the first time in what suddenly feels like one *very* short life, Tripp prays—begs—to a God he's never felt was listening before.

Please don't let me die here.

The radio clip on his shoulder crackles to life once again, and Tripp tips his head, prepared to digest whatever crap news Mickey has to share. But the voice that comes over the line has him pressing a fist to his forehead, eyes pinching shut against the burning pressure behind them. He swallows hard past the lump in his throat, and it goes down like needles.

"Tripp? Tripp, it's me," the deep, familiar voice says, and Tripp nearly chokes trying to reply, struggling so much that it takes him nearly three false starts to get a single word out.

"Hey, sunshine," is what he finally manages, trying hard not to sound anywhere near as wrecked as he feels. "What—what's the weather like where you are? Me, I'm in a bit of a heatwave. Could do with some rain."

"Oh, Tripp," Leander replies, huffing a reluctant laugh, and Tripp can just picture him—clutching the mic two-handed like a lifeline, like he might grab Tripp through it if he can hold on tight enough. Such a *Lee* thing to do that the mental image actually makes Tripp smile. He really is the light of Tripp's entire fucking life, and—oh.

Oh, shit. He *can't* go out like this, not without letting Lee know. Maybe that's not fair, not a *nice* burden to rest on his best friend's shoulders, but Tripp's the one who's about to be cut down in his early thirties, so fuck *fairness.*

"Lee, I gotta tell you something," Tripp begins, releasing the mic for a second so that Leander can acknowledge that he's listening, that he can hear. Wouldn't it be just Tripp's luck that he finds the stones to confess his stupid feelings, and the damn radio cuts out over it?

"No," Leander replies, and Tripp frowns, trying to press his mic's button, but Lee is still talking, the stubborn asshole. "I owe you an apology, Tripp. I owe you—"

"Holy shit," Tripp murmurs to himself, tensing as he processes Leander's voice on the other end of the line, near-sobbing and fighting a losing battle to gain control of his speech. He finds himself clutching his own radio just as tightly as he was previously making fun of Lee for doing.

"Tripp, I didn't mean to add to your distress today," Leander continues, teetering on the edge of hysteria. "I—Tripp, I just keep failing. Again and again. When you were dropping, I searched high and low and I couldn't find you. And then I screwed up with our aftercare, put you at risk, dropped on my own watch, and you bore the brunt of that fallout. And I just wanted—I *needed* to do this right, for this next step between us to be a *win* for you. For myself. For *us.*"

He pauses, must let his finger slip off the mic, and Tripp quickly jumps in. "You think you're the only one rolling snake eyes here? Lee, hello? Look where I am." Tripp can almost *hear* Leander's eyes rolling, and it makes him smile again, despite the circumstances. He sighs, leaving the button pressed so Leander can hear him do so. "I shouldn't have put you on the spot. I'm sorry. Or, hell, you know what? I *should* have, but only if I had the balls to put myself out there, too. And I'm not—I'm not gonna just...*let* this be it for us, not without—"

The words die in Tripp's throat, not because he's afraid to say them, not because he's unsure about his place in Lee's heart, but simply because it *hurts.* This shouldn't be the way this goes down for them, not after everything they've been through and all they've overcome. Lee deserves *flowers* and candles and a carefully curated, emotionally charged mixtape—all that girly, romantic shit Tripp secretly likes, too. He deserves Tripp in a collar and on his knees, and—and *fuck,* a goddamn ring, a house in the 'burbs, and their whole lives in front of them.

Not *here.* Not like this.

Life's shitty like that, though, sometimes. Tripp should have known better than to think that fate wouldn't pull the rug out from under them. It was too easy with Lee, too good *not* to expect they wouldn't be allowed to keep it.

"Tripp, I love you," Leander's voice crackles over the radio, and Tripp bursts into tears, the way his sobs have him sucking in polluted air quickly leading him to cough. "I would have gone with you into that building if I'd known, all the way, please know that. You don't need to say anything in return, I just—I was going to tell you tonight. It kills me to imagine you—" His voice breaks a little, and he struggles not to say what they're both thinking—*dying.* "—to imagine you not knowing."

This is it.

Fuck what they *should* have had, this is what they get. Tripp's heart is pounding, but he knows this is *right,* and now that it's time, he can't fucking wait to tell Leander how he really feels. Dragging a dirty sleeve across his face, Tripp inhales a deep, steadying breath and reaches to press the button on his mic once again.

Nothing happens, it doesn't even key up.

"No! No, no, no," Tripp mutters, ripping the mic from his jacket and sending the clip flying, but no matter how many times he presses down on the button, it stays silent. In fact, the radio doesn't even beep, the display dark and lifeless. Looking down at it, Tripp realizes with dawning horror that it's died, possibly from a drained battery or maybe from damage sustained during his fall.

"Oh, *hell* no," Tripp growls. "This is—*hell,* no."

Shoving a hand down into the pocket of the pants he's wearing beneath his bunker gear, Tripp fumbles out his phone. Murphy's Law—it was stuffed in his left pocket, likely positioned directly beneath his hip when he landed. Naturally, the screen is smashed, and when he tries to mess with the power button, the display flickers tauntingly back at him, offering nothing but a bunch of uneven, colored lines.

Useless.

Whipping his head around frantically, Tripp takes stock of his options. There's really only the one door out, and it's no secret that it just may lead him out of the frying pan and into the fire, literally. Still, what does he have to lose? If there's one thing Tripp is *not* going to do, it's sit around with his busted leg and his useless arm, waiting to die. Not when—not when *Lee* didn't even get to hear what Tripp has waited goddamn *years* to say.

A beat-up metal chair is sitting by its lonesome nearby, the kind that looks as if it belongs in a school room, and Tripp uses the frame to drag himself to his feet. Once standing, he leans on the seat back like a makeshift walker, clinging to the rail with both good hand and bad so as not to put unnecessary weight on his busted leg. There's no time to crawl, not with the way smoke is pouring through that hole he punched through the wall, so Tripp limps as quickly as possible in the direction of the door.

It takes longer than he'd like to get there. He's forced to alternate pausing to breathe through the pain with crouching low just to suck in slightly less sooty air. Sweat pours down Tripp's face, soaking the clothing layered beneath his gear and turning it sticky and uncomfortable, but that's the least of his worries. Summoning every ounce of his training, every survival instinct he's ever had, and all the crashing adrenaline left in his body, Tripp shoves both the chair and himself forward, one foot in front of the other, rinse and repeat until he *finally* reaches the door.

Slumping against it in relief, Tripp recoils immediately from the powerful heat seeping through the metal. That action sends him off-balance and stumbling, flopping heavily to the floor and leaving him sprawled out in fairly dramatic fashion. In the chaos, Tripp accidentally flings his makeshift walker halfway back in the direction he came from, cursing as he flails. He cries out as he lands roughly on his injured leg, tears springing to his eyes as he cradles his thigh and rocks compulsively until the searing pain abates enough for him to keep a coherent thought inside his head.

The door is scorching hot, and that can only mean one thing—there's fire directly on the other side, and Tripp can't risk opening it. He could cause a backdraft in the room that would burn him to a crisp, leaving him dead within seconds.

Defeated, Tripp slumps the rest of the way to the ground, letting his head drop back onto the concrete as he stares up into the increasingly dense smog swirling above. The warm glow of the flames from the other room reflects off the smoke and reminds him of one particular Fourth of July—feels like a hundred years ago, now—just him, Beau, and some fireworks. Tripp had saved up a little money from his after-school job and subsisted on dry cereal for an entire week just to get them, but the look on Beau's face made it all *so* worth it.

As Tripp slowly lifts his eyelids, the time between each opening grows longer and longer from blink to blink. In between, he can almost *see* the memory playing out in front of him. Feels like he's *in it,* like he's really there.

It's not so terribly hot, anymore.

"Bozo," he says softly, turning his head to the side and smiling down at his kid brother, who grins back happily with a popsicle smile.

"Come on, Tripp!" Beau takes off running across the open field, racing to light some more exploding rockets. Tripp follows behind, even though—even though there's *something* he's supposed to be doing, he's sure of it—but there's no pain here. No worries, no tightness in his chest, and no rising fear. The grass feels soft beneath his feet, and the air is cool, crisp.

Just as Tripp is about to call out for his little brother to wait up, there's a loud explosion to his right that doesn't sound at *all* like a firework. No, this particular blast sounds like rock crumbling, metal screeching, and—*people yelling?*

Tripp's eyes snap open and he whips his head to the side, clocking the most relieving sight he's ever laid eyes on, bar none. A handful of firefighters equipped with a Reeves stretcher, all of them packed up and making their way towards him as a group. *Is he dreaming?* Weakly, Tripp blinks against the tears and stinging smoke in his eyes, reaching up to pinch his own cheek. The action hurts his wrist as much as his face, so he decides that he's alive.

A firefighter with a white helmet, piercing, ice-blue eyes, and a *very* familiar gait crouches next to Tripp's head and cups the side of his face. "Good to see you, brotha," Gunnar manages, and while they'll likely never talk about it, Tripp can *hear* the relief in his voice, the stress of whatever he's been through over the last hour causing it to break. He grabs Gunnar's gloved hand on his face and holds on, nodding but not trusting himself to speak.

Gunnar takes care of that. "Let's get you outta here."

"My leg," Tripp finally says, as one of the other guys slips an oxygen mask over his face and the rest of them open and spread the collapsible plastic stretcher next to his body. "Think it's broke. Wrist too."

"Shit, if that's all that fall did you, I'd say you got someone lookin' out for you upstairs. Now don't talk anymore, sugar, you got soot all over your nose and mouth. Your throat hurt? Just nod, yes or no."

Tripp nods his 'yes' and Gunnar claps him on the shoulder, standing and turning away to speak into the mic on his shoulder. "My radio. My helmet," Tripp whispers, pointing over his head to where he tossed those items, not bothering to mention his airpack still in the other room—that thing is toast. As he's doing so, the crew rolls Tripp onto his side, shoving the Reeves underneath his body before rolling him back.

Being tipped onto his bad leg makes Tripp grimace and grit his teeth, but he doesn't say a word about it. Within seconds, he's being lifted into the air and carried through the gaping hole Gunnar and crew made in the wall with their tools.

Strangely, Tripp is kind of jealous—punching through walls is a good time, one of his favorite things to do. At least, when he's not trapped in a life-size EZ Bake Oven and trying to create an emergency exit. Or, you know, working against the clock to rescue a good friend and co-worker, probably. Maybe Tripp will just not ever mention that thought out loud.

The adjacent room is yet another windowless space, but Gunnar's team walks across it confidently now that they have Tripp safe and in tow. Right next to him, Gunnar's talking away on the radio, and if Tripp had to make a best guess, he's giving Mickey a countdown to starting surround-and-drown ops. Surround and drown means they're done trying to save the building—as soon as Tripp and his rescuers are clear, the pump-equipped fire apparatus will circle the entire thing and dump continuous streams of water from above until the fire is out.

From his position on the stretcher, Tripp's truly starting to struggle to breathe, but he keeps quiet about it. There's nothing his crew can do but get him out of here, and they're all moving as fast as they physically can. Instead of dwelling on the tightness in his chest, the sharp soreness in his throat, the wheeze even he can hear when he exhales, Tripp looks around and watches the scenery.

Turns out, his theory about being in a basement was correct, so he couldn't have tunneled his way to safety if he tried. The door they pass through in the second room has broken chains, and Gunnar picks up bolt cutters from the floor as they pass. All of that considered, Tripp hazards a guess that he wouldn't have faired very well on his own here, either, even if he had managed to break through a second wall.

After those doors, there's a right turn, a long hallway, a left, another hallway, and eventually, a staircase that leads to—*fucking finally*—an exterior metal door with a glowing red "EXIT" sign hanging above it.

Gunnar's team carries Tripp up the stairs.

One level higher and what feels like halfway down the block from where Tripp was trapped, the air seems clear and everything is wet, the walls still actively dripping with water. Vaguely, Tripp contemplates whether that damage is from the fire department's intervention or from the sprinklers, and then immediately wonders why he can't turn off his work-brain.

"Stop," Gunnar orders his crew. "Let's get him out of this gear before we head outside. Things are gonna get crazy fast, I don't wanna be taking bunkers off in the back of the rig. I have blankets to cover him." As the guys lower Tripp to the ground, Gunnar shoots him a meaningful look, and Tripp realizes that he's trying to help him retain his dignity.

Gunnar was right to worry, though—getting him out of his jacket, boots, and fire-rated pants is difficult, and Tripp screams more than once from the pain. They move quickly out of necessity, they aren't particularly gentle, and by the time Tripp is down to his duty pants and a t-shirt, he's shivering and tears are leaking from his eyes *again*. Defensively, Tripp cradles his sore arm to his chest.

"Alrigh', sugar, you're alrigh' now," Gunnar soothes, draping several hospital blankets over his shaking body. Nice gesture, but Tripp knows full well they aren't going to do shit for him out in the cold, especially with the way his skin is damp all over from sweat. "Boys, get him to the rig quickly, we don't need to be adding hypothermia to Tripp's list of troubles."

There's a low murmur of acknowledgement, and then the Reeves stretcher is being lifted again, the doors to the outside creaking as they're pushed open and Tripp is carried through.

The air is *frigid,* colder than Tripp remembers it being before, and his shivering ramps up immediately. Beneath the oxygen mask, Tripp's teeth chatter and he struggles to pull in a deep breath, the rapid shift in temperature more painful than relieving to his battered throat and lungs. When he opens his mouth to say so, his words come out in nothing but a croak, followed by a pained moan.

There's some kind of yelling commotion happening ahead of them, increasing as Tripp is carried down the length of the building and towards the street where the emergency vehicles are parked. Unfortunately, the way he's positioned, Tripp can only really see where they've come *from*, not where they're headed. That makes it difficult to decipher what's going on, but he nonetheless cranes his neck and tries his level best.

Eyes still bleary and stinging, Tripp has to blink several times before the line of people gathered at the caution-taped edge of the scene comes into any kind of focus. It does so just in time for Tripp to see Leander break through the line and come running towards them at full-speed. Not even thinking about what he's doing, Tripp immediately responds by sitting up and trying to stand.

That results in a predictable rush of, "Whoa, whoa there," responses and hands on his body, plus other, well-intended nonsense that's aimed at trying to stabilize the swaying and tilting stretcher *and* convince Tripp to lay back down, none of which he pays any attention to at all.

It only takes Leander twenty, maybe thirty seconds to reach them, but by then, the guys have given up on fighting Tripp. They lower the Reeves to the ground, muttering about how Lee is a medic anyway, and take the free moment to pull off their masks and breathe the fresh air.

"Lee," Tripp croaks, failing to get to his feet but not needing to because Leander skids to a stop in the mud and crashes to his knees at Tripp's side. Tripp's throat hurts like a *bitch,* he's shaking from head to toe, and his breath is coming short and sharp against his ribs, but he's *not* going to lose out on this. *Not again.* Throwing his arms around Leander's neck, Tripp drags him in close, basking in the solid, warm weight of his body, the thump of Lee's heartbeat in his chest, his own harsh and jagged breathing puffing right next to Tripp's ear.

"I love you," Tripp says plainly, though his voice is hoarse and scratchy and a cough stops him from saying it again right away. He hacks into his fist, chin still resting on Leander's shoulder while Lee thumps at his back and grips him like he can't bear to let go.

"Oh my god, his breathing," comes a familiar voice from somewhere above them, and Tripp glances up to see Marley peering worriedly down. "Lee, can't you hear—"

"I *know,* Marley," Leander says sharply, squeezing Tripp one last time before pulling back and cupping his face. "Tripp," he says seriously. "We need to get you to the truck, and then Zosia and I are going to put you under and put a tube down your throat. If we don't do it quickly, things could go very badly for you. Understand?" While he talks, Leander rocks back on his heels, motioning for the firefighters to pick Tripp up again, but keeping his big, warm hand on Tripp's face, right next to the oxygen mask, as they do.

Tripp's eyes widen, he can't help it, and he starts to shake his head—*no, no, he can't, anything* but that—

Leander sees his panic, slides his hand further around Tripp's head as they walk, tightening his grip on Tripp's hair at the scalp. "Listen to me," he says fiercely. "I will *not* lose you again. Let me help you, Tripp, so you can—" Leander breaks off abruptly and swallows roughly, only glancing away for a split-second to compose himself. "So you can tell me what you just said every damn day until you finally get sick of me."

The paralyzing fear gripping Tripp's chest starts to subside, and he nods, though his teeth still chatter away in the cold.

"Also, fair warning, Beau is here. He's in the rig, setting up. You'll be in good hands."

Tripp raises his eyebrows to protest but Leander just shrugs, reading him easily. "It's not like any of us were going to opt out of treating you voluntarily. They didn't have any luck keeping me away, and they won't have any with Beau."

Doing his best to relax, Tripp stares up at the starlit sky, trying not to worry that he's about to be put to sleep only to never wake again. After what he just went through, that's maybe the *most* terrifying news he could possibly have received. But Lee is right—if Tripp is going to put his life in anyone's hands, he couldn't ask for better options, even if they're both secretly as scared as he is.

The stars disappear, replaced first by hazy, ambient flashing red and white lights, and then the ceiling of the ambulance as Tripp is loaded inside. Beau's face materializes upside down in front of him, and Tripp does his best to smile weakly, though his tight, wheezy breathing is really taking its toll.

"Don't talk," Beau says immediately, grabbing Tripp's hand. "One for yes, two for no." Tripp nods. "Lee told you we're going to put you under, protect your airway?"

One squeeze.

"Kay," Beau nods. "Just until the swelling goes down. I'll be with you the whole time, the ICU nurses are going to *hate* my guts. I'll make sure you're sedated, that you're not in pain. We'll pull the tube just as soon as it's safe, I promise. Tripp, I promise. We're going to get you through this. You with me?"

One squeeze.

To Tripp's left, Leander's wrapped a tourniquet around his bicep and is poking around the inside of his elbow, looking for a place to start an IV. When Tripp catches his eye, he winks and slides the sixteen-gauge in like butter, before Tripp can even react. With practiced hands, he retracts the needle and adds a saline lock, tapes it down, and starts running some fluid that's already primed and hanging from the ceiling. Next to him on the bench seat are a neat row of syringes and vials that Beau must have set up, but Leander doesn't touch any of them yet.

Beau taps a thumb against the side of his hand. "Before I put you out, does anything hurt?"

One squeeze.

"His left leg," Leander interrupts. "Left arm. Anything else?"

One squeeze.

326

"Alright, let's do this." Beau passes Tripp's hand off to Leander and then starts running both of his own over Tripp's body, moving quickly from the top of his head to his toes. "Squeeze Lee's fingers when I touch something that hurts." As Beau works his way down, Tripp does as he's told, almost forgetting to do so at one point because he's busy staring into Leander's eyes, and isn't *that* fucking ridiculous?

Down by Tripp's feet, the doors slam shut and the ambulance rumbles into high idle as Marley prepares to navigate them away from the scene.

"Hey there, big boy," Zosia's voice declares brightly, and Tripp has never been happier to see her smiling face when she appears above him. Someone in this friggin' truck should be *not* closely related to or in love with him, that seems like a smart move. He waves tiredly, and coughs as a greeting.

Beside him, Leander glances at the cardiac monitor Tripp's now hooked up to, and even Tripp can understand the threat of his dropping oxygen level—eighty-two percent and holding, not great. When he holds his free arm up towards the light, the tips of his fingers look dusky, and it's not from soot. Leander catches him looking and squeezes his hand.

"It's time," he says, and when Tripp opens his mouth to try and reply, to do something stupid like say his final goodbyes, Leander knocks his oxygen mask out of the way just to clamp a hand over his mouth. "Don't you dare," he warns, stern and fierce, even though his eyes are shining. "Tell me again when you're better."

Against Leander's palm, Tripp coughs avidly until he removes it, swiftly replacing the mask. Above him, Beau and Zosia switch places, Beau taking his spot at Tripp's head, presumably because he's the guy that's going to actually stick the piece of plastic down Tripp's throat. Now there's a heartwarming, brotherly moment if Tripp's ever seen one. He snorts a little at the thought and promptly regrets it when his airway burns.

Glancing to the side again, Tripp notes that Leander is busy triple-checking his syringes and dosages, and so he takes advantage. He grabs Beau's arm, tugging it away from where he's messing around in the airway kit.

"Beau," he says, and everyone protests, but Tripp holds up a finger and they very reluctantly fall silent. "I love Lee," he says croakily but with a big grin, pleased that even now, he's managed to thwart Leander's rules.

"Jesus Christ, Tripp," Beau breathes, rolling his eyes and covering Tripp's face with a bag-valve mask that spews oxygen forcefully. "We *know.* Lee, put him out."

Lee's smile is the last thing Tripp remembers seeing before he slips under. What a way to go.

***

Leander

Watching Tripp's eyes flutter closed as the first sedative hits his veins is one of the hardest things Leander has ever had to do, never mind *cause*. He feels Zosia's reassuring hand on his shoulder, very nearly allowing himself to shut his own eyes and lean into it for strength.

The world spins madly on.

"Zosia, cricoid pressure," Beau instructs, and Zosia's hand disappears as she complies. She leans over to press gently but firmly on the cartilage rings in Tripp's throat, compressing his esophagus to tilt the trachea and make it easier for Beau to visualize sliding a tube between the vocal cords.

Beau doesn't pre-ventilate using the bag-valve-mask he's holding, just lets the high-flow oxygen do its thing, since Tripp is still breathing on his own. While he's not practiced working in a bumpy, swaying ambulance like this, the procedure is still something Beau has clearly done hundreds of times, and Leander is *glad* he's here. *So* glad, otherwise he'd have to use his own brain, and that's— well, Leander's brain is not one hundred percent online at the current moment.

"Lee," Beau snaps, and when Leander looks up, he gets the sense that it's not the first time Beau has called his name.

"I'm with you," he replies quickly, as Beau looks on uncertainly, hand poised and hovering over the Mac 4 blade he's set aside to use when intubating Tripp. Beau knows Leander's lying, knows he shouldn't be anywhere near Tripp's medical care right now, but needs must, and EMS is always about doing the best you can with what little you have. Always about saving lives and making things happen, *despite* your own feelings about the situation, or the permanent lack of other people to rely on.

After a fleeting, scrutinizing second, Beau nods, back to business. "Give that lidocaine. There's one hundred and twenty milligrams drawn up, check it if you want. I don't know how hard Tripp hit his head, but I'm not taking any chances. Go ahead and flush once that's in, then give the etomidate straight after. I started with thirty and we'll switch to ketamine if needed. He might go easy—let's see if we can avoid paralytics."

"Do you want to switch?" Zosia asks quietly.

Leander sincerely considers it, but shakes his head 'no' in the end. As hard as this might be, relinquishing Tripp's care to someone else sounds harder. If nothing else, Leander can take comfort in the fact that he's *doing* something, that he's actively working to keep the man he loves alive. He *needs* to be a part of that right now.

So he gives the medications Beau requested, making sure to push the etomidate slowly so as not to lock up Tripp's jaw and induce the need for a paralytic. It's an easy order to carry out, because Beau drew up both medications earlier while he was waiting in the truck—along with a few others—just in case.

Any other time, Leander would patently refuse to administer a syringe full of something that someone else prepared, but these aren't exactly normal circumstances. Even if Leander didn't trust him, or even defer to him as a physician, Beau's stakes in this might be even higher than his own. The bubble they're in right now is just that.

The ambulance hits a bump as it turns, sirens wailing in the background that Leander barely hears. He sees Tripp's sats on the monitor changing, watches him become even more floppy and lifeless than he previously was, watches as Beau springs into action when that happens. Smoothly and with practiced hands, Beau opens Tripp's mouth and slides the lighted blade inside, sweeping Tripp's tongue up and out of the way. He uses the handle of the blade to lift Tripp's jaw from the inside, opening his airway structures so they can be properly visualized as Beau bends to squint into his mouth.

Leander finds himself wincing, despite having performed the exact same procedure many, many times by his own hands. It's so much more brutal as a bystander, though—or maybe that's solely related to who is lying on the stretcher today.

"Tube," Beau says, extending his palm but leaving his eyes locked onto Tripp's vocal cords. Zosia grabs the endotracheal tube Beau previously selected, prepared, and left sitting on top of the airway kit, half out of its plastic wrapping and covered in lubricant. Leander swallows the lump in his throat and tries not to feel useless. He cycles the blood pressure cuff on Tripp's arm, not overly interested in the results, and tries not to feel worried about the way Beau grunts and struggles to get the tube situated.

After what feels like hours but was really only seconds, Beau exhales a sigh of abject relief as he removes the blade and inflates the balloon that'll hold the tube still in Tripp's trachea, prevent it from becoming displaced. Zosia threads a tube holder around the back of Tripp's head and screws it into place, ensuring their setup doesn't move while Beau test-ventilates. In sync with his team, Leander gets his stethoscope into his ears and checks Tripp's lung sounds.

"Pull it back a centimeter," he suggests, when he listens to the left side of Tripp's chest. "You're deep." Beau loosens the structures keeping the tube in place and does as Leander suggests, ventilating again as Leander listens and flashes a thumbs up. "It's perfect."

They go through the motions: attaching a carbon dioxide detection device that helps monitor for accidental displacement, checking Tripp's vital signs, and assessing his awareness level. The whole entire thing, from med push to matching sighs of relief, takes less than five full minutes, which is about the time the etomidate lasts in Tripp's system.

He starts to stir, groggy and irritated and lifting his hands up to his mouth almost immediately. Leander feels awful—while the meds they've administered mean that Tripp will likely have absolutely zero memory of this, he's still in pain *now*. The tube is inevitably irritating his already sore throat, and he's not awake enough to reason why it's necessary to refrain from yanking it out on the spot.

"He needs to be sedated again," is what Leander says out loud. Beau nods, standing and beckoning for Zosia to take his place with the bag ventilations while Leander restrains Tripp's wandering hands gently, down near his stomach.

Attempting to change positions in the small space has the two other medics doing an awkward dance that involves Zosia standing on the narrow seat across from Leander and Beau half-hanging from the pole that runs the length of the ceiling overhead. It's the kind of thing Tripp would have laughed at, would have cracked some kind of inappropriate joke about, just to break the tension and lighten the mood.

Once they're situated, Beau reaches over and takes the ketamine from next to Leander's hip, dosing it correctly and pushing it himself. "We'll get him through with this 'til we're inside. Probably start him on a propofol drip then, depending on how he does and whether or not he's going into surgery. Speaking of which…"

Bypassing the radio completely, Beau pulls his phone from his pocket and swipes it open. Choosing a contact, he dials, and within minutes is giving report and consulting with one of the ED physicians. When he hangs up, Leander has questions.

"You're the trauma surgeon on call," he says bluntly. "If it's necessary, will you..?"

"I don't think so," Beau answers, still poking at his phone but nevertheless anticipating Leander's concern without him having to voice it. "When I left to come down to the scene, they called Aliyah in—she's my boss, Chief of Trauma. Hey, you know she's Cornell's sister, right? Your medical director?"

Leander squints up at him in confusion and disinterest. Beau rambles when he's nervous. He's no less competent for it, though, crouching down to insert a second IV line in Tripp's other arm and securing it effortlessly, like it's second nature for him to do so.

"Anyway, I think they knew I'd be useless for the rest of my shift. Short of something crazy happening, if Tripp needs surgery, I won't scrub, but I'll watch from the balcony—keep you updated."

At that, Zosia leans over and touches Leander's shoulder again. "No one expects you back, either," she says gently. "We called in county support to hold down rehab at the fire, and I talked to Chief Maxwell personally. He's going to recall C Platoon to come in right away, tell them to bring one of the other trucks down to the scene. He said you can give him a call when you figure out what kind of time you need off."

"That's uncharacteristically generous of him," Leander mutters. "What is the catch?"

"I wouldn't make plans for Christmas," Zosia snorts, and Leander sighs, because she's probably right. The last time Maxwell was on an actual bus was when Leander was riding the yellow one. Being that out of touch tends to make him a particularly unreasonable negotiator when it comes to time off, but that's Future Leander's problem.

The truck's backup alarm sounds and Leander starts, surprised to look up and see that they're arriving at the hospital. He cycles Tripp's cuff so they can have fresh vitals for the trauma team, and then helps Beau prepare Tripp to be taken inside while Zosia continues to ventilate.

Oxygen tubing comes off the wall adapter and attached to a portable tank, the cardiac monitor goes in-between Tripp's legs. Since he continues to be well-sedated, Beau and Leander clip the stretcher's chest-level seatbelt over both of Tripp's arms so that they can't drop. All the while, Leander averts his eyes from Tripp's face, unable to decide whether it's harder to see him sedated and looking barely alive, or anxious, confused, and uncomfortable.

As their somber group wheels Tripp's unmoving form through the doors to the ER, security is waiting to direct them immediately into Trauma One, or "The Bay." Inside, a mass of gowned and gloved personnel are lined up and waiting, all kinds of equipment fired up and at the ready. Surprisingly—or maybe not so much—Leander feels nothing but relief at handing over Tripp's care for good.

Right now, he *needs* to be a nervous, scared family member, not a healthcare provider. He needs to hold Tripp's hand, to be spoken to slowly and kindly by professionals who use small words and careful phrases, who treat him like a lay person who doesn't understand what's happening and needs compassionate guidance to do anything.

Beau *very* clearly does not feel the same, transitioning immediately into full-on, hardcore doctor-mode. As Leander watches the trauma team descend on Tripp, Beau is in the thick of the fray, ordering films and a battery of blood tests, alongside an assortment of medications that EMS doesn't have access to in the rig. Having absolutely no desire to join him, Leander glances around.

He catches sight of Briana lingering just outside the wide, sliding glass doors to the trauma bay, and he makes his way over to her side. She doesn't say anything, just wraps his hand in hers and squeezes, resting her head on his shoulder as they watch the dramatic scene unfolding inside the room.

They're in an odd position, the two of them—not exactly members of this particular team, but not unwelcome, either. They stay out of the way.

In front of them, Tripp's clothes are swiftly cut away, his body is prodded this way and that, and Leander begins to go numb, with one minute quickly becoming indistinguishable from the last. Vaguely, he registers that the room is loud and bustling with commotion, but nothing translates into more than a low-level buzzing in Leander's mind.

The whole thing is a blur.

The F.A.S.T. ultrasound reveals some concerning bleeding in Tripp's belly, so he's taken to the O.R. for an exploratory laparotomy. Bri has to return to her shift on the unit, but Autumn shows up before she leaves—and thank God for that, because Leander is barely functioning.

While he spaces out, Autumn guides him around the hospital, wherever it is he needs to be. From the ED to the O.R. waiting room, to yet another, smaller waiting room outside the I.C.U., Autumn's steady presence by his side keeps Leander from simply curling up in a ball on the floor or possibly going catatonic.

She manages his phone, relays messages from Beau (*"everything is fine, bruised spleen, they're closing him up"*), and rubs his hand comfortingly, softer than Leander's ever seen her before. She puts coffee in his hand, inserts herself between Leander and nosy well-wishers who show up or text to find out what happened, and eventually, she walks Leander into the I.C.U. to see Tripp, once he's finally out of recovery.

Beau's status in the hospital has the I.C.U. bending the rules just slightly—Leander shouldn't even be allowed in, not technically. And yet, he finds himself welcomed, like a brother (*or a husband*), accepted by Beau's word alone that he's important enough to remain at Tripp's side.

Tripp is—well, that's hard to describe. When Leander first walks in, and despite being incredibly prepared for what he knows he'll see, it's a shock. His usually bright and vibrant friend is pale, small-looking in his hospital bed, buried under wires and multiple IV lines attached to assorted medication pumps. There's a cast on his left forearm, another running from thigh to ankle on his left leg, and a compression garment encouraging circulation on his right.

On top of all that, he's still intubated, the breathing tube now hooked up to a giant ventilator that hums and hisses steadily, but only beeps occasionally.

Each of those things, Leander expected. He knew that Tripp's left radius and ulna were both broken in the fall, that his left kneecap was cracked, too. He knew that Tripp was lucky enough to avoid surgery for both of those things—for now. He knew that Tripp had a couple of fractured ribs, still more that were badly contused, plus additional severely-bruised bones in his hips, pelvis, and a likely concussion in his head. He *knew* what a post-surgical ICU patient on a vent would look like. He *knew.*

But what he didn't anticipate was having to reconcile *Tripp* as that patient: still, vulnerable, *sick.*

When Leander steps to Tripp's bedside and takes his hand, Tripp's eyes flutter partially-open and he grimaces around the tube, which has Leander feeling a strange flood of relief. Not relief over him being uncomfortable, but over the proof that Tripp's *in* there, that he's still himself and still fighting. The moment is brief, though, with Tripp slipping back off into a medicated sleep almost immediately.

That slice of life, with very little deviation, is how the next few days pass by as well. Brief and marginal progress immediately followed by some setback, tiny victories that Leander is told he should celebrate as if they're big ones.

He just wants to take Tripp home.

Instead, he zombie-walks through the hours, assisting with Tripp's care as much as he's allowed, which mostly amounts to cleaning him up and changing his bed linens alongside the staff. Sometimes, he's permitted to help with cast care to Tripp's injured arm and leg, and with the frequent turning and repositioning of his limp body. He's not supposed to, but Leander is quick to do things like empty Tripp's catheter bag, and use the oral swabs Beau nicks from the supply room to carefully clean Tripp's teeth and tongue and around the tube.

He makes sure that everyone who enters the room knows how precious Tripp is and that they treat him as such, but mostly, Leander sits and waits. The white noise of daytime talk shows and the kind of trash that airs on TV at three a.m.

become the soundtrack to his life, overlaid with the ever-present beeping and hissing of multiple IV pumps and the vent.

The I.C.U. nurses and aides fuss over Leander nearly as much as they do Tripp, bringing him half-sandwiches and tiny plastic juices, ginger ale poured into sty-rofoam cups, and donuts from the nurse's station. They also come with chastise-ment for his lack of rest, admonishments to be 'careful,' and not 'wear himself out.'

"Tripp is going to need you even more in these coming days," they warn.

That sounds like heaven—Leander can't wait for Tripp to need him. To be fuck-ing *useful* again, instead of eternally occupying the comfy chair someone dragged into the room, acting like he's a tumor growing out of the seat cushion.

Beau is there often, too, of course, though he manages his well-being a lot better than Leander does, or perhaps that's Briana taking the wheel. It's probably Bri-ana. Either way, Beau actually leaves the hospital most nights to sleep at home, he showers and shaves and doesn't lose ten pounds in five days. He also con-tinues going to work—hanging out, signing orders, and doing his charting from the ICU where he can keep an eye on Tripp, which is almost suspiciously con-venient.

On day four, Tripp is supposed to be extubated, but instead is diagnosed with pneumonia. An aggressive course of antibiotics resolves the worst of that in ano-ther day and a half, but early on, Leander and Beau are told to "prepare them-selves," because infection after smoke inhalation is frequently fatal.

Tripp fights hard and beats the odds once again, not that Leander ever doubted him, even for a second.

(Maybe for a second. The dead of night is a lonely, painfully quiet time in the hospital.)

During their stay, Leander comes to learn the cracks in the wall of Tripp's I.C.U. room like the lines on his own face. Using his non-dominant hand, he could draw perfectly the borders of the small water spot marring the ceiling overhead. He knows all of the staff by name—from Kevin Lee, the environmental services kid who empties Tripp's trash most nights and is attending graduate school for physics, to Tripp's slightly strange, but clearly competent attending, Aliyah Read-ing.

By day five, Leander is sporting a beard that he thinks Tripp would absolutely *hate*. He'd probably demand it be dragged all over his thighs before insisting Le-ander shave, but he'd hate it.

On day six, Beau parks him in front of the mirror in the hallway bathroom and demands he do something about it. Eventually, Beau switches out with Bri, throwing his hands up in exasperation when Leander simply stands there with the razor in his hand and stares blankly at his homeless-looking reflection, glaring furiously at the bags under his eyes.

Bri shaves his face. She does so with the practiced, gentle, and non-judgemental touch of a nurse who is entirely used to caring for people who are unable to care for themselves.

As a thank you to Bri for his newly-shaven face, Leander takes a shower.

That evening, Tripp's treatment team stops the sedation, and Tripp wakes up.

They crank the head of Tripp's I.C.U. bed vertical so that he's sitting, and the "superior Doctor Reading," as Aliyah calls herself, pulls the tube free just as soon as Tripp makes it clear he's back with them. Once it's out, Tripp coughs and wheezes and makes a series of disgusted and irritated faces that Leander would find both amusing and adorable, if not for the current set of circumstances. His nurse swoops in to stick a nasal cannula under Tripp's nose and around his ears, and he looks as if he likes that even less.

Leander's chest feels tight, but his heart is full.

"Can I—" Tripp starts, but abruptly breaks off to cough, wincing and touching his fingers to his throat. Leander shifts where he's sitting on the side of Tripp's bed, looking around for something to offer him, but his nurse is already coming to the rescue. She holds out a cup of water, fixing the straw so that it's easy for Tripp to take a sip.

"Slowly," she cautions, as Tripp slurps gratefully, though it clearly hurts him almost as much to swallow. "You haven't had solid food in a few days, we've been bypassing your stomach completely. You can thank your brother for pulling *that* tube long before you woke up."

"I remember," Tripp mutters hoarsely, shrugging one shoulder before accepting another sip of water and then flopping back against his pillow. "Little. Sucked."

The fact that Tripp is already *joking,* as exhausted and uncomfortable as he must be, has Leander stifling a somewhat distressed laugh and covering his mouth. Hoping fervently that Tripp doesn't notice, Leander closes his eyes and squeezes, willing the tears that are welling up behind them to disperse.

No such luck.

When Leander opens again, Tripp's hand is on his thigh and he's gazing back at him with warm, if tired, fondness, and he winks.

"Alright, gang," Aliyah declares, after doing the world's quickest physical exam in history on Tripp. She turns and sweeps her white-coat-clad arms towards the doorway in a gesture that can only mean, *get the fuck out.* "Tripp needs to rest. *One* of you may stay, and I'll make that choice an easy one—Beau, come with me now and I'll let you consult on your brother's plan of care."

Beau's face lights up. After giving Tripp a gentle hug and murmuring some words of encouragement in his ear, he follows his Chief out the door like a puppy. He's hand-in-hand with Bri, who's just gotten off her own shift, and that takes care of half the room. It's just Leander and Tripp's nurse now, and he's relatively certain that direct care staff were exempt from the shooing.

Despite that, the nurse doesn't stick around. Briefly, she has Tripp rate his pain, adjusts a few things on the various IV pumps, administers a push medication, and warns Leander not to try and keep Tripp awake.

"I'm not an idiot," Leander mutters, sliding off the side of the bed and into his own chair, which, at this point, probably has the outline of his butt permanently imprinted on the cushion.

"No," the nurse agrees amiably, adjusting one of Tripp's infusions for the last time before heading for the door. "But you've been waiting for this since the moment y'all walked in. What he's been through and what you've been through are two totally different kinds of trauma, and you both need time to recover. Just... keep your expectations low for tonight." Before Leander can reply, she wiggles her fingers at them and slips away.

That leaves Leander alone with Tripp, but when he turns his attention back to the man, Tripp's already fast asleep. "Low expectations," Leander says softly. "Check." Still, he can't resist scooping up Tripp's hand just to feel the warm weight of it, the lines and bumps of Tripp's fingers interlacing with his own. Many times over the past several days, Leander has sat like this, pressing the pads of two fingers down onto Tripp's pulse point anytime he needed tangible proof of life.

Doing so makes Tripp stir, pretty long lashes batting against his cheek as his eyelids flutter open, just halfway. "Hey," he croaks, licking his lips, and Leander immediately holds up the water cup for Tripp to take a sip. He drinks slowly, head falling back heavily when he's done. Tripp looks positively drained, and once again, Leander wishes that there was something he could *do.*

He's so busy worrying about how useless he is, Leander forgets to *say* anything to Tripp, who tugs at his hand, weakly but impatiently. "Sorry," Leander tells him, when he realizes Tripp is trying to get his attention. "I just—" He stops, drops his head to where their hands are joined against the mattress, and presses his forehead to Tripp's knuckles, swallowing a treasonous sob before it can escape.

Against his skin, Tripp's hand turns, something it hasn't done in days, despite Leander doing this very thing *so* many times. Tonight, Tripp's hand cups his jaw, tries to encourage him to sit up. When he does, Leander knows he looks awful, probably red-eyed and with tears streaming down his cheeks, but Tripp still looks at him like he's the only person who matters in the world. The way his eyes crinkle and the corners of his lips curl up, it's so *Tripp,* and so fucking relieving, Leander can barely breathe.

"Come," Tripp says huskily, spreading his arms like he wants Leander to crawl into them. He can't—the bed is too damn small even if he wanted to, never mind all of Tripp's wires and tubes running into and over him. Still, hell if he isn't going to *try.* He'd *try* to lasso the moon and drag it into bed with them if Tripp asked him to.

When all is said and done, Leander has somehow managed to wedge his hip onto the side of the bed *right* next to Tripp's, and he curls forward, tucking his face into Tripp's neck, careful to avoid the central line in his chest that was placed way back on Day Two. Tripp isn't strong enough to do much more than drape his arms loosely around Leander's waist, but he tries—nosing in Leander's hair, humming a little and sighing with obvious happiness.

It's—it's *not* even remotely the way Leander imagined this moment playing out. Not how he dreamed the way their first time being alone together after sharing their feelings would be. They're worlds away from anything resembling fantasy, but Leander hasn't a single complaint. The moment may not be ideal, but it *is* real, and Tripp is *alive,* and right now, that's more than enough.

Remembering Tripp's doctor's warning and his nurse's reinforcement of it, Leander forces himself to pull away much sooner than he wants to—*he never wants to* —and when he does, Tripp's eyelids are heavy, barely staying open.

"I'm with you all the way here," Leander promises, squeezing both of Tripp's hands tight between his own, but Tripp just rolls his tired eyes. His easy, flippant response has Leander huffing a laugh, even as another tear escapes.

"Dramatic," Tripp scolds, his voice cracking in the middle of the word, but Leander gets the point.

"Alright," he concedes, raising his hands in surrender before sinking back into his stupid chair and regarding Tripp with untempered affection. "I understand. No 'chick-flick moments,' right?" Tripp's smile widens at Leander's use of air quotes, and he tips his chin up, presumably in agreement to the sentiment expressed.

Leander grins, beyond thrilled to have his asshole friend—*boyfriend?*—back. He clears his throat before gruffly saying, "Go to sleep, you incorrigible bastard."

Tripp salutes, barely getting the tips of his fingers to his temple before his eyes are closing the rest of the way, whether he wants them to or not. When Leander is *very* sure that he's passed out cold, Tripp surprises him by roughly murmuring, "Love you."

"Oh, sweetheart, I love you too," Leander replies immediately, surging out of his seat to press a kiss to Tripp's forehead, lingering to draw a hand down his cheek, fingers catching on the oxygen tubing. "My whole life, I've never loved anything else."

Even though he's stuck in the "comfy" chair, even though he gets jolted awake every hour *on* the hour when a nurse comes in to check on Tripp, Leander sleeps better that night than he has in *ages*. He dreams vividly about the day he'll do so next to Tripp, in his own apartment, in his own bed—*not* in the playroom.

Even fast asleep, Leander can't wait.

Chapter 12

"This is boring," Tripp complains from his place on Lee's couch. His back and his left leg are propped up with pillows from the playroom bed, his left arm is in a sling across his chest. Not a sling the hospital gave them, mind you, but one that Lee finally fashioned out of satin scarves when Tripp wouldn't stop trying to use his injured hand. It *might* be securing his arm to his chest a *touch* tighter than is strictly necessary.

"This is the worst," Tripp adds, when Leander doesn't rise to his bait, allowing his head to loll dramatically against the pillow behind him. To be fair, Leander doesn't disagree, especially regarding the misuse of BDSM equipment. All they're missing is the ball gag, not that he hasn't considered it.

"You're a terrible patient," Leander deadpans from the recliner next to Tripp, replying without so much as looking up from the book lying open in his lap. "I'm taking care of you. Catering to your every whim. You should be grateful. Falling at my feet to worship my benevolence in thanks. Instead, you're whining. You know how much I detest whining."

Tripp scoffs. "I'd *rather* do that first thing," he agrees, and Leander stifles a smile, still focused on the pages of his book but no longer actively reading. "C'mon, Lee," Tripp needles. "My limbs might be broken but my mouth ain't."

When Leander glances up and catches Tripp's eye, he knows that he's been caught. "Anymore," he says pointedly, trying and failing to not look amused at the way Tripp bites his lip and waggles his eyebrows suggestively. "God, you're awful."

"I think I'm adorable," Tripp retorts.

It's not as if Leander isn't planning to give in—*eventually*—but being unable to physically turn Tripp over his knee and spank him, he's had to get creative with keeping the bratty attitude in check. *Especially* now that Tripp's injured and stuck in one place, completely at Leander's mercy (though not exactly in the way they're used to). That dynamic shift has been... interesting, to say the least.

Unfortunately for both of them, dramatic, life-threatening events that end in sweeping romantic gestures only go so far towards softening *reality*, and theirs has been tough.

Three weeks have passed since Tripp's release from the hospital, and while Tripp might enjoy being Leander's submissive in the bedroom—and perhaps occasionally outside of it, when the mood strikes—he *hates* being *dependent* on anyone for anything. Which means that Leander is constantly walking an incredibly fine line between *caring* for Tripp and pissing him off. More than one evening has devolved into Leander storming out of the living room and onto his own balcony to cool off, shutting the sliding glass door behind him and knowing full-well that it's a dick move because Tripp can't follow.

Although, knowing Tripp, he'd crawl across the hardwood floors hand over fist if he thought it would drive home a point. That awareness has Leander perpetually ensuring that—even when he's angry—his phone remains charged and tucked in his pocket...*just in case*. Tripp always lets him have his space, though, and likely needs his own. It's such that usually, by the time Leander ventures back inside, Tripp is ready to push past whatever it is they were bickering about and let it go.

Usually. Sometimes he's not, choosing instead to ignore Leander and pout on the sofa like a beer-drinking toddler well into the early hours of the morning. Meanwhile, Leander retreats to their bedroom and screams his frustrations into a pillow.

Even then, he unfailingly plugs in his phone and leaves it on low volume by his bedside—just in case.

If Leander thought that he loved Tripp before, he's really beginning to understand what that *means,* and it's not all sunshine and roses.

Still, Leander wouldn't trade it. If anything, their struggles make the quiet, peaceful moments they share together taste that much sweeter. Life is not perfect, and Leander never expected it to be.

So they're fine. It's all temporary, and they'll get through this. In a few more weeks, Tripp's casts will come off, Leander will return to work, and Tripp will start intensive outpatient physical therapy in the name of eventually being cleared to do the same.

All in all, Leander has no regrets about this path he volunteered to walk—both personally and in regards to Tripp's recovery. In fact, he'd do it again in a heartbeat. He's not remotely sorry for shouldering the primary caretaker responsibility (*not* that he would ever admit to Tripp that's what it is), or for not passing Tripp off to Beau, back when he had the chance.

That's another thing Leander doesn't ever plan on admitting to Tripp—that he and Beau held a post-intubation conference with just the two of them regarding what would come next. A heated back and forth outside of Tripp's I.C.U. bay while he was still down for the count inside, snoring away on his painkillers. It's probable that Tripp would disown them both if he knew, and he *definitely* would do so if he found out that the argument involved who was best suited to care for him in his (however temporary) infirmity.

As far as the conversation itself went, it honestly surprised Leander that Beau even *wanted* the job, never mind the fact that he was willing to raise his voice to Leander in pursuit of it. Beau's aggressive insistence that he *needed* to bring Tripp home to the Truett's apartment, needed to look after his brother *himself,* raised Leander's hackles and resulted in him snapping off a comment or two about the inappropriateness of that entire scenario. It's possible that Leander implied that he was the obvious and *only* suitable choice, which only made Beau increasingly irritated and prickly.

The whole encounter felt strange and left Leander feeling completely off-balance, especially when Beau abruptly cut himself off and stormed away in a very *un*-Beau-like manner. Stomping down the hall holding one hand high, like he just *couldn't* with Leander anymore. It's the most Tripp-like Leander's ever seen him act, which was quite terrible, because Beau is definitely *not* Tripp, and Leander's usual tactics for coping with Truett dramatics would certainly not have been welcomed.

He briefly contemplated texting Beau to apologize, but in truth, Leander wasn't sorry in the least. Beau's actions didn't make any sense to him, outside of the theory that Beau perhaps didn't *trust* Leander to care for Tripp, which hurt too much to seriously consider. Why *would* a just-married young man want to postpone his entire life—*and his honeymoon*—to play nursemaid to his *brother?* Especially when there was a superior, sensible alternative for everyone involved?!

It was odd, no doubt, but Leander didn't dwell too much. He simply chalked his confusion up to a severe lack in both familial bonds *and* / or romantic awareness. It's not as if he was in any position to judge whatever worked for Beau in his relationship with Bri. Not when Leander's behavior was a solid part of the reason he and Tripp were so messed up in the first place.

Ultimately, Leander opted to let Beau storm off in his self-righteous huff without protest, only to watch him be escorted right back down the hallway by his ear—in spirit if not in practice—by his wife, less than sixty minutes later.

"Tell him," Briana demanded, flipping her curly blonde ponytail back over her shoulder and crossing both arms over a stained, white sundress. The outfit was jarring to Leander's eye, totally out of place for the cold weather, and only then did he realize that she was probably dressed to go to the airport. Dressed for her *honeymoon,* having changed out of her scrubs once her shift ended. The dried reddish-brown smear marring her torso caught his notice, but Leander didn't say so. It would appear that he and Beau weren't the only ones having a rough day.

Looking like a chastised puppy, Beau was busy averting his eyes and pulling at his own fingers, eventually revealing that he was *not* actually upset at Leander, he was feeling guilty. Apparently, he'd been planning to move out of the shared Tru-ett apartment and into a brand new condo with Briana within the next couple of months, but had never gotten around to telling *Tripp* that.

"Our lease is up soon," he mumbled. "Tripp can afford the place on his income alone, but I figured if he wasn't cool with me leaving, I'd just continue paying my share until he found somewhere new. I can't spring that on him *now,* though! We'll just have to stay. We'll lose our deposit on the condo, but that's not a huge deal. Tripp needs me, anyway."

With an exasperated grumble, Briana leaned in and used her elbow to nudge Beau's ribs, making him grimace. "And?"

"And… " Beau sighed, tipping his head back and rolling his neck. "And I feel like I owe it to him," he reluctantly explained, raising his hands before allowing them to drop and clap against his thighs. "Lee, Tripp practically raised me. Changed my diapers, got me dressed for school, always made sure I had something to eat, and that my homework was done. I can't just… " He shook his head. "I would *never* leave him like this, the one time he really needs me."

That, at least, made heaps more sense than whatever Leander was previously assuming, but if Beau expected unconditional support for his unnecessarily self-flagellation, he had another thing coming.

"Beau," Leander said gently, catching Briana's eye and receiving a reassuring nod. "Tripp *wants* you to live your life. You spoke to him this morning, he told you so himself. He would *hate it* if you skipped out on your honeymoon because of him, after he told you to go. In fact, I think you know that he would never forgive himself if you did, warranted or not. I do think you're probably right to be concerned about the apartment news, because you know how he hates change and loves you, but you can't possibly believe that Tripp would actually *want* you to give all that up?"

Somewhat sadly, Beau hung his head, lifting a hand to swipe somewhat angrily across his face before shaking his head in the negative. "No, I know," he replied softly.

"Guilt isn't logical, baby," Briana chimed in sympathetically, reaching out to rub Beau's arm. "You need to talk to him."

Leander held up a finger. "If you're open to it, I have another idea," he suggested, and unsurprisingly, Beau and Bri were all ears as Leander filled them in.

In the end, Leander is reasonably certain that Beau was glad to be let off the hook, no matter what he claimed. Both in regards to being Tripp's caretaker, and for the responsibility of breaking the news about moving out (at least, with no safety net in place). Instead, while Beau and Bri were calculatedly unreachable on their flight to Aruba, Leander approached Tripp *first* with a request of his own. One that he was *very* careful to frame clearly and accurately, and to not make sound like he was only offering because of the circumstances—even if Tripp only knew about half of them at the time.

"Will you move in with me?" put the ball in *Tripp's* court, and by the time he spoke to Beau the next morning, Tripp was practically glowing about it. Which meant that when Beau casually dropped his bomb in regards to moving, Tripp had already decided he didn't give two shits because *he was too.*

In the interest of full disclosure and honest communication, later that night, Leander did cop to knowing about Beau's plans, emphasizing that they weren't relevant—he'd already been anticipating asking Tripp to move in before they ever came up. Considering that his story had the benefit of actually being true, added to the fact that—at this point in their hospital stay—Leander was *way* too worn out to lie convincingly, Tripp believed him.

In true Tripp fashion, though, he *did* hold his forgiveness temporarily at bay— only agreeing to trade it for a blowjob, value to be cashed in at some point in the not-too-distant future.

That joke is on Tripp, though, as he never negotiated "to completion," a card which Leander intends to play to his full advantage just as soon as the opportunity arises.

With their immediate future settled, Leander had contacted EMS Chief Maxwell and gone on official leave from work, which strangely, the Chief didn't even question. It was almost like Maxwell expected him to do so, as if he already believed that Leander and Tripp were together *and* serious about it.

Leander chalks *that* up to his love declaration over the radio, as surely that moment had not remained sacred between himself and Tripp. A private channel only indicates that the band is for side communications, not that others can't listen in. With the way the emergency services community thrives on drama, Leander is sure that plenty of his co-workers were treating their crisis like some kind of reality soap.

Lifestyles of the Sexually Deviant and Emotionally Constipated, coming soon to a radio wave near you.

Thankfully, Leander is a workaholic whose social pursuits have essentially always been limited to BDSM and beekeeping, one of which he's never actually translated from copious research into any sort of practical effort. Therefore, the majority of his sick and vacation PTO have simply been accumulating. The department's administrative end took care of rolling his benefits over from year to year, at least until he hit the max hours allowed to bank. As Maxwell told it, Leander could finagle up to six full months of paid leave, if he chose to do so.

Not necessary, Leander told him. Tripp's doctors predicted that he would have the casts off in six to eight weeks, and after that, it would be physical therapy's job to decide when he might be ready to return to work. That *could* take several additional months, yes, but Tripp won't be bedridden any longer, not by that point. He won't need Leander to sit at home and tend to him twenty-four-seven.

Actually, Leander felt fairly certain in his belief that by then, it would be good for him and Tripp to have some scheduled time apart. To be working their way back into a regular routine.

… *Or* perhaps the idea of coming home from work to Tripp waiting for him was just *far* too tempting to dismiss outright.

Still, time off sorted and discharge location decided, there was plenty more to negotiate between the two of them, and not all of it went so smoothly. In fact, Tripp about blew a gasket when he discovered that Leander had been working on his '*caregiver skills*' the entire time Tripp was unconscious.

It hadn't come up in casual conversation, so Leander hadn't outright mentioned it, but Tripp's assumptions about what his discharged life would look like required swift correction. Before that, Tripp was under the false impression that when he was finally sent home, a nurse would be there *all* of the time—to take him to the toilet, to wash him in the shower, and generally, to help with everything else "humiliating" (his words) that came with being disabled and unable to care for oneself.

When Tripp found out that in actuality, the nurse would only be stopping by for an hour or so, two, maybe three times per week, he had been very confused. It was then that Leander helpfully pointed out that *he* would be there, that he was more than capable of doing all of the things Tripp listed in the nurse's stead, and in fact, that he had been doing much worse all along.

"You—you *what?*" Tripp had paled, face going slack in disbelief as the implications of what Leander was saying sunk in. "You can't—Lee, you—*please* tell me this is one of your weird jokes that I don't get. Tell me you're not serious."

Leander, for his part, didn't understand what the big fuss was about. After all, he's had his tongue *inside* Tripp's ass. Cleaning him up while he was *unconscious* and gravely ill wasn't something he even thought to blink at. In fact, if anyone was going to do it, it seemed only right for that person to be him.

In response to Tripp's marked horror, Leander furrowed his brow and tipped his head to the side, confused. "Believe me, it was not at all funny seeing you so helpless. Caring for your needs made me feel useful, which was a rarity that week. But yes, I am serious. I've already been doing those things, and then some. It doesn't bother me in the least."

Releasing a strangled noise that made him sound more like a dying cat than a human being, Tripp clawed his pillow out from behind his head and smashed it over his face, though not before Leander witnessed his cheeks beginning to turn bright red.

"Never tell me," Tripp said, into the pillow. "Lee, we have *sex!* Never, ever tell me."

"Tripp, I don't see you any differently, if that's what you're concerned about." Leander had reached out a hand to touch one of Tripp's, but his freckled fingers immediately curled into a fist and buried their way into the bedding as Tripp moaned in apparent agony.

Leander tried his best to provide additional reassurance, but that didn't go over well, either. "Many people, both men and women, watch their partners give birth to their children, which I can assure you is a *far* more graphic and disturbing event, and they still—"

"*Lee!*" Tripp whipped the pillow away from his face, looking up at him incredulously. "Not helping." He pushed his finger pointedly into Leander's chest and narrowed his eyes. "And I swear to God, if you finish that comparison, I will live to make you regret it."

Putting his hands in the air, Leander sank into the depths of the comfy chair, smart enough to know when to quit. As they both sat there in silence, the air between them remained stilted and awkward. Steadily avoiding eye contact, Tripp pretended to watch a *King of Queens* rerun that Leander knew for a fact he'd seen twice already that week. Central Hospital's media catalog truly left something to be desired.

To his own credit, Leander tolerated that atmosphere for over an hour before he broke. Genuinely upset that Tripp felt *so* uncomfortable over what *he* felt was simply the *least* he could do for the person he loved, Leander opted to try and explain his feelings one more time. For this round, though, he took a different approach.

"When we… " He paused to clear his throat, waiting as Tripp reluctantly tore his eyes away from the TV. "Before, on the day—well, you know. Earlier, at my home, you enjoyed yourself, didn't you?"

Clearly surprised and probably slightly confused at Leander's shift in tack, Tripp just blinked back at him for an extended moment before nodding slowly. "'Course," he replied, somewhat guarded, clearly harboring the suspicion that Leander was not *actually* changing the subject. Fair enough, he wasn't.

"You came out of the bedroom with your collar on. You…*we* maintained our roles in a purely non-sexual manner."

"Oh," Tripp said, and he sounded disappointed, maybe even slightly angry, flushing a little and scratching at the back of his neck. He gave a small shrug. "Yeah, I guess we should've discussed that or something first. What, you're going to tell me that made you uncomfortable?"

"Quite the opposite," Leander assured him, reaching out to brush fingers over his thigh. "I always enjoy having you as my sub. And to be frank, I enjoyed watching you be so at ease outside of the bedroom. You seemed… content, even though you were essentially acting as a service sub."

Tripp shrugged again, a small thing that barely disturbed his shoulder as his fingers fidgeted with the folds of the bedsheets pooled around his hips. "I like taking care of you," he admitted quietly.

"Some of the tasks I gave you were gross," Leander noted. "Stripping and washing all of our soiled linens, cleaning the toys we used by hand. I can't imagine you enjoyed that."

"Life is gross," Tripp retorted. "And I enjoyed it because it was for you. I knew it would make you happy or whatever. I didn't even think about—" Tripp stopped talking abruptly and snapped his mouth shut, dipping his chin to glare down his nose at Leander. "Not cool," he grumbled, waving a finger in Leander's smirking direction. "And *not* the same, either."

"Isn't it?" Leander pressed, scooting forward on his chair to grab Tripp's accusatory hand and cup it between his own while Tripp scowled. "Even if you were *just* my sub, it would be well within our relationship construct *and* my own ideals for me to care for you in your time of need. If you would allow it, of course. However," Leander paused, licking his lips and squeezing Tripp's hand for emphasis. "It is my understanding that you are no longer *just* my sub."

"Yeah," Tripp replied breathily, staring down at the sheets before chancing a glance up and meeting Leander's earnest gaze. "Guess not."

"It's not weird to care for someone you love," Leander added, only when he felt sure he was receiving Tripp's full and undivided attention. The resulting pink that spread down over his freckled neck and under the edges of his hospital gown was softer than his embarrassed flush, and entirely too rewarding. "Please don't be angry with me for wanting to take care of you. You have no idea how hard it was to just—to *sit* here and be useless to you."

"Lee," Tripp said with a sigh, head dropping back against his pillow. "I'm not pissed at you, alright? I'm just... " He waved his free, albeit casted, hand around in the air, presumably gesturing to his current situation as a whole. "I'm having the opposite fuckin' problem, and it sucks."

"Agreed," Leander said easily, squeezing the hand he's holding again. "So how about this. I *promise* to ensure that I do everything within my power to keep you independent once we're home. Whatever that may entail. We'll make modifications to the bathroom, the bedroom. We'll have occupational therapy get you every device and aid known to man, so that you can do as many activities as possible without requiring outside assistance. We'll work together, and if there is something you absolutely cannot stand to have me help you with, we'll figure a way around it."

Tripp was back to picking at his blanket, but he did look relieved. "I just—Lee, I don't want you to see me differently. When I'm all healed up and blowing you in the shower, I don't want you flashing back on washing my ass in a shower chair meant for eighty year olds in nursing homes."

Now, *that* remark came as a surprise. Caught off guard, Leander laughed loudly and Tripp startled. While he did feel somewhat bad for laughing, the idea was just— "Ludicrous," Leander said simply, with a shrug of his own. As Tripp opened his mouth to protest, Leander waved him off.

"Listen. You know that I am... not like other people. I process things differently, am frequently too logical, too blunt, too literal. In this particular situation, those things happen to work in your favor. I will never see you differently because of some physical limitation, or because you let yourself be weak in front of me. I just do not operate that way, Tripp. It's not something you have to worry about. I can try and reassure you more, if you like, but I'm hoping you'll trust me."

From beneath his lashes, Tripp was still looking at him skeptically, so Leander kissed the back of his hand and gave it a pat. "You know, sometimes I think that I was built to love you," he said casually, tracing the patterns imprinted on Tripp's skin, the remnants of superficial burns that were nearly all healed. "It's as if I was programmed to be one thing, one way, and then you came along and—"

Leander looked up, finding emerald green eyes already staring back, wide and unflinching. "Things that never made sense to me suddenly clicked. I am *happy* loving you, Tripp. Caring for each other's bodies is just *part* of that, but this is no different to me than what we do in the playroom, because it's what you need. Perhaps that doesn't make any sense to you, but there it is."

Suspiciously quiet for a moment, Tripp broke the heavy silence in the room by saying, "Alright, well, just so long as you don't develop some kind of diaper-play kink. That shit is still a hard no on my list."

"Noted," Leander replied with a smile, as he leaned back in his chair.

Surprisingly, though, Tripp isn't finished. "Thing is," he started. "I dunno if I can afford all that stuff, Lee. I mean, our insurance is decent, but we still have like, a fifty percent co-pay on D.M.E. So, you know. Your idea is great in theory, but buddy, I'm still waiting to hear how much rent I'm gonna owe before I can even *think* about that. Place like yours… "

From his chair, Leander just rolled his eyes, having tried and failed (multiple times by that point) to convince Tripp that moving in didn't automatically mean having to split expenses. Still, he should have known better than to be surprised when Tripp wanted to try and insist on doing that very thing.

"We don't need to do this right now."

"I think we do," Tripp challenged, sitting up a little straighter and attempting to cross his arms over his chest before remembering he had a cast on. Leander watched with one eyebrow lifted as Tripp struggled to wiggle into a comfortable, yet intimidating position, waiting him out. "You're obviously rolling in cash, dude. If I'm gonna come and be your kept boy—" Leander snorted. "—or whatever, I should at least get to know who's bankrolling my sugar daddy."

Tripp raised his own eyebrows pointedly, the unbelievable brat, and therefore, it was Leander's turn to scowl.

"Don't be crass, Tripp."

"Then just tell me, Lee, c'mon. We're—we're like, building a life together here, man. Aren't we? I mean, I'm not reading this wrong, am I? You love me, I love you, we're moving in together. You're talking about wiping my ass for me and saying you don't even care if I pay rent—shit, Lee, that's more than my own old man ever did for me."

The smug look disappeared from Tripp's face, his confrontational attitude bleeding away the more he talked, and Leander was in the wrong, completely. He knew it. Tripp deserved better than Leander's usual avoidance of all things personal. Despite that, he couldn't help teasing Tripp, just a little.

"For someone who supposedly hates the idea, you seemingly can't stop bringing up the ass-wiping—"

"Lee!" Tripp snapped, exasperated, snatching a crumpled straw wrapper from his overbed table and chucking it at Leander's head. "Start talking or I'm gonna call Beau and tell him I changed my mind on giving him his life back. Then he'll be my designated ass-wiper and the two of us will stay living together in that crummy apartment until we're old and gray and Briana divorces him, and it'll be all your fault."

"That is one polluted stream of thought," Leander remarked as Tripp threw up his hands. "Fine," he added quietly. "I'm rich."

"Yeah, no duh, Lee," Tripp replied sarcastically and Leander closed his mouth, folded his arms across his chest, and raised an eyebrow at Tripp, who almost immediately shrunk down into his bedding.

"Do you want to hear what I have to say, or not?"

"Yes, Sir," Tripp replied meekly, and internally, Leander found himself gloating. He quickly sobered up, though, when he remembered what, exactly, he was supposed to be explaining.

Swiftly, Leander wracked his brain for a starting point, trying to recall what he might've revealed to Tripp in the past and how many years he could skip over while still making sense. "I don't think I've ever told you that my mother died when I was young," he began carefully. "Not as young as you and Beau experienced, I was fourteen. Although, if I had to venture a guess, you likely spent more time with your mother in those four short years than I did with mine in triple that. Certainly, from what I've heard, your mother at least acted the part."

Leander paused, but Tripp didn't interrupt or make any jokes, just sat quietly and waited patiently for the story to continue.

"My mother was... unkind. More interested in 'fixing' whatever she perceived was wrong with me than finding out who I was, what I wanted out of life. As soon as I reached an age where there existed a boarding school accepting children that young, I was shipped off. Even when I was home, holidays and such, she was frequently traveling. You know my twin, Lawrence—Chloe's father—he and our older brother Lorenzo received similar treatment, except Lorenzo—I believe he goes by 'Loki' these days—was a difficult child.

"Expelled from school after school, to the point where he wasn't welcome home again, which is why we're not as close as we might be these days. We simply have very few shared memories and common experiences, save for the occasional holiday and Mother's funeral, plus he's several years our senior. Lawrence, at least—well, being kept together went a long way. But he would also like to pretend that our shared past doesn't exist. Understandable, considering that most would describe what we went through as 'abuse,' both at that 'Christian' school and at home.

"It's difficult for him to be around me, even so many years later." Leander could tell that Tripp had some sort of reaction to the casual way he referred to his mother's passing, but he wasn't going to apologize or make excuses for it. This was how he felt, and if Leander was going to be made to talk about his family, it was going to be on his terms. Parched from speaking, Leander reached out and stole Tripp's styrofoam water cup, sipping intently and then holding it in his lap, fiddling with the lid.

"My father left us. He was an extremely high-ranking military man. *Extremely* high," Leander emphasized, with a meaningful look at Tripp. "His relationship with our mother happened to be a second attempt at having a family, and he was much older than she was. Apparently, his experiment failed. He didn't enjoy raising children any more than he did the first time around, because I wasn't even out of diapers when he accepted a position serving the incoming Presidential administration and failed to invite any of us along."

"Jesus Christ," Tripp said softly, but beyond that, he stayed quiet. Of note, Tripp did leave his hand conspicuously palm-up on the bed, accessible and in easy reach should Leander have wanted to take it, but he didn't push the issue. It was a greatly appreciated gesture, even if Leander didn't take advantage—not yet, anyway. He was rooted in a particular state of mind at that moment, and touching wasn't something he felt especially warm and fuzzy about. He rarely did when reflecting on or recounting his difficult upbringing.

"You probably know him as Robert Grigori."

That definitely got Tripp's attention, and he dragged a hand over his mouth before pointing a finger in Leander's direction. "Hold up," he said, in obvious disbelief. "Your old man is General Grigori? The dude everyone called 'God' because of how much power he had over not one, but *two* different presidents? You don't look anything like him."

"He was SecDef for the better part of a decade, yes," Leander confirmed. "And... thank you, I suppose."

"Oh, definitely. Name should've been a clue, I guess, but we always called him —"

"God, I know. Everyone did."

"Yeah, so, God—uh, Robert? Whatever. He always kind of reminded me of a weirdly attractive squirrel." As Tripp's eyes went guiltily wide, Leander squinted and tilted his head to the side, suspicious. "And I see now how that was definitely not the right thing to say."

Rolling his eyes, Leander shifted in his chair and opened his mouth to continue, but Tripp cut him off again.

"You both have really nice eyes," he offered. "Super... uh, blue." Closing said eyes in vexation, Leander held up a silencing hand. "Right," Tripp added. "I'm done."

"The rest of the story is simple," Leander continued. "My emotionally and physically cruel mother *also* had an extremely high-paying job. She didn't need the child support my father sent, but certainly wasn't going to beget the satisfaction of allowing him to stop. Every penny went into an account that was meant to collectively fund each of our way through advanced higher education—medicine or law, preferably.

"But then she died, and control of that account went to me, along with all of her other accounts and assets, which were not paltry. Lorenzo—er, *Loki,* right— wasn't interested in any of it. He had our mother's knack for business, he's a globetrotter, and these days, a very wealthy man in his own right. Or so I've heard.

"And Lawrence—" Leander just shook his head. "There was a time when he would accept money to help with Chloe, but nothing else. We've talked about the way he turned towards religion to cope. I never understood that draw, not after...everything. Either way, today, as a pastor, he still has no interest in wealth. *Chloe* will never want for anything, not that I'm allowed to tell her so. I believe that's part of why Lawrence didn't fight her becoming a firefighter as much as he might have. At least the work is honest.

"Anyway, as you know, I opted out of a traditional four-year university to attend EMT and then paramedic school at the local community college. The end result, as it applies here, was an already significant amount of cash doing nothing except sitting in the bank earning more money." Leander stopped talking abruptly, and it took Tripp a full minute to apparently realize that the story was over.

"Wait, that's it? So you've got, what? Thousands of dollars saved up? What about when it runs out?"

"Millions," Leander corrected flatly, picking at the cuticle of one thumb. "It's not going to run out. I live modestly. Also, I make a mediocre living as a paramedic. I could almost definitely afford to move into the storage space in the basement of my apartment building, should the need arise."

That made Tripp laugh and then immediately wince and clutch at his ribs. Without asking for permission, Leander shot a glance at the clock before pressing the nurse's call button and requesting Tripp's pain medication over the intercom.

"Anyway," he said, flopping back into his chair. "The way I see things, it's not my money, either. I didn't earn it. In fact, this is probably a good time to disclose that Marley has full access to all of my accounts. She directs much of the overflow towards various progressive and social causes that would infuriate Robert Grigori if he ever discovered what his hard-earned cash was funding."

"I ain't no charity case," Tripp said gruffly, but he was smiling. "Though, now I understand why you're always picking up our bar tab."

Leander nodded in agreement. "The money allows me to do what I love without worry. The least I can do is assist my partner in doing the same."

Before Tripp had a chance to reply, the nurse bustled in, taking the opportunity to assess Tripp from head to toe before administering his pain medication through the IV. In truth, Leander thought it was opportune timing. No doubt, this was a hard concept for Tripp to accept—the idea of *anyone* providing for him, as if he was incapable of doing so for himself. Not that *Leander* thought anything of the sort—but that was just Tripp's nature.

With any luck, the morphine coursing through his veins would create some sort of Pavlovian effect, a positive feeling when Tripp eventually thought back on the conversation as a whole. Leander could only hope.

The nurse lingered by the computer attached to the step-down unit's wall to complete her charting, clicking rhythmically away at the keyboard. By the time she finished, Tripp's eyelids were looking heavy, and he was visibly fighting sleep.

"This isn't over," he slurred, while Leander busied himself pulling his chair closer to Tripp's beside and holding his hand while he drifted off.

"Of course, Tripp," Leander replied good-naturedly.

But Tripp hadn't brought up the discussion—*any* of it—ever again. Not the money situation, and not the "ass-wiping" one, either. There was no lack of opportunity for him to do so—discharge planning was taken as seriously as an Olympic sport at Central, so by the time they were walking (wheeling, for Tripp) out the front doors, not a single aspect of Tripp's continuing care was left to guesswork.

Despite that, Tripp didn't say another word about his misgivings, just accepted things as they came and allowed Leander to cleanly step into the role of "partner and caregiver" without further protest.

As far as Leander was concerned, *that* was a win, and one he wasn't about to question.

And so, they were discharged home to Leander's apartment. Between the visiting nurses, the physical and occupational therapists, the follow-up doctor's appointments, and everything that came with both transforming Leander's space and caring for Tripp in it, the following weeks flew by. Once Beau returned from Aruba, he came over frequently. His presence allowed Leander and Tripp to have some breathing room, under the guise of grocery shopping or some other errand, creating natural space so that neither had to actually admit they needed it.

On her off-nights from work, Bri came too, and the four of them would play poker and try their best to make Tripp feel as normal as humanly possible. They'd prop his leg on an extra chair and set him up with a nonalcoholic beer, and everything would seem like usual—at least, until Tripp began to nod off against his will right there at the table. Then Beau and Bri would bid them both goodnight, pretending not to look concerned as Leander wrangled Tripp into his wheelchair and carted him off to the bathroom to get ready for bed, both of them bickering amiably about it the whole way there.

It was fine, though. Leander kept his promises to Tripp regarding going the extra mile to ensure he stayed independent, and Tripp, while frequently grumpy and miserable about his situation, tried his best not to direct those frustrations at Leander.

Most importantly, nearly every night after returning home, they slept curled together in Leander's bed. Most frequently with Tripp on his right side, head resting on Leander's chest. The pillows from the playroom never made their way back, journeying only from the couch to the bedroom so that Tripp could stay comfortable no matter where he might be, and Leander didn't mind that, either.

The first time he woke to Tripp stuffing a pillow behind his *own* back and another behind his legs so he could more effectively position his injured limbs over Leander's body was a bit of a shock, but the end effect was entirely nest-like and not unpleasant at all.

So they adapted. More easily than Leander might have guessed, even.

The well-wisher brigade was another thing altogether. A never-ending stream of firefighters and EMTs knocking on the door began immediately the afternoon they arrived home, and didn't slow until well after two full weeks had passed. Only then because Reina stepped in and threatened to ban anyone who "kept Tripp from getting his rest" from her bar, and none of them could afford to drink anywhere else.

All of that said and done, Tripp was *exhausted* during that period of time. He was still taking powerful, 'round the clock narcotics, his various aches and pains fresh enough to keep him grumpy and uninterested in pushing his limits. For Leander and Tripp, this made things like learning each other's *romantic* interests and inclinations difficult, and for the most part, their non-platonic relationship ended up temporarily shelved.

It was for the best. Leander would be lying if he claimed he had the energy for sorting through *any* of that on top of everything else they were dealing with. At the end of any given day, all he wanted to do was *sleep*. While he missed the playroom and dominating in general, the drowsy, dopey kisses he and Tripp exchanged while they were both on the verge of passing out were *plenty* to keep Leander satisfied for the time being.

Right around the time Reina cut off his visitors, though, Tripp also began cutting back on his medications. That left him quite a bit more alert during the day, and *far* more reminiscent of his normal self. He stopped falling asleep while binging Netflix, started grabbing Leander's ass and winking whenever he walked by. He cracked jokes, and pushed Leander's buttons, and was both intensely frustrating and wholly charming to be around. He was *Tripp* again.

The newly-resurfaced but still very much the same *Tripp* also didn't pull any punches about what he wanted or what he thought he could handle. He had yet to be cleared by his doctor for sex, but that didn't stop Tripp from asking, begging, and then eventually, attempting to bait Leander into fucking him. Not being cleared didn't stop him from getting *pissed* when Leander wouldn't do it, either, and the first night Tripp spent on the couch and Leander spent alone in their bed was over that very thing.

The morning that followed the spat, Leander made Tripp an enormous stack of bacon as an apology, even though he didn't feel that he had done anything wrong. In turn, Tripp confessed that it was his own insecurities about himself, his body, and their somewhat-stalled relationship driving him to pick a fight more than anything else.

"I think it's very normal for there to be a learning curve in these situations," Leander replied gently, carefully lifting Tripp's legs and sliding onto the couch beneath them. He took Tripp's uninjured foot between his hands and began massaging the arch until Tripp's tense body relaxed and he laid back, staring somewhat dejectedly up at the ceiling. "I am well out of my depth here, too, Tripp. I've never *been* in a 'romantic relationship' before, and I have no idea what I should or shouldn't be doing."

"Won't catch me complaining about this," Tripp offered, wiggling his toes.

"Yes," Leander agreed, his tone edged with frustration. "But this—I would do this for a sub. I—sometimes when I see you, I just want to grab you and kiss you for no reason. But I have no idea whether that would be welcomed or not. Just because you were open to certain things as my submissive doesn't automatically mean you're interested outside of that context."

Tripp was silent for a moment and then he laughed. "Well, fuck if I know how to reply to that, Lee. I mean, sometimes I'd be into that, yeah. Cuddling and touching for no reason? Hell, yeah. But sometimes I just don't want to be touched. Gotta be honest, doesn't happen *often* when it comes to you, but, you know. Sometimes." Tripp shrugged. "It's just how I am."

Working his hands up Tripp's calf, Leander nodded slowly. "It is becoming apparent to me that both of us are very bad at this. Relationships. Romantic relationships, specifically—with all of our mounting failures, I think that it's possible we are the last two people on this planet who should be attempting one together. And yet, you are the only person I can imagine trying to do so with."

"So you're saying we're a couple of dumbasses?"

Leander smiled. "Just 'a couple' is fine. Less dumb, less ass. But also, yes."

"Could be a lot *more* ass, if you'd let me seduce you."

"Tripp."

"C'mon Lee," Tripp whined, reaching down to tug at Leander's sleeve, encouraging him to make eye contact. "I'm busted up, not dead. I haven't gone this long without getting off since before we started hooking up. Look, see?" Tripp opened his mouth wide and stuck out his tongue, as if that was going to prove something. "Huh? Looking good, right? No swelling. Totally good to go. You could just kneel on either side of my face, I'll suck you off, you do the same for me, everybody wins. I mean, if you *wanted* to, we could even scene. Not like I need all my limbs for that, anyway."

Hearing that remark, Leander pulled away, grabbing Tripp's wandering hands and relocating them to his own stomach. "This is not a rejection of you," he said bluntly. "But you've taken one too many narcotics if you think I'm going to scene with you while you're still healing."

"Lee," Tripp complained, tossing his good arm over his eyes. "You're killing me."

"I will, however, promise to take you to the club downtown once your casts are off and you are cleared for strenuous activity. I'll even let you help plan the scene. How is that?"

"Strenuous?" Tripp repeated, perking up significantly as he peeked out from underneath his arm. Because he's Tripp, he followed that with a gesture towards his crotch, using his casted hand. "Sounds awesome, but doesn't help me right now."

"I'm working on that," Leander agreed, moving Tripp's legs out of the way and getting up off of the couch. "Give me twenty minutes and I'll be back with you. Watch your *Real Housewives.*"

"I'm living *Real Housewives* now," Tripp replied gleefully, predictably reaching up to pinch Leander as he passed. "Got me a sexy sugar daddy to spank my ass and everything."

"He must be a very tolerant man," Leander deadpanned as he headed for the kitchen and his junk drawer.

Twenty minutes later had him returning to Tripp's side with a clipboard stolen from one of the ambulances and two matching, hand-written lists clipped to it. He passed one over to Tripp and asked, "What do you think?"

Squinting and bringing the paper close to his nose in order to read Leander's writing, Tripp's face scrunched in confusion as he processed. "Romantic kink negotiation?" he asked. "What—why?"

"Why not?" Leander quipped. "We both admit to feeling out of sorts in this department. This exercise will at least give us a starting point, a basis for communication and to build on. I also thought that we could use the stoplight system. If one of us initiates affection that the other isn't interested in at the moment, 'yellow' could help them to relay that. Just like in the bedroom, it's not personal, it's simply a boundary. Boundaries are healthy."

Tripp stared blankly down at the paper for a moment and then looked up. "Lee, this is actually kinda brilliant. You know what? You're awesome. Alright, let's do this."

Surprised, Leander just sat there and blinked. "I anticipated more cajoling would be needed. I had planned to offer you that blow job I owe you in exchange for your enthusiastic participation."

The laugh he got in reply was whole-hearted and bright. "I'll show you 'enthusiastic'," Tripp said with a grin, stretching up to wrap a hand around the back of

Leander's head and draw him in for a kiss. Just before their lips met, he paused, so close Leander could feel Tripp's breath on his face.

"Color?"

"Green," Leander replied with a smile, and Tripp finished closing the space between them, kissing him soft and thorough, with far more tongue, energy, and enthusiasm than his healthcare team would likely approve of being used. Too bad, because they're not the ones living with Tripp day in and day out, not the ones who have to decide when it's safer to just let him have something he wants. And on that note, honestly, Leander did see Tripp's point. After all the man has been through, he *should* be able to set his own limits.

Moreso, Leander should trust him to do so.

When they were done kissing—and one did lead to another—Leander managed to wrangle a very soft and affectionate Tripp back into filling out his list. There was some kind of irony to doing so while sporadically trading even more kisses and gentle touches, but he and Tripp have never been what anyone would call *typical,* anyway.

In the end, their lists were surprisingly (or perhaps not, considering) compatible, and whether the activity actually changed anything between them or not, Leander didn't care. He *felt* more comfortable moving forward with Tripp, like they were once again on level footing, the same way they were after filling out their kink lists. It's possible that this was a somewhat useless exercise in practice, but Leander couldn't be sorry for utilizing the communication tools that worked for him (and Tripp) in the past.

Not to mention, seeing Tripp dive in so readily was a turn-on. Realizing that Tripp would likely do just about *any* silly thing Leander proposed if he thought it meant something to him reminded Leander of why he was *so* attracted to Tripp in the first place. Once their pens were down, Tripp barely had the chance to flippantly remind him of his promise before Leander was knocking Tripp's good leg down off of the couch and crawling between them.

While he didn't end up caving to Tripp's pleas to fuck his mouth, he *did* give him a pretty stellar orgasm, if Leander does say so himself. Good enough that Tripp succumbed almost immediately to the hormones and residual pain medication floating around in his system, passing out cold for nearly three hours straight, right there on the couch.

Hard as a rock, Leander cleaned Tripp up and then took his ass directly to the shower. He finished himself off by stroking his cock to the memory of Tripp in there with him—*on his knees, at his feet*—and had not one fleeting regret about it.

The rest of their third week home unraveled in the same way, with Leander pacifying Tripp by blowing or jerking him off nearly anytime he asked, but nothing more, and no reciprocation. However much Tripp may have enjoyed what he was getting, it quickly became clear to Leander that those acts weren't doing anything to quell Tripp's desire for the "real thing."

… Which brings them to *today*, and Tripp's continued, relentless attempts to bait Leander and drag him down into the depths of depravity alongside him, whether it's in Tripp's own best interests or not. Oh, what Leander wouldn't give for that parade of visitors to start back up again, to provide him with an excuse for not letting Tripp goad him into what would inevitably be very *satisfying* but very dangerous sex.

Oh, how the tables have turned.

The truth is, he's *so* weak for Tripp. *God*, Leander loves him so much, wants to be near him and all over him in a way he's never experienced before and is only growing stronger. Even when Tripp is doing his best to saw away at the last string connecting him to sanity, Leander craves him. Ever since he cracked the door by blowing him on the couch, Leander knew he'd cave eventually.

It was only a matter of time.

Well, we behaved for a while, Leander thinks, sighing internally and deciding that if he's going to give in, he'd better do it right.

"Give me twenty minutes," Leander tells Tripp for the second time this week, patting his shoulder and exiting to the bedroom without another solitary word. The look of sheer excitement mixed with surprise on Tripp's face is *wholly* worth whatever fallout this questionable decision may bring, so much so that Leander wonders why, exactly, he's waited so long to relent.

Fear, probably. But Leander knows that he *can* navigate this safely and enjoyably for the both of them, of course he can. He's an experienced Dom, practiced in restraining various people in all manner of incapacitation. How many countless scenes has he guided himself and others through safely in the past? No one has *ever* left his care with injuries Leander didn't intentionally put there. No one has ever—to his knowledge—felt unsafe *or* unsatisfied in his hands.

And it's *important* to his and Tripp's developing relationship that Leander remember that fact. That he *not* lose confidence in himself or his abilities now. Tripp's deepest needs have not changed, despite his physical condition, and Leander *can* make this work. It was easy to become lost in caring for Tripp like a *caretaker,* enough that Leander might have accidentally forgotten how vital it is that he remain Tripp's Dom, too—his partner in *all* things, not just the ones that currently have the loudest presence.

That spiraling thought sparks another, and Leander suddenly knows exactly what he's going to do. Equally important, he knows *where* he's going to do it.

The playroom bed has always been symbolic of the boundaries he and Tripp have set between them, the ones they're rightfully breaking down now, and it's time to finish that off in a meaningful way. He and Tripp have had sex in the playroom, Tripp's submitted to him there. They've slowly but surely let that dynamic creep out into the rest of the apartment and even to the world, but never into Leander's—*their*—bedroom.

In that bedroom, they've slept platonically. They've been romantic and sweet, kissing until they fell asleep and holding each other all night long. They *haven't* bridged both worlds, not yet, and Leander thinks that it's about time he brought the pieces together.

Before setting the scene, Leander retreats to the bathroom. There, he showers, shaves, and cleans himself up. There's a bottle of lube that's made itself a home next to the shampoo and body wash, untouched since Tripp's accident. Leander picks it up to consider and shrugs, figuring it wouldn't hurt to prep himself ahead of time. The bathroom fills with misty steam, fogging the mirrors and the door handles as Leander's shower drags on, but beneath the hot spray, he's oblivious.

Two fingers deep in his ass, Leander's mind drifts easily into another world. His damp forehead presses against the arm he has braced against the tile wall, and he sighs. Imagining Tripp's fingers in place of his own helps move things along more quickly, though Leander resists touching his cock, insistent as it might be between his legs. Once he's deemed himself relaxed and ready, he lets his fingers slip free, finishing his shower routine before stepping out and toweling off.

From the drawer below the sink, Leander extracts a clean plug, lubing and inserting the metal piece before stepping into a fresh pair of cotton pajama pants. No need to ruin the surprise. Or, the mystique, anyway—with Tripp's current condition, there's pretty much only one reasonable way to go about honoring his request, and Leander is positive Tripp already knows that.

He still does the work of transforming their bedroom into something reminiscent of the playroom, but softer. There is absolutely no doubt in Leander's mind that if Tripp didn't want to get laid so badly, these efforts would result in relentless teasing, and not the sexy kind. The lighting of candles (*scented—summer campfire*), the mood music, the general outing of himself as a huge sap who has never done this before—Tripp is absolutely going to be dying internally over his inability to crack jokes.

But fuck Tripp, Leander's got a stake in this, too. He's *never* done a scene with someone for whom he has feelings, *and* who openly admits to loving him back. He's been in a variety of convoluted *alternate* versions of that scenario, but not this one in particular, and it has him fighting off a certain amount of anxiety.

Should he act differently? Will he *want* to act differently, once they're physically together? Will Tripp welcome those changes in Leander's approach, or red-light them out of hand?

Only when Leander finds himself standing at the foot of his bed, staring blankly into the middle distance while clutching a handful of quilt *so* tightly his knuckles have turned white, does it occur to him that he may be overthinking things.

With a deep breath, Leander forces his brain to turn off, strolling—in what he hopes reads as a confident manner—out of the bedroom and across the apartment. As he passes behind the couch where Tripp is lying, Leander doesn't so much as glance down at the man. Nonetheless, he can feel Tripp's eyes following his movements with poorly-disguised interest.

After retrieving the item he set out to get from the foyer, Leander returns to Tripp's side and presents the small box with all of the gravity it deserves. He lifts the hinged lid so that Tripp doesn't have to struggle, and drops down to one knee. "Would you like to put this on? No pressure."

The way Tripp's face lights up, one would have thought Leander had announced he'd gained magical powers with which to heal Tripp's injuries instantly. "Yes, Sir," Tripp replies softly, reaching out to run the fingers of his good hand along the pliable green leather in an almost reverent manner. "Damn, I missed this," he remarks, almost to himself.

It's the first time in recent memory that Tripp has voluntarily dropped the sassy, bratty front he's been putting on, and Leander is relieved to see it. He's also still annoyed that Tripp has been acting like such a punk to begin with, but now is not the time. *Or is it the perfect time?*

"Would you two like a moment alone?" he asks, unable to resist.

The glare he receives in return is worth it, but Leander holds up a hand and swallows his smile, plucking the collar from its case and holding it out so that their evening doesn't careen wildly off the rails by his hand. As peaceful as the apartment's balcony is, hanging out there alone isn't on Leander's agenda for tonight.

"May I?" he asks.

"I dunno, are you gonna keep being a dick about it? *Sir?*" Tripp pouts.

"No. I want you in it as much as you want to be in it. Lean forward."

Fitting the collar around Tripp's neck feels like a nearly-religious experience, but Leander is *not* a sap, is *not* going to ruin this moment by becoming emotional and accidentally flashing back on everything they've been through and all of the times he thought they might not ever make it back here. He's *not*.

Fuck.

The fact that Tripp is sitting here in front of him, perfectly alive and mostly-well, hair all disheveled and wearing Leander's rattiest white t-shirt and a pair of loose Batman boxers—it does nothing to take away from the gravity of the moment.

Tripp looks as if he's experiencing some of the same struggles inside his own head, his eyes turning glassy and red, so Leander does the mature thing and leans in to kiss him, *hard*. The intimate contact gives them both something to pour the confusing tension and energy into like a spillway, and it helps.

With his good hand, Tripp reaches up to cup Leander's face, holding him close and kissing back with everything he's worth. Still kneeling on the floor, Leander just wiggles his way in between Tripp's legs, gathers him close and holds on, letting his mouth convey what he absolutely can't bring himself to say out loud.

When the two of them finally part, they're both short of breath, lips swollen and shiny. Seeing Tripp like that is enough to bring Leander's mind roaring swiftly back to his original plans for the evening. Tripp seems to agree, his shorts tenting and his hands starting to wander of their own accord.

Briefly, though, Leander does catch him glancing over at his wheelchair with a scowl on his face—one that suggests he'd rather take a baseball bat to the thing à la *Office Space* than ever sit in it again. And Leander can understand that. Being wheeled into the sex dungeon is nothing to be ashamed of outright, but that's not for him to decide. These are Tripp's feelings to have, and clearly, the chair feels like something negative right now. That's fair, considering that the whole scene is going to be different by nature to their usual, full of similar-types of reminders, and it's apparent Tripp finds this one particularly humiliating.

Thankfully, Leander has an alternate idea.

One thing that he's been doing consistently ever since Tripp's release from the hospital is taking advantage of his building's gym. Running, lifting, working out with various weights—all of it, and he's been doing so daily without fail. It's been a useful form of stress relief, *and* a path to keeping up his physique now that Tripp is relying on him so much, physically speaking. The results are some seriously-toned muscles Leander didn't even know he could have. He's pretty sure they're up to the task he has in mind for tonight.

"Forget the chair and lean forward," Leander demands. "Wrap your arms around my neck and hold on." However skeptical he might be, Tripp complies without question. When he's situated at the edge of the couch, Leander grabs underneath Tripp's thighs, tightens his core muscles, and stands. As Tripp yelps and clings like a spider monkey, Leander chuckles and adjusts his grip so that he's cradling his ass.

Pressed flush against his chest, Tripp's breath is hot on Leander's neck, the air moving sharp and fast over his skin. Contrary to how it might seem at first glance, Leander is fairly certain he isn't scared or upset, considering Tripp's crotch is pressed directly against his stomach.

"I do enjoy your response to being manhandled," he says quietly into Tripp's ear as they walk. "I enjoy everything about you, regardless of your limitations, whether perceived or actual."

"And I enjoy these fuckin' biceps, holy shit, Lee," Tripp exclaims. "I gotta get back to the gym, can't have you showing me up like this. Hey, would you break up with me if I worked out my right side 'til I had a Popeye arm? Could be sexy," Tripp suggests. In response, Leander dumps him unceremoniously onto the bed, perhaps a bit more roughly than he might have otherwise.

"Oh, *yes*. Hell, yes. I fuckin' missed this," Tripp declares happily, spreading his legs as much as he's able with the cast in the way, restricting his movement. "Come on, Sir, make me beg for it."

"First of all," Leander remarks, stepping closer to Tripp's side and slipping fingers underneath the band of elastic around his waist. "It seems you've forgotten *who* is in charge here, and *whose* job it is to *listen* and *obey*." With deft hands, Leander works the boxers down over Tripp's hips and cast until they're off. By the time he's done, Tripp's gotten himself stuck in his shirt, grumbling from somewhere inside it about forgetting to untie the sling. Feeling merciful, Leander pulls the tie and releases his arm before moving to help tug the offending shirt the rest of the way gone.

When Tripp's face pops free, he at least has the decency to look abashed. "I'm sorry, Sir," he says immediately. "Really. I just—*fuck*, Lee, I really need this. I need you." With a faintly shaking hand, Tripp reaches out and touches Leander's bare side, right above where his pajama pants are slung beneath his hip bones.

"I know," Leander concedes, taking Tripp's hand and kissing the back before returning it palm-down to Tripp's stomach. He turns on his heel, walking over to the bedroom door in order to close it, hoping to maintain the atmosphere he's curated in the room.

Leander's bed is huge. It's a California King, it has an extremely expensive mattress, and it's stuffed to the brim with pillows and blankets. Not solely for Tripp's comfort, but because Leander enjoys them, too. Right now, Tripp is lying somewhere close to the middle, looking ridiculous with his neon pink arm wrap and bright green leg cast, and whether it's the size of the bed or the plaster, he actually looks small. He's *right* there, though, and that's what matters, equally looking like every missing piece Leander didn't know he lacked.

Tripp. In his bed. His submissive, Tripp. His partner, Tripp. His friend, his lover.

Leander shifts his gaze down for a moment, blinking at his bare feet until his vision clears. Once it's safe to do so, he advances towards the bed, stepping out of his pants in one fluid motion before crawling up and without hesitation in-between Tripp's legs.

"There are rules for tonight," Leander says bluntly, shifting on his knees. "You get only what I see fit to give you, no arguments. If you *do* argue, I will end the scene. As always, I am your Dom. I am responsible for your safety, your well-being. I will not be reckless with either, no matter how much you try and goad me into it. I *will* punish you for trying to push me in that direction, and it will not be a punishment you enjoy. Understand?"

"Fuck, yes," Tripp replies breathily, his eyes glazed over now for all the *right* reasons, and Leander loves him. "Sir."

"Safeword?"

"Halligan, Sir."

"And are you using it?"

"No, Sir."

Leander nods. "In addition to your safeword, please use the stoplight system for any discomfort—this is not a time to push through pain. You can safely assume that if you *do* feel pain tonight, it was not intentional on my part. I want you to say 'yellow' immediately if that occurs so that we may reassess together. I trust you to be wise about your limits." Leander arches an eyebrow, and for once, Tripp nods solemnly: he understands.

Business aside, Leander begins to feel like he can relax a bit more. He cracks a smile. "Everything else, I suppose I will let you discover as we go along."

Looking surprised, Tripp glances around. "That's it? No... restraints? No hot wax? No ball gags or dildos? Damn, Sir, you go all vanilla on me while I was out of commission? Should I be worried?"

"Shut up, Tripp," Leander retorts, leaning down to kiss him. He goes out of his way to pin Tripp's right arm to the bed when he does—no use in spoiling the game just yet.

With Leander's tongue down his throat, Tripp moans. He kisses back enthusiastically, and Leander lets him. They make out for a few minutes, amping up the arousal and the crackling energy between them until Leander starts to feel hot all over.

Eventually, *predictably*, Tripp rocks his hips forward, gliding his hard cock up against Leander's, and in response, Leander immediately freezes, going unexpectedly *stock still*.

It takes Tripp a second to catch on, but once he does, he relaxes his hips down and they go back to making out. The second time Tripp rocks his pelvis up, Leander pulls away, straightening his spine and wagging a finger at him. "Uh uh," he teases, but Tripp just looks confused, so Leander dives back in. This time, he leaves Tripp's uninjured hand free to do whatever it likes, and in seconds, it's tangled in his hair.

Leander sits up.

"Oh, no," Tripp groans. "Seriously?"

"Movement restriction," Leander explains, however unnecessarily. "By your own willpower. I'm going to give you what you want, what you've been asking for, but you'll have to stay perfectly still to get it. Move your body from where I position it or touch mine and everything stops. Disobey me enough and I *will* stop completely for the night. If that happens, you'll get to watch me jerk off onto your chest and face, and you will not be allowed to come."

Leander pauses for a moment and then adds, "and I *will* take a picture of you like that to commemorate the moment. Hmm. On second thought, do what you like. This is bound to end well for me, either way it goes. How convenient."

Tripp flushes, bites his lip, drags it slowly through his teeth as he contemplates Leander's words. *Stunning.*

As Leander pushes away and slides down off of the bed, he asks, "Color?"

"Green, Sir," Tripp replies quickly, and Leander can tell by his tone that he's still very excited, not disappointed in the least. *Good.* Standing by the side of the bed, Leander arranges Tripp's body so that he's on a diagonal, head very close to the edge, but not dangling off of it. From there, he's at the perfect height to rub the head of his cock over Tripp's lips, so he does.

"Is this what you want?" Leander asks, struggling not to become distracted by the way Tripp's lips part unconsciously. "What you've been begging me for all week?"

"Yes, Sir," Tripp replies, and almost accidentally, his pink tongue darts out and flicks over Leander's slit. It feels delicious, but Leander doesn't react as such, except to pull away.

"Uh-uh," he scolds, with a shake of his head.

"'M'sorry, Sir," Tripp replies breathily, and Leander believes him—he's slipping quickly into subspace and the look in his eyes is nothing but *pure,* unadulterated *want.* There is no doubt in Leander's mind that Tripp is trying to behave.

"You just want to suck my cock so badly," Leander commiserates, tapping the head against Tripp's lips once again.

"Yes," Tripp croaks, right hand flexing on the mattress, working against all of his instincts to be good, to be still. *Poor Tripp, he's got a long way to go, here.*

"If I let you suck my cock, you'll be my good boy, won't you? You'll be still. You'll raise your hand if you're in pain and say 'yellow' when you're able?"

"I'll be good," Tripp rushes to say. "Please, Sir."

"Open," Leander commands and Tripp quickly obliges. "Tongue out." As soon as it appears, Leander slides his cock along its slick surface, holding the side of Tripp's head tenderly as he moves maybe a third of his length in and out, letting Tripp taste, letting him adjust. Tripp just moans around whatever he's given, sucks happily, and lets his jaw go slack when Leander tries to move deeper.

The wet heat of Tripp's mouth after weeks of only having his hand and his memory translates to sheer, utter bliss, and Leander nearly forgets himself several times. It would be so *painfully* easy to get lost in Tripp this way, to fuck his face roughly and with abandon, to come hard down his throat—but he resists. Of course, he resists. Safety aside, Leander has designs about how this scene is going to end for him, too.

When he eventually pulls back, Tripp's face is sloppy—saliva trailing down his cheek and the side of his chin closest to the mattress. His lips are puffy and reddened and he's wearing a completely dazed expression that makes him look positively drugged.

"Color, Tripp," Leander says, gently but firmly, and Tripp *grins.*

"Green," he replies dreamily, very much himself, and Leander is relieved.

"May I—" he starts and then stops, hesitating. "I'm going to kiss you, because I love you so much and I can feel it spilling over inside of me. It's not because we're sceneing, and I just thought—perhaps you should have the opportunity to say no."

Below him, Tripp blinks a bit of the haze from his eyes, dragging the back of his hand across his wet mouth and shaking his head a little. "Sir—Lee—are you seriously worried that I don't want to kiss you right now? Or like, are you just trying to mess with me?"

"No," Leander replies defensively, folding his arms across his chest. "Our scenes are rooted in ongoing enthusiastic consent, and I am *asking* whether you consent to changing the dynamic for one kiss to—"

"Jesus Christ," Tripp murmurs. "Green, I consent, I love you too. Now kiss me already, so we can fuck. Wait—do scene rules apply? Can I touch you?"

Leander squints and thinks about it for a moment. "The rules do not apply for this one negotiated kiss."

Tripp just stares up at him, incredulous. "You are *so* fuckin' weird. I love you." He reaches up to tug at Leander's arm until he's close enough to yank down by his head, moving to cup Leander's freshly-shaven jaw with his good hand and drawing him close. Tripp is in control, bringing their mouths together deep and soft.

The way their lips move in sync, the way Tripp is careful in teasing with his tongue—Leander doesn't mind being judged a little, because *this* is what he wanted. This kiss feels different—it feels like *love*. Perhaps he won't stop a scene to make the distinction in the future, but right now, he's not even sorry.

"Alright, back to business," Leander asserts once he pulls away, and Tripp rolls his eyes but makes a sign with his hand that either means '*proceed*' or '*fuck you*', Leander's not entirely certain. Despite that, he presses on, climbing back up onto the bed and straddling Tripp's body, reaching behind himself to remove the plug that's nestled between his cheeks.

"Remember," he says sternly. "You must remain still."

To Tripp's credit, he's perfect. From the agonizing push of Leander sliding *ridiculously* slowly onto his cock, to the teasing way he lifts back up, nearly popping all the way off before dropping down again, Tripp behaves. Spread out on the mattress, he makes these enticing little moans Leander wishes he could swallow, fluttering his eyes open and shut and working the fingers of both hands into the linens.

Even when Leander begins to really move, Tripp stays nearly motionless. They catch each other's gaze and hold it, Leander circling his hips and Tripp very obviously wishing his hands were on them, though he remains compliant.

It's intense—this thing between them. Whether it's love or lust, domination, attraction, or something completely else, Leander's never felt so drawn to another human being in his entire life. He leans forward, planting his forearms on either side of Tripp's head for leverage, and continues staring into Tripp's eyes as he rides him.

"Put your arms above your head," he instructs, and Tripp complies, Leander lacing his left hand with Tripp's right once it's there.

"Sir," Tripp whimpers.

"You can finish," Leander assures him, digging a knee into the mattress to pick up the pace while dropping his free hand to stroke his own cock. The change puts him at the perfect angle to bite at Tripp's nipple, so he does, hanging on while the jolt of sensation has Tripp's hips stuttering and his head tilting back as he comes with a loud cry.

Leander's hips work him through it, circling lazily as he sits all the way up and focuses on reaching his own finish line. Flashes of Tripp sucking him off earlier make Leander smile, make heat pool in the depths of his belly, make him come messily all over Tripp's chest, just like he promised.

Once he's caught his breath and Tripp is slipping out (the rest of Tripp already practically unconscious beneath him), Leander makes good on his other threat and snaps a picture, though it's not a punishment. They'll enjoy that together, later.

He goes about his usual routine, cleaning both himself and Tripp with a warm cloth before propping Tripp up on some pillows and ensuring that he drinks his orange juice. In line with their new normal, Leander also provides Tripp with the handful of pills he takes at night and watches as they all go down. As he turns off lights and blows out candles, Leander can't help but feel like this is all *very normal*.

He's not sure what he expected to come from having sex with a Tripp who is in love with him, but it wasn't *normal*. It wasn't *routine*. Something life changing, perhaps, something profound. And maybe that's unfair, because those things were certainly there, too—they always are between them—but no more than any other time they've had sex. Or any time they've held each other through the night, or snuggled on the couch, or fought about whether Tripp *actually* needed help getting on and off of the toilet.

Huh.

As Leander slides into their bed beside Tripp, who promptly begins stuffing pillows around him like some kind of crazed bird, Leander thinks that it's actually better this way.

Nothing has changed, and that is a good thing.

"That was great," Tripp proclaims, around a very obnoxious yawn. "You feel amazing as fuck, Lee. But listen—no switching it up when we go to the club, deal? That night, you're fucking me. You doing me in a room full of people is like, maybe the hottest fantasy I've ever had."

"Fair enough," Leander agrees with a nod. "You know that in order to go to the club, you'll have to be able to stay awake for more than five minutes post-orgasm?"

"Shuup," Tripp mumbles into Leander's skin, nearly out.

It's perfect, Leander thinks, as he looks around his darkened bedroom and really lets himself feel the weight, the *presence* of Tripp *in* it with him for the first time.

He's home.

Chapter 13

Six Months Later

Tripp is itchy. Anxious in his own skin, unsettled, probably close to jittering right off the edge of the playroom bed if Leander wasn't standing, you know, right there, looking down at him with narrowed eyes.

"We can postpone," he suggests, and Tripp shakes his head vehemently.

"No way," he replies quickly, breath coming out in a rush. "No. Worked too hard for this, waited too long. I'm not—" He grimaces, hand dropping to his left thigh, where the ghosts of nerve pain still bother him occasionally. The flash he's having right now is there and gone—if it had been a strike from Leander's hand, Tripp would have called it a tease. As it is, he's just going to call it annoying. Lee looks worried, but before he can so much as open his mouth to react, Tripp holds up his other hand, still massaging with the left.

"I'm fine, it's not really pain, Lee. Just angry nerves."

If Leander looked any more skeptical, his eyes would be closed. "Our appointment isn't static. If you're having a bad day, we shouldn't—"

"There's no *we* about this, Lee!" Tripp explodes and then immediately regrets it when the hand Leander has stretched out towards him retracts and gets cradled defensively against his boyfriend's chest. "Shit," Tripp mutters, scrubbing his palm across his face before collapsing back onto the bed, leaving his legs dangling over the side. "You know I didn't mean that. It's just, babe—all the work I've done? Tonight is a big fuckin' win for me."

From somewhere above him, Leander's voice sounds calm and unaffected. That shouldn't be a surprise, Leander's more than used to dealing with Tripp's frequent tetchiness and mood swings when it comes to his injuries and rollercoaster recovery. For whatever reason, Leander somehow manages to not ever take his bullshit personally, even when Tripp's mad enough to wish he would.

Lee is a damn saint.

He's also annoying as fuck, especially when he's seeing straight through Tripp's hedging and shitty attempts to wall himself off. Or when Tripp's covering for being stupid under the guise of being brave.

"Tripp, I know that you view this as some sort of mile marker you have to pass in order to not fail. But as I've told you before, your goals are yours to set. The mile marker can be moved."

Tripp snorts. "That's a terrible analogy, who taught you that? You can't move mile markers, Lee. If you did, then they wouldn't, you know, mark the miles." The sting of Lee's belt snapping as it makes contact with Tripp's jean-clad thigh has him yelping and jerking on the bed, but also breaking out into a huge smile. Even a month ago, Lee wouldn't have dared mess with him so casually, and *definitely* not with pain.

They've both come a long way since then. Tripp with his physical rehab, and Lee with learning to let go and to trust that Tripp knows his own limits.

Initially, Lee's reservations were understandable, even if Tripp didn't like them. Causing intentional, recreational pain while he was still taking narcotics to manage his injuries just seemed like a really terrible idea and a recipe for disaster. And Tripp could even comprehend his reluctance as a Dom beyond that—his uneasiness with any kind of hardcore scening at all. After watching him suffer for so long, Leander had difficulty accepting that *pain* was something Tripp could still enjoy, had an even worse time accepting that it was something *he* could still administer without guilt (or traumatic flashbacks of his own, probably).

In the end, Tripp had to take a pretty hands-on approach towards guiding their relationship in the playroom, at least for a while. Not that they switched, per se, but Tripp insisted on a much more active role in planning scenes and staying alert during them. It was a bit of a reversal that neither of them ever saw coming, but looking back, Tripp feels like it's been good for them.

During that time, Leander really needed the validation, and Tripp needed the power. If he hadn't taken the bull by the horns, so to speak, Tripp doubts they would have been able to get back to the place they're in today. It didn't hurt his own self-confidence or his desire to take back some of the autonomy that relying on Leander for his day to day needs had snatched away, either.

History aside, the quick flash of—*welcomed*—pain across his thighs has Tripp near-giggling, relieved that Lee isn't going to try and turn his concerns into a genuine attempt to dissuade him from going out. Support is one thing, but Tripp's not being reckless—he's *this close* to being cleared for a full return to work, and he'll be damned if he puts himself in any kind of position to mess that up. He's ready, and he wouldn't say so if that wasn't the case.

"One last thing, and I'll be quiet about it," Leander says, and Tripp raises an arm in the air, waving it around like, *proceed, your Majesty*—God knows Lee is going to, anyway. "We *could* simply visit, or mingle. Spend time in the middle room with less pressure on you to perform."

"Dude, no," Tripp snaps, slightly less heated this time as he pops back up to a sitting position and gawks at Leander in disbelief. "No. Listen, buddy, you dragged me to that brunch mixer, we did the whole meet-and-greet, took the tour, did the voyeur thing—you know *full well* how much I thought it sucked having to watch from the front row while other people got to do the fun stuff."

Several paces away, Leander's just staring back at him blankly, pulling the leather belt through his hands like he can't figure out whether to thread it through his pants or whip it at Tripp again. "I thought that you enjoyed yourself at the Munch. You certainly enjoyed the snacks, and I don't recall any complaining when I blew you in the parking lot after—"

"Dude," Tripp protests, spreading his hands. "Totally missing the point. Also, you didn't let me come."

Leander smirks. "I did. Eventually."

"Yeah, well, I want this, Lee. Come on, don't taint this for me. I can't—" Tripp blows out a sigh of frustration and messes up his hair with his fingers, dropping his head. "This is about me," he tells his knees, "and it's *for* me, but I'm not gonna do it if you're not all the way on board. Or if I have to convince you that I'm ready. We ain't goin' into it like that." Tripp chances a glance up, but his Dom hasn't moved.

Raising his eyebrows, Leander steps to Tripp's side and straddles his legs, settling in his lap. The position is slightly awkward—Lee is six feet of muscle and Tripp's ass isn't fully on the bed, but knowing Lee, that's probably the point. As such, Tripp tenses his muscles and holds on, managing to balance Lee's weight fairly easily. Just to make his own point, Tripp leans up to catch Lee's mouth, distracting him with kisses before bracing himself and flipping them both over onto the mattress.

Entirely pleased with his work, Tripp grins down at a stunned Lee and tips his chin. "Squats are doing their job," he declares, referring to the ones Lee has been making him do to build back muscle in his legs and core. Tough but effective, the exercises Lee comes up with would probably make Tripp's quiet, mousy physical therapist stroke on the spot. But even she can't argue with results like these.

Considering that Lee is a fucking sadist towards his own body when it comes to working out, it probably should have occurred to Tripp that given even half the chance, he'd be one with *Tripp's* regimen, too. He likely should have considered that a bit more before inviting Lee to help him build strength, but Tripp wasn't thinking with his upstairs brain when he imagined them training together.

The thing is, Lee went into this knowing that unlike regular people, Tripp *can't* return to work with a half-healed leg. He has to pass the physical agility and endurance testing for the City all over again. It's no secret that getting back on that level after acting the part of a couch potato for months *and* suffering muscle wasting in his left leg has been *hard*.

Lucky for Tripp, Lee has been more than willing to get creative, both with workouts and the motivation to complete them. Lee was smart—giving him *other* things to focus on while strength training, and it's because of that creativity Tripp's come as far as he has. After all, no physical therapist worth their certification was ever going to suggest augmenting squats by doing them with his ass over a dildo. *Lee*, on the other hand…

In fact, Lee built an entire attachment for the spanking bench he already owned, one that allowed a dildo of choice to be placed vertically on the adjustable kneeler, *right* where Tripp's ass should end up in a properly-done squat. Hours of fun-slash-misery ensued, but Tripp's thighs are almost as thick as Lee's these days, and he's got the endurance of an actual cowboy for riding cock, so *take that, Lee*.

…alright, so maybe Lee stood to gain a few things from all of that, too.

Regardless, there were plenty of other ingenious exercises working alongside the pegging squat, all of which helped Tripp along in his journey back to being ripped. That includes Tripp's favorite, which is Lee himself lying with his mouth open beneath Tripp's hips while he does push-ups, and *dude*—Tripp's never been more motivated to feel the burn.

In retrospect, Lee's had a *lot* to do with Tripp's current state, both mental and physical, and maybe he should be a little less hard on the guy for trying to look out for his well-being.

It's just that Tripp has *plans*, and this night is important to him for more than one reason. Tripp's *nerves* are acting up for more than one reason. Really, it's got a lot less to do with the way he's about to get publicly flogged and railed, and a lot *more* to do with what he *hopes* Lee will be wearing when he does all of that to him.

The ring sits heavy inside the little box in Tripp's pocket.

About a month ago, Tripp nervously confessed his intentions to Beau, and both he and Bri (once everyone calmed down) pretty much instantly volunteered to help Tripp shop. It was a quick trip—they were inside the mall jewelry store for all of two whole minutes before the winner was spotted. There it was, perched on a blue velvet display inside a glass case, and the three of them excitedly freaked out about how *perfect* this particular band happened to be. Ironically, Beau and Bri didn't know *why*, exactly, the ring was perfect, but even so, they *were* right.

White gold with a line of sapphire running through the middle, the stones are a blue that Tripp will forever associate with his Dom, his friend, his—*hopefully*—future husband. The ring reminds Tripp very much of his emerald collar and the way it matches his own eyes. Imagining the band on Lee's finger, he very suddenly understood what Lee's undying affection for the collar itself was based upon, way back when.

Tripp wants Lee in this ring, wants him to *never* take it off. And he's in no way promising that he won't slobber all over it like a lovestruck idiot, exactly the way he hated Lee doing to him when they first got together. In fairness, Tripp didn't *get it* then. He does now. Wearing this ring, Lee is *his*.

If all goes as planned, Lee is going to have it on his finger tonight.

Even before he swiped his credit card at the store, Tripp had been wracking his brain trying to plan the perfect proposal, but nothing seemed right. What he *really* wanted was to make up for the shitty love confession that never should have been—to give Leander all the romance and emotional crap both of them secretly enjoy (sometimes), and that Leander deserves.

But the 'right time' never seemed to present itself, and any scenario Tripp tried to concoct felt forced, felt like it wasn't *them*. In fact, as recently as a couple of days prior, Tripp had gone so far as to *almost* pull the trigger.

While Lee was at work, Tripp went shopping. When he returned home, he pushed all of the furniture in the living room up against the walls. Space cleared, he built a pillow and blanket nest around a disgustingly adorable picnic set-up on the floor. He lit candles, strung fairy lights, put champagne on ice, and cooked Lee's favorite meal: the whole enchilada (not literally, he made burgers). Tripp even busted out his old boombox to curate a mixtape for Lee—thirteen of his most treasured classic rock songs, which *everyone* knows is as romantic a gesture as they come.

When it came down to the wire, though, Tripp just couldn't spit the words out. There was nothing wrong with his setup—hell, Lee was thrilled with it. Tipsy on champagne and elated to have a hot meal in his belly after a long day on the rig with virtually zero downtime, Lee had been handsy all throughout dinner. Not *just* by feeding Tripp, which he insisted on, but in general. In fact, they've both been uncharacteristically soft and affectionate with each other, laughing and exchanging kisses, murmuring sweet, gentle words like a couple of irredeemable saps.

Absolutely *nothing* was out of place, and no scene Tripp's able to imagine or dream up could have possibly set a more perfect tone. Despite all that, the moment just didn't feel right. Not that Tripp could give voice to *why,* it just didn't.

So the ring stayed heavy in his pocket, heavier on his mind. Ever since, Tripp's slowly starting to realize that if he keeps waiting for the 'perfect moment,' he and Lee are going to die of old age before they ever make it to the altar. And he *really* wants Lee to go into the club tonight *marked.* Possessive, maybe, but Lee was right when he said that they aren't *just* Dom and sub anymore, and Tripp—Tripp wants everyone else to know that, too.

So fuck romance, that's never really been their thing, anyway. It's fucking time.

"So, I'm gonna—" Tripp cuts himself off, swallows hard, and gestures towards the doorway. The reason they're in the playroom to begin with was practical—to gather supplies for tonight and then get Tripp ready, but his collar is still in its box out in the foyer. Tripp left it there intentionally, wanted the excuse to gather himself for a minute, to come back and get down on one knee for an entirely different reason. It's cliche, it's symbolic, it feels like *them*—as much as anything is ever going to.

"Of course," Leander acknowledges, failing to notice that anything is strange with Tripp's demeanor as he slides backward off of his lap. Lee stands, stretches, and then takes himself over to the middle armoire to continue rifling through it. Tripp lets his gaze linger on the way Leander's too-small t-shirt stretches taut across his upper back for a prolonged moment, eventually heaving a deep breath and turning to walk out of the room. His nervous left hand is flexing at his side, right next to the pocket with the ring.

This is it.

Contrary to his outward calm, Tripp's mind is racing a mile a minute. All manner of thoughts are tearing through it, barely staying long enough to terrorize him before being bumped away by the next horrifying thing. From second(*third, fourth*)-guessing his instincts on whether this is *really* the right moment, to imagining all the ways a proposal could go terribly wrong for him, Tripp wishes he could press pause and have a drink. Unfortunately, the club they're going to has a strict 'no alcohol / no intoxication' rule if you're playing, and come Hell or highwater tonight, Tripp is *fucking playing.*

When he makes it to the foyer and picks up the box with his collar inside, Tripp stops to take another deep breath. He closes his eyes and forcibly clears his mind, shoving all of those intrusive thoughts *way* the fuck to the back where they won't have a shot at derailing his plans. Once he's cool and composed again, Tripp jams the collar into his free pocket and pulls the other, smaller box free.

One more deep breath, and he's ready.

With a decisive nod to no one but himself, Tripp pivots on the balls of his feet back towards the bedroom, instantly yelping and recoiling, nearly falling on his ass when he turns to find Lee standing *right* behind him.

"Jesus—*Lee,* what the fuck?" Tripp slaps a hand over his chest. "I didn't survive being trapped in a burning building and recover from *two* broken limbs just for your creepy ass to give me a heart attack in my own damn house."

Leander squints in apparent confusion, eyes darting down to Tripp's chest like he can't tell if he's definitely joking, so Tripp exhales roughly and rolls his eyes. This isn't exactly the setup he was hoping for, but—

"I need to ask you something," Leander blurts out almost anxiously, which is un-Leander-like enough to be somewhat disconcerting. "I've been thinking about it all day. I feel it's imperative that I do so before tonight, however… there just never seems to be a *good* time." As Leander reaches a hand into his pocket, Tripp suddenly catches on, but Lee has the box out and is dropping to one knee before he can stop him.

"Oh, *hell* no!" Tripp declares vehemently, and only in retrospect does he realize what that must sound like to Lee. The impact registers all over Leander's face, though, and Tripp immediately feels like an ass. The guy looks like someone killed his puppy in front of him. "No, no—shit," Tripp adds, frustrated and a bunch of other emotions he's too surprised to parse out right now. "That's not— I'm not—*Lee,* you idiot."

Unsurprisingly, Tripp's poor attempt to backtrack goes over like a lead balloon. Fumbling with his hands, Leander tries and fails to quickly stuff the box he's holding back into his pocket. Tears well up around the waterlines of his bright blue eyes in a way that has Tripp wholeheartedly believing he'll be deserving every inch of the spanking he's set to receive later.

"Lee, I'm sorry," Tripp tries, reaching out to graze Leander's bicep as he awkwardly stands back up off the ground. Tripp just wants to touch him, but—and rightly so—Lee isn't interested, shrugging Tripp's hand off and turning away.

"You don't need to explain, Tripp," is all he says.

Increasingly alarmed, Tripp figures he has about ten seconds to set this thing right before the damage verges dangerously close to unfixable. *Thank God for hardwood floors.*

His own little box clutched tight in hand, Tripp sprints a few paces and then skids to cut Leander off before he can make it across the living room, sliding down onto one knee *almost* gracefully. Before Leander can so much as blink, Tripp pops the box open and presents it earnestly upward.

"I was just pissed because you got there first," he says honestly, with a little shrug and the smile he knows Lee is a sucker for. "Still kinda am, honestly. Dude, what are the fucking odds?" Above him, Leander is visibly struggling to process, squeezing his eyes shut and shaking his head before opening them again and peering down at Tripp in disbelief.

"Okay, yeah, I deserve that," Tripp admits. "But put yourself in my shoes."

"I *am* in your shoes, right now," Leander points out, still not addressing the box or the question, and—*oh, Tripp didn't actually ask the question, did he?*

"Shit," Tripp remarks again, wincing as the pressure of the hard floor on his bad knee starts to make it throb. He's healed, sure, but dropping his entire weight onto a recently fractured bone pressed against an unforgiving surface isn't exactly advisable. *Especially* if it's just to make a point, but too late now.

"Let me—" Leander murmurs, dropping down to thread an arm underneath Tripp's shoulder and around his back to help him stand, but Tripp resists.

"No," he says, pulling away slightly, as much as he can afford to do without winding up toppling over. "No, Lee, please. I wanna do this for you. You deserve one fucking thing that isn't tainted by—by my bullshit."

Finally, Tripp seems to have said the right thing, and Leander's face softens. "Alright," he says, withdrawing his arm and sitting back on his heels.

"Really? You're just gonna sit there?" In response, Leander raises his eyebrows, folds his arms across his chest, and waits. "Fine," Tripp sighs. "Guess I deserve that, too." He winces again as his knee cracks, holding up a dismissive palm when Lee's face shifts with concern. "At least give me your hand," he says, impatiently wiggling his own until Leander obliges.

"Lee," Tripp starts, and then immediately falters. He's confident, he's ready, but in all the commotion, every single thing Tripp's prepared and had ready to say has fled from his brain. "Son of a bitch. Maybe I should have just let you go first," he mumbles, suddenly embarrassed and ducking his head.

But Leander shuffles forward, takes both of Tripp's hands and the ring box between them and dips his head low so that Tripp is forced to look him in the eye. He's still teary, but Tripp's pretty damn sure it's not because he's feeling rejected —at least, he hopes not.

"I want to hear what you have to say," Lee says gently.

Staring down at their joined hands, Tripp takes a deep breath before letting it out and speaking from the heart. "Lee, I ain't got any fancy words for you," he chokes out past the lump in his throat. "I had this whole thing, but… " He shakes his head, blinking away his own tears. "I messed this all up." Pausing, Tripp sucks in yet another lungful of air—*boy, that's becoming a theme*—and composes himself. Voice shaky, he presses on. "Sweetheart, fuck up or not, all I want is you. I hope you know that by now. Marry me. Wear my ring. I want to wear yours."

It's not like he thinks Lee is gonna say no—not now, anyway—but for whatever reason, it's still damn hard for Tripp to lift his gaze and to meet Lee's eyes, to see his response. Maybe that's because then, it'll be real. Maybe it's because deep down, Tripp *still* feels like he isn't worthy of Lee's affection, his love. Those insecurities haven't reared their ugly heads in a while, but old scars run deep. Tripp is who he is.

When Tripp *does* raise his eyes, all he finds in Lee's face looking back is unflinching love and acceptance. Suddenly, Lee's emotional response to Tripp's presumed rejection feels all the more powerful, and Tripp's melting into his arms before he can stop himself.

"Lee," Tripp whimpers, when Leander catches him, "I'm sorry I made you think —even for a *second*—"

"I didn't really," Leander admits, stroking a comforting hand down Tripp's back. "I was confused. Let's not—"

"Okay," Tripp agrees readily, nosing at the space just below Lee's ear, breathing him in, clutching at his clothing, soothing his own rough edges. "Um… so?"

Against Tripp's chest, Leander's body shakes with quiet laughter, and yet, Tripp can feel him moving to wipe the back of his hand across his face. "Yes," he rumbles, and Tripp feels a rush of relief and excitement and just—*warmth*, like nothing he's ever experienced.

Tripp sits up and Lee is *right* there, big hands reaching to cup both sides of his face as he smiles, eyes crinkling and shining. "Yes."

"Yeah?"

"Yes!"

"Me too," Tripp exclaims, and then they're kissing and Lee is pushing him down to the floor, wrapping hands around the back of his head to cushion it and licking enthusiastically into Tripp's mouth. In the chaos, the ring box goes tumbling from Tripp's hand, but Lee recovers it quickly. He pulls away and Tripp chases him, trying to make Leander bring his mouth back, but he's insistent.

"I want my ring," Leander demands, and hell, Tripp can't argue with that. Hair and clothing mussed, they untangle their limbs from each other and haul themselves back to sitting positions. Tripp's box has snapped closed at some point, so Leander opens it again as Tripp watches, peering inside before tossing his head back and laughing.

Affronted, Tripp frowns, but Leander just continues to smile. He shakes his head, and pulls his own little box from his pocket, tossing it through the air for Tripp to catch. When Tripp flips it open, he understands very quickly what was so damn funny.

"Fuckin' Beau," Tripp curses, taking in the sight of an identical band to Leander's nestled in velvet, this one with an emerald inset instead of sapphire. It *is* really nice, though. Well, of course it is—Tripp has damn good taste.

"Briana, actually," Leander corrects. "Two weeks ago, and this ring just *happened* to be available in your size to take home that day. At the time, I thought it was some sort of cosmic sign. Turns out, we are merely victims of cosmic-level meddling from our well-meaning siblings."

That, of all things, brings Tripp up short, leaving him speechless, a little breathless, and feeling weirdly emotional. Lee casually referring to Beau as his brother? Tripp didn't think this moment had any possibility of becoming sappier inside his own head, but here he is. It makes Tripp determined to make more of an effort with Lawrence—hell, to make *any* effort with the elusive *Loki*—if it'll make Lee any kind of happy. They're going to be *family,* something Tripp's always wanted and never really thought he'd have.

Oblivious, Leander's busy trying on his ring. He stretches his hand out and admires the way the metal glints in the light, the way Tripp's usually seen girls do, which is stupidly adorable. Clutching his own ring in his fist, Tripp's unable to stop staring, unable to stop *thinking* about how goddamn lucky he is.

"Would you—" he starts, and then his voice cracks and he has to do a very unmanly throat-clearing cover-up. Leander doesn't say anything about it, though, just takes Tripp's hand and unfurls his fingers, plucking the ring out of his palm and sliding it easily onto Tripp's left ring finger.

Perfect fit.

"I love you," Tripp blurts out, and Leander beams, smiling that really wide, beaming smile he saves for special occasions—for when he's either sloppy drunk or *so* unbelievably happy the joy seems to bubble out of him. He leans in and kisses Tripp softly, still smiling when they pull away.

"I told you," he says simply. "My whole life, I've never loved anything else."

***

The BDSM club downtown is ultimately one big, converted warehouse. Inside, it's split into three different rooms: one for socializing where absolutely no play is allowed, one mixed space for light play *and* snacking (mostly naked people and sex swing antics, from Tripp's observations), and a third room, which Tripp has taken to calling "the Dungeon."

It's not an inaccurate description: some of the things he's seen go down in there make his own pain kink look almost laughably amateur. Nearly anything flies in that room, and almost everything *does*. As Tripp has learned from experience, the big-ass shower with a drain in the center? Not actually for getting clean.

The conclusion? These people are on another level, one that initially, Tripp wasn't sure he was interested in living up to.

Thankfully, though, that seems to be just fine with everyone that Tripp's met and interacted with from the membership. There's very little judgement here, and the more he's socialized, the more he's found plenty of people who seem to be more like *him* than the chick he saw wrapped in barbed wire with an entire fist up her ass.

Once he got over the initial shock, Tripp *did* think it was pretty cool that all levels of kink are welcome and defended in the place, and the more comfortable he's become, the more anxious he's gotten to really join in. After all, it's only *Lee* that Tripp really needs to trust—and that is a done deal.

Still, things at the club can be… intense. Considering that anything does go—within the confines of the rules—inside the Dungeon, Tripp's learned that if he's uncomfortable, well, there's always the finger sandwiches and music one room over. It's each attendee's own responsibility to know their boundaries and limits and to remove themselves from situations they aren't enjoying.

Between the two of them, Lee is all about Tripp taking the reins and setting both of their limits for his comfort, because not much bothers Lee at all. If the BDSM community had research nerds, Lee would have joined up immediately, sitting on the sidelines in the Dungeon with glasses and a clipboard, taking clinically impartial notes. The way he watches nearly *any* scene, *any* kink playing out live with barely a twitch of a facial muscle—it's almost supernatural. It's like he's already seen the entirety of humanity blossom, grow, and die in cyclical fashion and nothing can faze him.

Tripp on the other hand—Tripp's got limits, and he knows when to see himself out.

All-inclusive kink aside, what is absolutely *not* allowed or even tolerated in *any* room of the club is non-consensual touching. Clear, verbal consent must be both asked for and received, especially between members who aren't already paired off and didn't arrive together. Thanks to that rule, Tripp is pretty okay with being paraded through the space nearly naked, feels relatively safe in allowing himself to lean into the arousal that thrums through his system over the excitement of being watched.

Not that anyone is very likely to even speak to him, anyway—not with the leash trailing from the front of his collar to Leander's hand and the sharp, threatening smile anyone who even *skirts* the question of sharing Tripp gets from him in return. No, Tripp thinks the possibility of having to address that question himself is pretty damn unlikely, but he's well-prepared with a polite "no thank you," resting on the tip of his tongue, just in case.

This evening, as they walk through the windowless front doors to the club's lobby, Tripp feels *more* than ready for whatever they might encounter, but that doesn't mean he's anxiety-free. In front of him, Leander nods greetings to the two (*giant*) bouncers as they pass, both of whom smile back amiably and don't so much as move to check their IDs. Tripp might be offended about that if he wasn't so damn nervous, but his head is busy enough at the moment that he barely notes it happening.

Leander, on the other hand, is in his element. Tripp's leash *and* hand held firmly in his own, the Dom books it over immediately to sign-in and report to one of the hosts, as the two of them have reserved space in the Dungeon tonight. A demonstration on the schedule guarantees them not only time and apparatus, but an audience, though as Leander reminded Tripp earlier, it's just a plan— there's no hard obligation to follow through.

Tripp barely listens to Lee hashing out details with the club managers, leaning into the 'quiet submissive' role so that he doesn't have to answer friendly but ridiculous questions about how he's feeling, or whatever. Being a sub is definitely convenient that way, sometimes—here, more than anywhere. No one's going to think twice about a collared Tripp standing docilely behind his Dom, looking down at his feet and using his free hand to fiddle with the buttons on Lee's trench coat, the one he's currently wrapped in.

There's another thing Tripp secretly adores but will never admit to aloud.

In fact, when Lee suggested wearing it (for ease of covering up Tripp's skimpy outfit during the brief time they'd be outside), Tripp had resisted, declaring loudly and adamantly that if *Lee* wanted to go out in public looking like a flasher, that was fine for him, but he wasn't going to be "caught dead in that beat-ass thing."

Lee, naturally, had helpfully pointed out that Tripp was literally planning to get naked and perved on in a public place, which Tripp strongly resented being used so logically against him.

Anyway, he's wearing the damn coat. Not that Lee will *ever* enjoy the satisfaction of finding out, but Tripp has absolutely accepted that having Lee's clothes and smell all around him is comforting as hell, especially when things start to go haywire in his brain.

Discreetly, he dips his nose into the collar for a quick sniff, which is of course when Leander decides to turn back around, eyes alighting immediately on Tripp and his buried nose. The knowing grin that spreads across Lee's face upon catching him in the act pisses Tripp off something fierce, but he just rolls his eyes and straightens up. Here's to hoping that the low lighting in the entryway is enough to mask any redness tipping his ears.

Clearly letting Tripp off the hook, Leander doesn't say anything, just leads him over to the lockers lining the right wall. He opens one up, tapping Tripp's ankle with the toe of his boot, a signal for him to remove his shoes. Nerves returning in full force, Tripp complies and then moves on to unbuttoning the trench as slowly as humanly possible. As in, if he went any slower, the buttons would be doing themselves back up.

After patiently waiting for longer than Tripp would have guessed, Leander steps into his space and presses their foreheads together. "This is not something you *have* to do," he reminds Tripp, for probably the twentieth time today. "This is supposed to be *fun*. Sexy. Nerves are normal. Honestly, I believe embracing the fear and anticipation only makes it more exciting. But Tripp—the only person you need to impress here is me. The only person you have to be *good* for is me."

When Lee lifts their joined hands, his left to Tripp's right, up between their chests to press a kiss to his knuckles, the metal of Leander's brand new ring flashes under the light of an overhead sconce. Tripp's ring is safely at home—he has particular feelings about his collar filling that role, especially in *this* setting— but damn, if he doesn't love seeing Lee's in its rightful place.

"Damn straight, Sir," he replies, suddenly feeling a lot more confident.

Trust Lee, he reminds himself. You're not in this alone.

And Tripp *does* trust Lee, always has, which prompts him to realize pretty abruptly that he's being—*at best*—silly and extra. He *wants* to do this.

Resolved, Tripp promptly shucks the trench coat down his arms in one smooth motion, handing it over somewhat triumphantly. If any part of him still wasn't sure, Lee's reaction to him baring it all is validation enough. Heck, he's already seen what Tripp looks like—*fuckin' dressed him like a doll, in fact*—and yet, he's *still* standing there with open *want* painted across his face, near-drooling with the way he's got his lower lip trapped between his teeth.

To be fair, Tripp *knows* he makes quite the picture right now, and he's damn proud of it. The emerald green satin panties are back, complete with their lace trim and the little bow at the front. They match Tripp's collar *and* his eyes—*take that, Heidi Klum.* Tripp can Top Model with the best of them, especially with his newly-toned muscles, courtesy of Lee and his sadistic sexercises.

On top of *that*, Lee has tied a simple harness around Tripp's chest, something comforting but practical for what they have planned. It's the soft, bamboo silk Tripp favors—also emerald, for the aesthetic. Beyond the harness, Tripp's arms are free—for now. His legs, on the other hand, are not.

Both of Tripp's thighs are wrapped in custom triple-chain cilices Lee ordered online, though only one of them has the expected spikes on the inside, facing his skin. Tripp's left thigh is still too unpredictable with nerve pain, and strange as it may sound, he gets no enjoyment out of stoking that to life—not in his day-to-day, and definitely not during a scene. That he's wearing the cilice at all on the left is simply for appearances—it's no one else's business why he and Lee do what they do, or what limits Tripp may set for himself, but it's easier to not invite questions.

All of that aside, the cilice on his right leg is something Tripp *loves* and wishes Lee would work into the rotation more often. The malleable spiked garter has three rows of interlocking, thin, metal rings, tied in the back over his quadriceps with black ribbon. Tonight, it's cinched tight enough to be uncomfortable, to irritate the skin beneath it and to bother him when he moves, but not to cut into Tripp simply from being worn. Left alone, it'll leave his thigh red, lightly excoriated, but intact, similar to the way his ass looks after a spanking.

Tripp knows full-well that Lee has no intention of leaving it alone. Just the thought and possibility makes his left bicep tingle, has him reaching up to trace fingers over the scars marking the outline of Leander's handprint, still raised and plainly visible. Tripp adores those scars (and the memories that come with them) *almost* as much as he loves Lee himself.

Speaking of—Lee is still admiring him openly, uncaring that other people are trying to get to the lockers and having to skirt around the two of them ungraciously blocking the way.

"Take a picture, it'll last longer," Tripp snarks, and then immediately shrinks when Leander's gaze rises from his body to his face, full of fire and righteous fury. The hair on Tripp's arm stands on end, and he has to suppress a shiver at the sight. "Uh, *Sir*," he course-corrects, and Leander's eyes narrow, his smile absolutely predatory.

"I have," he says simply, taking the coat and leaving Tripp to wonder when the hell *that* happened and how he failed to notice.

Without another word, Leander locks their things away and drops the key into his pocket before shouldering his bag of supplies. Once again, he picks up the end of Tripp's brand-new leash and sets off into the depths of the club. While Lee is definitely wearing a *lot* more clothing than Tripp currently is, somehow he looks *just* as sexy, maybe more. Effortlessly so, and Tripp will probably never get over how unfair that is. The fact that he gets to sleep with the guy takes the sting out a bit, but *damn*.

If this *was* Top Model, Tripp has to be real—Lee would kick his ass all the way down the runway and back without even trying.

Not only that, but Lee is dressed the part of a Dominant tonight. The club has a dress-code standard for Doms, but Lee's personal style fits into it easily. Because of that, he just ends up looking like a hotter version of himself, which Tripp also thinks is very unfair. To him, specifically, because he has to sit back and *look* for God only knows how long. *Rude*.

Trailing behind like the obedient sub he is, Tripp's eyes are drawn to Lee's ass and the way the dark, tight black jeans he's wearing sculpt it perfectly. As if those weren't bad enough, Lee is rocking that black dress shirt and black waistcoat combo he wore to Beau and Bri's bachelor / bachelorette party, complete with the red tie. His hair is artfully-mussed with the right amount of gel, and as a sundae topper, he went with the giant combat boots that he usually wears to work, the ones that Tripp has definitely not begged Lee to fuck him in (more often).

Nearly every eye turns to gawk as they pass, and Tripp can't decide whether to be proud or jealous, so he settles on both. At least he can take comfort in the fact that Lee is going to be fucking him in front of all these people very soon (*and also fucking* only *Tripp for the rest of his life—holy shit*—a thought that doesn't hurt to savor, either).

Tripp's cock stirs in his panties. He does his best to will it down, but it fills out insolently anyway, *highly* interested in the pending proceedings and the images flashing through Tripp's mind. The cock ring Lee fit snugly around the base of his dick and balls is made to keep the wearer erect, so Tripp knows that it's either self-restraint or agony—though he can't actually decide which way he wants to go with that just yet.

He *kind* of regrets not taking Lee up on the vibrating plug offer and opting for the boring silicone variety. Would've made for a nice distraction, or at least, some friggin' stimulation.

His mistake.

Lee leads him through the first room pretty quickly: it's not overly interesting. This converted section of the warehouse holds a subdued mix of plush seating around coffee tables with food and drink on spreads at the edges, plus a collection of people, many in street attire, laughing and chatting. Not that he and Lee *can't* hang out here, but generally speaking, the socializing room stays relatively kink-free.

The mixed room, which is the second space Lee walks them into, makes much more sense for pairs or groups to 'warm-up' in, so to speak. That doesn't stop Tripp from grabbing a handful of the social room's cashews, nipped from one of the aptly-placed bowls that are on a table next to the doorway as they pass through it.

The mixed space is lively tonight. There's upbeat music playing, and Tripp finds himself bopping his head to the beat. The volume isn't loud enough to drown out conversations, but it does add to the party-like atmosphere in the room. Over in the far corner, a sex swing hangs from the metal rafters, currently occupied by a female sub who looks happy as a clam to be having her ass lazily turned red by several other club members standing around her. It's not an intense scene by any means, they all just seem to be hanging out and having a good time.

On the opposite side of the room from where they entered is the door to the Dungeon, the largest and most hardcore space the club has to offer. As such, the gateway to the room is blocked by thick, heavy, black curtains that don't move unless you *move* them. Tripp knows that it's not *really* a barrier, it's just another way the club works to ensure that if you're looking, you're informed and consenting to see whatever might lie beyond.

Soon enough, *Tripp* is going to be that thing beyond the curtain, that semi-terrifying-for-new-people personification of kink that someone may or may not want to experience second-hand. Maybe everyone will be into what he and Lee do in there tonight. Maybe some won't, but that's not what fazes him. For the first time ever, *Tripp* won't be able to turn around and walk away if his nerves win out.

It's probably totally ridiculous to think that way, when *Tripp* is the one who was pushing so hard for them to come here. When his own hands and mind helped to design their scene, when literally nothing is going to be a surprise, and—*for the thousandth time, Truett*—he *trusts* Lee beyond all matter of reason.

Tripp swallows hard and allows Lee to lead them towards the corner of the room directly across from the sex swing. An unoccupied area, where a ring of cushy, armless chairs surround a small table with a variety of snacks laid out. Notably, there are pillows on the floor, too. This place knows its audience, that's for sure.

Next to the seating circle is a wide soft-drink bar, since the club is substance-free, and Lee stops to grab a soda. The bartender hands over his Coke in a tall, icy glass with only one straw, and as the condensation drips tantalizingly down the side, Tripp desperately hopes that Lee is planning to share. His mouth is like the fucking Sahara.

Wordlessly, Leander tugs Tripp's leash as he relocates to one of the soft chairs, hanging onto his drink as he motions for Tripp to kneel on the pillow by his side. As soon as they're both settled, Lee drops Tripp's leash and focuses on offering him soda via the straw, which Tripp drinks down gratefully. When he's had his fill, he sighs and lets his head drop to rest on Lee's thigh.

"Thank you, Sir," he murmurs, allowing his eyes to drift shut.

Maybe the '*knows their audience*' award goes to Lee, after all. The second Tripp's head is down, Lee's hand is in his hair—stroking, soothing, calming, until both the world and Tripp's nerves begin to disappear. At some point, someone stops by to speak to Leander. Tripp can feel their presence above him, can hear the two men exchanging friendly words, feel the rumble of Lee's laugh and the sound of the music playing layered beneath that.

Tripp's in his bubble, though, well on his way to leaving all the things he normally carries, normally *worries about* at the door. *Trust* is so much more than the word—it's this, it's handing his fears over to Leander before he even asks Tripp to do so, before they even step foot into their play space for the evening.

They stay like that, with Tripp leaning on Leander for an indeterminate period of time wherein he swims and melts, drawing from his Dom's solid strength at his side. It could be hours or only minutes, Tripp doesn't care and doesn't try to figure it out. He only knows that when Leander taps his cheek and slides a hand around his bicep to help him stand, it's time to go.

And Tripp's ready.

Being led through the heavily draped curtains doesn't feel ominous or scary, not when he's following Lee, not when *Lee* is the one holding them open, guiding Tripp into a whole new world alongside him. His eyes stay focused on Tripp— *always on Tripp*—looking right through him and seeing every inch of every single thing Tripp tries so damn hard to hide from everyone else.

Oh yeah, he's ready.

The Dungeon is softly lit, bright enough that any Doms can easily see what they're doing, but nothing harsh. The music in here is different: still quiet and left for background noise in a way that won't interfere with commands or safe-words, but it's deeper, heavier, something with bass that pulses in Tripp's chest. This is a whole different kind of party from the social hour out front or the casual-kink in the mixed space, of that, Tripp is sure.

It's crowded in here, too. More so than Tripp's seen it in the past, but that doesn't faze him, because he only has eyes for Lee. Still, it's impossible not to notice the sheer number of people. Some are playing, most watching, and nearly everyone is touching someone besides themselves, though hardly any are doing so in the same way as whoever's standing beside them. Pairs are dwarfed by larger groups that seem to naturally dissolve into two-to-foursomes, but everything feels sort of fluid.

It's an enchanting thing to be a part of, Tripp thinks, feeling awed.

As magical as it might be, the one thing that isn't lacking back here in the Dungeon is communication. The "enthusiastic and continuous consent" rule is hard and fast, and something that's clearly taken seriously. Monitors with armbands drift amongst the crowd and hang at the edges, but they're less 'bouncer' than Tripp initially expected (although, they do that too, if necessary) and more "Ask Jeeves."

In fact, the first time Tripp was here, his longest conversation *not* involving Lee was with a dude named Cal who turned out to be the lead monitor for the whole operation. He was super cool, gladly answering all of Tripp's questions and explaining that the Dungeon monitors usually function to help. They keep an eye out for potential consent or rule violations and act kind of like the gym employees who explain weight settings to newbies so they don't hurt themselves or others.

If Tripp's being honest, he'll admit that Cal's a good-looking, silver fox type, one that he wouldn't have turned down if Lee wasn't already his entire world. And Cal *did* offer, though he was amiable and unoffended when Tripp politely declined. Even now, in his semi-subspaced daze, Tripp picks Cal and his piercing light eyes out of the crowd, finding him lurking unobtrusively in a shadowed corner next to some industrial piping. Tripp tips his chin and the guy raises a hand in acknowledgment, having apparently noticed him, too.

Tripp wonders if he'll watch their scene (likely, since he's working) and what he'll think. A thrill rips through his body just imagining that—and hell, that's allowed, right? That's the entire point of this thing, isn't it? It *is,* Tripp knows that, but it's also maybe something he didn't fully understand until right that second. The concept of going through with this is one thing, the reality is quite another, but he's *way* into it.

Moving in step behind Leander, Tripp follows him compliantly towards the back of the Dungeon, over to a spanking bench that's not currently in use. It's freshly wiped down and has a recovery couch just off to the side nearby, and Tripp's practically itching to be bent over it.

A sharp tug on the leash yanks Tripp from his reverie with a start, his gaze torn away from the equipment to land on Leander, who has now turned to face him. His Dom holds up a single finger, steps to the side, and gives the spanking bench a once-over, turning some knobs and repositioning the parts to his liking.

"Color, Tripp," Leander demands when he's done, dropping his bag to the ground and advancing, reaching up to unclip the lead from the ring on Tripp's collar.

"Green, Sir," he answers confidently and Leander nods, a slight smile playing at the corner of his mouth.

"And your safeword?"

"Halligan, Sir."

"Are you using it?"

"No, Sir."

"Are you going to be good for me?"

"So good, Sir," Tripp replies quickly, earning himself the soft graze of Leander's fingertips down his forearm.

"Then kneel," Leander commands, sweeping that same hand towards the piece of equipment he's just adjusted.

This is it.

With his heart pounding in his chest, Tripp does as he's told, climbing up onto the padded kneeler before bending forward and pressing his chest to the elevated portion of the bench. With Lee's adjustments, it now tips forward so that Tripp's upper body can take some of his weight, relieving the pressure on his knees. The position leaves him head-down with his ass fully displayed and in the air, and Tripp can feel his cock growing hard just from the positioning, from the *exposure*.

People are watching this.

Tripp's arousal only grows when Leander removes his hands from where they're resting awkwardly next to his ears, folding first one arm and then the other behind his back. Lee secures them deftly above the dip in his spine using new rope tied off to Tripp's existing chest harness. It's a snug fit, Tripp's fingers nearly touching his elbows, and forearms mostly overlapping. He tries, but can't so much as wiggle a half-inch of leeway in any direction.

He loves it.

"Color," Leander checks in softly, probably noting the way Tripp's fingers are flexing and his muscles are tensing as he tests his bonds. While he awaits a reply, Lee checks them himself, ever the responsible Dom that he is.

"Green, so green," Tripp assures him, his cheek sticking to the leather slightly when he goes to lift his head.

Leander pushes it back down. "Then stay there," he demands, fingers still pressing into the back of Tripp's skull. "And be still."

It's not like he doesn't know what's coming, but somehow, that makes it even harder to keep from moving. Tripp bites his lip, works hard at controlling his instinctual impulses to twitch and pull and wiggle. Instead, he takes a deep breath and counts to five before letting it back out.

"Good boy." Leander's gravelly voice filters down to Tripp's ears from somewhere behind him, one hand resting hot on the small of Tripp's back. It's *just* above his panties, taunting him.

"We're going to warm you up now," Leander advises, finally allowing his hand to drift down and tug at the lacy trim of the lingerie. Running two fingers just beneath the seam, Leander moves the fabric and tucks it into Tripp's crack, around the edges of the plug, which he taps firmly (and unexpectedly), making Tripp jump. His ass cheeks fully exposed, Tripp can feel the breeze from the ceiling fans above, and all he can think about is how he'll likely be grateful for that in very short order.

The first strikes from Leander's hand are nearly soft and teasing, but Tripp knows him well enough to recognize that's exactly what it is. A tease, maybe even *bait*, trying to rile Tripp up. It's interesting, though—Lee always switches hands when warming Tripp's skin, utilizing his non-dominant arm so that he doesn't accidentally hit too hard, which means that he's currently using his left.

His *left*—which is sporting a brand new ring, and Tripp can *feel* it. Every fall of Leander's palm against his skin, there's an extra spark of sensation from the metal —*and it's so good.*

Cheek pressed against the bench, Tripp's mouth drops open slightly, his eyes falling shut at the emotional ecstasy that comes sweeping over him alongside that physical feeling—he could never have predicted feeling *this* strongly about that damn ring, but here he is.

It's been less than two minutes, they're barely out of the starting gate, and Tripp's already thinking about begging Leander to fuck him. It would piss Lee off something fierce, but Tripp's not entirely sure how long he's going to be able to resist.

Here he is, splayed out like some expendable toy, and Tripp's *so* stupidly happy, that happiness is somewhat overshadowing his desire to be Lee's good, obedient sub. He fucking loves Lee. He loves being engaged. *And* he *loves* being dominated by his fiancé in front of any and everyone who cares to watch. Hell, at this point, the humiliation that might come with begging could actually be hot, but Lee would probably be disappointed, and that would suck the fun out of it.

It's those last few thoughts in the train that convince Tripp to remain quiet and compliant, to follow Leander's instructions and take whatever's being dealt his way.

Besides, the good part's next, Tripp thinks.

When Leander removes his belt, he does so while standing right in front of Tripp's face. The metal jingles as he tugs the buckle open, and the expensive material rustles as Lee pulls it free. Agonizingly slow, dragging the leather pointedly through each of his pant loops until there aren't any left.

"Color, Tripp."

"Green, Sir," Tripp replies dreamily.

Leaning down to get in Tripp's ear where no one else can hear, Leander softly reminds him, "I'm already proud of you. Don't think that you have something to prove to these people. Use your safeword or the colors if you need to, that's an order."

"Yes, Sir," Tripp acknowledges as Leander squeezes his ass and stands, moving to disappear again behind him where Tripp can't see his face. The belt cracks when Leander snaps it against itself, and Tripp jumps, *just* a little. He's still floating, but the anticipation is high and his blood is running hot through his veins.

Instead of focusing on what's coming, Tripp thinks about the reasons behind why he gravitated towards these elements when he and Lee were planning this scene.

For starters, Tripp got into this power dynamic thing first and foremost to get out of his damn head. Along the way, he's found both relief and strength in learning to reframe the way he approaches coping with his own perceived failings (whether real or imagined), *managing* them instead of repressing. He's turned both pain and pleasure into weapons wielded expertly by Leander's hand. Weapons that when used properly, have the power to carve Tripp into the person he's always secretly wished that he could be.

Someone stable. Healthy. Happy.

That pressure relief valve he always thinks about? It has to be opened every so often, Tripp knows that now. *This* kind of pain? It's the kind that sets Tripp free, and Lee is gonna take him there. Tripp squeezes his eyes shut, gathering all of the negative thoughts he's accumulated over the past few months and turning them loose.

Things like: he's a failure at his job for getting trapped and injured. That he put his crew at unnecessary risk, caused copious resources to have to be wasted and redirected because *he* was irresponsible. That he's a burden to Leander, a leech, a *regret.* That he's a disappointment to Beau, for all of the usual reasons, and now so much more. That he's *weak* for not returning to work sooner, that he'll never be up to par when he does, that he'll be putting his crew and the people he serves in danger by being back on active duty.

That he's a *mistake,* a loser, unwanted and unworthy.

When Lee's belt connects with his ass, tears spring to the corners of Tripp's eyes, and it's not from pain. In fact, he barely feels the hit—but it's as good an excuse as any.

The second impact, Lee aims to lay the leather down exactly where the first stripe was made, and that one smarts, but Tripp embraces it, welcomes it. Strike after strike, on his ass and across the tender skin of his thighs, and eventually, over the cilice. The barbed wrap digs in only on the right and causes *beautiful* stinging sparks where each of the spikes touches his skin.

The tears fall, Tripp *flies,* and one by one, hit by hit, Tripp lets each of those negative thoughts *go.*

When they're all gone (*and they are all gone*), it's just him and Lee and the throbbing pain in Tripp's backside, and then he can really enjoy himself.

As the scene continues on, Tripp drifts but still notices his surroundings. It's a hell of a rush to have his ass whipped in front of all these people. Some come and go, but many stay to watch their little demonstration from beginning to end, and Tripp watches them in return. Even from his limited view, he can see a femme sub wince as Lee lands a particular strike, and despite the tears in his own eyes, Tripp grins.

He's so good, Lee will be so proud. All of these people can see how damn good he is.

Between his legs, Tripp's cock is rock hard in its ring, even though his arousal has been simmering slow and steady, an afterthought to everything else going on. He supposes that's the purpose of those things, though, isn't it? He didn't pay attention, and now his dick is almost painfully engorged.

Lee ignores it, because of course he does. He just goes on turning Tripp's ass and thighs red and raw until the surface under Tripp's face is slick with his tears and he's more numb than anything else.

Through it all, Tripp stays quiet, save for an occasional cry or moan that he just can't help, and he remains still. Occasionally, Lee will lean down, cover Tripp's body with his own, grind against his sore skin with the rough fabric of his jeans. His actions are in contrast with his words, the way his lips brush gently against the shell of Tripp's ear and his words come soft and sweet. He whispers sweet nothings, tells Tripp how proud he is, how *good* he's being, how Leander could never ask for a better sub.

When Leander finally pulls the plug from his ass, Tripp's *spinning.* The crowd has dissolved into a bit of a blur and his hips have begun to twitch against his will, seeking friction. He bites his lip, trying not to groan as Lee's slick fingers press inside, teasing, adding more wetness, taking the opportunity to press unrepentantly against Tripp's prostate, making him buck and moan.

It's only in the back of his mind that he even *hears* Leander shushing him, feels the soothing hand in the middle of his back. His ass and thighs are one fiery mess, and Tripp thinks he can feel something dripping down the back of his right thigh, towards his knee.

Lee appears briefly in his sight range, adjusting the bench so that Tripp is more level, so that his ass is more accessible. And then he's back, a hand on Tripp's left hip and his cock nudging at Tripp's slick entrance. Dazed, Tripp glances up and suddenly remembers that they're being watched, that he's about to be fairly aggressively taken in front of God knows how many people.

Fuck, that's hot, he thinks, and then Leander's pushing inside and Tripp's closing his eyes, mouth dropping open at the intrusion. Leander isn't careful, isn't slow, and there's definitely an accompanying burn because he's quite a bit bigger than the plug Tripp's been wearing.

It's *good,* though, and while all Tripp can do about it is grab at his own arms, he has to stop himself from shoving back into the sensation.

Nearly as soon as Lee's hips hit Tripp's aching ass, Leander sets an intense pace that has Tripp whimpering with every thrust and struggling not to beg out loud for more. As if Leander can read his mind, he threads a hand into Tripp's hair, yanking it back by the roots and demanding what he wants with the kind of casual, unquestioned authority he so effortlessly commands.

"Beg."

It's perfect. It's exactly what Tripp wanted him to do, what he *needs* after the things they've done so far.

"Please, Sir, oh! God, please!"

The way Lee's body reignites the pain sensations with every slap of his skin meeting Tripp's is *exquisite.* Stoking the fire each time they come together, Lee takes care to hit Tripp's prostate when he can and reaches around to stroke his cock, making sure to bring some pure pleasure into the mix, too.

Tripp relishes every second.

At some point, Lee pulls out and takes the friction away completely, which makes Tripp finally crack, unable to remain *still* with everything ravaging his system. It's not a conscious choice at this point to squirm and cry and beg, even if that's exactly what Lee commanded he do earlier.

"Please, Sir, I need—"

"Tell everyone what a slut you are for my cock," Leander instructs coolly, even as he pushes fingers inside and toys with making Tripp's eyes roll back in his head. Doing that while simultaneously demanding Tripp talk, that he *make sense—* fucking *sadistic.*

"I—"

"Say it," Leander demands, leaning down to bite at the meat of Tripp's flank, hard enough that Tripp gasps and pants a little.

"I'm y-your slut," Tripp blurts out, having absolutely no reservations about declaring it to the entire world, just incredibly aroused and fuzzy and barely holding a coherent thought in his head. "All yours, Sir! I'd—" His voice breaks as Leander's mouth skims his rim, his left hand working Tripp's cock and the fingers of his right skating mercilessly over his prostate from the inside. "Oh, *fuck, Sir! Please,* please let me come on your cock, *please.*"

"Because you need it?" Leander prods, and Tripp's breath is coming short now, his wrists burning as he pulls against his own will at the ropes.

"Need it," Tripp repeats, "need you, please, Sir," he adds, letting out a moan when Leander withdraws his fingers and swiftly replaces them with his cock once more. This time, there's no break and no mercy, but there are no demands, either. Leander grabs Tripp's hair and fucks him hard, Tripp giving over fully to the sensations swirling around him, resisting the urge to tense up and instead going totally pliant.

Lee uses him like a toy and Tripp feels *so deliciously right.* His orgasm pools in his belly and spills over the *second* Leander says, "you may come," gritted out hard and rough because he's holding back, too.

As he spills hot cum onto the floor below, Tripp goes warm and flushed from head to toe while his orgasm ravages his body, clenching his ass and dragging Leander over the edge with him.

Vaguely, Tripp's aware of some cheering and applause, of Leander talking in the background, but he pays none of it any mind, slumping down over the spanking bench in exhaustion. He thinks the noise must be a good sign, though—people seem to have enjoyed his and Lee's display, *he* must have done a good job.

Lee will be proud, Tripp thinks, pleased, allowing a smile to creep over his face even as he's falling asleep still tied up.

He's half-delirious when his bonds are removed, when the pinching around his thighs disappears and he's coaxed upright. On legs like jello, Tripp nearly collapses backward when he tries to stand, but to his surprise, there are *two* sets of strong arms waiting to catch him. When Tripp shifts in the human safety net, blinking innocently up at his rescuers, he recognizes Lee and Cal staring down at him, one with concern, and one with poorly-concealed amusement.

"'Sup?" Tripp slurs, tipping his chin and doing his best to slap on a panty-dropper smile. In reality, he suspects that he probably looks like he's having a stroke.

"Tripp," Leander says, exasperated. "We need to get you to the couch. Help us out, it's just five steps to your left."

"What's left again?" Tripp asks blearily, leaning heavily on Lee as he struggles back to his feet. Cal doesn't so much as shift even a half-step away, though he allows Leander to continue controlling the situation as much as he's able and only puts his hands on Tripp when absolutely necessary. Even in his somewhat altered state, Tripp appreciates that.

Good dude, he thinks. They should hang out sometime, play poker. *What was he doing? Oh, right.* His ass is on fucking *fire.*

Together, the three of them stumble over to the couch, and Lee kicks back immediately, positioning himself the long way against the arm and motioning for Tripp to lay across his chest. Gladly, Tripp goes, face finding its way straight into the crook of Leander's neck. While it's probably not the most ideal way to tend to injuries, Tripp digs it.

Cal is nice enough to bring Lee's bag over and to offer to wipe down the equipment, which Tripp gets the distinct feeling is a personal nicety, not something the club generally offers. 'Take care of your own fluids,' kind of seems like a given, anyway.

As Leander extends his warmest thanks, Tripp allows himself to relax in his Dom's grip. He drifts again, but in a very different way. While he does, Lee smears cream from his bag onto Tripp's burning ass and thighs before wrapping some gauze around his right leg only, securing it with tape. The cilices are already gone, and there's not much blood that Tripp can see, but there must be *some* or Leander wouldn't bother with the bandage.

Awkward as it is to work from the angle they're positioned, Lee makes it happen without asking Tripp to move or sit up. Once he's finished, though, Tripp *is* made to lift his head, take some ibuprofen, and drink his juice, Leander reminding him gently that they can't stay here all night.

The haze of subspace has begun to burn off. It happens a hell of a lot quicker out here in public than inside their own playroom, a space where all Tripp has to do is roll over and let Lee cater to his every whim. By the time his bottle of OJ is gone, he's ready to get moving, ready to be back in their private cocoon where it's just him and Lee. All of the people surrounding them are less interesting, more irritating than anything else, now that the scene has ended.

It occurs to Tripp that the way he *needs* Lee post-scene is *much* more desperate and intense than he's had cause to realize in quite some time. Being in public and unable to *have* him the way that Tripp wants—it almost brings back memories of their first week together, when Tripp was dropping and alone.

But that's not what's going on here. He's not being denied anything he needs, only delayed, and only of his own making.

Still, Tripp's thinking that if they're going to come back and play here, maybe they'll stick to lighter kink in the future. Just mess around and have some fun, rile each other up, and then head home to finish their scene the way they *really* want to do in private and in peace.

Everyone else is just… superfluous. Not that Tripp has even contemplated the idea of wanting someone besides Leander in ages, but despite that, it shocks him to find out how completely disinterested he is in *anyone* else, in any way, shape, or form. He just wants Leander.

With that thought in mind, Tripp surfaces from the crook of Leander's neck, raising his gaze to find Lee already looking his way, smiling warmly. "I'm quite ready to go home and have you all to myself," Leander remarks, which has Tripp releasing an extremely relieved breath as he smiles back.

"Help me up?" Tripp asks, wincing when he shifts and his tender skin rubs against Lee's jeans. Ever the show-off, Lee scoops his way under Tripp's armpits and around his back, hauling him unceremoniously to his feet while Tripp squeaks in protest. "I said *help*, not manhandle, Jesus."

Leander just smirks. "You enjoyed it," he says, repositioning them both so that his arm is around Tripp's waist, casually supporting him while they walk. Tripp doesn't miss the way Lee eyes his left leg with suspicion, watching carefully for a limp or any sign that Tripp's in some kind of pain he's not supposed to be having. He's *not*, for the record. His ass hurts like hell and he's going to be feeling it for days, but it's the *good* kind of hurt, the kind he's been missing.

"Thank you," he says quietly as they move from the mixed room into the socializing one and on to the lockers.

"Thank *you*," Leander replies easily, pulling the key from his pocket and opening the lock. He removes his coat and slides it over Tripp's shoulder as he speaks. "You were stunning. I couldn't take my eyes off of you. I enjoyed myself immensely, and I hope you did, too."

Tripp hesitates. "I did, but—" Leander's eyes flash. He stops whatever he's doing in the locker to put his full attention on Tripp, all up in his space with both hands threading into Tripp's own and everything. "Whoa, hey, I'm cool, sweetheart," Tripp reassures him and Leander relaxes, but only minutely. His face still looks like he wants to smite whatever might have mildly inconvenienced Tripp, just on principle.

"You can tell me if I went too far, Tripp. Or if you didn't enjoy—"

"Pump the breaks." Tripp steps in, cutting Leander off before he can go on a tear. "That's not what I said, alright? It rocked, I had an *awesome* time. Hear me? I would tell you." He's careful to maintain eye contact, to touch Leander's chin gently to convey that he's sincere, that he's being honest. "C'mon, Lee, kiss me and tell me if I'm lying."

There's a pause where Leander narrows his eyes, considering, before leaning forward to close the scant space between them. This kiss is ridiculously soft, sweet and careful but still thorough and with an edge of heat. It has Tripp following after Leander's mouth for more when he pulls away.

"Alright," Leander concedes. "I believe you."

Tripp rolls his eyes. "What I was *saying,* is that playing in public is one thing, but I'm pretty sure I'm a 'private finish' kind of guy, if you catch my drift." His fingers wander down Leander's exposed forearms, stupidly longing to be wrapped in them, which is the whole damn point. "This feels—wrong, I guess. I wanna be doing what we usually do."

"Yelling at each other about who got cracker crumbs in the sheets?"

"Yes," Tripp replies seriously, and Leander laughs as he closes up the trench coat, leaning in to kiss Tripp again when he runs out of buttons to fasten near the top.

"I agree," he says simply. "Not to mention, I need to give your injuries quite a bit more attention before we go to sleep. If you only knew the anxiety I'm feeling over allowing you to walk around like this… " Lee's eyes go a little wide, so Tripp squeezes his hand reassuringly before grabbing and stepping into his boots, declining to lace them up before starting for the door.

"I'm okay," Tripp reassures, lifting their joined hands to press lips to Lee's knuckles, inadvertently catching the edge of his new ring. "Love you," he murmurs, and for whatever reason, that makes Leander flush.

"I love you very much," he says in reply, scrubbing a hand across his pink-cheeked face. The bouncers at the front doors hold them open so that Tripp and Lee can exit, and while they murmur polite goodnights, their eyes never leave each other's.

As the doors swing closed behind them, Tripp says, "Mushy shit aside, I'm *damn* glad we brought my car. No way your piece of shit would let me lay on my stomach in the backseat. Lee, you're rich, when the hell are you gonna upgrade that rust bucket?"

Leander just swats his ass in reply.

Epilogue

One Year Later

Whoever said that long-term relationships and marriage are boring, that chemistry dies and intimacy becomes increasingly dull and distant between partners as time goes by, never met Leander and Tripp.

The rust-stained sink of the strip club bathroom groans beneath Tripp's hands as he's forced to shift his weight forward, though not as loudly as Tripp himself does. Behind him, Leander has his fiancé bent nearly in half, legs kicked wide where he stands between them. This space is as nasty as Leander remembers it being from Beau and Bri's own pre-wedding party, but that only adds to the excitement. He and Tripp have been too spoiled for too long—they *need* this.

Biting down on his bottom lip, Leander doesn't even *try* to stifle his own noises of appreciation as he watches himself slide easily in and out of Tripp's ass. The soft, round cheeks bracketing his cock are still bright pink from the spanking Leander doled out before deciding to fuck him, and just for fun, he raises his hand and brings it down hard one more time.

The slapping sound his palm makes when it connects with Tripp's skin seems to echo off of the dingy tile, and Leander's grimy mirror reflection grins to hear Tripp's responding whimper.

"How badly do you need to come?" Leander asks casually, still thrusting, and in fact—he pulls Tripp's cheeks apart wide with both hands, growling in approval at both the improved view and Tripp's quiet grunt as he fucks him deeper.

"Mmrph," Tripp replies, and *truly,* he is feeding the beast tonight.

Leander's smile widens as he releases one ass cheek so that he can reach out and jerk Tripp's head back roughly by his hair. His submissive is sweaty and pliant, but of course, yanking his head around doesn't get Leander the reply he's after, because Tripp is extremely well-gagged. With his face tipped back, it can at least be confirmed that he still has the whole of Leander's favorite blue tie stuffed inside that smart mouth. It's ruined and he'll miss it, but this sight is well worth the loss.

"Shame you can't tell me," Leander muses, pressing his hips forward to bury himself as far inside Tripp as he can possibly get. Meanwhile, he's reaching around to finger the metal cock cage that's still holding his sub hostage, eliciting *quite* the whimper when he does.

"I imagine this must be exceedingly uncomfortable for you by now. You've spent, what? Two and a half, three hours receiving lap dance after lap dance? To think of all that sweet friction you must've endured."

Leander's teasing but not exaggerating—after all, this is *their* co-bachelor party, there wasn't a chance in hell he wouldn't do the most to make it fantastically memorable. A repeat of the stunt he pulled the last time they were here seemed perfectly in order, although this time, Leander topped it off with something Tripp never saw coming: a lap dance from Leander himself.

And Tripp is easy—Leander knew that he wouldn't even have to get naked to drive him out of his mind. It was easy as paying for half an hour in the Champagne room, but without the accompanying strippers. Surprisingly, not an uncommon request, according to the club's management. Worth every penny, at any rate, just to see the look on Tripp's face when *Leander* walked in and the music turned on.

While it's true that he and Tripp have done a great number of depraved and dirty things together—most of them twice and several with an accompanying audience—for whatever reason, this was different. Leander's never witnessed Tripp *so* obviously turned on as he was in *that* moment, and to see it was surprisingly relationship-affirming.

It made Leander feel powerful, *wanted*. Not that Tripp ever makes him feel otherwise, but his reaction was simply not what Leander would have expected *his* presence to provoke. Not when Tripp was undoubtedly expecting some hot young thing with assets his fiancé just doesn't have on offer to walk through the door. It's not a leap to assume that Tripp was anticipating professional, scantily-clad women, and instead, he got the guy who borrows his toothbrush—and he was *psyched* about it.

And Leander in his t-shirt and jeans, no less.

One wouldn't think—except, perhaps he *should*. Since the day they confessed their feelings for each other, Tripp's never made any bones about the fact that he only wants Leander. Appreciative as he might be for other form and function, whether it be porn or a particularly sexy display at the club, Tripp really does go out of his way to both show *and* tell Leander that *he* is the thing that lights his fire.

Those sentimental thoughts *almost* have Leander feeling guilty for torturing Tripp so badly. For lining up every dancer in the place to grind in his lap and then rounding out the party by doing the same. It makes his dick even harder than it already is—*inside Tripp's ass*—to think about how they played inside that private room together. It was certainly the catalyst to dragging Tripp in here and ripping his pants off.

The way Tripp put his hands on Leander's body as he rocked his hips with the beat, ass rolling teasingly over Tripp's thighs. The *possessiveness* with which Tripp yanked Leander's back flush against his chest, how Tripp tucked his face over Leander's shoulder and into his neck. Most of all, the way he spread his own legs wide and invited whatever havoc he knew Leander would wreak, all the while knowing that he was wearing that unforgiving cage, and that he'd pay for it.

In the present, Leander shivers, bracing his hand on Tripp's shoulder and finding the shirt that he's wearing damp beneath his palm. He slows his thrusts, contemplating his next move. It's hardly a break for Tripp—the position they're in just causes Leander's cock to drag more slowly over his prostate, and he whines through the gag, legs shaking a little as they struggle to continue holding him up.

It's a delicious feeling, all of that power and control. It's also a gorgeous sight, and one that Leander imagines he'll think about shamelessly tomorrow, when Tripp is standing across from him at the altar, dressed like a proper gentleman in his perfectly-fitting tux.

Sliding a hand up Tripp's neck and around his throat, Leander tightens his fingers, lightly restricting Tripp's ability to breathe freely, especially through the gag. "Color," he demands, and Tripp's hand fumbles for Leander's thigh, only to tap twice: *green.*

"Three to safeword," Leander reminds him, and then wraps an arm around Tripp's belly for leverage before hoisting him up by the neck and resuming fucking him hard and fast.

With that shift in mood, Tripp stops trying to restrain himself from making any noises. His head lolls back against Leander's shoulder, the edge of the sink digging into his thighs. He moans and cries and chokes, all of his sounds vaguely muffled by the fabric in his mouth as Leander chases his own orgasm and comes with several rough slaps of their skin and a low, satisfied moan.

The tie is pulled swiftly free from Tripp's mouth nearly the second Leander is done, even before he moves to recover the plug and shove it back inside Tripp's ass. He flips Tripp around, needing to grab his bicep to steady him on his feet, dazed and messy as he is. Leander's pretty sub is plied full of alcohol and raging hormones, and by some miracle, *still* so damn perfect in his willingness to please.

How on earth did he get so lucky?

Leander can't help but wonder that as he examines Tripp's throat, checking for marks or damage. Green eyes blink down at him slowly, squeezing shut for a protracted moment before lazily cracking open again, as Tripp's pink tongue darts out to wet his lips. In front of him, Leander 'accidentally' shifts his hips forward as he stuffs himself back into his pants and does up his belt, causing his thigh to rub against Tripp's poor, caged cock. Tripp winces.

"Tripp," Leander says casually, almost distractedly, making a show of proceeding to check him over before continuing. "Would you like your wedding present, now?"

Clearly somewhat out of it, Tripp just raises his eyebrows and shrugs. Leander doesn't fail to notice the way his left hand creeps repeatedly towards his crotch, being tugged surreptitiously away at the last second when Tripp's brain catches up to his aching body's demands. He has to be in *misery*.

"Just say yes," Leander encourages gently, cupping Tripp's jaw and pressing a chaste kiss to his lips. It's softer than anything else that's passed between them this entire night.

"Yes, Sir," Tripp replies weakly, slumping back against the sink. Very clearly, he is not expecting relief.

"Very well." With a smirk, Leander reaches down to free Tripp's cock, careful to remove the cage quickly and to give Tripp a moment to recover. He doesn't disappoint—groaning gratuitously and nearly doubling over. Both hands go flying to his groin, but Leander is there to catch him, to thread an arm around his back and hold him up.

"Oh, *God*," Tripp cries, legs trembling and breath coming in near-gasps when Leander gets a hand around his thickening length and gently gives him the contact he's been so desperately craving.

"Still Lee," he says mildly, outwardly unbothered by Tripp's absolutely ruined state. "Or Sir, to you."

Tripp makes a noise that could possibly be an attempt to say, *"Sir,"* or maybe, *"fuck you,"* but they'll never know, because it's muffled terribly against Leander's throat. As both of his hands fist wildly into Leander's shirt, Tripp's mouth stays open and wet on his skin.

Leander cradles him close, can feel the way his muscles jump, unsure as to whether he wants to lean into the (over)stimulation or rip his body away. Lost to sensation, Tripp's tongue darts out near Lee's pulse point, the heat of the air from Tripp's lungs puffing hot over the saliva it leaves behind.

In his arms, Tripp *moans*, flinching but rocking his hips forward anyway when Leander gathers precum from the tip of his cock and spreads it around. He's careful, and slowly, Tripp begins to relax, but Leander's not an idiot—this is not going to last. No man could be expected to, not after all he's been through tonight.

Idly, Leander considers what to do next—he'd let Tripp penetrate him, but he's not sure the man currently possesses the strength or the stamina to stay vertical on his own right now, never mind *fuck*.

No, Leander made this bed and will therefore need to help Tripp lie in it, or whatever that analogy would be.

While Tripp whimpers and sways, Leander quickly shoves him backward and onto the counter next to the sink, doing so before he has the chance to fall over completely. With both hands wrapped around his lovely thighs, Leander heaves Tripp up and spreads his legs before ducking between them and taking nearly all of Tripp's cock deep into his throat without reservation. Tripp's scent is musky from sweating through everything Leander's subjected him to tonight, and his taste on Leander's tongue is thick with salt, backed with the bitter tang of his release.

Apparently unable to stop himself, Tripp nearly sobs when he's abruptly thrust into the wet heat of his Dom's mouth, throwing his head back and hitting the mirror with a *crack,* though it doesn't seem to faze him in the least. He tightens his thighs around Leander's head, and Leander has to fight his arms through to pin them back down, lest he be suffocated.

It would not be a terrible way to go, he thinks.

When he glances up, Tripp has an arm thrown dramatically across his face, leaving tear tracks visible at the bottom of his cheeks. His chest is heaving and his free hand is hovering *just* above Leander's head, fingers flexing and releasing while he only barely resists the urge to grab, to *take,* to press down.

Leander pops off of him with a slurping sound, dips down to mouth at his balls and lick around the base of his cock. Satisfied with the way Tripp tenses but still doesn't touch him, Leander purses his lips and takes *just* the crown in between them, sucking gently.

Above him, Tripp's mouth drops open and his head tilts further back, and Leander's never been sorrier that he doesn't have a camera handy. The line of his sub's throat, long and damp with sweat, has never looked more enticing. Tripp's entire body shakes beneath him, and Leander refocuses, reaching up to grab Tripp's hovering hand and plant it firmly in his hair, pushing down and sending himself with it.

"Oh, *fuck yes, Sir,*" Tripp yells as he's given free rein to pull Leander's hair and shove his face down into his crotch. It's a reward that Tripp deserves, and Leander does his damndest to let him use it to his heart's content. He relaxes his jaw, breathes through his nose, and allows Tripp to fuck his face enthusiastically.

This whole night has essentially been foreplay, and Tripp has been perfection, the likes of which Leander hardly believed existed in the world. Because of that, it's no surprise when it's barely two minutes of action before his hips are stuttering, his muscles are clenching, and there's hot cum spilling violently down Leander's throat.

Calmly, while Tripp hollers and cries, Leander closes his lips around the width of him, simultaneously removing Tripp's hand from his head as he swallows and works him through the tremors. Devilishly, he also makes sure to lick the last drops of spend clean from Tripp's slit when he's done, flicking his tongue an extra pass around the head in the process. It's borderline cruel, but Leander can't be expected to resist an opportunity to torture Tripp just a *little* bit more, now can he?

After that, Leander relents, though he relishes the way Tripp jerks and thrashes at the mere threat of continued overstimulation. While he straightens up, Tripp doesn't even pretend to move, just stays splayed out provocatively on the countertop, his pants dangling haphazardly from one ankle. He's a sight: his neck is bent at a strange angle so that he can lean against the mirror, his shirt is rucked to high heaven, and he's breathing like he just ran a marathon, sweat sheen covering every inch of visible skin.

Again, Leander laments his lack of foresight with the camera—even his iPhone is out at the table with Beau, since he hadn't wanted to bring it into the Champagne room. Additionally, whatever happened to Tripp's phone is anyone's guess —Leander hasn't seen it all night, and that's a damn shame right about now.

"Good gift," Tripp croaks, flashing a thumbs up that gives Leander a glimpse of the collar wrapped around his left wrist, *and* the ring on his finger. Suddenly,

Leander's feeling warm for an entirely different reason, and he responds by leaning forward to scoop a disheveled Tripp up and hug him tight.

"I'm very grateful for you," he says gruffly, pulling back to find Tripp smiling dopily, staring up at him with an eyebrow raised.

"Gettin' sappy on me, Lee?"

"No," Leander denies, crouching down to grab the waist of Tripp's jeans and pull them back over his free foot. "Come, let's get you semi-presentable—I think 'fully' may be a lost cause at this point, but needs must."

"You should talk," Tripp snorts, pointing to Leander's hair.

With a start, Leander glances up and into the mirror, which he's mostly ignored until now, and *oh*. He looks nearly as bad as if he'd been intentionally styled to appear like he stuck a fork into a light socket. Abandoning Tripp to sort out his own pants, Leander scowls and runs the water in the sink, sticking his head underneath the tap until the top of his head is properly soaked. His hair is next-level unruly, but even it can't survive a drowning.

Once he's satisfied, Leander flips his head back sharply. The movement causes water to spray everywhere, including over Tripp. He yelps, flinches, and glares, but then seems to realize that the cool liquid feels good, and promptly hops off the counter to do the same with the tap. Leander pretends that he doesn't notice the way Tripp wobbles on his feet, still unsteady. It is, after all, the night before their wedding—he can give Tripp a break, just this once.

Freshly rinsed and (sort-of) coiffed, the two of them face each other, straightening out clothing and brushing away imaginary dirt and dust until they both look as presentable as they're going to get.

"What would you like to do now?" Leander asks, figuring he'll leave it up to Tripp whether they rejoin the party or sneak off to return home and fall into bed together. To *sleep,* this time. They do need to get *some*. It's late, and perhaps Leander should be more worried about that than he is, but they only get to do this once. That, plus their ceremony is scheduled for the evening—really, they should have plenty of time to rest and recover, even if they do continue partying for a while longer.

"Oh, ho," Tripp says triumphantly, like he knows something Leander doesn't. "Suppose you forgot, too busy making my night hell to remember your promises." He grins at Leander and waits, while Leander frowns and wracks his brain for whatever he's missing.

"I—*oh,* the shots."

"Yep!" Tripp declares happily.

"I completely forgot," Leander admits honestly. When they planned this night over three months prior, Tripp insisted on betting that Leander couldn't—*wouldn't*—make it through the night without succumbing to fucking Tripp in the strip club bathroom. The prize? Body shots, which Leander would absolutely *not* give Tripp the satisfaction of doing (in public) before.

Man enough to admit when he's been bested, Leander sighs and gestures for Tripp to head back out there. A man of his word, he's already preparing to pay up by untucking his just-fixed shirt once again.

"Fuck yes," Tripp hisses, pumping his fist and near-skipping out the bathroom door. Truly, Leander does not see the appeal of forcing the person you love to lie down on top of a sticky, gross bar so one can suck liquor from their various crevices. But a bet is a bet, and just between him and the moon, Leander wouldn't have done anything differently, had he remembered. He *will* maintain that it's stupid, though—they could just as easily go home, where Tripp could lick whatever parts of Leander he wishes to his heart's content.

Loving someone apparently means sacrifice, so Leander follows his *far* too giddy fiancé across the room, climbing up onto the bar without so much as having to be told. Beau and Marley are already there, refreshing drinks for the table, and Leander doesn't miss the way Beau wrinkles his nose when he sees the state (and maybe the smell) of both of them.

"I need to be *way* drunker for this," Beau mutters, signaling the bartender for an extra shot before high-tailing it back to their table.

"You gonna judge me too?" Tripp asks Marley, shooting her an epic serving of faux-grumpy side-eye as Leander obediently lies down and rucks up his shirt.

"Hell, no!" Marley exclaims. "I'm here to aggressively cheer all public displays of 'that gay shit' on. Also, I got next with Lee! The body shots, not the—"

"You most certainly do not," Leander replies flatly, shifting uncomfortably against the bartop before hollowing out his stomach in preparation for being a living cup. *Stupid.* "My hair is adhering to this surface. If I'm bald in our wedding photos, you cannot complain."

Down near his knees, Marley laughs so hard she snorts, choking on the sip of Coke she was attempting to swallow as the bartender appears on Leander's other side. In his hand, a tequila bottle is poised for action.

"We'll just make sure they shoot you front-facing," Tripp quips amiably, shaking some salt onto the bottom of Leander's rib cage and shoving a slice of lime pulp-side out into his mouth before he can protest.

"Mmph," Leander retorts.

"Now you sound like me," Tripp says quietly, tossing Leander a wink before dipping down and licking the salt in a stripe off of his chest. He follows quickly by lowering his lips to Leander's stomach and slurping out the liquor, taking the time to swirl his tongue around in a way that Leander is *almost* able to appreciate —give him another ten minutes. He hopes Tripp will be ready to head out of here by then, anyway.

When he's finished consuming the shot, Tripp leans up and pulls the lime slice from between Leander's lips with his own mouth, sucking the juice out noisily before letting the rind drop to the floor.

Across the bar, the bartender sighs and rolls his eyes, but Leander barely notices because Tripp's slipping a hand behind his head, pulling him close and kissing him with both fire and tenderness. His mouth burns with alcohol and acid, and Leander's a sucker for the way those things taste on Tripp. Unable to stop himself, Leander exhales his own little sigh and leans into the sweet display of affection, regretful when Tripp pulls away. His expression is soft when he does, though, and Leander just smiles dumbly up at him, truly in awe.

"Damn," Marley says, followed by a whistle. "Maybe I'm only ninety-nine percent gay, not one hundred and ten like I thought. That was *dreamy.*"

"Hmm," Leander murmurs happily, still gazing dazedly up at Tripp and cupping his face.

"Get off my bar," the bartender snaps. Leander quickly hops down.

Thankfully, his previous prayers are answered and Tripp *does* want to head out after that. Their whole entourage ends up leaving with them, which means that Leander and Tripp finally get to utilize the party bus they paid for, unlike the last time. The ride to drop everyone off at their various stops is fun at first, full of music and dancing (and more drinking). Bri and Autumn are a wild mess, continually trying to make out with each other, which Beau can't seem to decide if he wants to stop or encourage.

After several failed attempts to either separate the girls or insert himself in the middle, Beau ends up washing his hands of it completely and falls into a rather serious-looking conversation with Tripp near the front of the bus.

That leaves Leander stuck sitting in the back, wedged between two people he never thought he'd successfully wrangle into the same room together, never mind onto a *party* bus leaving a strip joint.

His brothers.

As the bus jostles them lightly around, Leander feels emotionally torn between seizing the moment to talk things out, and hoping desperately that one of his and Tripp's work friends picks that very moment to start vomiting violently. As a paramedic, it would be his sworn duty to tend to them and to *not* continue forcing uncomfortable small talk.

No such luck. Theo and Mac both look like they could go ten more rounds with a bottle of Jack, and Ro—well, Ro was always going to drink them all under the table.

At least Chloe had the decency to decline the courtesy invite to the club—she's an adult, of course, but as her uncle, Leander can't help the fact that he still sees the tiny, curly-haired little girl he helped raise every time he looks her way. He's grateful she didn't make him cope with that at his own bachelor party.

Although—there *is* another possibility. Chloe pretty much lives to seize opportunities to make him uncomfortable, so in retrospect, he thinks it's likely that her absence has more to do with the person currently sitting to his left. And perhaps, even, the one to his right.

"Great party, LeeLee!" Loki declares, slapping Leander's shoulder casually with the arm he has draped around his back. "That guy really loosened you up, made you *way* more fun than I remember. Hell, I might've come back years ago if I'd known you had strip club potential. You too, Law-Man," Loki adds, leaning over Leander's lap so that he can poke Lawrence in the ribs, the lollipop stick he has hanging haphazardly from his mouth nearly taking out Leander's eye.

"Yeah, well, I'm here for Lee," Lawrence mumbles.

Despite himself, Leander eyes his twin with concern. The guy is wearing his Reverend's collar and is almost completely sober. Still, he doesn't look *entirely* miserable, which is better than anyone might have expected in these circumstances. He reaches out to squeeze his twin's hand, hoping to convey his thanks.

"It wasn't too terrible?" he asks quietly. Lawrence glances over at him and smiles.

"Nah," he replies. "Everyone was very... welcoming. Friendly. And the dancers were very respectful."

Loki snorts and leans back against the leather seat, crossing one leg over the other by manspreading and setting his right calf obnoxiously on his left knee. "I take it back. You have not changed one damn bit, brother."

"It's not like I can't say the same about you," Lawrence retorts, but there's really no heat in his words. He slouches against Leander's side, but his expression isn't as hard as it might be, so Leander retains the hope that they'll all get through this relatively unscathed. *Perhaps,* if they can collectively manage to even temporarily stow their bullshit, they'll emerge better than they were going in.

God knows, Leander and Lawrence have been holding each other at arm's length for years now, and Loki—Loki's just been *gone.* It's clear that they all want to leave their tumultuous upbringing and the uncertainty of early adulthood in their past, but they're grown now. There's no reason they can't have a future together, one where they simply accept each other for who they are and meet each other where they're at.

A happy ending, Leander thinks wistfully, as the siblings across the way catch his attention and manage to hold it. The original Truetts are sitting on the bus' long bench seat, turned and tilted towards each other as they converse, the world around them seemingly forgotten. Now *that's* an aspirational bond between brothers.

After all, Beau and Tripp had far worse experiences growing up than any of the Grigoris—and they're as close as family can be. They carry their abusive father's name, a burden Leander can only partially understand, but they're unbothered by it. Leander finds that he admires their resilience even more now, wants to study how they've managed it, to learn and steal their secrets for himself.

For now, he'll just have to be grateful for what he has, which is as new a start as his blood family is ever going to get.

"Thank you both for being here," he says softly, reaching out to put a hand on each of his brothers' laps. He's never bothered to be vulnerable with either of them before, but if he's going to be taking his cues from Tripp, this seems like a good first step. "It means… it means a lot to me to have you both here, to have your support. I—I've been guilty of focusing on the wrong things, in the past. The money, I know that's a point of—of contention—"

Leander's cut off by Loki's snorting again and squeezing his shoulder, but his voice when he speaks is uncharacteristically soft. "Not like you had any kind of role model to teach you priorities," he says. On Leander's other side, Lawrence nods in agreement, and those two being on the same page is enough to render Leander speechless.

"You've done well for yourself," Lawrence chimes in. "I think we all have. The money is… " He shakes his head. "Well, I think we all know it's there if we need it."

"I'll never touch it," Loki declares. "Screw dear old Mommy and Popsicle, and all they never did for us." He raises his glass and nudges Leander until he picks up his half-empty bottle of beer and begrudgingly does the same. To his surprise, Lawrence joins in, though his glass is definitely filled with seltzer, maybe a twist of lime if he's feeling wild.

"Screw 'em," Lawrence declares solemnly, clinking his glass to Leander's force-fully enough that it hits Loki's, too. "To us," he adds. "To Lee."

"To Lee," Loki echoes enthusiastically. "And to that smokin' hot piece of ass he's somehow managed to brainwash into marrying him." Loki wiggles his eyebrows and laughs before tipping most of his drink into his mouth. Leander shakes his head, but he can't stop smiling.

On the other side of the bus, Tripp looks up in time to catch his eye and wink, raising his hand almost shyly in a wave, which Leander returns.

"You two are disgusting," Lawrence comments. "I'm so happy for you."

"Yes," Leander replies agreeably, glancing around to take in his drunken family and friends, truly beginning to absorb how lucky he really is. Would *any* of this be possible, would *any* of it be *his* if it weren't for Tripp? Leander's not a dramatic man, but he can't imagine that would be the case.

Being Tripp's best friend was always quite wonderful—skirting the edges of be-ing included in his family was bliss.

But this? This is *real,* and not only that, it's really *his.* Not something peripherally shared with him out of pity but to which he doesn't actually belong. This is *his* husband, his siblings—Beau and Bri included—his family, both blood and cho-sen, brought together *finally* in a way that Leander badly hopes will stay.

They'll work on it, *he'll* work on it. God knows, Tripp's shown him how, shown him why it matters so much that they try.

Feeling overwhelmed with love and appreciation for Tripp, Leander touches his fingers to his lips and mimes blowing him a small kiss. In response, Tripp looks as if his smile might break his face in half.

"*Disgusting,"* Lawrence reiterates, with feeling.

Yes, Leander believes they're all going to be just fine.

***

Lawrence's church is modest, an incredibly old building with very little funding and not as much community support as it deserves, considering how accepting they are of anyone who wishes to attend. Despite that, Leander's never made himself a home here, never *quite* been able to reconcile the God Lawrence believes in with the state of the world and how badly so many "Christians" treat both others and each other.

It's not that he doesn't *want* to believe, Leander just can't help feeling that God —if there really is one—left them all behind a long time ago, and that people like Lawrence are just talking to the empty sky.

The church itself is very pretty, though, with tall, elaborate stained glass windows that spill multi-colored light onto the worn pews, even in the early evening. There's also the fact that it means something to Lawrence to be able to marry his brother here, which Leander can't argue with.

Tripp could not care less either way—his exact words were, "that means it's free, right?"

So here they are.

Ceremony-wise, this wedding is nothing like Beau and Briana's ultra-traditional affair. Technically, they both have groomsmen and bridesmaids, but none of them are walking down the aisle. They're all already seated in the first two rows of pews facing the altar, and there are plenty of other people behind them who are just as important to both Tripp and Lee. Found family, friends, even co-workers they share.

This is one *big* family, coming together officially—but a family that already exists, nonetheless. There have never been "sides," and they're certainly not going to create any now.

The two doors that swing wide to the sanctuary are currently closed, leaving Tripp and Lee alone in the little foyer, awaiting their walking music to start. Since Mickey and Reina are the closest thing to parents either groom has anymore, the engaged duo also made the decision to forgo being escorted down the aisle (and subsequently, anyone waiting at the end). While both Mickey and Reina would have been more than happy to walk with either of them—one at a time, together, or whatever other mash-up they chose—even that touch of formality felt silly and ill-fitting to the vibe they were looking for today.

This, this hand-in-hand, "tackling it together" thing? This makes sense. What *doesn't* make sense is how Leander feels, standing here, waiting.

Truthfully, had someone been willing to take the bet, Leander would have put money on Tripp being the nervous one. Whenever he pictured this moment, it was with Tripp jittering out of his skin and Leander stepping briefly into Dom-mode to calm him back down.

But that isn't the case.

Beside him, Tripp is the very picture of strength and calm. He's been wearing the same serene, *happy* smile nearly constantly since they woke up this morning, and nothing seems to faze him in the least. Dressed in his perfectly-fitting tux with his hair neatly coiffed, he stands quietly with Leander's hand clutched firmly in his own, just waiting, patient as can be.

Leander can hardly believe his own eyes. Tripp's foot doesn't tap, his fingers don't pick, his teeth don't chew at his cheek and worry his bottom lip. Even with his collar around his wrist—tucked safely beneath his dress shirt—he's entirely *un-*Tripp-like, and Leander isn't entirely certain that he shouldn't be offended.

After all, *he's* a nervous damn wreck. So much so, that it's a wonder his palm doesn't slide right out of Tripp's from all the sweat.

Very sexy, very not repulsive. Exactly what you want from your fiancé on your wedding day.

"Relax, sweetheart," Tripp murmurs.

"How can I?" Leander huffs, yanking his hand away and folding his arms across his chest. The fabric of his tux jacket doesn't stretch very well, and standing this way is disagreeable. Still, Leander persists, because not only is he irritated, but he has a *point* to make to his *irrationally calm* almost-husband. "This is only one of the biggest moments in our entire lives. You were more nervous the day we picked out pie flavors for the reception!"

"Yeah, well, pie is life, Lee."

With a snort, Leander turns away, wondering what the hell is up with the delay in their music. The sooner they can get this over with, the sooner Leander can take Tripp into a closet and ensure that he leaves uncomfortable enough to avoid sitting for the remainder of the evening. Serves him right for being so damn ca-valier.

Alright, that's probably not the attitude he should be going into this with, but— *oh.*

A sudden, incredibly distressing realization brings Leander up short, and he's glad that he's facing the wall so that Tripp can't see his face. *Fuck. Oh, fuck.* As his breath quickens and his heart speeds up in his chest, Leander is forced to deal with the increasingly unavoidable awareness that *he* is the *Tripp* in this situation, today.

He hates it.

For all the time he's spent reassuring Tripp that anxiety and vulnerability are not weaknesses, that there is *no shame* in needing external support and an outlet, Leander has always prided himself on his ability to keep his shit together. On the way his cool head effortlessly prevails in a crisis, and how he never allows his *emotions* to rule his behavior, no matter how intense they might be or how tempting it may feel to lash out.

And yet, here he is, on their wedding day, not only *doing* that very thing but failing to even recognize it.

An apology is on the tip of his tongue when Leander turns back around, but Tripp is *right* there, smiling that goofy, calm smile and stepping into Leander's space like he's entirely sure of his welcome. Despite his knee-jerk desire to grumble and pull away, to lean into the discomfort he feels, Leander *knows—rationally,* anyway—that this is fear talking, and that the only way out is through.

So when Tripp cups his face, leans in and presses soft, comforting lips to his, Leander allows himself to relax into him.

"You're being stupid," Tripp says, right against his mouth, and Leander doesn't argue.

"The question is, why are you *not* being stupid?" he retorts. "I'm appropriately anxious to the situation and you—"

"—Have wanted to marry you for way longer than I let on," Tripp admits easily, sliding an arm around Leander's waist and pulling him in close, swaying them both gently back and forth. "Sorry, Lee," he adds with a little laugh and a shrug before trailing more kisses over Leander's jaw. "I ain't scared at all about tying myself to you. You know, all of my worst nightmares, back when we were running circles around each other? Every single one of them was about losing you. About what I'd have left when you were gone, when you decided it was time to move on."

"You never told me," Leander says softly, moving his grip on Tripp from his hips to his back and holding on tight. He drops his face to Tripp's shoulder and lets himself continue to be swayed.

Tripp hums thoughtfully in his ear. "Yeah, well, telling you now." He pauses, taking a deep breath that Leander can feel against his own chest.

"I'm not scared," Tripp repeats. "Because I know that you love me. I know we're going to continue building an awesome life together. Why the hell would I be scared? And on that note, I ain't worried about your nerves, either. You do whatever you need to do, feel your wrong fucking feelings, rock out with whatever silly shit you're gonna do. Just... walk down that aisle with me anyway, okay? Fucking come home with me tonight and let me—let me keep loving you, Lee. Alright?"

Tucked up against Tripp's shoulder, Leander blinks back tears, even as a little laugh escapes his mouth. "Of course, Tripp," he says softly. "There was never any question of that."

"I know," Tripp replies, roughly pressing another kiss to the top of his head and clearing his throat. "Yeah, I know."

Just beyond their private little space, the music starts, and to Leander's surprise, he actually feels a lot better. Tripp pulls back, holding him at arm's length by both shoulders and eyeing him with concern.

"You good?" he asks, before gesturing to the closed door. "'Cause I can—"

"I'm good," Leander assures him, to Tripp's obvious relief. He offers his hand again, and Tripp takes it, his smile even wider than before.

Their ceremony feels anticlimactic, after that. Of course, they go through the motions, exchanging their engagement rings as wedding bands after Lawrence bestows the blessing. It's lovely, but as far as Leander's concerned, Tripp was right, in more ways than one. They're already as married as it gets, there's nothing to *be* nervous about here.

Additionally, the things Tripp told him before they walked down the aisle, well —those are vows if Leander's ever heard any.

Tripp, apparently, feels the same.

When it comes time to exchange their official ones, as Leander stands by, Tripp reaches into his breast pocket and extracts a folded piece of paper with lots of messy, scratched out handwriting scrawled across it. He stares down at whatever's written there for a moment, hesitates, and then crumples the paper up, tossing it carelessly over his shoulder.

Leander cocks his head to the side in question, but when Tripp meets his gaze, he smiles and holds out both hands, which Leander gladly takes. When he speaks, Leander understands immediately.

"Lee, thank you for loving me," is all Tripp says, and all he needs to say.

Leander smiles widely. "Thank you for showing me how."

When they don't say anything else, a confused Lawrence eventually pronounces them married to a chorus of slightly-delayed cheers and clapping, but Leander is too busy kissing Tripp to pay anyone else any mind.

***

At the end of the night, after cake, pie, a *lot* of dancing both slow and wild, plus the removal of a garter from Echo's leg by Chloe—who won the right fair and square by jumping off of a chair and nearly onto Mac's head to catch it—that has both Leander and Lawrence wishing for eye bleach, the reception winds to its natural end. As Leander waits for Tripp to return from tipping their vendors, he scans the room and takes stock of their remaining guests.

Interestingly enough, Loki and Autumn seem to have struck up a familiarity that suggests neither will be ending the night alone. Leander vaguely considers warning his brother, but as well as he knows Loki, he's sure that he can hold his own. Anyway, if he's secretly hoping that an entanglement with Autumn might draw his nomadic family member closer to home, Leander can hardly be blamed for that.

Happy endings all around, he thinks, and then shudders at the accidental double entendre he'd be very pleased to never contemplate again where his family is concerned. Thankfully, Tripp picks that moment to appear out of nowhere and provide much-needed distraction, relaying that they're in the clear to start heading out.

There are so many people to *hug* before either of them are allowed to leave their own wedding reception. That's something Leander didn't plan for, but he's not sorry about it, either. Every person he embraces and thanks is a reminder of how *lucky* he is, how wide his roots really spread.

From Mickey, Reina, and Ro, to Beau and Bri—and Bri's barely-showing baby bump—to Zosia and Darla, Marley and Autumn, both of his brothers and his niece, and all of his and Tripp's many co-workers, everyone is lining the way out, waiting to wish them well.

Just outside the reception hall, Theo has Engine 15 parked and blocking the road with its emergency lights flashing. The exterior of the truck is decked out with string lights and crepe paper, among other shiny bells and baubles, plus a *giant* sign strung across the back that's sporting cartoon flames and proclaims, "Just Married!"

The station is right down the street, and the truck will carry them there. Tripp's car is packed and waiting, ready to whisk them away to a cabin in the mountains for a secluded, romantic honeymoon.

The two of them exit the building to a shower of rice and drunken hollering, and Leander's never been so damn happy. With arms wrapped around each other's waists, he and Tripp make a run for it underneath the spray, laughing and ducking their heads, lest they end up with rice in their eyes. Tripp climbs onto the back of the engine first and then holds out his hand, dragging Leander up with him and wrapping an arm around his back, presumably to keep him safe when they start to move.

As the truck pulls away, their family and friends wave and cheer, and Theo blasts the siren. It's all somewhat cheesy for Leander's tastes, but the way Tripp looks with rice in his messy hair and color in his cheeks, wearing the biggest smile he has in his arsenal plastered across his face, Leander wouldn't trade this memory for anything.

They hold onto each other as the truck picks up speed and the crowd gets smaller and smaller in their wake.

"So," Tripp says, raising his voice to be heard over the noise of the engine revving. "What's next?"

Leander thinks for a moment, and then grins. "What's your safeword, Mr. Truett?"

Tripp looks surprised, but quickly recovers. "Halligan, Mr. Truett, Sir."

God, that sounds good in Tripp's mouth. "And... are you using it?"

"Hell no, Sir!"

Onward.

Timestamp

"Happiness is distraction from the human tragedy."

Leander read that quote somewhere once and has always thought that it rang almost uncomfortably true in his own life. As a paramedic, he's been offered a front-row seat to the tragedy of human existence for years—and he loves his job, takes all sorts of pleasure in doing the work. Being a medic gives him a sense of purpose and self-worth, it makes him feel fulfilled.

On a good day, that means saving lives, perhaps even changing them. It means being able to shake his patient's hand or give them a hug, having effectively reversed whatever dire situation they were experiencing. It means stabilizing a serious injury, mitigating a life-threatening illness, or even just providing a bit of coveted relief from acute pain.

Some shifts, it's as simple as that, and there's nothing strange about enjoying an abject win.

On the other hand, occasionally, Leander finds himself enjoying his job at another human being's expense. Performing difficult, rare, or highly technical interventions is a rush, but such extreme measures are only called upon when a given patient is unfortunate enough to be experiencing their Very Worst Day.

The fact is, saving lives can and often *does* exact the need for a brutal procedure (or two) in the process. Sliding a tube deftly between spasming vocal cords, power-drilling a needle into *bone* for an urgent access line. Pressing syringes—one, two, *three*—into the negative space of a person's chest, holding your own breath while waiting to see if you've relieved the mounting pressure… *yanking* the distal section of a gray and pulseless limb to urgently reduce an unstable fracture.

All brutal, innately horrifying procedures, even in their frank necessity.

It's not that Leander gets off on his patients' pain—that would be disgusting. It's that he's *good* at his job, at performing those brutal procedures. It's that having the opportunity to *execute* those skills, to prove his competence and worth as a provider—that's both satisfying and gratifying. It's a strange line to walk, and not something generally discussed outside of provider circles.

Leander is self-aware enough to realize that those interventions are simultaneously a distraction and a means of taking control for the *provider*. They're tools, wielded against a terrible situation to create an empowering one. Leander also knows from experience that having to sit and *watch* those procedures being done, to have only your thoughts about what the patient—your loved one—is going through to entertain you, well, it's *far* worse than working the problem with your own two hands.

Distraction.

Truthfully, *this* is the genesis of why it is so hard for medical professionals to keep their hands off and their mouths closed when their friends and family are the patients. It's why doctors, nurses, therapists, and paramedics all make the *worst* patients themselves. The visceral need to insert themselves into care and care planning is frequently frustrating for the treating medical team, and is often mistaken for arrogance or ego.

Of course, sometimes that *is* the case, fair.

More often, though, it's simply the manifestation of a desperate need for that usual distraction, that clinical detachment, that provider is accustomed to having. Without those things, medical professionals are stuck with reality, and a reality they know *way* too much about to ignore.

Any medical professional facing a crisis does so with the increased knowledge and awareness that comes with being an educated and informed customer. They are eternally burdened by not having the *luxury* of taking comfort in ignorant bliss. Leander knows that most providers forget to account for this when treating their peers and their peers' family members—but he's been there. He can't ever forget.

Even now, years after Tripp's accident, Leander sometimes wakes in the middle of the night sweating and terrified. Images of the love of his life, pale and motionless in an ICU bed with a machine forcing air in and out of his lungs so that he continues to breathe, perpetually haunt his dreams. There was no blissful ignorance, no care-based distraction once the hospital took over for him and Beau, in those dark days. Just Leander, the brown water spot on the ceiling, and a kind of fear he never knew existed.

An event like that, or just looking down the barrel of your *own* mortality—it's not an easy thing for any provider to face. The idea that no matter how hard we work, sacks of meat with varying expiration dates are all we amount to at the end of the day. We are fragile, and life can hit us hard, can take all of our best laid plans and wipe them clean off the board when we're least expecting it.

Point being, a lack of distraction in any of those cases? It's the opposite of fun.

Of course, escape comes in many forms, and on-the-job distraction only lasts as long as the ambulance ride to the hospital. *Procedures* are not coping mechanisms, and they won't help chase away the ghosts of those whom Leander made every effort to save and it still wasn't enough.

It is an inarguable fact that if Leander didn't have the distractions he has *outside* of his job, it would be a much greater struggle for him to find happiness, to achieve inner peace, to shake those ghosts. Not to mention, his ability to continue getting up every morning, to step back onto the truck, to throw his heart and soul into what he does—Leander needs more than the job itself to keep him sane enough to *do* it.

Thus, Leander enthusiastically applies said quote about happiness and distraction to his extracurriculars, as well. The things he does outside of work to *forget,* to make his mind relievedly blank and his energy carefree, to unburden himself from the weight of all that—as described—human tragedy.

Uncomfortably true, but true nonetheless, and there are no ifs, ands, or buts about it: Leander loves a good distraction. *Loves* his very distracting husband, and everything they do together.

Having been a Dom in the BDSM scene for a very long time, Leander's never had as fulfilling and satisfying a relationship as he does with Tripp. *Before* Tripp —and without any regular submissive to turn to—Leander was struggling endlessly to get out of his own head, to leave work at work and to not take his professional failings to heart and into his home.

Without Tripp, Leander had frequent nightmares and difficulty sleeping. He drank too much and worked out too little, he wasn't nearly as healthy or well-composed. He coped, he kept it together, but he wasn't *thriving*. And Tripp was the same, probably worse—that's how they got together, after all.

And now, just over two years into their marriage, Leander's never been more sure that taking up with Tripp was the right thing to do. Perhaps it took longer than necessary (and required a life-threatening disaster) to force the two of them to admit to their mutual romantic feelings towards each other, but they *did* get there eventually. More importantly, they've been going strong ever since.

Today, Tripp is Leander's best friend, his confidante, his lover, and his submissive. As previously mentioned, he's also a delicious distraction of epic proportions, and Leander appreciates him all the more for it. Despite their intense relationship, though, Leander remains a professional at work. He is always extremely intentional about leaving said distractions at the door when he puts on his uniform, never allowing them to compromise his attention and focus.

As a frontline medical provider, dramatic as it may sound, Leander is *literally* the thing that is standing between life and death for his patients. Well—some days, anyway. Others, he's the thing standing between bad heartburn and a lack of cab fare. Still—allowing his mind to wander even *briefly* away from whatever emergency situation is at hand can easily meet with disastrous results. For the patient, naturally, but in some situations, for the provider, too.

So Leander takes care to ensure that doesn't happen—tempting as both his daydreams and the reality of Tripp himself may be.

On the other hand, he's only human, and perhaps it was simply a matter of time until he broke.

Tonight, Leander's not feeling particularly responsible.

He'll blame a number of things for that. His entire week, for starters—it's been a perfect storm for getting sucked into distraction at an inopportune time. For seeking that brief moment of respite from "the human tragedy," so to speak.

It's nothing so serious as many of the things he and Tripp have been through in the past, just an agonizingly slow slog of difficult days. Their schedules have been opposite, Tripp on dayshift and Lee on nights. That leaves precious little time to blow off steam together. Or even *be* in each other's company at all. Between the ridiculous human need to sleep and one of them being distracted by work or eating or showering while awake, it's been tough.

In an attempt to rectify their passing like ships in the night, earlier this particular evening Tripp came by Lee's station to visit. They had every intention of at *least* sharing a meal together, perhaps playing some poker if the EMS gods were on their side. On arrival, with greasy bags of burgers in hand, Tripp was fresh off his own shift, still clad in his navy t-shirt and duty pants. He walked up smelling enticingly like sweat and oil from working under the hood of Engine Fifteen, and Leander had a terrible, terrible time keeping his hands to himself. Tripp's hair was spiky and messy but his smile was easy, eyes crinkling at the corners when he lit up at the sight of Leander.

After all this time, the fact that his simple existence still provokes that reaction in Tripp makes Leander feel disgustingly warm and tingly inside.

"Sir," Tripp murmured in his ear when they hugged, just low enough that no one else wandering around the ambulance bay—namely Marley—could hear. Despite the angry grumble in his stomach, Leander couldn't think of a time when he cared about food less. He *misses* Tripp on weeks like this, misses him terribly. The feel of his body against Tripp's, whether it's sexual or just curling around him in the dead of night—it's not easy to be without his husband for any extended period of time.

Tonight, with Tripp's pointed, *"Sir,"* all sorts of dirty ideas flashed through Leander's mind, but he somehow—*barely*—managed to behave. With his hands firmly on Tripp's hips, Leander cleared his throat and smiled like he was perfectly fine.

Lies, said his dick.

In truth, he's never had such a wild urge to slam Tripp up against the wall and ravage him publicly more so than in that very moment.

Alright, that's a lie, too—but the desire *was* real, and strong.

Of course, while Leander managed to stave off his primal urges to bend Tripp over right there next to the industrial washer and dryer, the universe decided that wasn't enough torture to go around. The two of them relocated inside, had *just* settled down in the kitchen—boots overlapping under the table and burgers barely unwrapped—when the house system went off, dispatching Leander's truck to a cardiac arrest at the nearby nursing home.

Groaning, Leander reluctantly dropped his burger without so much as a bite, taking those five seconds instead to kiss Tripp a rueful goodnight. *Any* other type of call and he might have opted to pause and wolf down at least half of his meal, but with a code, seconds matter. Ethically, Leander couldn't justify it. Those bites might translate to the difference between being able to restart someone's heart—or not.

And so he went, out the door and leaving a disappointed Tripp behind.

Sweet as he is, Tripp had promised to wrap Leander's food up and put it in the fridge for when he got back. On the way to the call (while Marley drove), Lee had spoken to him some more over text. Even after working twelve hours himself, Tripp offered to stay at the station and wait for Leander to return so that they could still eat together. Naturally, Leander told him not to be ridiculous, to go home and eat, relax and get some sleep.

It wasn't until two calls later (and no break to return to the station) that Tripp texted and admitted he had been waiting there anyway, hoping Leander would make it back. At that point, Tripp was finally ready to admit defeat and head home, having to be back at work himself by six a.m. the next morning.

For whatever reason, that news and subsequent blow felt even more disappointing to Leander than their ruined dinner, just knowing that Tripp was trying *so* hard to see him, and that Leander had let him down.

Leander thinks about that all now, as he waits outside the E.R. for Marley to emerge with their restocking supplies. He fiddles with his silent phone and tries to think of ways to make this up to Tripp, once the week from hell is over. He struggles to come up with anything particularly inventive or enticing, which is unusual, but maybe he's just tired.

Sighing, Leander cracks his neck and closes his eyes against the unusually warm night wind, trying to steal a moment of peace. His radio crackles and beeps at his side, but the dispatch that drops isn't for him, thank God. He doesn't feel like himself. It's just one of those nights, though. Apathy and exhaustion catch up with everyone—what Leander needs is a damn break, a vacation, *something.*

Perhaps that's why—after Leander *finally* returns to station and scarfs his burger stone-cold straight out of the fridge because he's *that* hungry—he does what he does. It's harmless, really (or at least, that's what Leander tells himself), initiating something he would normally put a swift stop to, had Tripp tried it on him.

Both of us are lonely and miserable, more distracted than we should be because of it, Leander rationalizes, inside his own head. *We deserve this, after the week we've had.* Tapping his phone against his palm, Leander reasons that he'll be in a much less foul mood, that he'll be able to play the part of happy and focused provider more credibly if he caves to his craving for just a *little* distraction.

I need this, he tells himself. But he has work to do as well—he'll have to multi-task.

So, barely-chewed burger sitting painfully heavy in his stomach, Leander trudges down the hallway to begin making his way through the copious call documentation he needs to do in the charting room. On the way, he texts Tripp. It's nearly midnight, so Leander knows there's a possibility Tripp won't answer. He's still disappointed when that's what happens, but Leander keeps his screen unlocked and the message thread up, just in case.

The fluorescent lights overhead in the charting room are stark and violent, assaulting Leander's tired eyes as they compete with the blue glare of the desktop screen and the backlight on his phone. Sighing, Leander closes his lids for a long moment, rubbing his pointer and middle fingers into each eyelid and wishing that he could take a nap. When he opens them again, there's a message waiting from Tripp, and Leander wonders how tired he must be that he missed the vibrating alert.

> **Tripp:** Hey, Sunshine. Missing
> my ass that much?

If Tripp were in the room, Leander would roll his eyes and glare at him sternly, but he isn't, so there's no reason not to hide his delighted grin. Via text, though, he's all business.

> **Leander:** Tripp. Do you not
> want to play?

> **Tripp:** Sorry, Sir.

> **Leander:** Good boy.

Too damn easy. Leander settles back into his rolling chair, legs stretched out and crossed at the ankles in front of him, paperwork temporarily forgotten. His EKG strip printouts, signature sheets, and the hurried notes he took on each patient lay strewn about the counter next to the computer. It's out of character for him to be so scattered, but Leander feels as if he deserves it. Hell, he's responsible *every* damn day of the year and he's been "on" with no outlet for nearly an entire week—it's not crazy to want to take ten minutes with his husband to relax a little.

> **Leander:** I sent you your
> instructions. What's taking so
> long?

Leander's nearly positive that on the other end of the phone, in their shared apartment, Tripp is stretched out in bed running through the same reservations and concerns he himself has been battling. But with Leander's unambiguous go-ahead, he's hoping—*for once*—that Tripp won't want to talk about it. That he'll choose to trust that Leander needs this, that he knows what he's doing and what he's asking for. That he has everything under control.

True to form, Tripp doesn't disappoint. He never does.

> **Tripp:** Just tryna find my good side, Sir ;)

> **Leander:** There isn't an inch of you that doesn't qualify. You are beautiful, stunning perfection. Every feature carved by God himself to be my perfect ideal, both inside and out. Nothing you could do, no picture you could take, could ever be anything less than that. My sweet, sweet boy.

With a line like that, Leander knows he's really tempting fate for his unrepentantly bratty husband to send him an unflattering photo, something like—Tripp with a triple chin squashed down into his neck, eyes crossed and making a ridiculous face. After all, that is Tripp to his core, the sarcastic bastard. Not that Leander can punish him for an impulse, but the fact that Tripp is likely fighting it off is amusing enough.

Regardless, if Leander knows the man the way he thinks he does, Tripp will take the silly picture but resist sending it right away. Likely, Leander will wake up one morning in the coming week with it set as his lock screen. Tonight, though, he's fairly certain Tripp wants to play as much as he does. If that's actually the case, then he'll be good.

He's correct—Tripp makes no acknowledgement of Leander's cheesy sweet nothings, but less than two minutes later, a picture message appears in their texting thread. It's a good thing Leander is sitting, because even though he's expecting the provocative shot, the sight makes him fumble, dropping his phone into his lap.

He doesn't pick it up right away—instead, he closes his eyes and lets out a low groan at the wave of disappointment that he isn't there to enjoy Tripp's current state in person. *Oh, the possibilities.* Leander savors the mental image of everything he *could* be doing to Tripp for a long moment before sitting up and returning his eyes to the phone's screen.

The picture displayed shows Tripp (of course), dressed in nothing but Leander's favorite pair of emerald green, lace panties. They're not the originals (if memory serves, this is pair five—somehow, they keep getting ruined), but they look as mouth-watering as they did the very first time Leander saw Tripp wearing them.

The angled image Tripp sent is cropped from mid-torso to mid-thigh—such a tease, his sub. Leander finds himself biting his lip and zooming in—hey, he's allowed.

Oh, this will be fun, Leander thinks, entirely pleased. If there's one thing he and Tripp are good at, it's making the best of tough situations, and tonight will be no exception. Leander has a vague plan—something along the lines of instructing Tripp to tease himself mercilessly, dildo up his ass while he jerks himself off. Edging without relief will be involved, no doubt, made worse by the fact that Tripp will have to go to work and endure working his entire shift tomorrow before he can come home and get off.

Since they *are* both free tomorrow night and the two days following—the pain will be worth the delayed pleasure.

> **Tripp:** See something you
> like, Sir?

Leander sees something he *knows* he'll enjoy taking apart from afar, that's for sure. However, safety comes first.

While it's not necessarily sexy, Tripp is aware that if he winds up *too* worked over and distracted, Leander wants him to safeword out and get himself off. Tripp's well-being at work is paramount, period. *No* game, no distraction or escape from reality (entertaining as it may be) is worth putting that at risk. To ensure that they're definitely on the same page, Leander reiterates all of that over text and refuses to answer Tripp's teasing messages until he gets an acknowledgment of the same.

> **Tripp:** this part of your
> torture plan, sweetheart?

> **Leander:** Tripp.

Tripp: Oh, yeah, talk safety to me baby

Leander: Keep it up and you won't be coming tomorrow night, either

Tripp: 😳

Tripp: I understand the rules, Sir.

Leander: Very good. Then get on the bed. Bring the items I told you to collect. Arrange yourself as I described, and then send me a photo.

Leander: By the way, I love you and miss you and am terribly jealous of that vibrator, the sheets on our bed, and those panties.

Smiling as he presses *send,* Leander decides that it's well worth his time to get comfortable. He slides the chair back before kicking his feet up onto the counter where the computers are lined up. His boots thud heavily against the cheap laminate. It shakes, but Leander barely notices, eyes glued to his phone while he waits in high anticipation for Tripp to reply.

Unfortunately for Leander, just as his phone dings again, his pager opens with static and the house system flares to life. "*City Medic Two, assist the police in the area of Penn Street and South Fifth Street with a possible ALS Medical.*"

"Fuck," Leander swears, tipping his head back and closing his eyes. His luck just won't quit this week, apparently. With a sigh, Leander drops his feet and moves to pocket his phone, thinking better of it at the last minute. Knowing it's a mistake, he swipes the screen open and peeks at the photo that's waiting in the thread.

Naturally, the sight elicits another groan, and Leander bites down on his bottom lip until it hurts. Splayed out on their bed, Tripp is on his back with the panties pulled to one side, the camera likely somewhere down around his knees. His upper body and face are far enough away to be completely out of focus, but his ass cheeks are spread and the dildo is already pushed inside. Leander's guessing this still originated from a video, judging by the impossible angle.

As he reluctantly shoves his way out of his seat and heads for the ambulance bay where Marley has the truck up and running, Leander texts furiously. He gives Tripp both a litany of praise and a list of instructions, knowing that he'll be at least forty-five minutes until there's *any* possibility of replying again.

Leander: Love you and miss
you, my wonderfully good
boy.

Wearily, he tucks the phone away and hops into the truck.

"I put us responding," Marley tells him, her words barely discernible wrapped around a giant yawn as they are. Just seeing it makes Leander respond in kind, and he glares at her, annoyed.

"Thanks for reminding me of how tired I am," he says flatly, as Marley pulls the truck forward and out of the garage.

"Better wake up," she says, flipping on the lights via the switch in the center console and closing the bay doors behind them. "Dispatch says this guy is wild, giving police a really hard time. He's got a medical bracelet on but they can't get close enough to see what it says and he isn't keen on sharing, apparently."

Leander raises an eyebrow. "Interesting," he remarks, glancing out the window to watch their red lights bouncing off of the darkened buildings as they pass. Any other night, he *would* find this interesting, possibly even intimidating. Psych patients, intoxicated people, altered mental status of any kind (whether self-induced or medical, like with hypoglycemia) are often unpredictable and frequently difficult to manage. Leander supposes he should be glad the police called them for help and didn't just throw this poor sap headfirst into a cell to ride it out.

It's just that tonight, his interest lies elsewhere. His body and mind are exhausted and craving relief. Leander's almost itchy, the way he's so needy for Tripp and some quality, uninterrupted time together. He *never* lets himself get like this at work, but it is what it is. Leander is only human, and he's failing at working above that pay grade tonight. Superhero status: offline. The reality is, the best anyone is getting from him over the next five hours or so is second-string energy.

"Dispatch, Medic Two is on location with PD," Marley says into the mic as she smoothly guides the truck to a stop next to the curb. There are two city police cruisers and a supervisor's SUV parked ahead of them on the street, the SUV half-up on the sidewalk. All three vehicles have their emergency lights on, and between the reds and blues and the street lamps, at least the dead of night isn't hindering Leander's ability to see clearly what's going on.

They're somewhere in the middle of what amounts to the main drag of the city, darkened shops lining both sides of the street. Less than a block away, there's a bar with a lit neon sign and a small crowd gathered outside, the patrons' laughter and jeers drifting through the air as Leander cautiously exits the ambulance.

Between those onlookers and his truck, five police officers have a pretty built-looking white male effectively cornered up against a glass storefront. They're essentially holding a perimeter, surrounding him in a semi-circle but not attempting to move any closer. The guy *looks* like a caged animal, eyes wild and posture defensive, ready to strike at anyone at any time. No question, this situation is a ticking time-bomb.

"This isn't good," Leander mutters to Marley, unhooking his keys from his belt loop and handing them over to her. "Pull out the narc box, would you?"

"What, you don't think naked boy is going to come easy?"

"No," Leander deadpans, ignoring Marley's obvious sarcasm while he sizes up the scene in front of him. "I do not."

To be fair, *Naked Boy* is not an inaccurate descriptor—every inch of skin on all six-plus feet of their potential patient is on display, save for—thankfully—the parts hidden by a grime-streaked pair of boxers and the silver bracelet wrapped around his left wrist. He's shoeless, dirty, scraped all to hell, and his eyes remain wide and fearful. On his head, he's sporting a blond, messy mop that sticks up in all directions, reminiscent to Leander of the way Tripp laughs at the hair on his own head, and the way it behaves most mornings.

It's a good thing that the weather is unseasonably warm, oddly temperate for the dead of night in late fall. It could just as easily have been snowing, and then this would have been a whole different call. Hypothermia in agitated patients is never a fun time.

As Leander looks on thoughtfully, mentally formulating a plan, an officer appears at his side.

"Heya, friend," Darla Haanscomb greets him brightly, a wide smile on her face as a comforting hand squeezes Leander's shoulder. "Long time, no see. Sorry to be dragging you out like this, but I figured it was for the best..." She trails off and gestures vaguely in the direction of the cornered man, whose eyes have locked onto Leander in an entirely unnerving way. Naked boy's unblinking ice-blue stare is enough to send shivers down Leander's spine, and he's a six-foot, well-muscled man himself, so it's not as if he's easily shaken.

"Without being privy to further details, my educated guess is that you did the right thing," Leander offers, barely glancing at Darla. "What happened?"

As Leander listens (and continues to observe his patient), Darla recounts matching 911 calls from the bar and several patrons outside that described an unclothed man running around screaming in the streets. Thus far, by all reports and since police arrival, he hasn't actually been violent. Hasn't attacked any bystanders or officers, even when they attempted to isolate him.

Darla and the other officers *did* witness him yelling and rolling around on the ground in the roadway, pulling at his own hair and mumbling incoherently, but his agitation hasn't been directed at anyone besides himself. The man hasn't been able to answer questions or provide any useful information about who he is, which isn't a surprise, and no one at the bar recognizes him.

It isn't very much to go on. Leander wishes he could at least get a look at that bracelet, but his wish just may not be in the cards tonight.

Ultimately, because he doesn't know the man's medical history or have any idea about what might be going on, Leander decides to attempt a deescalation before resorting to chemical or physical restraints. Although, he does enact a Plan B. It's simple enough to draw up some Ativan and stick it in his pocket with a nasal atomizer screwed onto the tip. A quick squirt into the patient's nostril should lay him out pretty quickly if necessary, though Leander hopes it won't come to that.

At Leander's request, the police dissolve their line and step back, giving him a wide berth and space to speak to the patient alone. Thanks to Darla, the flashing emergency lights on all of the vehicles get turned off, too. In Leander's experience, they're a constant visual reinforcement to an agitated person that *something is wrong*. Rarely helpful.

In fact, without approaching, Leander studies the man's face as the lights go out and the cops visibly stand down. The change is subtle, but the man relaxes, if only minutely. The set of his jaw and the lines of his face lose just a *tiny* bit of their tension, and that's enough—Leander takes the opening.

"Hello," Leander says cautiously, and the man's eyes snap to him, still wild, but clear and somehow focused. It's a start. "My name is Lee, and I am not with the police. I'm a paramedic. I'm here to help you, to get you out of here safely. Would you like that? To leave?"

Still guarded, the man studies Leander for several long seconds. Arms tightly crossing his chest, blanched fingernails dig into flexed biceps, and the ball of one foot presses grinding into the cement, like he's stubbing out a cigarette. He swallows, and Leander watches the Adam's Apple in his throat bob. He's sweaty, much more so than the weather—or even his running-around antics—should have caused.

Over the next fifteen minutes, Leander doesn't move. He doesn't try to step forward or get into the man's space, doesn't touch him, or attempt physical contact of any kind. He just talks—and listens, when the man has something to say, which is infrequent, and laconic—and offers suggestions. Explains what will happen if the man chooses to come into the ambulance of his own free will.

Eventually, the man gives up his name. It's Bart, or at least, that's what he's calling himself. It's very obvious to Leander that Bart took something, something psychoactive that is having a fairly extreme negative impact on him. It's probable that Bart is nothing like this when he's sober, and Leander doesn't fail to remember that.

Which is why, when the police officers start grumbling and complaining about how long he's taking, Leander pays them no mind. What's best for Bart and what's comfortable for all of them aren't necessarily the same thing. It's his job to carry out the former, not cater to the latter.

Unfortunately, Bart can't or won't admit to what he took, or even the way he ingested it. He won't let Leander see his bracelet, or relay what's on it. Leander doesn't care about the morals and ethics of drug use, except that certain drugs interact with other drugs, and he'd like to know what his Ativan might do to Bart if administered.

Some days, he just doesn't get those answers, and this is looking like one of those times.

Regardless, after some careful coaxing, Leander manages to talk Bart into the truck. He doesn't touch the man as they walk over, and Bart keeps a careful distance. He continues to cling to himself, too, eyeing Leander with suspicion-laced-fear, but he goes. His bare feet leave dirt on the steel steps leading into the box, and Leander notes the way Bart doesn't flinch at all when his skin meets the sharp treads meant to stave off falls.

Whatever he's on, it's impairing every single one of his senses.

For that reason, Leander hesitates when Darla sticks her head into the back and asks if Leander wants an officer to ride with them. Despite his agitation, Bart has only been cooperative so far, if hesitant. But being scared is not a crime, and he seems to have formed a tentative trust with Leander. Right now, Bart is sitting quietly on the stretcher, finally dropping his hands from his biceps to worry the edge of the hospital sheet draped gently over his lap instead. His eyes dart around, but that's been consistent since EMS showed up, so Leander doesn't worry too much about it.

If Bart had showed *any* signs of aggression, Leander wouldn't hesitate to bring an officer into the back for his own safety. But he *hasn't,* and he's clearly distrustful of the blue uniforms. Hence, Leander's pause. It's a dilemma, for sure, one that has Leander glancing between his patient and Darla's face in the doorway with a lack of surety.

"It's Auriel, if that makes a difference," Darla offers.

"Maybe have him ride in the front? Just in case," Leander replies, trying to find a happy medium. If he weren't nearly as tall as Bart and as buff as he is, perhaps he'd be more inclined to risk his patient's current settled state, but as it is, keeping the peace seems more important. The risk is likely low—once again, Bart *hasn't* shown any interest in hurting him—and even if he tries something, Leander can undoubtedly handle himself until Auriel can climb into the back.

"Yes," he reiterates more firmly, in response to Darla's questioning eyebrow. "Let's do that."

The ride is uneventful, for the most part. They go quietly, lights and sirens off, easy listening music playing over the speakers, and Bart keeps to himself. He even lets Leander take a set of vital signs, which is more than Leander expected, honestly.

When they're about three minutes away from the hospital, Leander moves from his seat next to Bart so that he can grab the radio and have dispatch connect him with the ER. He gives his report standing just behind the stretcher, like he usually does. As he's talking, he inadvertently catches Bart's gaze in the reflection of the windows in the back doors, and that's when it happens.

It's all so fast, so unexpected, Leander can barely get his hands up to defend himself before Bart is on top of him.

It's strange, the things that pass through one's mind in such circumstances. In Leander's case, it's watching Bart grab the oxygen tank kept stored beneath the adjustable head of the stretcher that sets him off.

Why didn't I move that? He chastises himself internally, watching everything go to shit in what feels like slow-motion.

Out of *everything* Leander could have forgotten, every precaution he thought was taken, *why* didn't he think of the oxygen? Everything else—he was so careful, so sensitive, so thoughtful. He made all the right moves, all the right choices, did *all* the right things for Bart. Even the choice to only buckle him in at the waist—everything Leander did was carefully designed to keep his patient calm, to help him feel in control, safe, and to ferry them both to the hospital without incident.

Leander doesn't take the assault lying down, of course. He fights back, grapples for the oxygen tank, wrestling with it while hollering for Marley to pull over. Auriel moves quickly—he's a rock star. He's climbing in through the side door and coming to Leander's rescue seemingly before the truck has even fully stopped moving.

By then, though, his and Bart's squabble has Leander nearly pinned at the other end of the box. They're well-matched, in both body size and muscle, but Bart has something on his side Leander doesn't, and that's drugs fueling his system. It's what gives him the final burst of energy to yank the tank from Leander's hands for good, to haul it back, and slam it into the side of Leander's head—hard enough to make him see actual cartoon birds and stars.

Dizzily, as he slumps to the floor and weakly lifts his hand for protection against the onslaught, Leander thinks Tripp would find the cartoon birds funny, circumstances aside. He blinks, blood trickling down into his eye, and can only watch helplessly as Bart brings the tank up over his head again.

The last thing Leander sees before everything goes dark is Auriel pulling out his taser and firing, but he's not quick enough. The oxygen tank finds its target, and Leander's vision goes fuzzy, and then black.

***

Tripp

The soles of Tripp's shoes slap hard against the sleek, tiled floor as he races down the inner corridor leading from the parking garage to the emergency department's waiting room. The sound echoes off of the stark white walls with their generic art prints, mocking him. Tripp had thought briefly about pulling into one of the ambulance-only spots and walking into the ER directly, but in his haste to leave the apartment, he left his ID badge in the catch-all bowl on the sideboard.

Said bowl still sits next to the box meant for his collar, though it's been ages since Tripp's even bothered to return it there. Whether it's around his neck or circling his wrist, Tripp doesn't particularly enjoy being without the thin strip of emerald-dyed leather, doesn't see a reason that he should have to be.

With his heart thudding in his chest, his breath sharp like knives in his throat as he hurries, Tripp's right hand is drawn to the collar now. He takes comfort in tracing its edges, breathing into the way the collar curves and presses against the skin just above his left hand. In a way, the collar *is* Lee—surrounding him, keeping him steady. A constant reminder that he's *there,* that he loves and cares for Tripp, that he's always holding him tight.

The lump that rises in Tripp's throat is hard to push past, but he reminds himself again that he doesn't have any details, that maybe the situation is not as bad as he's imagining. It's a hard pill to swallow, though, thinking back on the panicked call he'd received on *Lee's* cell from *Darla,* of all people. Thinks about the audible chaos in the background, about Darla's rushed insistence that Tripp *get to the hospital immediately,* and the fact that she wouldn't put Lee on the line.

Tripp's not a total idiot. Nothing about this is looking good.

He bursts through the doors at the end of the hallway, rocketing out into the busy waiting room and turning nearly every head his way in the process. To Tripp's surprise, Beau is standing by the triage counter, clad in his disposable blue trauma gown and hat, mask off of his face but still tied and hanging around his neck. He looks exhausted and worried, biting distractedly at his fingernails while scrolling his phone, and Tripp's heart drops down somewhere near his balls.

Beau always has his shit together. *Always.*

The younger Truett glances up at Tripp's dramatic entrance, catching his brother's eye on sight. The expression on Beau's face wavers between relieved and pitying, settling on something carefully blank. *God,* Tripp doesn't like the way *any* of this is looking. Not at all.

"C'mon," Beau calls out, waving an anxious arm to encourage Tripp to pick up the pace, as if he ever stopped running. Without a word, Beau grabs Tripp by the bicep as soon as he's close enough to do so, slaps his ID badge against the wall sensor, and yanks Tripp sideways through the automatic double doors before they've even fully opened.

"He's already on standby in pre-op," Beau says as they hustle forward. "It's emergent, Tripp. I couldn't hold him in the trauma bay, Neuro's gotta get in his head like, ten minutes ago." They reach the end of the hall in the blink of an eye, dead-ending at an elevator bank that leads to the main hospital. Beau slams the "up" arrow angrily with this knuckles before rubbing the back of his wrist across his forehead.

"There are consents you need to sign, and if you want my opinion, I don't think you should see him right now—"

"What? Fuck that," Tripp interjects angrily, right as the doors slide open and Beau shoves him inside. In their haste, they nearly bowl over a tiny nurse who squeaks and turns sideways as she exits past them.

Beau holds up a hand to him—*wait*—then smashes "4" with even more emphasis than he did the call button. "Dude, relax. I never thought you'd listen to me. Just—ugh." Beau sighs, pauses, looks at Tripp pleadingly where he slumps tiredly against the wall. "You need to be prepared for what you're going to see, alright? I can't guarantee he'll be awake, he's been in and out. If he is, he might not be able to talk to you, might not know who you are. That's worst case," Beau quickly amends, seeing Tripp's stricken face.

"Okay but—Beau, what the *hell* happened?"

That brings Beau up short, has him blinking stupidly into the soft elevator lighting as Tripp waits impatiently for an explanation.

"Oh," is all Beau replies.

The elevator dings their arrival on the surgical floor. When they shuffle off, Beau finally slows down, looking completely lost in thought as he guides Tripp off to the side of the hallway. They move towards a window bank that looks out over the roof of the emergency department and the parking lot beyond. "I thought —"

"Darla didn't tell me shit," Tripp supplies and Beau exhales forcefully.

"We don't really have time," he says, all puppy-dog eyes and pleading tone. Tripp nods (*the fuck else can he do?*), gestures for him to get on with it. "Short version: agitated psych patient. Drugs on board, got hold of the oxygen tank and clocked Lee over the head with it. Twice." Beau breaks off for a second, allowing Tripp to digest the information.

Meanwhile, Tripp feels as if the floor has opened up below him and he's free-falling to his death. Stomach firmly lodged in his throat, he waits for the splat of his body hitting the pavement, but of course, it never comes.

"…Depressed skull fracture," Beau is saying, when Tripp tunes back in. "Epidural hematoma, smaller subdural, obviously a ton of contusion—we really won't know until he's out of surgery and recovering. Right now, he's looking pretty rough, and his prognosis—it's… it's—well, we just won't know until after the surgery."

"Won't know?" Tripp echoes faintly, reaching a hand out and leaning on the cool glass of the wide window pane for support. There's lube drying on the inside of his thighs. It's tacky and disgusting, and Tripp hasn't decided yet whether he regrets not taking an extra thirty seconds to clean himself up.

What a weird fuckin' thing to dwell on right now, but here he is. Tripp hates himself a little, is starting to hate Beau even more for keeping him from Lee.

Oblivious, Beau steps closer to squeeze Tripp's shoulder, his thin and no-longer-sterile gown fluttering around his baggy scrubs. "He has the best team," Beau emphasizes. "Dr. Nami is Chief of Neurosurgery, she's board-certified, she's basically magic with fixing and rewiring brains. We just need to move, okay? The most important factor here is time. If you insist on seeing Lee before you sign the consents, I'll bring you to him, and I'll bring the papers to you. Or I can take you to the waiting room, we'll do the consents there. But we have to go now, so decide. And Tripp, I know that you're stubborn. Most stubborn guy I know. But for your sake, think about whether you want to risk *this* being the last image of Lee you'll have."

That snaps Tripp out of his semi-dissociated reverie like a bucket of ice water to the head. "You can't be fuckin' serious," he retorts. He knows his eyes are wide with disbelief, and he's not sure whether he should be angry, or disgusted, or maybe begging. "Beau—it's *Lee*."

To Tripp's relief (because he doesn't have any of that in him at the moment), Beau doesn't put up a fight. With a tight nod of his head, Beau sighs in what feels like expected resignation. "Yeah. Yeah, I know. I know, Tripp. Alright, let's go."

Tripp can't help it, he slips back into that partially-dissociated state as Beau leads him through several double doors and over red-tape lines painted onto the floor. An "OR STAFF ONLY BEYOND THIS POINT" sign screams at Tripp to turn back more than once, but Beau's insistent grip on his arm buoys them onward.

It's surreal, walking through spaces he's clearly not meant to be in. That, and knowing *Lee* is somewhere back here, barely clinging to life. Tripp just wants to be with him.

As a firefighter, Tripp's assisted with the transport of a critical patient from the parking lot to the burn unit, or even the OR doors more than once. He's been on this floor, but he's always handed over care before this point. Never really been in charge of care to begin with, always there squeezing a ventilation bag, or holding pressure on something that spurts. Basically, a grunt. Doing something mindless, brainless, and to top it all off, Tripp's never been emotionally invested in the person on the stretcher.

Well, except for once, and let's just say—it's a *hell* of a lot easier to be the patient, of that Tripp is now certain. Sure, it's nerve-wracking thinking you might die or whatever, and having a tube jammed down your throat to help you breathe is no damn picnic. But on the other hand, you get to pass out a lot. The nurses give you good drugs that make reality feel distant, keep you from having to deal with any of it. That's not so bad.

Family, on the other hand—they get no drugs, no enhanced sleeps that help with coping and take them out of their own heads for a while. They just have to sit. And wait. And pray, or whatever. Count the seconds on the clock. Look at your busted, broken body doing whatever it's (not) doing, all still and unnaturally quiet in a hospital bed.

Yeah, no question, this is way fucking worse.

The room Lee is being kept in is more of a bay, really. Several "stations," for lack of a better word, identical areas curtained off from each other that resemble the trauma bays downstairs. Each has a monitor mounted to the wall, oxygen access, wire buckets of supplies mounted above where the head of a stretcher would go. There's only one bed in the room, though, only one station that's occupied. It's not a real hospital bed, either—it's a trauma stretcher, fitted with a haphazard flat sheet and not a soft, fitted one. In all likelihood, that sheet came directly off of the ambulance's litter.

It has blood all over it.

Why Tripp even notices the stupid details of the bed, he couldn't say. It probably has something to do with the way Lee is lying semi-lifeless on top, IVs running into both arms, wires and tubes everywhere. The nurses bustle around him like bees fighting over a pollen-heavy flower and just as busy. Except, that's adorable, a scene Lee would *love*, and that Tripp would love to watch Lee delight in seeing. It's something straight out of a daydream.

This, the true reality of it? This is a nightmare, and maybe Tripp isn't ready to look directly at it.

But Beau's words echo in his head, the bits about *time* and not having much of it. They carry him forward on numb feet, have him sinking into the chair that a kind nurse in a "Washington State Cougars" print surgical cap pulls up for him.

The nurse's bright blue eyes steal Tripp's attention, make him think about *Lee*, who he hasn't forced himself to focus on, not yet.

Not yet, because then it will be real, and there will be no going back.

God, when Lee is better, Tripp has *got* to tell him that he fuckin' gets it now. How goddamn *hard* this is. That he doesn't have any idea how Lee did it with him, how he functioned at all, never mind helped Beau to save his life.

Lee.

His smile flits across Tripp's mind, his laugh echoes in his ears.

Jennifer, the nurse's plastic ID tag says, and her expression in the picture seems friendly, compassionate. When Tripp raises his eyes to meet hers, she just looks concerned. Her lips are moving, and it takes Tripp an extended moment to realize that she's speaking to him.

"Make it quick," she's saying, tipping her head towards Lee, and Tripp finally understands that she's echoing Beau's earlier warning. She's firm, but her tone isn't unkind, just honest, no-nonsense. Tripp appreciates it, almost as much as the grounding squeeze he gets to his shoulder as she hurries away.

Slightly delayed and too late for her to see, Tripp nods, his eyes flicking reflexively in the direction she indicated and *finally* landing on Lee.

He's not prepared.

"Oh, sweetheart," he blurts out, unable to swallow the devastation. Even to Tripp's own ears, his voice sounds distressed, but it *feels* disconnected from him. Tripp reaches for Lee's hand where it's laying limply next to him on the bed, and scoops it up. Lee doesn't squeeze back, doesn't offer any sign that he knows Tripp is there, but his hand is big and warm and it fits perfectly inside Tripp's, just like it always has.

Lee's hand is perfect, undamaged, save for a few scrapes around the knuckles. His sapphire-inlaid wedding ring sits innocuously where Tripp slid it on, way back when, and Tripp's fingers go to it immediately. He swallows hard before forcing himself to focus on Lee's face.

It's hard to look at him. The Lee in Tripp's mind barely resembles the bruised and battered mess laid out on this bed. The entire right side of his husband's face is bruised and swollen, Lee's right eye sealed completely shut by the trauma. There's a ton of bloody gauze piled and taped atop his head, and there's a wire, or a drain, or *something* coming out from underneath the stack—who knows, Tripp isn't able to even *consider* checking that out too closely.

"Lee," he croaks, using his free hand to shake Lee's shoulder gently. Above them, the monitor beeps in a chastising way, and Tripp frowns. "Lee, please, man," he pleads, eyes filling up against his will, wasting no time in spilling over. He hardly cares, let people see. "Come on, baby, just—" He tightens his grip on Leander's hand. "*Lee.*"

Tripp brings Lee's hand to press against his tear-streaked cheek, holds it there for a prolonged moment while he chokes back a sob. "You gotta come back to me, sunshine. Alright? You gotta—"

It's nonsense talk, Tripp knows it, feels it in his bones. Lee hasn't moved a muscle since he walked in, never mind shown any remote signs of waking. Because of that, Tripp is definitely not expecting the grunt that follows his demand. He blinks the water from his eyes, straightens up a little and lowers Lee's hand in time to see Lee's left eye crack open, just slightly. The glimpse of dark blue beneath nearly has Tripp bursting into tears all over again, but he manages to control himself.

"Lee! Lee, I'm here. Stay with me, okay? Can you talk, or—" The corner of Lee's mouth twitches and he blinks his good eye twice. His mouth opens and closes shortly after, but no sound comes out, not even another grunt.

"Okay," Tripp tells him, carefully cradling the uninjured side of his husband's face. "It's okay, Lee, don't—don't stress about it, no worries. Beau's got a real good doctor ready to fix you all up, okay? And then I'll be there when you wake up. I'll be there and we'll go home, and everything is gonna be okay. You got that?"

Lee's mouth twitches again, and Tripp *swears* it ticks up into the ghost of a really shitty smile. He looks pained, but he closes his eye and opens it again, pointedly this time. "Was that... once for yes?" Tripp asks, and then waits, and Lee does the motion again. Slow, deliberate. The non-verbal exchange fills Tripp with incredible relief—Lee is *in there,* he's okay.

He's okay.

"Oh god, thank fuck," he says, sniffling. "Lee, I love you so much, okay? We're going to get you all fixed up. I'm here." Babbling, he's babbling—Tripp knows he is, but he can't help it. He thinks Lee is doing the "yes" wink again, but this time, his eye doesn't open back up.

Tripp squeezes his hand and tries not to sob.

"Take his wedding ring with you," the voice of the nurse from earlier says gently.

Jennifer, Tripp remembers. She's appeared out of nowhere by Tripp's side again, or maybe she never left the room. He really has no idea.

"I'll have to send it down to Security, otherwise. I'm sure you don't want that."

"No," Tripp replies gruffly, sounding less grateful than he means to be. He clears his throat as he robotically works Lee's ring down off of his hand. There's a tan line left behind, even this late in the year, and Tripp stares at it blankly. It's so normal, so *Lee,* that he can't quite reconcile its existence with Lee's current state. Instead of pocketing the ring, Tripp slips it on next to his own. Lee's fingers are slightly thicker, but not enough that it might fall off. Tripp clenches his hand into a protective fist anyway.

"Here," Beau's disembodied voice carries from somewhere behind him, and Tripp doesn't even bother to turn around. "Jenn, Nami changed some of his infusion orders, FYI. Anesthesia's right outside, we can roll over as soon as these are signed."

"Already on it," the nurse says with a dismissive wave. She leaves Tripp's side to go and fuss with one of the electronic pumps flowing medication into the IV inserted in Lee's right arm.

"Tripp, here," Beau says, his tone more pressed than it was before as he tugs at Tripp's sleeve. Reluctantly, Tripp lets go of Leander's hand, tucking it gently into his side and leaning down to kiss the corner of his mouth before complying. When he turns around, Beau's expression is downright pitiful as he watches, and that's maybe the worst thing Tripp's seen yet.

Over the next few minutes, Beau rambles and Tripp mindlessly scribbles every time his brother points. There's a whole sheet on advanced directives, and at least with *that,* Tripp knows what to do. He and Lee have had this conversation many times, like all of their provider friends. They've even had it with Beau and Bri, so when Beau scans Tripp's chosen check boxes and nods, Tripp knows that he's agreeing because he sees Lee's wishes reflected accurately back in black and white text.

At least he knows he got something right, here.

When they're done, Tripp steals one more kiss, one more soft whisper into Lee's ear that he *better fucking come back* to him, right before Lee is wheeled away and out of Tripp's reach. His heart feels like it's ripping apart inside his chest, but all he can fucking *do* is stand there like an idiot. So stand there he does, silently twirling Lee's ring and ignoring the way his tears fall off of his face and onto the ugly, green-tinged floor.

It's only when the bay is fully empty, not just of Lee, but Beau, and Jenn, and everyone else, too, that Tripp abruptly realizes his brother didn't tell him where to *go,* or what to do next.

He's about to full-on panic when suddenly, a familiar face appears in the doorway. Not a face Tripp expected to see, but then again, maybe he should have. Autumn's curly hair is pulled back and she's dressed in pink scrubs, so maybe she's working, or maybe she just got off shift. She's hardly Tripp's favorite person on the planet, but right now, he's never been happier to see someone.

"C'mon, loverboy," she says, stepping forward to loop an arm encouragingly through Tripp's. She's surprisingly strong, and Tripp lets himself lean into the support, just a little. "This is getting to be a pattern with you two." Autumn's free hand rubs Tripp's bicep in a very soothing, very *un*-Autumn type of way. "Let's go get you some coffee."

Tripp's heard *far* worse ideas in his life than that. Still, he can't help but ask, "Got anything stronger?"

Autumn laughs, and weirdly, that makes Tripp feel slightly better. At least he knows she understands.

***

Autumn stays. The hours that follow are some of the longest and most painful of Tripp's entire life. He can't focus enough to read a magazine or even listen to the TV that blares in the family waiting room. He has concerned texts overloading his phone from everyone and their mother, but Tripp just doesn't have the spoons to answer yet.

Sometime during that endless haze, Tripp finds out why Bri hasn't come to see him. He should have realized, but his brain isn't exactly working at full capacity. Thankfully, Autumn is there to relay that Bri was on duty until three a.m. in the ICU, and that she insisted on staying long past the end of her shift to care for Lee once he made it out of surgery. Not for the first time, Tripp feels goddamn grateful for his and Lee's little family (including Alfie, who's currently playing house at Beau's, watching Tripp's toddler niece Mary so that Bri *can* stay).

Absently, Tripp thinks about Mary and the little brother she has on the way. It makes him crush and crumble the empty styrofoam cup he's holding in his hand, has him dropping his head low between his shoulders and praying desperately to Lee, like he can somehow hear.

Lee, you gotta make it out of this, buddy. You gotta meet your nephew. He's gonna love you so damn much, Lee, just like we all do. Lee. I need you. Please be okay.

This time when Tripp looks up, he finds Autumn's eyes full of tears, too. As they begin to spill over, running slowly and silently down her cheeks, Tripp pulls her into a tight hug and they just cling to each other. The awkward plastic arm of the chair in-between them presses painfully into Tripp's hip, and the silence of the waiting room hangs heavily.

They stay like that for a very long time.

Eventually, Beau appears in the doorway beside Dr. Nami, a relieved smile gracing his tired face and barely any expression on hers. Tripp stiffens, but Autumn whispers in his ear that Nami is always like that.

According to both doctors, the surgery went well and Lee should be rolling into the ICU within the hour. Because of who Tripp is, he'll be allowed in right away. That's a goddamn relief, since Tripp was planning on fighting his way to Lee's side come hell or high water, and simply worrying about any consequences later.

When it's time, Autumn accompanies Tripp and Beau in the elevator to the unit, but she isn't allowed to actually come into the ICU. Tripp promises to update her frequently, hugs her, and thanks her sincerely. It's maybe the most genuine interaction he and Autumn have ever had.

"You guys have to stop this crazy death wish thing you have going," she jokes lightly, chucking him on the shoulder. The sentiment actually makes Tripp laugh, albeit a little bitterly. "Hang in there." She walks away without making him reply.

Exchanging a glance with his brother, Tripp answers Beau's raised, questioning eyebrow with a nod of his own; he's ready.

The ICU itself is too much like he remembers. Too-sterile air, the scent of disinfectant in his nose, a mediocre cover for metallic blood and stale body fluids. The incessant beeping of life-sustaining machinery to both his left and right. For a second, Tripp has to stop and take a deep breath, centering himself.

Maybe Autumn's comment wasn't such a joke, after all—Tripp has a feeling they're all going to need some very intensive therapy once Lee is better.

Maybe sooner.

Tripp smoothes down the front of his shirt, composes himself carefully before again following after Beau. His giraffe of a brother has graciously stopped in the middle of the hallway, averting his eyes and allowing Tripp the space he needs to gather his wits without comment.

Once he has, Beau tips his head towards a bay with sliding glass doors that are wide open, a blank whiteboard on the wall to the right.

Seeing Lee is easier this time. He doesn't look any better overall, but he doesn't look worse, and he's definitely less bloody, which Tripp thinks must be good. He's wired for sound, though. There's a drain coming out of the bandages on his head, a monitor in his scalp tracking the pressure in his brain, plus all of the IVs that were flowing before, maybe more.

So much equipment, dwarfing Lee and making him look small—not an easy task.

When they arrive, Lee is intubated and heavily sedated, and Beau rambles about why he'll stay that way while Tripp doesn't listen at all. Instead, he just pulls a chair into the space between the giant ventilator and the bed, and holds his husband's hand. Tripp hangs on for dear life, drops his head to the mattress, and keeps praying, praying like Lee can hear him.

Tripp hardly moves a muscle until the sun is high overhead in the sky.

***

As it turns out, that first night and all the trauma it wrought is only the beginning. Things get better at a snail's pace, so slowly that at times, Tripp feels as if they might actually be going backward.

Sometimes, they definitely are.

That first week, Leander is kept under sedation with the vent breathing for him for several days. *To help his brain heal,* is how it's explained to Tripp. When Dr. Nami finally removes the tube, Lee doesn't wake up the way Tripp did. No, Lee's return to consciousness is slow, measured, and frustrating for Tripp, who didn't understand that this is how it would be.

At first, Leander doesn't talk, and no matter how much Dr. Nami reassures Tripp that she isn't worried, it doesn't make Tripp feel any better. No amount of Lee squeezing hands on command or wiggling his toes indicates that *Lee,* the real Lee, and not some half-catatonic shell of who he used to be, is actually *in* there.

"His brain has been through a lot," Dr. Nami tells Tripp, in that matter-of-fact, condescending way that she speaks. Tripp is pretty certain she thinks she's being empathetic, and weirdly, he kind of respects that. She's an asshole, he's an asshole —assholes get things done, so, whatever on her bedside manner. "There's still quite a lot of swelling, and between the injury and my poking around in there, it's not surprising to discover that he needs some time to come back to himself."

Tripp tries to smile and nod, tries to hear her, to internalize the reassurances that Lee can still be okay. He forces himself to focus on the way Lee's eyes follow him, the way he answers yes or no questions by blinking without fail, the way he follows simple commands. The signs *are* there, if Tripp is willing to believe them, but it's hard.

The fear remains; hot, molten, and angry in his stomach. It comes up several times, when Tripp least expects it—once into the biohazard trash can in the corner of Lee's room, and once all over the "tranquility garden" that decorates the area between the parking structure and the entrance to the main hospital.

The day that happens feels like an all-time low. As Tripp sits back on his heels, surrounded by colorful flowers and wiping the bile from his lips, knees aching from being pressed into the pitted concrete, he lets himself cry. Out here, where Leander can't see, where no one will find out how goddamn weak he is.

It's just that he's so fucking *scared,* and everything feels so uncertain. *Maybe* Lee is okay, maybe he's just got a long, slow road ahead of him. Or maybe him waking up is just a delay in the inevitable, and Tripp is fooling himself.

He can't *allow* himself to believe, not yet. Good things don't happen to Tripp, and his time with Lee already feels like stolen bliss he didn't earn. Tripp always worried it'd be taken from him, someday when he least expected it, and now, here they are. It would be too goddamn hard to let himself relax and then find out he was wrong.

***

Three days since the tube came out, and Lee's silence is louder than any words could ever be. He still sleeps a lot, the doctors have him on all kinds of medications to help him relax and keep his pain under control. Around five in the evening, Lee's dinner shows up in the ICU on a tray, appetizingly pureed and smelling about as enticing as it looks. Tripp eyes the mess disdainfully before glancing over at Leander, who's been passed out cold for the last hour or so.

Tripp doesn't bother to wake him. Lee isn't allowed to eat without an aide or a speech therapist present—swallowing issues, just another thing that might or might not be temporary. Either way, Tripp's been warned; no matter how good Lee's prognosis (and Dr. Nami remains staunchly secure in her belief that he will fully recover), he has a long road ahead. Considering his speech deficits and his struggles with eating, apparently it's obvious that he'll likely have to relearn most of his basic functions.

Like a toddler.

Tripp doesn't care about that—he isn't remotely afraid to stand by Lee's side, however messy this is going to get. He'll be at every rehab session, he'll fucking go to nursing school if he goddamn has to. Learn to work a feeding tube, and a Hoyer lift, and crush meds and whatever else. Lee doesn't need to walk, doesn't need to be able to feed himself, or wipe his ass, or put on his own pants and tie his shoes for Tripp to love him.

Fuck all that.

No, all Tripp cares about is that Lee's *mind* is there. That underneath all of these issues, there's still *Lee*. The snarky, stubborn asshole Tripp fell in love with, the take-no-shit Dom who makes Tripp feel safe, secured, and loved. The personality, the passion, the brains and the empathy that make Lee who he is—as long as Lee is still *Lee*, they'll fuckin' figure out the rest.

Of course, he can't voice any of that. Not to Dr. Nami or Autumn or Beau, and *definitely* not to Lee, because this isn't about *Tripp* and what Tripp needs. So he keeps his crushing fear to himself.

But every hour that goes by and Lee doesn't talk, Tripp worries more. When Dr. Nami can't give him a good reason, when Lee's brain swelling dwindles to practically nothing and *still* he doesn't speak—Tripp's frightened, and trying hard for Lee's sake not to show it.

Maybe if Lee were more *awake*—not so sedated and uninterested in attempting to answer complicated questions. Maybe if he could *write,* or sign, then Tripp could have a clue, but the fact is, he can't do any of those things. All he can do is blink and squeeze hands.

While Tripp rarely leaves Lee's side, Beau comes and goes as often as he's able. He tries his best to reassure Tripp, but that goes over about as well as Beau trying to convince Tripp of anything ever has.

Same as it ever was.

Tonight, Tripp stares out the bay window at the setting sun, and waits. The speech therapist will be in at any moment and she'll wake Lee. Lee will eat and pass out again, and Tripp will be left alone with his whiny, selfish-ass thoughts. He scowls at his sallow-looking reflection in the glass.

Outside, there's ice on the ground, the first solid sign of winter coming on. It's late as hell this year. The pink in the sky is bright, reflecting prettily off the frozen surfaces, and Tripp gazes out over all of it longingly.

He thinks about their honeymoon in the mountains, thinks about the late anniversary trip they took back there at this very time, last year. They'd gone hiking and fishing despite the cold, even tried to fuckin' ski. Tripp can't ski for shit, spent more time on his ass and babying his bum knee in the hot tub than he did actually standing up on those godforsaken things.

The sharp stabbing of the cold across exposed skin, Lee's bright smile, the way he'd howled with laughter at Tripp's ineptitude on skis—it all flashes across his mind now, and Tripp smiles despite himself. He thinks about Lee massaging the pain in his legs away and then spanking his ass sore, just to put things in perspective.

Dick.

A morbid, depressing part of him wonders whether that was their last trip like that, and Tripp didn't even know it. He wonders, if Lee never gets back to the way he was, what their lives will look like going forward.

At the end of the day, Tripp only knows one thing—so long as Lee is *in there,* Tripp will make it fuckin' work.

The sound startles him. It comes from out of nowhere, really. Besides the beeping of ICU monitors and IVs, and Lee's occasional soft snoring, there isn't much noise in here at all. The sliding glass doors to the main ICU are usually closed, now that Lee is fairly stable and not giving everyone heart attacks every twenty minutes. Sealed off, to where even the relative bustle of the intensive care floor is kept to a minimum. People's conversations, even directly outside of Lee's room, usually sound muffled, distant.

This sound is clear as a bell, a voice Tripp would recognize anywhere, and he would swear his heart stops beating in his chest. If he were the one hooked up to monitors, no question—they'd be alarming like crazy. He definitely stops breathing—standing still as a statue at the window, afraid to turn around.

Lee, that goddamn beautiful asshole, says it again.

"Tripp."

Just like that, Tripp lets go of every fear he's been harboring, whirling around and making it to Lee's side in less than two long strides. The head of Lee's bed is raised a little, forty-five degrees like it usually is, and on it, Lee's face is turned in Tripp's direction.

He looks more wide awake than Tripp's seen him yet, and that sight alone makes his heart soar. Lee's blue eyes are wide open (or as wide as the right will go with the residual swelling), and clear.

"Tripp," he repeats, lips curling up into a small smile.

"Lee," Tripp chokes out, not even pretending that he's remotely okay. He knows there are tears making tracks over his cheeks, knows he's probably getting splotchy and pink, doesn't give one red cent about it. He sinks down on the edge of Lee's bed, grabs both of Lee's hands and cups them in his own. "Hey, sweetheart, hey. So we're, uh, talking now?"

In front of him, Lee's smile widens, making it clear he *fucking understands,* and Tripp loses it. Lee can't do much, can't lift his arms and wrap Tripp up in them, but he scrabbles with his fingertips until he can squeeze, weakly tugs at the fabric of Tripp's shirt. He shifts impatiently, making sounds that want to be words but don't quite get there. It's obvious to Tripp that Lee wants to hold him, and he gives in easily.

Tucking his face into Leander's neck, Tripp does the work of wrapping Lee's arms around his torso and his own around Lee's shoulders, snug between his husband and the bed.

"Tripp," Leander says brightly into his ear, clearly delighted with his efforts and the outcome of a totally undone Tripp all up in his business. Overwhelmed and fucking *happy,* Tripp can't find it in him to do anything but sob with relief, so that's what he does. Around his ribs, he can feel Lee's arms tighten with intention, and that's pretty damn good, too.

***

For every breakthrough, there's a setback, often two or more. But sometimes, Lee's steps forward are more like leaps, and those give Tripp hope that they *will* get there, eventually.

Mostly, though, his steps are small.

Nearly two weeks after being hospitalized, Leander leaves the ICU for a bed on the neuro floor. There's nothing small about that, in Tripp's opinion. The neuro floor is quieter, calmer. Absent of the anxious rushing of staff and the haunting cloud of fear and death constantly hanging overhead in the ICU. Having Bri in their regular rotation of nurses was great, but Tripp would trade her in a heartbeat for the easygoing atmosphere the regular neuro floor offers.

The police finally show up, now that Lee is able to put short sentences together, able to get his point across—for the most part. The cops don't need much in the way of corroboration since both Marley and Auriel were witnesses, just Lee's statement and his permission for the D.A.'s office to offer Bart a plea deal involving drug rehab and restitution. Everything else aside, Lee has no interest in going to court over this thing, so he's quick to agree.

Tripp privately thinks the guy's getting off too easily, but it's Lee's choice. Lucky for Bart, Lee has this thing about everyone being redeemable and worthy of a second chance. Apparently, the knock to the head didn't shake that overly idealistic bullshit loose, because he's still sticking to it.

Fine, only Tripp kinda hopes he runs into the guy on the street someday. In a dark alley outside of a bar, where nothing in the world could stop him from exacting some more fitting justice. Hey, the quality of mercy is not Tripp—he's never claimed it was.

Regardless, Lee is having a good day when the detectives come traipsing into his room, and he greets them warmly. He doesn't stutter or cut himself off (often) as he recounts what he remembers from that night (not a lot). To Tripp's ear, Lee sounds *almost* normal. To a stranger, they might not even guess that he's struggling. Might chalk his infrequent hesitations up to emotional trauma, or even missing memories.

It's a relief for Tripp to watch. Lee's speech isn't perfect yet, but it's heaps better than those first few nightmarish days when he said nothing at all. Both Dr. Nami and Lee's speech therapist, Eileen, are pleased with his progress, which is great. Even better, Tripp can now tell—with absolute surety—that Lee is *in there*, dry and stupid sense of humor and all, so what more can he ask for?

Patience, maybe. Yeah, Tripp wouldn't mind someone ponying up a little bit of patience to spread around, that's for sure. Not for *him,* mind you—Tripp has all the goddamn patience in the world for Lee. It's *Lee* himself who's easily frustrated, angry at his own slow trek back to wellness, and the persistent inability to do things the way he feels he should.

On the one hand, Tripp gets it. He's been where Lee is, though not as badly off. Sort of, anyway. True, he's never had to relearn moving words from the inside of his head down off the tip of his tongue, or forgotten how operate a fork, but he *did* have to let his brand-spanking-new boyfriend clean his butthole—and *not* in the sexy way. So, he's not completely without a reference point.

The thing is, Lee is a logical guy. In fact, he out-logics, out-analyzes, and out-smarts Tripp at every turn, every day of the week, just for kicks. He always has. He's the King of Rationale, the Tzar of Common Sense. He's deliberate, thoughtful, and always considers both the facts and any other points of view before becoming emotional.

Basically, he's the opposite of Tripp, and Tripp both loves and hates him for it.

These days, though, Lee is acting a *lot* more like Tripp, and a lot less like the Leander Tripp has become used to. It's understandable, of course, even without a potential brain injury complicating things. Whether or not this is a personality change that will wind up permanent hardly matters at the moment—Lee's feelings and frustrations are valid on their own.

…That doesn't make them any fuckin' easier to deal with, or throw Tripp any less off-kilter when Lee explodes over literally *nothing.*

And he does. When he can't find the right word or force it to come out of his mouth. When his hand won't cooperate and do what his head wants it to do. When his legs won't support his weight beneath him, or the space behind his eyes simply won't stop pounding. Any of those things happen, and Lee gets upset. He yells at nothing, cries out in disgruntled irritation, or maybe flings what he's holding across the room.

Sometimes even his anger doesn't go the way Leander intends, and naturally, that only makes things worse. All of the distractions in the world—games, Tripp reading from books, movies, pictures of Mary being her adorable self—some days, they just don't help. On days like that, the only thing Tripp can do is give his husband space.

Times like those, he'll leave the hospital and drive to the Roadhouse. He'll pick up burgers and shakes as a peace offering for something he didn't even do wrong. More often than not, he'll toss back a shot or two while he's there. More often than not, he pretends he doesn't see Reina and everyone else's pitying gazes, steadily watching him do so.

Sometimes, he sits in the parking lot below his and Beau's old apartment and just stares up at the balcony, thinking about how complicated he *thought* things were back then.

Whenever he returns, Lee apologizes. That never fails. Most times, Leander cries and tells Tripp how much he hates himself for getting so frustrated, how much he hates everything about this situation. If Tripp were more of an asshole than he is, he might be inclined to say, "I told you so," because Lee definitely thought it was a hell of a lot easier than *this* when Tripp was in his shoes.

And Tripp didn't even throw shit.

But the thing is, Tripp doesn't even care. Yeah, it's hard. Yeah, Lee drives him up the damn wall some (most) days. But he drove Tripp up the wall at home, too, *before* all this. Marriage is already hard, fucking *living* with some asshole who is *totally* different from you is hard, but Tripp *loves* him more than anything, knows that Lee feels the same in return. They've already done the world-ending bullshit, already faced down their own mortality and their limited time together.

So this—hard as it is—this is fucking easy. It's just a moment in time for them, something that *someday,* they'll look back on and hold each other a little tighter, glad that they made it through intact. Tripp never, not for *one* second, forgets that he nearly lost Lee. The fear and overwhelming sadness he felt as Lee was wheeled away from him, hurt and bleeding, stays with him permanently like a vice around his heart.

In fact, Lee's broken, unconscious face flashes across his eyelids nearly every time he closes them—Tripp *can't* forget.

So this? This is *nothing*.

Every time Lee apologizes, Tripp tells him so. He tells him he has a right to his anger, his frustration, but that he's got nothing to apologize for. And then he kisses him like they're alone in their apartment and making up after a dumb fight. Maybe slightly more gently, since the right side of Lee's face is still tender as hell, but the feeling remains the same.

"I'm not going anywhere," Tripp always says. "You can't chase me away."

***

The days turn into weeks. Lee is moved to a rehabilitation center that has a median age of senior citizen discount. Unsurprisingly, Lee hates it and resents having to be there very much. Tripp's out of his depth at this point, since he never went through this particular hell himself. All he can do is ride the wave and try to find ways to support Lee, to make this temporary nightmare easier for them both.

The problem and the reason Lee can't go straight home has nothing to do with Tripp's willingness to help or their ability to afford care. It's that Lee is still relearning basic functions, like walking and transferring, and it's not a quick process. He needs equipment that technically, Lee *could* afford to buy and install, but doing so would mean giving up their playroom.

Even if it would only be temporary, Lee nixes that idea on the spot, says he'll cope with the rehab center any day over *that*. Honestly, Tripp's sort of grateful. They've had enough of their lives turned upside down that losing the playroom —even if it isn't meant to be forever—feels like a step too far. Feels like an intrusion into something that *this*—this assault on Lee, this whole fucked up sidebar —shouldn't be able to touch.

Anyway, the rehab center is closer to their apartment than the hospital, and between those two places is the Roadhouse. So at the very least, Tripp's trips for burgers and shakes (and shots) become slightly more convenient. That's something, at least.

Tripp has to go back to work. He waits until Lee is out of the hospital, but with the looming knowledge that he'll likely have to take off again once Lee comes home, it only seems practical. Plus, Lee's days are busy right now, so it's not like he's sitting in a wheelchair staring at the wall, lonely by himself. If he's not being actively treated by a therapist, then he's working his programs with the aides or sleeping off the exhaustion that comes with doing exactly that.

The rehab center doesn't let Tripp sleep there, either—not like the hospital. As such, if he's on days, that means only seeing Lee for a few hours in the evenings, after work. If he's on nights, Tripp spends his daylight fighting sleep so that he can sit in on Lee's therapy sessions and actually *be* the support system Lee deserves.

Needless to say, Tripp's so chronically tired, he could fall asleep standing up more often than not. Weirdly, though, between Lee's schedule and his, he almost feels like they saw more of each other when Lee was working full-time. *That* realization sucks most of all.

The nights are the worst for Tripp. Even when they were on opposite shifts, four days tended to be the maximum he would ever have to go before sleeping in Lee's arms again. Now, it's been weeks. He spends the darkest hours of the night doing a lot of tossing and turning, plus a good amount of glaring at the ceiling, just to mix it up. Considering how tired he is all of the time, that says a *lot* about how used to having Lee next to him Tripp has become.

Tripp misses him more than he ever thought he was capable of missing anything at all.

Still, he presses on. It's not like there's any choice.

That hellacious routine drags on for *three months*. Three very long months after Lee has left the hospital. By the time they're finally working on discharge planning, outfitting Tripp and Lee's apartment with all the equipment and outpatient services they'll need, Tripp feels like a walking zombie. It's all worth it though—because Lee is improving.

He's still a bear, still miserable about not being able to do everything he thinks he should be at this point. On the other hand, at least now, Lee can walk and talk and write his name and (more or less) take a shower standing up without Tripp or an aide holding onto a gait belt so that he doesn't fall and smash his head and start this whole damn thing over again.

Lee's stubbornness is as relentless as Tripp's support. It's both his mortal enemy and greatest strength. He's fallen several times at the rehab, determined to take himself to the bathroom on his own or retrieve something he's dropped—dumb things, if you ask Tripp. Little acts of defiance are really what they are. Lee just wants to prove that he *can*. Unfortunately, he's not great at simply accepting that for right now, sometimes he can't. Thankfully, none of those incidents resulted in serious injury—just some cuts and bruises, mostly to Lee's ego.

In the last care meeting Tripp has with Lee and Lee's support staff in the days before discharge, they review all of the safety mechanisms and functional adjustments Lee knows he has to make at home. At this point, Tripp is well aware that

Lee will do or say just about anything to get the hell out of there, so he takes Lee's solemn promise to ask for help when he needs it with a *touch* of skepticism.

It's fine, though. Tripp's actually with Lee on this one—anything is worth having his husband home again. And Lee really has come leaps and bounds since the incident—he's *close* to his normal, he really is. Unsteady on his feet if he does too much, but hey, who the hell isn't? Tripp's never been more sure that Lee will get there. Not that *Tripp* even cares if Lee can climb mountains or ski or even ride on an ambulance—Lee is alive and he's himself. That's all that matters to Tripp.

But *Lee* cares. Lee loves his job, dreams desperately of getting back to it. The guy basically chose being a paramedic over his dead mother's dying wishes, so Tripp's pretty sure he gets how important it is to him. The thing is, Lee's improvement has been steady, predictable. He *will* get back there one day. Tripp isn't worried and neither is Lee's care team.

Lee, on the other hand—he's a damn nightmare about it. Pushing himself harder than he should, becoming frustrated and angry when small victories don't feel big enough inside his own mind. It's exhausting for Tripp to keep reassuring him, but Tripp keeps his opinions to himself and tries hard to shut up and do exactly that.

After all, Tripp knows what it's like to feel helpless, a useless burden on those you love, and Lee has had it way worse. Even after his release, Lee still has to take it easy. He can't do what Tripp did; working out like a maniac, pushing his body to its limits without fear. He *has* to relax, has to keep his blood pressure down, has to be the tortoise in the race, no matter how much he wants to be the hare. For someone like Lee, who is used to simply setting his mind to a goal and chasing it down without fear, it's gotta be awful.

The day Lee comes home, it snows. Fluffy, sticky flakes blanketing the ground, the kind that are perfect for snowball-making. They're still floating down from the grey sky as Tripp carefully brings Baby to a stop at the edge of the visitor's parking lot next to their building. Baby belongs inside on a day like this, but Tripp will just come back and move her later. It's far fewer steps to the lobby elevator than the one in the garage, and Lee has already had a long day.

True to form, Lee is half out of the car by the time Tripp makes his way around, already bucking the rules and breaking his promises to accept help, even if he doesn't strictly need it. Tripp doesn't say anything about it, though. Lee is a big boy, he can weigh his own risks. Plus, he looks so damn happy.

For the first time in months, Lee's smile looks truly genuine as he tips his face to the sky, blue eyes bright. The clouds reflect in his irises as Tripp steps into his space, drawn to him instinctively. Lee's lids flutter closed, soft white flakes landing and melting on his skin as Tripp looks on. The sight is so beautiful and Lee looks so *peaceful* that Tripp can't help but lean in and press his lips to Lee's jaw.

In response, Leander hums happily. When Tripp draws back, his husband's eyes are open and focused intensely on him, the sky forgotten. Lee's gaze is so fierce and familiar that it takes Tripp being pinned by it to realize that it's been *missing.*

Just like that, Tripp's carnal need for Lee comes flaring back to life, taking him by surprise. While he hasn't been actively suppressing those thoughts and urges, he hasn't been encouraging them, either. With everything that's gone on, sex has been pretty much the last thing on his mind.

It's weird, now that Tripp's thinking about it, that he *hasn't* been more horny and frustrated. Before this whole thing, he and Lee never went a day without at *least* teasing each other. Hell, Tripp was running down the ER hallways with lube in his ass, ready to be bent over the nearest surface for a reason.

Well, whatever—Tripp chalks their mutual dismissal of the subject up to stress and Lee's protracted recovery. There's also the matter of Tripp slipping into the caregiver role and Lee being barely able to hold a fork (never mind a dick) for like six whole weeks.

With the looks Lee is giving him now, Tripp's pretty sure they'll be back to acting like twenty-year-old newlyweds in no time. Maybe it was just a matter of opportunity. Fucking in the bathroom of the rehab center was never really an option, after all. Doesn't matter—they've got plenty of privacy now.

Lee barely lets the doors close behind them in the elevator before he's all over Tripp. And by all over, Tripp definitely means *all over.* Tongue down his throat, hands thrust into his still-buttoned pants, bodies grinding mercilessly. It's enough to leave Tripp panting, shaking, and halfway to Happy-Town by the time the elevator dings for their floor. Before Tripp can so much as grab his wits, Lee is yanking him out and down the hall by the front of his shirt.

"Take it easy," Tripp mutters, hardly meaning the words but feeling obligated to say them anyway, because safety and recovery and—honestly, his brain is too addled right now to remember what else. With his shirt half-undone and Lee's hard cock pressing against his hip, it's not like Tripp could slow things down, even if he wanted to. He's human, he's *so* in love with Lee, and he hasn't been laid in almost four months.

Lee looks equally undone—lips parted, hair messy from Tripp's hands, and his clothes all askew. But there's also a glimmer of *something*—some flash of disappointment or resignation that crosses Lee's handsome face and is gone before

Tripp can even fully register it. He figures it doesn't matter because a second later, Lee is back on him again and all rational thought leaves the building completely.

Tripp has no idea that in hindsight, he'll look back and realize—that's the moment it all went wrong.

***

It takes Tripp almost two entire months to figure it out. To be fair, Lee is damn good at hiding his emotions, when that's what he wants to do. Sure, Tripp gets glimpses here and there, but Lee's moods change faster than the wind these days, so Tripp is never one hundred percent sure whether what he's looking at is a serious concern or just a bad day.

The trouble is, the two of them never *quite* make it back to "normal." They get into a more normal routine, sure. Lee goes to outpatient therapy and Tripp goes to work. They both go to talk therapy, because it seems obvious at this point that any reasonable person would need it. They cook and clean the apartment together, and Lee participates more and more with each passing day. They fight and they fuck and they go back to ending every night in each other's arms, but *once again,* something is missing.

It's not like they haven't been down this road before—Lee was reluctant to return to the playroom after Tripp was hurt, too. Back then, Tripp thinks that had a lot more to do with Lee watching Tripp suffer and not wanting to *cause* suffering himself, but he's also fairly certain that's not the case here. In fact, the more hints Tripp drops and the more unaccepted offers he leaves open, the clearer it becomes.

Lee has lost his mojo.

If Tripp had to take a wild guess, he'd say it's a mix of Lee not believing he's worthy, and a straight-up self-confidence issue after all they've been through.

In retrospect, Tripp thinks he probably should have seen this coming. It's definitely in line with Lee's personality and who he is, Tripp just thought—well, he thought they were past distrusting each other as a couple. Past Lee thinking that Tripp *caring* for him undercut his authority and power as a Dom.

Even that, though—that's not exactly what this is, is it? Tripp's been there, he knows.

Relying on your partner for *everything* the way Lee has had to do is *hard.* It's demoralizing, humiliating, all those good things. Tripp gets that, it's just... he thought Lee would get *over* it. After all, he was the one telling Tripp to do the same damn thing when the roles were reversed. Pick yourself up by your boot-straps, Tripp. Accept help, Tripp. Don't be so whiny, I *love* wiping your ass, Tripp. And now here Lee is, throwing himself the same pity party in his own damn head. Doesn't even have the decency to admit he's *doing* it, either.

Whatever—Tripp knows Lee well enough to see through him, and to give him what he needs. Even if Lee isn't willing to ask for it like an adult. You know, the way he'd expect and demand for Tripp to do. If Tripp didn't want to be domi-nated so damn badly, he'd throw a fuckin' tantrum over it himself. But as it is... *choices.*

So instead of picking a fight, Tripp hatches a plan. He puts in to use up the last of his work vacation days in the middle of *March* (damn, this year is already painfully long) and secures a reservation at their honeymoon cabin. With a little help from a friend (and yes, after this, Tripp is *definitely* going to have to count Autumn in as his friend), he makes it happen.

When the big day rolls around, Lee has no fuckin' clue what's up, and that's the way Tripp wants it. In fact, when Tripp sits him blindfolded in Baby's passenger seat, Lee doesn't even realize there are suitcases in the back, alongside a giant cooler of food and drinks.

Part of Tripp still sort of worries that this is a terrible idea. That Lee is going to be incredibly pissed off and not receptive to what Tripp has planned, but hell. That's a chance he has to take at this point. He *misses* his Dom, knows that in the place that lies beyond Lee's fear and self-pity, Lee misses him too. Vanilla sex is nice and all, emotional connection is awesome. Life purpose, meaningful work, and recovery in general are important.

But *Lee* is a Dom and Tripp is a sub, and they *need* that aspect of their lives as much as anything else, down to the bone.

The first few minutes out on the road are peaceful. Or at least, they're quiet. Tripp told Leander they were going on a "surprise trip," and nothing more than that. Regardless of his surety about what Lee needs, Tripp's still flexing his hands on the wheel and trying hard not to act as nervous as he feels.

As they take the onramp out of the city and onto to the highway leading north, Tripp glances around, silently wishing goodbye (and good riddance) to all the re-minders of all of their bullshit, at least for a little while. Absently, Tripp clicks on the radio and begins humming along to the classic rock station Baby is default-tuned to. It's nice. With Lee beside him, he feels... almost normal.

Almost.

Above them, the midday sky is grey and full, the air outside Tripp's window heavy and with that particular winter smell that means a storm is on the way. Snow is definitely on the horizon, Tripp just hopes he can beat the worst of it to where they're going. Baby's no snow bunny, that's for sure.

The silence is broken by Leander, who has very quickly tired of *not* being in control of any given situation that concerns him. Tripp wishes he'd translate that stubbornness to their sex life, but if all goes as planned... "Where *are* we going, Tripp? Tell me right now, or I swear, I'm taking this ridiculous blindfold off."

"It's romantic," Tripp protests. "C'mon, sunshine, play along."

Leander grumbles something unintelligible under his breath, but he does cross his arms and sit back. To Tripp's amusement, he turns his head towards the window like he's staring out, despite the fact that he can't see a thing. Petulant son of a bitch.

"Love you," Tripp offers, a somewhat manipulative attempt at compromise that he knows Lee can't resist. Sure enough, a little smile tugs at the corner of Lee's lips. A minute later, his hand is feeling its way across the seat, tangling with the one Tripp has lying between them. "You can see?"

"Nope," Leander replies, entirely satisfied with his ability to predict Tripp's behavior. He squeezes Tripp's fingers for emphasis, and Tripp exhales, full of hope that this will actually work.

***

The drive is around two hours long and Lee begins to complain when they're still thirty minutes away that he needs to pee and can't hold it any longer. Considering how close they are, Tripp knows that if he takes the blindfold off now, Lee will definitely guess their destination. Maybe that wouldn't be the end of the world—it's definitely not the end of the surprises—but Tripp has an image in his mind of how he wants this to go.

He chews his lip for a bit while Leander starts threatening to pee on Baby's seats before taking the next exit off of the highway. They're well into the mountains now, and civilization is sparse. More trees than buildings or cars. Even still, there's a gas station and a general store not two hundred feet from the highway, but Tripp drives right past it.

Instead, he scans the trees for any break in the line, getting lucky fairly quickly. There's a dirt path that looks relatively clear and anyway—Tripp doesn't intend to drive very far down it. He pulls Baby off of the road until she's just hidden from sight before throwing her into park and taking a deep breath.

Here goes nothing.

"Sir," he says, very clearly and intentionally. "May I help you?"

There's a pause accompanied by a weighty silence that descends in the cabin of the car while Tripp holds his breath and waits for Leander to respond. If Lee isn't willing to play along now, *fuck*—this whole trip could turn out to be a bust. It's a gamble, for sure, but one Tripp is willing to try. The *old* Lee—he wouldn't fuckin' hesitate, and Tripp is *positive* his Dom is in there, somewhere.

From less than three feet away, Tripp can practically hear the gears turning in Lee's head as he slots the pieces of this not-so-complicated puzzle together. He waits for the refusal, the chastisement, the warning sigh and accompanied, "*Tripp…*"

It doesn't come.

"Alright," Leander says carefully, when he finally says anything at all. He doesn't sound hesitant, just measured, and Tripp's hope soars.

He takes a second to gather himself, trying to swallow down the excitement he feels at not being turned down, at even the *possibility* of having Lee back the way he wants him. As Tripp steps out of the car and rounds it, his heart thuds in his chest like a teenage boy picking up his prom date. Suddenly, Tripp's damn glad Lee is blindfolded and can't mock him for the smile that he's wearing and the way it stretches from ear-to-ear.

Or hell, maybe he wishes Lee *could* see it. Maybe that would be the friggin' incentive Lee needs to break and turn Tripp over his knee like Tripp's been dying for him to do for so long.

For the first time since Tripp realized Lee wasn't jumping headfirst back into dominating him, Tripp wonders if *he* has been clear enough. If Lee *knows* how badly Tripp needs him. He thought so, but—just maybe, the hints he *thought* were as loud as sirens were more like confusing whispers.

Maybe on top of Leander not feeling worthy, he hasn't realized how badly Tripp still wants him, too.

As Tripp opens Lee's door and helps him step out, Lee tenses underneath his hands. *Alright, so not* just *a misunderstanding, then.* He really is nervous. But he's willing to try, and Tripp can work with that.

"Thank you, Sir," Tripp says, when Leander takes his arm and allows Tripp to lead. It's only maybe three steps to the edge of the path, far enough that even if someone drives by, they wouldn't be able to see him with his dick out.

It's *freezing* out here, at least ten degrees colder than downtown in the city, and Leander shivers a little. He had his coat off in the car and didn't put it back on when they got out. Tripp's underdressed too—while his own coat is on his back, it's leather and not exactly weather-appropriate, but Tripp didn't think they'd be doing an impromptu sort-of-scene in the woods when he got dressed this morning. At least it isn't snowing yet.

It is beautiful, though, and quiet. Missing the hustle and bustle of traffic and people rushing around that plagues the city even in the darkest hours of the night. There's nothing like that here. Just giant trees towering overhead, branches rustling in the chilly breeze, and the sound of birds and squirrels hopping around in the brush beyond the path.

Leander shivers again and Tripp forces himself to suppress the nursemaid instincts—the impulse to cover his husband up or bundle him back into the car, piss break be damned. If Tripp wants to do this, to *really* do this, he has to let Lee be the boss of himself. Be the boss of both of them, really, not just when it comes to sex or when Tripp deems it convenient.

It occurs to Tripp that maybe Lee isn't the only one who's slipped pretty far out of their usual dynamic—it's not easy for him to step back and let Lee take the reins again.

Maybe they both need this trip more than Tripp thought.

He clears his throat and ignores the cold. "May I, Sir?" he asks, touching two of his fingers to Lee's belt buckle.

The smirk is back, ticking up the corner of Lee's mouth below the blindfold when he says, "You may, my sweet boy. My scheming, duplicitously sweet boy, who has brought me out into the—I'm guessing—*wilderness* using possible subterfuge and outright dishonesty."

"Geez, Lee," Tripp hedges, fingers faltering as he tries to undo Lee's belt. "It ain't as bad as all that."

"Hmm," Leander replies. "Lee?" His questioning tone is sharp and brings Tripp up short, snapping his head up the way he routinely does when Lee is expecting eye contact. Of course, Lee is still blindfolded and yet somehow, Tripp feels as if he's looking straight through him. When he licks his lips, he could *swear* Lee grin widens, just a hint.

"Sir," Tripp replies quickly, his brain belatedly catching up as it attempts to process everything that's happening in front of him. "I definitely, *definitely* mean Sir."

"I need to urinate very badly," Leander reminds him, as straight-faced as he can possibly be while still sounding entirely amused.

With renewed confidence, Tripp gets Lee's buckle undone before moving to stand behind him. While he reaches into Lee's boxers to tug him out, Tripp tucks his icy nose into the side of Lee's neck. He's definitely pushing Leander, trying to see how much control Lee wants to take back from him, how ready he is to really take this thing to the next level.

God, Tripp hopes he's reading this right. He hasn't been this excited about anything in *months,* and honestly, that has very little to do with the increased blood flow currently rushing to his dick.

Lee lets Tripp nose behind his ear while he pisses, and when he's done, he says so, without any indication that he's feeling any type of way. The manner in which his dick has filled out a little in Tripp's hand says otherwise, though, so instead of complying, Tripp gives it a stroke or two.

In an instant, Tripp finds himself laid out on the ground, hand that was just holding Lee's cock now twisted almost painfully tight against the small of his back. His cheek is flush against the gravel-studded dirt, and the way it digs into his skin *bites* and teases and feels *so* damn good. Lee's weight on his back, the heavy palm resting between his shoulder blades—*fuck, yes.*

Welcome back, Lee, Tripp thinks.

"What did I say, Tripp?" Leander growls from behind him. "Were my instructions unclear?"

Tripp can't help but grin happily, despite the bit of rock lodged in the side of his mouth. "No, Sir," he replies enthusiastically. Leander shifts against him so that he's straddling Tripp's thigh, pelvis pressing against Tripp's ass. He's hard now, and Tripp's never been so goddamn happy in his life.

As Tripp struggles to control his breathing and the urge to shiver from anticipation (and maybe a *little* bit from the incredibly cold ground), Leander's body blankets him almost completely. His lips run the shell of Tripp's ear and he hums softly. The vibrations against Tripp's sensitive skin have his eyes fluttering closed, hopeful.

"You think you can bait me?" Leander murmurs. "After all this time? You think you're in charge here?"

"God, no, Sir," Tripp replies honestly, working hard not to press back into Lee's groin. It's not a difficult instinct to fight, considering *this* is all Tripp *really* wants, and he'd do goddamn anything to keep it. "You're in charge, Sir. Always."

There's a short pause, and then Lee's weight vanishes from his back like it was never there. "Good," Leander replies, and the sound of his hands clapping together like he's dusting himself off reaches Tripp's ears. "You may stand up."

Somewhat shakily, Tripp gets to his feet. His insides feel like they're vibrating, and all he really wants to do is drop to his knees and beg Lee to fuck him up, right here in this half-frozen forest. Instead, he turns and faces Leander, only a little surprised to see that the guy still has his damn blindfold on.

Despite that, Tripp can see the cocked eyebrow Lee is sporting, read the way his arms are crossed over his chest. Like the good boy he is, he waits quietly until Leander decides to speak again. When he does, Tripp is pretty sure he looks pleased.

"You may finish escorting me to our destination now," Leander says, offering his arm and linking it through Tripp's when he steps into his side. "Shall we?"

"Absolutely, Sir," Tripp replies, happily accepting the offer and guiding Leander back towards the car in high spirits. Hey, he might not have gotten fucked in the middle of the woods, but overall, Tripp feels as if this dipping of his toe into the waters of submission went *far* better than even he could have hoped for.

The last leg of their journey flies, and there's a palpably different energy in the cabin of the vehicle than before by the time Tripp's exiting the highway again. Following his memory, Tripp pulls off of the main road running through the small town that sits at the base of the mountain they're staying on. The directions are easy, but navigating up the winding side street becomes difficult as the first fluffy flakes that started to drop fifteen minutes prior turn heavy.

As Tripp squints against the bright white curtain marring the view ahead, Leander begins to get restless at his side. It's almost as if he can sense Tripp's distress and really—that's very likely the case.

"Is everything alright?" he asks quietly. "Tripp, if you need my assistance, please don't feel like whatever plans you have will be ruined. Is it snowing?"

"Yeah," Tripp replies gruffly, taking Baby down to a crawl so that she doesn't slip and slide and send them careening off the side of the mountain. Baby's his pride and joy, but she's not an off-road vehicle by any means. Even now, her tires fail to grip the road through the inch or so of unplowed, slushy snow. Tripp silently praises his own foresight in packing food for them in a cooler, just in case. There's no way they're getting down into town tonight—*maybe* tomorrow if the snow stops and the plows do a decent job with clean-up.

"Are you ignoring me?"

"No," Tripp snips, not failing to note the way Lee's jaw clenches in his peripheral vision. "No, Sir," he amends, a lot more softly. Lee's jaw relaxes, and Tripp can almost imagine the pleased twinkle in his eye. "We're almost—"

Right on time, the stretching driveway that leads off of the road, down through the woods, and dead ends at their cabin appears to Tripp's right. He sighs with relief and takes Baby smoothly down the path. The snow here is a bit lighter, the tree cover protecting the ground just a bit. It's enough for Baby to make it through. With the weight of the flakes and the dense rate that they're falling, though, that definitely won't last. It's good they came when they did.

"We're here," Tripp announces, pulling Baby underneath the carport to the left of the cabin and noting with appreciation all the firewood stacked high against the wall. "No!" he yelps, as Leander raises his hand to remove the blindfold. "Please," he adds hurriedly. "Just—give me five minutes, alright? Sit tight and I'll walk you in. *Sir.*"

"Sit tight," Leander echoes, clearly amused. Even still, he tucks his hands obediently into his lap and settles back in his seat. "I trust you," he says, and Tripp exhales.

The next five minutes are a race, since he has *no doubt* that Leander is counting the seconds. Knowing the layout of the cabin is a plus, and Tripp makes good use of his advantage. Intent on not wasting time, he shoulders every bag they have *plus* picks up the cooler with a grunt and a huff. Tripp's fairly sure he hears a chuckle from the front seat, but it's not like he has the time to stop and check.

The wind and snow sting his face as Tripp makes the short trek from the carport to the front porch. It's cold, but it's beautiful here. The forest surrounds the cabin completely on this side, though looking out from the back, it gives way to an incredible view of the valley and mountains beyond. Above him, the tree branches sway and the snow falls and Tripp feels a thrum of excitement in his veins.

He sets the cooler down onto the wooden floor of the porch so that he can punch his code into the lockbox hanging on the door. It opens easily, dropping a key ring into his hand. Knowing that his time is dwindling, Tripp quickly unlocks the door and hauls all of their gear inside.

Bags to the master suite off to the left, cooler in the kitchen, small travel bag out in the living room for... *reasons.* Thermometer adjusted from the eco-heating the owner keeps it on between renters to a more comfortable seventy-two, and some lights.

As he moves through the house, Tripp checks on the modifications and additions he sent Autumn ahead of them yesterday to carry out. To his delight, everything seems to be in place. It's lucky the cabin has owners Tripp and Lee have become friendly with, people who didn't mind making a few permanent changes on a whim.

Well, they at least didn't mind taking Lee's money in exchange for those changes, anyway. Same diff, as far as Tripp is concerned. It's nothing that'll be noticeable to anyone who isn't looking for it, but still. Testing the strength of the two ropes hanging from brand new silver loops in the raftered ceiling of the living room, Tripp grins and makes a mental note to send Autumn her favorite pizza the next time she's at work. He owes her big.

With the seconds ticking down, Tripp strips quickly and moves his collar from his wrist to his neck. He ditches his clothes in the bedroom, grabbing his robe out of one of the duffles before stuffing his feet back into his boots. Laces still untied, he flies out the front door and down the porch, *barely* making it to the passenger side of the car before Lee is kicking the door open and stepping out.

"Time's up," Lee announces, presumably before he even knows for sure that Tripp is there.

Gasping, Tripp slaps one hand onto Baby's hood to brace himself, clapping Lee on the shoulder with the other. "I'm here," he wheezes. "'M right here, just hold your damn horses. Aw fuck," he mutters, not even having to look at Lee's face to see the eyebrow go up. "Just—trust me, alright? You can take all of your frustrations out on my ass in a hot second. Sir."

"Intriguing," Leander replies, slamming the door. He nearly walks into one of the posts supporting the carport, Tripp swooping in to guide him away right at the last second. As they stand in the clearing, the snow settles in Leander's hair, making him look unusually delicate, pretty, almost ethereal. If Tripp wasn't freezing his nuts off, he could look at that sight all day.

As it is, he's in a hell of a rush to get back inside.

When they take the steps up onto the porch together, Tripp's unlaced boots clomp loudly against the wood and he nearly trips and walks right out of one. Despite that, Tripp doesn't miss the way Leander inhales sharply, suggesting he's caught on to where they are. Not shocking, Lee isn't an idiot and Tripp definitely knew it was possible that he would. But what Lee *doesn't* know is the way all of Tripp's pieces are about to slot together for the big reveal.

The cabin isn't the surprise—*Tripp* is.

Of course, he wasn't counting on Lee being *quite* so easy to get on board. The fact that he's already demanding Tripp call him "Sir" and insisting Tripp stop bossing him around definitely takes the pressure off.

"Stand here one second, please, Sir," Tripp says. He squeezes Leander's hand affectionately before letting it go just as soon as they're inside. Closing the door behind them, Tripp quickly shirks his robe, tossing it over the back of the couch as he steps out of his boots. Once he's down to Lee's favorite panties and his collar, Tripp puts a hand on Lee's back and touches his elbow, leading him gently into the middle of the space.

The cabin is really just one large room and the master suite—an open-concept, rustic situation that Tripp kind of wishes he could live in year-round. To their left is the kitchen and eating area, fully-equipped and topped off with an antler chandelier that Tripp's not done begging Lee to let him install above their own dining room set.

To the right is the living room, wide and airy with glass on two sides and sixteen-foot ceilings that make Tripp feel short. The fireplace runs all the way up to the top, bold and imposing, the divider in an otherwise uninterrupted view of the forest and a bit of the view beyond. Filling the space are two worn and deliciously comfortable couches with cushy pillows and flannel blankets folded in a stack. Rounding out the seating is an awesome leather recliner, all of the pieces facing said fireplace and the TV mounted above it, plus the expected side tables and low-watt lamps.

A huge floor-to-ceiling bookcase next to the entrance offers movies, books, and board games, none of which Tripp expects will get much use during this particular trip. At least, not if all goes according to plan (*so far, so good*).

At the opposite end of the house and the front door are two large sliders that lead out onto the balcony. This is Tripp's *favorite* part of the place, hands down. The view is breathtaking and the sun sets behind the mountains they're facing, turning the whole view molten and glowing almost every evening.

Tripp and Lee have enjoyed that scene on many a peaceful night, kicked back and relaxing with a drink in the hot tub that sits out there, too. Or, alternatively, with Leander fucking Tripp roughly against the porch railing, shoving his tie into Tripp's mouth to stop him from screaming into the valley and making their distant neighbors wonder if Jason Voorhees is out there.

As far as looks, the traditional cabin exterior of the house isn't for show. This place is the real deal—hand-cut logs from casement to ceiling, the inside showcasing it too. Beyond the walls, the wooden accents, the custom kitchen table and chairs, even the cabinets all match the blond, knotty logs of the house's bones. In contrast, the towering fireplace is grey stone, and the wide island in the kitchen has the same aesthetic on three sides.

Tripp loves it.

This place is like a second home to him, and he hopes Lee feels the same way. Hopes this will be a safe and welcoming ground zero for them to find their way back to each other, the way Tripp knows they can be, the way they deserve. Good memories, new-start symbolism, and all that crap Tripp doesn't really buy into and yet is counting on pretty heavily to come through for him.

He takes a deep breath before letting go of Leander, stepping away and in between the dual ropes hanging from the ceiling. Letting his fingers caress the soft rope as he drops, Tripp falls to his knees and folds his hands demurely into his lap. It kills him to miss Leander's reaction, but this is part of it, and Tripp doesn't have a choice. He lowers his head, stares at the carpeted floor in front of Leander's feet.

Right now, he's the picture-perfect image of submission. There will be no mistaking this for anything other than what it is: an offering, from Tripp to Leander.

"Come back to me, Lee," Tripp says softly. "*Sir.* You can look, if you're ready."

Despite keeping his eyes down, Tripp still thinks he can *feel* the moment Leander sheds the blindfold, and not just because the bit of his body Tripp can see shifts a little. There's a quiet gasp, barely audible, but more importantly, the current in the air changes. Suddenly—and Tripp's *pretty* sure it's not just his own excitement—the room feels electrified.

As Leander steps forward slowly, Tripp licks his lips, tries to control his breathing. There are fingers under his chin then, lifting his face until he's blinking up into an ocean of familiar blue. Lee is biting his own lip, both thoughtful and excited as he turns Tripp's face this way and that.

"I'm sorry," Lee declares, finally, and he sounds like he means it. His eyes are soft and regretful, despite the amusement in their creases. Today, his voice is without the self-pitying edge that's been lacing so much of what he says lately. To Tripp's eye, he looks effortlessly confident, like the Lee he fell in love with in *every* way, and they've barely gotten started.

Tripp's heart aches in his chest. If he were the kind of guy who waxed poetic about his feelings, the shit that would spill from his mouth right now…

Thank fuck he's not.

Lee's thumb is dragging across his lips, dipping past them to caress Tripp's tongue and hook around his teeth. Tripp doesn't flinch, just holds eye contact and lets Lee do whatever he wants. *Please do whatever you want to me,* he thinks.

"I'm sorry for not being able to give you what you need lately," Leander continues, his thumb slipping free and leaving a wet streak down Tripp's chin. "I'm sorry for—" he pauses, searching Tripp's face with his eyes, dragging his own lip through his teeth again before shrugging. It looks to Tripp like he's shaking something off, letting some invisible stress roll off of his shoulders and back. Tripp hopes it's the pain and confusion of the past few months, the way his need to rely on Tripp has gotten him so down and depressed, so far away from who he really is and wants to be.

"C'mon, Lee, come back to me," Tripp thinks, pleading with his eyes when he does.

"Color, Tripp," Leander says gently, and Tripp's whole body floods with both endorphins and relief.

"Green, Sir," he replies eagerly.

Recent history has Tripp expecting a kiss next, has him closing his eyes and leaning forward, already feeling Lee's lips ghosting against his. That's all they've been doing, after all. Romantic shit. Lovey, affectionate sex where Lee rides him until he's shaking or fucks him nice and slow while they make out, all sloppy and life-affirming.

Not that there's anything *wrong* with mushy stuff—shit has its place and all. It's just that sometimes Tripp wants to be slapped across his face and spanked until he's black and blue. With everything that's happened, though, he's gotten used to putting his needs on the backburner. Gotten used to accepting whatever Lee feels up to giving him at the moment, which hasn't been anything close to *that.*

So to say Tripp isn't expecting the sting of Lee's palm against his cheek and the whipping of his head to the side in its wake—it's an understatement.

In fact, it's *so* surprising and *so* gratifying that even Tripp is shocked at his own physical response. Between his legs, his dick goes from "mildly interested" to painfully hard like lightning, and Tripp himself is left gasping and moaning like a chick in one of his favorite porn clips.

"Can't fake that kind of enthusiasm," Leander muses, somewhere above him. He chuckles a little as Tripp blinks the tears from his eyes, trying to focus on his Dom. His head is swimming, his body is thrumming, and as much as Tripp *wanted* things to go this way, he wasn't prepared. Maybe, just *maybe* he was bracing for a worst-case scenario where Lee turned him down.

Or maybe he just forgot how fucking *good* it is to be at Lee's mercy like this. Either way, Tripp is already overwhelmed and it's the absolute *best* feeling, so he leans into it fully. Subspace has been nothing but a distant memory for Tripp for too long, and Lee aside, he definitely forgot what a high it is. Now that he's falling swiftly back into it, he's pretty damn powerless to slow down.

"Up," Leander demands, and an already spinning Tripp hurries to comply. "Hands above your head." Tripp stands, balancing on shaky legs, forcing himself to stay vertical while Leander ties his wrists together with one of the ropes above his head.

"Oh, fuck," Tripp whimpers, when Leander leans down to tap his left calf, indicating he should lift it. They've done this exactly once, and it was *hell* for Tripp. One of the hardest scenes he's ever pushed through. Not because it hurt or because it wasn't something Tripp was into, just the *physicality* required—it was a lot.

So, of course, this is what Lee wants to do. Test and press his fuckin' limits right out of the gate. Well, Tripp *did* give him the ropes (literally and figuratively), he should have known Lee would use them to their fullest extent. Anyway, he's not complaining. Whatever Lee wants—anything at all—Tripp will happily take and thank him sincerely for it.

But he still is who he is, can't help that one bit.

He picks up his leg, touches his foot to the inside of his thigh the way he knows Lee wants. *Dammit,* he's so fuckin' out of shape and out of practice, he's already sore. No way is he getting out of this without a major cramp and at least one pulled muscle.

"What, am I too much for you to handle on two feet? Gotta ease back into it by tying me up? Lost your touch, huh?"

Without missing a beat, Leander shifts the rope he's using to secure Tripp's ankle just above his knee into his left hand. With his right, he delivers three swift, sharp swats to Tripp's ass.

Like the brat he is, Tripp just laughs, relishing the way his skin smarts in the shape of Lee's fingers.

"You're going to regret that," Leander says, almost conversationally, as he finishes tying Tripp's legs together. Once he's done, he toes at the back of Tripp's supporting knee, leaving him scrabbling with his fingers at the rope he's hanging from and frantically tightening his abdomen so that he can keep his balance.

Dick, Tripp thinks, but he keeps his mouth shut. "Sorry, Sir," is what he says out loud, but he's still smirking, and he knows Lee can see it. In response, Lee just shakes his head and rolls his eyes.

"You're *lucky* my skills are rusty at the moment," he tells Tripp. While Tripp grins and tries to look tantalizingly cocky while balancing on one leg like a sexy as fuck flamingo, Leander notices the bag Tripp left for him on the couch.

"I think you're doing pretty okay," Tripp remarks, tipping his chin in the bag's direction. "That's your stuff. You're *welcome,*" he adds petulantly, and Leander shoots him a glare.

"Keep it up, Tripp," he warns, unzipping the bag and rifling through its contents.

"And you'll, what? Spank me?"

"Edge you until your cock is purple and painful and you're screaming for release, for starters. Refuse to let you come for this entire trip. Take you down from where you're tied up like that only long enough to ensure your safety and then string you up again. Plug your ass with a vibrator and—"

"Alright, geez, we get it, Leeifer. Sir. You're a badass devil in an angel's body." When Leander looks up and quirks a questioning eyebrow at him, Tripp winks back. "Wreck me, baby," he teases, entirely full of himself, even knowing he'll pay for it.

"You're incorrigible," Leander replies, but he can't quite hide the smile that ticks up the corners of his mouth. "You know that I'm going to make you regret that."

"Please," Tripp breathes, shifting a little and adjusting his grip. "God, I hope so."

"So many goodies in here," Leander muses. "So many options. I could stuff you full at both ends, bind your cock, cut you, drip wax all over your body—oh, so many lovely choices. And yet… I feel like tonight, I want this to be just us." He drops the bag, having selected nothing from it but a bottle of lube. Waving it at Tripp, he flicks the cap open and drizzles some onto two fingers. "And this, of course. After all, my hands can do just as much damage as any… *toy.*"

Oh, fuck. There he is.

That's the Lee that Tripp has been missing. That's the Lee he knew was still in there, somewhere, dying to come back out. If ever Tripp's wanted to sappily confess his undying love for his husband, it's never been more so than in this very moment. He's deliriously, *stupidly* happy right now. Ironically, Lee is probably taking the smile that's slapped across his face as an insolent challenge, but really, Tripp's just fuckin' thrilled.

Lee gets in his face, then, kissing him roughly, biting at his bottom lip just a *little* too hard. Tripp doesn't doubt that he leaves the imprint of his teeth behind when he goes. "Delicious," Leander murmurs, when he's done trying to lick the back of Tripp's throat, when he's had enough of nipping at the soft skin of his neck, the shell of his ear.

Against the crease of Tripp's thigh, Lee is hard, but he doesn't make any move to acknowledge it or pull himself out. Instead, he just tugs Tripp close by the hip, causing him to grumble and have to re-stabilize himself when he sways and nearly loses his precarious footing.

Leander smirks. "When will you learn not to push me?"

Licking his dry lips, Tripp looks down at him dreamily and grins. "Hopefully never, Sir," he replies easily.

The surprise on Leander's face pleases Tripp a *lot,* but he barely has time to appreciate it before his panties are being tugged down to his thighs and Lee's two wet fingers are pushing past his rim without pretense.

"Ungh," Tripp grunts, trying and failing to not look as affected as he is.

After all, this *is* what Tripp wants—something rough, verging on painful. Something dirty and passionate and unsanitized. Sharp edges and no kid gloves, but he knows better than to demand anything specific from Lee. That's a surefire one-way ticket to getting the exact opposite thing, in Tripp's experience.

So he just hangs on, relishing the slight discomfort and the demanding stretch inside his own mind.

"Look at this," Leander says, reaching around and patting one of Tripp's cheeks with his free hand. "You're just so *accessible* to me this way." Without further comment, he draws back and spanks Tripp as he scissors the fingers inside him, and Tripp can't help but tip his head back and moan.

Leander chuckles and licks a stripe up his neck and back down, sucking a kiss over Tripp's collarbone while he kneads the skin he just warmed up. "More?"

"Yes, Sir," Tripp sighs, his face tipping sideways into his own bicep, conveniently pulled almost flush next to his ear. "Please, Sir."

"Oh, that's so much more like it," Leander replies approvingly, adding another finger. "There's my good boy."

He spanks Tripp again and again while his other hand keeps Tripp's body pressed ridiculously close and continues opening him up. By the time Lee is four fingers deep—something he *never* bothers with unless it's otherwise part of the scene—

Tripp is whimpering and moaning into Lee's neck, barely keeping himself upright. Somehow, Lee has found the right angle to hit his prostate, and he's not been gentle about it.

His thigh is between Tripp's legs now, helping to keep him standing, but Tripp's still doing a *lot* of the work. His stomach aches, he's exhausted, his ass is on fire, and Lee hasn't even fucked him yet.

With his spanking hand, Leander soothes a palm over the side of Tripp's face, pushing him upright, presumably so that he can get a good look at the damage he's wrought. Tripp knows he must be a wreck, sweaty and undone as he feels. He does his best to meet Leander's gaze head-on, but his sight is a little blurry from tears and drifting into subspace.

"Gorgeous," Leander tells him, and Tripp feels *so* good, *so* proud of himself. "So perfect for me."

Which is why, when Leander pulls away, Tripp *moans*, nearly fuckin' cries. "Stay there," Leander warns. "Don't move. Just for a moment."

With his dick curved hard and aching, drooling precum against his stomach, Tripp sways in his bindings and tries not to make undignified noises. He's slightly dissociated, but still with it enough to know he wants Lee in him, *now*. Lee knows it too, if the way he's washing his hands *painfully* slowly over at the island is any indication.

When he returns to Tripp's side, it's to trail light fingertips teasingly over his chest and down his ribs as Leander circles him. Once he's behind Tripp, his hands go to Tripp's hips, his mouth to the nape of Tripp's neck, leaving wet kisses and semi-gentle bites.

"You're beautiful," he murmurs. "Even when you're being a stubborn brat. I could look at your body for centuries and never tire of mapping every curve, every freckle. I'm disgustingly in love with you, so much so that it boils up and threatens to explode out of me if I go too long without seeing you, touching you." His hand snakes around and strokes Tripp luxuriously, too loose to get him off but still sparking with pleasure.

Distantly, Tripp hears Lee's zipper going down, feels the rustling of his clothes as Lee pulls himself out. The head of Lee's cock presses at Tripp's loose, wet rim, pressing inside easily and filling him fully, making him moan and clutch at the rope between his hands.

He doesn't have the leverage to push back, and that's torture in and of itself. The slow slide of Lee seating himself has Tripp gasping by the end, a broken *"please,"* rolling off of his tongue before he realizes that's what he's saying.

"Shhh," Leander soothes. "Shhh, darling. My good boy." Just like that, his hand leaves Tripp's dick and finds its way to his neck, squeezing around the soft flesh just *slightly* too hard, so that Tripp chokes a little, sees stars. And then Leander lets go, jamming his fingers into Tripp's mouth, instead.

"Filling you from both ends sounded too good to pass up," Leander says, thrusting slow and long into Tripp's ass, fingers dipping against his tongue. Without having to be asked, Tripp sucks, deep throats Lee's digits enthusiastically, practically drooling around them. The groan Leander makes in response is all the encouragement he needs and Tripp turns it up a notch, licking between Lee's fingers and really going to town.

"*Tripp,*" Leander moans. "Tripp, how could I have let this—let *you* go for so long?" He's fucking Tripp fairly roughly now, and with the intrusion in his mouth, Tripp can only grunt in response. "Thank you," Leander is saying, and Tripp barely hears, he's off his face with pleasure and happiness. "For reminding me who I am."

Tripp isn't expecting it when Lee pulls away, though he probably should have been. He cries out, practically sobs, his cock throbbing painfully between his legs. A blurt of cum bubbles out of the slit—he was *so* damn close to finishing, *so* desperate for it.

"Hush," Leander tells him as Tripp whines, and then suddenly, his bound ankle is free and Lee is working on his hands. Once they're loose, Leander doesn't mess around, just jerks one arm and then the other behind Tripp's back, securing them with what might be a zip tie.

Honestly, Tripp has no idea and doesn't much care—the relief he feels at being cut down is *nearly* as satisfying as his impending orgasm promises to be, although not quite.

Even on two feet Tripp is wobbly, but Leander is right there with him. "Come," Lee urges, marching Tripp forward. He moves him a few feet nearer to the couch, close enough that when he puts one hand on Tripp's abdomen and one on his back, bending him forward, Tripp's face winds up resting on the cushioned arm.

A tear leaks from his eye, running down the side of his cheek and soaking into the fabric. "Fuck, yes," Leander groans as he pushes back inside. "So tight. You feel like Heaven, Tripp."

As he picks up the pace, fucking Tripp pretty ruthlessly now that he has something to brace against, Leander's hand right hand reaches across, curving around Tripp's left shoulder. It wraps over the scarred imprint of its own shape, in the opposite direction. Lee's torso twists to let him do so, the angle changing to perfectly press against Tripp's prostate with every forward stroke. His left hand works Tripp's aching ass cheek, spanking it again occasionally.

Now that he doesn't have to hold himself up, Tripp lets himself really float. With Lee pounding on his prostate and all the teasing and edging he's been subjected to, Tripp knows he's not going to have a problem coming untouched so long as he can get himself into the right mindset. The praises and sweet words Lee is murmuring in his ear help, and Tripp rides the wave, letting himself be brought closer and closer. This time, he doesn't fight it, doesn't try to hold his pleasure at bay.

It's Lee letting go of his shoulder and threading fingers into his hair, scratching at his scalp, that sends him over the edge. Tripp's legs are shaking, there's sweat dripping off of him, and his whole body feels tense and hot. His muscles lock up when he comes and he drifts so far into subspace he barely feels connected to his body anymore.

Even still, he can feel Lee's slick skin sliding against his back, can feel the hot, wet spill somewhere deep inside of him and Lee's shudder of release when he comes. Tripp's own orgasm feels fucking *endless*. Tantric, he might say, if words were a thing he could grasp at all. It washes over him and out of him, eyes rolling back in his head as his cum spurts out, landing on the couch and the floor in violent splatters.

As Tripp pants and trembles and fights his way back to himself, he rubs his forehead against the arm of the couch, staring down blankly at the mess on the floor.

"…okay? Tripp, are you okay?"

Belatedly, Tripp realizes Lee is shaking his shoulder, trying to get him to stand upright. His arms are free but his legs are weak and Lee has already pulled out, so instead, Tripp half-rolls around to collapse down on the couch. Once he's there, he blinks up at Leander hazily, taking a deep breath before holding up the "OK" sign.

Lee is peering back with concern, but he seems to relax a little, at the familiar sign. Tripp closes his eyes for a moment, barely registering Lee advising him that he's going to grab juice. Tripp *wants* to tell him about the cooler in the kitchen, but his mouth isn't currently working with his brain, so instead, he just nods and enjoys the back of his eyelids.

It turns out to be irrelevant. Lee finds the cooler with ease and returns to the living room with Tripp's juice and a protein bar, which he proceeds to mother-hen down Tripp's throat. Tripp, meanwhile, is still subspaced-out and barely remembers how to chew like a human being.

When he finally begins to regain his senses and his limbs stop tingling, he's not where he remembers collapsing, half off of the couch. Now, he's arranged properly end-to-end with his legs draped over Lee's lap. To Tripp's delight, Lee is quietly but thoroughly massaging them toe to thigh with some sort of nice-smelling oil.

Tripp shifts, tucking an arm behind his head, between his hair and a decorative pillow that may not survive this encounter. As absorbed as he is in his task, Leander still notices, smoothing oiled hands up Tripp's thigh as he leans over to press a soft kiss to Tripp's lips.

"Hello, Tripp."

"Hey, Lee," Tripp replies, and even he can hear the affection laced through his own voice. He cracks a smile. He's never been good at hiding from Lee. "You good, sunshine?"

Eyebrows raising in surprise, Leander cocks his head, one hand still rubbing lazy circles into Tripp's muscles. "I believe that's my question," he protests mildly.

With a shrug, Tripp lifts his hand and lets it drift down the curve of Lee's face, over his stubbled jaw. "You're so damn good to me, Lee," he says. "Wanna make sure it's just as good for you, too."

Leander pauses for a moment, drops his head so that Tripp can't see his face. "I meant everything that I said while we were intimate," he admits, finally. "I don't say things in the moment that I don't mean." When he raises his face again, he looks more serious than Tripp would like. "You were right. I was hiding, I was… not myself, and I was doing us and our relationship an extreme disservice. Can you forgive me?"

Relieved, Tripp smiles widely, cups Leander's face with his tired hands and drags him in to kiss. "Nothing to forgive, sweetheart," he replies firmly. "Been there, done that, bought the t-shirt." Lee's scruff is rough under his fingertips, but Lee is warm and real and *his*. "We always come back to each other. Always bring each other back when one of us gets stupid, yeah?"

"Yes," Leander replies sincerely, eyes big and round and *way* too adorable and innocent-looking for who Lee is and what he does. "Thank you, all the same."

"You have and would do the same for my dumb ass," Tripp retorts, unable to stop himself from capturing Lee's lips once again. "C'mon, kiss me back, asshole," he demands when Lee is less than responsive. In response, he gets a hand in the middle of his chest slamming him back down on the couch, followed by a reproachful glare.

"The disrespect," Leander says, disapprovingly. Those words say one thing but his tone is light and he settles back into rubbing Tripp down without further complaint. Instead of returning to his legs, he takes Tripp's left hand and starts working the sore muscles in his wrist. "Any pain?"

Tripp shakes his head no. "You're all the medicine I need, baby," he teases, pleased when Leander fails at suppressing his smile. "Tired, though. How's the snow? Do I gotta make dinner or can the pizza guy make it up here?"

Leander straightens his back to check and Tripp follows, using his elbow to prop himself up enough to see out of all the glass surrounding them. The pure, nearly-opaque curtain of dimly-lit white that stares back tells him all he needs to know.

"I'll cook," Leander offers, though he looks unhappy about it.

"No worries," Tripp replies, settling down again and making himself comfortable. "What am I, new? Figured we'd end the day like this, so I whipped up a full meal while you were at therapy yesterday. Put it all in tupperwares. Just have to heat it up."

"Oh, thank God," Leander sighs, slumping back against the cushions. "You know I'm garbage with anything not frozen or pasta. I believe I can work the microwave just fine, though."

There's silence between them for a few moments as Leander finishes massaging Tripp's sore arms. "Lee?" Tripp ventures. "Are we—we're good, right? I know you said I was right and stuff, but… we're *back,* right? You want to be my Dom again?" Lee's head snaps up, staring back at Tripp like he can't believe his question and alright, fair. "I had to ask," Tripp adds weakly. "You know we don't assume shit."

"No, you're right to do so," Leander replies with a sigh, working the tension from Tripp's fingers before finishing up and folding them together in his lap. His own hands cover them. "Yes," he says firmly. "Yes, of course. You know I'll always be your Dom."

"Good," Tripp replies brightly, lifting his leg to tuck it under Lee's still clothed hip, prodding at him obnoxiously. "Then get your hot ass moving. Go make us food so we can eat before we crawl into bed and do this again. Or, hell, I'll get a fire going and we can get down and dirty right here. There's a restraint bench on the other side of that couch, I can watch the snow fall while you mess me up." He lifts his eyebrows in question.

"Don't tell me what to do," Leander snaps sharply, gaze fierce.

In response, Tripp just grins widely. "There he is."

Leander's answering smile is wicked.

About the Author

Robin Lynn is a 36-year-old queer, autistic mother of two, an unabashed fangirl sometimes known as "Wings," and a disabled former firefighter, paramedic, and registered nurse. She writes for queer audiences with the goal of reflecting and centering the lgbtqia2s+ community in more media, because everyone deserves to see relatable, imperfect main characters who mirror themselves simply existing and getting their happy endings.

Find out more and follow Robin for additional content and future projects by visiting: https://linktr.ee/castielslostwings

Glossary

Air Bottles—the compressed air tanks firefighters carry on their back to use with their SCBAs.

A.L.S.—Advanced Life Support, the level of care a Paramedic (or EMT-I / EMT-A, outside of this story) provides in the pre-hospital setting.

Aerial—a ladder truck that may or may not have a bucket. Some rescue trucks may also have ladders and buckets.

"Ambulance Driver"—A derogatory way to refer to an EMS provider, especially a paramedic. A reductive phrase that some advanced health care professionals who look down on EMS as a career use to be intentionally insulting.

Bag-Valve-Mask—a non-invasive manual ventilation device with a mask that fits over the patient's face (or an attachment for an endotracheal tube) and a bag that is squeezed to push air into the lungs. Often used in combination with other airway protection devices for someone who is not breathing or breathing inadequately.

Band / Channel—as it applies to radios, the frequency being used for communication. Different bands may be used for different purposes. Common bands are shared for dispatch and general response, specific bands are assigned for private communication or temporary usage such as fireground ops, landing a helicopter, or coordinating a search and rescue.

B.L.S.—Basic Life Support, the level of care an EMT-Basic provides in the pre-hospital setting.

Burn Building—A structure built specifically for training firefighters in various scenarios, fire suppression techniques and attack modalities, as well as team-building and rescue practice. Fires are intentionally lit inside and stoked to mimic real conditions. The burn building may mimic a residential or commercial structure and its integrity is carefully monitored and maintained by Fire Marshall and the Chiefs.

Bus—slang for 'ambulance'.

Calling report—the EMT or paramedic caring for the patient uses the radio system or phone to contact the emergency room staff and give report to the nurse or doctor in order to let the staff know that they are coming. This usually results in a bed being ready for transfer of care upon arrival and / or the necessary providers being ready to assume that care. Can also be used to request & receive orders from an E.D. physician.

Cardiac Tamponade—Cardiac tamponade is pressure on the heart that occurs when blood or fluid builds up in the space between the heart muscle and the outer covering sac of the heart. It is relieved by manually inserting a needle into that space and withdrawing the fluid.

Catheter bag—urine drainage bag for a bedbound or surgical / post-surgical patient

Central Line—a central venous catheter / central line is a tube that doctors place in a large vein in the neck, chest, groin, or upper arm to give fluids, blood, or medications or to do medical tests quickly. It is more stable than a peripheral IV and less likely to collapse as well as able to handle high volume and corrosive medications more easily or for a longer period of time.

Channel—see: Band.

"Charged"—descriptive word for when hose line that is hooked up to the fire hydrant or pumper is pressurized and filled with water.

Cilice—a spiked garter or other device originally worn by religious orders for penance and mortification, adapted by sadists & masochists for B.D.S.M. play and / or fashion aesthetics.

Contused / Contusion—bruised / bruising

Crew—A "crew" is the group of firefighters staffing one truck in order to fulfill the truck's role. Oversimplified, at a house fire, an engine crew would be focused on dousing the fire, ladder crew might be focused on ventilating the roof, and rescue crew might be focused on breaking down a difficult entry. These roles vary based on the emergency at hand and personnel are cross-trained, commonly rotating to fill them.

Cricoid Pressure—also known as Sellick's maneuver. A technique used in endotracheal intubation to try to reduce the risk of regurgitation and improve visualization of the vocal cords for placement. It involves the application of pressure to the cricoid cartilage at the neck, thus occluding the esophagus which passes directly behind it and tilting the voice box.

Dispatch—the 911 call-taking center responsible for coordinating agency responses to reported emergencies over the radio. There is usually one dispatch center per county and per city.

D.M.E. —Durable Medical Equipment, i.e. the adaptive and assistive equipment one might use at home (shower chairs, wheelchair, cane, etc).

Drafting / Drafting Engine—The process of raising water from a static source to supply a pumper (engine) is known as drafting. This type of operation may occur from any type of static water source including lakes, ponds, portable tanks, and water-carrying vehicles without pumps. An engine that has depleted its tank and has no hydrant to connect to will need to draft in order to keep supplying water to a fire. The engine conducting that process is the drafting engine.

E.D. —Emergency Department / Emergency Room

E.D. Code Red / Red Room Activation—Usually only found in Level 1 Trauma Centers, this team activation transforms the Trauma Bay or a dedicated room into an emergency operating suite to manage a critical patient that would not otherwise survive the trip up to the O.R. so that lifesaving surgical procedures can be urgently performed.

EKG—also known as ECG, electrocardiogram, a test done to analyze the heart rate, rhythm, and blood flow via electrical signals in order to determine whether there is any acute cardiac event happening.

Endotracheal Intubation—see: Intubation.

Epaulette—a type of shoulder piece or decoration used as insignia of rank. With bunker gear, it is a buttoned strap on the top shoulder where a radio mic is frequently clipped.

Essentials—Essentials of Firefighting, the staple "Intro" class at the Academy or otherwise.

Etomidate—a short-acting intravenous anesthetic indicated for the induction of anesthesia and intubation, as well as supplementation of less-than-effective anesthesia during short operative procedures. It is a hypnotic-type sedative.

Evolutions—During a live burn, an "evolution" is the time between when a fire is stoked to life, and when it's extinguished.

Extubated / Extubation—the removal of the endotracheal breathing tube.

F.A.S.T. Ultrasound—Focused Assessment with Sonography in Trauma (FAST) is an ultrasound protocol developed to emergently assess the abdominal and chest cavities for any abnormal bleeding so that rapid intervention can be initiated.

Fire Academy & "Probies"—Most paid fire departments send recruits through a series of classes with both academic and physical components they must pass in order to graduate. Fresh graduates are then placed on probationary membership ("probies") where they can continue training, further learn the ropes from experienced members, and prove to the department that they are capable as fully-fledged firefighters.

Fire bands—the radio frequencies designated for responding fire department communication with the dispatch center itself.

Fire Rehab—On an active fire scene (a fire that is actively being fought to extinguish), EMS will set up an area to triage and handle any injuries as well as assess the firefighters working the blaze. Usually, when rehab is active, one ambulance remains fully committed to the scene to provide it, and if a patient requires transport to the hospital, a second ambulance will do so. Firefighters will break to cycle through the rehab regularly, having their vital signs and lung sounds checked to ensure that it is safe for them to continue working. Frequently, a firefighter will have to be temporarily benched to cool down or relax until their vital signs return to normal limits. Fire rehab is intensely important but often very, very boring.

Rehab can also include the department's "Canteen," usually run by the auxiliary (a group of fire company members who are NOT active firefighters, often spouses or family members who do fundraisers and otherwise support the department) who bring supplies (often varying on the weather) to a fire scene to help support the effort. Usually water, towels, blankets, ice, food, fans, coffee, chairs, etc. This service may also be provided by a professional organization such as the Red Cross. Those orgs usually only come out for very large or protracted events.

Five-inch—Also referred to as LDH (large diameter hose), these are the large hose lines that connect directly to a hydrant or drafting source.

Fluids down—Motor vehicle accidents often result in oil, fuel, and other operating fluids being spilled from their tanks onto the roadway. Fire response is utilized to clean up so those things don't become a hazard to the public, usually by soaking them up with absorbents.

Gauged Needles—IV needles come in gauged sizes, generally, size 12 to 24, with the smaller number being a larger bore (width) needle & catheter. The larger the catheter, the faster fluid and medication can be infused, which can be important in critical illness / injury. Lee uses a 16 gauge IV on Tripp, which is a very large size, but Tripp certainly has the need (and his muscles have the veins) to support that.

Halligan—Halligan Bar, also known as a Halligan tool or Hooligan tool, is crowbar-like, multipurpose, forcible entry tool used by firefighters for prying, twisting, punching, or striking. It has a fork, a blade, and a tapered pick, and is considered a firefighting staple. The Halligan bar has become the most versatile hand tool to be used for the past seven decades for a multitude of fireground tasks. It is not uncommon for some firefighters to be possessive over their tools, or to name them out of affection.

High-Angle Rescue—a very specialized rescue unit that allows a particular type of truck to be used as braced leverage to recover victims from unusual, tight, or sharply-angled positions. Mountainsides, elevators, bridges, water towers, sewers, and ships are all possible examples. The related crew is highly-trained in those technical and specialized rescues but uncommonly activated, nearly always functioning as regular firefighters until the need arises. This team / truck may respond from much further away than would be standard. The crew is often much more highly-trained in climbing, rappelling, and confined-space rescue.

Hoyer Lift—A portable mechanical lift, often used in hospitals, rehabs, and care facilities to transfer patients who are unable to bear any weight.

Intubation / Endotracheal Intubation / "Tubing"—Inserting a breathing tube through the vocal cords and into the trachea of a person whose ability to breathe is at risk or has already ceased in order to support their respiratory efforts and protect their airway. With burn patients, this is often done prophylactically in anticipation of airway swelling from the heat and smoke. ET tubes come in a range of options based on the patient's age / size.

Ketamine—a dissociative anesthetic used medically for induction and maintenance of anesthesia. It is a controlled substance that can cause hallucinations.

Ladder Truck—also called an aerial. A ladder fire truck is a basic tool for rapid response, ventilation, extinguishment, and rescue operations in the fire service. An aerial ladder truck stands out in a fleet because of the highly visible ladder device on the top of the truck with either a mid-mount or rear-mount application. It may extend up to 100 feet and ninety degrees. It may have a bucket on the far end.

Laparotomy—a common surgical procedure performed to examine the abdominal organs and aid in diagnosis of any problems, including abdominal pain or identified bleeding on ultrasound, with the goal of fixing those problems at the same time.

Litter—a slang word for the rolling, collapsible main stretcher in the back of any ambulance.

Live Burn—an intentionally-created fire lit and maintained for practice purposes.

Mac Blade (or Miller Blade)—hinged metal device with a curved (Mac) or straight (Miller) "blade" and handle, used to scoop the patient's tongue out of the way and lift the jaw in order to visualize the vocal cords and place an endotracheal tube. Video-assisted intubation devices such as the King have made these less relevant in recent years. Beau uses a "Mac 4," which is for a "Large Adult." Blade choice is based on provider preference and the patient's jaw size.

Maltese Cross—A symbol adopted first by the FDNY in 1865, it is a symbol of protection as well as loyalty, bravery, and the willingness to defend the weak. It is commonly used with similar fire-service graphics and sometimes adapted slightly for an individual department but is universally recognized to represent firefighters.

Medical Director—Every licensed EMS agency must have an EMS agency medical director who acts as the ultimate clinical authority. A licensed physician (M.D. or D.O.) provides medical guidance, training and advice to the EMTs and paramedics working under their license and ensures provider awareness, compliance, and proficiency with protocols and regulations.

Nasal Atomizer—a syringe with an adaptor on the injecting end that allows certain medications to be sprayed directly into a patient's nose, allowing for super-quick absorption through the nasal mucosa for fast onset of action.

Nasal Cannula—plastic tubing that provides gentle, low-flow supplemental oxygen delivered to a patient's nostrils.

On-Status—Letting Dispatch / the 911 Center know the entity is available and ready to respond.

Partner dynamics—re: Lee "riding in [Marley's] four a.m. knee pain": In general, ambulances are staffed with either one EMT (BLS) and one paramedic (ALS) or two paramedics. When the providers are mixed, the EMT handles any BLS calls and the paramedic any ALS calls, the load is not split evenly. A paramedic CAN choose to handle a BLS call, but not vice versa. Driving is always considered the easiest gig, the provider in the back always does the paperwork. Leander is saying that he'll handle one of Marley's BLS calls so she can just drive, as a favor.

Paralytic—a neuromuscular blocking agent, a powerful muscle relaxant used to prevent muscle movement during surgical procedures or critical care. If sedation is not adequate to relax the patient enough to insert an ET tube, one may be needed to assist. Once a paralytic is administered, the patient will no longer be able to breathe on their own, so assistive ventilation must be continued / completed.

PASS device—The Personal Alert Safety System (PASS) devices are designed to alert aid using audible signal technology. Normal operation is for the PASS devices to activate a 95-decibel multiple-frequency alarm signal if the lack of motion exceeds a specific time period. A firefighter wears one outside their bunker gear and, when armed, it makes a very loud sound if they manually activate OR stop moving for more than thirty seconds.

Platoon—a group of personnel assigned to be on the same shift together. Platoons are typically made up of multiple crews. Each platoon normally has leadership (captain and lieutenants), and an assortment of firefighters of varying experience levels. An Asst. Chief may oversee one or multiple platoons, the Fire Chief oversees them all.

Probies—see: Fire Academy.

Propofol—a short-acting medication that results in a decreased level of consciousness and a lack of memory, relaxation and sleepiness before and during procedures and for ongoing sedation needs.

Q.A.—Quality Assurance, usually related to charting. Charts are often regularly reviewed by coworkers of the same or higher certification and / or rank to ensure the appropriate protocols are being implemented. Concerns are escalated to the service's Medical Director.

Red Room Activation—see: E.D. Code Red.

Reeves Stretcher—Used to immobilize patients with spinal or neck injuries and / or extricate patients from tight spaces, the Reeves Sleeve stretcher is pliable, durable, lightweight, and carries in excess of 1,000 pounds at a time.

Rehab—see: Fire Rehab.

Rescue Truck—A rescue vehicle is a specialized vehicle used in technical rescue. It is designed to transport and provide the specialized equipment necessary for various rescue situations. This truck carries an array of heavy equipment such as the jaws of life, wooden cribbing, generators, winches, hi-lift jacks, cranes, cutting torches, circular saws, and other items unavailable on standard trucks. Different departments may have further specialized rescue units. These trucks are not typically equipped with water tanks or pumping ability.

Resus—slang for "resuscitation," or intensive medical care provided to a person experiencing respiratory or cardiac arrest.

SCBA Gear—Self-Contained Breathing Apparatus. A type of respirator that contains breathable compressed air. Used by firefighters and others who may be working in areas filled with smoke, toxic gas, or other contaminants that are immediately dangerous to life and health.

Spinal Immobilization—a technique used to keep a person with a potential spine injury (usually suspected after a fall or high-impact event) quiet and still to minimize causing further injury or damage. This usually involves placing a cervical collar around the neck and securing the patient to a long spine board.

Stage and Identify—Bruises and injuries in general have predictable healing patterns that a professional would be able to observe at a glance. A red bruise is fresh, day one. A purple-blue one is a couple days old, green is just under a week, yellow is just over, and brown is old. These healing stages can be important and informative tools to providers. As a trauma surgeon, Beau would be especially proficient at assessing visible injuries, especially bruises, at a glance.

Taking a Unit / Company 'Off-Status'—Letting Dispatch / the 911 Center know that a crew or piece of apparatus or officer or an entire company is unavailable to respond to any emergency. This may be done to clean up or restock after a previous response, for training, or for lack of personnel.

Tones—also called "alert tones." A certain pattern of sounds that activates pagers and radios for a specific company or unit. Station Eleven's tones will not open Station Fifteen's pagers, although the sound can be heard over the same frequency band.

"Tubing"—see: Intubation.